RED PLANET BLUES

ROBERT J. SAWYER

Incorporating the Hugo and Nebula
Award–nominated novella 'Identity Theft'

The first ten chapters were originally published in a slightly different version as the novella 'Identity Theft' in *Down These Dark Spaceways*, edited by Mike Resnick, published by Science Fiction Book Club, 2005.

This edition first published in Great Britain in 2014 by
Gollancz
The Orion Publishing Group Ltd
Orion House
5 Upper Saint Martin's Lane
London, WC2H 9EA
An Hachette UK Company

A CIP catalogue record for this book
is available from the British Library.

ISBN 978 1 473 20008 1

Printed and bound by Clays Ltd, St Ives plc

www.sfwriter.com
www.orionbooks.co.uk
www.gollancz.co.uk

For

Sherry Peters

ACKNOWLEDGMENTS

In February 2004, Hugo Award–winning author **Mike Resnick** approached me with an offer I couldn't refuse: write a "science-fictional hard-boiled private-eye novella" for an original anthology he was editing for the Science Fiction Book Club called *Down These Dark Spaceways.*

That story, "Identity Theft," went on to win Spain's Premio UPC de Ciencia Ficción, which, at 6,000 euros, is the world's largest cash prize for science-fiction writing. It was also a finalist for the Canadian Science Fiction and Fantasy Award ("the Aurora"), as well as for the top two awards in the science-fiction field: the World Science Fiction Society's Hugo Award (SF's "People's Choice Award") and the Science Fiction and Fantasy Writers of America's Nebula Award (SF's "Academy Award")—making "Identity Theft" the first (and so far only) original publication of the SFBC ever to be nominated for either of those awards. In a slightly modified form, "Identity Theft" makes up the first ten chapters of this novel.

In 2007, my wife Carolyn and I spent the summer at Berton House, the former home of Canadian historian and author **Pierre Berton**. One of Canada's most prestigious writers' residencies, Berton House is in Dawson City in the Yukon Territory—the heart of the Klondike Gold Rush. Although I'd already established the Great Martian Fossil Rush as the backstory to "Identity Theft," it was my time in the Yukon—living across the dirt road from **Robert Service**'s cabin, and just a block from **Jack London**'s old home—that made me want to really explore the madness and greed that drives stampedes of prospectors. My thanks to the Berton House administrator **Elsa Franklin**, and to **Dan Davidson** and **Suzanne Saito**, who looked after us in Dawson City.

For other help and encouragement, my thanks go to **Ted Bleaney, Wayne Brown, David Livingstone Clink, Paddy Forde, Marcel Gagné, James Alan Gardner, Martin H. Greenberg, John Helfers, Doug Herrington, Al Katerinsky, Herb Kauderer, Geoffrey A. Landis, Kirstin Morrell, Kayla Nielsen, Virginia O'Dine, Ian Pedoe, Sherry Peters**, and **Alan B. Sawyer**.

My working title for this book was *The Great Martian Fossil Rush*, but my American publisher wanted something that played up the noir angle. I asked for suggestions online, and hundreds of possibilities were put forth. **Jeffrey Allan Beeler, Nazrat Durand, André Peloquin**, and **Mike Poole** each separately proposed the title we ended up using, *Red Planet Blues.* My thanks to them, and to the more than one hundred other people who made suggestions. As it happens, the same title was used in 1989 by my great friend Hugo Award–winning writer **Allen Steele** for a novella he later incorporated into his terrific 1992 Mars novel *Labyrinth of Night;* I'm using the title with Allen's kind permission.

Finally, huge thanks, as always, to the Aurora Award–winning poet **Carolyn Clink**, who helped in countless ways; to my father **John A. Sawyer**, who encouraged my early interests in both paleontology and other worlds; to **Adrienne Kerr** at Penguin Group (Canada) in Toronto; and to **Ginjer Buchanan** at Penguin Group (USA)'s Ace imprint in New York. And, of course, many thanks to my agents **Christopher Lotts, Vince Gerardis**, and the late **Ralph Vicinanza**.

There are strange things done 'neath the Martian sun
By those who seek the mother lode;
The ruddy trails have their secret tales
That would make your blood run cold;
The twin moonlights have seen queer sights,
But the queerest they ever did see
Was that night on the shore of a lake of yore
I terminated a transferee.

ONE

The door to my office slid open. "Hello," I said, rising from my chair. "You must be my nine o'clock." I said it as if I had a ten o'clock and an eleven o'clock, but I didn't. The whole Martian economy was in a slump, and even though I was the only private detective on Mars this was the first new case I'd had in weeks.

"Yes," said a high, feminine voice. "I'm Cassandra Wilkins."

I let my eyes rove up and down her body. It was very good work; I wondered if she'd had quite so perfect a figure before transferring. People usually ordered replacement bodies that, at least in broad strokes, resembled their originals, but few could resist improving them. Men got more buff, women got curvier, and everyone modified their faces, removing asymmetries, wrinkles, and imperfections. If I ever transferred myself, I'd eliminate the gray in my blond hair and get a new nose that would look like my current one had before it'd been broken a couple of times.

"A pleasure to meet you, Ms. Wilkins," I said. "I'm Alexander Lomax. Please have a seat."

She was a little thing, no more than 150 centimeters, and she was wearing a stylish silver-gray blouse and skirt but no makeup or jewelry. I'd expected her to sit with a fluid catlike movement, given her delicate features, but she just sort of plunked herself into the chair. "Thanks," she said. "I do hope you can help me, Mr. Lomax. I really do."

Rather than immediately sitting down myself, I went to the coffeemaker. I filled my own mug, then offered Cassandra one; most models of transfer could eat and drink in order to be sociable, but she declined my offer. "What seems to be the problem?" I said, returning to my chair.

It's hard reading a transfer's expression: the facial sculpting was usually excellent, but the movements were somewhat restrained. "My husband—oh, my goodness, Mr. Lomax, I hate to even say this!" She looked down at her hands. "My husband . . . he's disappeared."

I raised my eyebrows; it was pretty damned difficult for someone to disappear here. New Klondike was locked under a shallow dome four kilometers in diameter and just twenty meters high at the central support column. "When did you last see him?"

"Three days ago."

My office was small, but it did have a window. Through it, I could see the crumbling building next door and one of the gently sloping arches that helped hold up the transparent dome. Outside the dome, a dust storm was raging, orange clouds obscuring the sun. Auxiliary lights on the arch compensated for that, but Martian daylight was never very bright. "Is your husband, um, like you?" I asked.

She nodded. "Oh, yes. We both came here looking to make our fortune, just like everyone else."

I shook my head. "I mean is he also a transfer?"

"Oh, sorry. Yes, he is. In fact, we both just transferred."

"It's an expensive procedure," I said. "Could he have been skipping out on paying for it?"

Cassandra shook her head. "No, no. Joshua found one or two nice specimens early on. He used the money from selling those pieces to buy the NewYou franchise here. That's where we met—after I threw in the towel on sifting dirt, I got a job in sales there. Anyway, of course, we both got to transfer at cost." She was actually wringing her synthetic hands. "Oh, Mr. Lomax, please help me! I don't know what I'm going to do without my Joshua!"

"You must love him a lot," I said, watching her pretty face for more than just the pleasure of looking at it; I wanted to gauge her sincerity as she replied. After all, people often disappeared because things were bad at home, but spouses are rarely forthcoming about that.

"Oh, I do!" said Cassandra. "I love him more than I can say. Joshua is a wonderful, wonderful man." She looked at me with pleading eyes. "You have to help me get him back. You just have to!"

I looked down at my coffee mug; steam was rising from it. "Have you tried the police?"

Cassandra made a sound that I guessed was supposed to be a snort: it had the right roughness but was dry as Martian sand. "Yes. They—oh, I hate to speak ill of anyone, Mr. Lomax! Believe me, it's not my way, but—well, there's no ducking it, is there? They were useless. Just totally useless."

I nodded slightly; it's a story I heard often enough. I owed much of what little livelihood I had to the NKPD's indifference to most crime. They were a private force, employed by Howard Slapcoff to protect his thirty-year-old investment in constructing this city. The cops made a token effort to keep order but that was all. "Who did you speak to?"

"A—a detective, I guess he was; he didn't wear a uniform. I've forgotten his name."

"What did he look like?"

"Red hair, and—"

"That's Mac," I said. She looked puzzled, so I said his full name. "Dougal McCrae."

"McCrae, yes," said Cassandra. She shuddered a bit, and she must have noticed my surprised reaction to that. "Sorry," she said. "I just didn't like the way he looked at me."

I resisted running my eyes over her body just then; I'd already done so, and I could remember what I'd seen. I guess her original figure hadn't been like this one; if it had, she'd certainly be used to admiring looks from men by now.

"I'll have a word with McCrae," I said. "See what's already been done. Then I'll pick up where the cops left off."

"Would you?" Her green eyes seemed to dance. "Oh, thank you, Mr. Lomax! You're a good man—I can tell!"

I shrugged a little. "I can show you two ex-wives and a half dozen bankers who'd disagree."

"Oh, no," she said. "Don't say things like that! You *are* a good man, I'm sure of it. Believe me, I have a sense about these things. You're a good man, and I know you won't let me down."

Naïve woman; she'd probably thought the same thing about her hubby—until he'd run off. "Now, what can you tell me about your husband? Joshua, is it?"

"Yes, that's right. His full name is Joshua Connor Wilkins—and it's Joshua, never just Josh, thank you very much." I nodded. In my experience, guys who were anal about being called by their full first names never bought a round. Maybe it was a good thing this joker was gone.

"Yes," I said. "Go on." I didn't have to take notes. My office computer—a small green cube sitting on my desk—was recording everything and would extract whatever was useful into a summary file for me.

Cassandra ran her synthetic lower lip back and forth beneath her artificial upper teeth, thinking for a moment. "Well, he was born in Wichita, Kansas, and he's thirty-eight years old. He moved to Mars seven mears ago." Mears were Mars years; about double the length of those on Earth.

"Do you have a picture?"

"I can access one." She pointed at my dusty keyboard. "May I?"

I nodded, and Cassandra reached over to grab it. In doing so, she managed to knock over my "World's Greatest Detective" coffee mug, spilling hot joe all over her dainty hand. She let out a small yelp of pain. I got up, grabbed a towel, and began wiping up the mess. "I'm surprised that hurt," I said. "I mean, I *do* like my coffee hot, but . . ."

"Transfers feel pain, Mr. Lomax," she said, "for the same reason biologicals do. When you're flesh and blood, you need a signaling system to warn you when your parts are being damaged; same is true for those of us who have transferred. Of course, artificial bodies are much more durable."

"Ah."

"Sorry. I've explained this so many times now—you know, at work. Anyway, please forgive me about your desk."

I made a dismissive gesture. "Thank God for the paperless office, eh? Don't worry about it." I gestured at the keyboard; fortunately, none of the coffee had gone down between the keys. "You were going to show me a picture?"

"Oh, right." She spoke some commands, and the terminal responded—making me wonder what she'd wanted the keyboard for. But then she used it to type in a long passphrase; presumably she didn't want to say hers aloud in front of me. She frowned as she was typing it in and backspaced to make a correction; multiword passphrases were easy to say but hard to type if you weren't adept with a keyboard—and the more security conscious you were the longer the passphrase you used.

She accessed some repository of her personal files and brought up a photo of Joshua-never-Josh Wilkins. Given how attractive Mrs. Wilkins was, he wasn't what I expected. He had cold, gray eyes, hair buzzed so short as to be nonexistent, and a thin, almost lipless mouth; the overall effect was reptilian. "That's before," I said. "What about after? What's he look like now that he's transferred?"

"Umm, pretty much the same."

"Really?" If I'd had that kisser, I'd have modified it for sure. "Do you have pictures taken since he moved his mind?"

"No actual pictures," said Cassandra. "After all, he and I only just transferred. But I can go into the NewYou database and show you the plans from which his new face was manufactured." She spoke to the terminal some more and then typed in another lengthy passphrase. Soon enough, she had a computer-graphics rendition of Joshua's head on my screen.

"You're right," I said, surprised. "He didn't change a thing. Can I get copies of all this?"

She nodded and spoke some more commands, transferring various documents into local storage.

"All right," I said. "My fee is two hundred solars an hour, plus expenses."

"That's fine, that's fine, of course! I don't care about the money, Mr. Lomax—not at all. I just want Joshua back. Please tell me you'll find him."

"I will," I said, smiling my most reassuring smile. "Don't worry about that. He can't have gone far."

TWO

Actually, of course, Joshua Wilkins *could* perhaps have gone quite far—so my first order of business was to eliminate that possibility.

No spaceships had left Mars in the last twenty days, so he couldn't be off-planet. There was a giant airlock in the south through which large spaceships could be brought inside for dry-dock work, but it hadn't been cracked open in weeks. And, although a transfer could exist freely on the Martian surface, there were only four airlock stations leading out of the dome, and they all had security guards. I visited each of those and checked, just to be sure, but the only people who had gone out in the past three days were the usual crowds of hapless fossil hunters, and every one of them had returned when the dust storm began.

I'd read about the early days of this town: "The Great Martian Fossil Rush," they called it. Weingarten and O'Reilly, the two private explorers who had come here at their own expense, had found the first fossils on Mars and had made a fortune selling them back on Earth. They were more valuable than any precious metal and rarer than anything else in the solar system—actual evidence of extraterrestrial life! Good fist-sized specimens went for tens of thousands; excellent football-sized ones for millions. In a world in which almost anything, including diamonds and gold, could be synthesized, there was no greater status symbol than to own the genuine petrified remains of a Martian pentapod or rhizomorph.

Weingarten and O'Reilly never said precisely where they'd found their specimens, but it had been easy enough to prove that their first spaceship had landed here, in the Isidis Planitia basin. Other treasure hunters started coming, and Howard Slapcoff—the billionaire founder of the company that pioneered the process by which minds could be scanned and uploaded—had used a hunk of his fortune to create our domed city. Many of those who'd found good specimens in the early days had bought property in New Klondike from him. It had been a wonderful investment for Slapcoff: the land sales brought him more than triple what he'd spent erecting the dome, and he'd been collecting a life-support tax from residents ever since. Well, from the biological residents, at least, but Slappy got a fat royalty from NewYou each time his transfer process was used, so he lined his pockets either way.

Native life was never widely dispersed on Mars; the single ecosystem that had existed here seemed to have been confined to this basin. Some of the other prospectors—excuse me, fossil hunters—who came shortly after W&O's first expedition found a few excellent specimens, although most of the finds had been in poor shape.

Somewhere, though, was the mother lode: a bed known as the "Alpha Deposit" that produced fossils more finely preserved than even those from Earth's Burgess Shale. Weingarten and O'Reilly had known where it was—they'd stumbled on it by pure dumb luck, apparently. But they'd both been killed when their heat shield separated from their ship upon re-entry into Earth's atmosphere after their third expedition—and, in the twenty mears since, no one had yet rediscovered it. But people were still looking.

There'd always been a market for transferring consciousness; the potentially infinite lifespan was hugely appealing. But here on Mars, the demand was particularly brisk, since artificial bodies could spend weeks or even months on the surface, searching for paleontological gold.

Anyway, Joshua-never-Josh Wilkins was clearly not outside the habitat and he hadn't taken off in a spaceship. Wherever he was hiding, it was somewhere under the New Klondike dome. I can't say he was breathing the same air I was, because he wasn't breathing at all. But he was *here*, somewhere. All I had to do was find him.

I didn't want to duplicate the efforts of the police, although "efforts" was usually too generous a term to apply to the work of the local constabulary; "cursory attempts" probably was closer to the truth, if I knew Mac.

New Klondike had twelve radial roadways, cutting across the nine concentric rings of buildings under the dome. The rings were evenly spaced, except for the giant gap between the seventh and eighth, which accommodated agricultural fields, the shipyard, warehouses, water-treatment and air-processing facilities, and more. My office was at dome's edge, on the outside of the Ninth Circle; I could have taken a hovertram into the center but I preferred to walk. A good detective knew what was happening on the streets, and the hovertrams, dilapidated though they were, sped by too fast for that.

When I'd first come here, I'd quipped that New Klondike wasn't a hellhole—it wasn't far enough gone for that. "More of a heckhole," I'd said. But that had been ten years ago, just after what had happened with Wanda, and if something in the middle of a vast plain could be said to be going downhill, New Klondike was it. The fused-regolith streets were cracked, buildings—and not just the ones in the old shantytown—were in disrepair, and the seedy bars and brothels were full of thugs and con artists, the destitute and the dejected. As a character in one of the old movies I like had said of a town, "You will never find a more wretched hive of scum and villainy." New Klondike should have a sign by one of the airlocks that proclaims, "Twinned with Mos Eisley, Tatooine."

I didn't make any bones about staring at the transfers I saw along the way. They ranged in style from really sophisticated models, like Cassandra Wilkins, to things only a step up from the Tin Woodman of Oz. The latter were easy to identify as transfers, but the former could sometimes pass for biologicals, although you develop a knack for identifying them, too, almost subconsciously noting an odd sheen to the plastiskin or an unnatural smoothness in the movement of the limbs; *paydar,* it was called: the ability to spot a bought body.

Of course, those who'd contented themselves with second-rate synthetic forms doubtless believed they'd trade up when they eventually happened upon some decent specimens. Poor saps; no one had found truly spectacular remains for mears, and lots of people were giving up and going back to Earth, if they could afford the passage, or were settling in to lives of, as Thoreau would have it, quiet desperation, their dreams as dead as the fossils they'd never found.

I continued walking easily along; Mars gravity is just thirty-eight percent of Earth's. Some people were stuck here because they'd let their muscles atrophy; they'd never be able to hack a full gee again. Me, I was stuck here for other reasons—thank God Mars has no real government and so no extradition treaties. But I worked out more than most people did—at Gully's Gym, over by the shipyard—and so still had strong legs; I could walk comfortably all day if I had to.

I passed a few spindly or squat robots—most of whom were dumb as posts, and none of whom were brighter than a four-year-old—running errands or engaged in the Sisyphean tasks of road and building repair.

The cop shop was a lopsided five-story structure—it could be that tall, this near the center of the dome—with chipped and cracked walls that had once been white but were now a grimy grayish pink. The front doors were clear alloquartz, same as the overhead dome, and they slid aside as I walked up to them. On the lobby's right was a long red desk—as if we don't see enough red on Mars—with a map showing the Isidis Planitia basin behind it; New Klondike was a big circle off to one side.

The NKPD consisted of eight cops, the junior ones of whom took turns playing desk sergeant. Today it was a flabby lowbrow named Huxley, whose blue uniform always seemed a size too small for him. "Hey, Hux," I said, walking over. "Is Mac in?"

Huxley consulted a monitor then nodded. "Yeah, he's in, but he don't see just anyone."

"I'm not just anyone, Hux. I'm the guy who picks up the pieces after you clowns bungle things."

Huxley frowned, trying to think of a rejoinder. "Yeah, well . . ." he said, at last.

"Oooh," I said. "Good one, Hux! Way to put me in my place."

He narrowed his eyes. "You ain't as funny as you think you are, Lomax."

"Of course I'm not. Nobody could be *that* funny." I nodded at the secured inner door. "Going to buzz me through?"

"Only to be rid of you," said Huxley. So pleased was he with the wit of this remark that he repeated it: "Only to be rid of you." He reached below the counter, and the inner door—an unmarked black panel—slid aside. I pantomimed tipping a hat at Hux and headed into the station proper. I then walked down the corridor to McCrae's office; the door was open, so I rapped my knuckles against the steel jamb.

"Lomax!" he said, looking up. "Decided to turn yourself in?"

"Very funny, Mac. You and Hux should go on the road together."

He snorted. "What can I do for you, Alex?"

Mac was a skinny biological with shaggy orange eyebrows shielding his blue eyes. On the credenza behind his desk were holograms of his wife and his baby daughter; the girl had been born just a couple of months ago. "I'm looking for a guy named Joshua Wilkins."

Mac had a strong Scottish brogue—so strong, I figured it must be an affectation. "Ah, yes. Who's your client? The wife?"

I nodded.

"Quite the looker," he said.

"That she is. Anyway, you tried to find her husband, this Wilkins . . ."

"We looked around, yeah," said Mac. "He's a transfer, you knew that?"

I nodded.

"Well," Mac said, "she gave us the plans for his new face—precise measurements and all that. We've been feeding all the videos from public security cameras through facial-recognition software. So far, no luck."

I smiled. That's about as far as Mac's detective work normally went: things he could do without hauling his bony ass out from behind his desk. "How much of New Klondike do they cover now?" I asked.

"It's down to forty percent of the public areas."

People kept smashing, stealing, or jamming the cameras faster than Mac and his staff could replace them; this was a frontier town, after all, and there were lots of things going on folks didn't want observed. "You'll let me know if you find anything?"

Mac drew his shaggy eyebrows together. "Even Mars has to abide by Earth's privacy laws, Alex—or, at least, our parent corporation does. I can't divulge what the security cameras see."

I reached into my pocket, pulled out a fifty-solar coin, and flipped it. It went up rapidly but came down in what still seemed like slow motion to me, even after a decade on Mars; Mac didn't require a transfer's reflexes to catch it in midair. "Of course," he said, "I suppose we could make an exception . . ."

"Thanks. You're a credit to law-enforcement officials everywhere."

He smiled, then: "Say, what kind of heat you packing these days? You still carrying that old Smith & Wesson?"

"It's registered," I said, narrowing my eyes.

"Oh, I know, I know. But be careful, eh? The times, they are a-changin'. Bullets aren't much use against a transfer, and there are getting to be more of those each day, since the cost of the procedure is finally coming down."

"So I've heard. Do you happen to know the best place to plug a transfer, if you had to take one out?"

Mac shook his head. "It varies from model to model, and NewYou does its best to retrofit any physical vulnerabilities that are uncovered."

"So how do you guys handle them?"

"Until recently, as little as possible," said Mac. "Turning a blind eye, and all that."

"Saves getting up."

Mac didn't take offense. "Exactly. But let me show you something." We left his office, went farther down the corridor, and entered another room. He pointed to a device on the table. "Just arrived from Earth. The latest thing."

It was a wide, flat disk, maybe half a meter in diameter and five centimeters thick. There were a pair of U-shaped handgrips attached to the edge, opposite each other. "What is it?"

"A broadband disruptor," Mac said. He picked it up and held it in front of himself, like a gladiator's shield. "It discharges an oscillating multifrequency electromagnetic pulse. From a distance of four meters or less, it will completely fry the artificial brain of a transfer—killing it as effectively as a bullet kills a human."

"I don't plan on killing anyone," I said.

"That's what you said the last time."

Ouch. Still, maybe he had a point. "I don't suppose you have a spare I can borrow?"

Mac laughed. "Are you kidding? This is the only one we've got so far, and it's just a prototype."

"Well, then," I said, heading for the door, "I guess I'd better be careful."

THREE

My next stop was the NewYou building. I took Third Avenue, one of the radial streets of the city, out the five blocks to it. The NewYou building was two stories tall and was made, like most structures here, of red laser-fused Martian sand bricks. Flanking the main doors were a pair of wide alloquartz display windows, showing dusty artificial bodies dressed in fashions from about five mears ago; it was high time somebody updated things.

The lower floor was divided into a showroom and a workshop, separated by a door that was currently open. The workroom had spare components scattered about: here, a white-skinned artificial hand; there, a black lower leg; on shelves, synthetic eyes and spools of colored monofilament that I guessed were used to simulate hair. And there were all sorts of internal parts on the two worktables: motors and hydraulic pumps and joint hinges.

The adjacent showroom displayed complete artificial bodies. Across its width, I spotted Cassandra Wilkins, wearing a beige suit. She was talking with a man and a woman who were biological; potential customers, presumably. "Hello, Cassandra," I said, after I'd closed the distance between us.

"Mr. Lomax!" she gushed, excusing herself from the couple. "I'm so glad you're here—so very glad! What news do you have?"

"Not much. I've been to visit the cops, and I thought I should start my investigation here. After all, you and your husband own this franchise, right?"

Cassandra nodded enthusiastically. "I knew I was doing the right thing hiring you. I just knew it! Why, do you know that lazy detective McCrae never stopped by here—not even once!"

I smiled. "Mac's not the outdoorsy type. And, well, you get what you pay for."

"Isn't that the truth?" said Cassandra. "Isn't that just the God's honest truth!"

"You said your husband moved his mind recently?"

"Yes. All of that goes on upstairs, though. This is just sales and service down here."

"Do you have security-camera footage of Joshua actually transferring?"

"No. NewYou doesn't allow cameras up there; they don't like footage of the process getting out. Trade secrets, and all that."

"Ah, okay. Can you show me how it's done, though?"

She nodded again. "Of course. Anything you want to see, Mr. Lomax." What I wanted to see was under that beige suit—nothing beat the perfection of a high-end transfer's body—but I kept that thought to myself. Cassandra looked around the room, then motioned for another staff member to come over: a gorgeous little biological female wearing tasteful makeup and jewelry. "I'm sorry," Cassandra said to the two customers she'd abandoned a few moments ago. "Miss Takahashi here will look after you." She then turned to me. "This way."

We went through a curtained doorway and up a set of stairs, coming to a landing in front of two doors. "Here's our scanning room," said Cassandra, indicating the left-hand one; both doors had little windows in them. She stood on tiptoe to look in the scanning-room window and nodded, apparently satisfied by what she saw, then opened the door. Two people were inside: a balding man of about forty, who was seated, and a standing woman who looked twenty-five; the woman was a transfer herself, though, so there was no way of knowing her real age. "So sorry to interrupt," Cassandra said. She smiled at the man in the chair, while gesturing at me. "This is Alexander Lomax. He's providing some, ah, consulting services for us."

The man looked up at me, surprised, then said, "Klaus Hansen," by way of introduction.

"Would you mind ever so much if Mr. Lomax watched while the scan was being done?" asked Cassandra.

Hansen considered this for a moment, frowning his long, thin face. But then he nodded. "Sure. Why not?"

"Thanks," I said, stepping into the room. "I'll just stand over here." I moved to the far wall and leaned against it.

The chair Hansen was sitting in looked a lot like a barber's chair. The female transfer who wasn't Cassandra reached up above the chair and pulled down a translucent hemisphere that was attached by an articulated arm to the ceiling. She kept lowering it until all of Hansen's head was covered, and then she turned to a control console.

The hemisphere shimmered slightly, as though a film of oil was washing over its surface; the scanning field, I supposed.

Cassandra was standing next to me, arms crossed in front of her chest. "How long does the scanning take?" I asked.

"Not long," she replied. "It's a quantum-mechanical process, so the scanning is rapid. After that, we just need a couple of minutes to move the data into the artificial brain. And then . . ."

"And then?" I said.

She lifted her shoulders, as if the rest didn't need to be spelled out. "Why, and then Mr. Hansen will be able to live forever."

"Ah."

"Come along," said Cassandra. "Let's go see the other side." We left that room, closing its door behind us, and entered the one next door. This room was a mirror image of the previous one, which I guess was appropriate. Lying on a table-bed in the middle of the room was Hansen's new body, dressed in a fashionable blue suit; its eyes were closed. Also in the room was a male NewYou technician, who was biological.

I walked around, looking at the artificial body from all angles. The replacement Hansen still had a bald spot, although its diameter had been reduced by half. And, interestingly, Hansen had opted for a sort of permanent designer-stubble look; the biological him was clean-shaven at the moment.

Suddenly the simulacrum's eyes opened. "Wow," said a voice that was the same as the one I'd heard from the man next door. "That's incredible."

"How do you feel, Mr. Hansen?" asked the male technician.

"Fine. Just fine."

"Good," the technician said. "There'll be some settling-in adjustments, of course. Let's just check to make sure all your parts are working . . ."

"And there it is," Cassandra said to me. "Simple as that." She led me out of the room, back into the corridor, and closed the door behind us.

"Fascinating." I pointed at the left-hand door. "When do you take care of the original?"

"That's already been done. We do it in the chair."

I stared at the closed door and I like to think I suppressed my shudder enough so that Cassandra was unaware of it. "All right. I guess I've seen enough."

Cassandra looked disappointed. "Are you sure you don't want to look around some more?"

"Why? Is there anything else worth seeing?"

"Oh, I don't know," said Cassandra. "It's a big place. Everything on this floor, everything downstairs . . . everything in the basement."

I blinked. "You've got a basement?" Almost no Martian buildings had basements; the permafrost layer was very hard to dig through.

"Yes," she said. She paused, then looked away. "Of course, no one ever goes down there; it's just storage."

"I'll have a look," I said.

And that's where I found him.

He was lying behind some large storage crates, face down, a sticky pool of machine oil surrounding his head. Next to him was a stubby excimer-powered jackhammer, the kind many fossil hunters had for removing surface material. And next to the jackhammer was a piece of good old-fashioned paper. On it, in block letters, was written, "I'm so sorry, Cassie. It's just not the same."

It's hard to commit suicide, I guess, when you're a transfer. Slitting your wrists does nothing significant. Poison doesn't work and neither does drowning. But Joshua-never-anything-else-at-all-anymore Wilkins had apparently found a way. From the looks of it, he'd leaned back against the rough cement wall and, with his strong artificial arms, had held up the jackhammer, placing its bit against the center of his forehead. And then he'd pressed down on the jackhammer's twin triggers, letting the unit run until it had managed to pierce through his titanium skull and scramble the material of his artificial brain. When his brain died, his thumbs let up on the triggers, and he dropped the jackhammer, then tumbled over himself. His head had twisted sideways when it hit the concrete floor. Everything below his eyebrows was intact; it was clearly the same reptilian face Cassandra Wilkins had shown me.

I headed up the stairs and found Cassandra, who was chatting in her animated style with another customer.

"Cassandra," I said, pulling her aside. "Cassandra, I'm very sorry, but . . ."

She looked at me, her green eyes wide. "What?"

"I've found your husband. And he's dead."

She opened her pretty mouth, closed it, then opened it again. She looked like she might fall over, even with gyroscopes stabilizing her. "My . . . God," she said at last. "Are you . . . are you positive?"

"Sure looks like him."

"My God," she said again. "What . . . what happened?"

No nice way to say it. "Looks like he killed himself."

A couple of Cassandra's coworkers had come over, wondering what all the commotion was about. "What's wrong?" asked one of them—the same Miss Takahashi I'd seen earlier.

"Oh, Reiko," said Cassandra. "Joshua is dead!"

Customers were noticing what was going on, too. A burly flesh-and-blood man, with short black hair, a gold stud in one ear, and arms as thick around as most men's legs, came across the room; he clearly worked here. Reiko Takahashi had already drawn Cassandra into her arms—or vice versa; I'd been looking away when it had happened—and was stroking Cassandra's artificial hair. I let the burly man do what he could to calm the crowd, while I used my wrist phone to call Mac and inform him of Joshua Wilkins's suicide.

FOUR

Detective Dougal McCrae of New Klondike's Finest arrived about twenty minutes later, accompanied by two uniforms. "How's it look, Alex?" Mac asked.

"Not as messy as some of the biological suicides I've seen," I said. "But it's still not a pretty sight."

"Show me."

I led Mac downstairs. He read the note without picking it up.

The burly man soon came down, too, followed by Cassandra Wilkins, who was holding her artificial hand to her artificial mouth.

"Hello, again, Mrs. Wilkins," Mac said, moving to interpose himself between her and the prone form on the floor. "I'm terribly sorry, but I'll need you to make an official identification."

I lifted my eyebrows at the irony of requiring the next of kin to actually look at the body to be sure of who it was, but that's what we'd gone back to with transfers. Privacy laws prevented any sort of ID chip or tracking device being put into artificial bodies. In fact, that was one of the many incentives to transfer: you no longer left fingerprints or a trail of identifying DNA everywhere you went.

Cassandra nodded bravely; she was willing to accede to Mac's request. He stepped aside, a living curtain, revealing the synthetic body with the gaping head wound. She looked down at it. I'd expected her to quickly avert her eyes, but she didn't; she just kept staring.

Finally, Mac said, very gently, "Is that your husband, Mrs. Wilkins?"

She nodded slowly. Her voice was soft. "Yes. Oh, my poor, poor Joshua . . ."

Mac stepped over to talk to the two uniforms, and I joined them. "What do you do with a dead transfer?" I asked. "Seems pointless to call in the medical examiner."

By way of answer, Mac motioned to the burly man. The man touched his own chest and raised his eyebrows in the classic "Who, me?" expression. Mac nodded again. The man looked left and right, like he was crossing some imaginary road, and then came over. "Yeah?"

"You seem to be the senior employee here," said Mac. "Am I right?"

The man had a Hispanic accent. "Horatio Fernandez. Joshua was the boss, but I'm senior technician." Or maybe he said, "I'm *Señor* Technician."

"Good," said Mac. "You're probably better equipped than we are to figure out the exact cause of death."

Fernandez gestured theatrically at the synthetic corpse, as if it were—well, not *bleedingly* obvious but certainly apparent.

Mac shook his head. "It's just a bit too pat," he said, his voice lowered conspiratorially. "Implement at hand, suicide note." He lifted his shaggy orange eyebrows. "I just want to be sure."

Cassandra had drifted over without Mac noticing, although of course I had. She was listening in.

"Yeah," said Fernandez. "Sure. We can disassemble him, check for anything else that might be amiss."

"No," said Cassandra. "You can't."

"I'm afraid it's necessary," said Mac, looking at her. His Scottish brogue always put an edge on his words, but I knew he was trying to sound gentle.

"No," said Cassandra, her voice quavering. "I forbid it."

Mac's tone got a little firmer. "You can't. I'm required to order an autopsy in every suspicious case."

Cassandra opened her mouth to say something more, then apparently thought better of it. Horatio moved closer to her and put a hulking arm around her small shoulders. "Don't worry," he said. "We'll be gentle." And then his face brightened a bit. "In fact, we'll see what parts we can salvage—give them to somebody else; somebody who couldn't afford such good stuff if it were new." He smiled beatifically. "It's what Joshua would have wanted."

. . . .

The next day, I was sitting in my office, looking out the small window with its cracked pane. The dust storm had ended. Out on the surface, rocks were strewn everywhere, like toys on a kid's bedroom floor. My phone played "Luck Be a Lady," and I looked at it in anticipation, hoping for a new case; I could use the solars. But the ID said NKPD. I told the device to accept the call, and a little picture of Mac's face appeared on my wrist. "Hey, Alex," he said. "Come by the station, would you?"

"What's up?"

The micro-Mac frowned. "Nothing I want to say over open airwaves."

I nodded. Now that the Wilkins case was over, I didn't have anything better to do anyway. I'd only managed about seven billable hours, damn it all, and even that had taken some padding.

I walked into the center along Ninth Avenue, passing filthy prospectors, the aftermath of a fight in which some schmuck in a pool of blood was being tended to by your proverbial hooker-with-the-heart-of-gold, and a broken-down robot trying to make its way along with only three of its four legs working properly.

I entered the lobby of the police station, traded quips with the ineluctable Huxley, and was admitted to the back.

"Hey, Mac," I said. "What's up?"

"Morning, Alex," Mac said, rolling the *R* in "Morning." "Come in; sit down." He spoke to his desk terminal and turned its monitor around so I could see it. "Have a look at this."

I glanced at the screen. "The report on Joshua Wilkins?"

Mac nodded. "Look at the section on the artificial brain."

I skimmed the text until I found that part. "Yeah?" I said, still not getting it.

"Do you know what 'baseline synaptic web' means?"

"No, I don't. And you didn't either, smart-ass, until someone told you."

Mac smiled a little, conceding that. "Well, there were lots of bits of the artificial brain left behind. And that big guy at NewYou—Fernandez, remember?—he really got into this forensic stuff and decided to run it through some kind of instrument they've got there. And you know what he found?"

"What?"

"The brain stuff—the raw material inside the artificial skull—was pristine. It had never been imprinted."

"You mean no scanned mind had ever been transferred into that brain?"

Mac folded his arms across his chest and leaned back in his chair. "Bingo."

I frowned. "But that's not possible. I mean, if there was no mind in that head, who wrote the suicide note?"

Mac lifted those shaggy eyebrows of his. "Who indeed?" he said. "And what happened to Joshua Wilkins's scanned consciousness?"

"Does anyone at NewYou but Fernandez know about this?"

Mac shook his head. "No, and he's agreed to keep his mouth shut while we continue to investigate. But I thought I'd clue you in, since apparently the case you were on isn't really closed—and, after all, if you don't make money now and again, you can't afford to bribe me for favors."

I nodded. "That's what I like about you, Mac. Always looking out for my best interests."

• • • • • • • • • • •

Perhaps I should have gone straight to see Cassandra Wilkins and made sure we both agreed that I was back on the clock, but I had some questions I wanted answered first. And I knew just who to turn to. Juan Santos was the city's top computer expert. I'd met him during a previous case, and we'd recently struck up a small-f friendship—we both shared the same taste in Earth booze, and he wasn't above joining me at some of New Klondike's sleazier saloons to get it. I called him and we arranged to meet at The Bent Chisel, a wretched little bar off Fourth Avenue, in the sixth concentric ring of buildings. The bartender was a surly man named Buttrick, a biological who had more than his fair share of flesh, and blood as cold as ice. He wore a sleeveless gray shirt and had a three-day growth of salt-and-pepper beard. "Lomax," he said, acknowledging my entrance. "No broken furniture this time, right?"

I held up three fingers. "Scout's honor."

Buttrick held up one finger.

"Hey," I said. "Is that any way to treat one of your best customers?"

"My best customers," said Buttrick, polishing a glass with a ratty towel, "pay their tabs."

"Yeah," I said, stealing a page from Sergeant Huxley's *Guide to Witty Repartee.* "Well." I made my way to a booth at the back. Both waitresses here were topless. My favorite, a cute brunette named Diana, soon came over. "Hey, babe," I said.

She leaned in and gave me a peck on the cheek. "Hi, honey."

The low gravity on Mars was kind to figures and faces, but Diana was still starting to show her forty years. She had shoulder-length brown hair and brown eyes, and was quite pleasantly stacked, although like most long-term Mars residents, she'd lost a lot of the muscle mass she'd come here with. We slept together pretty often but were hardly exclusive.

Juan Santos came in, wearing a black T-shirt and black jeans. He was almost as tall as me, but nowhere near as broad-shouldered; in fact, he was pretty much your typical pencil-necked geek. And like many a pencil-necked geek, he kept setting his sights higher than he should. "Hi, Diana!" he said. "I, um, I brought you something."

Juan was carrying a package wrapped in loose plastic sheeting, which he handed to her.

"Thank you!" she said with enthusiasm before she'd even opened it; I didn't know a lot about Diana's past, but somewhere along the line, someone had taught her good manners. She removed the plastic sheeting, revealing a single, long-stemmed white rose.

Diana actually squealed. Flowers are rare on Mars; those few fields we had were mostly given over to growing either edible plants or genetically modified things that helped scrub the atmosphere. She rewarded Juan with a kiss right on the lips, and that seemed to please him greatly.

I ordered a Scotch on the rocks; they normally did that with carbon dioxide ice here. Juan asked for whiskey. I watched him watching Diana's swinging hips as she headed off to get our drinks. "Well, well, well," I said, as he finally slid into the booth opposite me. "I didn't know you had a thing for her."

He smiled sheepishly. "Who wouldn't?" I said nothing, which Juan took as an invitation to go on. "She hasn't said yes to a date yet, but she promised to let me read some of her poetry."

I kept my tone even. "Lucky you." It seemed kind not to mention that Diana and I were going out this weekend, so I didn't. But I did say, "So, how does a poet sneeze?"

"I don't know, how *does* a poet sneeze?"

"Haiku!"

"Don't quit your day job, Alex."

"Hey," I said, placing a hand over my heart, "you wound me. Down deep, I'm a stand-up comic."

"Well," said Juan, "I always say people should be true to their innermost selves, but . . ."

"Yeah? What's your innermost self?"

"Me?" Juan's eyebrows moved up. "I'm pure genius, right to the very core."

I snorted and Diana reappeared to give us our drinks. We thanked her, and she departed, Juan again watching her longingly as she did so.

When she'd disappeared, he turned back to look at me, and said, "What's up?" His face consisted of a wide forehead, long nose, and receding chin; it made him look like he was leaning forward even when he wasn't.

I took a swig of my drink. "What do you know about transferring?"

"Fascinating stuff," said Juan. "Thinking of doing it?"

"Maybe someday."

"You know, it's supposed to pay for itself now within three mears, because you no longer have to pay life-support tax after you've transferred."

I was in arrears on that, and didn't like to think about what would happen if I fell much further behind. "That'd be a plus," I said. "What about you? You going to do it?"

"Sure, someday—and I'll go the whole nine yards: enhanced senses, super strength, the works. Plus I want to live forever; who doesn't? 'Course, my dad won't like it."

"Your dad? What's he got against it?"

Juan snorted. "He's a minister."

"In whose government?"

"No, no. A *minister*. Clergy."

"I didn't know there were any of those left, even on Earth," I said.

"He *is* on Earth; back in Santiago. But, yeah, you're right. Poor old guy still believes in souls."

I raised my eyebrows. "Really?"

"Yup. And because he believes in souls, he has a hard time with this idea of transferring consciousness. He would say the new version isn't the same person."

I thought about what the supposed suicide note said. "Well, is it?"

Juan rolled his eyes. "You, too? Of course it is! Look, sure, people used to get all worked up about this when the process first appeared, decades ago, but now just about everyone is blasé about it. NewYou should take a lot of credit for that; they've done a great job of keeping the issue uncluttered—I'm sure they knew if they'd done otherwise, there'd have been all sorts of ethical debates, red tape, and laws constraining their business. But they've avoided most of that by providing one, and only one, service: moving—not copying, not duplicating, but simply moving—a person's mind to a more durable container. Makes the legal transfer of personhood and property a simple matter, ensures that no one gets more than one vote, and so on."

"And is that what they really do?" I asked. "Move your mind?"

"Well, that's what they *say* they do. 'Move' is a nice, safe, comforting word. But the mind is just software, and since the dawn of computing, software has been moved from one computing platform to another by copying it over, then immediately erasing the original."

"But the new brain is artificial, right? How come we can make super-smart transfers, but not super-smart robots or computers?"

Juan took a sip of his drink. "It's not a contradiction at all. No one ever figured out how to program anything equivalent to a human mind—they used to talk about the coming 'singularity,' when artificial intelligence would exceed human abilities, but that never happened. But when you're scanning and digitizing the entire structure of a brain in minute detail, you obviously get the intelligence as part of that scan, even if no one can point to where that intelligence is *in* the scan."

"Huh," I said, and took a sip of my own. "So, if you were to transfer, what would you have fixed in your new body?"

Juan spread his praying-mantis arms. "Hey, man, you don't tamper with perfection."

"Hah," I said. "Still, how much could you change things? I mean, say you're only 150 centimeters, and you want to play basketball. Could you opt to be two meters tall?"

"Sure, of course."

I frowned. "But wouldn't the copied mind have trouble with your new size?"

"Nah," said Juan. "See, when Howard Slapcoff first started copying consciousness, he let the old software from the old mind actually try to directly control the new body. It took months to learn how to walk again, and so on."

"Yeah, I read something about that, years ago."

Juan nodded. "Right. But now they don't let the copied mind do anything but give orders. The thoughts are intercepted by the new body's main computer. *That* unit runs the body. All the transferred mind has to do is *think* that it wants to pick up this glass, say." He acted out his example, and took a sip, then winced in response to the booze's kick. "The computer takes care of working out which pulleys to contract, how far to reach, and so on."

"So you could order up a body radically different from your original?"

"Absolutely." He looked at me through hooded eyes. "Which, in your case, is probably the route to go."

"Damn."

"Hey, don't take it seriously," he said, taking another sip and allowing himself another pleased wince.

"It's just that I was hoping it wasn't that way. See, this case I'm on: the guy I'm supposed to find owns the NewYou franchise here."

"Yeah?" said Juan.

"Yeah, and I think he deliberately transferred his scanned mind into some body other than the one that he'd ordered up for himself."

"Why would he do that?"

"He faked the death of the body that looked like him—and I think he'd planned to do that all along, because he never bothered to order up any improvements to his face. I think he wanted to get away, but make it look like he was dead, so no one would be looking for him anymore."

"And why would he do that?"

I frowned then drank some more. "I'm not sure."

"Maybe he wanted to escape his spouse."

"Maybe—but she's a hot little number."

"Hmm," said Juan. "Whose body do you think he took?"

"I don't know that, either. I was hoping the new body would have to be roughly similar to his old one; that would cut down on the possible suspects. But I guess that's not the case."

"It isn't, no."

I looked down at my drink. The dry-ice cubes were sublimating into white vapor that filled the top part of the glass.

"Something else is bothering you," said Juan. I lifted my head and saw him taking a swig of his drink. A little amber liquid spilled out of his mouth and formed a shiny bead on his recessed chin. "What is it?"

I shifted a bit. "I visited NewYou yesterday. You know what happens to your original body after they move your mind?"

"Sure," said Juan. "Like I said, there's no such thing as moving software. You copy it then delete the original. They euthanize the biological version once the transfer is completed."

I nodded. "And if the guy I'm looking for put his mind into the body intended for somebody else's mind, and that person's mind wasn't copied anywhere, then . . ." I took another swig of my drink. "Then it's murder, isn't it? Souls or no souls—it doesn't matter. If you wipe the one and only copy of someone's mind, you've murdered that person, right?"

"Oh, yes," said Juan. "Deader than Mars itself."

I glanced down at the swirling fog in my glass. "So I'm not just looking for a husband who's skipped out on his wife. I'm looking for a cold-blooded killer."

FIVE

I went by NewYou again. Cassandra wasn't in, but that didn't surprise me; she was a grieving widow now. But Horatio Fernandez—he of the massive arms—was on duty.

"I'd like a list of everyone who transferred the same day as Joshua Wilkins," I said.

He frowned. "That's confidential information."

There were several potential customers milling about. I raised my voice so they could hear. "Interesting suicide note, wasn't it?"

Fernandez grabbed my arm and led me quickly to the side of the room. "What the hell are you doing?" he whispered angrily.

"Just sharing the news," I said, still speaking loudly, although not quite loud enough now, I thought, for the customers to hear. "People thinking of uploading should know that it's not the same—at least, that's what Joshua Wilkins said in that note."

Fernandez knew when he was beaten. The claim in the putative suicide note was exactly the opposite of NewYou's corporate position: transferring was supposed to be flawless, conferring nothing but benefits. "All right, all right," he hissed. "I'll pull the list for you."

"Now that's service. They should name you employee of the month."

He led me into the back room and spoke to a little cubic computer. I happened to overhear the passphrase for accessing the customer database; it was just six words—hardly any security at all.

"Huh," said Fernandez. "It was a busy day—we go days on end without anyone transferring, but seven people moved their consciousnesses into artificial bodies that day, and—oh, yeah. We were having our twice-a-mear sale. No wonder." He held out a hand. "Give me your tab."

I handed him the small tablet computer and he copied the files on each of the seven to it.

"Thanks," I said, taking back the device and doing that tip-of-the-nonexistent-hat thing I do. Even when you've forced a man to do something, there's no harm in being polite.

. . . .

If I was right that Joshua Wilkins had appropriated the body of somebody else who had been scheduled to transfer the same day, it shouldn't be too hard to determine whose body he'd taken; all I had to do, I figured, was interview each of the seven.

My first stop, purely because it happened to be the nearest, was the home of a guy named Stuart Berling, a full-time fossil hunter. He must have had some recent success, if he could afford to transfer.

On the way to his place, I walked past several panhandlers, one of whom had a sign that said, "Will work for air." The cops didn't kick those who were in arrears in their life-support tax payments out of the dome—Slapcoff Industries still had a reputation to maintain on Earth—but if you rented or had a mortgage, you'd be evicted onto the street.

Berling's home was off Seventh Avenue, in the Fifth Circle. It was part of a row of crumbling townhouses, the kind we called redstones. I pushed his door buzzer and waited impatiently for a response. At last he appeared.

If I wasn't so famous for my poker face, I'd have done a double take. The man who greeted me was a dead ringer for Krikor Ajemian, the holovid star—the same gaunt features and intense brown eyes, the same mane of dark hair, the same tightly trimmed beard and mustache. I guess not everyone wanted to keep even a semblance of their original appearance.

"Hello. My name is Alexander Lomax. Are you Stuart Berling?"

The artificial face in front of me surely was capable of smiling but chose not to. "Yes. What do you want?"

"I understand you only recently transferred your consciousness into this body."

A nod. "So?"

"So, I work for NewYou—the head office on Earth. I'm here to check up on the quality of the work done by our franchise here on Mars."

Normally, this was a good technique. If Berling was who he said he was, the question wouldn't faze him. Unfortunately, the usual technique of watching a suspect's expression for signs that he was lying didn't work with most transfers. I'd asked Juan Santos about that once. "It's not that transfer faces are less flexible," he'd said. "In fact, they can make them *more* flexible—let people do wild caricatures of smiles and frowns. But people don't want that, especially here on the frontier. See, there are two kinds of facial expressions: the autonomic ones that happen spontaneously and the forced ones. From a software point of view, they're very different; the mental commands sent to fake a smile and to make a spontaneous smile are utterly dissimilar. Most transfers here opt for their automatic expressions to be subdued—they value the privacy of their thoughts and don't want their faces advertising them; they consider it one of the pluses of having transferred. The transferee may be grinning from ear to ear on the inside, but on the outside, he just shows a simple smile."

Berling was staring at me with an expression that didn't tell me anything. But his voice was annoyed. "So?" he said again.

"So I'm wondering if you were satisfied by the work we did for you?"

"It cost a lot."

I smiled. "It's actually come down a great deal recently. May I come in?"

He considered this for a few moments then shrugged. "Sure, why not?" He stepped aside.

His living room was full of worktables covered with reddish rocks from outside the dome. A giant lens on an articulated arm was attached to one of the tables, and various mineralogist's tools were scattered about.

"Finding anything interesting?" I asked, gesturing at the rocks.

"If I was, I certainly wouldn't tell you," said Berling, looking at me sideways in the typical paranoid-prospector way.

"Right," I said. "Of course. So, *are* you satisfied with the NewYou process?"

"Sure, yeah. It's everything they said it would be. All the parts work."

"Thanks for your help," I said, pulling out my tab to make a few notes, and then frowning at its blank screen. "Oh, damn. The silly thing has a loose excimer pack. I've got to open it up and reseat it." I showed him the back of the unit's case. "Do you have a little screwdriver that will fit that?"

Everybody owned some screwdrivers, even though most people rarely needed them, and they were the sort of thing that had no standard storage location. Some people kept them in kitchen drawers, others kept them in tool chests, still others kept them under the sink. Only a person who had lived in this home for a while would know where they were.

Berling peered at the slot-headed screw, then nodded. "Sure. Hang on."

He made a beeline for the far side of the living room, going to a cabinet that had glass doors on its top half but solid metal ones on its bottom. He bent over, opened one of the metal doors, reached in, rummaged for a bit, and emerged with the appropriate screwdriver.

"Thanks," I said, opening the case in such a way that he couldn't see inside. I then surreptitiously removed the bit of plastic I'd used to insulate the excimer battery from the contact it was supposed to touch. Without looking up, I said, “Are you married, Mr. Berling?” Of course, I already knew the answer was yes; that fact was in his NewYou file.

He nodded.

“Is your wife home?”

His artificial eyelids closed a bit. “Why?”

I told him the honest truth since it fit well with my cover story: “I’d like to ask her whether she can perceive any differences between the new you and the old.”

Again, I watched his expression, but it didn’t change. “Sure, I guess that’d be okay.” He turned and called over his shoulder, “Lacie!”

A few moments later, a homely flesh-and-blood woman of about sixty appeared. “This is Mr. Lomax from the head office of NewYou,” said Berling, indicating me with a pointed finger. “He’d like to talk to you.”

“About what?” asked Lacie. She had a deep, not-unpleasant voice.

“Might we speak in private?” I asked.

Berling’s gaze shifted from Lacie to me, then back to Lacie. “Hrmpph,” he said, but then a moment later added, “I guess that’d be all right.” He turned around and walked away.

I looked at Lacie. “I’m just doing a routine follow-up,” I said. “Making sure people are happy with the work we do. Have you noticed any changes in your husband since he transferred?”

“Not really.”

“Oh? If there’s anything at all . . .” I smiled reassuringly. “We want to make the process as perfect as possible. Has he said anything that’s surprised you, say?”

Lacie crinkled her face even more than it normally was. “How do you mean?”

“I mean, has he used any expressions or turns of phrase you’re not used to hearing from him?”

A shake of the head. “No.”

"Sometimes the process plays tricks with memory. Has he failed to know something he should know?"

"Not that I've noticed."

"What about the reverse? Has he known anything that you wouldn't expect him to know?"

Lacie lifted her eyebrows. "No. He's just Stu."

I frowned. "No changes at all?"

"No, none . . . well, almost none."

I waited for her to go on, but she didn't, so I prodded her. "What is it? We really would like to know about any difference, any flaw in our transference process."

"Oh, it's not a flaw," said Lacie, not meeting my eyes.

"No? Then what?"

"It's just that . . ."

"Yes?"

"Well, just that he's a demon in the sack now. He stays hard forever."

I frowned, disappointed not to have found what I was looking for on the first try. But I decided to end the masquerade on a positive note. "We aim to please, ma'am. We aim to please."

SIX

I spent the next several hours tracking down and interviewing three other recent transfers; none of them seemed to be anyone other than who they claimed to be.

After that, the next name on my list was one Dr. Rory Pickover. His home was in a cubic apartment building located on the outer side of the First Circle, beneath the highest point of the dome; several windows were boarded up on its first and second floors, but he lived on the fourth, where all but one of the panes seemed to be intact. Someone was storing a broken set of springy Mars buggy wheels on one of the balconies. From another balcony, a crazy old coot was shouting obscenities at those making their way along the curving sidewalk. Most of the people were ignoring him, but two kids—a grimy boy and an even grimier girl, each about twelve but tall and spindly in the way kids born here tend to be—decided to start shouting back.

Pickover lived alone, so there was no spouse or child to question about any changes in him. That made me suspicious right off the bat: if one were going to choose an identity to appropriate, it ideally would be someone without close companions.

I buzzed him from the lobby. A drunk sleeping by the buzzboard was disturbed enough by the sound to roll onto his side but otherwise didn't interfere with me.

"Hello?" said a male voice higher pitched than my own.

"Mr. Pickover, my name is Alex Lomax. I'm from the NewYou head office on Earth. I'm wondering if I might ask you a few questions?"

He had a British accent. "Lomax, did you say? You're Alexander Lomax?"

"I am, yes. I'm wondering if we might speak for a few minutes?"

"Well, yes, but . . ."

"But what?"

"Not here," he said. "Let's go outside."

I was pissed, because that meant I couldn't try the screwdriver trick on him. But I said, "Fine. There's a café on the other side of the circle."

"No, no. *Outside.* Outside the dome."

That was easy for him; he was a transfer now. But it was a pain in the ass for me; I'd have to rent a surface suit.

"Seriously? I only want to ask to ask you a couple of questions."

"Yes, yes, but *I* want to talk to you and . . ." The voice grew soft. ". . . and it's a delicate matter, deserving of privacy."

The drunk near me rolled onto his other side and let out a wheezy snore.

"Oh, all right," I said.

"Good chap," replied Pickover. "I'm just in the middle of something up here. About an hour from now, say? Just outside the east airlock?"

"Can we make it the west one? I can swing by my office on the way, then." I didn't need anything from there—I was already packing heat—but if he had some sort of ambush planned, I figured he'd object to the change.

"That's fine, that's fine—all four airlocks are the same distance from here, after all! But now, I really must finish what I'm doing . . ."

• • • • • • • • • • •

Of course I was suspicious about what Rory Pickover was up to and so I tipped Mac off before making my way to the western airlock. The sun was setting outside the dome by the time I got there to suit up. Surface suits came in three stretchy sizes; I put on one of largest, then slung the air tanks onto my back. I felt heavy in the suit, even though in it I still weighed only about half of what I had back on Earth.

Rory Pickover was a paleontologist—an actual scientist, not a treasure-seeking fossil hunter. His pre-transfer appearance had been almost stereotypically academic: a round, soft face, with a fringe of graying hair. His new body was lean and muscular, and he had a full head of dark brown hair, but the face was still recognizably his own. His suit had a loop on its waist holding a geologist's hammer with a wide, flat blade; I rather suspected it would nicely smash my fishbowl helmet. I surreptitiously transferred the Smith & Wesson from the holster I wore under my jacket to an exterior pocket on the rented surface suit, just in case I needed it while we were outside.

We signed the security logs and then let the technician cycle us through the airlock.

Overhead, the sky was growing dark. Nearby, there were two large craters and a cluster of smaller ones. There were few footprints in the rusty sand; the recent storm had obliterated the thousands that had doubtless been there earlier. We walked out about five hundred meters. I turned around briefly to look back at the transparent dome and the ramshackle buildings within.

"Sorry for dragging you out here, old boy," said Pickover. "I don't want any witnesses." There was a short-distance radio microphone inside that mechanical throat for speaking outside the dome, and I had a transceiver inside my fishbowl.

"Ah," I said, by way of reply.

"I know you aren't just in from Earth," said Pickover, continuing to walk. "And I know you don't work for NewYou."

We were casting long shadows. The sun, so much tinier than it appeared from Earth, was sitting on the horizon now. The sky was already purpling, and Earth itself was visible, a bright blue-white evening star. It was much easier to see it out here than through the dome, and, as always, I thought for a moment of Wanda as I looked up at it. But then I lowered my gaze to Pickover. "Who do you think I am?"

His answer surprised me, although I didn't let it show. "You're the private-detective chap."

It didn't seem to make any sense to deny it. "Yeah. How'd you know?"

"I've been checking you out over the last few days," said Pickover. "I'd been thinking of, ah, engaging your services."

We continued to walk along, little clouds of dust rising each time our feet touched the ground. "What for?"

"You first, if you don't mind," Pickover replied. "Why did you really come to see me?"

He already knew who I was, and I had a very good idea who he was. I had my phone on the outside of my suit's left wrist, and it was connected to the headset in my helmet. "Call Dougal McCrae."

"What are you doing?" Pickover asked.

"Hey, Alex," said Mac from the little screen on my wrist; I heard his voice over the fishbowl's headset.

"Mac, listen, I'm about half a klick straight out from the west airlock. I'm going to need backup.

"Lomax, what *are* you doing?" asked Pickover.

"Kaur is already outside the dome," said Mac, looking offscreen. "She can be there in two minutes." He switched voice channels for a moment, presumably speaking to Sergeant Kaur. Then he turned back to me. "She's north of you; she's got you on her infrared scanner.

Pickover looked over his shoulder, and perhaps saw the incoming cop with his own infrared vision. But then he turned back to me and spread his arms in the darkness. "Lomax, for God's sake, what's going on?"

I shook my phone, breaking the connection with Mac, and pulled out my revolver. It really wouldn't be much use against an artificial body, but until quite recently Joshua Wilkins had been biological; I hoped he was still intimidated by guns. "That's quite a lovely wife you have."

Pickover's artificial face looked perplexed. "Wife?"

"That's right."

"I don't have a wife."

"Sure you do. You're Joshua Wilkins, and your wife's name is Cassandra."

"What? No, I'm Rory Pickover. You know that. You called me."

"Come off it, Wilkins. The jig is up. You transferred your consciousness into the body intended for the real Rory Pickover, and then you took off."

"I—oh. Oh, Christ."

"So, you see, I know. And—ah, here's Sergeant Kaur now. Too bad, Wilkins. You'll hang—or whatever the hell they do with transfers—for murdering Pickover."

"No." He said it softly.

"Yes," I replied. Kaur was a sleek form about a hundred meters behind Pickover. "Let's go."

"Where?"

"Back under the dome, to the police station. I'll have Cassandra meet us there, just to confirm your identity."

The sun had slipped below the horizon now. He spread his arms, a supplicant against the backdrop of the gathering night. "Okay, sure, if you like. Call up this Cassandra, by all means. Let her talk to me. She'll tell you after questioning me for two seconds that I'm not her husband. But—Christ, damn, Christ."

"What?"

"I want to find him, too."

"Who? Joshua Wilkins?"

He nodded, then, perhaps thinking I couldn't see his nod in the growing darkness, said, "Yes."

"Why?"

He tipped his head up as if thinking. I followed his gaze. Phobos was visible, a dark form overhead. At last, he spoke again. "Because *I'm* the reason he's disappeared."

"What? Why?"

"That's why I was thinking of hiring you myself. I didn't know where else to turn."

"Turn for what?"

Pickover looked at me. "I did go to NewYou, Mr. Lomax. I knew I was going to have an enormous amount of work to do out here on the surface now, and I wanted to be able to spend weeks—months!—in the field without worrying about running out of air or water or food."

I frowned. "But you've been here on Mars for six mears; I read that in your file. What's changed?"

"*Everything*, Mr. Lomax." He looked off in the distance. "Everything!" But he didn't elaborate on that. Instead, he said, "I certainly know this Wilkins chap you're looking for. I went to his shop and had him transfer my consciousness from my old biological body into this one. But he also kept a copy of my mind—I'm sure of that."

"That's . . ." I shook my head. "I've never heard of that being done."

"Nor had I," said Pickover. "I mean, I understood from their sales materials that your consciousness sort of, um, hops into the artificial body. Because of that, I didn't think duplicates were possible at the time I did it, or I never would have undergone the process."

Kaur was now about thirty meters away, and she had a big rifle aimed at Pickover's back. I held up a hand, palm out, to get the cop to stand her ground.

"Prove it to me," I said. "Prove to me you are who you say you are.

Tell me something Joshua Wilkins couldn't know, but a paleontologist would."

"Oh, for Pete's—"

"Tell me!"

"Fine, fine. The most-recent fossils here on Mars date from what's called the Noachian efflorescence, a time of morphological diversification similar to Earth's Cambrian explosion. So far, twenty-seven distinct genera from then have been identified—well, it was originally twenty-nine but I successfully showed that both *Weinbaumia* and *Gallunia* are junior synonyms of *Bradburia.* Within *Bradburia* there are six distinct species, the most common of which is *B. breviceps,* known for its bifurcated pygidia and—"

"Okay!" I said. "Enough." I held up fingers to show Kaur which radio frequency I was using and watched her tap it into her wrist keypad. "Sorry, Sergeant," I said. "False alarm."

The woman nodded. "You owe me one, Lomax." She lowered her rifle and headed past us toward the airlock.

I didn't want Kaur listening in, so I changed frequencies again and indicated with hand signs to Pickover which one I'd selected. He didn't do anything obvious, but I soon heard his voice. "As I said, I think Wilkins made a copy of my mind."

It was certainly illegal to do that, probably unethical, and perhaps not even technically possible; I'd have to ask Juan. "Why do you think that?"

"It's the only explanation for how my computer accounts have become compromised. There's no way anyone but me can get in; I'm the only one who knows the passphrase. But someone *has* been inside, looking around; I use quantum encryption, so you can tell whenever someone has even *looked* at a file." He shook his head. "I don't know how he did it—there must be some technique I'm unaware of—but somehow Wilkins has been extracting information from a copy of my mind. That's the only way I can think of that anyone might have learned my passphrase."

"You think Wilkins did all that to access your bank accounts? Is there really enough money in them to make it worthwhile? It's gotten too dark to see your clothes but, if I recall correctly, they looked a bit . . . shabby."

"You're right. I'm just a poor scientist. But there's something I know that could make the wrong people rich beyond their wildest dreams."

"And what's that?" I said.

He stood there, trying to decide, I suppose, whether to trust me. I let him think about that, and at last Dr. Rory Pickover, who was now just a starless silhouette against a starry sky, said, in a soft, quiet voice, "I know where it is."

"Where what is?"

"The Alpha Deposit."

"My God. You'll be *rolling* in it."

Perhaps he shook his head; it was now too dark to tell. "No, sir," he replied in that cultured British voice. "No, I won't. I don't want to *sell* these fossils. I want to preserve them; I want to protect them from these plunderers, these . . . these *thieves.* I want to make sure they're collected properly, scientifically. I want them to end up in the best museums, where they can be studied. There's so much to be learned, so much to discover!"

"Does Joshua Wilkins now know where the Alpha Deposit is?"

"No—at least, not from accessing my computer files. I didn't record the location anywhere but up here." Presumably he was tapping the side of his head.

"But if Wilkins could extract your passphrase from a copy of your mind, why didn't he just directly extract the location of the Alpha from it?"

"The passphrase is straightforward—just a string of words—but the Alpha's location, well, it's not like it has an address, and even I don't know the longitude and latitude by heart. Rather, I know where it is by reference to certain geological features that would be meaningless to a non-expert; it would take a lot more work to extract that, I'd warrant. And so he tried the easier method of spelunking in my computer files."

I shook my head. "This doesn't make any sense. I mean, how would Wilkins even know that you had discovered the Alpha Deposit?"

Suddenly Pickover's voice was very small. "I'd gone in to NewYou—you have to go there in advance of transferring, of course, so you can tell them what you want in a new body; it takes time to custom-build one to your specifications."

"Yes. So?"

"So I wanted a body ideally suited to paleontological work on the surface of Mars; I wanted some special modifications—the kinds of the things only the most successful prospectors could afford. Reinforced knees; extra arm strength for moving rocks; extended spectral response in the eyes so that fossils will stand out better; night vision so that I could continue digging after dark. But . . ."

I nodded. "But you didn't have enough money."

"That's right. I could barely afford to transfer at all, even into the cheapest off-the-shelf body, and so . . ."

He trailed off, too angry at himself, I guess, to give voice to what was in his mind. "And so you hinted that you were about to come into some wealth," I said, "and suggested that maybe he could give you what you needed now, and you'd make it up to him later."

Pickover sounded sad. "That's the trouble with being a scientist; sharing information is our natural mode."

"Did you tell him precisely what you'd found?"

"No. No, but he must have guessed. I'm a paleontologist, I've been studying Weingarten and O'Reilly for years—all of that is a matter of public record. He must have figured out that I knew where their prime fossil bed was. After all, where else would a bloke like me get money?" He sighed. "I'm an idiot, aren't I?"

"Well, Mensa isn't going to be calling you anytime soon."

"Please don't rub it in, Mr. Lomax. I feel bad enough as it is."

I nodded. "But if he suspected you'd found the Alpha, maybe he just put a tracking chip in this new body of yours. Sure, that's against the law, but that would have been the simplest way for him to get at it."

Pickover rallied a bit, pleased, I guess, that he'd at least thought of this angle. "No, no, he didn't. A tracking chip has to transmit a signal to do any good; they're easy enough to locate, and I made sure he knew I knew that before I transferred. Nonetheless, I had myself checked over after the process was completed. I'm positive I'm clean."

"And so you think he's found another way," I said.

"Yes! And if he succeeds in locating the Alpha, all will be lost! The specimens will be sold off into private collections—trophies for billionaires' estates, hidden forever from science." He looked at me with imploring acrylic eyes and his voice cracked; I'd never heard a transfer's do that before. "All those wondrous fossils are in jeopardy! Will you help me, Mr. Lomax? Please say you'll help me!"

Two clients were, of course, always better than one—at least as far as the bank account was concerned. "All right," I said. "Let's talk about my fee."

SEVEN

After Rory Pickover and I went back into the dome, I called Juan, asking him to meet us at Pickover's little apartment at the center of town. Rory and I got there before him, and went on up; the drunk who'd been in the entryway earlier had gone.

Pickover's apartment—an interior unit, with no windows—consisted of three small rooms. While we waited for Juan, the good doctor—trusting soul that he was—showed me three fossils he'd recovered from the Alpha, and even to my untrained eye, they were stunning. The specimens—all invertebrate exoskeletons—had been removed from the matrix, cleaned, and painstakingly prepared.

The first was something about the size of my fist, with dozens of tendrils extending from it, some ending in three-fingered pincers, some in four-fingered ones, and the two largest in five-fingered ones.

The next was the length of my forearm. It was dumbbell-shaped, with numerous smaller hemispheres embedded in each of the globes. I couldn't make head or tail of it, but Pickover confidently assured me that globe on the left was the former and the one on the right the latter.

The final specimen he showed me was, he said, his pride and joy—the only one of its kind so far discovered: it was a stony ribbon that, had it been stretched out, would have been maybe eighty centimeters long. But it wasn't stretched out; rather, it was joined together in a Möbius strip. Countless cilia ran along the edges of the ribbon—I was stunned to see that such fine detail had been preserved—and the strip was perforated at intervals by diamond-shaped openings with serrated edges.

I looked at Pickover, who was chuffed, to use the word he himself might have, to show off his specimens, and I half listened as he went on about their incredible scientific value. But all I could think about was how much money they must be worth—and the fact that there were countless more like them out there of this same quality.

When Juan finally buzzed from the lobby, Rory covered his specimens with cloth sheets. The elevator was out of order, but that was no problem in this gravity; Juan wasn't breathing hard when he reached the apartment door.

"Juan Santos," I said, as he came in, "this is Rory Pickover. Juan here is the best computer expert we've got in New Klondike. And Dr. Pickover is a paleontologist."

Juan dipped his broad forehead toward Pickover. "Good to meet you."

"Thank you," said Pickover. "Forgive the mess, Mr. Santos. I live alone. A lifelong bachelor gets into bad habits, I'm afraid." He'd already cleared debris off one chair for me; he now busied himself doing the same with another, this one right in front of his computer, a silver-and-blue cube about the size of a grapefruit.

"What's up, Alex?" asked Juan, indicating Pickover with a movement of his head. "New client?"

"Yeah. Dr. Pickover's computer files have been looked at by some unauthorized individual. We're wondering if you could tell us where the access attempt was made from."

"You'll owe me a nice round of drinks at The Bent Chisel," said Juan.

"No problem," I said. "I'll put it on my tab."

Juan smiled and stretched his arms out in front of him, fingers interlocked, and cracked his knuckles, like a safecracker preparing to get down to work. Then he took the now-clean seat in front of Pickover's computer cube, tilted the nearby monitor up a bit, pulled a keyboard into place, and began to type. "How do you lock your files?" he asked, without taking his eyes off the monitor.

"A verbal passphrase," said Pickover.

"Anybody besides you know it?"

"No."

"And it's not written down anywhere?"

"No, well . . . not as such."

Juan turned his head, looking up at Pickover. "What do you mean?"

"It's a line from a book. If I ever forget the exact wording, I can always look it up."

Juan shook his head in disgust. "You should always use random passphrases." He typed keys.

"Oh, I'm sure it's totally secure," said Pickover. "No one would guess—"

Juan interrupted. "—that your passphrase is 'Those privileged to be present—'"

I saw Pickover's artificial jaw drop. "My God. How did you know that?"

Juan pointed to some data on the screen. "It's the first thing that was inputted by the only outside access your system has had in weeks."

"I thought passphrases were hidden from view when entered," said Pickover.

"Sure they are," said Juan. "But the comm program has a buffer; it's in there. Look."

Juan shifted in the chair so that Pickover could see the screen clearly over his shoulder. "That's . . . well, that's very strange," Pickover said.

"What?"

"Well, sure, that's my passphrase, but it's not quite right."

I loomed in to have a peek at the screen, too. "How do you mean?"

"Well," said Pickover, "see, my passphrase is 'Those privileged to be present at a family festival of the Forsytes'—it's from the opening of *The Man of Property,* the first book of the Forsyte Saga by John Galsworthy. I love that phrase because of the alliteration—'privileged to be present,' 'family festival of the Forsytes.' Makes it easy to remember."

Juan shook his head in you-can't-teach-people-anything disgust. Pickover went on. "But, see, whoever it was typed even more."

I looked at the glowing string of letters. In full it said: *Those privileged to be present at a family festival of the Forsytes have seen them dine at half past eight, enjoying seven courses.*

"It's too much?" I asked.

"That's right," said Pickover, nodding. "My passphrase ends with the word 'Forsytes.'"

Juan was stroking his receding chin. "Doesn't matter," he said. "The files would unlock the moment the phrase was complete; the rest would just be discarded—systems that principally work with spoken commands don't require you to press the enter key."

"Yes, yes, yes," said Pickover. "But the rest of it isn't what Galsworthy wrote. It's not even close. *The Man of Property* is my favorite book; I know it well. The full opening line is 'Those privileged to be present at a family festival of the Forsytes have seen that charming and instructive sight—an upper middle-class family in full plumage.' Nothing about the time they ate, or how many courses they had."

Juan pointed at the text on screen as if it had to be the correct version. "Are you sure?"

"Of course!" replied Pickover. "Do a search and see for yourself."

I frowned. "No one but you knows your passphrase, right?"

Pickover nodded vigorously. "I live alone, and I don't have many friends; I'm a quiet sort. There's no one I've ever told, and no one who could have ever overheard me saying it, or seen me typing it in."

"Somebody found it out," said Juan.

Pickover looked at me, then down at Juan. "I think . . ." he said, beginning slowly, giving me a chance to stop him, I guess, before he said too much. But I let him go on. "I think that the information was extracted from a scan of my mind made by NewYou."

Juan crossed his arms in front of his chest. "Impossible."

"What?" said Pickover, and "Why?" said I.

"Can't be done," said Juan. "We know how to copy the vast array of interconnections that make up a human mind, and we know how to reinstantiate those connections on an artificial substrate. But we don't know how to decode them; nobody does. There's simply no way to sift through a digital copy of a mind and extract specific data."

Damn! If Juan was right—and he always was in computing matters—then all this business with Pickover was a red herring. There probably was no bootleg scan of his mind; despite his protestations of being careful, someone likely had just overheard his passphrase and decided to go hunting through his files. While I was wasting time on this, Joshua Wilkins was doubtless slipping further out of my grasp.

Still, it was worth continuing this line of investigation for a few minutes more. "Any sign of where the access attempt was made?" I asked Juan.

He shook his head. "No. Whoever did it knew what they were doing; they covered their tracks well. The attempt came over an outside line—that's all I can tell for sure."

I nodded. "Okay. Thanks, Juan. Appreciate your help."

He got up. "My pleasure. Now, how 'bout that drink?"

I opened my mouth to say yes, but then it hit me—what Wilkins must be doing. "Umm, later, okay? I've got some more things to take care of here."

Juan frowned; he'd clearly hoped to collect his booze immediately. But I started maneuvering him toward the door. "Thanks for your help. I really appreciate it."

"Um, sure, Alex," he said. He was obviously aware he was being given the bum's rush, but he wasn't fighting it too much. "Anytime."

"Yes, thank you awfully, Mr. Santos," said Pickover.

"No problem. If—"

"See you later, Juan," I said, opening the door for him. "Thanks so much." I tipped my nonexistent hat at him.

Juan shrugged, clearly aware that something was up but not motivated sufficiently to find out what. He went through the door, and I hit the button that caused it to slide shut behind him. As soon as it was closed, I put an arm around Pickover's shoulders and propelled him back to the computer. I pointed at the line Juan had highlighted on the screen and read the ending of it aloud: "' . . . dine at half past eight, enjoying seven courses.'"

Pickover nodded. "Yes. So?"

"Numbers are often coded info," I said. "'Half past eight; seven courses.' What's that mean to you?"

"To me? Nothing. Back when I ate, I liked to do it much earlier than that, and I never had more than one course."

"But it could be a message."

"From whom?"

There was no easy way to tell him this. "From you to you."

He drew his artificial eyebrows together. "What?"

"Look," I said, motioning for him to sit down in front of the computer, "Juan is doubtless right. You can't sift a digital scan of a human mind for information."

"But that must be what Wilkins is doing."

I shook my head. "No. The only way to find out what's in a mind is to ask it interactively."

"But . . . but no one's asked me my passphrase."

"No one has asked *this* you. But Joshua Wilkins must have transferred the extra copy of your mind into a body, so that he could deal with it directly. And that extra copy must have revealed your passphrase to him."

"You mean . . . you mean there's another me? Another *conscious* me?"

"Looks that way."

"But . . . no, no. That's . . . why, that's *illegal.* Bootleg copies of human beings—my God, Lomax, it's obscene!"

"I'm going to go see if I can find him," I said.

"It," said Pickover forcefully.

"What?"

"It. Not him. I'm the only 'him'—the only real Rory Pickover." He shuddered. "My God, Lomax, I feel so . . . so violated! A stolen, active copy of my mind! It's the ultimate invasion of privacy . . ."

"That may be," I said. "But the bootleg is trying to tell you something. He—*it*—gave Wilkins the passphrase and then tacked some extra words onto it, in order to get a message to you."

"But I don't recognize those extra words," said Pickover, sounding exasperated.

"Do they mean anything to you? Do they suggest anything?"

Pickover re-read the text on the screen. "I can't imagine what," he said, "unless . . . no, no, I'd never think up a code like that."

"You obviously just *did* think of it. What's the code?"

Pickover was quiet for a moment, as if deciding if the thought was worth giving voice. Then: "Well, New Klondike is circular in layout, right? And it consists of concentric rings of buildings. Half past eight—that would be between Eighth and Ninth Avenue, no? And seven courses—in the Seventh Circle out from the center? Maybe the damned bootleg is trying to draw our attention to a location, a specific place here in town."

"The Seventh Circle, off Eighth Avenue," I said. "That's a rough area. I go to a gym near there."

"The shipyard," said Pickover. "Isn't it there, too?"

"Yeah." Dry-dock work was so much easier in a shirtsleeve environment, and, in the early days, repairing and servicing spaceships had been a major business under the dome. I started walking toward the door. "I'm going to investigate."

"I'll go with you," said Pickover.

I shook my head. He would doubtless be more hindrance than help. "It's too dangerous. I should go alone."

Pickover looked for a moment like he was going to protest, but then he nodded. "All right. But if you find another me . . ."

"Yes?" I said. "What would you like me to do?"

Pickover gazed at me with pleading eyes. "Erase it. Destroy it." He shuddered again. "I never want to see the damned thing."

EIGHT

I had to get some sleep—damn, but sometimes I do wish I were a transfer—so I took the hovertram out to my apartment. My place was on Fifth Avenue, which was a great address in New York but a lousy one in New Klondike, especially out near the rim; it was mostly home to people who had tried and failed at fossil hunting, hence its nickname "Sad Sacks Fifth Avenue."

I let myself have six hours—Mars hours, admittedly, which were slightly longer than Earth ones—then I headed out to the old shipyard. The sun was just coming up as I arrived there. The sky through the dome was pink in the east and purple in the west.

Some active maintenance and repair work was still done on spaceships here, but most of these hulks were no longer spaceworthy and had been abandoned. Any one of them would make a good hideout, I thought; spaceships were shielded against radiation, making it hard to scan through their hulls to see what was going on inside.

The shipyard was a large field holding vessels of various sizes and shapes. Most were streamlined—even Mars's tenuous atmosphere required that. Some were squatting on tail fins; some were lying on their bellies; some were supported by articulated legs. I tried every hatch I could see on these craft, but, so far, they all had their airlocks sealed tightly shut.

Finally, I came to a monstrous abandoned spaceliner—a great hull, some three hundred meters long, fifty meters wide, and a dozen meters high. The name *Skookum Jim* was still visible in chipped paint near the bow, which is the part I came across first, and the slogan "Mars or Bust!" had been splashed across the metal surface in a paint that had survived the elements better than the liner's name. I walked a little farther alongside the hull, looking for a hatch, until—

Yes! I finally understood what a fossil hunter felt when he at last turned up a perfectly preserved rhizomorph. There was an outer airlock door and it was open. The other door, inside, was open, too. I stepped through the chamber, entering the ship proper. There were stands for holding space suits but the suits themselves were long gone.

I walked to the far end of the room and found another door—one of those submarine-style ones with a locking wheel in the center. This one was closed; I figured it would probably have been sealed shut at some point, but I tried the wheel anyway, and damned if it didn't spin freely, disengaging the locking bolts. I pulled the door open, then took the flashlight off my belt and aimed it into the interior. It looked safe, so I stepped through. The door was on spring-loaded hinges; as soon as I let go of it, it closed behind me.

The air was dry and had a faint odor of decay to it. I headed down the corridor, the pool of illumination from my flashlight going in front of me, and—

A squealing noise. I swung around, and the beam from my flashlight caught the source before it scurried away: a large brown rat, its eyes two tiny red coals in the light. People had been trying to get rid of the rats—and cockroaches and silverfish and other vermin that had somehow made it here from Earth—for mears.

I turned back around and headed deeper into the ship. The floor wasn't quite level: it dipped a bit to—to starboard, they'd call it—and I also felt that I was gaining elevation as I walked along. The ship's floor had no carpeting; it was just bare, smooth metal. Oily water pooled along the starboard side; a pipe must have ruptured at some point. Another rat scurried by up ahead; I wondered what they ate here, aboard the dead hulk of the ship.

I thought I should check in with Pickover—let him know where I was. I activated my phone, but the display said it was unable to connect. Of course: the radiation shielding in the spaceship's hull kept signals from getting out.

It was growing awfully cold. I held my flashlight straight up in front of my face and saw that my breath was now coming out in visible clouds. I paused and listened. There was a steady dripping sound: condensation, or another leak. I continued along, sweeping the flashlight beam left and right in good detective fashion as I did so.

There were doors at intervals along the corridor—the automatic sliding kind you usually find aboard spaceships. Most ships used hibernation for bringing people to Mars, but this was an old-fashioned spaceliner with cabins; the passengers and crew would have been awake for the whole eight months or more of the journey out.

Most of the door panels had been pried open, and I shined my flashlight into each of the revealed rooms. Some were tiny passenger quarters, some were storage, one was a medical facility—all the equipment had been removed, but the examining beds betrayed the room's function. They were welded down firmly—not worth the effort for scavengers to salvage, I guess.

I checked yet another set of quarters, then came to a closed door, the first one I'd seen along this hallway.

I pushed the open button but nothing happened; the ship's electrical system was dead. There was an emergency handle recessed into the door's thickness. I could have used three hands just then: one to hold my flashlight, one to hold my revolver, and one to pull on the handle. I tucked the flashlight into my right armpit, held my gun with my right hand, and yanked on the recessed handle with my left.

The door hardly budged. I tried again, pulling harder—and almost popped my arm out of its socket. Could the door's tension control have been adjusted to require a transfer's strength to open it? Perhaps.

I tried another pull and, to my astonishment, light began to spill out from the room. I'd hoped to just whip the door open, taking advantage of the element of surprise, but the damned thing was only moving a small increment with each pull of the handle. If there was someone on the other side and he or she had a gun, it was no doubt now leveled directly at the door.

I stopped for a second, shoved the flashlight into my pocket, and—damn, I hated having to do this—holstered my revolver so that I could free up my other hand to help me pull the door open. With both hands now gripping the recessed handle, I tugged with all my strength, letting out a grunt as I did so. The light from within stung my eyes; they'd grown accustomed to the darkness. Another pull, and the door panel had now slid far enough into the wall for me to slip into the room by turning sideways. I took out my gun and let myself in.

A voice, harsh and mechanical, but no less pitiful for that: *"Please . . ."*

My eyes swung to the source of the sound. There was a worktable with a black top attached to the far wall. And strapped to that table—

Strapped to that table was a transfer's synthetic body. But this wasn't like the fancy, almost perfect simulacrum that my client Cassandra inhabited. This was a crude, simple humanoid form with a boxy torso and limbs made up of cylindrical metal segments. And the face—

The face was devoid of any sort of artificial skin. The eyes, blue in color and looking startlingly human, were wide, and the teeth looked like dentures loose in the head. The rest of the face was a mess of pulleys and fiber optics, of metal and plastic.

"Please . . ." said the voice again. I looked around the rest of the room. There was an excimer battery, about the size of a softball, with several ca-

bles snaking out of it, including some that led to portable lights. There was also a closet with a simple door. I pulled it open—this one slid easily—to make sure no one else had hidden in there while I was coming in. An emaciated rat that had been trapped inside at some point scooted out of the closet and through the still-partially-open corridor door.

I turned my attention to the transfer. The body was clothed in simple black denim pants and a beige T-shirt.

"Are you okay?" I said, looking at the skinless face.

The metal skull moved slightly left and right. The plastic lids for the glass eyeballs retracted, making the non-face into a caricature of imploring. *"Please . . ."* he said for a third time.

I looked at the restraints holding the artificial body in place: thin nylon bands attached to the tabletop, pulled taut. I couldn't see any release mechanism. "Who are you?" I asked.

I was half prepared for his answer: "Rory Pickover." But it didn't sound anything like the Rory Pickover I'd met: the cultured British accent was absent, and this synthesized voice was much higher pitched.

Still, I shouldn't take this sad thing's statement at face value—especially since it had hardly any face. "Prove it," I said. "Prove you're Rory Pickover."

The glass eyes looked away. Perhaps the transfer was thinking of how to satisfy my demand—or perhaps he was just avoiding my eyes. "My citizenship number is AG-394-56-432."

I shook my head. "No good," I said. "It's got to be something *only* Rory Pickover would know."

The eyes looked back at me, the plastic lids lowered, perhaps in suspicion. "It doesn't matter who I am," he said. "Just get me out of here."

That sounded reasonable on the surface of it, but if this *was* another Rory Pickover . . .

"Not until you prove your identity to me," I said. "Tell me where the Alpha Deposit is."

"Damn you," said the transfer. "The other way didn't work, so now you're trying this." The mechanical head looked away. "But this won't work, either."

"Tell me where the Alpha Deposit is," I said, "and I'll free you."

"I'd rather die," he said. And then, a moment later, he added wistfully, "Except . . ."

I finished the thought for him. "Except you can't."

He looked away again. It was hard to feel for something that appeared so robotic; that's my excuse, and I'm sticking to it. "Tell me where O'Reilly and Weingarten were digging. Your secret is safe with me."

He said nothing, but my mind was racing and my heart was pounding—those fabulous specimens the other Rory had shown me, the thought of so many more of them out there to be collected, the incalculable wealth they represented. I was startled to discover that my gun was now aimed at the robotic head, and the words "Tell me!" hissed from my lips. "Tell me before—"

Off in the distance, out in the corridor: the squeal of a rat and—

Footfalls.

The transfer heard them, too. Its eyes darted left and right in what looked like panic.

"Please," he said, lowering his volume. As soon as he started speaking, I put a vertical index finger to my lips, indicating that he should be quiet, but he continued: "Please, for the love of God, get me out of here. I can't take any more."

I made a beeline for the closet, stepping in quickly and pulling that door most of the way shut behind me. I positioned myself so that I could see—and, if necessary, shoot—through the gap. The footfalls were growing louder. The closet smelled of rat. I waited.

I heard a voice, richer, more human, than the supposed Pickover's. "What the—?"

And I saw a person—a transfer—slipping sideways into the room, just as I had earlier. I couldn't yet see the face from this angle, but the body was female, and she was a brunette. I took in air, held it, and—

And she turned, showing her face now. My heart pounded. The delicate features. The wide-spaced green eyes.

Cassandra Wilkins.

My client.

She'd been carrying a flashlight, which she set now on another, smaller table. "Who's been here, Rory?" Her voice was cold.

"No one," he said.

"The door was open."

"You left it that way. I was surprised, but . . ." He stopped, perhaps realizing to say any more would be a giveaway that he was lying.

She tilted her head slightly. Even with a transfer's strength, that door must be hard to close. Hopefully, she'd find it plausible that she'd given the handle a final tug and had only assumed that the door had closed completely when she'd last left. Of course, I immediately saw the flaw with that story: you might miss the door not clicking into place, but you wouldn't fail to notice that light was still spilling out into the corridor. But most people don't consider things in such detail; I hoped she'd buy Pickover's suggestion.

And, after a moment's more reflection, she seemed to do just that, nodding her head, apparently to herself, then moving closer to the table onto which the synthetic body was strapped. "We don't have to do this again," said Cassandra. "If you just tell me . . ."

She let the words hang in the air for a moment, but Pickover made no response. Her shoulders moved up and down in a philosophical shrug. "It's your choice," she said. And then, to my astonishment, she hauled back her right arm and slapped Pickover hard across the robotic face, and—

And Pickover screamed.

It was a long, low, warbling sound, like sheet metal being warped, a haunted sound, an inhuman sound.

"*Please* . . ." he hissed again, the same plaintive word he'd said to me, the word I, too, had ignored.

Cassandra slapped him again, and again he screamed. Now, I've been slapped by lots of women over the years: it stings, but I've never screamed. And surely an artificial body was made of sterner stuff than me.

Cassandra went for a third slap. Pickover's screams echoed in the dead hulk of the ship.

"Tell me!" she demanded.

I couldn't see his face; her body was obscuring it. Maybe he shook his head. Maybe he just glared defiantly. But he said nothing.

She shrugged again; they'd obviously been down this road before. She moved to one side of the bed and stood by his right arm, which was pinned to his body by the nylon strap. "You really don't want me to do this," she said. "And I don't have to, if . . ." She let the uncompleted offer hang there for a few seconds, then: "Ah, well." She reached down with her beige, realistic-looking hand and wrapped three of her fingers around his right index finger. And then she started bending it backward.

I could see Pickover's face now. Pulleys along his jawline were working; he was struggling to keep his mouth shut. His glass eyes were rolling up, back into his head, and his left leg was shaking in spasms. It was a bizarre display, and I alternated moment by moment between feeling sympathy for the being lying there and feeling cool detachment because of the clearly artificial nature of the body.

Cassandra let go of Pickover's index finger, and for a second I thought she was showing some mercy. But then she grabbed it as well as the adjacent finger and began bending them both back. This time, despite his best efforts, guttural robotic sounds did escape from Pickover.

"Talk!" Cassandra said. *"Talk!"*

I'd recently learned—from Cassandra herself—that artificial bodies had to have pain sensors; otherwise, a robotic hand might end up resting on a heating element, or too much pressure might be put on a joint. But I hadn't expected such sensors to be so sensitive, and—

And then it hit me, just as another of Pickover's warbling screams was torn from him. Cassandra knew all about artificial bodies; she sold them, after all. If she wanted to adjust the mind-body interface of one so that pain would register particularly acutely, doubtless she could. I'd seen a lot of evil things in my time, but this was the worst. Scan a mind, put it in a body wired for hypersensitivity to pain, and torture it until it gave up its secrets. Then, of course, you just wipe the mind, and—

"You *will* crack eventually, you know," she said, almost conversationally, as she looked at Pickover's fleshless face. "Given that it's inevitable, you might as well just tell me what I want to know."

The elastic bands that served as some of Pickover's facial muscles contracted, his teeth parted, and his head moved forward slightly but rapidly. I thought for half a second that he was incongruously blowing her a kiss, but then I realized what he was really trying to do: spit at her. Of course, his dry mouth and plastic throat were incapable of generating moisture, but his mind—a human mind, a mind accustomed to a biological body—had summoned and focused all its hate into that most primal of gestures.

"Very well," said Cassandra. She gave his fingers one more nasty yank backward, holding them at an excruciating angle. Pickover alternated screams and whimpers. Finally, she let his fingers go. "Let's try something different," she said. She leaned over him. With her left hand, she pried his right eyelid open, and then she jabbed her right thumb into that eye. The glass sphere depressed into the metal skull, and Pickover screamed again. The artificial eye was presumably much tougher than a natural one, but, then again, the thumb pressing into it was also tougher. I felt my own eyes watering in a sympathetic response.

Pickover's artificial spine arched up slightly as he convulsed against the two restraining bands. From time to time, I got clear glimpses of Cassandra's face, and the perfectly symmetrical synthetic smile of glee on it was sickening.

At last, she stopped grinding her thumb into his eye. "Had enough?" she asked. "Because if you haven't . . ."

As I'd said, Pickover was still wearing clothing; it was equally gauche to walk the streets nude whether you were biological or artificial. But now Cassandra's hands moved to his waist. I watched as she undid his belt, unsnapped and unzipped his jeans, and then pulled the pants as far down his metallic thighs as they would go before she reached the restraining strap that held his legs to the table. Transfers had no need for underwear, and Pickover wasn't wearing any. His artificial penis and testicles now lay exposed. I felt my own scrotum tightening in dread.

And then Cassandra did the most astonishing thing. She'd had no compunctions about bending back his fingers with her bare hands. And she hadn't hesitated when it came to plunging her naked thumb into his eye. But now that she was going to hurt him down there, she seemed to want no direct contact. She started scanning around the room. For a second, she was looking directly at the closet door; I scrunched back against the far wall, hoping she wouldn't see me. My heart was pounding.

Finally, she found what she was searching for: a wrench, sitting on the floor. She picked it up, raised it above her head, and looked directly into Pickover's one good eye—the other had closed as soon as she'd removed her thumb and had never reopened as far as I could tell. "I'm going to smash your ball bearings into iron filings, unless . . ."

He closed his other eye now, the plastic lid scrunching.

"Count of three," she said. "One."

"I can't," he said in that low volume that served as his whisper. "You'd ruin the fossils, sell them off—"

"Two."

"Please! They belong to science! To all humanity!"

"Three!"

Her arm slammed down, a great arc slicing through the air, the silver wrench smashing into the plastic pouch that was Pickover's scrotum. He let out a scream greater than any I'd yet heard, so loud, indeed, that it hurt my ears despite the muffling of the partially closed closet door.

She hauled her arm up again, but waited for the scream to devolve into a series of whimpers. "One more chance," she said. "Count of three." His whole body was shaking. I felt nauseous.

"One."

He turned his head to the side, as if by looking away he could make the torture stop.

"Two."

A whimper escaped his artificial throat.

"Three!"

I found myself looking away, too, unable to watch as—

"All right!"

It was Pickover's voice, shrill and mechanical.

"All right!" he shouted again. I turned back to face the tableau: the human-looking woman with a wrench held up above her head and the terrified, mechanical-looking man strapped to the table. "All right," he repeated once more, softly now. "I'll tell you what you want to know."

NINE

"You'll tell me where the Alpha Deposit is?" asked Cassandra, lowering her arm.

"Yes," Pickover said. "Yes."

"Where?"

Pickover was quiet.

"Where?"

"God forgive me . . ." he said softly.

She began to raise her arm again. *"Where?"*

"Head 16.4 kilometers south-southwest of the Nili Patera caldera. There are three craters there, each just under a hundred meters wide, forming a perfect equilateral triangle; the Alpha starts just past the twin fossae about five hundred meters east of them."

Cassandra's phone was doubtless recording all this—as was my own. "I thought it was here in Isidis Planitia."

"It's not—it's in the adjacent planum; that's why no one else has found it yet."

"You better be telling the truth," she said.

"I am." His voice was tiny. "To my infinite shame, I am."

Cassandra nodded. "All right, then. It's time to shut you off for good."

"But I told you the truth! I told you everything you need to know."

"Exactly. And so you're of no further use to me." She took a multi-pronged tool off the small table, returned to Pickover, and opened a hatch in his side.

I stepped out the closet, my gun aimed directly at Cassandra's back. "Freeze," I said.

She spun around. "Lomax!"

"Mrs. Wilkins," I said, nodding. "I guess you don't need me to find your husband for you anymore, eh? Now that you've got the information he was after."

"What? No, no. I still want you to find Joshua. Of course I do!"

"So you can share the wealth with him?"

"Wealth?" She looked over at the hapless Pickover. "Oh. Well, yes, there's a lot of money at stake." She smiled. "So much so that I'd be happy to cut you in, Mr. Lomax—oh, you're a good man. I know you wouldn't hurt me!"

I shook my head. "You'd betray me the first chance you got."

"No, I wouldn't. I'll need protection; I understand that—what with all the money the fossils will bring. Having someone like you on my side only makes sense."

I looked over at Pickover and shook my head. "You tortured that man."

"That 'man,' as you call him, wouldn't have existed at all without me. And the real Pickover isn't inconvenienced in the slightest."

"But . . . *torture,*" I said. "It's inhuman."

She jerked a contemptuous thumb at Pickover. "He's not human. Just some software running on some hardware."

"That's what you are, too."

"That's *part* of what I am," Cassandra said. "But I'm also *authorized.* He's bootleg—and bootlegs have no rights."

"I'm not going to argue philosophy with you."

"Fine. But remember who works for who, Mr. Lomax. I'm the client—and I'm going to be on my way now."

I held my gun rock-steady. "No, you're not."

She looked at me. "An interesting situation," she said, her tone even. "I'm unarmed, and you've got a gun. Normally, that would put you in charge, wouldn't it? But your gun probably won't stop me. Shoot me in the head, and the bullet will just bounce off my metal skull. Shoot me in the chest, and at worst you might damage some components that I'll eventually have to get replaced—which I can, and at a discount, to boot.

"Meanwhile," she continued, "I have the strength of ten men; I could literally pull your limbs from their sockets, or crush your head between my hands, squeezing it until it pops like a melon, and your brains, such as they are, squirt out. So, what's it going to be, Mr. Lomax? Are you going to let me walk out that door and be about my business? Or are you going to pull that trigger, and start something that's going to end with you dead?"

I was used to a gun in my hand giving me a sense of power, of security. But just then, the Smith & Wesson felt like a lead weight. She was right: shooting her with it was likely to be no more useful than just throwing it at her—and yet, if I could drop her with one shot, I'd do it. I'd killed before in self-defense, but . . .

But this wasn't self-defense. Not really. If I didn't start something, she was just going to walk out. Could I kill in cold . . . well, not cold *blood*. And she *was* right: she was a person, even if Pickover wasn't. She was the one and only legal instantiation of Cassandra Wilkins. The cops might be corrupt here, and they might be lazy, but even they wouldn't turn a blind eye on attempted murder under the dome.

"So," she said, at last, "what's it going to be?"

"You make a persuasive argument, Mrs. Wilkins," I said in the most reasonable tone I could muster under the circumstances. And then, without changing my facial expression in the slightest, I pulled the trigger.

I wondered if a transfer's time sense ever slows down, or if it is always perfectly quartz-crystal timed. Certainly, time seemed to attenuate for me then. I swear I could actually see the bullet as it followed its trajectory from my gun, covering the three meters between the barrel and—

And not, of course, Cassandra's torso.

Nor her head.

She was right; I probably couldn't harm her that way.

No, instead, I'd aimed past her, at the table on which the *faux* Pickover was lying on his back. Specifically, I'd aimed at the place where the thick nylon band that crossed over his torso, pinning his arms, was anchored on the right-hand side—the point where it made a taut diagonal line between where it was attached to the side of the table and the top of Pickover's arm.

The bullet sliced through the band, cutting it in two. The long portion, freed of tension, flew up and over his torso like a snake that had just had 40,000 volts pumped through it.

Cassandra's eyes went wide in astonishment that I'd missed her, and her head swung around. The report of the bullet was still ringing in my ears, but I swear I could also hear the *zzzzinnnng!* of the restraining band snapping free. To be hypersensitive to pain, I figured you'd have to have decent reaction times, and I hoped that Pickover had been smart enough to note in advance my slight deviation of aim before I fired.

And, indeed, no sooner were his arms free than he sat bolt upright—his legs were still restrained—and grabbed one of Cassandra's arms, pulling her toward him. I leapt in the meager Martian gravity. Most of Cassandra's body was made of lightweight composites and synthetic materials, but I was still good old flesh and blood: I outmassed her by at least thirty kilos. My impact propelled her backward, and she slammed against the table's side. Pickover shot out his other arm, grabbing Cassandra's second arm, pinning her backside against the edge of the table. I struggled to regain a sure footing, then brought my gun up to her right temple.

"All right, sweetheart," I said. "Do you really want to test how strong your artificial skull is?"

Cassandra's mouth was open; had she still been biological, she'd probably have been gasping for breath. But her heartless chest was perfectly still. "You can't just shoot me," she said.

"Why not? Pickover here will doubtless back me up when I say it was self-defense, won't you, Pickover?"

He nodded. "Absolutely."

"In fact," I said, "you, me, this Pickover, and the other Pickover are the only ones who know where the Alpha Deposit is. I think the three of us would be better off without you on the scene anymore."

"You won't get away with it," said Cassandra. "You can't."

"I've gotten away with plenty over the years," I said. "I don't see that coming to an end." I cocked the hammer, just for fun.

"Look," she said, "there's no need for this. We can all share in the wealth. There's plenty to go around."

"Except you don't have any rightful claim to it," said Pickover. "You stole this copy of my mind, and you committed torture. And you want to be rewarded for that?"

"Pickover's right," I said. "It's his treasure, not yours."

"It's *humanity's* treasure," corrected Pickover. "It belongs to all mankind."

"But I'm your client," Cassandra said to me.

"So's he. At least, the legal version of him is."

Cassandra sounded desperate. "But—but that's a conflict of interest!"

"So sue me."

She shook her head in disgust. "You're just in this for yourself!"

I shrugged amiably and then pressed the barrel even tighter against her artificial head. "Aren't we all?"

"Shoot her," said Pickover. I looked at him. He was still holding her upper arms, pressing them in close to her torso. If he'd been biological, the twisting of his torso to accommodate doing that probably would have been quite uncomfortable. Actually, now that I thought of it, given his heightened sensitivity to pain, even this artificial version was probably hurting from twisting that way. But apparently this was a pain he was happy to endure.

"Do you really want me to do that?" I said. "I mean, I can understand, after what she did to you, but . . ." I didn't finish the thought; I just left it in the air for him to take or leave.

"She *tortured* me. She deserves to die."

I frowned, unable to dispute his logic—but, at the same time, wondering if Pickover knew that he was as much on trial here as she was.

"Can't say I blame you," I said again, and then added another "but," and once more left the thought incomplete.

At last Pickover nodded. "But maybe you're right. I can't offer her any compassion, but I don't need to see her dead."

A look of plastic relief rippled over Cassandra's face. I nodded, and said, "Good man."

"But, still," said Pickover, "I would like *some* revenge."

Cassandra's upper arms were still pinned by Pickover, but her lower arms were free, and they both moved. I looked down, just in time to see them jerking toward her groin, almost as if to protect . . .

I nodded in quiet satisfaction.

Cassandra had quickly moved her arms back to a neutral, hanging-down position—but it was too late. The damage had been done.

Pickover had seen it, too; his torso had been twisted just enough to allow him to do so.

"You . . ." he began slowly, clearly shocked. "You're . . ." He paused, and if he'd been free to do so, I have no doubt he would have staggered back half a pace. His voice was soft, stunned. "No woman . . ."

Cassandra hadn't wanted to touch Pickover's groin—even though it was artificial—with her bare hands. And when Pickover had suggested exacting revenge for what had been done to him, Cassandra's hands had moved instinctively to protect—

It all made sense: the way she plunked herself down in a chair, the fact that she couldn't bring herself to wear makeup or jewelry in her new body, a dozen other things.

Cassandra's hands had moved instinctively to protect *her own testicles.*

"You're not Cassandra Wilkins," I said.

"Of course I am," said the female voice.

"Not on the inside you're not. You're a man. Whatever mind has been transferred into that body is male."

Cassandra twisted violently. Goddamned Pickover, still stunned by the revelation, had obviously loosened his grip because she got free. I fired my gun and the bullet went straight into her chest; a streamer of machine oil, like from a punctured can, shot out, but there was no sign that the bullet had slowed her down.

"Don't let her get away!" shouted Pickover, in his high, mechanical voice. I swung my gun on him, and for a second I could see terror in his eyes, as if he thought I meant to off him for letting her twist away. But I aimed at the nylon strap restraining his legs and fired. This time, the bullet only partially severed the strap. I reached down and yanked at the remaining filaments, and so did Pickover. They finally broke, and this strap, like the first, snapped free. Pickover swung his legs off the table and immediately stood up. An artificial body has many advantages, among them not being dizzy after lying down for God-only-knew how many days.

In the handful of seconds it had taken to free Pickover, Cassandra had made it out the door that I'd pried partway open, and was now running down the corridor in the darkness. I could hear splashing sounds, meaning she'd veered far enough off the corridor's centerline to end up in the water pooling along the starboard side, and I heard her actually bump into the wall at one point, although she immediately continued on. She didn't have her flashlight, and the only illumination in the corridor would have been what was spilling out of the room I was now in—a fading glow to her rear as she ran along, whatever shadow she herself was casting adding to the difficulty of seeing ahead.

I squeezed out into the corridor. My flashlight was still in my pocket. I fished it out and aimed it just in front of me; Cassandra wouldn't benefit much from the light it was giving off. Pickover, who, I noted, had now done his pants back up, had made his way through the half open door and was now standing by my side. I started running, and he fell in next to me.

Our footfalls drowned out the sound of Cassandra's; I guessed she must be some thirty or forty meters ahead. Although it was almost pitch-black, she presumably had the advantage of having come down this corridor several times before; I had never gone in this direction, and I doubted Pickover had, either.

A rat scampered out of our way, squealing as it did so. My breathing was already ragged, but I managed to say, "How well can you guys see in the dark?"

Pickover's voice, of course, showed no signs of exertion. "Only slightly better than biologicals can, unless you specifically get an infrared upgrade."

I nodded, although he'd have needed better vision than he'd just claimed in order to see it. My legs were a lot longer than Cassandra's, but I suspected she could pump them more rapidly. I swung the flashlight beam up, letting it lance out ahead of us for a moment. There she was, off in the distance. I dropped the beam back to the floor.

More splashing from up ahead; she'd veered off once more. I thought about firing a shot—more for the drama of it than any serious hope of bringing her down—when I suddenly became aware that Pickover was passing me. His robotic legs were as long as my natural ones, and he could piston them up and down at least as quickly as Cassandra could.

I tried to match his speed but wasn't able to. Even in Martian gravity, running fast is hard work. I swung my flashlight up again, but Pickover's body, now in front of me, was obscuring everything farther down the corridor; I had no idea how far ahead Cassandra was now—and the intervening form of Pickover prevented me from acting out my idle fantasy of squeezing off a shot.

Pickover continued to pull ahead. I was passing open door after open door, black mouths gaping at me in the darkness. I heard more rats, and Pickover's footfalls, and—

Suddenly something jumped on my back from behind me. A hard arm was around my neck, pressing sharply down on my Adam's apple. I tried to call out to Pickover but couldn't get enough breath out . . . or in. I craned my neck as much as I could, and shined the flashlight beam up on the ceiling, so that some light reflected down onto my back from above.

It was Cassandra! She'd ducked into one of the other rooms and lain in wait for me. Pickover was no detective; he had completely missed the signs of his quarry no longer being in front of him—and I'd had Pickover's body blocking my vision, plus the echoing bangs of his footfalls to obscure my hearing. I could see my own chilled breath but, of course, not hers.

I tried again to call out to Pickover, but all I managed was a hoarse croak, doubtless lost on him amongst the noise of his own running. I was already oxygen-deprived from exertion, and the constricting of my throat was making things worse; despite the darkness I was now seeing white flashes in front of my eyes, a sure sign of asphyxiation. I only had a few seconds to act.

And act I did. I crouched as low as I could, Cassandra still on my back, her head sticking up above mine, and I leapt with all the strength I could muster. Even weakened, I managed a powerful kick, and in this low Martian gravity, I shot up like a bullet. Cassandra's metal skull smashed into the roof of the corridor. There happened to be a lighting fixture directly above me, and I heard the sounds of shattering glass and plastic.

I was descending now in maddeningly slow motion, but as soon as I was down, Cassandra still clinging hard to me, I surged forward a couple of paces then leapt again. This time, there was nothing but unrelenting bulkhead above, and Cassandra's metal skull slammed hard into it.

Again the slow-motion fall. I felt something thick and wet oozing through my shirt. For a second, I'd thought Cassandra had stabbed me—but no, it was probably the machine oil leaking from the bullet hole I'd put in her earlier. By the time we had touched down again, Cassandra had loosened her grip on my neck as she tried to scramble off me. I spun around and fell forward, pushing her backward onto the corridor floor, me tumbling on top of her. Despite my best efforts, the flashlight was knocked from my grip by the impact, and it spun around, doing a few complete circles before it ended up with its beam facing away from us.

I still had my revolver in my other hand, though. I brought it up and by touch found Cassandra's face, probing the barrel roughly over it. Once, in my early days, I'd rammed a gun barrel into a thug's mouth; this time, I had other ideas. I got the barrel positioned directly over her left eye and pressed down hard with it—a little poetic justice.

I said, "I bet if I shoot through your glass eye, aiming up a bit, I'll tear your artificial brain apart. You want to find out?"

She said nothing. I called back over my shoulder, *"Pickover!"* The name echoed down the corridor, but I had no idea whether he heard me. I turned my attention back to Cassandra—or whoever the hell this really was—and I cocked the hammer. "As far as I'm concerned, Cassandra Wilkins is my client—but you're not her. Who are you?"

"I *am* Cassandra Wilkins," said the voice.

"No, you're not. You're a man—or, at least, you've got a man's mind."

"I can *prove* I'm Cassandra Wilkins," said the supine form. "My name is Cassandra Pauline Wilkins; my birth name is Collier. I was born in Sioux City, Iowa. My citizenship number is—"

"Facts. Figures." I shook my head. "Anyone could find those things out."

"But I know stuff no one else could possibly know. I know the name of my childhood pets; I know what I did to get thrown out of school when I was fifteen; I know precisely where the original me had a tattoo; I . . ."

She went on, but I stopped listening.

Jesus Christ, it was almost the perfect crime. No one could really get away with stealing somebody else's identity—not for long. The lack of intimate knowledge of how the original spoke, of private things the original knew, would soon enough give you away, unless—

Unless you were the *spouse* of the person whose identity you'd appropriated.

"You're not Cassandra Wilkins," I said. "You're Joshua Wilkins. You took her body; you transferred into it, and she transferred—" I felt my stomach tighten; it really was a nearly perfect crime. "And she transferred *nowhere;* when the original was euthanized, she died. And that makes you guilty of murder."

"You can't prove that," said the female voice. "No biometrics, no DNA, no fingerprints. I'm whoever I say I am."

"You and Cassandra hatched this scheme together," I said. "You both figured Pickover had to know where the Alpha Deposit was. But then you decided that you didn't want to share the wealth with anyone—not even your wife. And so you got rid of her and made good your escape at the same time."

"That's crazy," the female voice replied. "I *hired* you. Why on—on *Mars*—would I do that, then?"

"You expected the police to come out to investigate your missing-person report; they were supposed to find the body in the basement of NewYou. But they didn't, and you knew suspicion would fall on you—the supposed spouse!—if you were the one who found it. So you hired me—the dutiful wife, worried about her poor, missing hubby! All you wanted was for me to find the body."

"Words," said the transfer. "Just words."

"Maybe so," I replied. "I don't have to satisfy anyone else. Just me. I will give you one chance, though. See, I want to get out of here alive—and I don't see any way to do that if I leave you alive, too. Do you? If you've got an answer, tell me. Otherwise, I've got no choice but to pull this trigger."

"I promise I'll let you go," said the synthesized voice.

I laughed, and the sound echoed in the corridor. "You promise? Well, I'm sure I can take that to the bank."

"No, seriously. I won't tell anyone. I—"

"Are you Joshua Wilkins?" I asked.

Silence.

"Are you?"

I felt the face moving up and down a bit, the barrel of my gun shifting slightly in the eye socket as it did so. "Yes."

"Well, rest in peace," I said, and then, with relish, added, *"Josh."*

I pulled the trigger.

TEN

The flash from the gun barrel briefly lit up the flawless female face, which was showing almost biological horror. The revolver snapped back in my hand, then everything was dark again. I had no idea how much damage the bullet would do to the brain. Of course, the artificial chest wasn't rising and falling, but it never had been. And there was nowhere to check for a pulse. I decided I'd better try another shot, just to be sure. I shifted slightly, thinking I'd put this one through the other eye, and—

And Joshua's arms burst up, pushing me off him. I felt myself go airborne and was aware of Joshua scrambling to his feet. He scooped up the flashlight, and as he swung it and himself around, it briefly illuminated his face. There was a deep pit where one eye used to be.

I started to bring the gun up and—

And Joshua thumbed off the flashlight. The only illumination was a tiny bit of light, far, far down the corridor, spilling out from the torture room; it wasn't enough to let me see Joshua clearly. But I squeezed the trigger, and heard a bullet ricochet—either off some part of Joshua's metal internal skeleton or off the corridor wall.

I was the kind of guy who always knew *exactly* how many bullets he had left: two. I wasn't sure I wanted to fire them both off blindly, but—

I could hear Joshua moving closer. I fired again. This time, the feminine voice box made a sound between an *oomph* and the word "ouch," so I knew I'd hit him.

One bullet to go.

I started walking backward—which was no worse than walking forward; I was just as likely to trip either way in this near-total darkness. The body in the shape of Cassandra Wilkins was much smaller than mine—but also much stronger. It could probably grab me by the shoulders and pound my head up into the ceiling, just as I'd pounded hers—and I rather suspect mine wouldn't survive. And if I let it get hold of my arm, it could probably wrench the gun from me; multiple bullets hadn't been enough to stop the artificial body, but one was all it would take to ice me for good.

I decided it was better to have an empty gun than a gun that could potentially be turned on me. I held the weapon out in front, took my best guess, and squeezed the trigger one last time.

The revolver barked, and the flare from the muzzle lit the scene, stinging my eyes. The artificial form cried out—I'd hit a spot its sensors felt was worth protecting with a major pain response, I guess. But Joshua kept moving forward. Part of me thought about turning tail and running—I still had the longer legs, even if I couldn't move them as fast—but another part of me couldn't bring myself to do that. The gun was of no more use, so I threw it aside. It hit the corridor wall, making a banging sound, then fell to the deck plates, producing more clanging as it bounced against them.

Of course, as soon as I'd thrown the gun away, I realized I'd made a mistake. *I* knew how many bullets I'd shot, and how many the gun held, but Joshua probably didn't; even an empty gun could be a deterrent if the other person thought it was loaded.

We were facing each other—but that was all that was certain. Precisely how much distance there was between us I couldn't say. Although running produced loud, echoing footfalls, either of us could have moved a step or two forward or back—or left or right—without the other being aware of it. I was trying not to make any noise, and a transfer could stand perfectly still, and be absolutely quiet, for hours on end.

I'd only ever heard clocks ticking with each second in old movies, but I was certainly conscious of time passing in increments as we stood there, each waiting for the other to make a move. And I had no idea how badly I'd hurt him.

Light suddenly exploded in my face. He'd thumbed the flashlight back on, aiming it at what turned out to be a very good guess as to where my eyes were. I was temporarily blinded, but his one remaining mechanical eye responded more efficiently, I guess, because now that he knew exactly where I was, he leapt, propelling himself through the air and knocking me down.

This time, both hands closed around my neck. I still outmassed Joshua and managed to roll us over, so he was on his back, and I was on top. I arched my spine and slammed my knee into his balls, hoping he'd release me . . .

. . . except, of course, he didn't have any balls; he only thought he did. *Damn!*

The hands were still closing around my gullet; despite the chill air, I felt myself sweating. But with his hands occupied, mine were free: I pushed my right hand onto his chest—startled by the feeling of artificial breasts there—and probed around until I found the slick, wet hole my first bullet had made. I hooked my right thumb into that hole, pulled sideways, and brought in my left thumb, as well, squeezing it down into the opening, ripping it wider and wider. I thought if I could get at the internal components, I might be able to tear out something crucial. The artificial flesh was soft, and there was a layer of what felt like foam rubber beneath it—and beneath that, I could feel hard metal parts. I tried to get my whole hand in, tried to yank out whatever I could, but I was fading fast. My pulse was thundering so loudly in my ears I couldn't hear anything else, just a *thump-thump-thumping,* over and over again, the *thump-thump-thumping* of . . .

Of footfalls! Someone was running this way, and—

And the scene lit up as flashlights came to bear on us.

"There they are!" said a high, mechanical voice that I recognized as belonging to the bootleg Pickover. "There they are!"

"NKPD!" shouted another voice I also recognized—a deep, Scottish brogue. "Let Lomax go!"

Joshua looked up. "Back off!" he shouted, in that female voice. "If you don't, I'll finish him."

Through blurring vision, I saw Mac say, "If you kill him, you'll go down for murder. You don't want that."

Joshua relaxed his grip a bit—not enough to let me escape, but enough to keep me alive as a hostage, at least a little while longer. I sucked in cold air, but my lungs still felt like they were on fire. In the illumination from the flashlights I could see Cassandra Wilkins's face craning now to look at McCrae. As I'd said, most transfers didn't show as much emotion as biologicals did, but it was clear that Joshua was panicking.

I was still on top. I thought if I waited until Joshua was distracted, I could yank free of his grip without him snapping my neck. "Let go of him," Mac said firmly. It was hard to see him; he was the one holding the light source, after all, but I suddenly became aware that he was also holding a large disk. "Release his neck, or I'll deactivate you for sure."

Joshua practically had to roll his one good eye up into his head to see Mac, standing behind him. "You ever use one of those before?" he said. "No, I know you haven't. I work in the transference business, and I know that technology just came out. The disruption isn't instantaneous. Yes, you can kill me—but not before I kill Lomax."

"You're lying," said McCrae. He handed his flashlight to Pickover, and brought the disk up in front of him, holding it vertically by its two U-shaped handles. "I've read the specs."

"Are you willing to take that chance?" asked Joshua.

I could only arch my neck a bit; it was very hard for me to look up and see Mac, but he seemed to be frowning, and, after a second, he turned partially away. Pickover was standing behind him, and—

And suddenly an electric whine split the air, and Joshua was convulsing beneath me, and his hands were squeezing my throat even more tightly than before. The whine—a high, keening sound—must have been coming from the disruptor. I still had my hands inside Joshua's chest and could feel his whole interior vibrating as his body continued to rack. I yanked my hands out and grabbed onto his arms, pulling with all my might. His hands popped free from my throat, and his whole female form was shaking rapidly. I rolled off him; the artificial body kept convulsing as the keening continued. I gasped for breath, and all I could think about for several moments was getting air into me.

After my head cleared a bit, I looked again at Joshua, who was still convulsing, and then I looked up at Mac, who was banging on the side of the disruptor disk. Now that he'd activated it, he apparently had no idea how to deactivate it. As I watched, he started to turn it over, presumably hoping there was some control he'd missed on the side he couldn't see—and I realized that if he completed his move the disk would be aimed backward, in the direction of Pickover. Pickover clearly saw this, too: he was throwing his robot-like arms up, as if to shield his face—not that that could possibly do any good.

I tried to shout "No!," but my voice was too raw and all that came out was a hoarse exhalation of breath, the sound of which was lost beneath the keening. In my peripheral vision, I could see Joshua lying face down. His vicious spasms stopped as the beam from the disruptor was no longer aimed at him.

But even though I didn't have any voice left, Pickover did, and his shout of *"Don't!"* was loud enough to be heard over the electric whine of the disruptor. Mac continued to rotate the disk a few more degrees before he realized what Pickover was referring to. He flipped the disk back around, then continued turning it until the emitter surface was facing straight down. And then he dropped it, and it fell in Martian slo-mo, at last clanking against the deck plates, a counterpoint to the now-muffled electric whine. I hauled myself to my feet and moved over to check on Joshua while Pickover and Mac hovered over the disk, presumably looking for the off switch.

There were probably more scientific ways to see if the transferee Joshua was dead, but this one felt right just then: I balanced on one foot, hauled back the other leg, and kicked the son of a bitch in the side of that gorgeous head. The impact was strong enough to spin the whole body through a quarter turn, but there was no reaction at all from Joshua.

Suddenly the keening died, and I heard a self-satisfied *"There!"* from Mac. I looked over at him, and he looked back at me, caught in the beam from the flashlight Pickover was holding. Mac's bushy orange eyebrows were raised, and there was a sheepish grin on his face. "Who'd have thought the off switch had to be pulled out instead of pushed in?"

I tried to speak and found I did have a little voice now. "Thanks for coming by, Mac. I know how you hate to leave the station."

Mac nodded in Pickover's direction. "Yeah, well, you can thank this guy for putting in the call," he said. He turned, and faced Pickover full-on. "Just who the hell are you, anyway?"

I saw Pickover's mouth begin to open in his mechanical head, and a thought rushed through my mind. This Pickover was bootleg. Both the other Pickover and Joshua Wilkins had been correct: such a being shouldn't exist and had no rights. Indeed, the legal Pickover would doubtless continue to demand that this version be destroyed; no one wanted an unauthorized copy of himself wandering around.

Mac was looking away from me and toward the duplicate of Pickover. And so I made a wide sweeping of my head, left to right, then back again. Pickover apparently saw it because he closed his mouth before sounds came out, and I spoke as loudly and clearly as I could in my current condition. "Let me do the introductions," I said, and I waited for Mac to turn back toward me.

When he had, I pointed at Mac. "Detective Dougal McCrae," I said, then I took a deep breath, let it out slowly, and pointed at Pickover, "I'd like you to meet Joshua Wilkins."

Mac nodded, accepting this. "So you found your man? Congratulations, Alex." He then looked down at the motionless female body. "Too bad about your wife, Mr. Wilkins."

Pickover turned to face me, clearly seeking guidance. "It's so sad," I said quickly. "She was insane, Mac—had been threatening to kill her poor husband Joshua here for weeks. He decided to fake his own death to escape her, but she got wise to it somehow and hunted him down. I had no choice but to try to stop her."

As if on cue, Pickover walked over to the dead artificial body and crouched beside it. "My poor dear wife," he said, somehow managing to make his mechanical voice sound tender. He lifted his skinless face toward Mac. "This planet does that to people, you know. Makes them go crazy." He shook his head. "So many dreams dashed."

Mac looked at me, then at Pickover, then at the artificial body lying on the deck plating, then back at me. "All right, Alex," he said, nodding slowly. "Good work."

I tipped my nonexistent hat at him. "Glad to be of help."

. . . .

Three days later, I walked into the dark interior of The Bent Chisel, whistling.

Buttrick was behind the bar, as usual. "You again, Lomax?"

"The one and only," I replied cheerfully. Diana was standing in her topless splendor next to the bar, loading up her tray. "Hey, Diana," I said, "when you get off tonight, how 'bout you and me go out and paint the town . . ." I trailed off: the town was *already* red; the whole damned planet was.

Diana's face lit up, but Buttrick raised a beefy hand. "Not so fast, lover boy. If you've got the money to take her out, you've got the money to settle your tab."

I slapped two golden hundred-solar coins on the countertop. "That should cover it." Buttrick's eyes went as round as the coins, and he scooped them up immediately, as if he were afraid they'd disappear—which, in this joint, they probably would.

"I'll be in the booth in the back," I said to Diana. "I'm expecting Juan; when he arrives, could you bring him over?"

Diana smiled. "Sure thing, Alex. Meanwhile, what can I get you? Your usual poison?"

I shook my head. "Nah, none of that rotgut. Bring me the best Scotch you've got—and pour it over *water* ice."

Buttrick narrowed his eyes. "That'll cost extra."

"No problem," I said. "Start up a new tab for me."

A few minutes later, Diana came by the booth with my drink, accompanied by Juan Santos. He was looking at her with his usual puppy-dog-love eyes. "What can I get for you?" Diana asked him.

He hesitated—it was clear to me, at least, what he wanted—but then he tipped his massive forehead forward. "Gin neat."

She nodded and departed, and he watched her go. Then he slid down into the seat opposite me. "This better be on you, Alex. You still owe me for the help I gave you at Dr. Pickover's place."

"Indeed it is, my friend."

Juan rested his receding chin on his open palm. "You seem in a good mood."

"Oh, I am," I said. "I got paid."

The man the world now accepted as Joshua Wilkins had returned to NewYou, where he'd gotten his face finished and his artificial body upgraded. After that, he told people it was too painful to continue to work there, given what had happened with his wife. So he sold the NewYou franchise to his associate, Horatio Fernandez. The money from the sale gave him plenty to live on, especially now that he didn't need food and didn't have to pay the life-support tax anymore. He gave me all the fees his dear departed wife should have—plus a healthy bonus.

I'd asked him what he was going to do now. "Well," he said, "even if you're the only one who knows it, I'm still a paleontologist. I'm going to look for new fossil beds—I intend to spend months out on the surface. Who knows? Maybe there's another deposit out there even better than the Alpha."

And what about the other Pickover—the official one? It took some doing, but I managed to convince him that it had actually been the late Cassandra, not Joshua, who had stolen a copy of his mind, and that she was the one who had installed it in an artificial body. I told Dr. Pickover that when Joshua discovered what his wife had done, he destroyed the bootleg and dumped the ruined body that had housed it in the basement of the NewYou building.

Not too shabby, eh? Still, I'd wanted more. I'd rented a surface suit and a Mars buggy and headed out to 16.4 kilometers south-southwest of Nili Patera. I figured I'd pick myself up a lovely rhizomorph or a nifty pentapod, and never have to work again.

Well, I'd looked and looked and looked, but I guess the duplicate Pickover had lied about where the Alpha Deposit was; even under torture, he hadn't betrayed his beloved fossils. I'm sure Weingarten and O'Reilly's source is out there somewhere, though, and the legal Pickover is doubtless hard at work thinking of ways to protect it from looters. I wish him luck.

"How about a toast?" suggested Juan, once Diana had brought him his booze.

"I'm game," I said. "To what?"

Juan frowned, considering. Then his eyebrows climbed his broad forehead, and he replied, "To being true to your innermost self."

We clinked glasses. "I'll drink to that."

ELEVEN

TWO MONTHS LATER

I had my feet up on the desk when a camera window popped open on my monitor. The guy on my screen had obviously pushed the doorbell—that's what activated the camera—but had then turned around. New clients rarely showed up without booking an appointment first, so I reached for my trusty Smith & Wesson, swung my feet to the floor, and aimed the gun at the sliding door. "Intercom," I said into the air, then: "Yes? Who are you?"

The jamoke looked back at the camera—and I saw that half his face was dull metal with only traces of artificial pinkish beige skin still attached. But the voice! I recognized that cultured British accent at once. "Good afternoon, Mr. Lomax. I wonder if I might have a word?"

I placed the gun on the desk and said, "Open." The door slid aside, revealing the transfer in the—well, not the *flesh*. "Jesus, Rory," I said. "What happened to you?"

There was movement on the surface of the metal forehead—little motors that would have lifted eyebrows had they still been there, I supposed. "What? Oh. Yes. I need to get this fixed."

"Get into a bar fight?" I thought maybe the old broken-beer-bottle-in-the-kisser routine could slice through plastiskin.

"Me?" he replied, as if astonished by the notion. "No, of course not." He extended his right hand. "It's good to see you again, Alex." His handshake—controlled by the artificial body's computer—was perfect: just the right pressure and duration.

With the skin half blasted away, his face looked almost as robotic as that of the unauthorized copy of him I'd rescued from the *Skookum Jim*. I went back to my seat and motioned to the client chair. Pickover was carrying a boxy metal case with a thick handle attached to the lid. He placed it on my threadbare carpet then sat.

"What can I do for you?" I asked.

"I'm hoping to engage your services, old boy."

"You want me to get whoever did that to you?" I said, making a circular motion with my outstretched hand to indicate his damaged face. "A little revenge?"

"It's not that. Or, at least, it's not *precisely* that."

"What, then?"

Pickover rose and effortlessly picked up the metal case he'd just put down. "May I?" he said, gesturing with his free hand at my desk. I nodded, and he placed the box on the surface—and from the thud it made, the thing must have weighed fifty kilos. Memo to self: never arm-wrestle a transfer.

He unlatched the box, and I stood to survey its contents. The interior was lined with blue foam-rubber pyramids, and sitting inside was a hunk of gray rock, half a meter at its widest and shaped vaguely like Australia. Although it was mostly flat, there were five indentations in its surface. "What's that?" I asked.

"The counter slab to two-dash-thirteen-eighty-eight."

"Counter slab?"

"The negative to a positive; the other side. If you split rock that has a fossil within, there's the actual fossil—a shell, say—on one side, and there's a negative image, or mold, of the same thing on the other side. The part with the fossil is the slab; the other part is the counter slab. Collectors sometimes take the former and discard the latter, although a real paleontologist sees value in both."

"And two-dash-whatever?"

"The prefix two denotes O'Reilly and Weingarten's second expedition, and thirteen-eighty-eight is the catalog number of the type specimen of *Noachiana oreillii*—a kind of pentapod—that's now in the Royal Ontario Museum back on Earth. This is the other part of that piece of matrix; I know the slab like—well, like the back of the hand I originally had."

"Ah," I said.

"I knew I'd found a rich bed of fossils—but, of course, there might be several of those; there was no reason to think that what I'd discovered actually was Weingarten and O'Reilly's Alpha Deposit. Until I found this counter slab, that is—that's proof that I'm actually working the Alpha."

"Fair enough," I replied. "But what's that got to do with you getting your face blown off?"

Pickover reached into the box and lifted the counter slab about half a meter using both hands—I doubt it required the strength of both, but he was likely being careful with the specimen. He set it down and then removed a large square of bubble wrap. With it gone, I could see what was at the bottom of the box: a flat metal disk about forty centimeters in diameter and six centimeters thick. The device was broken open, its mechanical guts gummed up by Martian sand—but there was no mistaking what it was: a land mine.

"Holy crap," I said.

"Exactly," replied Pickover. "Someone booby-trapped the Alpha."

I gestured at Pickover's damaged face. "I take it there's more than one land mine, then?"

"Unfortunately, yes. One of those damn things went off near me. If I'd been right on top of it, it would have blown me to—and here's a word I've never had cause to use hitherto in my life—smithereens."

That's the difference between Pickover and me: I'd never once used "hitherto," but "smithereens" came up often in my line of work. He went on. "As is, it took out a wonderful specimen of *Shostakia* I'd been working on."

"What set the mine off?"

"I was jackhammering a few meters away to remove a piece of matrix, completely unaware of the mine buried under the sand. The vibrations from the hammer must have triggered it."

I frowned. The New Klondike Police Department wouldn't care about this. Keeping order—more or less—under the dome was all that mattered to them; what happened outside it interested Mac and his crew about as much as the opera did. Still, I said, "Have you spoken to the NKPD?"

If he'd had a nose left, Pickover might have wrinkled it in disgust. "I can't involve that lot. I'd have to show them where the Alpha is, and they're corrupt. And so I came to you."

Process of elimination; one way to get work. "Thanks. But what's the mystery, then? Surely it was Weingarten and O'Reilly who planted the land mines, no? After all, if they were leaving Mars for an extended period—"

"—they might want to protect their find," Pickover said, finishing for me. "That's what I thought at first—and certainly this thing has been in the ground for a long time." He'd already set the counter slab on my desktop, and he now reached into the metal box and pulled out the ruined land mine. "But I searched to see who had manufactured this device." He pointed to some incised markings on the disk's perimeter. "Of course, it wasn't *sold* as a land mine; those are illegal. It's described as a mining explosive that just happens to have a pressure-sensitive trigger switch; it could also be detonated by remote control, by a coded radio signal. Anyway, this was made by a company in Malaysia called Brisance

Industries. The particular model is the Caldera-7, and the Caldera-7 was introduced eighteen months *after* O'Reilly and Weingarten were killed. No way it was part of the supplies brought along on any of their expeditions here."

"Then who booby-trapped the Alpha?"

"Ah! That's the question, isn't it? O'Reilly and Weingarten were killed at the end of their third voyage. They'd gone on their first voyage alone—just the two of them, two crazy adventurers thumbing their noses at all the moribund government space agencies by coming here on their own. It was on that first voyage that they'd stumbled on the Alpha. But working a dig is hard; it takes a lot of effort. And so on their second voyage, they brought an extra man with them, Willem Van Dyke. But once the second expedition got back to Earth, Weingarten and O'Reilly ripped Van Dyke off, giving him only a fraction of the proceeds from selling the fossils they'd collected."

"What about the third expedition?"

"The relationship with Willem Van Dyke was irreparably soured. Weingarten and O'Reilly didn't take anyone else along on the third."

"Ah," I said. "But obviously this Van Dyke knew where the Alpha was. You think he returned at some later point and placed land mines around the site?"

"He must have. After Weingarten and O'Reilly were killed, he was the only one left alive who knew the location of the Alpha. But the trail on him goes cold thirty-six years ago. He's had no public presence in all that time."

I went to fix myself a drink at the small wet bar on the wall opposite my tiny window. I didn't bother to offer Pickover one, although if I'd had an oil can, I might have told him to help himself to a squirt. "And so you want me to find Willem Van Dyke?"

"Exactly. Van Dyke may well know what happened to the specimens from the second expedition—which private collectors they were sold to. And when he later came back to Mars on his own, he might have worked the Alpha Deposit, at least some, and shipped more specimens back to collectors on Earth. I want to find those collectors and convince them to let me properly describe their specimens in the scientific literature. I'll never get the fossils *from* them; I understand that. They belong in public museums, but I know that's a lost cause. But perhaps I can at least do science on them, if I can find whoever the fossils were sold to. And the path to them begins with Willem Van Dyke."

"But you say he dropped out of sight thirty-six years ago? Hard to pick up the scent at this late date."

"True," said Pickover. "But the land mines provide a new clue, no?" He looked at me: two very human eyes set in that ravaged face. "Still, I guess it *is* what people in your profession call a cold case."

I thought about quipping, "They're all cold cases on Mars," but that wasn't up to my usual standard of repartee so I kept my yap shut. Still, it wasn't like I had any other work, and a cold case was win-win: if I didn't solve it, no one could blame me, and if I did, well, even better. "As you know, my fee is three hundred solars an hour, plus expenses." That was the same as I'd charged him the last time; it was a hundred more than what I'd quoted the transfer I'd thought was Cassandra Wilkins, but I have a soft spot for damsels in distress.

Pickover didn't look happy. Then again, with his current face, he probably *couldn't* look happy. "Deal," he said. "When can you begin?"

"Not so fast. There's one more thing."

"Yes?"

"I need to examine the evidence, as you paleontologists would say, *in situ*."

"You want to see the Alpha Deposit?"

"Can't do the job otherwise."

Pickover looked at me the way Gollum would have if you'd asked to try on his ring. "But I have to protect those fossils."

"Don't you trust me?" I said, batting my baby blues.

"I was going to say—and you'll forgive me—'about as far as I can throw you,' but given how low Martian gravity is and how strong I am now, that's pretty darn far." He was quiet for a time, and I let him be so. "But, yes, I suppose I *do* trust you."

To which my inner voice said, "Idiot"—but my outer voice said, "Thanks."

"You do understand how precious the fossils out there are?" he asked. "To science, I mean?"

"Oh, yes," I replied. "They're invaluable." And I, at least, could still flash a killer smile. "To science, I mean."

TWELVE

After Dr. Pickover left my office, I settled in for some research. I started by confirming what he'd told me. He was right about the land-mine model, and that it had been made in Malaysia. I'd been to a lot of places on good old Mother Earth before I—*ahem*—had to leave, but that wasn't one of them.

I found a useful site that gave instructions for disarming Caldera-7 mines, and I took note of the procedure. In the exact center of each circular disk, there was a hole three centimeters in diameter. Pushing a probe into that would depress the disarm switch; pressure anywhere else on the surface would blow the mine up.

I had been hoping to somehow gain access to Brisance's customer database; I thought maybe Juan Santos could hack into it for me. One *could* access Earth computer networks from Mars, but the time lag varied from three minutes to twenty-two when we had line of sight to Earth, and was even longer at conjunction, when the signal had to be relayed behind the sun. Hacking that way would have driven Juan crazy, so he'd have probably farmed the work out to some Earthside black hat. But Brisance had gone out of business eleven years ago, and, given the kind of equipment it had made, I suspected all its customer records had been wiped back then.

And, anyway, they might not have sold direct to consumer. Indeed, the land mines might have been purchased here on Mars. Judging by the dilapidated condition of the mine Rory had brought to my office, it'd been in the ground a long time. So many Martian businesses had gone bankrupt, though, that I didn't hold out much hope for finding out who might have bought anything decades ago. But it was the best lead I had, and so I headed into the center of the dome and dropped in on New Klondike's Finest to see if they had any records of busting someone for selling land mines here.

Sergeant Huxley was behind his long red counter when I came in, and I did the tip-of-the-hat thing in his general direction. "Well, well, well, Hux, fancy meeting you here!"

"Ain't my lucky day," Hux said. "Seeing you."

"No sirree," I replied. "Your lucky day would be one on which flabby came back into style."

"And yours," said Hux, for once rising to the occasion, "would be one on which people decided that beady eyes look good on anything other than a weasel."

"Hey," I said, "my eyes are private. Says so right on my business card."

"You're a dick," Huxley said.

"In the nonvulgar sense. But you're one in the other sense."

I'd literally seen gears move in Pickover's head earlier today; here, I only got to figuratively watch them as Huxley tried to process this. Finally, he came back with, "Gumshoe."

"Flatfoot."

"Shamus."

"Pig."

"Gunsel."

I was surprised he knew that one—and I wondered if he knew both its meanings. If he did, my next jab would have to be even harsher. While I was phrasing my reply, Mac came in the front door of the station. I turned to him. "Why, Mac! You actually went outside?"

He smiled. "Well, no. I'm arriving at work for the first time today. My daughter had an appointment with the pediatrician."

"P.D. attrition?" I said, raising my eyebrows. "You mean the police department might actually lose old Huxley here at some point?" This one played better in my head than spoken aloud, and they both just looked at me. Crickets were one of the few Earth bugs that *hadn't* made it to Mars, which was probably the only reason I didn't hear any chirping just then. I cleared my throat. "Anyway, Mac, can I talk with you?"

"Surrrre," he said, his brogue rolling the *R*. He nodded at Hux, and the sergeant pushed the button that slid the black inner door open. Mac and I walked down the narrow corridor to his office, and we took chairs on opposite sides of his desk; the desktop looked like polished wood, but was fake, of course—either that, or Mac was even more corrupt than Pickover thought.

"What can I do for you, Alex?"

I fished out my tab and showed him a picture I'd taken of the Caldera-7 Pickover had brought in. "A client of mine came across one of these on the claim he was working. It's a land mine."

Mac squinted at the image. "Looks more like it *was* a land mine. How old is that thing?"

"Might date right back to near the beginning of the Great Martian Fossil Rush. Anybody ever sell devices like this here on Mars? It was officially marketed as a mining explosive."

"Well, not openly, that's for sure. But let me check." He spoke to his computer, asking it to display all records in the police database about land mines or mining explosives. "Bunch of accident reports involving explosives," he said, reading from his monitor, "but nothing of—no, wait a sec. This one's sorta interesting. Copy to wall." The wall opposite the door, which had been showing the green Scottish countryside, changed to a blowup of the report Mac had on his own monitor.

"Thirty years ago, just after the dome went up," said Mac. "Ship arrived here bringing a load of stampeders in hibernation, plus their supplies. Cargo was being offloaded, but one of the carrying cases had become damaged in transit—wasn't anchored properly in the hold, I guess. The worker who'd been unloading the ship could see inside, and recognized the objects within as land mines." Mac pointed at the wall, and a portion of an image expanded, showing a flat disk like the one Pickover had brought to my office, but in pristine condition. "Same kind of device, right?"

I nodded.

"It was in one of the last cases offloaded from the ship," Mac said. "All of the other cargo had been collected by that point. Could well have been more of the same kind of mines in other cases, but no way to tell—and no record of who collected them. And, of course, no one ever claimed the three mines that had been found."

I nodded. "What's the status of that ship?"

He made motions in the air, and the wall changed to show the answer. "The *B. Traven,*" he said. "Decommissioned in—no, check that. It's still in service, but under a new name, the *Kathryn Denning.* Owned and operated by InnerSystem Lines, a division of Slapcoff Interplanetary."

The ship's original name rang a faint bell, but I couldn't place it. "Can I get a list of who was on it when it arrived with the land mines?"

I expected Mac to want his palm greased, but he was in a generous mood; I guess his daughter's appointment had gone well. "Sure." He gestured at the wall some more, and a passenger manifest appeared.

I scanned the names, checking under V and D, and even W, for a Willem Van Dyke, but none was listed. Well, this clown hardly would have been the first person to come to Mars under an alias. "How many names are there?" I asked.

“One hundred and thirty-two,” Mac’s computer said helpfully; it always amused me that it had a brogue as thick as Mac’s own.

“How many males?”

“Seventy-one.”

“Can you download the full list into my tab—males and females?” I said to Mac.

He spoke a command to his computer, and it was done.

A gender change was possible, of course, but Rory himself would doubtless tell me that the simplest hypothesis was preferable, so I’d start by assuming there were only seventy-one suspects—if one could apply the word “only” to so many. I had my work cut out for me.

THIRTEEN

I'd returned to my office and was leaning back in my chair, feet once more up on my desk. Since I wasn't expecting anyone, I had my shoes and socks off, letting the dogs air out. I'd copied the seventy-one male names from the *B. Traven*'s passenger manifest onto my wall monitor, replacing my usual wallpaper, which looked like, well, wallpaper—alternating forest green and caramel stripes, like in the house Wanda and I had lived in all those years ago back in Detroit. It'd be too much to have a picture of her on display, but the pattern subtly reminded me of her, and I liked having it in my peripheral vision.

No distinction was made between biologicals and transfers on the passenger manifest, but the *B. Traven* had completed this voyage back when uploading into an artificial body cost, as the saying goes, the Earth. Anyone who could afford to transfer back then wouldn't have been rushing to Mars to try to make a fortune; he or she already *had* one. So it was a safe bet that all these men had been flesh and blood.

In the intervening years, thirty-two had gone back to Earth, and thirteen others had died; neither condition exonerated them from really being Willem Van Dyke, but it did make it hard to question them in the former case and impossible in the latter. And so I started with the twenty-six who were still here. One name immediately leapt out at me: Stuart Berling; I'd interviewed him during the Wilkins case. He was the full-time fossil hunter who had transferred the same day Joshua Wilkins supposedly had—the guy who'd opted to have his new face look like holovid star Krikor Ajemian. I'd told him I worked for NewYou's head office when I'd questioned him then; he'd been the first transfer to pass my patented where-do-you-keep-your-screwdrivers game—the Turning Test, if you will.

I decided to start by speaking to him, so I put my footwear back on. When I'd been a kid, I'd thought "gumshoe" referred to getting chewing gum stuck to the bottom of your shoe because you'd been skulking in unsavory neighborhoods; it actually refers to the soft-soled shoes favored by those in my line of work, because they make it easier to follow people without being heard. My pair was taupe, a color name I'd learned from the box the shoes had come in.

I opened my office door, hoofed it to the hovertram stop, rode over to Third Avenue and Seventh Circle, went over to Berling's redstone, pressed the illuminated door buzzer, and—

And *wow*.

"Why, it's—it's Mr. Lomax, isn't it?" said the voice from the perfect bee-stung lips on the flawless heart-shaped face.

I blinked. "Lacie, is—is that you?"

She smiled, showing teeth as white as the polar caps. "Guilty."

Berling's wife had been a plain Jane who'd looked every one of her sixty-odd years when I'd last seen her. But, well, if he was going to upload into a beefcake holo star's likeness, it did make sense that she'd opt for this. My fondness for old 2D movies made me think first of Vivien Leigh, but I'd be surprised if there were more than three people under the dome who knew who she had been. It came to me that Lacie's new face—and her supernova-hot body—had been patterned after that of Kayla Filina, who had starred as Brigid O'Shaughnessy in last year's horrid remake of *The Maltese Falcon.*

"You look stunning," I said.

Lacie spun around, a perfect gyroscopically balanced pirouette. "Don't I, though?" she replied, flashing her pearly whites again. "Won't you come in?"

She stepped aside, I crossed into the townhouse, and the door slid shut behind me. "Is your husband home?" I asked. As before, the living room was filled with worktables covered with hunks of reddish rock.

"No. He's outside the dome, working his claim." She smiled broadly. "He won't be back for *hours.*"

"Ah. I was hoping to ask him some questions."

She was wearing a light blue dress that could have been painted on—and perhaps was. Its plunging neckline revealed the tops of two large perfect breasts. "What about me?" she said, placing exquisite hands on rounded hips. "You work for NewYou, right? Quality assurance? Well, I just transferred. Don't you have some questions for me?"

I had thought I'd have to come clean with Berling to get answers about his trip out from Earth on the *B. Traven* all those mears ago, but one doesn't blow a good cover unnecessarily. "I can see," I said, "that we did a magnificent job."

She tipped her head down, appraising her own body. "Oh, it looks great. Exactly what I was hoping for. But I do want to be sure that everything is functioning properly." She looked back up at me, aquamarine eyes beneath long dark lashes. "You know, while the work is still under warranty."

"Surely you and Mr. Berling have, um, tested things out."

"Yes, yes, of course—but he transferred first. I haven't yet had an opportunity to, ah, put this new body through its paces with a biological." She lifted her perfect eyebrows, and her forehead didn't crease at all as she did so. "It's like I'm a virgin again."

It's at moments like this that a man's morals are truly tested, and I asked myself the question that needed asking: could I actually bill Pickover for the time I spent making love with Lacie?

She took my hand, and I let her lead me to the bedroom. If you keep in good shape, sex on Mars is amazing, thanks to the low gravity. Zero-g, I'm told, is no fun: it's too easy to send your partner spinning across the room. But a third of a gee—well, that's just perfect. You can do acrobatics that put Earth-based porn stars to shame. And it's even better if, as Berling and his wife did, you have some handles mounted on the ceiling above the bed.

This wasn't my first time with a transfer, but Lacie was the best-looking one I'd ever been with, and she was a *very* generous lover. I'd heard it said that among biologicals, beautiful women got cheated on more often than plain ones, because the plain ones did all the things to keep their partners happy that the beauties wouldn't. Lacie still had the mind of someone who had had to work to interest men—and the body of someone who could have anyone she wanted. It was a very appealing combination.

When we were done—and it *was* a good thing that Berling was gone for hours—I had a sonic shower, and she buffed her plastic skin with a chamois.

I couldn't question her about Berling's arrival on Mars without telling her I wasn't with NewYou. I doubted she'd really be upset, but given that she might be able to pull my head off, I didn't want to risk it. Instead, I simply asked her to have him give me a call when he got home. But just as I was leaving, he called her. I stood out of view and listened. He'd had a good day out by the Reinhardt dunes, he said, and was heading to Ernie Gargalian's fossil dealership to sell his finds. I hadn't seen Gargantuan Gargalian for a few weeks, and so I made my way over there to intercept Berling; it was more seemly, I thought, to question him somewhere other than where I'd just banged his wife.

The sun was setting over Syrtis Major way, and the sky was growing dim. But Ye Olde Fossil Shoppe stayed open after dark every night: that's when the prospectors came back inside with their booty, and many wanted to sell immediately rather than storing fossils overnight in their homes and inviting thieves to come get them.

The walk over was pleasant—and not just because I was still grinning from my encounter with the now-lovely Lacie. Walking on Mars was virtually effortless, as long as you didn't have to wear a surface suit.

Ernie's shop was in the center of town near NKPD headquarters, which said a lot about who was really in charge here. "Mr. Double-X!" he proclaimed with his usual precise enunciation as I entered. "To what do I owe the pleasure?"

Ernie Gargalian was sixty-five and hugely fat, with man boobs that were only perky thanks to Mars's low gravity. His thinning silver hair was slicked straight back from his forehead, and his pale face had been puffed out enough to fill in most of the wrinkles. His brown eyes were close together and deeply set.

"Hey, Ernie," I said. "Has Stuart Berling been in yet?"

"Today? No. I haven't seen him all week."

"Well, he's on his way here. Mind if I wait?"

Gargantuan spread his giant arms, encompassing his showroom. "Fossils are fragile things, Alex. I don't want any rough stuff in the shop."

"Never fear, Ernie, never fear. Besides, Berling has transferred—and I'm not fool enough to get into a fistfight with someone who's presumably had mods for surface work."

"Oh, right," said Gargalian. "He's got that actor's face now, doesn't he? I don't hold with that." He made a circular motion in front of his own round visage. "If I were ever to transfer, I'd want to go on looking exactly as I always have. You aren't the same person if you change your appearance."

Ernie liked to call me "Mr. Double-X" because both my names ended in that letter, but he'd need an artificial body in Triple-X at least, and I doubted such things were stock items. But I didn't say that aloud; some jokes are best kept to yourself, I'd learned—after two broken noses.

A prospector came in, a woman in her thirties, biological, pulling a surface wagon with big springy wheels. Little wagons on Earth were traditionally red—I'd had one such myself as a kid—but they tended to get lost outside here if they were painted that color. This one was fluorescent green, and it was overflowing with gray and pink hunks of rock, including one on top that I recognized, thanks to Pickover's little lesson, as a counter slab.

Our town's name harked back to the Great Klondike Gold Rush, but at the end of a good day those stampeders had carried their bounty of dust in small pokes. Fossil matrix was bulky; extracting and preparing the specimens was part of what Ernie and his staff did for their thirty-five percent of every transaction they brokered for prospectors with Earth-based collectors. It was much too expensive to ship rock to Earth that was going to be thrown away there. The tailings were discarded outside our dome; there was a small mountain of them to the east.

Ernie went to tend to the female prospector, and I looked around the shop. The fossils on display were worth millions, but they were being watched by ubiquitous cameras, and, besides, no one would try to steal from Gargantuan Gargalian, if they knew what was good for them. Ernie was one of the richest men on Mars, and he had on retainer lots of muscle to help guard that wealth. On Earth, a multimillionaire might own a mansion, a yacht, and a private jet. There was no point in owning a yacht on Mars, but Ernie certainly had the big house—I'd seen it from the outside, and the damn thing had turrets, for God's sake—and he had the airplane, too, with an impossibly wide wingspan; it was one of only four planes I knew of here on the Red Planet.

There was a chart on one of Ernie's walls: side-by-side geologic timelines for Earth and Mars. Both planets were 4.5 billion Earth years old, of course, but their stories had been very different. Earth's prehistory was broadly divided into Precambrian, Paleozoic, Mesozoic, and Cenozoic eras—and I knew a few were pushing for a new era, the Transzoic, to have begun the year Howard Slapcoff had perfected the uploading of consciousness. But on a meter-high chart, that slice wouldn't have been thick enough to see without one of the microscopes that dotted Ernie's shop.

Martian prehistory, meanwhile, was divided into the Noachian, Hesperian, and Amazonian eras, each named, the chart helpfully explained, for a locale on Mars where rocks characteristic of it were found (and yes, ironically for a time scale that stretched back billions of years, the place that gave us the term Noachian had been named by Schiaparelli in honor of Noah's flood).

Both worlds developed life as soon as they'd cooled enough to allow it—some four billion Earth years ago. But Earth life just twiddled its—well, its *nothings*—for the next three and a half billion years; it was mostly unicellular and microscopic until the dawn of the Paleozoic, 570 million years ago.

But Mars produced complex, macroscopic invertebrates with exoskeletons within only a hundred million years. All of the fossils collected here dated from the Noachian, which covered the first billion years. By the time multicellular creatures appeared on Earth, life on Mars had been extinct for hundreds of millions of years: two ships that didn't quite pass in the cosmic night . . .

Ernie and the woman were exchanging words. "Surely these are worth more than that!" she declared.

"My sincerest apologies, dear lady," he replied, "but *Longipes bedrossiani* is the most common of finds; they were everywhere. And see here? The glabella is missing. And on this one, there are only three intact limbs—not much of a pentapod!"

They went back and forth like that a while longer, but she eventually agreed to the price he was offering. He gave her a receipt, and she left, muttering to herself.

Since Berling hadn't yet shown up, I took the opportunity to ask Ernie a question. "So," I said, doing my best to sound nonchalant, "do you think anyone will ever rediscover the Alpha Deposit?"

Ernie's eyes, already mostly lost in his fleshy face, narrowed even further. "Why do you ask?"

"Just idle curiosity."

"You, Mr. Double-X, are curious about women. You are curious about liquor. You are curious about sports. You are *not* curious about fossils."

"But I *am* intrigued by money."

"True. And, to answer your question, I doubt it'll happen anytime soon. In an unguarded moment many years ago, after perhaps one too many glasses of port, Denny O'Reilly said to me that the Alpha was only the size of a football field—an Earth one, that is."

"But why hasn't anyone else found it yet? I mean, it *has* been twenty mears."

"All we know is that it's somewhere here in Isidis Planitia—and Isidis Planitia is the flat bottom of the remains of a giant impact crater fifteen hundred kilometers in diameter. It's as big as Hudson Bay on Earth; you could fit over three hundred million football fields in it. Even with all the stampeders who've come here, there are still huge tracts of the plain that no one has ever set foot upon, my boy. Hell, no one's even found *Beagle 2*, and that presumably isn't even buried."

"*Beagle 2?*" I said.

"A British Mars probe. It was supposed to touch down on Isidis Planitia in 2003, but no signal was ever picked up from it."

"Is it worth something?"

"Sure, to a space buff, assuming it's not smashed to bits. I'd be glad to find a buyer for the wreckage, if someone brought it in."

"Maybe I should look for it. I was never any good at spotting fossils, but wreckage—that's something I understand."

"By Gad, you might make a decent sideline of it, at that," said Ernie. "There's even bigger salvage out there."

"Oh?"

"Tons of it. Denny and Simon landed on Mars in two-stage ships, like the old *Apollo* lunar modules, but much bigger. Each had a lower descent stage and an upper ascent stage. Unlike the old lunar modules, though, both stages were habitable. Anyway, the ascent stages are gone, of course—they all flew back to Earth. Two of them did indeed sell to collectors—the first crewed ships that had gone to Mars, after all! The third burned up on re-entry, as I'm sure you know."

"Yeah. What happened to the descent stages?"

"Two of three have been accounted for. You may have seen the original one. It's still out there on the planitia, where they first landed—although it's just a skeleton now; looters have taken all the good parts. The fact that it's here in Isidis is how we know the Alpha must be somewhere around here—Denny and Simon, of course, never said where it was. But it could be—and probably is—many hundreds of kilometers from that original landing site. They had Mars buggies on that mission that had a thousand-kilometer range."

"And the descent stage from the second expedition?" I asked.

"They crashed it in Aeolis Mensae."

"That's a long way from here."

"Exactly. See, Denny and Simon used *in situ* fuel production; they made their rocket propellant here from local material. Not only did they fill the ascent stage's fuel tanks here, but they reloaded the descent stage's tanks, at least in part, as well. After the ascent stage took off to bring them home—it had been perched atop the descent stage—they had the computer in the descent stage fire its engine and fly horizontally as far as the fuel would take it, just to disguise the location of where it had originally touched down. As I said, the first lander didn't necessarily touch down near where the Alpha was located. But the second lander had presumably been set down right by the Alpha, to serve as a base station while they mined it."

I nodded. "So they had to move it."

"Precisely."

"And the descent stage from the third mission?"

"God only knows what they did with it. But if it's intact, it would definitely be worth something."

Just then, Stuart Berling entered the shop. He had a memorable face now, but I guess I didn't, at least to him, because although his wife had recognized me at once, he didn't seem to know me at all. Oh, he looked at me suspiciously, but it seemed just typical prospector paranoia. The woman who'd been here earlier had glared at me the same way; no fossil hunter wanted another to know where his or her bounty had been found.

"Mr. Berling," I said, extending a hand that had recently been touching his wife's perfect new body. "What a pleasant surprise."

"Do I know you?"

"Alexander Lomax. I visited you at your home and asked you about your satisfaction with your transference."

Ernie was looking on in quiet amusement but said nothing.

"Oh," said Berling. "Right."

"I'd like to ask you some questions on another topic, if I may?"

"I told you I was happy with the work NewYou did. We really don't have anything else to discuss—and I've got business with Mr. Gargalian here."

"I'll gladly wait."

His brows drew together. "There's something fishy about you, Lomax."

This from a guy who was wearing somebody else's face. "Not at all," I said. "I'm just a contract researcher. I did some work for NewYou, and now I'm doing some for the New Klondike Historical Society." I didn't actually know if such a thing existed, but I figured it sounded plausible.

"About what?"

"I understand you came here early on, aboard a ship that was called the *B. Traven*, and—"

He lunged at me. I deked sideways, and he went sailing past, crashing into one of Ernie's worktables and tilting it backward a bit. A slab of rock slid toward the edge and started falling in Martian slo-mo. But Gargantuan Gargalian, moving with surprising speed for a man of his bulk, caught it before it hit the floor. "Stop it!" he demanded as he placed the fossil back on the table, which had now righted itself.

It wouldn't be much use, but I whipped out my gun anyway and pointed it at Berling—who, in turn, was pointing an artificial arm at me. "He started it!" Berling barked.

"What?" I said. "What did I do?"

Berling glared at me with the best approximation of rage his movie-star mask could muster. "How dare you bring that up? Damn you, how *dare* you?" His fists were balled, but they were rock-steady as he held them down by his hips; I guess transfers didn't quake when they were furious.

Even Ernie was on his side now. "You should know better than to mention the *Traven* to a survivor, Alex. I think you should leave."

I looked at them: the dashingly handsome transfer and the old fat biological. They both had expressions normally reserved for those who'd caught someone farting in an airlock. I holstered my gun and headed outside.

FOURTEEN

During the day, all sorts of people walked New Klondike's streets, although even more took hovertrams. But at night, decent folk mostly stayed indoors, especially as you got farther out toward the rim. Of course, I wasn't decent folk. There were hookers plying their trade and teenage hoods—the kids of failed stampeders who had nothing much to live for—hanging around, looking for anything to relieve their boredom, and if that happened to be rolling a drunk or breaking into a shop, so much the better.

Still, I didn't expect any trouble as I headed along Fourth Avenue toward my 11:00 p.m. date with Diana. After all, a good percentage of the lowlifes in town knew me on sight—and knew to avoid me. And even those who didn't know me could hardly assume I'd be an easy mark: I was muscular in the way most Martians weren't. But as I crossed the Third Circle, I was accosted by a tough-looking punk: biological, male, maybe eighteen years old, wearing a black T-shirt, with an animated tattoo of a snake with a rattling tail on his left cheek. "Gimme your money," he said.

"And if I don't?" I replied, my hand finding the Smith & Wesson.

"I cut you," he said, and a switchblade unfolded.

"Try it," I said, drawing the gun—for the second time in an hour; not a record, but close—"and I shoot you."

"Fine," said the punk. "Do me a favor." And he astonished me by spreading his arms and dropping the knife, which fell with typical Red Planet indolence to the fused regolith of the sidewalk.

"Okay," I said, keeping my gun trained on him, "I'll bite. How would that be doing you a favor?"

"I got nothing, man. Nothing."

"Been on Mars long?"

"Six weeks. Spent everything to get here."

"Where you from?"

"Chicago."

That was a place I *had* been to back on Earth; I could see why he'd wanted to get out. Keeping him covered, I bent over and picked up the knife. It was a beautiful piece, with a nicely carved wine-colored handle—I'd been admiring one like it a while ago in a shop Diana and I had visited over on Tenth. I retracted the blade and slipped it into my pocket.

"Man, that's mine," the punk said.

"Was yours," I corrected.

"But I need it. I need to get money. I gotta eat."

"Try your hand at fossil hunting. People get rich every day here."

"Tried. No luck."

I could sympathize with that. I reached into my other pocket, found a twenty-solar coin, and flipped it into the air. Anyone who had been on Mars long could have caught it as it fell, but he really was new here: he snatched at air way below the coin.

"Get yourself something to eat," I said and started walking.

"Hey, man," he said from behind me. "You're all right."

Without turning around, I gave him a hat tip and continued along my way.

• • • • • • • • • • •

As I'd said, Diana and I weren't exclusive—and I was detective enough to pick up the signs that she'd been routinely seeing someone else for well over a month now, although I had no idea who. But that was fine.

My encounter with the punk had delayed me a bit, and by the time I got to The Bent Chisel, she'd already put her top on. "Hey," I said, leaning in to give her a quick kiss.

"Hey, Alex."

"All set to go?"

"Yup."

We walked back to her place, which was four blocks away. There was no sign of the kid who'd accosted me, so I didn't feel any need to mention it, but when we got into Diana's little apartment—it was even smaller than mine—and I'd pulled her into an embrace, she said, "Is that a gun in your pocket, or are you just happy to see me?"

I wondered if she knew she was paraphrasing Mae West. "Actually," I said, smiling, "it's a switchblade." I brought it out and told her the story of how I'd acquired it.

"Wow," she said. "It's nice."

"Yeah. My lucky day, I guess."

It was her turn to smile. "And now it's going to be your lucky night."

We headed into her little bedroom. My earlier encounter with Lacie had been athletic indeed, but Diana and I always had gentle, playful sex. She'd been here on Mars for a dozen years, and that had taken its toll; she had the typically weak musculature of the long-term inhabitants of this world. I couldn't go back to Earth for legal reasons; Diana was stuck here because she'd never be able to hack a full gee again. But, still, we made do; we always did. And I *was* happy to see her.

. . . .

Turned out there wasn't any New Klondike Historical Society, but I guess things like that are never created while the history is being made. In the morning I headed over to the shipyard. I started by checking in at the yard office, which was little more than a shack between two dead hulks. The yardmaster was Bertha, a husky old broad with a platinum blonde buzz cut.

"Hey, gorgeous," I said as I entered the shack. I wondered briefly why whenever you said, "Hey, gorgeous," people thought you were being serious, but if you said, "Hey, genius," they thought you were being sarcastic.

"Hi, Alex. What's up."

"Just some research."

"No rough stuff, okay?"

"Why does everyone say that to me?"

"I've got two words for you: *Skookum* and *Jim*."

"Okay; true enough. But it's a different ship I'm interested in this time."

She gestured at her computer screen. "Which one?"

"Something called the *B. Traven*."

"Jesus," she said.

"What?"

"You don't know?"

"Know what?"

"The *Traven*."

"What about it?"

"It was a death ship."

I looked at her funny. "What?"

"How'd you get to Mars?"

"Me? Low-end liner. I forget what it was called. *Saget*, *Saginaw*—something like that."

"*Sagan?*"

"That's it, yeah."

"Good ship. Made eight round trips to date."

"If you say so."

"And how long was the journey?"

"Christ, I don't remember."

"Right. You literally don't—because the *Sagan,* like most of the ships that come here, uses hibernation. They freeze you when you leave Earth and thaw you out when you arrive here. That kind of ship employs a Hohmann transfer orbit, which takes very little power but a whole lot of time to get here. Transit time if you leave at the optimum moment is 258 Earth days, but it all passed in a blink of an eye for you. The *Traven* was supposed to do the same thing—all of the passengers in deep sleep, with just a bowman to keep things running."

"Bowman?"

"That's what they call the person who stays awake during a voyage when everyone else is hibernating. After a guy named Bowman in some old movie, apparently."

"Ah, right," I said; I knew which one. "But something went wrong?"

"Crap, yeah. The bowman went crazy. He thawed out passengers one at a time and terrorized them—abused them sexually. By the time one of the people he'd awoken managed to get word out—a radio message to Lunaport—there was nothing anyone could do. Orbital mechanics make it really hard to intercept a ship that's several months into its interplanetary journey. The whole thing was quite a sensation at the time, but—how old are you?"

"Forty-one."

"You'd have been just a kid."

"The name of the ship didn't seem to ring a bell with Dougal McCrae at the NKPD, either." I said it to defend my ignorance; I probably *should* have known about this. But maybe we'd studied it in school on a Friday. Memo to all boards of education everywhere: never schedule crucial lessons for a Friday.

"Yeah, well, Mac's about your age," Bertha said, exonerating him, too.

"Anyway, that explains why a guy lunged at me when I brought it up. He'd been on that ship."

"Ah," said Bertha. "But what's your interest? I mean, if this is news to you, you can't be like the other person who was asking about it."

Needless to say, my ears perked up. "What other person?"

"A couple of weeks ago. The writer-in-residence."

I blinked. "We have a writer-in-residence?"

"Hey, there's more to New Klondike culture than The Bent Chisel and Diamond Tooth Gertie's."

"And Gully's Gym," I said. "Don't forget Gully's Gym."

Bertha made a harrumphing sound, then: "You know who Stavros Shopatsky is?"

"One of the first guys to make a fortune from fossils here. After Weingarten and O'Reilly, I mean."

"Exactly. He bought a ton of land under the dome from Howard Slapcoff. But he was also a writer—adventure novels; my dad used to read him. And so he donated one of the homes he built here to be a writer's retreat. Authors from Earth apply to get an all-expenses-paid round trip to Mars, so they can come and write whatever they want. They usually stay six months or so, then head back."

"Okay," I said.

"And the current writer is doing a book about the *B. Traven*."

"I understand it's still in service, but under a different name," I said.

"Really?" replied Bertha. "What name?"

"The *Kathryn Denning*."

"Oh, is that the *Traven*? Interesting. Yeah, she's still active." Bertha looked at a monitor. "In fact, she's on her way here. She's due to arrive on Friday."

"Can you let me know when she touches down? I'd like to give her a once-over."

"You didn't tell me why you were interested in this."

She said it in a way that conveyed if I expected her to help satisfy my curiosity, I had to satisfy hers. And so I did: "I'm tracking down what became of some cargo she brought here, back when she was called the *Traven.*"

"It's been thirty years since she last sailed under that name. Surely you don't expect to find a clue aboard her at this late date?"

I smiled. "Can't hurt to have a look."

. . . .

My office was on the second of two floors. Instead of the rickety elevator, I always took the two half flights of stairs up. As I came out of the stairwell, I spotted a man at the end of the corridor. He could have been there to see anyone on this floor, but—

Jesus.

Well, not exactly. This guy was better-looking than Jesus. But he had the same longish hair, short beard, and lean face you saw in stained-glass windows.

It was Stuart Berling—unless the real Krikor Ajemian had come to Mars for some reason. I figured he was either here to beat the crap out of me for bringing up the *B. Traven,* or to beat the crap out of me for sleeping with his wife. Either way, discretion seemed the better part of valor, and I turned around and headed back to the stairwell. But—damn it!—he'd spotted me. I heard a shout of "Lomax!" coming from down the corridor.

I leapt, going down the whole flight at once. The thud of my landing echoed in the stairwell. I turned around and took the second set of stairs in a single go, too—but Berling could run like the wind, his transfer legs pumping up and down. Looking up the open stairwell from the ground floor, I saw him appear at the second-floor doorway. I hightailed it through the dingy lobby, almost colliding with an elderly woman who tossed a "Watch it, sonny!" at me.

The automatic door wasn't used to people approaching it at the speed

I was managing, and it hadn't finished sliding out of the way by the time I reached it; my right shoulder smashed into it, hurting like a son of a bitch, but I made it out onto the street. I could head either left or right, chose left, and continued along.

Running on Mars isn't like doing it on Earth: if you've got decent legs, you propel yourself several meters with each stride, and you spend most of your time airborne. The street wasn't particularly crowded, and I did my best to bob and weave around people, but once you're aloft you can't easily change your course, and I finally did collide with someone. Fortunately, it was a transfer; the impact knocked him on his metal ass, but probably did him no harm—although he threw something a lot less polite than "Watch it, sonny!" after me as I scrambled to my feet. While getting up, I'd had an opportunity to look backward. Berling was still in hot pursuit.

I'd chosen left because it led to a hovertram stop. My lungs were bound to give out before Berling's excimer pack did; if I could hop a tram that pulled away before he could get on it, I'd be safe but—

—but there's never a hovertram handy when you need one. The stop was up ahead, and no one was waiting at it, meaning I'd probably just missed the damn thing.

I continued along. There was a seedy tavern on my right called the Bar Soom—a name somebody must have thought clever at some point—and who should be coming out of it but that kid who'd tried to rob me last night. I was breathing too hard to make chitchat as I passed, but he clearly recognized me. He looked behind me, no doubt saw Berling coming after me like a bat out of Chicago, and—

And the kid must have tripped Berling as he passed, because I heard a big thud and the kind of swearing that could have made a sailor blush, if there had been any sailors on Mars.

I halted, turned around, and saw Berling trying to get up. "Damn it, Lomax!" he called, without a trace of breathing hard. "I just want to talk to you!"

Even though it seemed I now had an ally in this alley, I still didn't like my chances in a fight with a high-end transfer. Of course, maybe he'd spent all his money on that handsome face—I wondered if Krikor Ajemian got a royalty? But when in doubt it was safest to assume that a transfer had super strength, too. "About . . . what?" I called back, the two words separated by a gasp.

"The—that ship," he replied, apparently aborting giving voice to the cursed name.

I had my hands on my knees, still trying to catch my breath. Doesn't anyone phone for appointments anymore? "Okay," I managed. "All right." I walked back toward him, several people gawking at us. I nodded thanks at the punk as I approached. Berling's clothes were dusty—Martian red dust—from having skidded on the sidewalk when he'd been tripped, but otherwise he looked great, with not a hair out of place; I wondered how they did that. "What do you want to say?"

He turned his head as he looked left and right, noting the people around us, then moved his head side to side again, signaling "No." "Somewhere private," he said. And then, a little miffed: "I had been hoping for your office."

The number of my colleagues back on Earth who had been shot dead in their own offices was pretty high. "No," I said. "The Bent Chisel—you know it?"

"That rat hole?" said Berling. He *did* know it. But he nodded. "All right."

I figured we both needed some time to cool off figuratively, and I needed to do so literally, too. "Twenty minutes," I said. "I'll meet you there."

He nodded, turned, and departed. I looked at the kid.

"What's your name?"

"Dirk," he said.

"Huh," I said. "Your name is Dirk, and you came at me with a knife."

"Yeah. So?"

I shook my head. "Forget it. You still need money?"

He nodded.

"I'm a private detective. I could use some backup for this meeting with Berling at The Bent Chisel in case things get ugly. Twenty solars for an hour's work, tops."

The snake's rattle shook on his face. "Okay," he said. "I'm in."

FIFTEEN

Buttrick looked up suspiciously as Dirk and I entered the bar. He opened his mouth, as if to issue an automatic complaint about me needing to pay off my tab, but closed it, presumably realizing I was uncharacteristically up-to-date.

"A pretty-boy transfer is gonna come in here in a few minutes," I said. "Long hair, short beard. Send him to the booth in the back, would you?"

"All right," Buttrick said as he polished a glass in classic bartender mode. "But no rough stuff."

I threw up my hands. "You wreck a joint one time . . . !"

Dirk and I headed to the back. I chose this booth because it was near the door to the kitchen, which had its own exit into an alleyway; it was always good to have an escape route in mind. This booth also had my favorite bit of graffiti carved into the tabletop: "Back in ten minutes—Godot."

Shortly after we sat—side by side, both of us facing the rest of the bar, Dirk on the inside of the booth and me on the outside—Diana appeared, and I got up and gave her a hug. She stretched up to kiss me on the cheek. "Hey, baby," I said.

Dirk, I noticed, was content to look at Diana's killer rack while she and I spoke. "Hi, honey," she replied, smiling warmly at me; she had a great smile. I brushed some of her brown hair away from her brown eyes. "Good to see you."

"Good to see you, too," I replied, and I kissed her briefly on the mouth. Diana stole a look over her shoulder to see if Buttrick was watching. He was. She turned back to me, flashed her smile again, and said, "The usual?"

I nodded, and she tipped her head down to look at seated Dirk. "And for you, tiger?"

Dirk hesitated. I'd been there before: the moment when you're supposed to order something but can't really afford to.

"On me," I said, returning to the booth.

"Beer," he replied.

"Domestic or imported?"

"Domestic," I responded. No need to go crazy.

There were only three domestic choices, all synthetic. Diana rattled them off in what I realized was descending order of crappiness. Dirk hesitated again; he clearly hadn't been on Mars long enough to know the brands. "Bring him a Wilhelm," I said—which was a cute name for a beer, if you knew Mars history; Wilhelm Beer and his partner produced the first globe of the Red Planet back in 1830.

Diana headed off, hips swaying. I watched, and I imagined Dirk did, too. Blues was playing over the speakers—I think it was Muddy Waters. "When Berling gets here," I said to the kid, "watch him like a hawk. I don't know what his game is, but he's one angry man."

"Here he comes," Dirk replied.

It hadn't been twenty minutes, and that made me even more alert; Berling might have been getting here early to plan his own escape after an altercation. Buttrick pointed in our direction; Berling nodded and headed this way. He passed Diana, but he didn't spare her a glance; well, he *was* sleeping with Vivien Leigh. When he reached us, he sat down. I liked having the wide table between us; he couldn't grab my neck or punch me across it.

"Who's this?" he said, indicating Dirk with a movement of Krikor Ajemian's head.

"My assistant," I said, and before Berling could object to his presence, I pressed on. "You wanted to talk about—that ship."

He nodded. "You just startled me, is all, when you brought it up at Gargalian's." He looked past me, more or less at the door to the kitchen, which I knew had a round window in it. "You know, when I went to NewYou, I asked them if there was any way to edit out portions of my memories as they did the transfer, but they said that's not possible. I'd trade all my fossils to get rid of those memories, those flashbacks."

At that moment, Diana reappeared, depositing my gin and Dirk's beer. "And for you?" she said to Berling.

He looked at her with a blank expression. Alcohol was wasted on transfers, and most of them soon gave up paying for it; they could get a buzz or deaden their pain in other ways. Buttrick could rightly say, "We don't serve their kind in here"—but only because they almost never came in.

"Nothing," he said. Diana headed off. This time I didn't watch her depart; I didn't take my eyes off Berling.

"I didn't know the history of that ship when I brought it up," I said. "I'm sorry."

Berling scowled. "What happened aboard the *Traven*"—here in the darkened back corner, he was willing to utter part of the name—"was horrific."

I took a sip of my gin.

"You've got to understand," Berling continued. "We were young kids, most of us." He glanced at Dirk. "Kids like you. Some looking to make a fortune, some looking for adventure, some just looking to get away from Earth. We knew it'd be harsh, but we assumed it would be harsh *after* we got here." He shook his head. "You know why I'm still here? After all these mears? Because I'm terrified of spaceships—couldn't ever bring myself to fly on one again. Not after what happened on the *Traven*."

I tried to make light of it. "Turned out okay," I said. "You must have finally struck it big to buy new bodies for you and your wife."

"Yeah, I've had some luck at last. A couple of new species of rhizomorphs; previously unknown taxons always fetch top coin."

"Good for you. Never had much luck hunting fossils myself."

He placed his perfect hands on the scratched tabletop, palms down. "So, what exactly is it that you're investigating?"

"Some cargo that had been brought here aboard the *Traven* has turned up."

Berling narrowed his eyes. "Cargo?" But then he nodded. "You mean the land mines."

I kept an impassive expression. "What do you know about them?"

"I first heard about them after we landed—somebody discovered some in the cargo hold, or something like that, right?"

"Yes," I said.

"Christ, if I'd known about them while we were still in transit, I'd have set them off. Anything to put an end to it all."

I'd wondered if it had been Berling himself who had brought them on that voyage. After all, he clearly had access to high-quality fossils—which might mean the Alpha. But, judging by the deteriorated state of the unexploded mine Pickover had brought to my office, I'd assumed they'd been planted many years ago, and Berling had apparently only recently come into wealth. "Do you know who smuggled them aboard?" I asked.

"I didn't at the time. Like I said, I didn't even know they were there. But after we got to Mars, yeah, I figured it out. It was . . ." He trailed off.

"Yes?" I prodded, lifting my eyebrows.

Berling tilted his head. "How did you know my wife had transferred, too?"

Oh, crap. "I do quality-assurance follow-ups for NewYou," I said.

"You know that. She's on the list the franchise here gave me to interview next week."

"No, you don't," said Berling. "I was at NewYou a few days ago, getting a couple of minor adjustments made. I asked the new owner there, Fernandez, about you. He said, sure, he *knows* you, but he doesn't employ you. Said when you'd talked to me before you were investigating the disappearance of the previous owner, Joshua Wilkins, who I guess had transferred the same day I had. But when you came to see me about that, Lacie hadn't transferred yet."

"I work for the head office on Earth," I said. "I stopped by your place, but you weren't home."

His eyes narrowed. "Lacie never mentioned that."

"Anyway," I said lightly, "you were saying the person who brought the explosives aboard the *Traven* was . . . ?

But it was too late. Berling was on his feet. He didn't have enough to justify attacking me right there—but he certainly had his suspicions. "I knew I shouldn't trust you, Lomax," he said and stormed out.

I downed the rest of my gin. Dirk, wisely, didn't say a word.

SIXTEEN

I gave Dirk the twenty solars I'd promised him, and we exited The Bent Chisel and went our separate ways. I did not, however, give him back the switchblade I'd taken from him, even though I had it with me; it looked like it'd be a useful thing to carry, along with my phone, my tab, and my revolver.

I was sorry not to have gotten the information Berling had, but if this writer-in-residence fellow was doing a book about the *Traven,* he might know who had brought the land mines onboard. I decided to head out to see him; a little culture never hurt anyone. I took a hovertram since Shopatsky House, the writer's retreat, was way up by the north airlock station.

I'd expected the writer-in-residence to be a mousy academic, like Pickover. But when the green door slid open, it revealed a statuesque biological woman in her late twenties with flawless chestnut skin, sexy brown eyes behind long lashes, and a gorgeous mane of brown hair tumbling over her shoulders. The only thing remotely writerly about her appearance was that she wore honest-to-goodness eyeglasses, something I don't think I'd seen on anyone since leaving Earth.

"Hi," I said, smiling broadly. "I'm Alexander Lomax. I hear you're writing a book."

"I'm trying to," she said, without warmth. "I came here for peace and quiet." She crossed long arms in front of a lovely pair of breasts. "But people keep disturbing me."

"Sorry. I wanted to call ahead—but there's no listing for Shopatsky House in the directory."

"That's rather the point."

"You're writing about the *B. Traven,* right?"

She warmed a little at that. "Yes."

"I'm a private investigator. I'm looking into a matter that involves the *Traven.*"

"I really do jealously guard my time, Mr. Lomax. But as a writer, I often impose on others for help with my research—professors, doctors, scientists, what have you. And so, to keep the karmic balance, I'm always willing to help others who are looking for information, *if* they've done their homework." She peered at me over the top of her glasses; it was a look that was sexy when I'd seen it in old movies, and it was sexy here, too. "It's rude to just waste somebody's time asking them questions you could have answered on your own. So, let's see if *you've* done *your* homework. Why was that ship called the *B. Traven?*"

There's a pub trivia league that meets at The Bent Chisel. I used to make fun of its members—why bother to *remember* stuff, when your phone could *tell* you the answer to any question? But the name *did* faintly ring a bell, and—

And those who said I spent too much time watching old movies can suck it. "After B. Traven," I said, "who wrote the novel *The Treasure of the Sierra Madre,* the basis for the movie of the same name."

Luscious lips curved in a smile, and we both spontaneously said in unison, "'Badges? We don't need no stinkin' badges!'" She was grinning broadly now, and I added, "Of course, that's a misquote. What Gold Hat actually said was, 'Badges? We ain't got no badges. We don't need no badges! I don't have to show you any stinkin' badges!'"

She nodded. "Just like no one actually said, 'Play it again, Sam.'"

I did my best Bogey—an impression that hardly made an impression on anyone these days. "'Play it, Sam. You played it for her, you can play it for me. If she can stand it, I can stand it.'"

"Mr. Lomax," she said, stepping aside and gesturing, "won't you come in?"

It was too early to say, "I think this is the beginning of a beautiful friendship," so I didn't—but I *thought* it.

Shopatsky House looked very comfortable. Most furniture on Mars was printed here, rather than shipped in from Earth, but a couple of these pieces looked like real wood—including the . . . the . . . I dug through my memory for the term; I'd only ever seen such things in movies before: the roll-top desk. Sitting on it was a red cube about ten centimeters on a side; a household computer. Damn things didn't have to be that big, but people tended to lose them if they were smaller.

There was also another piece of furniture I'd never seen in real life: a filing cabinet. If I had one, I'd keep bottles of booze in it; I didn't know anyone who had paper files.

I realized I'd lucked out with her little test. I'd seen that movie a hundred times, and back when it was made, it was normal for only a few names to appear on the credits, instead of every damn catering assistant and holography technician. The author's name had caught my eye because it had included just a single initial: "B. Traven." That film—about the quest for gold in Mexico—*did* have interesting resonances for the hunt for fossils on Mars.

But if this gorgeous writer's trivia question had been a more prosaic one—"What's my name?"—I would have failed. My detective skills quickly came to the rescue, though, because there was a third piece of furniture I'd never seen used for its intended purpose before: a bookcase. Every set of boxed-in shelves I'd ever encountered simply displayed curios, *objets d'art,* or—here on Mars—interesting rocks or fossils. But this one, made of reddish brown wood that had a warmth to it that none of the reddish things native to this planet had, was partially filled with real printed books—doubtless the single biggest repository of such things on all of Mars.

The first two shelves contained volumes by Stavros Shopatsky with lurid titles like *The Wanton Savior, The Shores of Death,* and *Pirates in the Wind.* The subsequent shelves had books grouped by authors—but not alphabetically. First Hayakawa, then Chavez, then Torkoff, then Cohen. "Are these the other writers who have been in residence here?" I asked.

"That's right," she said, nodding that lovely head of hers. "We're each supposed to bring at least five kilograms of our own books as part of our personal mass allowance. If our books are only in e-editions, we're to have leather-bound copies produced to bring with us."

My eyes tracked to the second shelf from the bottom, which was partially full. An odd little L-shaped thingy pressed against the last book to keep them all from toppling over. The name on the spines of the last three books was Lakshmi Chatterjee. I reached down and extracted the final volume; its title was *Lunaport: Valor and Independence.*

"And now you're writing about the *B. Traven?*"

"Exactly."

"I'm trying to find out who smuggled the explosives aboard the *Traven.*"

"Ah, yes," she said. "The land mines." She headed into the living room and motioned for me to sit down. I'd hoped she was going to take the green couch, meaning I could move in next to her, but she took the matching chair instead.

I leaned into the corner of the couch and swung my legs up, leaving my feet projecting off the cushions into the air. "How much longer will you be on Mars?" The question had nothing whatsoever to do with the investigation.

"Another seventy-one days."

I smiled. "Not that anyone's counting."

"The next writer is coming in then; I go back on the ship that's bringing him."

"You looking forward to going home?"

"Somewhat. I like it here."

"Where *is* home for you?"

She crossed her long legs. She was wearing tight-fitting pants that looked like black leather and a tight-fitting black top. "Delhi." She looked at a wall clock—an *analog* wall clock; it always took me forever to decode those. But the point was plain; I should move things along. "Do you know who brought the land mines aboard the *Traven?*"

"Sure. It was Willem Van Dyke—the same guy Weingarten and O'Reilly had taken along on their second voyage."

I shook my head. "I've seen the passenger manifest. He wasn't on the *Traven,* at least not under that name."

"He wasn't a passenger," Lakshmi said. "He was crew."

"You mean—you mean *he* was the monster? The one who thawed out passengers and terrorized them?"

"No, no. He was the backup bowman; the spare. He was supposed to be kept on ice the whole voyage, and only thawed out in an emergency."

"Ah," I said. "And do you know what became of him?"

"Of course. I'm covering that in my book."

I looked at her expectantly. "And?"

She tilted her head and brushed lustrous hair out of her eyes. "I'll send you an invitation to the book-launch party."

I smiled my most-charming smile. "Please, Lakshmi. I'd really like to know."

She considered for a moment, then: "I don't know how much you know about the history of human space flight."

"Some. What they taught in school." Except on Fridays.

"Well, did you know that some space scientists used to say it was *impossible* for humans to safely come to Mars, or live here?"

"When did they say that?"

"From the 1970s to, oh, say, 2030 or so."

"Why?"

"Radiation."

"Really?"

"Yup. Earth's magnetosphere and atmosphere protect people on Earth's surface from solar and cosmic radiation. And they argued that without those shields, you'd get too big a dose coming to Mars or staying on its surface."

I smiled. "Shall we turn off the lights and see if we glow?"

"Exactly. It was a risible contention. The scientists who were making it were either talking outside their field of expertise or were deliberately misleading people."

I lifted my eyebrows. "Why?"

"A turf war. Sure, here on Mars we get more radiation than people on Earth do—enough for each year living under the dome to increase by a whopping *one percent* your chance of getting cancer sometime in the next thirty years. The scientists saying cancer was a showstopper were all either in the business of unmanned probes or wanted to spend forever hanging in Low Earth Orbit." She paused. "You know anyone who smokes tobacco?"

"My grandmother used to."

"Yeah. Well, if she'd moved to Mars but left her cigarettes behind on Earth, she'd have *reduced* her chances of getting cancer."

"Okay," I said. "So?"

"So, getting cancer via space travel or while living on Mars is a vanishingly slim chance. But, then again, so is striking it rich finding fossils here. That happens, and so does the cancer thing—just very, very rarely. Well, Willem Van Dyke didn't discover fossil riches—Weingarten and

O'Reilly did that, and they just brought him along for the ride. But he *did* win the other lottery, poor bastard: he's the one in a thousand who got cancer by traveling in space."

"And then what?" I asked.

"I'm still trying to find out. There are references thirty years ago to him having a terminal diagnosis, and I haven't turned up anything after that. Of course, he knew where the Alpha mother lode was, and even though Weingarten and O'Reilly ripped him off, he probably kept a few good fossils. I suspect he's long dead, but with the money those fossils would have fetched, he probably went out in style."

"Could he have transferred?"

"He might have possibly had enough money, yeah, but I doubt he'd have done that. This was decades ago, remember. Van Dyke was very religious. He believed he had an immortal soul and didn't believe that soul could be transferred into an artificial body. There were a lot of people like that back then. Even today, there are still some who want to overturn *Durksen v. Hawksworth* in the States."

I'd been all of twelve when that case had begun. A crazed gunman had shot President Vanessa Durksen. There had been no way to save her body, but Howard Slapcoff had successfully urged the president's chief of staff to have her mind transferred, and have the transfer serve out the rest of her term, instead of having the vice-president, who everyone agreed was a disaster, sworn in as her successor. Durksen had been well into her second term then, so there was no way she could stand for re-election, but a lot of pundits said the transfer could have won if she'd been eligible to run again. It had been a brilliant coup for Howard Slapcoff. Durksen had been scrutinized minutely by the whole planet—her every word, her every decision—to see if she'd changed in the slightest after transferring, and most people (except a few ideologues in the opposing party) agreed that she hadn't; mainstream acceptance of transfers really still being the same person began with that.

"Okay," I said. "Thanks. I appreciate the help."

She unfolded her long legs and rose. "Now, was there anything else? I really do have to get back to my book."

"No," I said. "But thank you." I tipped my nonexistent hat and, with considerable regret, left her and headed out into the dreary world under the dome.

· · · · · · · · · · ·

I spent the rest of the day searching for information about Willem Van Dyke. Although the Privacy Revolution of 2034 had made it a lot easier for people to not leave tracks wherever they went, most people still had pretty extensive online presences. But not Willem Van Dyke—or, at least not the Willem Van Dyke in question; it turned out to be an irritatingly common name. He really did seem to go off the grid thirty years ago, just as Rory Pickover and Lakshmi Chatterjee had said. I suppose he could have just headed out into the wilderness to die—but there was no death notice that I could find.

Once night fell, I went to see Rory Pickover at his apartment at the center of the dome. After he'd let me in, and we were seated in his yellow-walled living room, I dove into what I wanted. "You promised to take me to see the Alpha."

Pickover looked at me unblinkingly. I stared him down as long as I could, but his acrylic peepers weren't affected even by direct exposure to the desiccated Martian atmosphere, so he won. But I wasn't going to give up. "Seriously," I said. "I need to see it."

"It's nothing to look at," he replied.

Pickover himself was nothing to look at either, at the moment; most of the skin was still gone from his face. "I understand that. But I'm having no luck tracing Van Dyke—and there may be a clue to his whereabouts there."

"All right," Pickover said, surprising me; I'd expected the argument to last longer. "Let's go."

"Now?"

"Sure, now." He stood up. "It's dark out—that's my first line of defense in keeping you from recognizing landmarks. Second line of defense will be having you polarize your surface-suit helmet for the journey, meaning you'll barely be able to see out of it in the dark. Third line of defense will be my taking a circuitous route to get us there. Fourth line of defense is that by this late you must be tired, meaning you might even fall asleep on the journey—indeed, you'll want to, since it'll take hours, and we won't be able to accomplish much until dawn."

I'd kind of hoped to make it over to The Bent Chisel tonight to see Diana, but at least he was agreeing to take me. "All right," I said, getting up as well.

"Great. Bathroom's down there, old boy—better avail yourself before we head out, and . . ."

"What?"

"Oh, nothing. Haven't used it myself in months—not since I transferred. I hope I remembered to flush."

SEVENTEEN

Since the episode with Joshua Wilkins, I'd researched ways to kill a transfer, just to be on the safe side. Sadly, except for using a broadband disruptor, there didn't seem to be any reliable method. That made sense, of course: the bodies were designed to cheat death—they were highly durable, with vital components encased in protective armor. I'd tried to find a way, but it seemed kryptonite was hard to come by on Mars.

Even so, Pickover made me leave my gun in a locker at the western airlock station—I guess he was afraid I might try to do him in once he'd shown me where the riches were located. He didn't know I'd acquired a switchblade from Dirk, though, and he was too naïve to give me a pat-down before we headed out, so I kept that in my pocket.

My detective's brain was hard at work trying to figure out precisely where he was taking me. First clue: we'd exited through the western airlock, and this was the one bit of information that couldn't be misdirection for my sake, since it was where he'd parked his privately owned Mars buggy when he'd last returned from the Alpha.

Thank God Pickover had bought the buggy prior to transferring, because it was the expensive kind that had its own life-support system. If he'd been buying one today, he'd doubtless have opted for the cheaper—and more reliable—ones that simply provided transportation.

Pickover rented me a surface suit. He paid for it directly, since he would have ended up being expensed for it, anyway—but I didn't have to wear it for the long drive, although he did make me put the fishbowl over my head. On Earth, that would have been uncomfortable—normally, the suit's collar bore the weight of the helmet—but the thing wasn't heavy enough here to be bothersome. Pickover did make it opaque, though, before we started tooling along.

A planitia is a low plain, and just like their counterparts on Earth, they tended to be nothing but miles and miles of miles and miles. We chatted a bit at first, but having to listen to Rory's voice echo in the fishbowl was unpleasant, and after a time we both fell silent. I confess I wiled away the hours thinking about Diana, Lacie, and Lakshmi, separately and in various permutations.

I possibly did doze on the trip—tough guy like me doesn't often think about his childhood, but when my mom wanted me to sleep and I wouldn't, she used to take me for a drive. Pickover had also made me leave my tablet computer and phone behind; I had no tools that might help me calculate our location. But by the time we got to where we were going, the sun was rising in the east. I'd been hoping it would be coming up over jagged peaks or broken crater walls that I could match to topographical maps, but the illuminated part of the horizon—and, as I saw as the sun climbed higher, the horizon all the way around—was just more smooth ground, with one exception: to the west, there was the crumbling wall of a small crater.

I used the buggy's toilet then got into the rented surface suit—this one was kind of a drab olive green—and exited the vehicle. The buggy had springy wheels almost a meter across, and a boxy clear passenger cabin; the Martian atmosphere was tenuous enough that streamlining didn't matter for surface vehicles.

Pickover went to the buggy's trunk and pulled out a device that looked a bit like an upright vacuum cleaner with no bag attached.

"What's that?" I asked.

"A metal detector. I just got it yesterday."

"I'd have thought those would be useless on Mars," I said, "because of all the iron oxide in the soil."

"Oh, it's easy to tune metal detectors to ignore iron. But I did have a devil of a time finding one to rent. They're of no help in fossil hunting, of course, and the standard uses for such things—beachcombing, searching for archeological artifacts, and so on—simply don't apply here."

He handed it to me.

I raised my eyebrows. "You want me to do the minesweeping?"

"I can't," Rory said. "I tried—but the metal in my body interferes too much with the detector. You, on the other hand . . ."

The guy was more clever than I'd given him credit for. He hadn't brought me out here because I wanted to see the Alpha; he'd brought me out here because he needed the help of a biological.

He went back to the trunk and brought out another device: a tank of compressed gas with a flexible hose attached. "For blowing sand," Rory said, evidently anticipating my question.

"Okay," I said. "Show me where you found the first land mine."

"This way. Follow in my footsteps precisely. I've used this path numerous times; it's either free of land mines or they've all corroded like that one I brought to your office."

He led, dust rising from his footfalls. I still found it bizarre to see a person in street clothes walking unprotected on Mars. Pickover was wearing what I imagined paleontologists wore back on Earth: brown work boots, heavy khaki pants, and a flannel work shirt. He'd also put on a baseball cap with the logo of the Toronto Blue Jays; I guess transfers needed something to keep the sun out of their eyes, too.

We headed out about fifty meters—I counted the paces—and came to an area that had been marked off into a grid of meter-wide squares by monofilament. The strands were almost exactly the same color as the red dust, and I mentioned that they were hard to see. "Not in the infrared," Pickover replied. "I'm running a small current through them from that excimer pack, there. To me, they're bright white, but the average prospector won't notice them at all unless he trips over them."

He stepped over one of the strands, and I gingerly did the same. We did this five more times and then stopped. "We're still a ways from where the land mine went off," he said crouching, "but let me show you this. It's the spot where I found the counter slab for two-dash-thirteen-eighty-eight."

"The fossils are lying right out on the surface?"

"Occasionally," said Pickover, "but they're usually a short distance down—but only a short distance. See, on Earth, sedimentary rocks have been forming for billions of years. But on Mars, sedimentation came to an end over three and a half billion years ago, when the open bodies of water dried up. So, instead of ancient sediments being deeply buried, they're right on the surface—or just about. The water ice close to the surface here at the Alpha long ago either dissociated or sublimated, leaving eight or ten centimeters of loose, dry sand overtop of the ancient matrix. At the Alpha, that matrix is made out of areslithia—Mars stone. It's really just sand and silt fused with water ice; the ground here is as much as sixty percent water ice by weight. Do you see what that means, Alex?"

I didn't. "What?"

"Well, on Earth, most fossils are permineralized: the spaces in the original organic material have been filled in by minerals percolating through the ground; that new material replaces the original biological specimen, which ultimately disappears. But here at the Alpha, the fossils *are* the original material, simply embedded in the matrix. You can often get an Alpha fossil out of the matrix just by bringing the areslithia up to room temperature and letting the ice melt. That's why the fossils from here at the Alpha are so good—they're the actual ancient exoskeletons, unaltered, preserved in a dense slurry that's been frozen solid for over three billion years."

"Not completely, I bet. That land mine you brought in was corroded."

Pickover nodded. "Yes, true. Something—maybe a micrometeoroid impact a couple of decades ago—heated a patch of the soil enough that there was a small pocket of running groundwater, and that's what rusted out that mine. But most of the rest of this whole field"—he gestured expansively—"has been completely frozen since the Noachian."

"But that counter slab you brought to my office was solid, even at room temperature."

"Only because I'd infused it with a stabilizer, replacing the water content with thermoplastic."

"Ah."

He rose and continued walking. After about forty meters we came to a spot where there was a big divot out of the ground. "That's where the mine that blew up was," he said pointing. "And over there's where I recovered that one that was rusted through." He indicated a much smaller defect in the surface.

I began a slow minesweep of all 6,000 square meters of what Pickover had identified as the Alpha Deposit; he walked behind me.

While we walked along, I tried to commit landmarks to memory; this was my first time here at the Alpha, but I suspected it wouldn't be my last, and knowing the terrain is halfway to winning a battle. Going right back to the first *Viking* landers, people had been giving whimsical names to various Martian boulders. Off to my left was a big one that looked like the kind of car I'd seen in 1950s movies—it even had a couple of fin-like projections; I mentally dubbed it "Plymouth." And to my right was a head-shaped rock with craggy good looks; the old-movie buff in me felt "Hudson" was the perfect name for it.

It turned out the Alpha wasn't surrounded by land mines—which, after all, would have required a lot of them. But there was an extant line of twelve, each about eight meters from the next, along the eastern perimeter of the Alpha; the one that had exploded, and the one that had rusted out, would have been two additional points along that line. I guess that meant New Klondike was indeed east of here, and Willem Van Dyke had assumed anyone out looking for the Alpha would come from that direction.

If this were an old battlefield, we'd just lob rocks at the remaining land mines and blow each of them up in turn. But that might damage precious fossils, and so instead we set about carefully clearing them. The mines were mostly buried under a couple of centimeters of dry sand. Rory used his blower at a shallow angle to remove the sand from on top of one of the mines, and sure enough, the deactivation hole was visible right in the middle of the disk. The hole was actually plugged with sand, which is something neither of us had anticipated but we both probably should have. But after a moment, a thought occurred to me. I had transferred the knife to the equipment pouch on my surface suit. I pulled it out.

"What's that?"

"A switchblade, I said.

He frowned, clearly unhappy that I'd brought a weapon along. But I handed it to him, and showed him the button that caused the blade to spring out. He had better balance than me, better reflexes, and had already proven he could survive a land-mine explosion. And so he stood over the mine, one leg on either side of it, and he bent over, positioned the closed switchblade above the deactivation hole, and pressed the button.

The blade shot out, nicely slicing through the sand, and its tip must indeed have hit the button down below because a little mechanical flag on the top of the mine, near the center, flipped over from red to green—just as the material I'd read said it would.

Rory couldn't let out a sigh of relief, but I could, and did. He then pried the mine up; it seemed stuck a bit in the permafrost beneath it, but it finally came free. We repeated the process eight meters farther along, deactivating and liberating another Caldera-7.

We could have continued on, deactivating all the other mines, but by this point I needed something to eat. And so we each picked up one of the deactivated mines and headed back toward the buggy; I'd bought some sandwiches from the little shop at the airlock station but needed to go inside the pressurized cabin so I could take off my fishbowl to eat them.

Before we did that, though, Pickover opened the buggy's trunk again, and we put the deactivated mines inside; on the way back home, we'd find someplace to dispose of them. There were brown fabric sacks in the trunk; part of a paleontologist's kit, I guessed. Pickover used some of them to make nests to carefully cushion the mines, just in case.

While he was doing that, I looked out at the area, which, to my eye, seemed no different from anywhere else on this part of Mars: endless orange plains under a yellow-brown sky, and—

Oh, Christ.

"Rory," I said, over my helmet radio, "do you have telescopic vision?"

He closed the trunk, straightened, and faced me. "Sort of. I've got a twenty-to-one zoom built-in. It helps when working on fossils. Why?"

I pointed toward the horizon. "Is that what I think it is?"

I watched as he turned his gaze. Nothing happened on his face, making me wonder what mental command he used to access the zoom function. "Who could that be?" he asked.

Damn. So it *was* another Mars buggy, sitting out on the planitia. We'd been tailed through the dark, all the way here from New Klondike. Normally, I'd have spotted a tail almost at once, but I'd had this stupid polarized fishbowl over my noggin for the whole ride out.

And Pickover had made me leave my gun behind.

EIGHTEEN

"I think we should get out of here," I said into my headset microphone.

"We can't leave the Alpha exposed to looters," Pickover replied.

"Rory, we're defenseless."

"The fossils are defenseless."

"Damn it!" I intended the curse for him, but as I said it, the distant Mars buggy started moving in, kicking up a plume of dust as it did so, and Pickover took the words as a response to that.

"Yeah," he said. "They're barreling directly toward us."

The radio we were using was supposed to be encrypted, but whoever was coming at us now might have bribed the guy I rented my suit from to reveal the encryption code. The person or persons in that Mars buggy might well be listening in on everything I said to Pickover, and so now knew that they'd been spotted.

When two biologicals didn't want to use radio on the surface, they touched their helmets together and let the sound pass between them. Pickover wasn't wearing a helmet. I wondered if he'd opted for super hearing as well as super vision—although I couldn't imagine what use the former would be for a fossil hunter. I turned off my radio and shouted, "They might be listening in on our communications."

The Martian atmosphere was only about one percent as thick as Earth's; it conducted sound, but not very well. Pickover was looking at me but it was clear that he hadn't heard what I'd said. I walked over to him and motioned for him to stand still. I then leaned my helmet against his artificial head.

"I say!" he exclaimed as I did so.

I spoke only slightly louder than normal. "They may have been listening to our radio. Turn yours off." I pulled my head away, and he nodded but didn't do anything else, again making me wonder how that worked for a transfer—what did he do inside his mind that deactivated the transmitter? But although I could make noise—my helmet was pressurized—his jaw was flapping in the tenuous Martian air and wasn't making any sound I could hear. I was good at reading lips—a marketable skill for a detective—but the restrained movements of his were different enough from those of a biological that I wasn't able to make out what he was saying.

I touched my helmet to his forehead—the only time in recent memory that I'd done something similar was head-butting a drunk at The Bent Chisel. "I can't hear you," I said loudly. "Let's separate. They can only come after one of us in that vehicle. You stay here. I'll see if I can draw them away from the Alpha, okay?"

He nodded his head; it slid against the helmet. It was fortunate that his hair was synthetic; the last thing I needed was a smear of oil obscuring my vision through the fishbowl. Having finished quarterbacking our next play, I snapped, "Break!" and started running in a direction perpendicular to the incoming buggy.

I could run like the wind inside the dome—but the surface suit and air tanks added fifty kilos to my normal ninety, and the layer of dust on the plain made it hard to get good footing. Still, I put everything I had into it, hoping the intruder would go after me: it was the nature of all predators, human or otherwise, to chase after someone who was trying to escape. Looking to my right, it did seem the buggy—still some distance off—was veering toward me.

Of course, I had no idea what I'd do if whoever it was *did* intercept me. Even if they didn't have a gun, anything that would smash my helmet would do to finish me off out here.

My heart was pounding, and I was sweating inside the suit—which was not a good thing: I was fogging up the fishbowl. The suit did have dehumidifier controls, but I'd have to stop running to fiddle with them, and I didn't want to do that. And since the fog was on the inside of the helmet, I couldn't wipe it away with my hands, either, and—

And *damn!* The surface of Mars was littered with rocks, and my boot caught on one, and I went flying. At least I came back down in slo-mo; I had plenty of time to brace myself for the impact. I looked toward the buggy and could make it out in more detail now. It was yellow—not an uncommon color for such things—and it had a pressurized habitat, meaning whoever was chasing me was more likely biological than not.

I scrambled to my feet and started running again. There was no doubt now that the buggy was coming at me, rather than Pickover. I'd expected it to rush right up to me, but it skidded to a stop about seventy meters away, spinning through a half turn. Ah, it had come to the periphery of the Alpha, and the driver had slammed on the brakes; either they knew about the land mines, or they didn't want to risk damaging any exposed fossils by driving over them.

The buggy's boxy habitat swung backward on hinges, and I saw the white cloud of condensation that occurs when breathable air is vented into the Martian atmosphere. Coming through the cloud were two figures in surface suits. The helmets were polarized, so I couldn't see who was inside, but the person on my left, wearing a red suit, was a curvy female, and the one on my right, in a blue suit, had the bulk of a man. The woman was carrying what might have been a pump-action shotgun, although where someone would get such a thing on Mars, I had no idea; it's not like they were needed to kill varmints here.

They started running toward me, and I now weaved left and right as I ran. I wasn't sure what I was running *for*—there was no shelter, although I thought hills were starting to peek over the horizon, which suggested we might be near Syrtis Major.

I looked to my left, trying to spot Pickover, but couldn't make him out. I looked back to my right and saw the woman in red fire the shotgun. There was almost no report from the blast in this thin air, but I saw the lick of flame. She didn't come anywhere near to hitting me—suggesting she wasn't experienced with a gun.

When they weren't weighed down by surface suits, you could see at a glance if a runner was new to Mars or not; it took a while to get the hang of sailing so far with each stride. But I couldn't tell about this woman. The man, though, was an old hand; he was close enough now that I could make out details of the suit he was wearing. It had an old-fashioned helmet that was glass only at the front. No one rented suits like that anymore, so this guy probably owned his—and had for at least ten mears.

Another blast from the shotgun. If they hit me in the suit, it probably wouldn't kill me; the pressure-webbing in the fabric would double nicely as a reasonably bulletproof lining. But although the helmet was impact resistant, it wasn't shatterproof; alloquartz did a great job of screening out UV, and wouldn't break if you dropped it—especially in Mars's gravity—but the warranties specifically disclaimed micrometeorite damage, and I imagined lead shot coming in at high speed was a good approximation of such impacts.

I decided to reactivate my radio. I did that by hitting a control in the suit collar with my chin; it was just to the left of the tube that snaked around from behind, bringing air into the fishbowl. "Pickover," I said, "remember, they may be listening in. Don't tell me where you are—but I'm heading west, and they've opened fire on me."

The cultured English accent: "Roger."

Another male voice on the same circuit, half out of breath from running. "Professor Pickover, is that you?"

Pickover, surprised: "Yes. Who is this?"

"Professor, my name's Darren Cheung. I'm with the United States Geological Survey. We thought you were someone looting the fossil beds."

"It's a trick, Pickover!" I shouted.

But the little paleontologist wasn't as naïve as I feared. "The girls can flirt and other queer things can do," he said. If it was a code for me, I didn't know it. He added, "What's that mean?"

"Professor," said the same male voice, "we're wasting time."

Pickover's voice was harsh. "Get him, Alex."

I appreciated his faith in me, but I didn't have any idea just then *how* to get him—or the woman who was also closing rapidly. There was another blast—visual, not aural—from the shotgun, and this time I was hit in the shoulder. The impact knocked me sideways, and I sent up a dust cloud when I fell. Beneath the dust, there were loose rocks. I grabbed one about the size of a grapefruit, scrambled to my feet, and continued running. My shoulder hurt, but the suit seemed intact, and—

And, no, damn it, there was a chip out of my helmet. It hadn't broken all the way through, but the structure had doubtless weakened; another hit, and I'd be sucking in nothing but thin carbon dioxide.

The man was slightly outpacing the woman, and that was working to my advantage—she seemed reluctant to shoot again with him in front of her; perhaps she was worried about going wide enough of her mark to hit him instead of me.

I had no such compunctions. The man was now close enough that I could throw my rock at him. All that bench-pressing at Gully's paid off, and I had plenty of experience throwing things under Martian gravity—as Buttrick at The Bent Chisel could testify. I hit the man right in the faceplate, and it cracked in a spider-web pattern that probably obscured his vision but I didn't think was going to result in him gasping for breath, unfortunately.

Still, it slowed him down enough that the woman was now in front again, and she brought the shotgun up to her red-suited shoulder. She was clearly about to fire when Pickover's voice burst into my helmet, and hers, too, presumably. "Look out, Alex!"

I swung my head to the right and saw our Mars buggy rushing toward us, a great cloud going up behind it. As I leapt to one side, I was touched that Pickover was willing to drive over his precious fossil beds to rescue me. He slammed the brakes in a way that would have made a screeching sound in a real atmosphere, and popped the clear habitat roof open. I leapt in, and he put his metal to the pedal. I thought he was going to take us through a wide one-eighty, but instead he aimed directly for the woman in red. I struggled to pull the lid down over the habitat as he continued to roar toward her, clearly aiming to mow her down. But she was aiming, too—right at us.

That the woman was reasonably new to Mars was now obvious. The best way to stop a car on Earth was to shoot out the pneumatic tires, but we favored springy wiry things. The angle between the spokes changed constantly under computer control, and each spoke led not to a continuous rim but to a separate pad. A camera up front watched for obstacles, and the spokes configured themselves to make it possible to go over most rocks without even touching them. Trying to shoot such wheels out was useless, but she nonetheless fired at our left front tire—and it didn't slow us down at all.

The man in the blue suit started running back toward their yellow Mars buggy. He wasn't going as fast as he'd been before; I suspect he'd slowed down not so much out of fatigue—having a guy hurtling toward you in a motorized vehicle tended to get the old adrenaline going—but because he was having trouble seeing through the cracks in his faceplate.

Pickover had to make a choice: go after the woman with the gun or after the apparently unarmed man who had a chance of getting back to his buggy. I could think of arguments for either selection, and didn't gainsay the one Rory made: he decided to pursue the woman, who was running like the wind.

There was no way she could outrace us on a flat surface, but even a planitia has some craters on it, like God had peppered it with his own shotgun. She was heading straight for the one I'd noticed before; it was maybe thirty meters across. The crater wall rose in front of us. To get up it, she had to drop the shotgun, and it skittered with Martian indolence down the crater face. She scrambled up, gloves clawing for purchase. Damn, but I wished I had my gun! It would have been easy to take her out while her back was to us. Our springy wheels did their best, but when the slope exceeded forty-five degrees, they weren't able to get enough traction, and we started backsliding.

I unlatched the habitat lid, and it fell open, letting me hop out. The buggy managed to reverse its slide and climb back up a bit farther after the weight of me and my surface suit was no longer in it. But soon the slope proved too much again, and Pickover abandoned the buggy, too; the vehicle came to rest half-on and half-off the sloping, crumbling crater wall. I flipped open the trunk, exposing the land mines. The activation knob was on the underside of the mine, dead center, behind a little spring-loaded safety door. I reactivated both mines, and saw that the flags on their upper surfaces turned red. I then picked up one of the mines, supporting it underhanded by its rim.

The man had succeeded in his retreat; I could see him in the distance clambering into their buggy. I'd thought he was going to hightail it away from here, but he came charging toward us again. I chinned my radio: "One warning only: get out of the buggy!"

It was possible that the damage to his helmet had wrecked his microphone in addition to impairing his vision. Or maybe he just didn't feel inclined to take orders from me. Either way, he kept racing my way at a clip I couldn't outrun. I took a bead on the approaching vehicle, and flung the land mine the way you'd toss a discus. It spun through the air and—

Ka-blam!

—hit the flat front of the buggy's habitat, exploding on impact. The canopy was reduced to crystalline shards that went flying. I saw the man in the blue suit throw up his arms, trying to cover his face—

His *exposed* face: the glass visor of his helmet was gone. He gasped for breath—and I imagine he felt the linings of his lungs seizing up in the wicked cold of an equatorial Martian day.

His vehicle was still moving, though—the habitat was wrecked, but the chassis was intact and those big wheels kept on rolling, propelling it at high speed along the wall of the crater and—God damn it!—straight toward me and our Mars buggy.

I ran as fast as I could, but the incoming vehicle plowed into our buggy, and the other land mine I'd activated in preparation for throwing it went off, and I watched as the axles snapped on the incoming yellow buggy and our buggy burst into flames that almost immediately were snuffed out by the carbon dioxide atmosphere.

We were all marooned in the middle of nowhere.

NINETEEN

I rushed over to the man in the blue surface suit. He'd tumbled out of the wreckage and was still desperately trying to cover his face. I looked around for anything that could help him do that: tarpaulin, plastic sheeting, even paper. But there was nothing.

I doubted he could still hear me, given that the air was out of his helmet, but I said, "Hold on!" anyway. I used my gloved hands in addition to his own to try to make a new front for his helmet. For a moment, I thought it was working, but even though clouds of air were still coming out of the tubes attached to his tank, his fingers went slack and his arms dropped down, and there were now huge gaps that I couldn't cover.

And so at last I got a good look at his face. His nose had bled—low air pressure or the impact—but the blood had now frozen onto his face, a narrow face that was Asian, perhaps sixty years old, with thick gray hair. I didn't recognize him. His mouth worked for a few moments—gasping for air, or hurtling invective at me, I couldn't say which. And then it just stopped moving, about half open. I took no pleasure in watching this man expire, even though he'd tried to kill me—but I didn't waste any tears over it, either.

I'd lost track of Pickover during all this, and, swinging my head in the fishbowl, I saw no sign of him—which meant he must be inside the crater, along with the lady in red. I looked around for the discarded shotgun and found it. Damn thing had gone barrel-down into the dust and probably had a bunch of it in the bore now. Still, I grabbed it and scrambled up the crater's rim, which was about three meters high, and peered over the edge.

I'd expected to see Pickover having captured her at this point. After all, she was now unarmed and he was much more nimble as a transfer than she—whoever she was—could possibly be in a surface suit. But Pickover was—well, I couldn't exactly say he was a lover not a fighter . . . but he definitely wasn't a fighter. Although it was true she no longer had a gun, she did apparently have a lasso: a loop of what, judging by its dark color, were fibers made of carbon nanotubes, meaning it would be almost impossible to break even with a transfer's strength. And she'd managed to get it around his ankles and had pulled it tight. While I watched, she gave the lasso a yank, pulling Pickover's legs out from under him. He tumbled backward—a body slam, not a slo-mo fall—landing flat on his back and sending up a cloud of dust.

As it happened, Pickover was facing my way; she had her back to me. I could make it two for two, pumping shot into her from behind, but her suit might protect her. And, besides, I had questions I wanted to ask. I hauled myself up over the crater rim and clambered down the crumbly incline. The two of them were just shy of the crater's central bulge.

Pickover tried to get to his feet. The woman yanked the lasso again, and he tumbled backward once more. I think she'd have preferred to hog-tie him, but she didn't have enough rope for that—I imagine she'd improvised the lasso out of line she'd brought along to help with climbing; she must have thought the Alpha might have been deep in some crevasse, and—

Yes, that was it. She didn't have another real gun, true—but she had a piton gun attached to her suit's belt, and she bent over now and positioned it against the center of Pickover's artificial chest. She presumably hoped that firing a metal spike into his innards would damage *something* that would incapacitate him. She pulled the trigger.

Pickover screamed and his torso convulsed. It was like watching a biological getting defibrillated, but the intent was the opposite. I had made it down to the reasonably flat bottom of the crater. There was hoarfrost along this part of the wall, since it hadn't yet been touched by the rising sun.

The woman, who was straddling Pickover, moved the piton gun farther down his chest and fired again. Once more, Rory convulsed from the impact. I brought the shotgun to my shoulder and Pickover seemed to be tucking his knees up toward his torso, maybe to protect his nuts and bolt.

I fired, the recoil pushing me backward a bit—and Pickover got his knees through the woman's spread legs and kicked her in the chest with his bound feet. She went flying up a good two meters, and the bulk of my shot flew through the gap that had appeared between her and Pickover before she came down again.

Rory rolled onto his side so she wouldn't fall on top of him, and I hurried in. She hit the ground before I'd closed all the distance and was in a push-up posture, trying to get to her feet, by the time I got there. I grabbed her shoulder and flipped her onto her back, then loomed over her with the shotgun aimed right at her helmet.

"Can you hear me?" I said into my suit radio.

I gave her time to weigh whether she wanted to reply—and, after a moment, she did, although the connection was staticky and hard to make out. "Yes."

"I want to see your face. There are two ways that can happen. One is I blast open your helmet. The other is you depolarize it. Your choice."

She just lay there. Maybe she was hoping blue boy would come to her rescue, jumping me from behind. I wanted to see her face when I broke the news—not out of any sick desire to watch her feel hurt, but because her reaction would be a useful clue to the nature of their relationship.

"Five seconds, lady," I said. "One. Two. Three."

She moved her right hand to the bank of buttons on her left forearm, and the bowl went from reflecting a distorted image of me to being transparent.

And that face I did know, a gorgeous symphony in chocolate shades: brown skin, brown hair, brown eyes. Lakshmi Chatterjee, New Klondike's writer-in-residence.

"Sweetheart," I said, "I thought we had something special."

"We still could," she replied. She indicated Pickover, who was lying on his side. "With him out of the picture, you, me, and Darren split it three ways."

"Just two ways, honey. Darren is dead."

Her brown eyes went wide, but she didn't seem too broken up by it, and, after a moment, she said, "Even better."

I looked over at Pickover, and, yeah, I thought about it for half a second. Now, you could say that all things being equal, it made more sense to share the wealth with Rory, who'd never tried to kill me, than with Lakshmi, who'd happily shoot pitons into my chest, too, if given the chance. But old Dr. Pickover wasn't going to let these fossils be sold, so there was no sharing to do with him.

Still, I *liked* the guy.

"No dice," I said. I reached down and wrenched the piton gun from her and sent it flying—it was easy enough to toss it clear over the crater's rim. "Roll over," I said. "Face down."

Lakshmi hesitated, so I pushed the shotgun muzzle right up against her fishbowl. She nodded within and turned onto her stomach. "Don't move," I said.

I went over to Pickover. If he'd been knifed, the standard advice would be to leave the blades in, lest removing them exposed gaping wounds through which he'd bleed to death. But I thought in this case the metal spikes might be causing electrical shorts inside him, and so I grabbed them—my suit's gloves insulating me—and pulled them free. One came out clean; the other was covered with black machine oil. I tossed them aside.

"You okay?" I asked.

He looked no worse for wear—although the workings of his face were still exposed. "I think so."

I glanced at his bound ankles. "You still have my switchblade?" He'd kept it after using it to disarm the two mines.

"In the pouch," he said.

I opened his equipment pouch and took out the knife. I tried to cut through the material, but my guess had been right: it was carbon nanofiber; the knife didn't even make a mark on it. Still, that didn't mean we were out of luck. I went over and kicked Lakshmi none too gently in the thigh. "Up," I said.

She got to her feet.

"You made the lasso," I said, pointing. "Untie it."

She hesitated for a moment then bent over to do so. It took a particularly good figure to look attractive through a surface suit, but, admiring her from behind, it was clear that that was precisely what she had.

"Come on!" I said. "Hurry up!"

"I can't," she said after trying for a bit. She held up her hands. "The gloves are too thick."

"Take them off, then."

"It's fifty below zero!"

I considered. "All right. Rory, can you manage it?"

He sat up. A jet of oil squirted from one of the holes in his chest, but he didn't seem to notice. His fingers were unencumbered, and I imagined he'd opted for a super-high degree of dexterity, since part of his job was preparing minute fossils. I kept the shotgun trained on Lakshmi, while he struggled to loosen the loop—and, at last, he succeeded.

He surprised me by holding out a hand so I could help him get up—but that might just have been the natural thought of the middle-aged mind within the transfer body; I was counting on him not actually being severely injured. I put my gloved hand in his naked one and pulled him to his feet. He nodded his thanks and stepped out of the lasso. I bent over, picked it up, and slipped it over Lakshmi's head and shoulders, pulled it down past her breasts, then cinched it tight, binding her arms below the elbow to her waist—which, again, emphasized her remarkable figure.

I took the other end of the cord, holding it like a leash. I gave her a little shove, and she started walking in front of us. Pickover fell in next to me. I had to let go of the cord to let her, and then me, scramble up the inner crater wall and down the outer one. We'd come out about thirty degrees around the rim from where I'd gone in, and—

"Oh, yeah," I said. "I probably should have mentioned that."

Pickover's artificial jaw had dropped to half-mast. Lakshmi stopped dead in her tracks. "How are we going to get home?" she exclaimed, looking at the two wrecked buggies.

"That's a very good question," I replied. Mars had no telephone system outside the dome, no global positioning system, and no string of communications satellites—it was the frontier. And the planet's weak and wonky ionosphere was no use for bouncing signals, so radio worked only more or less over line of sight—meaning there was no way to call all the way back to New Klondike for help. "Given how long it took to get here," I continued, "and even allowing for Rory possibly not having taken the most direct route out, I'd guess it'd take days to walk home." In this gravity, even in the suit, I could easily manage it—and I suspected Lakshmi was in good enough shape to do it, as well. Except for one thing: I looked at the air gauge built into my suit's inner left sleeve. "I've got five hours left."

Lakshmi was still bound with the lasso. I rotated her arm in a way that probably wasn't pleasant and read her gauge. "And she's got three." I didn't add, but I certainly thought, *Which means if I take her tanks, I've got a total of eight.* I looked at Pickover. "We should head out."

"You're not abandoning me here!" Lakshmi exclaimed.

I turned to her. "Why not? You were prepared to kill me, and you just tried to kill Dr. Pickover."

"Not kill him, just disable him—with damage that would be easy to repair."

"Well, tell you what, sweetheart: you can start walking; you, at least, should more or less know the way."

"I'm new to Mars; you know that. Darren was navigating. I honestly don't have a clue which way to go."

"If you ask him nicely, Rory might point you in the right direction."

He was looking down at his chest, probing the holes in it with his fingers, and—

And, no, actually, he was probing the holes she'd made in his work shirt. I hadn't paid much attention to it until now, but it was a somewhat tattered flannel number sporting a light and dark gray plaid and pockets over both breasts. Above his left breast was a logo showing what I was pleased with myself for recognizing as a trilobite, and beneath that, some words that were too small for me to read.

"This was my lucky shirt," he said. "Got it when I was doing field-work at the Burgess Shale; I brought it all the way from Earth." He looked at her. "And you wrecked it."

The upper hole was merely a rip; the lower one was now badly stained by oil.

Lakshmi took on a desperate tone. "Please, tell me which way to head."

"It doesn't make any difference," I said. "You won't get anywhere near the dome before your air runs out. At least if you stay here, we'll know where your body is, and can come back and give you a decent burial."

"You bastard," said Lakshmi.

"I'm just telling you the truth."

Rory looked around, getting his bearings. "That way," he said, pointing in a direction somewhat more northerly than what I would have guessed but not so much so that I doubted his word. "Walk that way."

"Thank you," she said to Rory. Then, to me: "You're going to die, too, Lomax. Yes, you've got more air than I do—but it's still nowhere near enough."

I smiled. "It wouldn't be if I were going to walk it. But I'm not."

"You expect a rescue?" She looked relieved. "Then I'm waiting right here with you."

"Oh, no. I'm heading out, too. But Rory's going to carry me."

"I am?" said Pickover.

"You are. Bend over a bit."

He did so, putting his hands on his knees. I climbed onto his back piggyback style. It was easy for him to take the weight—the combination of low gravity and a transfer's strength. "And you're going to run," I said. I thought about digging in my heels as if they were spurs and yelling, "Giddyap," but I didn't think the paleontologist would appreciate that. So instead I simply said, "Let's go."

Lakshmi looked furious, but Pickover did indeed start running, leaving her behind. It took Pickover a hundred meters to find the right gait with me on his back, but he finally did. The horizon went up and down as he ran along, his powerful legs sailing from one footfall to the next. Holding on to him wasn't difficult. The miles and miles of miles and miles shifted one by one from being in front of us to behind us, and soon enough Lakshmi's cursing faded away as we moved out of radio range.

TWENTY

Dr. Pickover and I reached the vicinity of New Klondike by mid afternoon. To his credit, Rory had taken a straight path all the way back, with no attempt to disguise the route. Polarizing the fishbowl at night had rendered me almost blind, but here in broad daylight it just made looking out at the world comfortable—so I now had a rough idea of where the Alpha Deposit was.

"Almost there," said Pickover, via radio. It was astonishing listening to someone who had been running at high speed for hours but wasn't out of breath. I looked at my air gauge; I still had twenty-odd minutes left. I'd never thought of the dome as pretty before, but it sure looked that way as it came into view, glistening in the sunshine.

"Okay," I said to Pickover. "No point in making a spectacle of ourselves. Let's walk the rest of the way."

The scientist stopped and bent his knees, lowering himself a bit. I hopped off his back. It felt good to not be bouncing up and down anymore.

"We have to go back for her," Pickover said, as I fell in beside him. "Get more bottled air, get another buggy. Go rescue her."

I reached over and held his forearm with my suit glove. "Rory, she's dead by now. She has to be."

"But if—"

"If what? She had less air than me, and I'm almost empty. Even if she did manage to conserve her oxygen, there's no way she could still be alive by the time we got back out there."

"Yes, but . . ."

"But what? She tried to kill both of us."

"I know. I just don't want it on my conscience, I guess."

"I had mine removed years ago," I said. "Makes things easier."

We walked on in silence. The dome in front of us was an impressive feat. Building it would have been impossible even forty years ago, but nanoassemblers had constructed the whole thing molecule by molecule, extracting the source silicon dioxide from the Martian soil, modifying it into ultraviolet-opaque alloquartz, and laying it down in the pattern Howard Slapcoff's engineers had programmed. Its rim was anchored into the permafrost, and its great weight was borne by curving struts and the central support column, all made of carbon nanotubes.

We went through the airlock, and I returned the surface suit. The person who had rented us the suit wasn't on duty anymore—which was a good thing, since I would have felt obliged to clock him for having revealed the radio-encryption key to Lakshmi. Adding insult to injury, Pickover lost his damage deposit because of the chip out of my helmet.

I collected my little tablet computer, phone, shoulder holster, and gun from the locker, put the tab in my right hip pocket, slipped the phone around my left wrist, placed the pistol in the holster, and draped the holster over my shoulder. My clothes were clean, but Pickover was covered with dust, and he'd gotten a fair bit of it in the exposed workings of his face. I used the john while he went through the cleaning chamber, where air jets blasted dust off him, and vacuum hoses sucked up the stuff that wouldn't blow away.

When Pickover was done, we headed out onto Ninth Avenue. "What now?" he asked.

I gave him an appraising look. "You've been missing most of your face for God knows how long, and you've got two holes in your chest. I'm thinking it's time you visited NewYou."

He shuddered. "I get so angry when I think about what they did. A bootleg copy of me!"

"I know. But the people who did that are gone, and so is the bootleg—and you *do* need to get fixed up, and they're the only game in town."

"All right," he said. "But will you come with me?"

"You're the client; I charge by the hour. You really want to pay someone to hold your hand?"

"Please, Alex."

I'd been hoping to go home, have a shower, change, and then maybe go see Diana. But I said, "Okay."

"Thank you."

I made Pickover wait for me while we stopped at a shop so I could buy a sandwich; the ones I'd bought before had gone up with the buggy. Meat was synthesized directly—no need for messy, smelly animals—and the place we went into printed a passable roast beef on an algae bun. I ate it as we walked along. We had to cross right through the center of town, since NewYou was on Third and about halfway out to the other side of the dome. Before we went in, I think Pickover would have liked to have taken a deep breath to steel himself—so to speak—but he couldn't.

We were greeted inside by Horatio Fernandez, he of the massive arms. "My God," he said, looking at Pickover, "what happened to you?"

I spoke before Pickover could answer. "Little accident with some climbing gear."

"And your face?" asked Fernandez.

"Cut myself shaving," Pickover replied.

"Jesus," said Horatio. "Let's get you into the workshop."

Pickover looked at me. "I'll wait," I said. "Don't worry."

Fernandez called out, "Reiko!" A woman came through a doorway to mind the store. Fernandez headed into the back, and Pickover followed.

I remembered Reiko Takahashi from the Wilkins case, and so I went over to say hello. She was petite, about twenty-eight, and very pretty for a biological.

"Hello, Mr. Lomax," she said, smiling perfect teeth.

I was pleased she remembered my name. "Alex," I said.

"Alex, yes. Hi."

"Hi."

She moved closer and looked around, making sure we were alone, I guess. "Are you working on another case?"

"My friend needed some maintenance, and I'm keeping him company."

"Ah."

Reiko had long black hair that went halfway down her back. Three streaks of orange went through it, one behind each ear, and the third exactly down the center. She had brown eyes, and eye shadow that matched the streaks, and was wearing a dark gray pantsuit over a silky blouse that was also the same shade of orange. "What brought you to Mars?" I asked, making conversation.

She smiled mischievously. "A spaceship."

"Ha ha. Seriously, though?"

She looked at me for a moment, as if trying to decide whether she wanted to confide something. But then she simply said, "Something to do."

I turned on the patented Lomax charm. "Well, I'm glad you came." I gestured at the front window. "This planet is so dreary; we can use all the beauty we can get."

She dipped her head a little, pleased. Then she looked up at me without straightening her neck back out. "I'm glad you dropped in," she said.

"Thank you." I dialed it up a notch. "I'm certainly glad I did, too."

Her voice grew tentative. "I'd been thinking of coming to see you, actually."

"Oh?"

"Uh-huh."

"Why didn't you?"

"I'm . . . forgive me, but I just wasn't sure you were the right man."

I put a finger under her chin and lifted her lovely face. "Of course I am. Why don't we go somewhere and talk?"

She looked around. "No, this will do. We're alone."

"We are indeed," I said.

"You see, there's a matter I need help in investigating."

Oh. "And what might that be?"

She looked at me for several seconds, sizing me up. "Okay," she said. "But you have to promise not to tell anyone."

"Tell anyone what?"

It was amazing how many people would ask you to pledge silence then go on even when you hadn't. I was feeling pleased about that insight when she started speaking, but by the time she'd finished, I'd found myself taking a step backward.

"It's just this," she said. "Denny O'Reilly was my grandfather."

TWENTY-ONE

I'm sure my poker face cracked; that was *quite* a claim. "Really?" I said.

She nodded. "My mother was his daughter; his only child. And I'm his only grandchild."

I'd seen photos of Denny O'Reilly. He'd been a white guy, and Miss Takahashi had exquisite Asian features. She'd obviously previously encountered surprised expressions like the one I must have been wearing. "My grandmother was from Kyoto," she said. "And my mother married a man from Tokyo. Despite that, I was hoping I'd still have a little bit of the luck o' the Irish in my genes. I thought I could retrace my grandfather's steps and find the Alpha."

"But you didn't."

"I didn't."

"And now you work here?" I raised my eyebrows. "Forgive me, but, well, if you're Denny O'Reilly's granddaughter, shouldn't you be, you know, rolling in it?"

"My grandmother was his mistress, not his wife."

"He didn't leave anything to your grandmother?"

"He didn't leave anything to *anyone.* He died intestate. And in the jurisdiction he lived in, that meant it all went to his actual wife. She had no children—and, for that matter, neither did Simon Weingarten. I'm the only surviving heir of either of them—except the courts did me out of my due."

"Ah. And when you failed to find riches here, you had to get a job."

"Exactly." She gestured at one of the floor models. "Have you ever thought about transferring, Mr. Lomax? A man in your line of work, it might come in handy."

"You on commission, Reiko?"

She smiled. "Sorry."

"So, what exactly were you hoping I could help you with?"

"Well, like I said, I wasn't sure if I needed a detective, or what. But someone broke into my apartment last week."

"What did they take?"

"Nothing. But the place was ransacked. I called the police, and they took my report over the phone, but that's all."

"Do you know what the thief was looking for?"

She said, "No," but I could tell she was lying.

There was still no one else in the shop. It was my turn to decide if I wanted to confide in her. "You asked if I had a case. I'm actually investigating an old one: the fate of Willem Van Dyke."

Her eyes opened wider.

"I see you know the name," I said.

"Oh, yes. He came to Mars on the second expedition with my grandfather and Simon. Horrible man; tried to sell all the fossils out from under them."

"That's what your grandfather said?"

"Yes. Why do you care what happened to Van Dyke?"

"I have a client who doesn't like loose ends."

"Was that him? Your client? Going into the back?"

I nodded.

"He looked in bad shape."

"He'll be okay."

"What's his name?"

"Rory Pickover."

"*That* was Mr. Pickover? Wow."

"Yeah. His face needs a little work."

"I'll say. Why's he interested in this?"

"You know he's a scientist, right? He wants to find any fossils from the Alpha that might have gone into private collections, and he figures Van Dyke might be the key to that."

"Ah," said Reiko. "Well, maybe I can help, too. The diary mentions some names."

"Whose diary?"

"My grandfather's."

"He kept a diary of the second expedition?"

"Yes, I believe so. And of the first, as well. I've never seen those, but . . ."

"But what? What diary are you referring to?"

"There was one of the third mission."

"Really?" I said. "But wouldn't that have been lost when their ship burned up on re-entry?"

"No. My grandfather beamed it home to my grandmother just before he and Simon left Mars. Of course, they were going to spend the months of the return voyage in hibernation, and only thaw out to handle re-entering Earth's atmosphere. But he broadcast the diary just before he left Mars—in terms of his conscious time, that was less than a day before he died."

"And you have copies of this diary?"

"Well, *a* copy, yes. A bound printout of it."

I felt my eyebrows go up. "On paper?"

"Uh-huh. My grandmother never wanted it to get out; parts of the diary are very personal, and you know how things take on a life of their own once they get online. But she wanted me to know where I'd come from, and who my grandfather had been. So about a year ago, just before she died, she had a bound printout of it made, then erased the files. I have the one and only copy."

"And it's here on Mars?"

She didn't answer.

"Is it?" I said.

Another hesitation, then a small nod.

"That's what the thief was looking for," I said. There was no point in raising my tone to make it a question; it was obviously true.

She nodded again meekly.

"Does the diary reveal the location of the Alpha?"

"No. If it did, I wouldn't be working here. But, as I said, he mentions some collectors he'd done business with in the past."

"Who else knows about—"

Just then, the front door slid open, and an elderly man shuffled in. "Excuse me," Reiko said, and she went over to speak to him. From what I overheard, he was a prospector trying to decide between spending the money he'd made from his finds either on transferring or on passage back home.

I pulled out my tab and looked at the encyclopedia entry on Denny O'Reilly, particularly the stuff on his personal life. There was no mention of a mistress, although he had indeed been married at the time he'd died, and that woman, who had been dead herself for a dozen years, had inherited his estate; she'd doubtless had the money to transfer at some point, but had been killed unexpectedly in a plane crash.

The elderly customer was looking at a sample body in the window display. The man happened to be black and the body was white, but its build was similar to his own.

Since she was still busy, and since Rory would probably be a while longer, I stepped outside onto the street and used my wrist phone to call Dougal McCrae.

"Hello, Alex," he said from the tiny screen.

"Hey, Mac. Did you guys investigate an incident at the home of a Reiko Takahashi recently?"

He looked away from the camera. "Two secs." Then his freckled face turned back to me. "Yeah, a B&E. Kaur handled it. Strange; nothing taken."

"What can you tell me about Miss Takahashi?"

He looked off camera again. "No wants, no warrants. Life-support tax paid in full. Came here three months ago. Works at NewYou—you've met her, remember?"

I nodded. "Thanks, Mac. Talk to you later."

"One thing while I've got you, Alex."

"Sure."

"We've had a couple of missing-persons reports."

"Oh?"

"Yes. A woman named Lakshmi Chatterjee and a man named Darren Cheung. Logged out of the dome, but apparently never returned. They rented a Mars buggy, and she rented a surface suit; the rental firm wants them back."

"I can imagine so."

"Same log shows that you and Dr. Pickover went out shortly before them."

"I brought my suit back."

"With a cracked helmet."

"Shoddy workmanship," I said.

Mac looked at me dubiously.

"Anyway," I said, "I'll let you know if I see them."

"You do that, Alex."

I nodded, shook the phone off, and started to head back inside. I was startled by the door sliding open before I'd reached it—it was the old man, coming out. "What did you decide?" I asked amiably.

He narrowed his eyes, as if wondering what business it was of mine. But he answered nonetheless. "I'm going home."

He didn't look like he was in good enough shape to hack the gravity on the mother world. "Really?" I said.

"Yup. Going back to Lunaport. No damn fossils anywhere there; I've had my fill of dead things."

I nodded; he'd do fine there. *"Bon voyage,"* I said. I'd once made the effort here on Mars to see Luna without a telescope; it's about as bright as Mercury is as seen from Earth's surface, which is to say not very bright at all. I squeezed past the old codger and went inside.

"Sorry you didn't make a sale," I said to Reiko, jerking my thumb toward the front door.

"So am I," she replied. "Sure I can't interest you?"

I looked at her pretty face and thought that she interested me just fine. But what I said was, "About your grandfather's diary . . ."

"Yes?"

"The thief didn't find it. I trust you've got it somewhere safe."

"Oh, yes."

"Here at NewYou?"

"No."

"Then where?"

She compressed her lips, and the color went out of them.

"Reiko, if you want me to investigate this, you have to trust me."

She considered. "There's a writer here, doing an authorized biography of my grandfather. She's got it."

I seriously doubted we had more than one writer, but I asked anyway. "Who?"

"Her name's Lakshmi Chatterjee. She's staying at Shopatsky House."

"I thought she was doing a book about the *B. Traven,"* I said.

"What's that?" asked Reiko.

It occurred to me that being a writer—or even just claiming to be one—was a great cover. You could tell people you were doing a book on just about anything, and they'd take you into their confidence. Still, if Lakshmi had the diary already, she obviously wasn't the one who'd searched Reiko's place. "Who else besides Lakshmi knows about the diary?"

"No one. At least, no one here on Mars. Lakshmi promised to keep it a secret."

At that moment, Pickover came out of the back room. His face had been repaired, and although there were still two rips in his favorite shirt, I had no doubt that whatever damage there'd been underneath had also been fixed. He was followed by Horatio Fernandez. The two of them went over to the cash station to settle up.

"Okay," I said to Reiko. "I'll see if I can figure out who broke into your place, and, if I do, I'll lean on them a bit—make sure they leave you alone in future."

"Thank you, Mr. Lomax."

"Alex. Call me Alex."

She smiled, showing the perfect teeth again. "Thank you, Alex."

Pickover was finished. I said goodbye to Reiko, and he and I headed outside. As soon as the door slid shut behind me, I turned to him. "You okay?"

"Good as new," he said.

"Did he put a tracking chip in, do you think?"

"I watched him like a hawk—easy to do when someone is working on your face. I don't think so. But I'll get myself checked, as before."

"Good, okay. Don't forget." I paused, then: "Here's a shocker for you. Miss Takahashi is Denny O'Reilly's granddaughter."

"Oh, really?"

"No," I said, unable to resist. "O'Reilly." I waited for him to laugh—but I guess he was only laughing on the inside. "Anyway," I said. "Yes, she is. Her grandmother was Denny's mistress. That mechanical ticker of yours ready for another shock? There's a diary of Weingarten and O'Reilly's last voyage. Denny transmitted it to Miss Takahashi's grandmother before they left Mars."

Rory's plastic face lit up almost—almost literally. "Oh, my God! If he recorded any paleontological details—I have to see it! There's no known record of what they'd found on the third expedition. Who knows what treasures the Alpha yielded that were lost when their ship burned up?"

"Don't sweat it," I said. "I'll get it for you. It's at Shopatsky House, and, as we both know, the position of writer-in-residence is now vacant. I'll go retrieve it."

"And what about me?" asked Pickover.

I smiled my most reassuring smile. "Go home and clean some fossils. I'm going to swing by my office, then head out to get the diary. This shouldn't take long."

TWENTY-TWO

There was a sign outside Shopatsky House that I hadn't seen the last time, because I'd approached it then from the opposite direction. It was a white rectangle with dark green lettering, and it talked about who Stavros Shopatsky had been and explained that although some might view this site as a tourist attraction—as if Mars got many tourists—it was actually a private home with a hardworking author within, and people should be quiet and respect the writer's privacy.

But the sign, like so much in New Klondike, had been vandalized. Someone had carved "Books Suck" into it. Everybody's a critic.

Most homes had their front doors well secured—and some other potential entrance that was easy to break in through. I went around back. The grounds were covered with ferns that did well in the dim sunlight we got here.

It used to be people left a spare key under a rock—and Mars had *plenty* of rocks. But unless you were a transfer, you probably used a biometric lock these days, and few people stored a spare finger somewhere in their backyard. I did a cursory search anyway but didn't find anything.

Still, there was a big window in the back—writers, I hear, like to stare out into space, which must be good work if you can get it. The window was probably alloquartz or shatterproof glass, but the molding around the window might, I thought, be made of less-stern stuff, and indeed that turned out to be the case.

Fortunately, Shopatsky House was on the outer rim, with a backyard that no one could see unless they happened to be right on the other side of the dome, looking in. I used the switchblade I'd gotten from Dirk to cut through the molding on all four sides of the window. Pressing in at the bottom made the heavy pane angle out at the top, and I managed to get it to fall toward me. I jockeyed it the half meter down to the ground.

There was no way short of wearing a full surface suit to avoid leaving DNA and other identifying things behind, and so I didn't even bother to try to cover my tracks. After all, I'd been in the house earlier with Lakshmi's permission; if Mac's people ever did investigate this break-in, that fact would exonerate me.

I looked around the small home and quickly found the writing station. Lakshmi apparently wrote with a keyboard; there was one sitting on a little table next to a recliner chair, opposite a monitor wall. I understood that those who were serious about words and how punctuation was wielded preferred keyboards to voice-recognition.

I looked everywhere in this room that might conceal a paper diary, but it clearly wasn't here. I moved into the living room, which had the roll-top desk, and started looking through its cubbyholes and drawers but, again, *bupkes.*

I went to the wall that had the bookcase leaning against it, and looked at each of the spines in turn. As I'd noted before, they weren't alphabetical but chronological, with Lakshmi's own books at the end. There were about eighty books in all, and—yes, yes, there it was: a short hardcover volume, with no printing on the spine, inserted at the far right of the second shelf from the top.

The thick front cover was blank, too, but the title page said, "Journal of Denny T. O'Reilly." The pages were filled with text in a nice font—a proper little book.

I heard a sound, wheeled around, and saw the front door sliding open. There was no way for me to make it out the same way I'd come in without crossing the line of sight of whoever was coming in. I ducked farther into the room with the bookcase, then peered around the jamb of that room's open doorway to see who was entering.

My heart jumped. It was as if I were seeing a ghost.

A beautiful, brown-haired, brown-eyed, brown-skinned ghost.

It was Lakshmi Chatterjee, back from the dead.

I moved deeper into the room. The entryway wasn't carpeted, and I could hear what sounded like hard-soled shoes being dropped. I didn't hear anything else for a bit, which might have meant she was just standing there, but more likely meant she was now walking barefoot. I didn't know how she'd been rescued, but she was probably sweaty and tired; if she was like me, she'd head for the shower—and I wasn't sure where that was in this house. If it was off the other room, no problem—I could make good my escape while she was in there. But if it was off this room—and there *was* another closed door opposite the one I'd just come through—well, then, I was in trouble.

She took a right, not a left, and I let out my held breath—but she was going first to the kitchen, not the bathroom, damn it. Still, if she buried her head in the refrigerator, I might be able to sneak past her. I heard sounds that I couldn't quite identify, and then some sort of machine started up. I ducked back out of view and waited. It took her a few moments to emerge from the kitchen, and when she did so, she was magnificently, totally, wonderfully nude. The washing machine must have been in, or just off of, the kitchen; I recognized now the sound of electrostatic spin cleansing.

She turned left, facing me in all her curvy perfection, and her mouth dropped open in absolute shock.

"Hello, Lakshmi," I said, stepping toward her, my gun in my hand.

"What are you doing here?" she demanded.

"I might ask you the same thing. How'd you get home?"

"None of your damn business." She noticed that I was holding the diary. "Put that back."

"Not a chance."

"You walk out of here with it, and I'm calling the police."

"Let's call them right now. Tell them what you tried to do to Dr. Pickover and me."

"Let's do that," she said, hands now on her lovely hips. "Tell the whole solar system where the Alpha Deposit is."

I considered my options. I could just shoot her—but the body would eventually be discovered, and Mac would have no trouble tracing the bullet to my gun. I could simply run for it—she doubtless had no idea yet that I'd removed the back window, and so would be surprised when I headed that way instead of toward the front door. Or I could stay here and see what developed; it is, after all, not my norm to run out on a beautiful naked woman.

I decided, somewhat reluctantly, to simply leave. I walked slightly toward her, pointing the gun at her, then headed for the little office, now backing away from her. I made it most of the way to the hole where the window had been, reholstered the gun so one of my hands would be free to climb out, turned around, and—

Pow!

She'd grabbed something heavy—I didn't know what—and thrown it at me. On Earth, she'd have needed a baseball pitcher's arm to hurl whatever it was so far, but here it was easy. She might have been a lousy aim with a shotgun, but she hit me right between the shoulders. The impact sent me tumbling over her windowsill, and I went headfirst into her backyard—my noggin, sadly, not hitting soft ferns but rather the large sheet of alloquartz I'd removed earlier. It took me a second to regain my senses. I was scrambling to my feet when I heard Lakshmi shout, "Freeze!"

I didn't exactly do that. Instead, I rolled onto my butt and sat looking up at her as she leaned out the window, perfect breasts hanging down.

"Or what?" I said. There was no way she had a concealed weapon.

"Or you die."

"How?"

"The self-destruct device in that book you're holding."

"Oh, come on!"

She shrugged as if it were of no real concern to her. "Look inside the back cover."

I did so and, lo and behold, stuck there was a piece of plastic about the size of an old-fashioned business card and several millimeters thick—the kind of explosive someone had cleverly nicknamed "cardite." Such things had transceiver chips inside them and could indeed be detonated by remote control. I tried to rip the back cover off the book, but the hardcover binding was too tough.

"You don't have the remote," I said, looking back at Lakshmi.

"Wanna bet?"

"Reiko Takahashi has it."

"No, she doesn't. It's geared to my computer."

"You're bluffing."

"Try me. It'll blow the book to bits—and take off your arm, at least, it if doesn't outright kill you."

"Let's call Miss Takahashi and find out," I said, lifting my left arm to bring my wrist phone closer to my face.

"You seem to think you're in the driver's seat here, Mr. Lomax. You're not." She spoke over her shoulder: "Persis?"

It was hard to make out from here, but her computer—that red cube I'd seen before sitting on the roll-top desk—replied in a female voice: "Yes, Lakshmi?"

"In thirty seconds from my mark, detonate the explosive in the book—and please do a countdown."

"Mars seconds or Earth seconds?" asked Persis. Since the Martian sol was 1.03 times the length of an Earth day, Martian seconds were 1.03 times as long as Earth ones.

"Oh, for Pete's sake!" declared Lakshmi. "Mars seconds!"

Nothing happened for a moment, and then Lakshmi realized she had to say, "Mark." She did so, and I heard Persis counting down.

"Thirty. Twenty-nine. Twenty-eight."

"Toss the book aside, Lomax."

I drew my gun. "Abort the countdown, Lakshmi."

I was hoping she wouldn't think of the obvious. But she did; she crouched down beneath the windowsill, out of my line of fire.

"Twenty-two. Twenty-one. Twenty."

But since she was crouching, she wasn't looking. I scrambled forward, just below the sill, surged to my feet standing on the alloquartz pane, grabbed Lakshmi by her wrists, hauled her out through the window, rolled back on my spine, and flipped her past me onto the bed of ferns.

"Seventeen. Sixteen. Fifteen."

I tossed the book aside; unlike cordite, cardite wasn't finicky about such things.

"I don't think either of us wants that destroyed," I said, jerking my head toward it as I pulled my gun again and aimed it at Lakshmi, who was now appealingly spread-eagled with her tushy facing up.

"Persis," she said, "abort!"

There was only one problem. Persis apparently couldn't hear Lakshmi now. *"Eleven. Ten."*

"Oh, crap," I said.

"Eight. Seven."

Lakshmi rolled onto her back and leapt to her feet, jumping a good meter off the ground as she did so. "Abort!"

"Five."

"Abort!" she shouted as gravity slowly pulled her down.

"Four."

"Abort!" she shouted again.

"Three."

"Abort!" she shouted once more as she lunged toward the window. I was back on my feet and danced out of the way to let her do so.

"Two."

"Abort!"

"Aborted," said Persis calmly.

Before Lakshmi could make it in through the window, I jumped over and grabbed her wrists. We struggled for a bit, but although she was strong—recent arrivals from Earth tended to be, by the standards of most Martians—I was stronger. When it ceased to be fun, I pushed her toward the dome, and said, "Keep walking." I made sure she went three times as far as I'd thrown her—well out of Persis's earshot, or whatever you called it when a computer was listening. "Stand there," I said. "Don't do anything. Just stand there."

She did so, although now that she'd lost the upper hand, she seemed moved to modesty. She used one arm held horizontally to cover the nicest parts of her breasts and another held vertically with fingers splayed to partially conceal what I'd already seen plenty of down there.

I fetched the book from where I'd tossed it, then pulled out the switchblade and started carving through the thick back cover, separating it from the spine. When the back cover was free, I flung it as far as I could—which meant it went sailing clear out of sight.

"And now," I said, still keeping the gun trained on her, "I'm going to leave, taking this book with me."

"You won't be able to make sense of it," she said. "It's a personal diary, full of Denny's own private shorthand. Why do you think they needed a historian to write the authorized story?"

"Well, if it turns out that I require your help, I know where to find you. And don't plan on any more trips out to the Alpha. Not only is it fortified, but I killed your buddy Darren Cheung, and I'll kill you, too, if need be, to protect it. You might be able to count on police protection here under the dome—although you'd be a fool to stake your life on that—but you go out on the planitia again, and you're *mine*, understand?"

She was staring at the ground, but at last she nodded. I used the barrel of my pistol to lift her chin up and said into her dark eyes, "Here's looking at you, kid." And then I headed on my way.

TWENTY-THREE

I decided it was prudent to not go where it would be *too* easy for Mac to find me, just in case Lakshmi did call in the break-and-enter. He wouldn't look for long, but he'd certainly try my office and apartment, so I went by Gully's Gym, had a sonic cleaning there, and changed into the blue track pants and black muscle shirt I kept in my locker. I checked the mirror to make sure I was kempt and sheveled, then headed over to Pickover's place.

When I got there he was doing precisely what I'd suggested he do: cleaning a fossil. "Goodness!" he said, looking at me. "What happened to you?"

"What?"

He pointed at my forehead. "That's a hell of a goose egg."

I probed the area he'd indicated. "Oh. Yeah. I took a fall."

He might not have been a detective, but he *was* a scientist. "Falling in this gravity doesn't cause injuries like that."

"True. I went flying onto a piece of alloquartz."

"My God."

"Anyway," I said, "the good news for that conscience of yours is that Lakshmi Chatterjee is alive."

"And kicking, apparently," he replied—but he did look relieved. "How'd she get back here?"

"I have no idea. But I got the diary from her."

He held out his hand, and I gave it to him. "Sorry about the back cover," I added.

Pickover flipped it open to the first page and began reading. After a few moments, he looked up. "That's O'Reilly's voice, all right—his tone."

"I'm going to have to work my way through it," I said.

"I want to read it, too," Pickover replied. We considered for a moment. I couldn't recall the last time the fact that I wanted to read something prevented somebody else from simultaneously reading it, too. I suppose *somewhere* in New Klondike there might be a paper scanner, but I had no idea where.

"All right," I said. "It'll probably make more sense to you than me, anyway—you go first. Just, for God's sake, keep your door locked, and don't let Lakshmi Chatterjee anywhere near it."

"She drove stakes into my heart like I was a vampire," Pickover said. "She's the last person I'd allow in here."

"Good. Start reading. How long do you think it'll take you?"

He riffled the pages, gauging the density of content. "Two or three hours, I suppose."

"Did you get yourself checked for tracking chips?"

"Yes. I'm clean. I'm sure Fernandez wanted to put one in, but I didn't give him an opportunity."

"Okay. I'll be back."

"Where are you going?"

"To get some dinner. You may not have to eat, Rory, but I do."

• • • • • • • • • • •

And I did precisely that, going over to The Bent Chisel. Buttrick was his usual nasty self. I headed back and waited for Diana to come and offer me service. Truth to tell, what I wanted wasn't on the menu, but she wasn't off for several more hours, so that would have to wait. I ordered a drink, plus steak and green beans; the former would be vat-grown, the latter, synthesized.

Diana returned with my Scotch on the rocks, and I made short work of it. There weren't many other customers this time of day, so she motioned for me to scooch over a bit, and she placed her shapely bottom next to mine. "Whose husband whacked you on the forehead this time?"

"It wasn't like that," I said.

"Riiiiight," she replied and she squeezed my thigh.

"Seriously," I said. "Hey, you're a cultured gal. Do you know anything about the writer-in-residence here?"

"Lakshmi Chatterjee? Sure."

"Is she any good?" It was the first time in my life, I think, I'd asked that about a woman and didn't mean for the words "in the sack" to be understood.

"She's great. I read her book about Lunaport when I heard she was coming here. She's like the Shelby Foote of that war."

"Ah," I said. I'd never heard of him, but I imagine with a name like that he got beat up a lot as a kid. "Seems like a sweet deal, getting an all-expenses-paid trip to Mars."

"Well, she has to work for it," Diana said.

"Oh, yeah. She's writing a book on the *B. Traven*." Or maybe she's doing an authorized biography of Denny O'Reilly. Or something.

"Not just that," said Diana. "She has to meet with beginning writers in the community and critique their manuscripts."

"Really?"

"Yeah. That's how these things go: most of the time is the writer's own, but some of it has to be spent working with newbies."

"How does that work?"

"You make an appointment, send in a manuscript in advance, and she meets with you for an hour to go over it."

"At Shopatsky House?"

"I guess."

"You write poetry," I said.

She winced. "I write bad poetry."

There are some things even I couldn't dispute with a straight face, so I let that pass and simply said, "You could make an appointment to see her."

"Oh, God, no. I couldn't show my poetry to her. She's *excellent.*"

"That's what she's there for. To help beginners."

"I can't, Alex."

"Please, baby. I need you to get into that house."

"Why don't you go yourself?"

"I've been there." I pointed to my forehead. "That's where I got the goose egg."

Diana was suddenly huffy. She started to get up.

"It's not like that, babe," I said. I lowered my voice—not because anyone could listen in on us in the back, but so Diana, in her topless splendor, would have to lean in to hear me. "I, ah, let myself into her place. She had a, um, document that I needed to access."

"Let yourself in?" Diana said coldly. "So her locks were programmed to recognize you?"

"No, sweetheart—honest. I removed the back window and snuck in. We fought, but I got away with the document. But prior to that, she attacked me and Pickover out on the surface—tried to kill us both."

Diana frowned. "Pickover is a transfer."

"Didn't stop her from shooting spikes into his chest—or coming at me with a shotgun."

"God!" A beat. "But what's this all about?"

"She thinks we know where the Alpha Deposit is."

"And do you?"

This time, my poker face didn't fail me. "Of course not."

"But she tried to kill you."

"Uh-huh."

"And you want to send me off to be alone with her?"

"Well, um, she doesn't have anything against *you*."

"Why do you need to get me into her house?"

"So you can plant a bug there, so I can listen in on her conversations. She's got at least one more accomplice—someone helped her out today, I don't know who, but I need to find out."

"Why? What difference does that make?"

The difference was that at least one more person apparently knew the location of the Alpha Deposit—the person who had come to Lakshmi's rescue there. Also, a bug in Lakshmi's place might let me know if she was ignoring my warning and planning another trip to the Alpha. But I simply said, "Please, baby. I need you to do this."

Diana sat back down but a little farther on the bench from me than before.

"Well?" I said, after she'd been quiet for a bit.

"Okay," she replied. "But you've got to take me out."

"I'd be happy—"

"To Bleaney's."

I frowned. Bleaney's was the pricey nightclub where prospectors who had struck it rich went to celebrate. "Deal," I said, leaning over and kissing her on the cheek.

I'd just put it on the expense claim I was going to give Pickover.

• • • • • • • • • • •

After leaving Diana at The Bent Chisel, I actually went most of the way back to Shopatsky House, since the Windermere Clinic was near there. Old Doc Windermere—a walrusy-looking biological with a handlebar mustache—would dig out a bullet or patch up a knife wound without feeling a need to involve those pesky folks at the NKPD; taking care of the bruise on my forehead was nothing by comparison, but I figured I might as well give him this bit of business, too. Gloria, his receptionist/nurse—a breathy little pink-haired bundle of energy—was always glad to see me, and, frankly, I rather liked seeing her, too. I think the doc watered his anesthetic down the same way Buttrick watered down his booze, but a gander at Gloria was usually enough to take the pain away, at least for a few minutes.

It was a slow night for fights, I guess; I didn't have to wait to get in. Doc Windermere played a couple of healing beams over my forehead, and, as I could see in the cracked mirror opposite me, the swelling went down, and the purple color faded away.

I thanked the doc, paid Gloria in cash, and then headed over to Pickover's place, figuring he should be finished reading Denny's journal by now.

"Well?" I said after he let me into his apartment. "Anything exciting in the diary?"

"Yes, indeed," he replied, taking a seat; I did the same. "Weingarten and O'Reilly contacted several people back on Earth, trying to arrange the sale of fossils in advance; the diary includes descriptions of some of the fossils—and it's got the name of the collector they'd previously sold the decapod to!"

"The what?"

"The decapod! There's only one known specimen—they brought it back on their second mission." He held the diary up triumphantly. "My guess is that they were ancestral to the pentapods that came to dominate later—and now I know whose collection it's in! I tell you, Alex, we may not even need to track down Willem Van Dyke!"

That sounded like my fees were about to dry up, so I quickly protested. "There are still some leads for him I'd like to follow up on."

Rory was in an expansive mood. "Oh, of course, my boy, of course! Your field and mine, we both say the same thing: leave no stone unturned!"

"Good," I said. "Now what?"

"Now, we should head out to the Alpha again. We can't leave those wrecked buggies there; someone's bound to spot them sooner or later. And we need to finish clearing out the land mines. Are you up for another road trip, old boy?"

Driving to the Alpha took a lot of hours, and that meant a lot of solars for me. "Why not?" I said. "But we'll need another buggy to get there."

"Do we rent or borrow one?"

"Borrow," I said. "I don't know how Lakshmi and that Darren Cheung fellow managed to tail us in the dark the last time, but it's possible our rental had a tracking device in it."

"That's illegal," Rory said. I made no reply, and finally he nodded. "Okay," he said. "So who do you know who has a clean buggy we could borrow?"

There were only two reasons to own a buggy: you spent a lot of time prospecting far from the dome, or you liked to race. Isidis Planitia is a plain, after all—it was great for racing. And my buddy Juan Santos liked machines of all types, not just computers. I called him. "Juan," I said to the little version of his face that appeared on my left wrist, "can I borrow your buggy?"

"Wow, Alex," he replied. "We must have a bad connection. It sounded like you said, 'Can I borrow your buggy?'"

"I know I dented it last time, but—"

"*Dented?* You call that a dent?"

"I had it fixed."

"We should have *you* fixed—make sure those defective genes of yours don't get passed on."

"How 'bout if you loan it to me, but I don't do the driving?"

"Who's going to drive it?"

"Dr. Pickover."

"That little mouse?"

"Standing right here," said Rory.

"Oh!" said Juan. "Um, sorry. I mean—um, yeah, sure, I guess you guys can borrow my buggy. But, God's sake, be careful this time, would you?"

• • • • • • • • • • •

Juan's buggy was white with jade green pinstriping. As I'd promised, Rory Pickover did the driving as we made the trip out to the Alpha Deposit again in the dark. This time he didn't ask me to polarize my helmet, and he let me bring my gun, tab, and phone along. There are only so many times you can have a man save your life before you have to start trusting him, and I guess Rory finally trusted me. It was nice that at least one of us had faith in my good intentions.

I watched through the canopy as first Venus and then Earth set. The sky was breathtaking. Even on the highest mountaintop on Earth, the atmosphere is still much denser than it is here on Mars, and Mars's two tiny captured-asteroid moons never reflected much light. On a clear night like tonight, the Milky Way was dazzling as it arched overhead.

"There's one other thing," Rory said, "that the diary revealed."

I looked at him, a dark form illuminated only by the stars and the blue dashboard indicators. "Oh?"

"Yes. O'Reilly said he'd left a large paper map of the Alpha in the lander's descent stage—with the precise locations of where they'd found the fossils they'd excavated marked on it. That sort of information is crucial scientifically."

"Why'd they leave the map behind, then?" I asked.

"They were planning to return. The diary said they were going to pick up excavating where they'd left off." He looked briefly at me. "I've got to have that map, Alex."

"I'm sure," I said. "But Ernie Gargalian told me nobody knows what became of the third lander."

Rory's voice was soft. "I do."

"Really?"

"Yes. I didn't want to tell you back at New Klondike. You never know who's listening, or where there's a microphone. But, yes, I'm pretty sure of where it is."

We hit a bump that was enough to lift me from my seat a bit. I cinched the shoulder belt tighter. "How'd you find it?"

"Satellite photos."

I frowned. "Lots of people must have looked for it that way."

"Yes, I'm sure they did. But they didn't know what to look for or where to start. I knew it had to be near the Alpha Deposit—and I had the advantage of knowing where that was."

"Ernie thinks they might have moved it," I said.

"Like the second lander? No. If they *had* crashed it somewhere else, somebody would have found the wreckage."

"Then what?"

"They buried it, right where they'd touched down."

"The Martian permafrost is rock-hard," I said. "It'd take forever to dig a hole big enough for a spaceship."

Pickover took on the lilting tone I imagined he normally reserved for talking to students. "And why do we call it permafrost, Alex?"

"Because it's permanently frozen."

"*What's* permanently frozen?"

"The soil."

"You can't freeze something that's already a solid."

"Oh, right, okay. Well, the water in the soil, then."

"Exactly. Isidis Planitia is a giant, shallow impact basin. Billions of years ago, it was filled with water. That water didn't disappear; most of it is now locked into the soil. As I told you, core samples show the ground around the Alpha is as much as sixty percent water."

"So they melted it?

"I think so, yes. Weingarten and O'Reilly had to have had a plan to hide their descent stage. I think they had the onboard computer fire its big landing engine until the frozen water melted, turning the soil into mud. The down blast would have blown the mud aside, creating a pit. The descent stage would have settled down into that, and, after the engine was cut, the mud would have flowed back in, burying it."

"Neat. But what would that look like from orbit?"

"Well, any surface rocks would have sunk into the mud. So, what you'd see is a circular area free of such things, maybe forty or fifty meters across. To the untrained eye, it'd look pretty much like a crater. Even at a one-meter orbital survey, it would be hard to tell from one; you'd have to look at multiple lighting angles to notice that it was a circle that didn't have any concavity."

"And you've found such a thing?"

"Yes."

"Because you had the Alpha as a starting point," I said. But then I shook my head. "No, no—it's the other way around, isn't it? You found this circular thingamajig first—and *that* led you to the Alpha."

"You *are* a good detective, Alex. That's right. I knew there was no way to just stumble upon the Alpha, not in all the vastness of Isidis Planitia. And I knew that the prospectors here mostly lacked the geological training to interpret orbital-survey images. I'd suspected they'd buried the descent stage—the one they took on the third mission would have made a great part of a permanent habitat. And so I started looking at satellite photos. There aren't that many that have been made in the last forty years; most of the Mars photo-survey maps are much older than that, and nobody has bothered to update them, because, after all, Mars is a dead world. But there *was* a Croatian satellite survey about fifteen years ago, and I accessed those images. Took me months of poring over photographs, but I finally found it."

"Nice work," I said.

"Beats hiking around endlessly, looking for the Alpha."

"Did you ever meet Dougal McCrae?" I asked. The bootleg Pickover had, of course, but I didn't recall this one ever having the pleasure.

"No."

"You'd like him. Chief detective at the NKPD. He doesn't like to have to get up from his desk to investigate, either."

"I've logged over five thousand field hours on Earth and Mars," Pickover said, sounding slightly miffed with me.

"Sorry." I turned to look through the canopy at the darkness. On long car trips, I sometimes felt a duty to help keep the driver alert. But Pickover was in no danger of falling asleep, although I supposed he might get bored with no one to talk to. "Do you mind if I nod off?"

"It's fine," he replied. "I'm listening to music."

. . . .

When I woke, the sun was coming up and we were pulling in near where we'd been before: the ruins of Lakshmi's buggy and the one we'd rented were about thirty meters to our right. I got into the surface suit I'd rented—it was brown this time—and Pickover swung the blockish canopy back. We headed outside.

"First things first," Rory said. "Let's see if we can find that map." He paused. "How meta! Looking for a map without a map!"

"Where do we start?" I asked.

Pickover pointed past the crater he'd tussled with Lakshmi in. "About five hundred meters that way. I don't want to drive in again—tire tracks take too long to disappear."

We started walking. It felt good to stretch my legs. "Oh, say," I said, "there's something I've been meaning to ask you about. You said something odd to that guy, Darren Cheung—something about flirty girls?"

Rory rattled it off: "'The girls can flirt and other queer things can do.'"

"Yeah. What's that mean?"

"It's an old mnemonic for Mohs scale of mineral hardness. If he'd really been with the US Geological Survey, he'd have known it."

We continued on. Soon enough, Pickover gestured at the terrain in front of us. "*Voilà!*"

I didn't see what he was referring to. "Yes?"

He sounded disappointed in me. "Right there—see? A circle, forty meters in diameter?"

I tried to make it out, and—

Ah. It was almost exactly the same ruddy color as the surrounding terrain and it was covered with dust—but nothing else; it lacked the usual litter of small rocks, and had no little craters marring its surface.

I said, "How do we get at the descent stage?"

"Well, it can't be very far down; the permafrost gives way to bedrock at a depth not much greater than the height of the descent stage, and its engine couldn't blast through that. Its top is probably just below the surface."

"Okay," I said.

"There were two hatches in the descent stage," Rory said. "One was on the outside of the hull for getting out onto the surface, and the other was on top, for connecting to the ascent stage. The upper access hatch should be right in the center of the circle." He'd brought along his geological equipment, including a big pickax. "The descent stage is circular in cross-section, and about ten meters wide." After taking a bead on a couple of distinctive rocks outside the circle, he assuredly made his way to its exact center.

I followed behind him. If I understood what Pickover had said, this whole round area had briefly been a massive quagmire of soil and water twenty mears ago. The footing didn't seem any different from the rest of the plain.

He swung his pickax. The point only went in maybe ten centimeters before it clanged against something metallic. Pickover dropped to his robotic knees and started digging into the permafrost with his bare hands. I wasn't strong enough to be of any use, so I simply watched, gloved hands on my surface suit's hips.

It took him a few minutes to expose a circular metal hatch about eighty centimeters wide. It was slightly convex and had a wheel set into its center. Pickover gestured at it. "Be my guest, Alex." I gripped the wheel with both of my gloved hands and tried to turn it, but it wouldn't budge; it was either locked from the other side, or the works were gummed up with Martian dust.

Pickover loomed in and grabbed the wheel with his naked fingers. It was odd watching a man exert himself without, you know, visibly exerting himself. He didn't grunt or screw up his face; he just calmly did what I'd been incapable of doing: turning the wheel. He spun it through 180 degrees, then pulled on it to swing the hatch open.

It was dark inside, but a ladder with rungs that curved to match the circumference of the opening descended into the ship. He scrambled down into the blackness. I was startled a moment later when light started coming up at me. I hadn't seen him take a flashlight with him, and—

No. It wasn't portable lighting; it was the spacecraft's internal system. Well, excimer batteries *did* hold charges for a long time . . .

I looked around for something to keep the hatch from closing. There wasn't anything suitable at hand but, then again, the Martian zephyrs couldn't possibly blow it shut. I made my way down the ladder.

The interior of the descent stage was maybe five meters tall, with that height divided into two levels. The ladder continued all the way down to the bottom, which is where Pickover was, so I got off on the upper floor and started looking around. This floor was a disk divided into six pie-shaped wedges.

The first wedge contained cupboards and lockers filled with mining equipment and medical supplies. I checked for the map, but it wasn't there.

The second wedge—moving to the right—was a small galley, but the cupboards here were bare; well, running out of chow was one of the reasons their expedition would have come to an end.

Wedge three was a sleeping compartment with a wide foam mattress on the floor. I looked around, but, again, no map.

Wedge four was a toilet of a kind I had no idea how to use.

Wedge five was a little work area, with tools for cleaning fossils, much like the stuff I'd seen at Ernie's shop or in Rory's apartment.

I'd thought wedge six might be the other stateroom, but I guess that was down below; it was a storage room. A white space suit, streaked with Martian dust, was slumped way over on a chair. I tried to pick it up to get at the cabinets behind it, and—

Oh, my God! "Rory!" I shouted. "Up here!"

I felt the deck plates vibrate as he scrambled up the ladder from below. He was soon standing behind me, looking over my shoulder.

"It's not empty," I said, pointing at the space suit. "There's a body inside."

The suit was an old-fashioned one, with a gold-mirror-finish helmet visor that had been flipped down. There was no nameplate on the suit, nor any national flag or logo. "It must be Willem Van Dyke," I said. "He'd have known they were planning to bury the third lander, maybe. When he came here to plant the land mines, he must have taken refuge down here—maybe there was a dust storm, or something?"

Rory loomed in and looked for the release that would let him flip up the visor to expose—what? Rotted flesh? A skull? I didn't know what to expect after all these years. He found the release, and—

Rory gasped and staggered backward. I peered at the face—which seemed to be remarkably intact. The eyes were closed, and the chestnut hair was disheveled—but it was all still attached to the head. True, the skin was an ashen shade, but I'd seen people who were alive with worse complexions.

"My . . . God," said Rory. He was now holding on to a ledge jutting from the wall. "My God."

"What?" I said.

Rory's mechanical eyes were wide. "That's not Willem Van Dyke."

"Then who is it?"

Rory shook his head slightly, as if he himself couldn't believe what he was saying. "It's Denny O'Reilly."

I looked back at the corpse. "But—but he died on re-entering Earth's atmosphere . . ."

Rory's voice became a little sharp. "That's O'Reilly, I tell you."

"You mean . . . he was marooned here?"

"Apparently."

"By Simon Weingarten?"

"It sure looks that way." Rory pointed at a thick cable going from a red connector on the front of the suit to a similar connector on one of the straight walls. "He was plugged into the ship's life-support system."

"Surely they weren't on bottled air all the time they were on Mars," I said. "Shouldn't he have been able to recycle it, or manufacture more?"

"Yes," said Pickover. "For a time. The equipment was rated for months of use, but it would have given out at some point." He shook his head. "Poor blighter."

I don't think I'd ever actually heard anyone say that before, but it certainly applied here. It must have been terrible for O'Reilly: abandoned alone for weeks, or maybe even months, on Mars, and then finally asphyxiating.

Suddenly there was a great clang audible even via the thin Martian air as—

Jesus!

—as the hatch overhead came crashing shut.

I looked up and saw the wheeled locking mechanism on this side of the hatch rotating. We were being sealed inside the same metal coffin Denny O'Reilly had been left in all those years ago.

TWENTY-FOUR

I scrambled for the ladder—as much as one could scramble in a surface suit—but Dr. Pickover, unencumbered by such a thing, beat me to it. Probably just as well; he *was* stronger than me.

Pickover struggled to keep the locking wheel from being turned any further, but, damn it, whoever was on the other side managed a massive jerk of the wheel, knocking Rory off the ladder. He was now dangling from the wheel by both arms, with a two-story drop below. The twisting of the wheel had put the ladder behind him, and he seemed to be having trouble re-engaging with it. The wheel jerked once more, and—

Holy crap!

—Pickover was dislodged or let go, but either way, he came falling down the shaft in Martian slow motion.

I thought about reaching out to grab him, but there didn't seem to be much point; it'd probably just bring me tumbling down on top of him. He hit the floor, bending at the knees as he did so, but he still collapsed into a heap.

"Rory!" I called, and I slid down the ladder. When I reached the bottom—my first time on the lower level—I helped him to his feet.

Newcomers to Mars often did themselves injuries because they felt superhuman but were still flesh and blood. But Pickover *was* superhuman. Still, it was a nasty height to fall from, even here. Pickover's plastic face winced in pain as he rolled up his pant leg to expose his right ankle. Biological injuries were easy to spot: blood, bruising, swelling. There was no sign of any of that as Pickover probed the ankle with his fingers. "It's bent," he said, at last. "I can barely flex it."

I thought of Juan's Mars buggy up on the surface. Even if we could get out of here, if whoever had sealed us in had stolen or wrecked the buggy, there was no way Pickover could run me all the way back to New Klondike this time. I looked at my wrist air gauge; Rory could stay in here indefinitely, but I couldn't. We'd been sealed in by somebody stronger than Pickover, meaning it was either a transfer or a biological who'd had something to help him turn the wheel. Even if we could undo the seal, anyone on the outside with a gun could easily pick me off as I tried to haul myself up out of the hatch.

"Is it Lakshmi again?" asked Pickover, as he rolled his pant leg down. "Or do you suppose someone else followed us this time?"

I'd been alert while we were leaving the dome, and hadn't had my visor polarized on this trip. "No one could have," I said. "I'm sure of that."

He looked up at the hatch. "Could they have tracked Juan's buggy?"

"I don't see how. He said he'd swept it for bugs before we picked it up. And it's a lot harder to track vehicles here than people think; there's no GPS equivalent, and . . ."

"Yes?"

I blew out air—a luxury I might not have much longer. "And I'm an idiot," I said. I reached into my equipment pouch and pulled out the switchblade I'd gotten from Dirk. I pushed the button that caused the blade to spring out. Rory looked alarmed as I turned the knife around so that the blade was aiming toward my chest.

"Hang on, old boy!" Pickover said. "We're not done for yet."

But I was just maneuvering the knife to hand it to him. "You've got super strength," I said. "Can you break the haft open?"

He took the knife from me, looked at it for a moment, and indicated that he was going to snap the wine-colored handle by flexing it with his hands, as if to give me a chance to stop him. But I nodded for him to go ahead, and he did so.

The handle broke in two, and Rory split the pieces open. There was the channel for the blade, the spring mechanism—and the tracking device. I reached over, prized the little chip out, let it drop in slow motion to the deck, and ground the heel of my boot into it until it was crushed. Dirk, or whoever had hired him, had known it would be impossible to plant a tracking device on me—but having one in a knife I'd be bound to seize was another matter.

"Lakshmi Chatterjee must have hired the punk I got the knife from," I said. "That's how she managed to follow us out here in the dark, but . . ." I frowned.

"What?" said Pickover.

"Well, I—hmmm. How'd she know that *I* would be heading out to the Alpha? Did you tell anyone you were hiring me, Rory?"

"No, of course not."

"Still, you could have been seen coming to my office. Back when half your face was missing, you'd have been quite conspicuous."

"I—I hadn't thought about that," Rory said. "I'm not used to being clandestine."

"Well, what's done is done," I said.

Pickover was trying hard to be unflappable, but, despite his reserved face, his voice had become higher, and he was darting his eyes about nervously. "So, what now?" he asked. "We seem to be prisoners."

I looked around the lower level. It had a smaller interior diameter than the upper one, implying there was a donut of equipment or tanks surrounding us. "What about blowing the hatch?" I said. "Aren't spaceship hatches supposed to have explosive bolts?"

"I'll check," said Pickover. He headed up the ladder, hauling himself up with his arms and letting the foot with the damaged ankle dangle freely. Once he was at the top of the shaft, he looked around. "I don't see any controls for that," he called down. He tried the wheel again, but it didn't budge.

I moved off the ship's centerline into one of the four compartments on the lower floor, found a bucket seat, and dropped myself into it. I looked down at the deck plating, pissed at myself for having been so easily duped with the switchblade. Pickover was banging around up at the top of the shaft, trying various things to get the wheel moving again.

After a time, I looked up. The chair I was in was facing the curving bulkhead in front of me, but it was on a swivel base, and I slowly rotated it toward the central shaft; my instincts wouldn't let me keep my back to people, even though there was no one here but dead-as-a-doornail Denny and stainless-steel Rory. I looked more or less in the middle distance, at where the ladder began, but after a time my attention fell on the opposite bulkhead—which had a red door with a locking wheel in its center. Of course: the other exit—the one that would have led outside had the lander been sitting on the surface. But, damn it all, it *wasn't* sitting on the surface. It was buried in the Martian permafrost.

What goes down must come up.

"Rory!" I said into my fishbowl's headset.

"Yes?"

"Come down here."

It didn't take him long. "What?" he said, when he was standing between me and the red door.

"This is the descent stage, right?"

"Yes."

"So beneath our feet," I said, tapping the hull plating with my boot, "there are fuel tanks."

"They're actually in a torus around this level."

"Ah, okay. But below us, there's the descent engine, right? A big engine cone; a big landing rocket?"

"Yes."

"So, assuming there's any fuel left, what happens if we fire that engine?"

Pickover looked at me like I was insane. I get that a lot. "The engine cone is probably totally plugged with soil," he said.

"Would we blow up, then?"

He frowned in a subdued transfer way. "I . . . I don't know."

"Well, let's find out. There's got to be a control center."

"It's here," said Pickover, pointing to his right. I came over to the room he was standing next to. It had a curving control console, following the contour of the outer bulkhead. There was a bucket seat in front of it identical to the one I'd just vacated. I looked at Pickover.

"I don't know how to fly a spaceship," he said.

"Neither do I. And I bet Weingarten and O'Reilly didn't really, either. But the ship should know." I waved my arm vaguely at the ceiling lights. "The electrical system is working; maybe the ship's computer is, too." I lowered myself into the seat, and Pickover took up a position behind me. I scanned the instruments, but Pickover spotted what I was looking for first and reached over my shoulder to press a switch.

There was a big square red light on the console that flashed in what looked like a random pattern—but I knew it wasn't; it was one of those lights that robots in old sci-fi flicks used to have that flashed in time with spoken words, once per syllable. Such lights didn't really serve any purpose on robots, but they *were* handy to indicate that a computer was talking in a spaceship cabin that might or might not be pressurized. There wasn't much air in the lander, and all of it was unbreathable, but it was sufficient to convey faint sound. I cranked up the volume on my suit's external microphones. "Repeat," I said.

"I said, can I be of assistance?" replied a male voice; in the thin air, I couldn't say much more about it than that, although I thought it sounded rather smug.

"Yes, please," I said. "Can you open the hatch?"

"No," the computer replied. "Both egress portals are manually operated."

"Can you blow the top hatch?"

"That functionality is not available."

"All right," I said, crossing my arms in front of my chest. "We'd like to take off."

"Ten. Nine. Eight."

"Wait!" I said, and "Hold!" shouted Pickover.

"Holding," said the voice.

"Just like that?" I said. "We can just take off? You know we're buried in Martian permafrost."

"Of course. I engineered the burial."

"Um, is it safe to take off?" asked Pickover.

"Well, safe-ish," said the computer.

"What kind of answer is that?" I asked.

"An approximate one," replied the prim voice.

"I'll say," I said. And then it occurred to me to ask another question. "Do you know how long you've been turned off?"

"Thirty-six years."

"Right," I said. "Do you know why Simon Weingarten marooned Denny O'Reilly here?"

"Yes."

"Spill it."

"Voiceprint authorization required."

"Whose?"

"Mr. Weingarten's or Mr. O'Reilly's."

"They're both dead," I said.

"I have no information about that."

"I can show you O'Reilly's body. It's upstairs."

"Be that as it may," said the computer.

I frowned. "What other information has been locked?"

"All navigational and cartographic records."

I nodded. If the lander ever was moved, no one but Simon or Denny could ask the computer how to get back to the Alpha. "All right," I said. "We need to get out of here. That door"—I pointed to the other side of the ship—"is it an airlock?" I couldn't see the computer's camera, but I was sure it had one, and so it should have known what I was indicating.

"Yes."

"The outer door is sealed?"

"Yes."

"Does it swing in or out?"

"Out."

I motioned to Pickover. He walked over and worked the wheel that opened the inner door, which swung in toward him. There was a chamber with curving walls between the inside and outside hulls of the ship, big enough for one person. "Is there a safety interlock that will prevent us from opening the outer door while the inner one is open?" I asked.

"Yes," said the computer.

"Can it be defeated?" I assumed there must be a way to turn it off, since it'd be a pain in the ass to have to cycle through the airlock during testing back on Earth.

"Yes."

"Do so."

"Done."

"Okay. I propose that you fire the engine to lift the ship up out of the ground so that the airlock is just above the surface. Can do?"

"Can do," said the computer.

"All right," I said. "Rory, are you ready?"

"As ready as I'll ever be."

I got out of the chair and moved over to stand behind him. "Nothing personal," I said, "but if whoever is outside opens fire, you've got a better chance of surviving than I do."

The paleontologist nodded.

"Computer," I said.

"My name is Mudge," the machine replied.

I heard Pickover snort; the name must have meant something to him. "Fine, Mudge," I said. "We're ready."

"Ten," said Mudge, and he continued in the predictable sequence.

There was a wheel set into the outer door, which was also red. Pickover moved over and grabbed it with both hands, ready to start rotating it as soon as it was above the ground. I grabbed onto a handle conveniently set into the wall of the airlock, in case it turned out to be a rough ride.

"Two," said Mudge. "One. Zero."

The whole ship began to shake, and I heard the roar of the engine beneath my feet and felt it transmitted through the deck plates and the soles of my boots. We did not explode, for which I was grateful. But we didn't seem to be going anywhere, either.

"Mudge?" I called.

The computer divined my question. "The permafrost is melting beneath us and, by conduction, at our sides, as well. Give it a moment."

I did just that, and soon did feel us jerking upward. I tried to imagine what the scene looked like outside: perhaps like a cork working its way slowly out of a wine bottle.

There was a rectangle in front of Pickover, above the wheel, that I'd stupidly taken as decorative, but it was a window in the outer airlock door. Light was now streaming in from the top of it, and the strip of illumination was growing thicker centimeter by centimeter as the ship rose out of its muddy tomb. I couldn't make out any details through the window, though: it was streaked with reddish brown muck.

If whoever had locked us in had been standing guard, I hoped—old softy that I am—that he or she realized what was going on, since I imagined the superheated rocket exhaust would spray out in all directions once the cylindrical hull was fully above ground.

Soon the entire height of the window was admitting light. Our ascent was still slow, though. Pickover was craning to look out the port, presumably to see when the bottom of the door was above ground—

—which must have been *now,* because he gave a final twist to the locking wheel and hauled back and kicked the door outward with the leg that had the uninjured ankle.

Suddenly we popped higher into the air—free now from the sucking wet melted permafrost. Pickover threw himself out the airlock with a cry of *"Geronimo!"*

I scrambled to follow suit, but by the time I got to the precipice, we were already dozens of meters above the ground; even in Martian gravity, the jump would surely break my legs and probably my neck, too.

"Abort!" I yelled over my shoulder. "Mudge, lower us back down!"

The vibration of the hull plating changed at once, presumably as the computer throttled back the engine. We hung in the air for a moment, like a cartoon character after going off a cliff, and then started to descend.

Pickover had ended up spread-eagled in the mud, but was now getting to his feet and trying to run, despite his bad ankle. The cylindrical habitat had reduced its altitude by half. Pickover was having a terrible time gaining traction in the mud; I didn't want to singe him. "Cut the engine!" I called to Mudge. The hull suddenly stopped vibrating, and we began dropping like a rock. I was afraid the ship would fall right back down into the hole it had previously occupied, especially since it was probably widened now by the rocket exhaust. When I figured my chances were at least halfway decent for surviving, I leapt out of the airlock, trying for as much horizontal distance as I could manage.

When I landed, my legs went like driven piles into the muck. No sooner had they done so than a shock wave went through the melted permafrost as the massive lander impacted the surface behind me. I twisted my neck to see. The lander had hit half-on and half-off the hole, and now was teetering toward me; it looked like it was going to topple over any second. I tried to pull myself up and out of the mess, but it was going to take some doing—and the chances of the ship falling precisely so that I ended up poking safely through the open airlock doors instead of being crushed seemed slim. It was too bad we hadn't brought along the lasso that Lakshmi had used on Pickover earlier; he could have employed it to haul me out of the quagmire.

That is, if he himself could get solid footing. Behind me, the tottering ship was making a groaning sound, conveyed through the attenuated atmosphere and picked up by my still-open external helmet microphones.

I was pushing myself up out of the mess as fast as I could, but a surface suit really wasn't designed for those sorts of gymnastics. For his part, Pickover was staggering away from me like Karloff fleeing the villagers, the mud still sucking at his every step.

Suddenly—it was always suddenly, wasn't it?—a shot rang out, audible because my external mikes were still cranked way up. The bullet whizzed past me and impacted the mud. I swung my head within the fishbowl, trying to make out the assailant. There: about ten o'clock, and maybe thirty meters away—a figure, probably a man, in an Earth-sky-blue surface suit, holding a rifle aimed at me.

TWENTY-FIVE

Pickover finally reached solid ground, it seemed, but as soon as he did, he threw himself down, presumably to make a harder target for whoever was shooting at us. As proof that he was back on *marsa firma,* the belly flop sent up not a splash of mud but a cloud of dust.

I pulled myself a little farther out of the muck, removed the Smith & Wesson from my shoulder holster, then took a bead on Mr. Blue Sky. There was no way to call "Freeze!" to him, so I just squeezed the trigger, setting off the oxygenated gunpowder, and watched with satisfaction as he slumped over.

But speaking of freezing, I think the mud was starting to do that again. I didn't want to end up as one of Pickover's fossils, and so, with a final Herculean effort—as in the Greek hero, not the Agatha Christie detective—I hauled myself out of the thickening sludge.

And just in time, too! With a dinosaurian groan, the ship came tumbling down. I spun around in time to see it hit, and it splashed me from helmet to boot with filth. I used my gloved hands to wipe the front of my fishbowl clean, although it was still streaked with mud, and looked at the fallen lander. The sealed circular hatchway stared out at me like a cyclopean eye.

There was no way anyone could enter through the airlock again; it was face down and buried. I hadn't seen it happen, but I suspected that the outward-opening door had been slammed shut when the curving hull had hit the muck. If we were going to get back inside, we'd have to find a way to unseal the top hatch. But that was a problem for later; for now, I made my way over to Pickover. "It's safe to get up," I said once I'd reached him. His bum ankle was making it hard for him to do so, so I gave him a hand. While walking over, I'd scanned around for anyone else—but Mr. Blue Sky seemed to be alone. We headed over to see him.

"You okay?" I said to Pickover, as we closed the distance.

"Yeah, but that jump didn't do my ankle any favors; it's worse than before."

The sun was high, and there were a few thin clouds overhead. We got those naturally sometimes, although I wondered if they were actually our rocket exhaust or water vapor from the melted permafrost. Phobos is hard to see during the day, and catching sight of Deimos is a good sign that you don't need your eyes fixed; I managed the former, but not the latter, although who knew if the little terror was up, anyway.

I still had my gun out. Blue Sky looked like he was slumped over unconscious, but he could just be playing possum, waiting until we were near enough that he couldn't miss. But as we got closer, he really did seem out of it, and when I knelt next to him, I could see why. "Ooops," I said.

Pickover sounded aghast. "You just killed a man, and the best you can manage is 'Ooops'?"

"Well, he *did* try to kill us," I said. My bullet had gone a little higher than I'd intended and had shattered his helmet, exposing him to the subzero cold and the razor-thin atmosphere. It was an odd sight: the youthful face was clearly dead, the eyes were locked open and staring straight ahead, and a trickle of blood, already frozen, extended down from a corner of his mouth. But the snake tattoo on his left cheek was still animated, the rattle on the tail moving back and forth. It was Dirk.

"I know him," I said.

"Oh?"

"Yeah. Dumb punk, recently arrived from Earth." I shrugged a little.

"Ah," said Rory, I guess because he needed to say something. But, then, after a moment, he went on. "Hello, what's this?"

Lying on the ground nearby was an excimer-powered jackhammer, like the one Joshua Wilkins had used to fake the suicide in the basement of NewYou.

"He must have used it to push the locking wheel against your strength, Rory."

"Ah, right. But what should we do with this poor devil? We can't just leave him here."

"No," I said softly. "We can't."

For once, Rory was being more mercenary than me. "It's the color of his surface suit," he said. "Anyone coming this way is bound to spot him. We don't want people stopping near the Alpha for any reason."

I pointed back the way we'd come. "But even if we bury him, that giant lander lying on its side is bound to attract some attention."

"Then we've got to move it."

"How? Juan's buggy can't haul that."

"There's no reason to assume the ship is no longer flightworthy," Pickover said. "Let's get Mudge to fly it back to New Klondike."

Normally, I'd have had Pickover carry the corpse, since it would have been no hardship for him, but he was still limping. I put Dirk in a fireman's carry, and we took him back toward the pit left by the lander. We could have used the jackhammer to dig a grave through the permafrost, but the pit, and the area for a bunch of meters around it, was still mushy enough to make it possible, though difficult, to inter him by hand, so we did that instead. When it was done, I stood over the spot for a few minutes, trying to think of something appropriate to say. But, for once, I was at a loss for words.

I assume it was Dirk who had rescued Lakshmi when we'd abandoned her here. She hadn't seemed like she expected the cavalry to come charging over the hill—so my guess was that while she and Darren Cheung had followed us, via the tracking chip in the switchblade, he had tailed them, hoping for his own crack at Alpha riches. And, to his credit, when he came upon Darren dead and Lakshmi getting that way, he'd rescued her rather than left her to die. Maybe there was *some* honor among thieves after all.

It wouldn't do to leave Dirk's buggy here. I knew from the old movies I liked that the terms "manual" and "automatic" used to refer to types of automobile transmissions, but the switch on the buggy's dashboard labeled with those two words simply selected whether the vehicle drove itself or not. I had Rory help me rotate the buggy so that it was facing northeast—vaguely toward Elysium—and then set it on its way; the buggy's excimer battery showed a three-quarters charge still, so the damn thing should go thousands of klicks before running out of power.

We then turned our attention back to the lander—and discovered we had another difficulty. If there was a way to talk to Mudge from the outside, we had no idea what it was. I doubted there was an external microphone; that sort of thing got burned off on entering an atmosphere, even one as thin as Mars's.

Still, Pickover could probably manage a decent volume, so I suggested he shout. He called Mudge's name a few times, but there was no response—although, even if the computer heard, it was also unlikely that there was a loudspeaker on the outside of the ship.

The cylindrical hull was partially buried in the mud, and the mud was congealing fast. The engine cone and a portion of the lower hull—but not enough to reveal the airlock door—was overhanging the original hole in the ground. The top hatch, now facing outward, was a couple of meters up; somewhat more than half of the ship's diameter was still above the surface. We moved close, and I boosted Pickover onto my shoulders so he could look at the locking wheel. He was having a hard time perching himself on me since he couldn't really flex his right ankle.

"It's been jammed with a crowbar," he said—or transmitted; I picked it up over my suit radio rather than the external mike. I felt Pickover's weight shifting on my shoulders as he struggled with the crowbar, but at last he got it free. He tossed it aside, then struggled a bit more and soon had the hatch open. "Mudge!" he called out.

My suit mike picked up the faint voice. "Can I be of assistance?"

"Can you get this ship airborne from its current posture?" Pickover asked.

"Most likely," Mudge replied.

"How much fuel do you have in reserve?"

"The sensor isn't designed to operate on its side," said Mudge, "but I estimate that the tank is about one-fifth full. Not nearly enough to make orbit, let alone escape velocity, I'm afraid."

"Can you fly to New Klondike?"

"Where is New Klondike?"

Right. The damn computer had spent the last four decades asleep.

"About 300 kilometers east of here," said Pickover.

"I would require a navigator," replied Mudge, "but the ship is capable of covering that distance."

"You fly it back, Rory," I said, craning my neck upward. "I'll get Juan's buggy and use it to tow the two wrecked ones away."

"Sounds like a plan," said Pickover, and he scrambled up into the access hatch; I was glad to have his weight off my shoulders. "Okay," he said. "I'm inside and—Jesus!"

"What?"

"Scared me half to death!"

"What?" I said again.

"Old Denny's corpse got dislodged when the lander toppled. I backed down the access tube right onto it."

"Yuck," I said, because he expected me to say something. I headed back toward Juan's buggy, following the footprints Pickover and I had left earlier. The buggy was intact, thank God. I'd faced murderous transfers before—but I didn't want to face an angry Juan Santos ever again. I didn't pressurize the cabin, though. "Rory?" I said into my headset.

"Here, Alex."

"Buggy's in good shape. You can take off whenever you're ready. I want to watch the launch, though. Give me a couple of minutes to get in position."

"Copy," said Pickover, in good astronaut fashion. I tooled around the rim of the crater and headed toward the dark bulk of Syrtis Major Planum. We weren't far north of the equator, and the sun was now nearly overhead. I did an S-shaped maneuver in the buggy and stopped short before I got to the part of the surface that had been melted; I didn't know how the springy tires would do on a kind of muck they'd never been designed for. I could now see the descent stage from a three-quarters view, favoring the top. "Okay," I said into the radio.

"Roger," replied Pickover, clearly still enjoying the notion of piloting a spaceship. But then he had to turn the reins over to the real pilot. "Mudge? We're all set."

I couldn't hear Mudge's reply, but after a moment, Pickover said, "Oh, right. Go ahead."

I saw a small hatch open on the side of the ship, and a thruster quad emerged—a cluster of four attitude-control jets. Another cluster emerged ninety degrees farther around the ship's circumference; I imagined there were two more at the other cardinal points.

On the quad close to me, the jet that was pointing down came to life, and the corresponding one on the other visible unit, near the top, did so, too. The cylindrical stage vibrated for a bit, and then, slowly at first and then more rapidly, it started to roll. I didn't want to think about Pickover—let alone the corpse—being rotated around like they were on the spin cycle.

The upper level of the descent stage was still partially hanging out over the pit, but by pumping the attitude-control jets off and on, and supplementing the rotational force with a little backward *oomph* from the jets that were facing forward, Mudge managed to at last dislodge the ship and half push and half roll it completely onto muddy ground, so that no part of it was jutting over the pit. After a few more adjustments, the ACS quads stopped firing. I heard Pickover talking again to Mudge. "Yes, I'm holding on. Whenever you're ready."

Apparently Mudge was raring to go, because as soon as Pickover said that, the big engine cone at the rear ignited, shooting out a plume of flame. The massive cylinder pushed forward, sliding at least twice the ship's length along the ground, digging a furrow as it did so, before it started to angle up toward the butterscotch sky. I watched it lift higher and higher and then streak toward the eastern horizon.

Once it was gone from view, I spun the Mars buggy around and headed back to that small crater with the two other wrecked buggies. And, of course, Dirk's excimer jackhammer was waiting for me there. I had no idea *which* fossils were the most valuable, but I wandered around and used the hammer to remove four choice-looking slabs, which I put in the trunk of Juan's buggy, along with the jackhammer. If I understood what Pickover had said correctly, it was best to keep the slabs frozen; I'd drop them off at a secret locale of my own on the way back.

Before removing each slab, I'd used my tab to take photographs of the specimens in the ground, and wider shots that established their precise locations and orientations; I'd placed my phone in the shots, so that dimensions could be worked out, too.

I couldn't literally cover our tracks—or the buggy's—but the ever-shifting Martian dust would do that soon enough. Still, I did make an effort to hide the wounds I'd just made in the soil.

Juan's buggy, like most models, had a trailer hitch, and I hooked up a line so that I could drag both wrecks, one behind the other. I wouldn't take them back to New Klondike because people would ask awkward questions about how they'd come to be destroyed, and because hauling that much weight all the way would make the journey take forever. But I did drag them thirty kilometers—not back east, in the direction we'd come, but south. They'd doubtless be stumbled upon at some point, but they would be nowhere near the Alpha.

I then finally got to give Juan's buggy a workout. This part of Isidis Planitia wasn't quite as good as the Bonneville Salt Flats, but it still let me pull some great skids, and I spun the buggy through a couple of three-sixties, just for fun. And then, at last, I headed home. I had no really good map of how to get there—and I wouldn't have been able to retrace the course to return here—but I knew the dome was to the east, and so I just started driving that way, confident I'd eventually pick up the New Klondike homing beacon. And, indeed, after about ninety minutes, I did.

The sun had reached the western horizon behind me by the time I was approaching New Klondike. When I was back in phone range, I checked in with Pickover; he was safe in his apartment and happier than I'd ever heard him. He'd found the map aboard the descent stage—it had been rolled up for storage, he said, but was as big as a kitchen tabletop, a fact he knew because he now had it covering his own and was poring over it excitedly.

As I got closer to the dome, I saw that Mudge and Pickover had put the descent stage down vertically on one of the circular fused-regolith landing pads; it was resting on articulated tripodal legs that must have been previously stored within the hull. The pads were numbered with giant yellow painted numerals at three places on their rims; this one was number seven.

There'd be some paperwork to take care of before the descent stage could be brought inside to the shipyard. I drove on to the garage building near the south airlock and returned Juan's buggy, pleased to see that although it was mud-splashed, it was otherwise no worse for wear.

I then entered the dome, returned my rented surface suit—getting the damage deposit back this time—and headed to my little windowless apartment. On the way, I listened to the voice mail that had accumulated while I was out, including a message from Diana that said Lakshmi Chatterjee had had a cancellation and could see her to talk about her poetry tomorrow at 2:00 p.m. It was less necessary now, I suspected, to bug Shopatsky House; Dirk had almost certainly been her accomplice. But it was still probably worth finding out if Lakshmi had revealed the location of the Alpha to anyone else or was planning another trip out to it.

Despite all I'd been through today, I was totally clean—the surface suit had kept all the dust and mud out. But I definitely needed a shower. Once I got home, I stripped and headed into the stall, opting to treat myself to a water rinse. (The irony was that it was water showers that were noisy; sonic showers were ultrasonic and didn't interfere with your hearing—not a lot of people sang while taking sonic showers.)

But while other sounds were being drowned out by the jets of H_2O, someone must have jimmied the lock on my apartment door. Or maybe they'd broken in earlier, and had simply been hiding until now. Either way, when I turned off the nozzles, what I heard was not the *drip-drip-drip* that I really needed to get fixed, but rather a low, unpleasant voice that said, "Freeze."

TWENTY-SIX

The door to my shower stall was alloquartz—not bulletproof, but, as they used to say about watches that you could get wet, bullet-*resistant.*

I turned slowly in the little stall so that I was facing the intruder, and so he might feel a little intimidated. The air was steamy, and there was the transparent door between us, with beads of water on it, but I'd lay money that the mug facing me was a transfer. Unfortunately, my money was in my wallet, in the other room, along with my pants.

The guy was big, the kind of bruiser that people would have called "Moose" on a planet that had any. He was aiming a gun at me—and, in-dignity of indignities, I soon recognized that it was my own.

"What can I do for you?" I said, as amiably as I could manage. He hadn't told me to stick my hands up, so I hadn't.

"You have something I want." His voice was slow, thick.

I looked down. "That's what all the boys say."

"Stow it," said the man. "I'm talking about the diary. We can do this

one of two ways. You tell me where it is, I get it, I leave, and you go towel off and put baby powder on your butt. Or you make me rip this joint apart looking for it, and I leave powder burns right above that six-pack of yours."

"You make a tempting case for the former option," I said.

It clearly took him a moment to digest this, but then he nodded. "Good."

"It's in a safe in my living room. The safe opens to simultaneous scanning of my fingerprint and me uttering a passphrase—a combination lock, if you will."

He jerked the Smith & Wesson to indicate I should step out. If he'd been standing closer, I might have been able to slam the alloquartz door into his arm—my bathroom wasn't much bigger than a closet—but that wasn't going to work. As I opened the door, he moved out into the living room. I dripped my way across to join him.

"Where's the safe?" he asked.

"In the wall. Behind the couch."

The couch was a threadbare affair upon which I'd pursued many a threadbare affair. It was heavy—it pulled out into a bed, for those occasional times I had an overnight guest who wasn't going to share mine—but not so heavy that I couldn't easily move it in Martian gravity. Still, I indicated for Moose to take an end, in hopes that his doing so would destabilize the situation enough that I could recapture my gun. But he *was* a transfer: he bent and put his left hand under the bottom of the couch and swung it away from the wall all by himself, without once taking the gun off me.

The safe couldn't be installed flush with the wall, of course; that would have made it protrude into my neighbor's apartment, and Crazy Gustav and I made a point of staying out of each other's way. Instead, it jutted from the wall at floor level. It was about forty centimeters tall and wide, and half that deep. Moose looked disappointed: he'd probably been hoping for a standalone unit he could just grab and run off with, but the safe's back was clearly fused to the wall. "Open it," he said in the same cow's-moo voice he'd used before.

I crouched next to it, making it look like a random choice that I happened to be between the safe and him. I placed my thumb on the little scanning plate, which of course not only read the pattern of ridges but also checked the temperature and looked for a pulse. I then uttered my favorite quote: "'Experience has taught me never to trust a policeman. Just when you think one's all right, he turns legit.'"

The lock moved aside with a *chunk*, I grabbed the pistol from within—one should always have a spare of anything vital to one's profession—rolled onto my side, swung the gun around, and aimed it at Moose.

The big transfer stared at me. "What are you going to do?" he said. "Shoot me? It'll just bounce off." He lifted his gun higher, as if taking a bead. "I, on the other hand—"

"—still don't have what you came for." I jerked my head toward the safe. He could see it had a few things in it—I kept some mementos of Earth in there—but the diary was conspicuously absent. I was still more or less supine, and he was towering over me from the other side of the couch. I shifted my aim from his chest to the ceiling-mounted lighting unit and squeezed off a shot. The room was plunged into darkness. I was hoping he didn't have the infrared-vision upgrade, whereas I knew the layout of my apartment intimately. I sprang to my feet and worked my way along the wall my place shared with Crazy Gustav's unit to the wall that separated this room from my bedroom.

My neighbors might call the police at the sound of a gunshot, and the police might come if they were called—but I was surely on my own for at least the next few minutes. I was betting Moose didn't have much experience with a revolver; the safety had still been on, I'd noted, when he'd been aiming it my way. Still, if he did get hold of me, he doubtless had strength enough to snap my neck.

Being naked, my footfalls weren't making any noise on the carpetless floor, whereas Moose's clodhoppers were coming down with thuds. If I could get to the bathroom, I could lock the door behind me and hole up in the alloquartz shower stall until help arrived—an ignominious way to survive, but what the heck.

But before I'd gotten that far, the damn main door to my apartment swung open, emitting light from the corridor. Of course: Moose had broken the lock on it when he'd let himself in. Silhouetted on the threshold was Dr. Rory Pickover. Moose swung around and fired—I guess he *did* know how to use the gun after all. Pickover was propelled backward by the impact and stumbled into the opposite corridor wall. He winced in pain as he looked down at his torso, then looked up with his plastic features drawn together. His voice was full of barely controlled rage. "I am getting really tired," he hissed, "of people shooting bits of metal into my chest." He crouched low then leapt, all his transfer's strength against Mars's feeble gravity. It was impressive—you fall in slow-mo on Mars, but you leap even faster than you can on Earth—and he slammed into Moose's chest, knocking him backward onto the couch.

I had never seen a transfer hit another transfer before, and, to be honest, Pickover fought like a girl: like a super-strong, excimer-powered girl. He smashed Moose in the face, and the sound was like two metal buckets crashing together. Moose was now seated on the couch, and I got my arm around his neck from behind. I couldn't cut off his air supply, but I could flip him over the back of the couch, and I did so. Pickover, meanwhile, grabbed the bottom of the couch in the little gap between it and the floor caused by the stubby couch legs, and he flipped the thing right over, and then he pushed it like a snowplow blade against the wall, trapping Moose in the triangular space.

I'd danced out of the way just in time and got to my feet, aiming the gun at the opening nearest Moose's head, in case he tried to come out. Pickover sat on the couch, and after a moment I clambered on it, too—which was quite uncomfortable for me, since my butt had to rest on the right angle between the couch's back and the unupholstered bottom.

Our combined weight was more than Moose could push off him, at least starting in a cramped space where he couldn't get any leverage. As we sat there—me naked, Pickover with a smoking bullet hole in his chest (and another favorite shirt ruined, I imagined), furniture upturned—Crazy Gustav happened to appear in the corridor, heading to his apartment. His sandy hair, as always, was askew, and he looked at me from his pinched, stubbly face. "Hey, Lomax," he said, "you really know how to class up a joint."

I crossed my legs demurely. "Thanks." I thought about asking him to call the cops, but Crazy Gustav had no fondness for them, and we seemed to have the situation under control. So instead, I just tipped my nonexistent hat at him, and Gustav went into his apartment, shaking his head.

TWENTY-SEVEN

I wanted to go get some clothes, but my weight was part of what was keeping Moose trapped. "Okay, big fellow," I called out. "Let's start with the basics. Who are you?"

"Nobody," he rumbled from beneath us, his voice muffled.

"Captain Nemo was nobody," I said. "Everybody else is somebody."

"Not me."

"What's your name?"

"Don't have one."

"Come on. People have to call you *something.*"

"Trace."

A cool name for a copy, I thought. "I take it you're hired muscle, Trace. But hired by who?" If he corrected me to "Hired by whom?" I'd fire a shot through the couch at him.

"Actual."

"Who's that?"

"That's all I ever call him. Actual."

"He a good boss?"

"You kidding?"

"No. If he sucks, maybe you want to change allegiance. Is he a good boss?"

"He's skytop."

I knew a lot of old-fashioned slang—old movies did that to you—but I hadn't heard that one for a while; Trace might as well have called him "groovy."

"And where is this . . . this skytop gentleman? Down on Earth?"

"No."

"Here on Mars?"

"No."

"Where then?"

"Figure it out."

I took a breath. "Fine, be that way—but don't say I didn't give you a chance. Anyway, the professor and I can't very well sit here all day. So, first things first: toss the gun out from under there."

Trace didn't do anything.

"Well?" I said.

"I'm thinking."

His transfer brain operated at the speed of light, instead of the pokey chemical-signaling rates used by biologicals, but stupid had its own velocity, and I waited while he weighed his options.

And, at last, he reached a conclusion. The Smith & Wesson went skittering out from underneath and came to rest beneath my framed *Casablanca* movie poster. I couldn't go retrieve the gun just now, but at least we were making progress.

But then I heard that annoying *ping* that I could only hear when the front door to my place was open: the elevator had arrived. There were the sounds of people moving along the corridor, and then Detective Dougal McCrae and Sergeant Huxley were standing there in the open doorway, looking at us. Mac was in plain clothes and had his piece out, and Hux, in his dark blue uniform, was carrying that garbage-can-lid thing that I knew was the broadband disruptor. "We had a report of two gunshots," Mac said, rolling the *R* in "report." "And I recognized the address."

It didn't seem the time to point out that all gunshots make a report—well, unless a silencer is used.

Mac went on. "We sometimes let one go. But two?"

"Thanks for dropping by," I said. "There's a transfer behind the couch. A thug. He broke in here."

"While you boys were having some fun," said Huxley.

"While I was in the shower, you cretinous pinhead."

Mac raised his voice. "This is the New Klondike Police. Come out with your hands up. And I should warn you, we have a broadband disruptor. Don't make us use it."

Trace had two options, neither of which was particularly dignified. He could crawl out head first on my right, or he could worm his way out feet first on my left. I could tell that he'd opted for the former by the way the couch was now shaking beneath us.

When he was no longer behind the couch, he rose and held up his hands; the galoot was big enough that his fingertips were touching my ceiling.

"If you gentlemen will excuse me," I said, and I headed to the bedroom, pausing along the way to pick up my S&W. I quickly threw on some clothes—by this point, the dry air we had under the dome had sucked up all the moisture, and I was no longer wet. I put on black jeans and a T-shirt that was so dark blue you'd have thought it was also black if you didn't have the jeans to compare it to.

I thought about taking a moment to comb my hair; in my business, it didn't hurt to have a slightly wild-and-crazy look, but right now I was downright Gustavian. But no sooner had I picked up the comb than I heard an all-too-familiar electronic whine. I ran out of the room and saw, in the stark light spilling in from the corridor, Trace standing spread-eagled with all his limbs vibrating and a look of agony on his face. "Jesus!" I shouted. "Rory, get out! Get out right away!"

The paleontologist looked puzzled but he knew by now to heed my advice. He dashed out into the corridor. Huxley was holding the disruptor in both hands, with the disk aimed squarely—or roundly—at Trace.

Mac could have intervened but he didn't; he simply kept his own gun trained on the transfer. After about ten more seconds, Huxley pulled out the control that deactivated the disruptor, and Trace collapsed like a skyscraper undergoing controlled demolition.

"Why'd you do that?" I demanded.

Huxley sounded defensive. "He came at us," he said. "He came right at us."

"Aye," said Mac. "He did. I'd warned him we had a disruptor, Alex—you heard me. But . . ." He lifted his hands philosophically.

Normally, one of us might have rushed in to look at a downed man to see if he was still alive, but I doubted any of us knew how to tell with a transfer. Huxley put down the disruptor, leaning it against the wall that had the poster for *Key Largo.* I called out, "Rory! It's safe to come back!"

Dr. Pickover appeared in the doorway a moment later. "Is he—" But even the transfer hesitated over whether "dead" was the right word.

I prodded Trace with my foot—I hadn't had time yet to put on shoes or socks. He didn't move. "I think so."

"All right," said Mac. He lifted his left arm and pointed at his wrist phone to let me know we were now on the record. "We had reports of two weapons discharges. Who shot first?"

"I did."

"Then you'll have to—"

I cut Mac off and pointed up. "I did—but I shot out the light, see? I agree hitting the switch would have been more genteel, but there's actually no regulation against shooting inanimate objects. I thought my chances were better in the dark."

Huxley appeared dubious—but then, he appeared dubious when he looked at a waffle iron, as if he suspected there must be some trick involved in getting bumps to make dents. But it was Mac's opinion that counted, and Mac nodded. "All right," he said slowly, looking at the downed transfer. "What was he doing here?"

"He broke in. Looking for money, I guess. I happened to be in the shower and startled him when I came out."

"Okay," said Mac. "And the second shot?"

"Dr. Pickover here showed up, and this goon fired at him."

Mac looked thoughtfully at the massive heap on the floor. "Never quite sure what to do with a dead transfer, but if we keep frying them at this rate, my coroner is going to need to find another job."

"Take him to NewYou," I suggested. "See if they can ID him."

Mac nodded. He began to look around my apartment. "Sorry," I said, interposing myself between him and the wall unit he'd been about to examine. "Not without a warrant."

"It's a crime scene, Alex."

"Only because Huxley fried the guy. You can't manufacture crimes just so you can nose around a man's home."

"Guns were fired."

"True. But I haven't filed a complaint, and neither has Dr. Pickover."

Mac scratched his left ear. "All right," he said. "You'll at least let me take some pictures of the body before we move it?"

I gestured toward it. "Be my guest." While he was doing that, I spoke to my phone, asking it to find an electrician who could come in and fix my ceiling light. By the time I was done with that, Mac was ready to go. He had taken Trace's arms, and Huxley had his legs, and they'd balanced the disruptor on Trace's belly, and were carrying him out my door into the corridor. "Mind if I tag along?" I asked.

"About as much as you minded me searching your apartment," Mac said.

Touché, I thought.

But Pickover spoke up. "We're heading to NewYou, anyway, Detective. I've got a damaged ankle, not to mention *this.*" He indicated the bullet hole. "And Mr. Lomax is being paid to be my bodyguard."

"I can see he's doing a wonderful job," said Huxley, pointing at Pickover's chest.

But Mac knew when he was beaten. "All right," he said. "Let's all go there."

TWENTY-EIGHT

Mac and Huxley had come to my apartment in a police car, but it was much smaller than a prowl car would have been on Earth, and, try as the four of us might, we couldn't get Trace stuffed into the back seat. My neighborhood was rough, but we had to go through classier parts of town to get to NewYou, and so just lashing him to the roof wasn't going to do. Mac finally gave up and called for the paddy wagon. I had no fondness for that particular vehicle—twice people had thrown up on me inside it—so Pickover and I headed out on our own while Hux and Mac waited. Normally, I'd have hoofed it, but Pickover's ankle was still a problem; we hopped on the hovertram.

They say you can judge a city by the quality of its public transportation. New Klondike's trams were covered with graffiti and filled with garbage; things were nasty around the edges in a frontier town, and, frankly, I liked it that way. It took us about ten minutes, with all the stops, to get as close to NewYou as the tram would take us.

We hadn't been able to talk about anything of substance on the tram—too many people listening—but now that we were out on the street, I said, "Any idea who the big guy was working for? Who 'Actual' might be?"

Pickover frowned, then: "The big bloke referred to him as 'he,' so it's presumably not Lakshmi." We were very near the center of the dome now. Overhead, all the supporting struts came together in a starburst pattern around the central column.

"Yeah, I don't think it's Lakshmi, either—but not because of that. Lakshmi knows where the Alpha is, and presumably Trace was after the diary because he *doesn't* know where the Alpha is and thinks it might tell him."

"Who else knows about the diary?" Pickover asked.

We continued along. "I only told you, but God knows how many people Miss Takahashi told." There was a pebble in front of me. I kicked it, and it skittered ahead for most of a block.

We beat Mac and company to NewYou. When we entered, Reiko Takahashi was on duty. I would normally look at her with honest admiration; she was, as I have perhaps mentioned once or twice, quite lovely. But I found myself averting my eyes. She'd long known that her grandfather was dead; I didn't have to be the bearer of *that* bit of news. But that her grandfather's body was here, on Mars, would come as a shock. Pickover limped up to the counter Reiko was standing behind, and they spoke for a few moments. She said Mr. Fernandez was in the workroom and could doubtless make him right as rain; I frowned, trying to remember the last time I'd seen rain. Reiko pointed to the door to the back. Pickover looked over at me, I gave him a thumbs-up, and he disappeared.

Reiko crossed the floor. Her long hair was gathered into a ponytail today, so the orange stripes were only partially visible. "Hello, Alex," she said, smiling. Her demeanor gave no hint that she'd heard anything from Lakshmi about my having made off with the diary.

"Hi, Reiko. I like your hair like that."

She tipped her head demurely. "Thanks." She indicated the doorway

Pickover had gone through. "Does everyone who spends time with you end up in that sort of shape?"

"Actually, he got off lucky. The NKPD will be here shortly with—ah, here they are now."

The front door slid open, and Mac and Hux came in. They'd gotten a stretcher somewhere along the way, and Trace's giant body was on it, covered from head to toe by a thin gray sheet.

Miss Takahashi's perfectly manicured fingers went to her mouth. "Oh, God!" she said, moving over to stand next to Mac. "What happened?"

"This gentleman," Mac said, "attacked us, and we had to, um, deactivate him."

Reiko's eyebrows drew together. "Let me get Mr. Fernandez." She hustled into the back, her high heels clicking. Moments later, she reappeared, followed by her boss.

"Detective McCrae?" Fernandez said. "What's up?"

Mac repeated what he'd said to Reiko, and then he pulled back one end of the sheet, revealing Trace's face. A transfer's skin color didn't change after death, and the eyes didn't necessarily close; Trace's green eyes were wide-open, although whatever the disruptor had done to his circuitry had caused one pupil to contract to little more than a pinpoint while the other was so dilated it looked like he'd just come from an eye exam. Of course, he was absolutely still, but he looked like he could leap back into action at any moment. At least with a human stiff, you knew they were out of the game for good.

"How'd this happen?" Fernandez asked. He looked ashen—worse than the dead guy; maybe he was worried about a liability suit if one of his uploads had failed.

"We used a broadband disruptor on him," Mac said.

Fernandez nodded. "Right, right. I'd heard that you guys had a prototype unit."

"Anyway, do you recognize him?"

"Sure," said Fernandez. "That's Dazzling Don Hutchison."

I'd heard the name before, so I had another look. "It is?"

"Well, it's not really him," Fernandez said. "But that's his face. Licensed and everything. The estate gets a royalty each time we use it. Don't get much call for it, though—nobody remembers him anymore."

"Who the hell is Dazzling Don Hutchison?" asked Mac.

I opened my mouth to reply, but so did Hux—and he had so little in life, I decided to let him beat me to it. "He was a football player," he said. "With the Memphis Blues."

"And he's dead?"

"Twenty years, at least," said Hux.

"But this isn't him uploaded?" said Mac to Fernandez. "This is someone else who bought his face?"

"I'd assume so."

"Can you identify who this is—was?"

"People who choose to use something other than their own face usually want to guard their anonymity."

"Sure," said Mac. "But you must have some way to tell who's who, so you can see if they're still under warranty or whatever. A serial number or something."

Fernandez went into his back room and returned a moment later holding a small scanning device. He aimed it at the body. "No transponder, meaning he opted for an anonymizer package. I'll have to open him up to have a look."

"Do that, please," said Mac.

"I've already got Mr. Pickover opened up. Let me finish his repairs then I'll take care of this."

"How long for an ID?" asked Mac.

"I'll need another hour on Pickover."

"All right," said Mac. He turned to me. "A drink, Alex?"

"Another time."

Mac looked at Miss Takahashi then back at me and gave me a knowing wink. "Right, then. Come along, Sergeant Huxley." The two of them left the shop, and Fernandez went into the back room, closing the door behind him. Nobody had bothered to cover up Trace again, so I did—leaving just me and Reiko alone in the showroom, the two of us biologicals surrounded by unoccupied transfer floor models of various body types and colorations.

"Disconcerting," she said, "seeing a dead transfer like that."

"Yes." I took a breath, then: "Reiko, I have something to tell you that—"

The alloquartz outer door slid open, and a filthy, ancient prospector came in. "You got a washroom?"

Most retail staff had a pat answer along the lines of, "Sorry, it's for customer use only." Apparently, NewYou had a canned response, too. "Sir," Reiko said, flashing her brilliant smile, "we can set you up so that you never have to use a washroom again! Come on in and let me show you the very best that modern science has to offer!"

The old fossil hunter looked like he was going to call Reiko an unkind name but then he caught sight of me and thought better of it. He turned around and beetled outside.

"You were about to say, Alex?"

"You might want to have a seat."

Her expression suggested she thought this was unnecessary—and, indeed, it probably was; even if you fainted on Mars, you likely wouldn't break anything. But she went to the stool behind the cash desk, sat, and looked at me expectantly. "Well?"

"First, your grandfather is dead. Unequivocally so. I don't want to say anything that gets false hopes up, so let's be clear about that up front."

She nodded.

"But," I continued, "he did *not* die re-entering Earth's atmosphere all those years ago. He died here, on Mars. I know, because Dr. Pickover and I have recovered his body."

"My . . . God." Her eyes were wide. "Are you sure? I mean, I don't doubt you've found *someone's* body, but—"

"I'm sure. Or, more to the point, Dr. Pickover is sure; he's the one who identified the corpse."

"My God. Where . . . where is the body now?"

"In the descent stage."

"Pardon?"

"We found the descent stage that was left here on Mars at the end of their third mission."

"Take me to it. I'll rent a surface suit."

"No need—or, at least, there won't be any need shortly. We've moved the descent stage here, to New Klondike. It's outside the dome now, but I'm going to get it hauled into the shipyard. You can come down once that's done and have a look."

She seemed dumbfounded and more than a little shaken; perhaps she was now glad she'd taken my advice to sit down. "I don't get it," she said, delicate hands folded in her small lap. "Why was he still on Mars?"

"It looks like he was marooned here."

"By who? By—by Simon Weingarten?"

"Pretty much the only suspect."

"Wow," said Reiko. "Wow."

I wanted to go take care of getting the lander brought inside. "I've got an errand to run. I should be back in time to hear whatever identification details Mr. Fernandez can give us."

Reiko nodded, and I went out through the alloquartz sliding door. Just past it, there was a big wet spot on the wall; perhaps Reiko should have let the old prospector use the john after all.

I headed to the shipyard in the Seventh Circle between Eighth and Ninth Avenues, and made my way to Bertha's shack. She was hunched over like an albino gorilla, looking at work orders. "Hey, dollface," I said.

"Oh, Alex, I was just about to text you. The *Kathryn Denning* has touched down outside the dome. They're offloading its cargo now."

"Thanks," I said. I reached into my pocket and pulled out a fifty-solar coin. "You'll let me know when I can get aboard to poke around?"

She took the money and nodded her jowly head.

"Great," I said. "Until then, I've got a ship I want hauled inside."

She looked at me blankly. "You have a ship?"

"Uh-huh."

"Where'd you get a ship?"

"Found it abandoned. Salvaged it."

"It'll cost to have a tractor bring it in, and you'll have to pay rent on a berth for as long as it's here."

"I have an alternative proposal," I said.

She narrowed her pig-like eyes. "Yeah?"

"Yeah. You haul it in for free, and you let me keep it here for free."

"Funny," she said. "I don't smell booze on your breath."

"Hear me out. You do that, and we'll charge people to tour the ship—say, twenty solars a head, which we'll split fifty-fifty."

"Ain't no one gonna pay to see some dead hulk," Bertha said. She gestured out the shack's tiny window. "We're knee-deep in them here."

"They'll pay to see this one. It's Weingarten and O'Reilly's lander from their final expedition."

"Holy crap," she said. "Really?"

"Uh-huh."

"Fifty-fifty, huh?"

"Right down the middle—with one condition. I get two days of exclusive access before we open it to the public."

"What for?"

"I'm looking for clues."

"I've always said you were clueless, Alex."

I thought about asking her if she knew Sergeant Huxley; it seemed like a match made in heaven. But I simply smiled and said, "Do we have a deal?"

"Deal."

"How soon can you have it hauled inside?"

"Portia—the gal who operates the tractor—is out getting a bite to eat. But I'll get her to do it when she comes back."

"Great, thanks. The ship's on pad seven. You'll make sure no one comes near it?"

"Yes, of course." She gestured at the shipyard. "Keeping away looters is half my job; I'm good at it."

"I know. Thanks."

"Fifty-fifty, remember," Bertha said, holding up her left arm and tapping the face of her wrist phone with a sausage-like finger to let me know that it had recorded the arrangement.

I feigned a hurt tone. "After all we've been through, you don't trust me?"

"Would you?" she asked simply.

"I see your point."

TWENTY-NINE

I'd have enjoyed watching the descent stage being hauled inside by the tractor—I don't care how big a boy gets, he still loves watching large machines at work. But I'd seen the process before. The giant south airlock was over 300 meters wide and fifty deep. If a ship could fit in—the *Skookum Jim* barely would have squeezed in sideways—it could be brought inside the dome; if it didn't, there was no other way to get it in. The whole process of filling or draining the lock took about an hour.

I headed back to NewYou, grabbing some synthetic sushi on the way. I got there just as Pickover was coming out of the workroom. His shirt still had a rip in it, but I presumed his chest was repaired, and he was no longer limping. I let him settle up with Fernandez—at this rate, Rory was going to have to sell a pentapod or two to stay afloat. And then I turned to Fernandez. "Can we take a crack at Dazzling Don now?"

"Absolutely," he replied.

Just then, Mac came through the front door. Mercifully, Huxley was no longer with him; Mac himself was carrying the disruptor disk under one arm—maybe he was afraid that Trace wasn't really dead.

"Okay," Fernandez said generally to the room. "Come along."

I'd assumed Pickover was going to join us, but he waved me off and went to have a word with Miss Takahashi. Maybe he wanted to try his luck—or maybe, as someone who had bought and paid for immortality, the notion of attending the autopsy of a transfer was too unsettling. In any event, only Mac and I followed Fernandez into the workroom. Given his massive arms, I had no doubt Horatio had been able to carry Trace here on his own. In fact, I suspected he'd done it as soon as we'd left; having a fried transfer in the middle of his showroom probably wasn't good for business.

Dead humans always looked smaller than they had in life, but for whatever reason that effect didn't apply to transfers. Doubtless Fernandez was used to dressing and undressing transfers—people might be born naked, but no one wanted to pop into a new body that wasn't wearing clothes. He undid the buttons on Trace's shirt, exposing a chest that was surprisingly doughy. I found myself thinking the guy should have worked out—but then realized how ridiculous that was.

Fernandez got a small cutting laser and aimed it at the top of the chest, just below the Adam's apple. With practiced efficiency, he played the beam downward. I'd once seen a biological autopsy and had been impressed by all the blood that had spilled out when the chest was opened, but there was none of that here, although the melting plastiskin gave off an odor like burnt almonds.

Fernandez put on blue latex gloves, and as he pulled the chest flaps apart, I could see why: the melted skin was tacky, and some of it stuck to the gloves.

Beneath the skin was a layer of foam rubber, and beneath that was a skeleton that had the purplish pink sheen of highly polished alloy. There was nothing corresponding to organs inside the chest. Indeed, a lot of it seemed to be empty space.

Fernandez got a tool—like pliers, but with oddly shaped jaws—and he attached it to one of a pair of cylinders positioned more or less where the lungs should have been. The tool seemed to unlock something; there was a loud click, and the cylinder came free. Fernandez pulled the cylinder out and placed it on the table next to the body. The cylinder was covered with lubricant, which he wiped off with a green cloth, and then he got a large magnifying glass with a light attached and looked at the metal casing. "This is a ballast unit," he said. "Gives heft to the torso. We don't advertise the fact, but they've got serial numbers on them."

He said the word "Keely," then spoke a string of numbers into the air.

His computer responded in a pleasant female voice. "Transfer completed—" and it named a date two years ago.

"Where was the transfer done?" Fernandez asked.

"The body was assembled here," said Keely, "at this NewYou franchise."

"That was before I started working here," Fernandez said to me. He spoke to Keely again. "And what's this person's name?"

"Unknown," said Keely.

Fernandez frowned. "There has to be a record of the transference," he said—but whether he was telling me, or reminding his computer, I didn't know. He tried rephrasing his question. "Who came in for a transfer that day?"

"Nobody."

I frowned, thinking of what Trace had said: "I'm nobody."

"There had to be a source mind copied into this body," Fernandez said into the air. "Whose mind was scanned that day?"

"No one's."

"Then how was the transfer made?"

"I don't know," said Keely.

"You're sure it was done here?" Mac asked.

"That ballast unit was taken from our stock," the computer replied.

"Curiouser and curiouser," I said, looking at Fernandez. "You said the face was off-the-rack, so to speak. What about the rest of the body? Did it have any special modifications?"

The female voice answered. "Option package five selected: superior strength. No other modifications to standard body."

"He said he was hired muscle," I said. "I guess he was. But who hired him?"

"Who indeed?" asked Mac. He looked at Fernandez. "What *do* you do with a dead transfer? A funeral for a transfer seems like an oxymoron."

"Yeah," said Fernandez. "Transfers do get destroyed every once in a while, of course, but not often; I don't think we've had more than a couple of cases here on Mars." He paused. "Well, with no record of who transferred into this body, there's no way to contact next of kin. I guess I'll just strip him down for spare parts." He looked at the body stretched out before him. "Although I gotta say, I rarely need any so big."

• • • • • • • • • • •

When Mac and I went back through the sliding door into the showroom, I was surprised that not only was Pickover gone, but so was Reiko Takahashi.

Fernandez, who came out a moment later, was angry; he didn't like that his shop had been left unattended. Then again, it wasn't as if anyone was going to steal a transfer body; there was nothing you could do with one until it had had a consciousness moved into it, and that was hardly a do-it-yourself affair.

I asked my phone to get hold of Pickover. He didn't answer, which could mean he was in trouble, or it could mean he was indeed getting it on with Miss Takahashi; even I had eventually learned that you don't answer your phone when you're in bed with a lady.

Reiko had been anxious to see her grandfather's body, but I doubted Pickover would go to the descent stage without me, and only teenagers went to the shipyard to make out. I looked around the showroom for any sign of a struggle; there couldn't have been a loud one or we'd have heard it in the next room. But there was no indication of anything amiss—excepting for the missing miss.

I looked at Fernandez, who was using his own phone, presumably to call Reiko. "No answer?" I said.

"No." He shook the phone off. "She wouldn't just disappear. She's not like that."

"Alex," said Detective McCrae. "What's going on?"

I took a deep breath; I needed to give him something so he wouldn't shut me down. "Reiko Takahashi is Dennis O'Reilly's granddaughter."

Fernandez's eyeballs looked like they were going to pop out. I went on. "Dennis O'Reilly didn't die when his ship burned up on re-entry. Rather, he was marooned here by Simon Weingarten. Reiko had a hard copy of a diary written by her grandfather, which he transmitted back to Earth before he was marooned, but she loaned it to Lakshmi Chatterjee, who is the writer-in-residence here in town."

Mac sounded incredulous. "We have a writer-in-residence?"

"That's what I said! They have to advertise these things better."

"So, this Lakshmi person has the diary?" asked Mac.

"No. Not anymore. It's somewhere safe—but that big bruiser, Trace, thought I had it; that's why he broke into my apartment." I turned to Fernandez. "I was told during the Wilkins case that there were no security cameras upstairs."

"That's true," he said.

"But do you have them down on this floor?"

"Yes, of course."

"Can we see a playback?"

"This way." He led us through the sliding door again; beyond the workshop there was a small office. He turned on a wall monitor and spoke to Keely. "Camera two playback, quad speed, starting thirty minutes ago."

The camera was obviously mounted above the cash desk and showed the transparent door that led outside. The door slid open and—well, the expression "I thought I saw a ghost" perhaps didn't apply when a transfer was involved, but there, in the doorway, illuminated rather dramatically from behind, was Trace—or rather an exact duplicate. There wasn't just one Moose; there were Meese.

"Well," said Fernandez, "it *is* an off-the-shelf face. Keely, normal speed."

I'd been so intent on the mug's mug I hadn't initially noticed that he was packing heat. But Miss Takahashi clearly did, for she froze in the video. Moose the Second rapidly closed the distance between him and her and signaled for her to be quiet.

Pickover had initially been oblivious, but he soon spotted the man and then the gun. The big transfer couldn't do much to Pickover, but he could kill Reiko, and Pickover clearly realized that. He looked back at the door to the room we'd been standing in, as if wondering whether to call for help, but after a second he decided against it. The camera had recorded audio, too, but none of them said a word. Pickover was flexing his legs ever so slightly; now that his ankle was fixed, I think he was trying to decide if he could leap across the room and tackle the other transfer.

But just then the door slid open again, and a *third* transfer with Dazzling Don Hutchison's face came in. That was enough to make Pickover think better of trying to be a hero; either one of the giants could rip his metal skull off his titanium spine. It was galling that all of this had been going on just meters away from me. The transfer who had entered first gestured with his gun, and Reiko headed out the door, followed by Pickover.

Mac was already on his phone, calling the police station to see if the strange party—two giant twins, a transferee paleontologist, and a hot little biological—had been seen by any of the public security cameras, but, of course, most of those had long ago been smashed.

"Who'd want to kidnap Professor Pickover?" Fernandez asked.

"Maybe they wanted Miss Takahashi instead," Mac said.

"Why would anyone kidnap her?" asked Fernandez.

"Ransom?" I suggested. "If they knew she's Denny O'Reilly's granddaughter, they might have figured there was money to be had." I turned to Fernandez. "Did you know?"

He crossed his massive arms in front of his chest. "Are you accusing me?"

"No. No. I'm just asking. You looked surprised when I mentioned it."

"I *was* surprised. I mean, she's Japanese; he was Irish. I'd never even suspected."

"Right," I said. "I doubt anyone did. But she told me." I walked closer to the wall. "And she told me when I was standing right about there." I pointed to a spot in the image, which now showed the empty showroom. "Which means a record of her telling me *was* made, by the same security camera that made this picture. You could have reviewed it and found out."

"I had no reason to go over the security recordings," Fernandez said.

"Does anybody else have access to them?" asked Mac. "Any of the other employees able to call them up?"

"Well, the Wilkinses could, of course—the previous owners. But Cassandra's dead, and Joshua has gone off to be a fossil hunter."

"Anyone else?" asked Mac.

"Reiko has access, too, but she'd hardly be spying on herself. None of the other employees can unlock the security footage, though, and I swear I didn't know who Reiko's grandfather was."

Mac pulled out a handheld sensing device and headed into the showroom. Transfers didn't leave behind DNA, but they might still shed cloth fibers or have unusual dirt in their footprints that could be useful. While he busied himself with that, I gestured toward the staircase. "Horatio," I said, "there's something I want to see up in the scanning room."

Fernandez shrugged. "Okay." I let him lead the way to the second-floor landing. He went into the left-hand room, and I followed him, closed the door behind me, pulled out my gun, and, as he turned around to face me, I aimed it at the middle of his chest.

THIRTY

All right," I said to Horatio Fernandez. "Spill it. Where is Rory Pickover?"

His eyes were wide, but he was showing commendable composure for a guy with a gun trained on him. He spread those massive arms. "I have no idea."

"You know what he does for a living, right?"

"Sure. He's a paleontologist."

"And you know he recently came into some wealth."

"I don't know anything about that."

"Little academic suddenly had the money to transfer."

"Well, yeah, I guess."

"And you just opened up his chest to do repairs."

"Uh-huh."

"And while you had him open, you put in a tracking chip."

"That's illegal."

"Yes, it is. But you did it."

"Why would I?"

"You figure he's found the Alpha Deposit, or some other major cache of fossils, and you want to know where it is. Rory had himself scanned for tracking chips after he initially transferred, but he'd all but told Joshua Wilkins that he was going to do that, and so Wilkins hadn't put one in. And he could clearly see what was in your hands as you worked on his face before, so you couldn't put one in when you were doing those repairs—but he had himself checked, just to be sure. But this time you were working in his torso, and he hasn't had a chance to be scanned since leaving here, which means the chip you just put in is active. So where is he?"

"I tell you, I did no such thing."

"You may, or may not, give a damn about Dr. Pickover. But Reiko was your coworker, and maybe your friend. Tell me where they are."

"Mr. Lomax, honestly, I swear to you—"

"This argument ends now. There's no security camera up here, is there? That's what you said. So, I'll tell the NKPD that you went nuts and came at me, and I had to shoot you in self-defense. It'll get sticky for a while, sure, but I'll get off—and you'll be dead. Unless you tell me right now where Dr. Pickover is."

I let him think for a few moments, then cocked the hammer. "Well?"

He blew out air then spoke over his shoulder. "Keely? Locate Rory Pickover."

A portion of the wall nearest us changed to a map of New Klondike, with the radial avenues in red and the circular roads in blue. It took a few moments, but soon a set of crosshairs appeared over the map, with a glowing white point at their center. Rory—and presumably Reiko and the two meese—were located on Sixth Avenue and heading south. "Zoom in," Horatio said to Keely, and the view expanded to show just the single block of Sixth Avenue between the Fourth and Fifth Circles. The dot was moving quickly; they must have been on a hovertram.

"Do you have a portable tracking device?" I asked.

Horatio went to a cupboard and got a small disk-shaped dingus. He made a few adjustments on it and handed it to me. One of its faces was a viewscreen showing a miniature version of what was on the wall. "All right," I said. "You stay up here for five minutes, do you hear me? Start counting Marenerises, and don't stop until you've hit three hundred." I backed away, opened the door while keeping my gun on him, closed it behind me, and headed downstairs.

Mac was bent over, running his scanner along the floor.

"Pickover has a tracking chip in him." I held up the device that Fernandez had given me.

Mac straightened. "Is that a fact?" he said, in a tone that conveyed he knew there was a story to tell.

"Aye," I said, imitating his brogue. "'Tis."

Mac had left the disruptor disk leaning against the cash counter. He retrieved it, and he and I headed out of the shop.

The little one-seater police car Mac had returned here in didn't have a place for me, but it did have a rear bumper and a couple of handholds on the back that could be used to transport a standing person. I positioned myself there, Mac placed the disruptor in the little gap behind the seat, he got in, and we took off down the street, Mac navigating using the device I'd gotten from Fernandez.

From my perch at the back, I couldn't see the tracking device, and I pretty much had to concentrate on holding on for dear life as Mac sent us careening along. But from what I'd seen on the display before I'd given Mac the tracking device, Rory, and likely Reiko and the meese, were heading toward the south airlock—or some point between it and here. The three transfers could just walk right out onto the Martian surface, but Reiko would have to be stuffed into a suit, and that would take time; if they'd actually wanted Rory instead of Reiko, I suspected they'd dump her before reaching the airlock.

Mac could call ahead to the airlock station and ask the guards there to try to detain the meese, but there wasn't a lot biologicals could do against two giant transfers programmed for super strength, and Mac's principal job was protecting Howard Slapcoff's investment; the last thing old Slappy would want is the airlock station being wrecked.

Pedestrians were gawking at us, and at one point when we had to pause to avoid hitting a recycling truck, I gave them a jaunty wave.

The road we were on took us by the shipyard. It was possible that that had been the meese's destination, but Mac was giving no sign of slowing down. I looked over at the sea of dead hulks—shattered dreams, broken lives, abandoned hopes. I just barely made out the descent stage we'd recovered off in the distance.

Mac hit the siren just then, and it startled me enough that I almost lost my grip. But as soon as the vehicle in front of us got out of the way, he shut it off. The dome was never far overhead anywhere in New Klondike, but it had now dipped quite a bit lower; we were at the outer ring where only one- and two-story buildings were possible.

Mac brought us to an abrupt stop. I hopped off the bumper and came around to the side of the car. The gullwing door rose, and Mac clambered out. He retrieved the disruptor, and we headed over to the complex of airlocks.

"They're stationary," Mac said, holding up the tracking dingus so I could see its circular display. "Outside—about half a klick southeast of here. I tried calling for backup, but the other three cops who are on duty today are dealing with a small riot over by the east airlock—somebody accused somebody else of claim-jumping, and it's gotten out of hand."

I nodded and started making my way to the suit-rental counter when Mac motioned me through a door labeled "Official Use Only." Inside was a change room for the police, with four suits hanging from racks. Two were navy blue and bore the initials NKPD across the back and had the police crest on each shoulder; the other two were nondescript plainclothes affairs. We suited up. Mac opted for one of the blue suits, and I took one of the plain ones, in a drab gray.

We went through a personnel airlock and came out on the Martian sands. The sky was dark, and the stars were out in all their glory. Off in the distance was a spaceship, lying on its side. In the dim light, it was hard to make out its contours, but it was a small vessel—a hibernation ship, not a luxury liner with cabins like the *Skookum Jim,* and—

Of course. It was the *Kathryn Denning,* formerly the *B. Traven,* the infamous death ship, recently returned to the Red Planet.

And, judging by the display on the tracking device Mac was holding, the meese had taken Rory Pickover right to it.

THIRTY-ONE

If a ship needed dry-dock repairs it was hauled inside, but most vessels that came to Mars were never brought into the dome—rather, they were prepped for turnaround out on the planitia. Mac and I started walking the 500 meters to the *Kathryn Denning.* Bertha had said earlier that the ship's cargo—which presumably consisted mostly of people in hibernation units—was being offloaded. It looked like that had been completed; we could see the wheel ruts made by the vehicles that had been involved.

Also visible in the dust were footprints. There were two sets of large running shoes and a smaller set of work shoes, but no space-suit boots. The meese had indeed disposed of Reiko at some point; I hoped she was okay.

From the look of the tracks, Rory had been walking in front, with a moose behind and to either side of him. I doubted he'd been leading the way, though; rather, they'd been propelling him along, and—

"See that?" I said over the suit radio.

"Aye," replied Mac.

The tracks told the story. Rory had tried to run: you could see the place where he'd leapt up, and where he'd impacted ten meters farther ahead. The meese had leapt as well, and there were clear signs that they'd all ended up tussling on the ground. And then for the rest of the way, there were only the two large sets of tracks, but one had adopted a shorter gait; I assumed a moose had picked up and carried Rory—who might well have been screaming and kicking—from that point on.

The spaceship was a stubby spindle, with its front and rear points lifted above the ground. Cargo hatches—some open, some closed—were visible, and there was a ramp coming down from what looked to be an airlock door. We walked closer, and I shined my suit's chest light up at the hull, which was a yellowish beige.

Along the bow, in script letters, were the words *Kathryn Denning.* My light was hitting the hull obliquely, revealing just beneath and behind that name some slightly raised lettering that had been painted over; under normal full-on lighting conditions I doubt it would be visible at all, and if I hadn't already known it said *B. Traven,* I probably couldn't have made it out.

A spaceship was a good place for a hostage-taking: it was designed to survive micrometeoroid impacts, which meant it could take a hail of bullets, too. It also had its own life-support system—and it could take off if need be.

Mac walked up the ramp, which was pretty steep, and he tried the door. It was locked. Mac told his phone to get him the New Klondike office of InnerSystem Lines; this close to the dome, his phone worked fine, and I could hear his conversation over our shared radio link.

The phone rang four times, and I thought perhaps everyone had gone home for the day. But then a woman's voice said, "InnerSystem. How can I help you?"

"I'm Detective Dougal McCrae of the New Klondike Police Department, and this is an emergency. I'm standing outside the *Kathryn Denning,* and need access to the interior."

"Just a second," said the woman, then: "I'm told I need an authorization code word from you."

"The code word is 'jasper,'" said Mac.

"Yes, right, okay," said the woman. "Well, to get in, you just need to punch in the master skeleton-key combination code on the keypad next to the airlock; it'll open any door on the ship, including the airlock one. Let me know when you're in position, and I'll recite it to you."

The keypad was behind a hatch helpfully labeled "Keypad" in English; there was also some Chinese, which doubtless said the same thing. Mac opened the little hatch and said, "Go."

"Five zero four," said the woman, then, "three two nine, three one seven, five one zero."

Mac pressed keys and the door slid about fifteen centimeters to the left; presumably it had been spring-loaded but held in place by the lock. The slight displacement revealed a recessed handle. Mac put his gloved fingers into it and pulled the outer door the rest of the way, revealing a chamber no bigger than an old-fashioned phone booth—something I'd seen in plenty of movies but never in real life.

Mac was still carrying the disruptor as he entered the tiny chamber. I pushed myself inside. It belatedly occurred to me that the surface suit Mac was wearing was probably bulletproof. I wondered if the plain one I'd chosen was similarly equipped.

Mac turned around and pulled the outer door shut. He then pressed the one large button on the airlock's left wall; it was labeled "Cycle" in English, and again presumably the same thing in Chinese. I couldn't hear air being pumped into the chamber, but I felt the growing pressure of it on my suit. When the pressure reached that of the ship's interior, a green light went on above the inner door, and, for good measure, it popped aside fifteen centimeters, revealing a recessed handle just like the one on the outer door.

Mac shimmied around—it really *was* meant to be a one-person airlock—and pulled on the handle, sliding the door all the way aside.

He still had the tracking device, but it was hard for him to operate it and hold the disruptor, so he handed the tracker to me. I tried to use finger gestures on the display to zoom in, but it wasn't responding to the touch of my glove. Since we were now at normal air pressure, I pulled off my right glove and tried again. The dot indicated that Rory was about thirty meters toward the stern, and I gestured to Mac that we should start walking in that direction.

The interior of the ship was well lit—in fact, *too* well lit. We tended to keep things a bit dimmer on Mars, since we only got about one-quarter of the sunlight Earth did. I found myself squinting. But I also peered around, trying to picture the horrors that had occurred aboard this ship all those years ago, and my mind started playing tricks. I was still breathing the same bottled air I had been out on the surface, but it now had an iron tang to it, as though it smelled of blood.

I assumed the meese hadn't counted on being tracked here and so wouldn't be expecting us. Still, the broadband disruptor wasn't easily aimed. If they'd kept Reiko rather than Rory, Mac could have fired the disruptor blindly into a room. But we couldn't risk taking out Rory, too.

Mac and I walked stealthily down the corridor, me in true gumshoe fashion and him in flatfoot mode. We soon heard voices up ahead and made an effort to be even quieter. The voices were muffled not because they were coming from behind a closed door—they weren't—but rather because Mac and I were still wearing our fishbowls. I undogged the fasteners, lifted mine off, and tucked it under my arm.

In reality, the air inside the ship *did* smell different: it was musty and stale. Without the helmet, I could hear the voices more clearly. It must have been the two meese: they had the same thick-and-slow speech Trace had had. They occasionally interrupted each other, which was strange and hard to parse: two identical voices overlapping.

Rory, if he was still with them, wasn't saying anything. I consulted the scanner and tried to judge the location the voices were coming from. It looked like the meese and Rory were now in separate rooms: the two thugs sounded like they were ahead but to the left and Rory was showing as ahead and to the right. I indicated that Mac should head off to immobilize the meese, and that I'd rescue Dr. Pickover; my phone had recorded the lock-override code that had been dictated to Mac and could play it back to me if I needed it for another door.

Sure enough, the little corridor we were in had come to its end, and there were two doors in front of us. The one on the left had its door open, and I could actually see the broad back of one of the meese through it; he was wearing the same clothes as before. The door on the right was closed. It had a sign on it, and although I couldn't make out the writing the symbol above it was clear: a caduceus; this was the sickbay.

I put my glove back on and looked at Mac. This was almost too easy. If Rory was safe behind the closed door on the right, Mac could take out the meese on the left, then we could spring the professor and be on our way. Except for one thing: Mac probably thought the kidnappers deserved due process, blah, blah, blah. Fine; he could use the disruptor to hold them at bay until the cavalry finally finished with the riot and showed up.

We didn't have a lot of time to think. The meese hadn't yet detected us, but if either of them happened to look out the open door of the room they were in, they'd see us. And so, while we still had the element of surprise, Mac shifted the disruptor so that he was holding it like a shield, and he surged forward, shouting through his surface suit's speaker, "NKPD! Freeze!"

THIRTY-TWO

The visible moose turned to face us, looking startled. I ran toward the door on the right and hit the keypad, and pounded out the skeleton-key numbers as fast as my phone read them back to me. I had my gun out, just in case Rory wasn't alone, and—

And he wasn't. The paleontologist was lying on his back on the one and only examination bed in the sickbay. He'd been strapped down, doubtless with the aid of the meese, and his work shirt removed—small consolation, I'm sure, that this time he wasn't going to lose another favorite garment. Looming over him was a scrawny, pale man with shoe-polish-brown hair in his mid-thirties—younger than me, but a toothpick; there was no question which of us would win in a fight. Still, the man was holding a cutting laser, which he'd been in the middle of using to make a vertical incision in Rory's chest, not unlike the one I'd seen Horatio Fernandez carve in Trace's corpse. A deepscan was displayed on the wall; it took me a second to realize that it was showing the interior of Rory's torso.

I gestured with my gun at the pale man. "Drop the laser and put your hands up."

"Alex!" said Rory, lifting his head to look at me.

"Hands up!" I said again to the scrawny man, who had ignored me. Meanwhile, next door, Mac shouted, "I said, freeze!" I was torn; if he needed backup, I should perhaps go help him. But a moment later, I heard Mac say, "That's better. This is a broadband disruptor. It's already taken down one of you today. Don't make me use it again. Keep your hands above your heads."

I cocked my pistol and aimed it at the thin man's face. "Make like your goons," I said. "Reach for the sky."

The man set down the laser and did so. His arms were skeletal.

"Who are you?" I demanded.

"Take a hike," he replied in a reedy, weak voice.

I turned my phone, attached to the suit's left wrist, so that it could see his face. "Identify this person."

"Error twenty-three," replied the device, which I had programmed to use Peter Lorre's voice. "No probable match."

I shook the damn thing off and looked back out into the corridor. Mac was now marching the meese toward the airlock. I turned back to the emaciated man. "What the hell are you doing opening up Dr. Pickover?"

Rory answered that: "I told the goons the diary is sealed inside my torso."

I made an impressed face. "And is it?"

"Yes. I had Fernandez put it in there for safekeeping." I looked at the deepscan. There was indeed the ghostly outline of an object the right size next to one of the ballast cylinders. "The goons threatened to kill Reiko if I didn't give them the diary. I *had* to tell them where it was."

There were two chairs in the room, padded enough to be comfortable even under Earth gravity. I set my fishbowl on one of them, then pointed to the other one; the scrawny man sat on it and lowered his hands. I moved back to Pickover. The restraints were built into the medical bed, but although a patient couldn't undo them once strapped in, the release mechanisms were plainly labeled. I lifted the latch for each of the four restraints, and Rory sat up, the incision on his chest opening a bit as he did so. A biological would be rubbing his wrists and ankles now to restore circulation, but Rory just sat there, looking daggers at his captor.

"Let me have the diary," I said.

Rory hesitated for a moment then did what the skinny man had been about to do before I'd interrupted him: he stuck a hand through the plastiskin and foam rubber just below his metal sternum, rummaged around, and pulled out the diary—still missing its back cover, but sealed now in a plastic bag. He handed it to me.

The bag was slick with clear lubricant. I didn't want the damn thing slipping around, so I removed the little bound volume from the bag and shoved it into my surface suit's hip pocket.

"What's become of Miss Takahashi?" I asked.

Rory's face lit up. "She escaped, Alex—with my help; I created a diversion. Those big blokes wanted to get rid of her; they want to get rid of everyone they think knows where the Alpha is, and they figured she must know, because she's read the diary." Rory was now putting his work shirt back on. "I kept telling them the diary doesn't disclose the location, and Reiko told them the same thing, but they didn't believe us."

I spoke to my phone while keeping my gun aimed at Rory's captor. "Call Reiko Takahashi."

"Shunted to voice mail," said Peter Lorre.

"Call Horatio Fernandez at NewYou."

Three rings, then: "Hello, Alex."

"Horatio, has Miss Takahashi returned?"

"No."

"She escaped"—I looked at Rory—"how long ago?"

"Forty minutes, I'd say."

"She escaped forty minutes ago. And I'm with Dr. Pickover."

"I'll let you know when she arrives here."

I shook the phone off. "Who are you?" I said again to the seated man.

"Get stuffed."

"My phone would know you if you were a longtime Mars resident—so you aren't. I'll assume you came here on this ship, and you're too chicken to go out into the dome. That's probably wise: New Klondike is a rough place, and it wouldn't be long before someone there decided to snap you in two." I took a step closer. "I might even decide to do it myself, and—"

I hadn't paid any attention to his clothing until now, but the shirt he was wearing was burnt orange with a circular patch over the left breast, a patch bearing the "ISL" logo of InnerSystem Lines; it was a uniform top. "Christ, you're part of the *crew*." I spoke to my phone again. "How many crew on the *Kathryn Denning?*"

"Two," wheezed Peter Lorre. "A primary bowman and a backup bowman. The former normally travels awake, while the latter makes the voyage in hibernation and is only thawed out in emergencies."

"So which are you?" I demanded.

"Go climb a tree," said the man.

"There aren't any for a hundred million kilometers," I replied. I looked at the phone again. "Get the names of the two bowmen from the InnerSystem office here."

"A moment." Then: "The primary bowman is Beverly Kowalchuk. The backup is Jeffrey Albertson."

"So you're Albertson," I said. I gestured with my gun for him to get to his feet.

He hesitated for a moment then did get up. It was the exact opposite of the effect one normally observed with someone newly arrived from Earth. Usually, the freshly thawed stand with way too much energy and actually lift themselves off the ground a bit; I'm tall enough that I'd bumped my head on ceilings a few times shortly after my own arrival here. But Albertson got slowly to his feet, wincing as he did so; if he was weak here, movement back on the mother world must have been excruciating for him.

"Those thugs of yours," I said. "One of them has already been fried—by the broadband disruptor you just heard that police officer talking about. We haven't identified him yet, but we will—same with whoever it is inside the other two."

The thin man shrugged. "Uno and Dos are the only names they've got."

Pickover brightened. "Oh, I get it! Alex, the third one wasn't called Trace; rather it was *Tres*—Spanish for three; sounds the same, but spelt different. *Uno, Dos, Tres.*"

"Huh," I said. "How high do the numbers go, Jeff?"

"Jump off a cliff."

"So what the hell's the matter with you, anyway?" I asked, not expecting an answer.

Rory was now standing beside me. "My grandfather looked the same way," he said. "It takes a lot out of you."

"What does?"

"Well, I suppose it could be anything, but . . ."

I waved the gun. "On the examining bed."

Albertson glared at me, but then did as I'd commanded. He simply sat on the bed's edge, but it was enough. The ship's computer obviously recognized him, even if my phone hadn't, and his medical records came up on a monitor in the room. I scanned them quickly. "'Stage-four lymphatic cancer.' And *those* numbers *don't* go any higher." I looked at him. "Tough luck. I wouldn't want to die in jail."

Albertson crossed his arms defiantly in front of his chest. I idly wondered if I could bring myself to rough up somebody in such bad shape, and—

"Oh, my," said Pickover. He'd been looking at Albertson's medical record in more detail; I imagine the scientific gobbledygook meant more to him than it would have to me. "Alex, look at this."

He was pointing at some text on the screen. I squinted to make it out, and—

And I guess this wasn't Albertson after all. Not only was the date of birth given, but the computer had also helpfully calculated his age and placed it in brackets after the date: "78 years."

I turned back to him, and—

And—

God.

And he was the *backup* bowman. He—Christ, yes. I'd never heard of anything like this, but . . .

He *looked* like he was in his thirties. Biologically, he probably *was* in his thirties.

"You've been doing this forever," I said. "For decades. You keep making trips back and forth between Earth and Mars—spending eight months or more each way in hibernation. I didn't know it was possible to do that many stints in deep freeze, but—"

Cancer.

A man who'd been diagnosed with terminal cancer decades ago.

"You're Albertson, all right," I said. "But that's not the name you were born with—was it, Willem?"

"Why don't you—"

"Take a long walk off a short pier? The nearest one of those is back with the trees."

Rory was staring at the man now, his eyes wide. "My . . . God," he said. "Willem Van Dyke—I never thought I'd see you in the flesh, but . . ." He shook his head. "The disease has taken a lot out of you, but, yes, I can see it now. Well, well, well. There are a million things I'd like to ask you about the second expedition, but . . ." He drew his artificial eyebrows together, and his voice turned angry. "Christ, you almost killed me!"

Van Dyke slid off the examining bed. "I did no such thing. That incision in your torso can be sealed easily enough. And besides, you can't be killed."

"Not here," said Rory. "Not now. *Before.* You're the one who brought the land mines along on the *B. Traven.* You're the one who booby-trapped the Alpha. Damn it, you blew half my face off! You could have killed me!"

"You can't be killed," Van Dyke said. "You're not alive."

Rory spluttered in a mechanical way. I looked at Van Dyke. "Those mines were passive protection," I said, "and you planted them long ago. But when you learned that Denny O'Reilly's granddaughter was coming to Mars, you decided you had to take active steps, right?"

Van Dyke said nothing. I let out a theatrical sigh. "You're not getting how this works, Billy-boy. I ask you questions, you answer—or you die. It's really not a difficult concept."

Van Dyke was looking not at me but at the wall where a freeze-frame of the deepscan of Rory was still being displayed. I suppose it galled Van Dyke that Rory could have comfortably taken the scanner's radiation forever, when it was radiation exposure that had given Van Dyke cancer. But he said nothing.

"All right," I said. "I'll tell you. You knew Denny O'Reilly had a mistress whose last name was Takahashi, of course. And you work for InnerSystem Lines—you get to see the passenger manifests for all their ships; you check them each time you return to Earth. When you saw there was a Reiko Takahashi booked to come to Mars, you got curious. It didn't take much digging to find out who she was. And, well, a collector of one sort knows collectors of other sorts: she'd doubtless made inquiries about selling the only extant copy of her father's diary—and you figured it might note the location of the Alpha. Couldn't have something like that kicking around. And so you sent in the clones."

"They're not clones," Van Dyke snapped.

"Work with me," I replied. "You've spent most of the last thirty-plus years on ice. Physically, you're—what?—thirty? Thirty-two?"

Van Dyke glared at me defiantly for a moment, and I raised the gun higher. "Thirty-eight," he said at last. And then, acknowledging that he didn't even look that old despite the ravages of cancer, he added, "I stay out of the sun."

"I guess it's a good deal for InnerSystem Lines," said Rory. "Your training stays fresh. From your point of view, it's been only a couple of years since you first started your job. You just thaw out for a few days or weeks between each journey, while this ship is prepared for its next voyage."

"I usually don't even bother coming out of deep freeze here on Mars," Van Dyke said. "When I do come back to living here, I'm going to come back in style."

"You're going to transfer," I said.

Van Dyke snorted.

"What?" I said.

"Like I would ever do *that*."

"But that's the cure for cancer. Hell, that's the cure for *everything*."

"No," said Van Dyke. "It isn't—but there *will* be a cure for cancer."

"That's what they've been saying *forever*," said Pickover. "But it seems like it's always twenty years in the future."

"The *are* making progress," Van Dyke said. "I check, every time I come out of hibernation. I'm guessing it's just ten years off now . . ."

"And if you can stay on ice for most of that time," I said, "you can get the cure." I shook my head. "But why not just transfer? I know it was hellishly expensive back when you were first diagnosed, but—"

"That's not the reason."

I frowned and it came to me. "Lakshmi—the writer-in-residence here—told me that you're devoutly religious. Is that why you haven't transferred?"

"Transferring," he said. "Such crap. It's *not* the same person."

Rory tilted his head to look at the man who'd been slicing him open. "People feel differently about it now."

"God doesn't," said Van Dyke.

Rory couldn't dispute that and so he fell silent.

"And what are you going to do when they find a cure?" I asked. "When you're well again?"

"Go fly a kite."

"Okay. I'll tell you. Weingarten and O'Reilly promised you a share of the proceeds from the Alpha. And you want what you think is coming to you. When you're well, you're going to work that claim."

"And you're out to stop anyone who might exploit it first," said Rory.

"Hence hiring the thugs with Dazzling Don Hutchison's face," I added. But then I found myself taking a step backward. "No," I said. "No, wait a minute. You didn't hire those guys." The word "skytop" was echoing in my head—the decades-old slang Tres had used. "Christ, you *are* those other guys. You're—my God—you're all three of them. You *have* transferred. That's why Tres called you 'Actual'—you're the actual Willem Van Dyke, and they're copies."

Van Dyke looked like he was going to deny it. But someone who had gone to such extraordinary lengths to stay alive doubtless had a certain appreciation for what my Smith & Wesson could do to him. "I've made proxies, that's all," he said, in his thin, disease-ravaged voice. "I'm the real me; I'm the one with the soul. Those are just knockoffs. I made a deal with the guy who runs NewYou here to produce them in secret."

"Horatio Fernandez?" Rory asked.

"No, no. His name is—"

"Joshua Wilkins," I supplied.

"That's him. Nasty man, but he could be bought. I had him create the three Dazzling Dons a couple of years ago."

"It's illegal to make multiple versions of the same person," Rory said. "It's *obscene* to do so."

"They were disposable—and they aren't people."

"What do they think about that?" I asked.

"Same thing I do, of course."

"Why three guys who look the same?"

Van Dyke lifted his eyebrows as if it were obvious. "To remind them that they *aren't* real people. They're ersatz; interchangeable; disposable."

I nodded. "And I bet they were supposed to be each other's alibis—one would be seen in public while the others did whatever needed to be done to protect the Alpha; they were never meant to all be seen in the same place at the same time. But then one of them was shut down, and so you figured a bigger force was needed next time."

And that explained why Tres had rushed Huxley, even though Mac had told him they had a broadband disruptor. Tres was probably as ignorant of what one could do as Willem Van Dyke had been; they all had minds three decades out-of-date.

"Okay," I said. "Let's go."

"Where?"

"Prison, ultimately, I imagine."

"I'm not going to jail," Van Dyke said.

"No? You roughed me up, shot Dr. Pickover, and then kidnapped him and Miss Takahashi with the intention of murdering them."

"I did no such thing. Uno, Dos, and Tres did all that, not me. And Tres is deactivated, and Uno and Dos are already in police custody."

"You masterminded it all."

"You'd have a hard time proving that."

I stole a line from Mudge the computer. "Be that as it may."

"Regardless," said Rory, "you booby-trapped the Alpha."

"Even if I did—and I admit nothing—that's outside the police's jurisdiction."

I gestured with the gun. "Walk." I picked up my helmet and got him out into the brightly lit corridor, followed by me and then Rory. I continued to speak: "If I were you, I'd do a deal with the police. You said it yourself: you've only got a couple of years left. Don't waste them in court. Cop a plea, pay a fine, forget about the Alpha, and get back to being on ice—and, who knows, maybe someday they *will* find a cure for cancer."

The corridor switched from carpeted to uncarpeted as we approached the airlock, and our six footfalls were now making a fair bit of racket.

The airlock door was closed. I wondered how Mac had managed to get through; there's no way he could have crammed himself and the two meese in all at once. It was a puzzle in logic—the kind Juan Santos enjoyed.

There were also three of us, but there was no reason we had to all go through at once. It was a toss of a coin whether Rory should exit first, or Van Dyke and I should. Of course, Van Dyke needed to get into a surface suit to do so, but there was a surface suit hanging by the door, and—

Ah, and it had the name Jeff Albertson on it. Well, he *was* part of the crew.

The light above the inner airlock door suddenly changed from green to red: someone was coming through from the other side. I supposed Mac could be returning, after having handed over the meese to other cops. Or it could be Bertha or someone else from the shipyard, or Beverly Kowalchuk or one of the local InnerSystem staff. Without knowing who it was, it seemed premature to get Van Dyke into a surface suit; maybe there was a moose out there named Cuatro, and having Van Dyke suited up would be playing right into his giant hands. "Don't bother changing," I said. "Not yet."

I held my gun in front of me with both hands and aimed it at the airlock door. It wasn't long before the light above it changed back to green, the door popped open that fifteen centimeters to reveal the recessed handle, someone pulled the door aside the rest of the way, and—

And a transfer with holovid star Krikor Ajemian's face was standing there in front of us.

THIRTY-THREE

"Berling?" I said, looking at the transfer framed in the airlock doorway. "Stuart Berling?"

He scowled. "Lomax? What the hell are you doing here?" But then his gaze shifted to Willem Van Dyke, and his brown eyes went wide. "My God," he said shaking his handsome head. "My God, it's true. You haven't aged a day."

"Do I know you?" Van Dyke replied. He gave no hint that he recognized the famous face in front of him, and, indeed, if he'd spent most of the last three decades on ice, he probably didn't.

"I'm Stu Berling," the transfer said.

Van Dyke spread his arms slightly. "Should I know you?"

"I was on the—on this damned ship."

"When?"

"Thirty years ago. The last time it sailed under the name—" He swallowed, then managed to get it out: *"B. Traven."*

"Oh," said Van Dyke, softly.

"I'd had questions about that for decades," said Berling. "But now I've got money—and money buys answers. A guy at InnerSystem's office here in New Klondike told me you were aboard. I couldn't believe it—couldn't believe you were still part of the crew after all these years."

"I don't know who you are," said Van Dyke.

"I'm the one who woke you. During the flight. All those years ago."

"No, you're not."

Berling seemed pissed that this was being disputed. "I am, damn you."

"I don't know what that geeky kid—he was just eighteen or nineteen—grew up to look like, but you're not him. You're a damn transfer, a *nothing.*"

Berling's tone was venomous. "I'm more of a man than you ever were. It was four days before I was able to get past that madman, get to your hibernation chamber, wake you up. And you didn't do a thing to stop him."

"There was nothing I could do," said Van Dyke. "He had guns; I was unarmed."

"You were the backup bowman," snapped Berling. "You were the only other crew member. You should have stopped him."

"I tried," said Van Dyke. "That kid saw me try."

"You had smuggled land mines aboard," said Berling.

"The official report said it was Hogart Pierce, the primary bowman, who had done that."

"Pierce was dead," said Berling. He gestured behind himself. "They shot him as he came out that airlock here on Mars. When they found the land mines, they said he'd been smuggling them for some client here. But it wasn't him; it was you."

Van Dyke looked like he was going to utter a reflexive denial, so before he could, I asked Berling, "How'd you figure it out?"

"Like I said, money unlocks things. I started digging into this." He pointed at the scrawny man, but looked at me. "Van Dyke had come to Mars once before that hellish journey, did you know that?"

"On Weingarten and O'Reilly's second expedition," I said.

Berling nodded. "And why didn't he come back on the third?"

"He'd had a falling-out with Weingarten and O'Reilly," I said, "over how to split profits, and—ah. As you greased enough palms to dig into Van Dyke's past, you discovered—what? That he was a munitions expert? Former bomb-disposal guy?"

"Black-market arms dealer," said Berling.

Van Dyke sneered, apparently offended by the term. "My expertise was in putting high-powered buyers in touch with those who had things of great value to sell. That's why Simon and Denny brought me aboard . . . literally."

"But then they double-crossed you," I said. "Or you double-crossed them."

Van Dyke said nothing.

"And, my God," I said, taking a half step backward. "You—God, yes, of course! You sabotaged their ascent stage on the third expedition. You couldn't have used the same model of land mine to do it—those were introduced after that ship left Earth. But an earlier model would have worked just as well—or some other explosive you had access to, as an arms dealer. You killed Simon Weingarten."

"And Denny O'Reilly," said Berling.

"No," I said, "but only because Weingarten marooned O'Reilly here." Berling looked surprised at this bit of news, but before he could speak, I went on. "So you're a murderer," I said to Van Dyke. "No wonder you're in no hurry to meet your maker."

"You could have halted the insanity," Berling said, also to Van Dyke. Pickover, wisely, was staying out of all this.

"No, I *couldn't!*" Van Dyke shouted at him. "The land mines were locked in a cargo hold; there was no way to get at them during the flight."

"You could have detonated them by remote control," said Berling.

"That would have blown up the ship!"

"It would have stopped him."

"It would have killed us all."

"It would have stopped *him.*" Berling was reaching his boiling point; he looked like he was going to explode.

"Stuart . . ." I said gently.

He wheeled on me. "That madman abused us. He tortured us. And Van Dyke could have stopped it. He could have stopped him. Instead it went on for another two months. Two months before we reached Mars, two months of horrific abuse."

"I'm sorry," Van Dyke said.

"Sorry!" shouted Berling. "That's not enough. I can't go home. I can't go back to Earth. I'm rich now—but there's nothing to spend it on here. I could never lock myself aboard another spaceship for months. And it's your fault." He didn't take a deep breath; he couldn't. But he did stop and look around—and then he shuddered. "Right over there—right down that hallway? See? That's where he first . . . where he first . . ."

"Stuart," I said again, as gently as I could. "It was thirty years ago."

"It's *not* thirty years for me! I relive it over and over again."

"I am sorry," Van Dyke said again. "There really was nothing I could do, and—"

Berling moved with a transfer's speed, and with the same violent temper I'd experienced from him at Ye Olde Fossil Shoppe. He leapt forward, landing less than half a meter from Van Dyke, and he rammed Van Dyke back against the wall—hard.

Maybe a healthy man could have taken it. And, of course, if this Van Dyke had been one of his transfer copies, he'd have survived it easily. But he wasn't—and he didn't. Berling's open palm crushed Van Dyke's chest. Berling took a step back, a look of horror on his face—as dramatic as a transfer's expression could get. "Oh, God . . ." he said.

Van Dyke crumpled to the floor. I rushed in and felt for a pulse. "His heart's stopped."

"Oh, God . . ." Berling said again, very softly.

I stretched Van Dyke out on his back and placed hands over his sternum to start chest compressions, but—

But his sternum was caved in and it felt as though the heart beneath it had been crushed. There was nothing to lose by this point, and so I did the compressions, but I could feel bone breaking further and an appalling squishiness beneath it all.

"Oh, God . . ." Berling said for a third time. "I didn't mean—I didn't want . . ." His jaw dropped. "I—I just wanted to *talk* to him."

"You killed that man," said Rory, speaking at last, his voice faint.

"I—I'm sorry. I—"

Rory did a series of body and facial movements that I guess were akin to taking a deep breath; he was clearly composing himself, and thinking about what to say. "All right, okay, I understand that you were a victim of abuse, but . . . but *he* wasn't the abuser, and . . ." He paused and shook his mechanical head slightly. "I'm sorry, you poor blighter, but you must know that even the NKPD won't be able to turn a blind eye to your killing him. InnerSystem is a division of Slapcoff Interplanetary; they'll demand to know what happened to their crew member, and the police will have to investigate."

Berling spun on his heel. I'd seen biologicals take hostages before: they often put an arm around someone's neck from behind—but even a broken neck could be repaired on a transfer. Instead, Berling had reached around from behind to clasp Pickover's forehead. His other arm had grabbed one of Rory's own just below the elbow. He propelled the paleontologist into the airlock.

"Don't take him," I said. "Take me. I'm the better hostage—you can easily overpower me."

"No dice," said Berling. "The police have that disruptor thing. They won't dare use it on me so long as I'm next to this guy."

"Alex . . ." said Rory, pleadingly.

Berling squeezed, and I saw indentations, like the beginning of finger holes for a bowling ball, appear in Rory's forehead. "Shut up!" snapped Berling. Rory did so. Berling released his grip on Rory's arm just long enough to pull the inner airlock door closed. There were a couple of minutes until the cycling process would finish, so I went down on one knee next to Van Dyke to see if there was anything at all that could be done, but he was gone.

I put on my fishbowl. The light above the airlock door turned green: Berling and Pickover had exited and were presumably now making their way down the ramp to the ground. Neither of them needed to eat or drink, and they could go months without charging up; my guess was that Berling would drag Rory out into the Martian desert. Of course, Rory still had a tracking chip in him, unbeknownst to Berling. But it would be better to stop them on the open planitia, rather than let them get somewhere that could be defended.

I cycled through the airlock as quickly as I could, and—

And whatever combinations of people Mac had chosen to get him and the meese out of the *Kathryn Denning* hadn't worked as intended. Berling and Rory were halfway down the ramp that led from the airlock to the ground, Berling still holding Rory's arm and clutching his skull. One of the meese was sprawled face down about twenty meters to the right—Mac had apparently used the disruptor on him—and the other moose and Mac were facing off against each other about forty meters farther along.

THIRTY-FOUR

Merely resisting arrest wasn't cause to use deadly force, and Mac, who ultimately worked for Howard Slapcoff, would be the last guy in the solar system to say a transfer was entitled to less than a biological was; the first moose must have actively attacked him.

Right now, Mac's back was to me. He had the disruptor disk aimed at the second moose, and they seemed to be at an impasse: the moose was refusing to move, and Mac's only recourse would be to kill him if he didn't.

Mac and I were still on the same radio frequency, and so I spoke to him. Rory should be tuned in as well, but his captor, Stuart Berling, wouldn't be able to hear. "Mac, it's Alex. I'm in the open airlock of the *Kathryn Denning* behind you. A transfer named Stuart Berling came storming in, and he's killed Van Dyke and taken Dr. Pickover captive; they're on the ramp in front of me."

There was silence long enough that I thought Mac's radio must be on the fritz. But then Mac's brogue came through, punctuated by some static; I wondered if the fact that he'd recently fired the disruptor had anything to do with that. "Aye, Alex, I saw the transfer coming toward the ship. I tried to stop him, but had my hands full with the two goons."

"Only one goon left," I said.

"You noticed that," said Mac. He and the moose were now slowly circling each other; I think Mac had started the movement so that he could change his perspective and get a glimpse of me. The transfer he was holding at bay would have already seen me and Berling and Pickover. "One of the goons took the opportunity to run back toward the ship," Mac said. "He went after the incoming transfer—Berling, did you say his name was? The goon wouldn't halt, and I had to fry him."

"Yeah. He must have figured that Berling was coming after Van Dyke—which he was."

Mac and the moose had rotated 180 degrees; Mac was now looking right at me. Berling and his captive Pickover were standing motionless halfway down the ramp.

"Mac," I said, speaking again after a pause, "are you in radio communication with the transfer thug?"

"Aye, I can be."

"What frequency?"

"Thirty-seven."

"Switching," I said, touching controls on my wrist. Then: "Okay, big fella. This is Alex Lomax. Which one are you? Uno or Dos?"

There was a pause while he thought—presumably not about what the answer was, but rather about whether to answer at all. But at last, he did. "Uno."

"Okay, Uno, I want you to consider something. Sorry to be the bearer of bad news, but the guy you call Actual—the actual Willem Van Dyke—is dead."

"You'll pay for that!"

"Hang tight. *I* didn't do it. But he is gone; sorry about that. And you know Tres got wasted at my apartment, and Dos is lying in a heap over there." I pointed. "No Actual. No other duplicates. Just you. That means *you* are Willem Van Dyke. Under *Durksen v. Hawksworth*, under the laws of just about every country: the biological original is gone and one transfer exists. You are Willem Van Dyke now. Sure, maybe Detective McCrae can pin a few petty things on you, and maybe he can't—he'd have to prove that you personally, not Dos or Tres, were responsible, and that'd take some doing. But even if he can, you're potentially immortal now; don't squander that. We can all walk away from this."

Uno had his back to me now, but he stopped and turned around; Mac could have zapped him with the disruptor, but I guess Uno trusted him not to by this point. He was clearly looking over at me—which meant he was looking in the general direction of Berling and Rory, too.

I thought that if Uno could be won over, he might help in saving Rory; there wasn't much I could do, armed with a gun, against a strong transfer. And as long as Rory and Berling were locked together there was nothing Mac could do with the disruptor. But Rory was strong, too—and if Uno and Rory both went against Berling, Berling might go down.

I couldn't see Uno's expression from this distance—although I suspected he could see mine, and so I tried a kindly smile. It seemed to work. He nodded—I could make out that much—and slowly lifted his arms into the classic "I surrender" pose.

"Very good," I said. Below me on the ramp, Berling was craning his neck to look back my way while still holding Rory as a shield in front of him. I doubted I could as easily talk him into letting his hostage go, but I held up fingers to indicate a new radio frequency—two and five—in hopes that Berling might want to parley for Rory's release.

Berling tilted his head, presumably doing something internally that switched radio frequencies. "Okay, Lomax," he said. "Talk."

"We all want to walk away from this, Stuart," I said. "Think about what's on the line. You've uploaded—you can live forever. You've found great fossils, and you'll find even more—you're rich." I paused, wondering if bringing Lacie into it was wise or not, but decided I needed every bit of persuasion I could muster. "And you've got an amazingly beautiful wife waiting for you. You don't need to throw all that away."

I wanted some feedback—some evidence that this was making sense to him—but he said nothing and so, after a time, I went on. "And you *don't* have to throw it away," I said. "If Uno, over there, accepts the role of the real Willem Van Dyke, then Van Dyke isn't dead, see? No homicide. No need for you to take a hostage. No need for *any* of this. All you—"

Motion caught my eye. Uno—in the body of Dazzling Don Hutchison—still had his hands held up, but he must have just crouched low, and then snapped those powerful legs straight, because he was flying up, up, up into the dark sky. He kept his right arm bent, but then stuck his left arm straight out from the shoulder; he looked, for all the world, as he flew higher and higher, like he was going to throw a Hail Mary pass. But he wasn't holding anything in either hand, and—ah—he was actually twisting around his vertical axis as he went up, and now was starting the slow descent. I'm sure he wanted to come down faster, but—

Yes, he'd angled backward a bit. He was going to come down right on top of Mac. Mac was fumbling to get the disruptor disk aimed up over his head, but soon abandoned that notion and simply scrambled to get out of the way. Even under Martian gravity, having 150 kilos of mass conk you on the head could do a lot of damage.

As Uno came down onto the planitia, he flexed his knees, and they bore the brunt of the impact. Still, a cloud of dust went up, and for a moment I wasn't sure what was happening. But soon Uno came barreling out of the cloud, heading straight toward Mac, who was hunched over and scuttling away. And then this Dazzling Don did what the real Dazzling Don had done countless times—he tackled the other player, driving Mac face first into the dirt. Mac landed on the disruptor; Uno pushed himself up off Mac, then grabbed Mac's shoulders and tossed him aside. He seized the disruptor disk and started running toward me.

No, *not* toward me. Toward Rory Pickover and Stuart Berling. "You killed Actual!" Uno said, no sign of exertion in his mechanical voice—just raw fury. I realized that he, too, must have selected frequency twenty-five; even from forty meters away he could make out the finger signs I'd presented to Berling.

He was closing the distance fast. "Uno, don't!" I yelled. "Don't!"

Uno slowed a bit, but only to get a good look at the disruptor and find its controls. And although I knew from experience that turning it off was harder than it should be, turning it on had never been a problem . . .

There were now only about fifteen meters between Uno and the Berling/Pickover pair, still on the ramp. It was my turn to jump. The airlock was higher up than I'd have liked, but I stepped onto the ramp, then leapt off. "Berling!" I shouted, as soon as I'd landed on the planitia. "Let Pickover go. Get back into the airlock! You'll be safe inside."

Berling didn't move.

"For God's sake!" I called. "Lock yourself back inside the ship!"

He stood there. Of course he couldn't do that; he could never lock himself in that death ship again.

Uno had come to a stop now. He held the disruptor in front of him, one hand in each of the grips on the opposite sides of the disk.

"Uno, for God's sake, let Dr. Pickover go! You don't want to do this!"

But he did. He must have pressed the twin triggers, because suddenly both Berling and Rory went stiff and then their bodies started spasming and—

And—Christ!—Berling was still gripping Rory's forehead, and his hand was clenching.

The high-pitched whine of the disruptor was barely audible in this thin air, but its effects were obvious. Both transfers looked like they were receiving massive electrical shocks.

"Stop!" I shouted, and "Stop!" shouted Mac.

But Uno kept holding down the triggers, and the two transfers kept vibrating, and—

And I saw Rory's head being deformed—as if the broadband frequencies coursing through his system weren't doing enough damage.

"For God's sake!" I yelled.

Uno didn't seem to know how to turn off the device, but he did twist his giant body, aiming the disk away from Berling and Rory. They both stopped jerking. Berling toppled sideways and fell off the ramp, his limbs stiff. He landed with a small thud and a big puff of dust next to me. Rory fell forward and skidded down the ramp, his partially crushed head leading the way.

"You didn't have to do that!" I said. "You didn't have to take out Dr. Pickover!"

Uno's voice had an infinite calmness. "That wasn't Dr. Pickover," he replied. "That was nobody." And then he stretched out his arms and began to slowly flip the disk end over end, and, as it was facing up, he said, "And I'm nobody, too—and with Actual gone, I have no reason to be." The disk continued to flip around, and the emitter side ended up facing toward Dazzling Don Hutchison's face. The giant body started to convulse as Uno's fists clenched shut on the twin triggers. He kept spasming for about twenty seconds as Mac and I rushed toward him from opposite directions. And then he toppled backward, still convulsing as he went down in slo-mo, until he was lying on his back, the disk held up over him.

Mac loomed in and pulled out the off switch, and suddenly everything was very, very still.

THIRTY-FIVE

I walked slowly over to where Mac was standing, and we stood wordlessly for a time: two weary biologicals in surface suits amid four dead transfers lying there on the Martian sands in nothing but street clothes.

Finally, backup arrived in the form of Huxley, Kaur, and another cop, rumbling out onto the surface in a pressurized van. Mac conferred with them, and the three newcomers set about photographing the bodies and taking various scanner readings and measurements. While they were busy with that, I took Mac up into the *Kathryn Denning* and showed him the corpse of Willem Van Dyke.

There wasn't much to say, and so Mac and I barely spoke. I left him inside the ship, taking readings with his scanner, and I trudged slowly down the ramp. All of this action had taken place by the south airlock. I had plenty of bottled oxygen, and so I decided to walk around the dome to the west airlock—just to clear my head a bit, and to avoid human company.

It was a little over three kilometers to that airlock, and I shuffled along, raising dust clouds as I did so, like Pig-Pen in the old *Peanuts* animated cartoons. After about a kilometer, I decided to try calling Reiko

Takahashi again, and I was relieved when her lovely face popped up on my wrist.

"You're okay?" I asked into my fishbowl's headset.

Her orange-striped hair was mussed. "Exhausted," she said. "My God, it was terrifying."

"But you're okay now?"

She nodded. "How's Mr. Pickover? Have you found him yet?"

She'd had enough of an upset for one day; I'd tell her later that Rory was dead. "He's with Detective McCrae right now."

"Oh, good."

"Rory said he created a diversion so you could get away."

"He did indeed, the sweet old fellow. He started singing 'God Save the King' at the top of his lungs—or, well, at top volume anyway. Those two giant jerks were mortified, and I managed to run off." She paused. "If you see him, won't you thank him for me?"

"Of course."

"Thanks," she said. "Look, I'm still pretty shook up. I'm going to take something and go to bed."

"I don't blame you. But can you let Fernandez know you're okay? He's been worried, too."

"I'll call him now," she said, and she shook off from her end.

I continued walking slowly. My shadow, falling to my right, walked along with me. The silence was deafening.

I had genuinely liked Rory Pickover, strange little man though he had been. He'd had something I'd seen all too rarely on Mars: selfless devotion to a cause rather than to personal gain.

The dome was on my right. I was walking about thirty meters away from it; I had no particular desire to make eye contact with anyone within. Earth was hanging above the horizon, brilliant and blue. My phone could have told me which hemisphere was facing me right now, but I didn't ask. I liked to think it was the side with Wanda on it. And although I couldn't tell what phase it was in, I wanted it to be a crescent

Earth, with the part Wanda was on in nighttime, too. I wanted her to be looking up, looking across all those millions of kilometers, at the red planet in her sky. I wanted her to be thinking of me.

I continued slowly along. For the first time ever, in all the mears I'd lived here, I felt heavy.

When a man's client is killed, he's supposed to do something about it. It doesn't make any difference what you thought of him. He was your client and you're supposed to do something about it. And it happens I'm in the detective business. Well, when someone who's hired you gets killed, it's bad business to let the killer get away with it, bad all around, bad for every detective everywhere.

Of course, the killer *hadn't* gotten away with it. Uno was dead. Still, Pickover had come to me for protection, and I'd failed him.

I'd never get paid for the work I'd done on this case, but that didn't matter. And there was no one to bill for any further work. But Rory had wanted to track down the fossils Weingarten and O'Reilly—and no doubt Van Dyke—had sold on Earth, not for gain, not for profit, not to line his own pockets, but so they could be described for science, for posterity, for all time, for all humanity.

And there were surely other paleontologists who could do that work, if I could locate those fossils. Maybe there'd even be a previously unknown genus amongst the specimens. And maybe whoever described that new form in the scientific literature might be persuaded to name it *Pickoveria*.

I arrived at the western airlock and left the police-department surface suit there. My office was near here, and I walked over to it. I went up to the second floor and made my way down the corridor. Once inside my office, I used the sink at the wet bar to wash my face and hands, and then I collapsed into my chair.

I sat for a few moments, thinking, then called Juan Santos on my desktop monitor. Juan's wide forehead and receding chin appeared on the screen. "You put a lot of kilometers on my buggy," he said.

I tried to rally some of my usual spirit. "A shakedown. Good for it. Keep it running smoothly."

"You could have at least filled the gas tank."

"It doesn't *have* a gas tank."

"That's beside the point."

"Hey," I said, "at least I brought it back in perfect condition."

"You mean I just haven't found the damage yet. Not surprising, considering how much mud it was covered in."

"You wound me, Juan."

"Not yet. But if I can find a baseball bat . . ."

This could go on for hours—but I wasn't in the mood. "Look," I said, "I've become acquainted with a computer that's almost forty years old. Problem is, files on it are locked to someone long dead. Can you help me out?"

"Do you know the make or model?"

"No, but it was installed in a Mars lander."

"That long ago?"

He was going to find out soon enough, anyway: "It was installed in Weingarten and O'Reilly's third lander."

"And you've found the computer?"

"More than that."

"You've found the *ship?*"

"Uh-huh. The descent stage."

"Where is it?"

"I had it brought to the shipyard. I was hoping you could meet me there."

"All right."

"In about half an hour?"

"Um, yeah. Yeah, okay."

"Thanks," I said and broke the connection. I got a spare gun from the office safe and brought it and my usual piece with me as I headed over to the hovertram stop. I had a sinking feeling that we hadn't seen the last of the day's excitement, and if Juan was going to be my backup, I wanted him armed.

A tram pulled up, and I hopped on. I changed trams at the transfer point outside the Amsterdam, a classy gym that appealed to nicer people than those I liked to hang out with, and took another tram to the stop closest to the shipyard. I got off and hustled over to the yardmaster's shack, but Bertha wasn't there. Still, it was easy enough to spot the descent stage, sitting vertically on its stubby trio of legs, with the airlock on the side and the access hatch on top, and the whole thing streaked with mud. I headed over to it.

One of the landing legs was aligned with the airlock door, and had ladder rungs built into it. I climbed up and cycled through the airlock.

"Welcome back," Mudge said, as soon as I was in. "Can I be of assistance?"

"You defeated the overrides before so that both the inner and outer airlock doors could be kept open simultaneously," I said. "Do that again, please."

"Done."

I heard a faint calling of my first name. I headed back into the airlock chamber and saw Juan Santos wandering among the hulks. "Over here!" I shouted through the open door and waved.

He caught sight of me, jogged over with the typical Martian lope, and climbed the ladder. I made room for him, and he stepped inside, put his hands on his hips, and looked around the circular chamber. "Like a page out of history," he said.

"Or a cage with a mystery."

"You should leave the poetry to the lovely Diana," Juan said. His face took on a wistful look as he contemplated his favorite waitress, but after a moment, he narrowed his eyes. "The computer is still active?"

"I am," said Mudge. "Can I be of assistance?"

Juan stretched his arms out, fingers interlocked, until his knuckles cracked. "Okay," he said into the air. "Now listen carefully. Everything I say is a lie." He paused, then: "I am lying."

"Puh-leeze," said Mudge.

Juan looked at me and shrugged good-naturedly. "It was worth a try. Is there a terminal I can use?"

"In there," I said, pointing to one of the four rooms on the lower level. Juan entered, and I slipped off my phone and placed it on a piece of equipment, with the lens facing him, just to keep an eye on him. The whole point of coming back here was to get the secret Mudge must now know—the precise map of how to get between the Alpha and New Klondike, and, therefore, the reverse—and I'd be damned if I let Juan extract that info for his own uses. Of course, there was no reason to think he suspected Mudge, or I, knew where the Alpha was; the wreck of Weingarten and O'Reilly's second lander had been salvaged from Aeolis Mensae, and he probably assumed this one had been recovered from somewhere equally far from the mother lode.

I climbed up the interior ladder; I wanted to give O'Reilly's space suit a more thorough examination for signs of foul play. But it wasn't in the room we'd left it in. Well, the ship had come crawling out of the mud, fallen over, rolled around, flown halfway across Isidis Planitia, gone from vertical to horizontal to vertical again, and been hauled by a tractor. Being tossed around like a rag doll wasn't quite the fate one of the richest men in the solar system had anticipated, I'm sure.

"Mudge," I said into the air, "what happened to Denny O'Reilly's body?"

"A combination of eating too much and not exercising enough."

"I mean, where is it now?"

"In the room on your right."

I entered that wedge-shaped compartment, and—

And that was odd. Yes, O'Reilly's suited body was in here, sprawled on the floor, but the cupboard doors were hanging open. I was sure they'd been closed when I left the ship. I suppose they could have been knocked open during the flight, but—

I entered the next room. Its cupboards were open, too. As were the ones in the next chamber, and the next one. There could be no doubt: someone had searched the ship.

"Alex?" called Juan from below.

I hustled down the ladder, entered the chamber he was in, and stood behind him. "Yes?"

He swiveled in his chair to face me. "I've unlocked the computer."

"That fast?"

"Sure. Like you said, it's a forty-year-old machine. Most security systems get hacked within *weeks* of being released. Ask it whatever you want."

I'd wait until I was alone to get the instructions to return to the Alpha. "Mudge," I said, "the ship has been searched since I left it. Did someone beside Dr. Pickover enter?"

"Who is Dr. Pickover?" asked the computer.

"Rory. The person who flew here with you earlier."

"Yes. After this ship was hauled through the airlock by a tractor, someone came aboard."

"Who?"

"I don't know."

"Biological or transfer?"

"I don't know what you mean." Damn. No, he wouldn't. Transferring had been something for only the insanely rich that long ago.

"Male or female?"

"Female."

"Age?"

"Perhaps twenty-eight or twenty-nine."

"Skin color?"

"Brown."

"Eye color?"

"Brown."

"Hair color?"

"Brown."

"Straight or curly?"

"Straight."

I thought about asking if she was hot, but I doubted Mudge would have an opinion. Of course, there were hundreds of women on Mars who fit that description, but I'd lay money he was describing Lakshmi Chatterjee.

"The woman was alone?" I asked

"Yes," said Mudge.

"Did you overhear her speak to anyone—on her phone, maybe?"

"Yes."

"Who was she talking to?"

"I don't know, and I could not make out the voice."

"What did she say?"

"She said, 'Hello.' There was a pause, then she said, 'Absolutely.' Another pause, then—"

"Did she say anything *important?*"

"I don't know what qualifies."

"List all the proper nouns she used in her phone conversation."

"In the order she first used them: Shopatsky House, Dave Cheung, Persis, Isidis Planitia, Dirk, Lomax, Mars—"

"Stop. What did she say about Lomax?"

"'If we can't take Lomax out, then we need an insurance policy.'"

"Continue the conversation from that point on."

"There was another pause, then: 'No, Dirk saw them together at The Bent Chisel; they're clearly an item, and she's coming to see me in a couple of hours; she's tailor-made for the part.' Another pause, then—"

"Stop." I looked at my wrist phone; it was 2:08 p.m., and Diana's appointment had been slated to start at 2:00. My heart started pounding. "Juan, we've got to go. Diana's in trouble."

THIRTY-SIX

Juan Santos looked up at me, piecing it together. "Diana?" he said. "*My* Diana?"

"Yes, yes," I replied. "She's at Shopatsky House right now." I headed through the descent stage's open airlock door and scrambled down the exterior ladder; Juan followed. As soon as we were both out on the shipyard grounds, I swore. "It'll take forever to get to Shopatsky House from here by tram."

"We won't take a tram," Juan said. "We'll take my Mars buggy."

"It'll take even longer to go get that."

"It would if the buggy was still outside. But it's not. I had it brought in for a thorough cleaning after I got it back from you—I've never seen mud on a buggy before." It was impossible to wash a car outside the dome; the atmosphere was too thin for sonic cleaning, the low air pressure caused water to boil away, and the ubiquitous dust dirtied things up again immediately anyway. "The sonic car wash is just inside the south airlock," continued Juan. It meant running in precisely the opposite direction from where we wanted to go, but he was right: using his buggy would get us to the writing retreat much faster than the tram would. I thought about calling the NKPD, but I didn't want a repeat of the fiasco that had occurred at the *Kathryn Denning.*

We ran to where the buggy was parked; it was indeed now clean, its white body glistening and not a speck of dirt obscuring its jade pinstripes. Juan was about to get into the driver's seat, but I said, "Let me." He frowned, but went around to the other side. He knew I'd been to Shopatsky House before.

I put the pedal to the metal. The lack of streamlining on Mars buggies was no impediment out on the surface, but in here I could feel the drag on the cubic habitat cover. Still, we were making great progress, and were soon on the heels of the very hovertram we'd have otherwise taken. I swerved around it. If the tram had had a driver, said driver might have given me the finger, but the computer that ran the thing seemed to take my maneuver with equanimity.

As I cut in front of the tram, a pedestrian was crossing the street ahead of us. It was hard to tell at the speed we were going, but he looked biological—meaning I might kill him if I hit him, instead of just knocking him flying. I slapped the flat of my hand against the center of the steering wheel, and—

Holy crap!

The sound almost burst my eardrums. Apparently a horn designed to be used in a thin atmosphere shouldn't be used in a thick one. The guy in front of me leapt a good meter and a half straight up.

"*Sorry!*" Juan shouted at the guy. "*Sorry!*"

We continued on, the dome getting higher and higher above our heads as we made it closer to the center.

"*Stop! Police!*"

It was a cop in a blue uniform. I ignored him; the worst thing he could do is give chase on foot.

But in the next block, another cop caught sight of us. Why is there never a police officer around when you want one, and they're everywhere when you don't? This guy was more ambitious than the first cop. He stepped into the middle of the street and stood, legs spread, in our way. He had a gun, and he held it in both outstretched hands aimed right at us. I hit the horn again, spun the buggy in a one-eighty, then took a right-hand turn onto the Third Circle. The cop didn't fire—probably didn't want to deal with the paperwork that followed a weapons discharge—and if he shouted anything after us, my ears were still reverberating too much from the horn blast for me to make it out.

This close to the center, the curvature of the concentric roadways was obvious, and I had to bank the buggy so much that the left-hand wheels actually lifted from the ground. More people were crossing the street in front of us, and I careened right then left then right again to miss them—one by just centimeters.

This route took us by NewYou. I tried to look in the showroom window as we raced past, but there was too much glare. After hurtling along a quarter of the arcing road, we took off down Third Avenue, heading out toward the dome's edge again. Suddenly a dog—one of the handful on the planet, an honest-to-goodness Mars rover—was chasing us. We bipeds could manage a good clip in this gravity, and quadrupeds could move like the wind. This one—a lab, it looked like—was running at a speed a cheetah on Earth would have envied, and—

"Son of a bitch!" I yelled—rather aptly, I thought. The damn thing had leapt onto the buggy's short hood, making it hard to see what was up ahead.

"Slow down!" Juan shouted.

I stole a glance at him. He looked terrified—but whether over what I was doing to his buggy or what was about to happen to us, I couldn't say. The dog was yelping something fierce, but seemed to be enjoying the ride. I craned my neck, trying to see around his bulk. We hit something small in the road—rubble or rubbish of some sort—and the car bounced, and Juan let out a yelp of his own.

This wasn't the street I wanted to be on, so I made a hard left at the next intersection, but there was a hovertram dead ahead. I slammed on the brakes. The buggy started spinning. The dog decided this was a good time to get off, and he did so. I was pressed over into Juan's side in a way that pushed the boundaries of a good bromance. When the car stopped spinning, we were facing in precisely the wrong direction. I did a quick U-turn, then headed on toward Shopatsky House, out at the rim. We were on the correct radial artery now—and it looked like smooth sailing for most of the rest of the way. Ah, the open road! All this rig needed was stereo speakers blaring out classic 2040s rock 'n' roll.

I ran the buggy right up onto Shopatsky House's fern-covered lawn and popped the canopy. Juan and I jumped out, and we bounded over to the building, sailing three meters with each stride. I left the buggy running, just in case we needed a fast getaway.

I thought about kicking the front door in, but that's actually hard to do, and my ankle couldn't be fixed as easily as Pickover's had been. And, anyway, I didn't have to do it. If Lakshmi had been as busy with underhanded stuff as things seemed to indicate, she wouldn't have had time to replace the back window I'd so carefully removed earlier.

I gave Juan the spare gun I'd brought for him, and we ran around to the rear, me taking out my own gun as I did so. Juan probably wasn't the best choice for backup—he was a thin guy with typically underdeveloped Martian musculature—but he was better than nothing. I motioned for him to stay out of sight; I wanted Lakshmi to think I'd come alone.

There weren't any winds or precipitation under our dome; the main reason for fixing the window would have been to keep nasty folk out, but with the window hidden back here, facing toward the dome's edge, no one probably even knew that it was gone. I crouched low and made my way over. I'd hoped to overhear something that would give away the situation within—either "actually, for your rhyming scheme, you need a word with emphasis on the penultimate syllable" or "and so, before you die, it's only fitting that you know exactly how I plan to take over this entire planet." But instead I heard precisely nothing, and so I rose up enough to peek into the hole where the window had been.

The room had been straightened a bit since my struggle with Lakshmi—but only a bit. I clambered over the sill and entered the house, holstering and then unholstering my gun as I did so. I walked out of that room into the living room, and there was Diana. She was seated at one end of the cushioned green couch and had a serene look on her round face. Her makeup was tasteful, her brown hair was up, her brown eyes were open, and, all in all, she looked perfectly fine—except for the bullet hole in the middle of her forehead.

THIRTY-SEVEN

My heart was jackhammering, and my eyes were stinging. I took a step toward Diana's body, but then Lakshmi's voice said, "Freeze."

I froze as much as I could, but I was quaking with fury.

"Drop your gun," Lakshmi said.

I had no proof that Lakshmi herself was holding a gun, but the hole in Diana was pretty good evidence that someone around here was packing. I let my Smith & Wesson go, and it fell gently to the floor.

"God damn it," I hissed. "You didn't have to kill her."

"She was dead when I got here," Lakshmi said.

"Oh, come on!"

"She was dead when I got here," Lakshmi repeated. "I'm not going down for this."

"How'd she get in, if you weren't here?" I demanded.

"Same way you did, I suppose. Through the rear window."

"I'm not buying that," I said. "And neither will the NKPD."

"Persis?" Lakshmi said into the air.

But there was no response from the Shopatsky House computer. I heard Lakshmi moving around behind me. I imagine she'd ducked her head into the room with the roll-top desk. "Someone took Persis," she said.

"How convenient," I replied. "No record of what went down. But you won't get away with it."

"I didn't shoot her," Lakshmi said again. "She was already dead when I arrived."

"Bull!" I said. "She had an appointment to see you!"

"And I was running late for it. She let herself in—through the hole where my window used to be, which she could only have known about because you must have told her. And someone else must have been in here, having gained access the same way—someone who'd come to rob me, I suppose—someone looking for the O'Reilly diary, perhaps. Whoever it was clearly was startled by Diana and let her have it."

"It's a neat story, sister. But it doesn't hold water."

"*Mister* Lomax," she said sharply. "I'm a professional writer. My plots most certainly *do* hold water."

"May I turn around?" I asked.

"All right."

I did so. She was dressed in red slacks and a tight-fitting silver top that showed a little cleavage. And she did indeed have a gun—a Morrell .28 revolver that seemed larger than it really was because her hands were dainty. Or maybe all guns look bigger when they're aimed at you.

"I should put a bullet through you right now," she said. "You've already broken into my place once before, and now you're here again."

"I'd advise against it," said Juan calmly from behind her. "In fact, if I may be so bold, I suggest that you drop the gun." I doubt Juan had heard any of our previous conversation from outside. His tone, although excited, didn't contain the rage that I knew would be in it if he were aware of what had happened to Diana.

Lakshmi had nerves of steel, I'll give her that. "I don't know who you are," she said, still facing me, "but you can't shoot me fast enough to prevent me from firing at Lomax first."

Juan was new to this sort of thing. Of course, he should have shot her without announcing his presence—what I get for bringing an amateur along. And I doubted he had it in him to fire at Lakshmi—under normal circumstances, that is.

"Nobody needs to die here," I said. You get good at calculating other people's lines of sight in my game. We were all pretty much in a row: Juan in the room with the missing window, Lakshmi in the open doorway to that room, me facing them both, and behind me, not yet really visible to Juan, Diana's dead body, seated on the couch.

I went on: "I mean, nobody *else* has to die here." I was speaking to Lakshmi but looking beyond her at Juan. "Diana was a good woman, Lakshmi. You had no right to kill her."

That did it. Juan's normally calm face twisted in rage. Just as he pulled the trigger, I dove for the floor—there was a good chance that the bullet would go right through Lakshmi, after all, and it could have gone on to take me out, as well. The moment she was hit, Lakshmi squeezed her own trigger, but I was already out of her line of fire, and the projectile sailed past where I'd been and lodged in the green couch next to Diana. Juan's bullet didn't make it all the way through Lakshmi's body—which was a good thing; poor Juan wasn't made of particularly stern stuff, and he'd have been tortured if one of his slugs had gone into Diana even though she was already dead.

Lakshmi, though, was still alive. Juan's aim was lousy; he'd merely hit the writer in the shoulder. Still, she was discombobulated enough that I was able to spring up from the floor, retrieve my gun, and then wrest hers from her. I then knocked her down and stood over her, my pistol aimed right between her breasts.

Juan rushed over to Diana, in some desperate hope that she was only injured and not dead. I heard him making small sounds.

Lakshmi looked like she was falling into shock from the gunshot wound. If I was going to get any additional information out of her, it would have to come soon. "Stick with me, sweetheart."

But she didn't. Her eyes fluttered up into her skull.

I didn't want to plug Lakshmi if it wasn't necessary, not because she didn't deserve it but because it would result in too much of a hassle with the cops—not to mention the administrators of the writer-in-residence program. She could have been faking being in shock, but the ever-widening pool of blood behind her suggested she wasn't. I shoved Lakshmi's little gun into my waistband, then looked for something to tie her up with. I supposed I could use my belt, but I'd spent enough of this case running around naked; I didn't want to end up in a big chase with my jeans around my ankles.

Juan was still on bended knee in front of Diana, as if he couldn't believe she were dead. "Cover Lakshmi," I said to him. He seemed a bit shocky himself, but he nodded, rose, and lifted his weapon. I saw he wasn't really pointing it at Lakshmi, but about a half meter from her; amateurs like Juan always found it hard to pull the trigger again after they'd seen up close the sort of damage a bullet could do.

I stepped into the other room and found a white terry-cloth bathrobe hanging in the closet. I pulled the sash out of the loops, brought it to the living room, and used it to bind Lakshmi's wrists. The cloth soaked up blood from the surrounding puddle, the red stark against the white fabric.

Then, as it often does, fate took a hand. The doorbell sounded. A portion of the living-room wall changed to the view from the front-door camera. Standing on the stoop was none other than Sergeant Huxley of New Klondike's Finest.

THIRTY-EIGHT

I motioned for Juan to follow me, and we hustled into the back room of Shopatsky House. The doorbell sounded again as we climbed through the missing window. My first thought had been that the cops had pieced together Lakshmi's involvement in all this, but then it occurred to me that Huxley was perhaps simply following up on the buggy joyride; Juan's vehicle was still sitting on the fern-covered lawn.

I didn't have time for the cops right now. Yes, Lakshmi needed medical attention, but even Hux would have the good sense to walk around the house when no one answered, and he'd doubtless find the hole where the window had been and go in to investigate.

Juan and I made our way along the edge of the dome, the alloquartz cool to the touch. I knew the clear wall next to me was curved, but from here it seemed completely flat. Juan kept saying, in a shaky voice, "My poor Diana."

We had gone a hundred meters or so counterclockwise along the edge of the dome. Outside, on our right, we could see rocks casting shadows beneath the yellow-brown sky. In the distance, a couple of Mars buggies were going along at low speed.

To our left now was a warehouse, with cracked walls and a couple of boarded-up windows. Rent tended to be cheap out on the rim, despite it being the only place where you could get uninterrupted views of the vast Martian plain—people preferred to live near the center, if they could afford it, so that they could see something human instead of the vast unchanging monotony of the world that had crushed their dreams. "Let's go," I said, gesturing for Juan to pick up the pace. We headed down one wall of the warehouse and exited out onto the radial street.

A horn sounded—not as loud as the one on Juan's buggy, but still jarring; we'd come out onto the road in front of a tram. "Come on!" I said.

We ran the short distance to the tram stop, passing a few other people as we did so: a dour middle-aged male prospector dragging a wagon that had nothing in it but mining tools; a teenage girl who glared belligerently at me, but then thought better of starting anything; and a thirty-something woman who was dressed like a banker or a lawyer—encounters with either of which usually spelled trouble for me.

We got on the tram. There were five other biologicals onboard and one transfer. The biologicals were staring at little screens; the transfer was looking off into space—or, more precisely, I suspect, was watching a movie or something that only she could see. It was generally better not to sit on the filthy tram seats. Juan knew that, but he was so shaken he plunked himself down. We were soon passing the Windermere Medical Clinic.

I managed to get Juan, who was still mostly out of it, to change trams at the appropriate point, and when that tram reached the stop closest to the shipyard, I tapped him on the shoulder. He got up, and we headed over. But Juan was still shaky, and he looked nauseous. "Take a few minutes," I said. "There's a kybo over there." I pointed to the outhouse past Bertha's shack. "Join me when you're ready."

He nodded and headed over to the small structure. I hustled over to the descent stage and clambered back aboard the cylindrical vessel.

"Can I be of assistance?" Mudge asked as soon as I was inside.

"Yes," I said, to Mudge, "you can be of assistance."

The computer sounded awfully pleased. "What can I do for you?"

"Has anybody entered since I last left?"

"No."

"Good. First things first, then: you flew here from the Alpha Deposit."

"Yes."

"So you must know the way back."

"Of course."

"Display written instructions for returning there, please."

"That information is locked."

"I'm sure it *was* locked. And I'm sure it isn't anymore."

"Well, well, well," said Mudge. "I'm surprised."

There were four monitors in a row along the curving outer wall. The far left one lit up with black text on a pale green background. If Mudge hadn't been so old, there'd probably have been a way to transmit the instructions to my tablet computer, but I didn't have time to fool around figuring out how. Instead, I just pulled out the tab and took a picture of the text, checked to make sure the photo was legible, then slipped the device back in my pocket.

"Okay," I said. "Now, erase that information—permanently."

"Are you sure you want me to do that?"

"Yes. Wipe it. Use the strongest possible erasure method."

"Done."

I blew out air. "Good. Now to the matter I asked you about before. Denny O'Reilly was marooned here on Mars. Correct?"

"Yes," said Mudge.

"Simon Weingarten took off without him. Correct?"

"Yes."

"On purpose?"

"Yes, that's right."

"How long did O'Reilly survive after being marooned?"

"He turned me off to conserve power for the life-support systems after seven days. I don't know how much longer he lived after that."

"Why did Weingarten abandon O'Reilly?"

I was leaning back against one of the walls of the wedge-shaped room. I'd expected the answer to be the prosaic one: "He wanted all the money for himself." But what Mudge said surprised me. "The love affair between Simon and Denny had taken a turn for the worse."

"Love affair?" I repeated.

"Yes."

I was down on the lower floor; I stepped into the central shaft and did a quick three-sixty: there was indeed no second bedroom down here.

"What went wrong?" I asked.

"Denny had promised to leave his wife when they returned to Earth, but Simon had discovered that Denny was involved with another woman on Earth, and that he had a young son by her and intended to take up with her upon his return."

"And who was the other woman?" I asked.

"Katsuko Takahashi."

I nodded. Reiko's grandmother. "Why didn't O'Reilly blow the whistle on Weingarten?" I asked. "All he had to do was radio Earth and blab that he'd been left behind."

"Sending a radio signal to Earth is a tricky matter," said Mudge, "and, as onboard computer, I was in charge of such things. Before he left, Simon programmed me to not allow Denny to send any such messages."

"Are you aware that this ship's ascent stage was destroyed re-entering Earth's atmosphere?"

"No," said Mudge. "But that explains why I have been unable to contact Currie."

"Who?"

"My counterpart; the computer aboard the ascent stage."

"Simon Weingarten perished on re-entry, too," I said.

"Noted," said the computer dispassionately.

A thought occurred to me. "Mudge, did you arrange the transmitting of Denny O'Reilly's diary back to Earth?"

"Yes."

"When?"

"Three hours before Simon departed in the ascent stage."

"So, Denny didn't know he was going to be marooned at that point?"

"I assume not."

"Then why did he send the diary?"

"Space voyages are risky. There was always a chance the return trip might fail. And, of course, Denny believed that he and Simon were going to spend that voyage in hibernation. He was afraid he was about to go to sleep and never wake up."

"Who did you send the diary to?"

"Katsuko Takahashi. It was encrypted; she alone had the decryption key."

"Did you—" I stopped and turned around. Juan was coming through the airlock. A little color had returned to his face. He nodded at me but didn't say anything. I turned back to face Mudge's console. "Did O'Reilly send copies to anyone else?"

"No."

"Not to his wife?"

"No."

"Did you keep a copy of the diary?"

"No. Denny ordered it wiped after it was sent. He was cognizant that someday this descent stage might be found."

I looked at Juan. "Could you recover it?"

"How did you delete the file, Mudge?" Juan asked.

"Blastron protocol 2.2b," the computer replied.

Juan shook his head. "It's gone for good."

Which meant that I had the one and only copy in my pocket. It belonged, of course, to Reiko Takahashi, who was still my client. I'd return it to her—after making a copy for myself, of course.

My phone played "Luck Be a Lady" from *Guys and Dolls.* The little screen showed Dougal McCrae's face, the signal presumably making it in through the open airlock door. I was surprised it had taken this long for that shoe to drop. Huxley must have reported the shooting of Lakshmi Chatterjee, not to mention the discovery of Diana's body, some time ago. I accepted the call. "Hello, Mac."

"Ah, Alex," said the freckled face. "Just thought I'd touch base. Make sure you're doing okay."

I tried not to look or sound puzzled. "Well as can be expected."

"Dr. Pickover's body is at the station now, along with those of the other three transfers." He paused. "I'm so sorry it turned out this way, Alex."

"Me, too." I peered at him, waiting for him to go on, but he didn't. "Um, Mac, did—has Sergeant Huxley called anything in?"

"Since when?"

"Last hour or so?"

"No. After he'd finished out by the *Kathryn Denning,* he went home. His shift was over."

"Ah," I said. "Um, he's not a wannabe writer or poet, is he?"

Mac laughed. "Huxley? God, no. I don't think he even *reads,* let alone writes."

"Okay," I said.

But Mac's eyes had narrowed. "What's up?"

"Nothing. Thanks for the call." I shook off.

The Windermere Medical Clinic was indeed near Shopatsky House; it seemed like a good bet, so I had my phone call it. Hot little pink-haired Gloria answered. "Hey, babe," I said, "just calling to check up on Lakshmi Chatterjee. That was a nasty gunshot wound to the shoulder. She still there?"

Pay dirt. "Oh, hi, sexy," she replied in that breathy voice of hers.

"Didn't know she was a friend of yours. Might have sterilized the scalpel if we'd known that."

"How's she doing?"

"We got her all cleaned up and sent her on her way."

"She was a bit shocky earlier."

"Oh, we took care of that, of course. She's fine now."

"Thanks. Is the man who brought her in still there, by any chance?"

"No. No, he left even before she did. Said he had some business to take care of."

"Thanks, angel." I shook my wrist again, and the screen went dark.

"Alex?" said Juan, looking at me. Of course, he'd overheard the conversations.

"It looks like Lakshmi has a friend on the police force," I said. "And I'd bet money that the business he had to take care of was . . ." I trailed off, not wanting to upset Juan.

"Yes?" he said. "What?"

"Well, it wouldn't be the first time the NKPD had lost a body," I said gently. "I bet Huxley went back to dispose of Diana's."

THIRTY-NINE

Doubtless Huxley would have the body moved before I could make it back to Shopatsky House. And I was so tired, if I did run into him there, even he might get the jump on me. Yes, I wanted revenge—but I wouldn't get it if I didn't get some sleep.

But sleep didn't come easily, not in a bed I'd shared with Diana. I took some melatonin, which usually puts me out, but it didn't work. Instead, I mostly lay on my back, staring up at the ceiling, which had a slowly rotating fan hanging from it.

My gut was churning, and my head was whirling—it was an odd sensation; I think perhaps it was what they call feeling guilty. If I hadn't sent Diana to see Lakshmi, she'd still be alive, still waiting tables, still writing poetry, still laughing and smiling and thinking about a better tomorrow.

Even if Huxley was on the take, even if Diana's body was now disposed of, I'd find some way to make Lakshmi Chatterjee pay—or, on the slim chance that she'd been telling the truth (I suppose there was a first time for everything), I'd make whoever *had* done it pay.

I got up in the morning, showered, and was eating synthesized bacon and eggs when my phone started playing its ringtone. I looked at my wrist; the ID said "NewYou." I accepted the call, and Horatio Fernandez's face appeared. "Alex, I'm worried. Reiko was supposed to be here almost half an hour ago, so I headed over to her place, just to see if she was okay. She's not there."

"She took something to help her sleep last night. Maybe she's just out like a light."

"No, no. She's *gone.* The door had been broken open, and the place was empty."

"Damn!" I'd assumed she was safe, what with Willem Van Dyke and all three meese dead. But—

Christ. Lakshmi Chatterjee. I'd warned that bitch not to go back to the Alpha—but maybe she thought if she had my client as a hostage, she'd be able to get away with it. One good day raiding the beds there would make her insanely rich, after all; I wouldn't be surprised if she was planning to head back on the *Kathryn Denning* with a steamer trunk full of fossil loot as soon as that ship was ready to go.

"Okay," I said. "I'll see if I can find her." I said goodbye, then called Mac, who had just gotten into the police station.

"Morning, Alex."

"Mac, Reiko Takahashi is missing again. Her place was broken into. I suspect she's been taken outside the dome. Can you check for me?" There were only four airlock stations; Lakshmi had to have taken her through one of them. I could have hoofed it to each one, but that would have taken all morning, and the security guards didn't have to take my bribes, but they *did* have to answer Mac's questions.

"I'll get Huxley to check," Mac said.

"No!" I said. Then, more calmly, "No. I'd take it as a personal favor, Mac, if you could make the inquiries yourself."

"What's going on, Alex?"

"Oh, you know me and Huxley."

Mac frowned dubiously.

"Please, Mac. I'll owe you one."

While I waited for Mac to call back, I got ready to go out the door. I was just doing up my shoelaces when my phone rang again.

"She went out of the north airlock," Mac said. "And she wasn't alone. She was with that writer-in-residence woman, Ms. Chatterjee."

"Ah. Did they rent a Mars buggy, by any chance?"

"No," said Mac. I was relieved; that meant they couldn't have gone far, and—

"No," Mac said again. "They drove up to the airlock in one, and they took it outside."

Oh, crap. "What color was it?"

"The buggy? Jesus, Alex, I didn't ask. What difference does that make?"

"None. When did they leave?"

"They logged out of the dome at 5:57 a.m."

I looked at my wall clock; four hours ago. And if they were outside the dome, they weren't the NKPD's concern.

"Thanks, Mac. I'll be in touch." I shook the phone off. Shopatsky House was near the north airlock, and I'd bet solars to soy nuts that the Mars buggy Lakshmi had taken Reiko outside in was white with jade green pinstripes—the one I had conveniently left running on the front lawn of the writing retreat.

If it had only been Lakshmi heading to the Alpha, I'd have been half tempted to just let her drive right on out there. The deposit was still guarded by a row of land mines, and I'd shed no tears if she was blown sky-high. But Reiko was my client, and I couldn't take having another one of those die on my watch.

I made another phone call. Juan Santos looked like he'd gotten even less sleep than I had. "Hey," I said, "you're a hacker. You must have a way to shut off your Mars buggy by remote control, no?"

He yawned, then, "Sorry. Yeah. I was thinking about that. You left it running at Shopatsky House, right? I figured I should go collect it this morning. The excimer battery should last for weeks, but—"

"Lakshmi has taken it outside the dome."

"Hell, Alex. I can't afford to lose that vehicle."

"I know, I know. I'll get it back for you. What's the remote shutoff code?"

He told me, and my phone recorded it. "But if you're using your phone to send it, you'll have to be within a hundred meters or so for it to be picked up," he added.

"Right, okay. And the code to turn it back on?"

He told me that, too.

"Thanks."

"Alex, I need—"

But I shook the phone off, grabbed my gun, and ran out my apartment door.

• • • • • • • • • • •

It would eat up half a day getting to the Alpha by Mars buggy; that would never do. And although O'Reilly and Weingarten's descent stage could fly there quickly, assuming it had enough fuel left, I'd have to get the damn thing hauled onto the planitia first, and that would take forever. And so I went to see the one person I knew who had every luxury item, including an airplane: Ernie Gargalian of Ye Olde Fossil Shoppe.

"Mr. Double-X!" Gargantuan exclaimed as I came into the empty store.

"Hey, Ernie."

"I hear you've had some adventures of late, my boy."

"Oh?"

"They say you've recovered Simon and Denny's third lander."

"Who would 'they' be?"

"I keep my ear to the ground, my boy."

I suspected if Ernie ever actually adopted that posture, he wouldn't be able to get back up. "Well, yeah," I said.

"There might be a market for it."

"For the ship?"

"There's a collector for everything," he said. "Would you like me to see what I can arrange?"

"I guess, sure. So, listen, can I borrow your airplane?"

Ernie had a hearty laugh, I'll give him that. "By Gad, my dear boy! You do have gumption."

"You can't spell gumption without P-I." Actually, maybe you could—but you'd have to do it phonetically.

"And just where might you take my plane, Alex?"

"To the Alpha Deposit."

Ernie's demeanor changed instantly. "You know where it is?"

"Yes."

"Very well. When do we leave?"

I'd expected this to be the price I'd have to pay. Rory wouldn't have liked it—but Rory was dead. Reiko, on the other hand, was probably still alive, but quite likely wouldn't be for much longer. "Right now," I said.

Just then a customer tried to enter. "No, no," said Ernie, hurrying to the door. "We're closed."

The customer—a woman in her forties—pointed at the laser-etched sign. "But the sign says . . ."

"A typo!" declared Ernie. "I'll get it fixed."

Crossing the room had been enough to set Ernie to huffing and puffing; there was no way he could walk all the way out to the edge of the dome; his plane, I knew, was parked outside the north airlock, coincidentally the same one Lakshmi and Reiko had exited through. But a man of Gargalian's stature—literal and figurative—did not trifle with public transit. He went into his back room and emerged floating on a hoverchair—and I saw that he'd also fetched a rifle.

It was a tight fit to get the hoverchair out through the shop's doorway, but he did it. I followed, and he spoke a command that locked up his store.

The chair zipped along so quickly that I was huffing and puffing myself by the time we got to the north exit. Ernie had a surface suit stored there that looked like the bag Phobos had come in. It was a struggle for him to get into it—it was a struggle for him to do pretty much anything—but he eventually managed it.

I had to rent a suit yet again. This time, it was the shade of green people used to associate with money. Ernie's was deep purple; he resembled an enormous eggplant in it.

Ernie's plane was one of three currently parked here. It was dark gray and had a gigantic wingspan—close to forty meters, I'd say. The front part of the cockpit looked like it had originally been designed to hold two side-by-side seats but had been modified for a single double-wide chair. I was relegated to the back; the habitat was teardrop-shaped, tapering toward the rear, so there'd only ever been one chair there. Once we were inside, Ernie set about powering up the plane.

Not only did you need big wings to fly on Mars, you needed a long runway to take off. The one here was a solid kilometer of Isidis Planitia that had been cleared of rocks. We made it almost to the end before I felt us rising.

I'd flown in small planes on Earth but never before on Mars, and I'd been in hibernation when I'd come here, so this was my first aerial view of New Klondike and environs. I craned my neck to see the city as we sped away from it: a large, shallow dome, glistening in the sun—looking for all the world like God had dropped a contact lens. Then there was nothing but Martian landscape stretching to the horizon below and the yellow-brown sky above. I pulled my tab out of my suit's equipment pouch and dictated the directions I'd gotten from Mudge to the back of Ernie's great loaf of a head.

The plane moved quickly but silently. I kept looking down, hoping to spot the white Mars buggy. Of course, it was always possible that Lakshmi had headed somewhere else, in which case I'd kick myself for letting Ernie know where the Alpha was, and—

—and there it was, up ahead, tooling along. We were arriving just in the nick of time; they were now just a few kilometers shy of the Alpha Deposit.

Airplanes on Mars need clear open stretches to touch down, just as they did to take off, and although Isidis Planitia was a plain, it wasn't a plain plain, and landing our plane was going to be a pain. Ernie was circling, looking for a place to set down. Not much sound carried in the thin Martian air, but our giant wingspan would make us impossible to miss if Lakshmi or Reiko happened to look up.

Ernie swore in Armenian, and his massive head swung left and right as he continued to search. Finally, he muttered, "Here goes nothing!" and we started to descend.

The patch of ground he'd picked didn't have any boulders, at least, but there were still plenty of rocks up to and including basketball size. The plane had the same sort of adaptive wheels that buggies had, although larger in diameter. Still, when we hit, we bounced several times as the wheels encountered rocks they couldn't negotiate. My breakfast gave an encore performance at the back of my throat.

We skidded a considerable distance, with Gargantuan yelling *"Yeehaw!"* When we at last came to a stop, Ernie and I dogged down our helmets, and he made the canopy swing open. He needed both hands to climb down, and so he dropped his rifle overboard, then used the rungs built into the side of the plane to lower his bulk to the surface. Once he was down, he bent over—with great difficulty—and picked his rifle back up.

I followed him down, then looked out at the wide expanse of Martian terrain in front of me. Ennio Morricone's "The Ecstasy of the Gold" was running through my head. It was, after all, greed that had driven the Great Martian Fossil Rush, the Great Klondike Gold Rush, and the Great

California Gold Rush, and Morricone's haunting theme captured that madness well.

Juan's Mars buggy was on the horizon, coming toward us; the plane had landed in a kilometer-wide strip between it and the eastern edge of the Alpha—the edge that was salted with land mines.

I walked out past the wing tip and told my phone to transmit the OFF code Juan had given me.

The white buggy continued to barrel in. At this distance, I couldn't see if it had green pinstriping; I suppose it was always possible that this was a different Mars buggy.

I told the phone to transmit again . . . and again . . . and again.

The damn thing was still closing, and Lakshmi must have had the accelerator right down to the floor. She was veering to the south a bit, clearly intending to go around our airplane. I had the phone send the OFF sequence once more, wondering if somehow Juan had made a mistake when he gave it to me; he had looked like he'd just woken up, after all, and—

—and, at last, the buggy was slowing. It skittered to a stop about seventy meters ahead of me. I could see movement within the canopy; of course, when the power went off, the life-support shut off, too. I imagine Lakshmi and Reiko were hustling to get their surface-suit helmets on. I had briefed Ernie on the way here, so he understood what was going down. He had his rifle butt against his shoulder and the barrel aimed at the buggy.

I'd put my holster on the outside of my suit. I pulled out my gun and ran toward the stalled vehicle—and the sight of me charging in with weapon drawn had the effect I wanted. Lakshmi popped the canopy on Juan's car—it opened mechanically rather than electrically, for safety reasons—and she and Reiko scrambled out.

My legs were longer than theirs, and I soon overtook them. We stood facing each other with just five meters of rusty, dusty plain between us. Reiko was in a suit of a darker green than my own and Lakshmi again had on a red one. All of us still had our fishbowls polarized, meaning the women might not have yet identified me; I, of course, could tell which of them was which by their heights.

Behind me, as a glance over my shoulder confirmed, Gargantuan Gargalian was waddling in, and he was now raising his rifle. It looked like Lakshmi Chatterjee's stint as Shopatsky House writer-in-residence was about to end with a bang.

FORTY

I looked down at my wrist controls to see what frequency my radio was using, then held up my left hand with three fingers raised, then changed it to four fingers.

Lakshmi dipped her opaque helmet slightly in a nod. Both she and Reiko touched their own wrist controls, presumably punching in frequency thirty-four. But neither of them said anything, instead waiting for me to speak. And so I did: "All right. The jig is up. Let her go."

I glanced over my shoulder again, just to get a sense of where Ernie now was, and—

Oh. He'd never met either of them, and their helmets were polarized. He'd had to choose which woman to take a bead on, and he'd mistakenly chosen Reiko. I opened my mouth to say something, but stopped when a pair of hands reached for the butterscotch sky. One of the raised hands, I saw now, was holding a tiny pistol. But the person raising her hands in surrender wasn't Lakshmi Chatterjee—it was Reiko Takahashi.

Lakshmi reacted instantly, her right arm lashing out to seize the gun, which she promptly pressed into Reiko's side. In the second it took for that to happen, it hit me: it hadn't been Lakshmi who had kidnapped Reiko; it had been Reiko who had kidnapped Lakshmi, so that she could force Lakshmi to show her where the Alpha was. Reiko must have broken her own door lock before going to get Lakshmi—preparing an alibi for when she returned home alone; no one would blame her if she'd had to off her captor to get away.

"Back off, Lomax," Lakshmi said, "or the little bitch gets it." She must have recognized my voice, since all four of us still had polarized fishbowls—which was half the reason I hadn't figured out the dynamic between Lakshmi and Reiko; I hadn't been able to see their expressions.

I kept my gun aimed at Lakshmi. "You won't shoot me. I'm the only one who knows the code to turn your buggy back on."

"If I shoot you," Lakshmi said, "a seat opens up on that airplane—so I don't need the code."

I chinned the control that depolarized my helmet; the sun was high enough now that it wouldn't be in my eyes facing this way. Lakshmi must have decided it was indeed better that we see each other, because her fishbowl grew transparent, too.

Ernie was on the same radio frequency as me, of course. He spoke for the first time. "My dear lady," he said, "we're all after the same thing. But the Alpha Deposit has wealth galore, enough to satiate the desires of each of us. There's no call for anything disagreeable to happen here."

"Who are you?" Lakshmi said.

"Ernest Gargalian," he replied, with a portly, courtly bow. "Proprietor of Ye Olde Fossil Shoppe." He depolarized his own helmet, revealing his round face and slicked-back hair.

Judging by her expression, Lakshmi recognized neither his name nor that of his establishment, which was too bad because no one who did know Ernie would ever threaten him. His operatives would avenge his death—and some of them were transfers. "Just so you know," I said to Lakshmi, "if this godforsaken planet has a Mister Big, he's it."

Reiko must have chinned her polarization control, too, because her helmet also grew clear. Her voice was filled with wonder. "You're Ernie Gargalian?"

"At your service."

"I—I didn't know you were on Mars. I didn't know you were even still alive."

Ernie scowled. "Yes?"

"You . . . you knew my grandfather," said Reiko.

"Ah, yes, indeed," replied Ernie. "Alex here told me that you're Denny's granddaughter. I was just a pup when I first met him and Simon at the Tucson Gem and Mineral Show. I was one of the first dealers to do business with them."

"What . . . what was he like?"

"An astute businessperson. As it appears, if I may be so bold, you yourself are. Why did you kidnap the lovely lady here?"

"She double-crossed me," Reiko replied. "She told me she was going to write a book about my grandfather. I gave her access to my grandfather's diary. I'd hoped she'd find a clue in there that would help us locate the Alpha Deposit, but when she did—"

"She didn't figure out where the Alpha was from the diary," I said. "Did you, Lakshmi? You had that punk, that kid—Dirk—you had him plant a tracking chip on me. And then you followed me here."

Lakshmi nodded. "That's right. The diary was useless. I found the Alpha without it." She looked at Reiko. "So why should I cut you in?"

"Because it's *mine,*" Reiko said. "My grandfather found it, so it belongs to me."

Reiko still had her hands in the air. Lakshmi still had a gun pressed into her side. Ernie still had his rifle aimed at the two women. Ennio Morricone was still playing in my head.

There was movement in the distance. It might have been a dust devil; they were common on Mars. I wasn't sure, though, and I knew better than to give away that I'd noticed anything. I kept my eyeline toward Lakshmi. Whatever I'd seen was still far away, so I sought to stall: "All right, then; okay. We have a little misunderstanding here, that's all. But there's no reason we can't all just walk away from this."

Lakshmi shook her head, brown hair brushing first one then the other side of her fishbowl. "Reiko told me on the way here that you've recovered her grandfather's body, isn't that right?"

I nodded.

"That's the way that *had* to go down," Lakshmi continued. "Even back then, when only three people knew where the Alpha was. First Denny O'Reilly and Simon Weingarten decided to cut Willem Van Dyke out of the picture. Then Weingarten decided to get rid of O'Reilly. It's the *only* way something like this can go down—with one person taking everything. That's human nature."

"My dear woman," said Ernie, "there are riches enough over yonder"—I don't think I'd ever heard anyone say "yonder" before in real life, but something about being out here, at the edge of the frontier, seemed to lend itself to using that word—"to satisfy even my appetite, and yours as well. We can all profit here. You'll need a sales agent, after all."

I didn't often wish I was a transfer, but I did just then, if only for the telescopic eyes. The thing—whatever it was—was still indistinct, but I thought for sure that it was getting closer. Still, maybe it *was* just a dust devil or—

—or maybe it was something moving so quickly that it was kicking up a plume of dust behind it.

Ernie's conciliatory comments had been directed toward Lakshmi—after all, she was the lady holding a gun—but it was Reiko who answered. Not many women could still look pretty while sneering, but Denny's granddaughter pulled it off. "She double-crossed me," Reiko said. "No way she walks out of this with anything."

The Martian landscape was infuriatingly fractal: that crater there might be a meter across or a hundred; that rock might be man-sized or mountainous. It really was hard to gauge the size of the thing that was approaching—or how far away it still was. But it was getting nearer, I was sure of that, and it now filled enough of my vision that I could assign it a color: turquoise, a thoroughly un-Martian hue.

"Double-crosses happen all the time on Mars," I said to Reiko. "Ernie here calls me Mr. Double-X. Shrug it off."

"Really?" said Lakshmi. "I thought he called you that because you don't have any balls."

By now the turquoise object was even closer. It was still beyond my ability to resolve in detail—maybe I needed to see an optometrist, or maybe no one with biological eyes could have made it out—but it had moving parts, of that much I was certain.

I still wanted Lakshmi to go down for killing Diana, but with Huxley having presumably removed the body, I didn't see how to make that stick, at least not yet. I'd figure a way, though, if—*when*—I made it back to New Klondike. And getting there meant getting the writer-in-residence to lower her gun. "Lakshmi," I said, "what happens on the planitia stays on the planitia. Let Reiko go, then head back to Shopatsky House and work on your book—whatever it really is about."

The turquoise object was getting ever closer. It was . . . yes, yes! It was a person. But a biological couldn't run that fast; it had to be a transfer. I stole a glance at Ernie. His expression gave no hint that he'd seen anything, and, indeed, he seemed intent solely on the women in front of him.

The runner shifted his course slightly; he was now mostly eclipsed by Lakshmi and Reiko. I could have changed my own position or craned my neck, but Lakshmi would doubtless notice that; I now regretted having depolarized my helmet.

Of course, there was no reason to assume that whoever was barreling in was coming to rescue Ernie and me. Just as likely, he was coming to help Lakshmi, who perhaps had somehow managed to get a signal out that she'd been kidnapped, or to help Reiko—or maybe it was a free agent and would do us all in and seize the riches for himself. If any of us had been transfers, that might have been difficult without a broadband disruptor, but if the runner had a pump-action shotgun or a machine gun—not that I'd ever seen one of those on Mars—he could easily take all four of us out.

Ernie decided to weigh in. "Young lady, Mr. Lomax is right. I have connections that could make any difficulties disappear, and—"

And Ernie must have felt the ground shaking slightly beneath his feet; a guy like me doesn't have much that jiggles, but he was a walking distant-early-warning system, and Lakshmi had clearly seen something in his face. She suddenly turned around, swinging Reiko around with her. My view of the incoming transfer was restored—and my jaw dropped in astonishment.

Rushing toward us was a stunningly beautiful woman—a gorgeous transfer with a supermodel's face and long blonde hair bouncing behind her. I didn't recognize her, but she was wearing a turquoise tracksuit that hugged her curves. Her large breasts were bouncing delightfully as she ran, but there was no sign that her chest was heaving. She wasn't breathing hard; she wasn't breathing at all.

And perhaps in a few seconds, none of the rest of us would be, either.

FORTY-ONE

It was hard to tell while looking at Lakshmi from behind, but I think she'd pulled her gun out of Reiko's side and was now aiming it at the gorgeous apparition, who was sailing ten meters closer with each stride. I was all set to jump Lakshmi from the rear when the blonde transfer leapt, flying through the almost nonexistent air. She slammed into the writer, knocking her on her back. Reiko danced out of the way just in time to avoid being bowled over, too.

Lakshmi swore; it doubtless hurt to be knocked over, especially when wearing a backpack with oxygen tanks. She was flat on her back but still had her little gun. I kicked the hand that held it. The weapon went up, up, and up some more. Lakshmi was trying her best to throw the blonde bombshell off her, but the transfer had grabbed her wrists.

Blondie looked at Ernie even as she was struggling with Lakshmi, and she made some beckoning motions with her lovely head. Gargalian seemed baffled for a second, but then got it. It took some doing, but Blondie managed to get up, and Ernie managed to get down without Lakshmi escaping. He took the simple expedient of sitting on her chest.

Lakshmi beat at him with gloved fists, but her suit didn't allow her arms to move fast enough for the blows to really hurt, I imagined.

Blondie smiled at me, but then her perfect mouth dropped open in surprise, showing the porcelain pearly whites within. It took me a second to realize she was now looking past me. I turned, and—

Damn. I really did need to do something about my eyes. Once again, there was something off in the distance. I squinted, and—yes: it was someone else running this way, this time coming in from the north.

Blondie's baby blues were wide. She probably had that bionic-vision thing going on; I wondered if there was a reticle over her retina. Reading a transfer's expression was hard, but I don't think she recognized whoever it was.

I didn't know if this interloper was friend or foe, but it pays to prepare for the worst. Since Blondie, at least, seemed to be an ally, I grabbed her hand—my glove in her naked plastiflesh—and led her perpendicular to the newcomer's travel, running west toward the Alpha, meaning he'd have to choose whether to come toward me and Blondie, or toward Lakshmi and Ernie. It was soon apparent that the newcomer had altered his trajectory to come after the two of us.

Blondie fell in next to me, matching my stride, and we continued on for a few hundred meters. Although the dust covering Isidis Planitia shifts over time, I could still make out two divots in the surface, and I maneuvered us between them. Then I scanned around for the automobile-shaped rock I'd dubbed Plymouth and the more jagged one I'd nicknamed Hudson. And so I figured stopping *here* was just right, with Plymouth at about ten o'clock and Hudson standing guard at 3:30.

The intruder was now just a hundred meters away. He was either wearing a beige surface suit, or was a transfer in beige clothes, or—less likely—a naked transfer with beige skin.

I was suddenly distracted by Ernie shouting into his helmet microphone. "Alex! Alex!"

I turned. Somehow, Lakshmi had managed to push Ernie off, or—no, no, that wasn't it. Reiko had a gun pointed at Ernie. Damn it! While I'd been busy maneuvering Blondie and me to just the right spot, and Ernie had been busy trying to flatten out all the appealing bumps on Lakshmi, Reiko must have gone off to retrieve the piece I'd sent flying earlier. Back on Earth, when people get surges of adrenaline, they sometimes manage to lift cars off trapped pedestrians; the sight of Reiko again packing heat must have been enough to give Lakshmi the jolt she needed to heave Ernie off herself, and she now had hold of his rifle.

Blondie flexed her fingers, disengaging her hand from mine, and in a blur of motion she scooped up a rock about the size of a softball, hauled back, and let loose a pitch worthy of the major leagues. The rock tore through the thin air and made it a good fraction of the distance, but it fell short, and I couldn't tell which of the three people she'd been aiming at. Ernie was on his feet, and the two women were facing off against each other, perhaps a dozen meters between them, Reiko aiming her pistol at Lakshmi, and Lakshmi pointing Ernie's rifle at Reiko.

If this had been the Old West, I would have heard the shot ring out, but the air was too thin for that, and instead all I heard was a feminine *"Oomph!"* over the radio as one of the women was hit, and I waited breathlessly to see which of them would crumple to the ground.

And, after about three seconds, one of them did, with graceful Martian indolence: the shorter of the two, the lady in dark green, the heiress who seemed to have inherited nothing but her grandfather's obsession with wealth.

Blondie suddenly sprang into action, running toward them. She'd yet to say a word, and I had no reason to think she was listening to the same frequency I was using, but I shouted anyway: "No! Stop! Go back the way we came!"

And either she *was* tuned into that channel, or else she had bionic ears in addition to bionic eyes, because she skidded to a halt, changed direction, and followed the precise path out that we'd taken in.

Meanwhile, the beige intruder was still coming straight for me. If I moved, he'd alter his course—and so I stood my ground.

Blondie was damn near flying, yellow hair a cloud around her head as she hurried toward Reiko and Lakshmi. Lakshmi aimed the rifle at Blondie, and I guess Blondie and I were thinking the same thing—that perhaps a gun that big *would* do real damage to a transfer; the blonde goddess started bobbing and weaving as she continued to race in. Lakshmi's first shot was a clean miss. The second got Blondie somewhere in the torso—hard to tell exactly where when watching from the rear—but it didn't slow her down.

I turned back to the intruder. It was a male transfer in khaki slacks and a khaki long-sleeved shirt, and he was still coming straight at me. As his shoulders worked up and down, I glimpsed that he had on a backpack—surely not air tanks, but rather a rucksack with equipment. Ah, and at last he was close enough that I could make out his face, and—

God, no!

I shouted, even though he almost certainly couldn't hear me through my helmet in this thin atmosphere. *"Rory, stop!"*

I hadn't seen the bootleg Pickover since shortly after I'd rescued him from the torture room aboard the *Skookum Jim*, but I had no doubt that this was him; the face was the one the bootleg had adopted to take on the identity of Joshua Wilkins. He was now just thirty meters from the line of land mines—and closing.

Even in a surface suit, I should be able to do at least as good a long jump as I could have back on Earth. I started running straight for him—meaning I was also running straight for the buried mines. When I got close to the line, I kicked off with all my strength and went sailing horizontally toward him, arms outstretched. He had the most astonished expression I'd ever seen on a transfer's face as I sailed closer, and—

—and, *damn!*, my Smith & Wesson flew out of my holster and dropped behind me. It must have hit one of the mines, because I was suddenly propelled forward by more than just the strength of my initial kick. The explosion was deafening even in the thin air. Something tore into my right leg as I collided with the bootleg Pickover and knocked him on his stainless-steel butt.

It took me a second to recover from the impact, but then I pushed myself to my feet and reached down to give Pickover a hand. As I pulled him up, I felt a stabbing in my calf. Land-mine shrapnel had sliced through my suit and the jeans beneath. A piece of skin about as long and wide as a banana was exposed to the subzero air, and blood was flowing down the suit's leg, although it would soon either freeze or boil off. I opened the suit-repair kit on my belt, pulled out the largest adhesive patch, and positioned it over the cut. Pickover and I were so close now that I could hear him speak. "My God!" he exclaimed. "Someone's booby-trapped the Alpha!"

I nodded as much to myself as to him; the legit Pickover had discovered that only after this bootleg had been spun off. I changed my radio's channel. "Channel twenty-two," I shouted. The transfer nodded, but didn't do anything visibly to indicate he'd selected that radio frequency. I went on at a normal volume. "What are you doing here?"

The bootleg's voice—which didn't sound anything like that of the real Rory—came through my helmet speakers. "I've been working a bed twenty kilometers north of here," he said. "I saw an airplane fly by, and it looked like the damn thing was coming down near the Alpha. I thought I should investigate—and then I caught sight of you."

"Good to see you, Rory. Some of those people over there want to steal fossils from here. Are you up for a fight?"

His eyes narrowed. "Hells yes."

Lakshmi, Reiko, Blondie, and Ernie were fifty meters east of us. Blondie was now kneeling next to the fallen Reiko. "The woman on the ground is the granddaughter of Denny O'Reilly."

"Oh, really?" he said, just as the other Pickover had when I'd first told him.

I wasn't in the mood for the "No, O'Reilly" schtick, although it *is* rare that you get to use a joke twice on more or less the same person. "Yes," I said. "The woman in red is Lakshmi Chatterjee. She's a writer, and has tried to kill me more than once. As for the transfer babe in turquoise, I have no idea who she is, but she seems to be on our side, or at least not actively against us. And the big guy is—"

"Ernie Gargalian." Sneering is more effective with a British accent, but even without it, Rory's contempt was plain.

"Yes," I said, looking out at the tableau. I suppose it *was* debatable which of us was the Good and which the Bad, but there was no way Reiko, Lakshmi, or Blondie could qualify as the Ugly—which left Ernie, Rory, and me to vie for that title. "But that's Ernie's airplane. He brought me here. The real threat to the Alpha, at least right now, is Lakshmi."

"I—I don't want to kill to protect the secret," Pickover said.

"I don't see another way," I replied. "Lakshmi is certainly willing to kill us." As soon as I said it, I realized that Ms. Chatterjee really wasn't much of a threat to Rory. Indeed, he could just run off—he could move faster than Lakshmi; for all I knew, he could even outrun her in the buggy, if she ever got it going again. But I'd saved him from that torture room, and I'd saved him again when I hid his identity from the legitimate Pickover, who, had he known of this one's continued existence, would have demanded he be terminated. I doubted he was going to take off on me. And, after a moment, he confirmed that. "All right. What now?"

"See those two pits, there? That's where your, ah, brother and I removed two of the land mines. You can safely move in and out if you go between those pits." The bootleg nodded, and I went on. "So, let's go. Our first order of business: disarm Lakshmi."

"Okay," said Pickover. "But how?"

"Improvise," I replied as I started running toward the others: sailing forward, kicking off, sailing forward again. Pickover must have hesitated for a moment, but he soon fell in beside me.

It didn't take long for Lakshmi to react. She assumed a marksman's spread-legged stance and aimed her gun at me, which was precisely what I was hoping for, because it meant she could no longer cover Ernie. As soon as she swung the gun away from the big man, Ernie did the best leap he could manage. He might have weighed only a third as much here as he would have on Earth—a fact that let him clear the ground by half a meter and come forward a meter and a half—but he *massed* exactly the same, and he slammed into Lakshmi from behind with a lot of inertia. While Pickover and I continued to close the distance, Lakshmi pitched forward, legs still splayed. Ernie landed on her suit's backpack, and although my view was bouncing as I ran, it looked like he was trying to disengage her air tanks.

Pickover suddenly surged in front of me, his artificial legs pistoning in a way mine never could. Despite doubtless having the wind knocked out of her, Lakshmi was struggling to lift her head and get the gun up again, and she squeezed off a shot at Pickover. I thought the paleontologist was hit—he did a headfirst roll into the ground—but then I realized it was a deliberate evasion tactic, and he somersaulted perfectly, Lakshmi's bullet flying above him while he rolled. He sprang back into a running posture and continued in.

I was now close enough to make out more detail. Blondie was still kneeling, and—no, no. That wasn't it. She wasn't kneeling; she was sitting cross-legged on the sand, and Reiko Takahashi's helmeted head was cradled in her lap.

Ernie was still doing things on Lakshmi's back, and—yes!—he managed to disengage her tanks and toss them aside. Doubtless there was still some air in her helmet, but the writer couldn't have more than a couple of minutes left to live.

Suddenly my own helmet exploded around me. Lakshmi had shifted her aim from Pickover to me and had squeezed off another shot. I couldn't see for a moment—the atmosphere that had been in my fishbowl turned into a white cloud of condensation—but as I continued running forward, I left the cloud behind. The tanks on my back were still working, though, and oxygen was being pumped though the tube from them. I stopped running for a moment, hoping that Lakshmi had shot her last, and yanked on the tube, pulling it farther up; they were designed to have some play for just such emergencies.

I felt the skin on my face freezing, my eyes hurt from the cold and the exposure to near vacuum, and my sinuses were seizing up. But there was warm air coming through the tube, which I'd now stuck in my mouth and was clamping onto with my teeth. I continued to run because I didn't know what else to do. I think I was bleeding from my scalp; shards from the fishbowl must have sliced into it.

I needed another helmet and fast. Ernie was clearly conscious of my plight: he was trying to undog Lakshmi's fishbowl. I was having trouble seeing now—I think my eyeballs were freezing in place, and—

And everything went dark and I went plowing face first into the ground. I managed to lift my chin and spit out the oxygen tube just in time to keep it from bashing my front teeth out. And then I felt the weight of someone on my back, and strong hands grabbed the sides of my neck and squeezed, strangling the life out of me.

FORTY-TWO

Still face down in the dirt, I brought my own hands up and tried to yank away the constricting ones, which were—

—which were naked, gloveless, exposed to the elements, and . . .

. . . and my vision *hadn't* failed. Rather, someone had thrown some sort of bag over my head, then tackled me, driving me to the ground, and now these strong artificial hands were sealing the bag as tightly as possible around my neck.

I felt the bag inflating, filling out like a balloon, as air continued to flow through the tube from my backpack tanks. Pickover must have taken a fabric specimen bag out of his rucksack and thrown it over my head to create a makeshift helmet; it was him on my back now. "Alex!" he shouted, so that I could hear him without the radio, the headset for which had fallen away with the shards of my fishbowl. "For Christ's sake, stop fighting me!"

I hadn't been aware that I still was—but I guess panic had taken over. I took a deep breath in the darkness and was delighted that I could actually *smell* the musty bag. And although I couldn't see anything, I could feel my eyeballs swiveling in their sockets again.

Pickover released his too-tight grip on my neck. The bag loosened, and I felt a blast of cold air, which was actually refreshing by this point. I brought my hands back to my neck, one to each side, and took over holding the bag in place.

"I'll be back!" Pickover shouted, or at least I think that's what he said; it was quite faint and muffled.

My cheeks felt like they were burning; I suspected they were getting frostbitten. And the sack did seem to be sticking to the top of my head, lending credence to my theory that I was bleeding there. It didn't seem likely that any of the damage was life-threatening, but I wasn't happy being out of the action. I lifted my neck and tried to pull the bag tight to my face, in hopes that I might be able to see through its weave, but there was no way to do so and maintain the air seal, and so I finally risked pulling the bag up off my face for a second and—

—and Pickover had run to Juan's white-with-green-trim buggy. He was now in the driver's seat, the canopy still up, and I saw him pound the dash, probably with balled fists, in frustration; the damn thing wouldn't start.

I brought my left forearm up into the bag and spoke to my phone, telling it to transmit the ON sequence. Nothing happened; the bag had all but emptied of air, and my phone couldn't hear me speaking, or, if it did, it didn't recognize my voice. I tried with my one free hand to keep the bag's mouth reasonably tight around my neck and wrist, and I waited for enough oxygen to be pumped out of the tube for the fabric to puff out a bit, and then I tried again. "Send the ON code to Juan's buggy!"

I hoped I was close enough. I was still lying on the ground, and would have a devil of a time getting to my feet without using my hands. "Send the ON code to Juan's buggy!" I shouted again.

The ground shook a bit beneath my chest. I thought perhaps Ernie was running—and that's a sight I'd have paid to see—but then I heard the Mars buggy's horn. I arched my neck and risked pulling the bag up enough to see out for a second. Again, there was a cloud of condensation and a blast of arctic air, but through the cloud, I made out Pickover in Juan's buggy, about a dozen meters in front of me. He still had the canopy up. I pulled the bag down, held it around my neck again, and stumbled toward the vehicle.

I soon felt Pickover's hands on me—he must have exited the buggy—and he helped me into its driver's seat, and then he slammed the canopy down from the outside. I emptied my lungs, then pulled the bag up—tugging hard to separate it from the frozen blood on the top of my head—reached forward, hit the switch labeled "Pressurize Cabin," and waited to breathe until I could feel and hear that there was enough air in the little chamber for me to do so.

I looked through the canopy and tried to take in everything that was happening. The situation had definitely changed: Ernie was standing with his hands held over his head. Lakshmi was back on her feet, air tanks attached and fishbowl securely on, and she had Ernie's rifle aimed at him. Blondie, meanwhile, was still tending to the fallen Reiko—which I presume meant that Reiko was alive, even if she wasn't moving.

Pickover was now standing beside the Mars buggy. He waved to catch my attention, then pointed straight ahead. I nodded and floored it, sending the buggy hurtling toward Lakshmi. It was three seconds before she realized what was happening, and when she did, she swung the rifle to fire at me. She managed to hit the windshield three times, each impact sending spider webs of cracks throughout the alloquartz, but she soon realized that she wasn't going to be able to stop me that way. She bolted in the opposite direction.

I already had the accelerator flush with the floor and just kept going, confident I could mow her down. She was weaving left and right, and I had to yank repeatedly on the steering wheel to keep her dead ahead, but at last the inevitable happened: I was upon her, and—

And she did indeed still have Earthly muscles. She leapt up, up, up just as I was about to run her over, and came down feet first on the little hood of the buggy, her back to me. The springy front wheels compressed as she hit.

We were still speeding forward; I slammed on the brakes in hopes of dislodging her, but she leapt up again as I did so, did a neat half twist in the air, and came down once more, this time with her calves bent back so that she landed on her knees facing me, denting the hood. The buggy had stopped, and she placed the rifle's muzzle against the center of one of the spider-web patterns her previous shots had made and she swiveled the barrel so she was aiming at my chest. Lakshmi was betting that a point-blank shot at a weak spot would go right through the alloquartz and into me—and that was a bet I didn't want to take.

Suddenly there was an impact behind me and the car was rocking up and down. I swung my head around to discover that Pickover had jumped onto the trunk, and now was leaping up onto the top of the canopy. He leapt again, this time landing on the hood right in front of Lakshmi, her rifle barrel between his legs. She pulled the gun away from the alloquartz so she could shoot up at him.

There wasn't room between the canopy and Lakshmi for Pickover to get enough leverage for a decent kick, but he brought his hands down, grabbing her arms just below the shoulders. His left arm worked its way down her right one until it was over the hand holding the rifle, and he tore it from her. He then maneuvered the gun around so that it was aimed at her face, and I waited for her own fishbowl—not to mention the gorgeous head within—to explode.

But Pickover couldn't bring himself to shoot, and after a few seconds the terror ebbed from Lakshmi's exquisite features as she realized that. She rolled backward onto her rump, her spine flat against the buggy's hood, and kicked her legs up into Rory's armpits, flipping him into the air and sending him sailing over so he came down headfirst toward the planitia. The fall was slow enough that he managed to break it by getting his hands splayed out, but that meant dropping the rifle. Lakshmi spun around on her butt, vaulted from the hood, and scooped up the rifle once more. She didn't aim it at Rory, but rather at me, and although the canopy might protect me, it also might not, and given that I didn't have a helmet, Rory clearly decided not to chance rushing her.

Lakshmi hurried around the side of the buggy. I was all set to gun it in reverse, but she stopped before she got behind the vehicle, and—

—and, crap, she reached into the side battery compartment and disconnected the excimer pack. The car's electrical systems—including life support—shut down just as surely as if I'd sent the OFF code again. Lakshmi then hauled back and threw the battery with all her might as far behind the buggy as she could—which was pretty damn far, thanks to her Earthly muscles, the almost nonexistent air drag, and the feeble Martian gravity.

There was enough oxygen in the canopy to keep me alive for some time, I supposed, but if I cracked the lid to go retrieve the battery, I'd lose it. Lakshmi took off running in the opposite direction from where she'd thrown the excimer pack, and Rory hesitated, trying to decide whether to go after the battery or after her. I guess he decided it was more important to get my air circulating again, and he ran toward the rear.

A movement to the right caught my eye. It was Ernie Gargalian, making a beeline for his airplane. He wasn't running, but he was walking fast, his arms working back and forth at his sides as he did so. He'd clearly decided to get away, and, in good Simon Weingarten fashion, apparently was content to maroon his partner here at the Alpha Deposit.

FORTY-THREE

Lakshmi, having apparently noticed what Ernie was up to, took off after him, presumably with an eye on the plane's passenger seat.

The bootleg Pickover hadn't seen precisely where Lakshmi tossed the excimer pack, and he was now searching around for it. With the buggy's power off and my fishbowl radio wrecked, I couldn't give him verbal instructions, although if he would just look back at me, I could at least point in the right direction.

I swiveled my head again to the front. Ernie was standing beside the plane now, turning it around by pulling on the tip of its port wing.

Blondie suddenly picked Reiko up and cradled her in bent arms. Reiko's body was limp; it reminded me of the poster for *Forbidden Planet* with Robby the robot holding Altaira. Blondie began running, carrying Reiko. The Amazonian transfer clearly had her sights set on the airplane, too, doubtless realizing it would be the quickest way to get the injured Reiko to the dome.

I turned the other way, and Rory finally looked back at me. I pointed emphatically, and he at last started looking in the right spot. Excimer packs don't get warm, so I guess his infrared vision was of no help, but—

Finally! He scooped the pack up and jogged back toward the buggy. Lakshmi had left the battery-compartment door open, but it took Rory a while to get the pack seated properly—one of the leads must have gotten bent. When he finally got it in place, I hit the power switch, and the dashboard indicators came to life. I then put my foot on the accelerator. I didn't want to ram the plane, but I could at least prevent Ernie from immediately taking off. I drove directly into the middle of the bit of open terrain he and I had used as a landing strip. Ernie had finished rotating the airplane to his satisfaction but now saw that I was in his way.

Blondie had covered most of the distance to the plane already, and Lakshmi had arrived at it. Ernie and Lakshmi started arguing, both gesticulating wildly. But the lady *did* have the rifle, and after a moment, he waved a hand resignedly at the cockpit, and she clambered into the rear passenger seat.

Ernie was getting in, too, although that took some doing in his eggplant suit. When he was aboard, the teardrop-shaped canopy slid shut over him and Lakshmi, and he started revving his engines; I could see the turbines spinning to life. I moved the buggy even closer, blocking him in. But he seemed willing to try taking off anyway—and, who knows, carbon nanofibers are pretty much indestructible; maybe the plane *could* survive ramming into the buggy.

The blonde goddess still had a few dozen meters to go. I couldn't imagine all the bouncing up and down was good for Reiko. The transfer bent down and gently laid Reiko on the ground again. She then did precisely what Ernie had done earlier: she grabbed the tip of the port wing and started rotating the airplane, turning it to face some nasty boulders. The two people aboard probably doubled the weight of the craft, but Blondie seemed to have no trouble with the task. Ernie might have thought his plane could take plowing into a buggy, but he had to realize that having a transfer hanging off the wing would screw up the aerodynamics that were already chancy in this meager atmosphere. He cut the engine and, rather than have Blondie rip the canopy open, he cracked the seal himself and let it slide to the rear.

Ernie knew he didn't have to get out—he was the trained pilot, after all—but Lakshmi looked like she wasn't going to budge, either. Blondie had her hands on her hips, annoyed. After about five seconds, she started moving toward the cockpit.

Pickover had now run up to the plane, and was on the opposite side of it from Blondie. Lakshmi's gun couldn't do much against either of their artificial bodies, and she at last seemed to think better of being stubborn; after all, if Pickover grabbed her on the left and Blondie on the right, the two transfers could probably rip her in half. Lakshmi lifted herself up out of the rear passenger seat and dropped to the ground. Blondie gestured for Pickover to come around to her side of the plane, and the two of them gently got Reiko into the vacated passenger seat.

I drove the buggy off to one side, Blondie realigned the airplane with the makeshift runway, Ernie gave a jaunty thumbs-up from the pilot's seat and he set the plane rolling along, the preposterously long wings bouncing up and down a bit as it did so, almost as if they thought flapping might help.

At last, the bird lifted off, climbing into the sky and heading east. I had served as navigator on the way out, but I supposed New Klondike couldn't be that hard to spot from the air, and soon enough Ernie would be able to lock in on the town's homing beacon.

That left two transfers and two biologicals here by the Alpha: Pickover and Blondie from Team Silicon and me and Lakshmi on the Carbon side. While I'd been getting the buggy out of the way, Lakshmi had given up her gun. This time, I think she had simply handed it to Rory rather than have him wrench it from her grip; a writer with a broken wrist was going to have a hard time typing, after all.

Rory then came over to the buggy. He and I exchanged discreet hand signs to agree on a frequency so we could have a private chat; I used the buggy's dashboard radio.

"I guess that's it for me," he said.

"Aren't you coming back to the dome?"

He shook his head. "I won't go back until I need to recharge; there's nothing for me there."

I blew out air. There were things we had to discuss, but this wasn't the time. "Come see me tomorrow, would you?" I said. "Maybe 2:00 p.m. at my office? There are a few, um, interesting developments you should know about."

"Not tomorrow. I'm in the middle of excavating a delicate specimen."

"The day after, then?"

"Fine." And then he walked the dozen or so meters over to Blondie, gave her Lakshmi's gun, and headed off, his back to me, walking slowly toward the northern horizon. I watched him go for a bit, thinking.

But my thoughts were interrupted by Blondie rapping knuckles on the canopy. She had propelled Lakshmi over to the other side of the buggy. I figured now that she was unarmed, I could easily take the writer, if need be. Except of course that I was confined to the interior of this buggy by my lack of a helmet. And, it seemed, Blondie wanted Lakshmi to be confined here, too. She was gesturing for me to open the canopy. I'd be just as happy to leave Lakshmi out here to eventually asphyxiate, but Blondie was pretty much in charge now; she had both guns and could force the canopy open from the outside—which might prevent it from ever sealing properly again. I complied with her wish and swung the transparent cover back. The interior atmosphere escaped. I didn't want to put the sack back on my head—I had my dignity!—and this should only take a second.

The blonde transfer shoved Lakshmi toward the car. Lakshmi glared defiantly for a moment but then acquiesced and pulled herself into the passenger seat. I immediately lowered the canopy and hit the "Pressurize Cabin" button.

"Might as well take off your helmet," I shouted once the interior was filled with air again. "We've got a long ride ahead of us."

Lakshmi made a small nod. She undogged then pulled off her fish-bowl and shook out her glorious hair. She held the helmet firmly on her lap rather than putting it in the little storage space behind her; she clearly didn't trust me not to grab it then crack open the canopy again. Smart girl.

Outside, Blondie slapped a palm against my side of the buggy, urging me to get going. I pressed my foot down, and we began moving forward. The blonde bombshell started running, and I drove behind, letting her set the pace as we headed into the darkness.

FORTY-FOUR

The buggy continued to roll through the night. I looked over at Lakshmi, dimly illuminated by the dashboard. A couple of times her chin dropped toward her chest, but she shook herself awake; she was probably as exhausted as I was but terrified of falling asleep.

"You're going to have plenty of time to sleep, sister," I said. "Icing Diana—that wasn't right."

"I told you before, I didn't kill her," she said, looking at me.

"If you didn't, who did?"

"I don't know. She was dead when I got there."

"I need something better than that. Your phone call from inside Weingarten and O'Reilly's descent stage was overheard by the ship's computer. You said Diana was your insurance policy."

"Exactly!" Lakshmi exclaimed "She was no good to me dead. But, as I said to Reiko in that conversation, if I had Diana alive, I could control you."

"But then you discovered that Diana was planting a bug for me at your place, and so you let her have it."

"I didn't, I swear."

"I don't have a lot of reasons to trust you."

"Maybe not. But look at it this way: if I'm lying, fine—you've got her killer. But if I'm not, then somebody who wanted Diana dead is still out there—and you could be their next target."

"I can take care of myself," I said.

"The way you took care of her?"

That stung, but I refused to let it show. More kilometers passed by.

• • • • • • • • • • • •

At last, we reached the vicinity of the dome. Blondie had effortlessly run the whole way. We headed to the north airlock station, since that was the one Lakshmi had logged the buggy out through, and, sure enough, Ernie's ungainly airplane was parked near there, safe and sound.

Normally, I'd have left the buggy outside, but I still didn't have a helmet, and so I drove it into the airlock tunnel. The outer door closed behind us, and we waited while the tube was brought up to one standard atmosphere; Blondie, meanwhile, went through the personnel airlock, which cycled much more quickly. By the time the door in front of me slid up, she was already on the other side waiting, along with, I was surprised to see, Dougal McCrae.

I swung back the buggy's canopy and clambered out of the vehicle. Mac moved quickly to the passenger side. "Lakshmi Chatterjee?" he said.

"Yes?"

"You're under arrest."

"What for?"

"One of our leading citizens, Mr. Ernest Gargalian, says you pulled a gun on him."

Lakshmi gestured dismissively. "What if I did? If it happened at all, it was outside your jurisdiction."

Mac stood firm. "You'll come with me," he said. I was grinning. Lakshmi probably had thought herself clever buying Huxley's support, but

Ernie could afford to buy himself the top dog. The writer protested a bit more, but there really wasn't anything she could do, and Mac soon had her cuffed. He turned to me. "Alex, I'll expect a full report on everything."

"Of course, Mac. I'll drop by the station later."

"You do that," he said, and he led Lakshmi away—which left just me and Blondie alone here. The gorgeous transfer rushed over to me, and—

Wow!

She threw her arms around me and drew me close, and with that lovely mouth of hers, she planted a long, hard kiss on my lips. There was no doubt I deserved some thanks after all of this, and if this was to be the payment, I couldn't really complain, but—

But the kiss went on and on, and when Blondie finally drew away, a giant grin spread across her stunning features. And now that we were in real air again, she could speak. I didn't recognize the voice at all; it was sultry, sexy, and totally captivating. "Thank you so much!" she said. "As soon as we got close enough to phone, I contacted Ernie. He said Reiko went into surgery hours ago and is already out and in recovery; she's going to be fine." She gave me another kiss on the lips, then added, "Thank you, Alex!"

I noted, in good detective fashion, that she was on a first-name basis with Gargantuan, not to mention with me—but I still had no idea who this blonde goddess was. "You're welcome," I said. "But you have me at a disadvantage, Miss, um . . ."

I'd never seen a transfer's eyes twinkle before, but hers seemed to just then. "Oh, Alex! It's *me.*"

I shook my head slightly, baffled, and she took a half step back to appraise me. "Look at you! You're a mess! Cut, frostbitten, filthy. Go off and get yourself fixed up, get some sleep, and be ready to go by 6:00 p.m."

"Go where?" I said.

"Dinner, silly. You still owe me dinner at Bleaney's."

My jaw dropped, and it was a few moments before I could get it working again. "Diana?"

Her smile was a mile wide. "The one and only."

My heart was pounding, and I'm sure I was grinning, too, but there'd been enough twists and turns in this case that I had to be sure. "Prove it," I said.

"Your left testicle—"

"Fine! Fine. Fine. Diana! But—no, no. I saw your dead body."

"You saw my *discarded* body."

"With a bullet hole in the middle of its forehead."

She waited for me to get it, and I did. "A frame-up," I said. "You were framing Lakshmi for murder." I thought about it. "Her gun, doubtless with her fingerprints, the body at her place—well, at Shopatsky House." I nodded. "But why? And how? You couldn't possibly afford to transfer."

"It pays to have friends in the right places," Diana said.

I'd been aware that she'd been seeing someone else of late, of course, but . . . well, well, well. "I didn't even know you knew Reiko Takahashi."

"Isn't she adorable?" Diana gushed. "I fell for her the first night she came into The Bent Chisel."

"But why frame Lakshmi?"

"She and Reiko were working together at first," Diana said. "You knew that: Reiko willingly loaned Lakshmi her grandfather's diary because Lakshmi supposedly had made a study of the Weingarten and O'Reilly expeditions; if there was a coded reference to the location of the Alpha in the diary, Lakshmi said she'd figure it out and split the riches with Reiko. But Lakshmi wasn't going to do that at all; she had learned where the Alpha was, but kept telling Reiko she didn't know its location—a double-cross. We had to get Lakshmi out of the picture, and, well, we *did* have a spare biological body that we had to dispose of somehow . . ."

"But if Lakshmi knew where the Alpha was, why frame her for murder before you'd found the location?"

"Because, my darling Alex, I knew that *you* knew where it was."

"How?" But then it came to me. "Dirk. The switchblade. You figured if Rory Pickover was back to being my client, I was bound to eventually learn where the Alpha was, and so you arranged for me to acquire something that had a tracking chip in it."

Diana nodded. "Sorry, baby, but, well, it *was* Reiko's rightful claim, not yours and not Dr. Pickover's. Lakshmi was already working with Dirk, and every time you returned to the dome, the tracking chip uploaded its data to the Shopatsky House computer—so Reiko and I took it when we planted the body."

"Clever," I said.

"Yes, but Lakshmi must have been anticipating something, because by the time we got it, she'd wiped the data from the computer. And, of course, by that point you'd figured out about the tracking chip and destroyed it."

"Ah, and so you decided it would be easier to just force Lakshmi to show Reiko where the Alpha was than it would be to get the secret from me—and so you kidnapped her."

"I didn't; Reiko did. But I *did* tail them, running a couple of kilometers behind, just in case Reiko needed help—which, of course, it turned out she did."

My head was spinning. She'd betrayed me, she'd used me, she'd outsmarted me. I took a step back and looked at her, absolutely stunned.

"You . . ." I said, my voice quavering, and I raised my right hand, pointing a finger at her. "You are . . ."

The blue eyes blinked. "Yes?"

"You are *amazing*," I said.

"I am that," she replied, and smiled. "Sorry, honey."

"So what happens now?"

She lifted her blonde eyebrows and grinned lasciviously. "Now? Why, we go to Bleaney's, of course."

"But you don't need to eat."

"No, of course not. But I love to dance."

"And after?"

She indicated her amazing new body with a sweeping motion of her hands. "A night we'll both remember."

FORTY-FIVE

Transfers weren't supposed to die. I'd never heard of a funeral for one, and, anyway, there couldn't be much of a funeral for Rory Pickover here on Mars. Whatever family he had was back on Earth, and he had few friends here. In fact, I think he had only one.

Dougal McCrae had released the dead transfer bodies, including that of the legitimate Rory Pickover, to NewYou. After the bootleg had come to see me at my office, as promised, he and I headed over there. We came through the front door, and that must have triggered a signal, because Horatio Fernandez immediately appeared from the workroom. His eyes went wide the moment he saw the bootleg Pickover. "Joshua!"

I scratched my ear. "Ah, yes. Um, this is going to take a little explaining. This isn't actually Joshua Wilkins. It's a bootleg copy of Dr. Rory Pickover."

"Good God," said Horatio. "Seriously?"

"Yes," I said.

"Then—then where's Joshua?"

"He's dead," I said. "He was mixed up in some bad stuff, and the police fried him with their disruptor."

"My . . . God. Really?"

"Yes," I said. Then: "Is Reiko in?"

"No," replied Horatio. "No, and she won't be coming back. I had to let her go. She was performing unauthorized transfers after hours."

"Transfers, plural?"

"Well, at least one."

"Are you going to bring charges?"

Horatio lifted his massive shoulders. "No cameras upstairs, remember. Hard to make an airtight case against her. And, besides, I've got a business to run. Going after the granddaughter of Denny O'Reilly isn't going to make me popular."

"Ah."

Horatio was looking at the bootleg. "I guess lots of things were going on here that I didn't know about."

"Yeah," I said. "I understand the body of the legitimate Pickover is here?"

"In the back room. Along with *three* bodies that look like Dazzling Don Hutchison, and one that looks like Krikor Ajemian." Horatio shook his head. "I honestly don't know what to do with them all."

Rory spoke for the first time since we'd come into the shop. "May I—can I—have a moment with . . . with the other me?"

Horatio nodded, and he led us into the workroom. Uno, Dos, and Tres—not necessarily in that order—were on their backs on the floor by the far wall. Stuart Berling was up on one worktable, his chest open; fiber-optic cables were running from the cavity to some equipment. And on the other table, the body of Professor Rory Pickover, Ph.D., was lying on his back, face up. His mouth was slightly ajar, revealing a strip of artificial dentition, and his acrylic eyes were open. They weren't staring straight ahead, though. Rather, they were looking to the right, frozen in a sideways glance.

As I've said, it's hard to read a transfer's expression, and so all I could do was guess at what the bootleg Pickover was thinking as he regarded his dead brother. It couldn't have made things any easier that the legitimate Pickover had opted to keep his original face. Oh, he'd had it cleaned up a bit, and he'd taken a lot of the gray out of his hair and had most of the wrinkles erased, but it was still recognizably Rory Pickover, mousy paleontologist.

The bootleg Pickover stood over him, unblinking. I'd have thought blinks were autonomic even for a transfer. Maybe he was trying not to cry—not that he *could*—and that was keeping his eyelids from moving.

"Give us a minute, won't you, Horatio?" I said.

Fernandez nodded and returned to the showroom. When he was gone, the bootleg lifted his head and looked at me, while indicating the dead transfer. "He knew about me, didn't he?"

"He didn't know you were still around, but, yes, he knew you'd been created."

"What did he say about me?"

What the legit Pickover had said was, "If you find another me, erase it. Destroy it. I never want to see the damned thing." Looking now at the bootleg, I found it hard to give voice to those words. "What would you have said in the same position?"

More silence, then the slightest of nods. "I don't blame him."

We stood quietly for a while, then the bootleg Rory said, "Okay. I'm ready."

We went back into the showroom. Horatio was at his cash station. We approached him and when he looked up, I said, "I ask for *fal-tor-pan,* the refusion."

If it had been my fellow old-movie-buff Lakshmi, I might have gotten the response, "What you seek has not been done since ages past—and then, only in legend." But all Horatio managed was, "Excuse me?"

"Let's go upstairs."

At least that generated a smile from Horatio. "I thought you'd never ask." He headed for the staircase, and I followed, with the bootleg Pickover making up the rear. Once upstairs, I pointed at the scanning room, Horatio opened the door, and we all went in. "You said there were no security cameras up here," I said. "Was that the truth?"

Horatio nodded.

"Good," I said. "We want you to open up this bootleg's skull, take out the artificial brain, and transplant it into the legitimate Rory's body."

Horatio looked stunned for a moment, but then he slowly nodded. "Yes, I guess—yes, I can do that. Of course, there are a bunch of systems in the body that will have to be recalibrated, but—"

"Whatever it takes," I said. "Do it."

"But . . . but Pickover is officially dead now."

"Only the cops know that—the cops and you. It does your business no good to have word getting spread around that transfers aren't in fact immortal, so I know you'll keep your trap shut. And the cops are in Ernie Gargalian's back pocket—or, at least the top cop is. Ernie owes me a favor; he'll get the report about Pickover to disappear."

We went back down to the workroom. Horatio and I moved Stuart Berling's dead husk to the floor to clear a worktable, then Horatio set about examining the corpse of the legitimate Pickover.

Soon enough, the top was off the legit Pickover's head, and Horatio removed the disruptor-fried and slightly squished brain. Apparently a transfer brain was normally spherical, rather than the, well, brain shape of a biological brain. It was about the size of a softball, but was teal in color and seemed completely rigid. At the bottom was a complex connector that I guess plugged into the artificial spinal cord. Horatio put that dead brain on the tabletop, the spine-plug keeping it from rolling away, and then he took a moment to hammer out the dents in the metal skull.

When he was satisfied, he turned to the bootleg Rory and said, "Okay, take your shirt off and have a seat on the edge of this table."

The bootleg unbuttoned and removed his khaki work shirt, then boosted himself up. I couldn't see any jack on Pickover's side, but Horatio managed to attach a fiber-optic cable terminating in a metal plug there, ninety degrees to the right of his plastic belly button; maybe it clamped on magnetically. "All right," he said. "First things first. I'm going to dial down your pain response."

"You can do that?" Rory replied. "Where were you when I needed you?"

Horatio, I'm sure, didn't understand, but he smiled anyway and turned to a control console. "Okay. That should do it; this shouldn't hurt. Tell me if it does." He picked up a laser cutter and sliced through the plastiskin above the bootleg's eyebrows; there was indeed no sign of discomfort from Rory. Horatio continued right around the head. The incision separated, just like a cut in real flesh would, but there was no blood. The metal skull it revealed had a seam around it, not unlike the ones you sometimes saw on anatomy-class skeletons.

It was strange watching surgery with the surgeon using bare hands and not wearing a facemask. The top of the skull came neatly off after Horatio did something to unseat it, and he placed it upside down on the table—a titanium cranium covered with artificial hair; it looked like half of a bionic coconut.

"Wait," said Pickover. "Give me a second." He tilted his head down—and I was afraid his teal brain might roll out of his skull as he did so, but it seemed to still be firmly attached. I guess he just wanted one last look at this body. I knew how he felt. Every time I'd left an apartment for the last time, I'd had one final look around, committing the place to memory—and saying my farewell.

"Okay," Rory said softly. "I'm ready."

Horatio made a couple more adjustments on his console then he placed his hand on the top of the brain and gave it a quarter twist, which disengaged it. He then pulled it up and out, and moved over to the other worktable, where the corpse of the legitimate Dr. Pickover was still lying on its back. There must have been an orientation mark on the brain that I couldn't see, because he rotated it until he had it facing a particular way. And then he placed it in the vacant skull, gave it a ninety-degree twist, and—

And the transfer's eyes, which had been stuck looking askance, shifted left and right a few times, taking in the scene, and then the mouth opened all the way, and the only remaining Dr. Rory Pickover in all the world said, in his inimitable fashion, "Thanks so much, old chap!"

I imagine the first time you transferred from a biological existence to an electronic one there was some disorientation. But Pickover was already used to what it was like to be a transfer, and he seemed comfortable. He sat up with ease, swinging his legs over the edge of the table.

"Your arms are four centimeters longer in this body," Horatio said, "so pay attention for a day or two while you reach for things. Oh, and you'll have to relearn how to activate your telescopic and infrared vision. These eyes are from a different manufacturer and operate slightly differently."

Pickover nodded—effortlessly, it seemed. And then he tipped his head down and looked at the back of his hand; I guess he figured he should get to know it. "The colors are a bit different," Rory said, looking up. "Your skin, Alex's hair."

"Oh?" said Fernandez.

"They're all a little more . . . golden."

"We can adjust that easily enough."

"It's kind of nice, actually." He brought his hands up and patted his chest. I thought he was exploring his body, but that wasn't it. "And it's so good to be wearing my own clothes again!" When he'd died, the legitimate Pickover had been wearing a dark blue work shirt with a silhouette of a dinosaur on one of the pockets.

Fernandez picked up the top of the skull and set about reattaching it. While he was doing that, I said, "Now, there's just one more task." I jerked my thumb at the empty form on the other table. "The world thinks that's Joshua Wilkins, who, of course, has really been dead for months. We've got to dispose of the corpse."

"I—he—was supposed to be hunting fossils," offered Pickover, as Horatio used a tool to lay down new plastiskin, sealing the skullcap in place. "You could just dump the body out on the planitia—make it look like he malfunctioned and expired out there."

"No," said Horatio, stopping in his work. "Absolutely not."

I looked at him.

"I've got a business to run here," he said, "and, like you said, it's based on the notion that I'm selling immortality—or, at the very least, durability. It can't be that his body just failed—not under anything approaching normal circumstances. You owe me that much."

"Okay," I said. "We'll find another way."

FORTY-SIX

Rory wanted to go home, and I could hardly blame him for being anxious to finally get there. After all, this version of him hadn't been to his own place since he'd been created. He had woken up in a primitive robotic body, had endured torture aboard the *Skookum Jim*, had upgraded that body to assume the identity of Joshua Wilkins, and had retreated for the past couple of months out onto the planitia to look for fossils, all without ever once seeing his own place. And so we parted company at NewYou. I headed to Gully's for a workout, then went to my apartment—and slept clear through to 10:00 a.m. the next morning.

When I awoke, there was voice mail from Ernie Gargalian, requesting my presence for a noon meeting at Ye Olde Fossil Shoppe.

I got there bang on time; one doesn't keep Mars's Mister Big waiting. I was surprised to find two other people already inside: Reiko Takahashi and Dr. Rory Pickover. Reiko was leaning against one of the display tables but looked no worse for wear; Ernie, of course, had gotten her the best medical treatment when his plane had arrived back at the dome—no Windermere Clinic butchery for Denny O'Reilly's granddaughter.

"Ah, Alex, my dear boy, good to see you!" Ernie said. "Come in, come in!" He gestured expansively. "Can I get you something? I have a hundred-year-old Scotch you might like."

"Maybe later," I replied.

"Later," agreed Ernie. "Yes, yes—propriety, my boy! One doesn't start business with alcohol; one concludes it. We'll save it for a toast."

Ernie's showroom didn't have any seats in it, but he led us to his opulent office, a room I'd never been in before. It had three wine red chairs that I imagined were upholstered with real leather. Ernie took the one behind the wide, ornately carved desk. Reiko took another, crossing her lovely legs. I took the final one. Rory, of course, could stand comfortably for hours.

"Alex, you've created a problem for me," Ernie said, "and we need to sort it out."

"A problem?" I repeated.

"Yes, my boy, yes. You've led me to the promised land; you've shown me Denny and Simon's mother lode. Riches beyond imagining, one might think."

"And that's a problem how?"

"Back on Earth," Ernie said, pointing vaguely at the sky, "they synthesize gold, they manufacture diamonds, they replicate rubies. Those things have no value—virtually no material object does. But actual fossils of extraterrestrial life—ah, *those* collectors will pay dearly for! And why, my dear Alex, why?"

"Their provenance," I said.

Ernie's fat face exploded in laughter. He looked at Pickover. "Did you hear him, my good professor? 'Provenance,' he said. Such a highfalutin word for him to know!" He turned his attention back to me. "Yes, absolutely—the fact that they're demonstrably genuine, that they haven't been synthesized or replicated, yes, indeed, my boy, that's one reason they're so valuable. But there's another criterion. After all, you can't make any money selling genuine moon rocks anymore, even though their provenance is easy to establish; it's hard to even give them away. But in days of yore, they used to be the most valuable stones on Earth. And do you know why that was?"

I had an idea, but you learn more by letting people tell stories their way rather than trying to beat them to the punch. "No."

"Because between 1972, when the last *Apollo* astronaut walked on the moon, until humans finally returned there, there were only 382 kilograms of moon rocks on Earth. Scarcity, my boy! Supply and demand! There were *tons* of diamonds then, but—well, my lad, I'll say it because I know you're thinking it! You know that surface suit of mine? The purple one? You could fit *all* the *Apollo* booty into it. And so of course those stones were highly valued."

"Right," I said. "Okay."

"But it's *not* okay, dear Alex. Not at all. I now know where a huge cache of wonderfully preserved Martian fossils is located—the best of the best, and not just quality, but quantity! I simply can't reveal that fact to the public. Oh, if I started selling a lot of material from there, yes, for a short time, I might realize spectacular prices, but soon Alpha fossils would be ubiquitous, and not just directly via me but on the secondary market, too. Alphas will be a drug on the market—everybody selling alphas; there will be alphas everywhere."

"So what are you going to do?" I asked.

Ernie smiled, his grapefruit cheeks moving up as he did so. "That's the question! And the answer is this, my boy: we're going to *curate* the Alpha. Dr. Pickover here will get to select the specimens to work on, studying them, scanning them, learning from them, describing them for science. He works at a slow pace; I know that, and that's fine. And when he's finally done with each specimen, he'll release it to me, and I will bring it to market; we'll find an appreciative buyer. And Miss Takahashi, here, the descendant of my dear old friend Denny, will share in the profits; I will send her a cut from every sale."

"But . . . but that could take years."

"By Gad, Alex, yes, it might! But so what? We not only live in an age of material abundance, my boy, we live in an age of immortality! Dr. Pickover has already made the transition, and surely none of the rest of us intend to ultimately join his fossils in the ground! I'm the oldest one in this room by a good piece, but I've just barely begun my life! And, as any good businessperson knows, an asset that pays steady dividends over time is far more valuable than one consumed quickly."

I looked up at Pickover. "And you're okay with this, Rory?"

Rory shrugged a bit. "It's not ideal; not even close. But I've got the site map that Weingarten and O'Reilly made, and Ernie here has been plugged into the black market for fossils since the very beginning; he's going to help me locate the collectors who have those old specimens. Now that Willem Van Dyke is gone, Ernie is just about the only lead I have for ever getting access to those fossils and describing them in the scientific literature. And I *do* get to scan and describe every new specimen that's excavated."

I turned to Reiko Takahashi. "And what about you? This works for you?"

She nodded her lovely head. "It'll do."

"But what about Lakshmi?" I said. "She knows where the Alpha is, too."

"My dear boy, please don't worry about that. She's no longer a problem."

"She's going back to Earth?" I asked.

Ernie's eyebrows climbed toward his slicked-back hair. "So unfortunate. She really shouldn't have resisted arrest."

I frowned; she hadn't.

"Of course, the *body* will be shipped back," he said. He tilted his fat head. "I hear our next writer-in-residence will be a playwright."

I looked over at Pickover, but it *was* hard to read a transfer's expression.

"And so that just leaves you, Mr. Double-X." Ernie shook his massive head. "I knew Stuart Berling, as you know—he was selling his fossils through me. Found some fabulous specimens not that long ago, and they made him a rich man, but he couldn't bring himself to return to Earth—that nasty business aboard the *B. Traven* had scarred him for life. And you're in much the same situation, aren't you, my boy? Berling couldn't return to Earth and neither can you; his reasons were psychological and yours are legal, but the effect is the same, isn't it?"

I crossed my arms in front of my chest. "And your point is?"

"My point is that for all this to work, the Alpha will still need protection—and nothing so clumsy as land mines. It will need someone to look after it. And that someone can be you. Insane wealth will do you no good, not here, not on Mars, but you'll make enough to have your life-support tax always paid, and your tab at The Bent Chisel always settled, and, when the time comes, you'll be able to afford to have yourself transferred into the finest of bodies." He raised a beefy hand. "It won't be full-time work, of course; you'll still have plenty of opportunities to ply your usual trade. But it will keep you nicely in the black for many mears to come."

"And you think that'll be enough for me?" I asked.

"My dear Mr. Double-X, I would not presume to speak for you. But it strikes me as win-win all around. What do you say?"

I thought about the four fossil slabs I'd jackhammered out of the Alpha and then hidden outside the dome. But my own little pieces of the stuff that dreams are made of had waited billions of years—they could wait a while longer . . . perhaps, even, until the day when I might be able to go back home.

And so I looked at each of the faces in turn: at the broad countenance of Gargantuan Gargalian, who had always known how to get what he wanted; at the exquisite, delicate features of Reiko Takahashi, who had perhaps gotten what I had wanted; and at the inquisitive visage of Rory

Pickover, who would walk naked into a live volcano if he thought he could learn something that no other man knew.

I turned back to Ernie. "I want my own Mars buggy. My own surface suit."

"Of course," said Ernie. "Consider it done."

"And I need a new gun."

"Naturally."

"And my own broadband disruptor."

Ernie laughed heartily. "Alex, my boy, that's thinking ahead, by Gad, it is. Yes, certainly, we'll get you one of those, too."

"All right," I said, nodding slowly. "We'll drink on it. Get that Scotch."

• • • • • • • • • • •

Because of speed-of-light delays, it's impossible to interact in real time with people on Earth. You can't chat with them by video; you can't speak with them on the phone; you can't swap instant messages. And so I hadn't spoken to Wanda—really spoken to her—in the ten years I'd been on Mars.

I didn't regret my choice, I didn't regret it at all. Wanda had done the only thing she *could* do. That abusing bastard had to be stopped, and she had stopped him, simply, cleanly, and for all time. But when you love someone, you look after them—and I looked after her. I took the rap for her, and, rather than face decades in jail, I escaped to a sealed dome on a red, barren rock; sometimes, it was hard to tell the difference.

Despite everything that had gone down these last few days, a man needs routines in his life, he needs order, he needs something to hold on to. Every week—every seven Earth days—I would record a video message for Wanda and pay to have it transmitted to Earth: Howard Slapcoff got his fee whether you were coming or going, whether you were living or dying, or whether you were just one of the living dead. I always found it awkward making the videos; it wasn't like me to talk about what was going on in my life. But a few days after she received mine, she'd send one of her own in reply, and when I got those, when I saw how happy she was, how at peace, how full of joy, it made everything worthwhile; it made me, at least for a time, feel alive.

And so I sat in the chair in my office, the wallpaper displaying the alternating green and caramel stripes of our house from all those years ago, and I straightened my collar, patted down my hair, cleared my throat, activated my camera, and spoke to it. "Hello, sis . . ."

FORTY-SEVEN

Diana, with her gorgeous new body, drove by my place to pick me up in Juan's buggy.

"How'd seeing Juan go?" I asked.

She smiled, and although it wasn't the smile of hers I was used to, it was still very pleasant. "He's such a sweetheart," she said. "He was so relieved that I was still alive."

"I bet."

"But—funny. I knew he liked me; I mean—come on—it was painfully obvious. But he didn't look at me the same way this time. I know I'm ten times better-looking now than I was before, but . . ." She shrugged a little. "Maybe there *is* something to be said for people who like you just the way you are . . . or were."

"Maybe," I said softly.

We drove to NewYou and collected the dead transfer body that had housed the bootleg Rory. Horatio Fernandez, per my instructions, had put the fried brain of the legitimate Pickover into the empty skull. In good mobster fashion, Diana and I stuffed the cybercorpse into the trunk. We then headed to the western airlock and drove through the tunnel there and out onto the surface.

I'd said before that newcomers to Mars sometimes hurt themselves because they feel invincible in the low gravity. I imagined something similar could happen with transfers: the combination of enhanced strength and feeble gravity makes them feel like comic-book superheroes. And Joshua Wilkins—poor, grieving Joshua Wilkins, who had recently lost his doting wife Cassandra—would quite plausibly have felt more reckless than most.

There were amazing places on Mars, and if a tourist industry ever develops here, I'm sure the brochures will feature Valles Marineris and Olympus Mons—respectively, the solar system's longest canyon and its largest volcano. Either of those would have done well for our purpose, but unfortunately they were both clear around the globe from Isidis Planitia. But Rory—who, of course, knew his geology—suggested a suitable spot closer to home. There was a dried lava flow extending thirteen kilometers from a mountain peak in Nili Patera. The sides of the flow were steep, and in some places featured an eighty-meter sheer drop.

Diana and I had brought along some climbing gear—carbon-fiber rope, a piton gun, and so forth—to make it look like old Joshua-never-Josh had decided to try his luck rappelling down the lava flow. We found the steepest edge we could along its length, opened the trunk, and carried the body to the precipice. I took one leg, Diana took the other, and we dangled it headfirst over the edge. "Count of three," I said. "One, two, three."

We let it go and watched it fall in that wonderful Martian slow motion, down, down, down, descending a height equal to that of a twenty-seven-story office tower. Mars, being Mars, served up a Wile E. Coyote falling-off-the-cliff-style puff of dust when the body hit.

It might be years or mears, or decades or mecades, until the body was found, but, when it was, I'm sure the coroner's report will read "death by misadventure." If my time ever comes, I'd like the same thing, I think—

beats all hell out of being gunned down by an ex-wife, strangled by a creditor, or knifed by a disgruntled client.

The trip back to the dome took the better part of a day, and that gave Diana and me plenty of time to talk. And, after several hours, with the sun low behind us and the sky ahead purpling, I decided to pop the question—the one that had been swirling at the back of my mind ever since I discovered that she was still alive. But getting to it required some setup, so, as we continued east, I said, "I think it's time to change things around a little."

"Oh?" replied Diana, turning her lovely head to look at me.

"Yeah. I'm tired of being the only private detective on Mars."

"What would you do instead?"

"No, no, no. I'm not talking about quitting. I love my work; to quote one of my predecessors, this is my métier. But I'm thinking about taking on a partner."

"Maybe Dougal McCrae would like to join you," Diana offered. "I imagine he gets tired of all the paperwork that goes with being a cop."

"No, not him." I took one hand off the steering wheel and swept it back and forth in front of me, as if indicating lines of text. "Can't you just see it? Light streaming through a window with two names painted on it, and the names visible as shadows on the floor: 'Lomax and Connally, Private Investigators.'"

She looked surprised, but whether at the vocational suggestion or at the discovery that I knew her last name, I wasn't sure.

"Well?" I said. "You certainly can't keep working at The Bent Chisel. No one wants to be served booze by a transfer; it's like having a Mormon bartender—the vibe is all wrong. And, sure, I know you don't need to pay the life-support tax anymore, but surely you still want to make some money."

She looked at me with lustrous acrylic eyes, and her voice was soft. "Oh, Alex . . ."

"Yes?"

"Alex, baby, don't you get it? I transferred for a reason."

"Of course. Immortality. Eternal youth."

"Not that; none of that matters to me. But, honey, I've been here twelve years, and, unlike you, I haven't been going to the gym. I wanted strength."

"You've certainly got that," I said. "That's one of the reasons you'd make a great partner."

She shook her head gently, the blonde hair glistening as she did so. "Stop for a second."

I did, and she turned around in her seat and pointed through the clear canopy. At first I thought she was referring to the body we'd disposed of—as if *that* was an impediment to being a private eye—but then I realized she was indicating the evening star, a sapphire glowing low in the western sky.

"Earth?" I said.

"Earth. I'm going home, and I'll weigh three times there what I weighed here. I could never have managed it in my old body. But in *this* body, I'll do just fine."

"But what's Earth got that Mars doesn't?"

The question was facetious, of course; the list was almost endless. But, still, her answer surprised me. "Reiko."

"She's here."

"For now. But she wants to go home; she never intended to settle here permanently—and, frankly, neither did I; it just sort of happened. Reiko and I are booked on the return flight of the *Kathryn Denning.*"

"But Reiko's still biological, no? And she'll weigh three times as much there, too."

"Sure. But she's only been on Mars for a couple of months, and she's been working out. She'll have no trouble readjusting to a full gee."

"I've never seen her at Gully's."

"That dump? Alex, she works out at the Amsterdam."

"I'm going to miss you," I said.

"Come see me. Surely that's why *you've* been working out, right? So you could go home someday?"

"Someday," I said quietly. "Maybe." I looked again at the blue planet, slowly setting behind us, then turned and started the buggy up. We drove in silence for the next hour or more, and when we did start talking again, it was about nothing of consequence.

Finally, we made it back to the New Klondike dome. We parked Juan's buggy, and I returned my rented surface suit, and, of course, I escorted Diana back to her place; it was, after all, almost 4:00 a.m.—although, realistically, she was in a better position now to protect me than I was to protect her. I wondered if she was going to invite me to spend what little was left of the night, but, as we headed up the rickety stairs to her apartment, she said, "Reiko's staying over, although I'm sure she's sound asleep by now."

I nodded, accepting that.

"But if you can wait for just a minute . . ." She unlocked her door and went in without turning on the lights; perhaps she was using infrared vision to do whatever she wanted to do. She came out again carrying a plain white bag, and she moved in and gave me a hug—a gentle one, as if she still wasn't sure of her own strength. "It's been fun, Alex."

She then reached into the white bag and pulled out another bag, one with a shiny rainbow-sheen finish and U-shaped handles secured by a red satiny ribbon. "I got you a little gift," she said. "Something to remember me by." She handed it to me. "Go ahead. Open it."

I was no better with the knot in the ribbon than Dr. Pickover had been with the knot in Lakshmi's lasso. Diana, who had longer fingernails, laughed a little and took the package back briefly to undo the bow. She then handed it to me, and I opened up the bag and pulled out its contents—a crisp gray fedora.

"Now you've got a real hat to tip at people," she said.

I picked it up by the crown and positioned it carefully on the top of my head. The fit was perfect. I lifted it and gave its inaugural tip to Diana.

"Thank you, sweetheart," I said, and I leaned in and kissed her on the lips one last time.

"My pleasure," Diana replied. "Take care of yourself, won't you, Alex?"

"Always have," I said. "Always will."

I walked down the stairs and out into the lonely night.

ABOUT THE AUTHOR

Robert J. Sawyer's novel *FlashForward* was the basis for the ABC TV series of the same name, and he was a scriptwriter for that program.

Rob is a lifelong space buff. In 2007, he participated in the invitation-only workshop The Future of Intelligence in the Cosmos at the NASA Ames Research Center. In 2010 and again in 2012, he was the only science-fiction writer invited to speak at the SETI Institute's first two SETIcon conferences on the search for extraterrestrial intelligence. In 2011, he became an invited contributor to the 100 Year Starship initiative, sponsored by the US Defense Advanced Research Projects Agency (DARPA). A thirty-year member of the Royal Astronomical Society of Canada, a member of both The Planetary Society and The Mars Society, and a graduate of the NASA-sponsored Launch Pad Astronomy Workshop, Rob has published in *Archaeology, Nature, Science,* and *Sky & Telescope,* and has done science commentary on-air for both the CBC and the BBC.

Rob is one of only eight writers ever to win all three of the world's top awards for best science-fiction novel of the year: the Hugo (which he won in 2003 for *Hominids),* the Nebula (which he won in 1996 for *The Terminal Experiment),* and the John W. Campbell Memorial Award (which he won in 2006 for *Mindscan).* According to *The Locus Index to Science Fiction Awards,* he has won more awards for his novels than anyone else in the history of the science-fiction and fantasy fields.

He's also won an Arthur Ellis Award from Crime Writers of Canada, and *The Globe and Mail: Canada's National Newspaper* named his previous SF/mystery crossover *Illegal Alien* "the best Canadian mystery novel of the year."

Rob hosts the Canadian skeptical television series *Supernatural Investigator.* He has been writer-in-residence at The Merril Collection of Science Fiction, Speculation and Fantasy in Toronto; at the Canadian Light Source, Canada's national synchrotron research facility, in Saskatoon (a position created specifically for him); and at Berton House in Dawson City.

Rob has received an honorary doctorate from Laurentian University and the Alumni Award of Distinction from Ryerson University, and he was the first-ever recipient of Humanist Canada's Humanism in the Arts Award. *Quill & Quire,* the Canadian publishing trade journal, calls him "one of the thirty most influential, innovative, and just plain powerful people in Canadian publishing." His website and blog are at **sfwriter.com**, and on Twitter and Facebook he's **RobertJSawyer**.

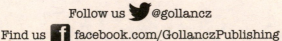

Conveyancing

Priscilla Sarton
LL.M
Principal Lecturer in Law
at the College of Law

Law series editor: Marise Cremona
Senior Fellow, Centre for Commercial Law Studies
Queen Mary and Westfield College
University of London

Second Edition

MACMILLAN

First published 1991 by
THE MACMILLAN PRESS LTD
Houndmills, Basingstoke, Hampshire RG21 2XS
and London
Companies and representatives
throughout the world

ISBN 0–333–59374–X

A catalogue record for this book is available
from the British Library.

First edition reprinted twice
Second edition 1993
10 9 8 7 6 5 4 3 2
02 01 00 99 98 97 96 95 94

Printed in Great Britain by
Mackays of Chatham PLC
Chatham, Kent

Contents

Preface

It has been surprisingly difficult when writing this book to decide on the correct words to use. A professional conveyancer can be either female or male, and to add to the complexity of the matter, either a solicitor or a licensed conveyancer.

There has been no wish to imply that every legal adviser is a male solicitor, but the pressing need for brevity has meant that 'he' has had to be used for both sexes and 'solicitor' for both professions. It is hoped that readers will not take offence. Another difficulty has been the replacement of the traditional words 'vendor' and 'purchaser' by the modern 'seller' and 'buyer' in the new form of contract for sale. 'Seller' is used throughout this book, but the word 'purchaser' is not so easily displaced, as in the context of the Land Registration Act 1925, the Land Charges Act 1972 and other property legislation, 'purchaser' has a technical meaning that 'buyer' does not. The choice was either to use 'purchaser' in some chapters and 'buyer' in others, or stick consistently to 'purchaser'. The second course has been chosen.

The Law Society has helpfully given permission for the use of questions from its past examination papers. The answers are the author's, and are in no way connected with the Society. Thanks are due to the Law Society and the Solicitors' Law Stationery Society Ltd for their permission to reproduce the protocol documentation, including the form of contract for sale, and to the Law Society for its permission to quote from its 'Introduction to the Protocol'.

The book is dedicated to Mark Sarton, for without him it would never have been written, yet he has suffered so much through its writing.

PRISCILLA SARTON

Table of Cases

Table of Statutes

Table of Statutory Instruments

1 Stages in a Conveyancing Transaction from the Seller's Point of View

1.1 Introduction

This chapter introduces you to the stages of a conveyancing transaction from the point of view of the seller's solicitor. It does not attempt to set out everything that needs to be done, but does detail the major steps and serves to put the other chapters into context.

At one time, this would have been an easy chapter to write, for a transaction trod a stately measure, the order of the steps never varying. Searches were always made by the purchaser, and title deduced and investigated after the contract for sale was made. In recent years things have changed. Sellers now sometimes do things traditionally done by purchasers. Things are now done pre-contract that used to be done post-contract. In the last two years there have been two editions of the Standard Conditions of Sale. We live in exciting times.

In March 1990 the Law Society introduced the National Protocol for the sale of domestic freehold and leasehold property. The protocol sets out procedures which the Society recommends all solicitors to use. The purpose is to speed the transaction through, and particularly to reduce the time lag between the parties coming to an agreement and the formation of the actual contract. Use of the protocol also involves the use of standardised documentation, namely a form of agreement for sale, property information forms and a 'fixtures, fittings and contents' form.

The protocol relates only to domestic transactions and even then it is not compulsory for a solicitor to use it, but its use is described by the Law Society as 'preferred practice'. It does anyway reflect procedures that were already becoming fairly widespread. Every solicitor acting in a domestic transaction should notify the solicitor on the other side whether or not the protocol will be used. Once the protocol has been adopted for that transaction it must be followed, except that a solicitor may depart from it provided that he gives notice to the other side of his decision to do so. The protocol only governs procedures between the two solicitors. It does not affect matters between the solicitor and his client, or third parties such as mortgagees. It is anticipated that the protocol will also be used between solicitors and licensed conveyancers.

It is stressed again that a solicitor who uses the protocol might find himself doing little different from what he would have done anyway. The only departures from his previous practice might be the use of the standardised forms, and the amount of documentation (what the protocol calls 'the package') supplied to the purchaser's solicitor before the contract. Nor is the protocol designed to be an exhaustive list of steps to be taken, and the Law Society in its introduction to the protocol states that 'at all stages the solicitor's professional skills, knowledge and judgement will need to be applied in just the same way as it has been in the past'.

This chapter describes a protocol transaction, but also attempts to explain how the transaction would proceed if it were not governed by the protocol. Exclusive attention to the protocol is discouraged by the fact that it is not exhaustive as to what steps must be taken, and that the Law Society states that the protocol is 'evolutionary', that 'some changes might be necessary', and that the Society is receptive to 'constructive criticism'.

1.2 Your Client

Imagine that Robert Oates is planning to sell his present home. The house is freehold and is mortgaged to the Potteries Bank plc. He is also planning to instruct you to act for him. In what it calls the first step, the protocol suggests that Robert should call on you as soon as he decides to put his home on the market, so that you can immediately start to put together the pre-contract 'package'. It can then be sent without delay to the prospective purchaser as soon as he is found.

You probably have only a slender hope of Robert coming to you at this stage. The first person Robert will approach is the estate agent, and he will not approach you until the prospective purchaser is actually found. When this happens Robert will instruct you to act for him.

1.3 Gathering Information

(*a*) *General*

Your first task is to gather information. You need this in order to draft the contract. You also need it to complete the Seller's Property Information Form which you will be sending to the purchaser's solicitor. This form is in the Appendix to this book. Read it, and you will know the sort of information you need to collect.

This gathering of information is what the protocol calls 'preparing the package: assembling the information' (the 'package' being the documents that you will send as soon as possible to the purchaser's solicitor). It is nothing new; a seller's solicitor has always needed this information. The sources of information include your client, possibly the estate agent, and the documents of title. So imagine you have Robert sitting in your office.

(*b*) *Interview with Client – Gathering Information about His Title*

(i) You must ask your client where his title deeds or land certificate are as you need to investigate his title in order to draft the contract. The deeds might be in the possession of your client, but if the house is mortgaged, the lender will have them. Robert's deeds are with the Potteries Bank, his mortgagee. The Bank may, when it learns of the proposed sale, be prepared to instruct you to act for it in the redemption of the mortgage. It will then send you the original deeds or, in the case of registered title, the charge certificate. The Bank will expect an undertaking from you to the effect that you hold the deeds on its behalf, and if the sale falls through, will return the deeds in the same condition as they were when you received them.

If the Bank will not be instructing you, then it may be reluctant to let you have the originals. If the title is unregistered, the Bank will send you an abstract or epitome of the deeds.

If the title is registered, you only need to be given the title number of the property. You can then obtain an office copy of the entries on the register and of the filed plan from the District Land Registry. (Note that it is always possible for you to discover if a title is registered, and the title number, by making a search in the public index map at the District Land Registry. See Chapter 5; 2 (d).

(ii) Ask Robert if his neighbours have any sort of rights over his property, such as a right-of-way. The point is that easements do not always appear on the deeds or on the register of title. They may have arisen from long use. (If a house is one of a terrace there is often a right-of-way for each owner over the backyards of the houses, for access to a side entrance.) Similarly, does your client exercise rights over a neighbour's property? Does he obtain his gas, electricity, water, etc., directly from the public road, or across a neighbour's property?

If the last-mentioned, you have to find out if the pipes, etc., are there merely by the permission of the neighbour, or if Robert has easements over the neighbour's land (see question 5 on the property information form).

(iii) Does Robert live in the house with his wife? If so, is she a co-owner? Has she agreed to the sale? (If the answer to these questions is 'yes' you need instructions from her (see Chapter 11).

(iv) Could anyone else have a claim to own part of the house? For example, did anyone contribute to the original purchase price with the intention of owning a share? If the answer is 'yes', it will affect the provisions put in the contract, (see Chapter 11) and the answer to question 8 on the property information form.

(*c*) *Interview with Client: Completing the Property Information Form*

The property information form has to be completed partly by the seller and partly by you on the basis of information supplied by your client. You can go through the form with him now. Alternatively, you can give Robert the form to take away with him to complete at home.

(*d*) *Interview with Client: Completing the Fixtures, Fittings and Contents Form*

This form (which is part of the protocol documentation) lists most of the items likely to be found in an average house and about which there could possibly be an argument as to whether or not they are included in the sale. The items range from aerials to door-knockers. You may hand this form to Robert at the interview, but you will doubtless ask him to complete it at home. He will have to indicate which of the items are to be sold with the house.

(*e*) *Interview with Client: His Financial Position*

What is your client's financial position? The mortgage to the Bank must be redeemed. The Bank should be asked for a redemption figure, on the basis that completion will take place in, say, six weeks time.

Ask Robert if there is a second mortgage. He may have borrowed money some time ago, signed a paper and not realised its significance.

If Robert's title is unregistered, a second mortgage may be revealed by a search against his name at the Land Charges Registry, where it would be registered as a CI or CIII land charge. If his title is registered, a search at HM District Land Registry may reveal a registered charge or an entry protecting an informal mortgage.

Robert, by virtue of an express or implied condition in the contract, will be promising that all mortgages will be redeemed. You need to check that the purchase price will be sufficient to discharge all the mortgages. If it is not, then he will have to find other funds with which to redeem them, or abandon the idea of selling the house. Usually, if your client is selling his house, he will be buying a new one. An example of the calculation of a client's financial position in such circumstances is given in Chapter 17.

(*f*) *Your Charges*

Robert may ask you for an estimate of your charges for acting for him in the sale. You must calculate the disbursements that you will have to make, and your fees. You might wish to make it clear that you are giving an estimate only, and that you are not bound to the figure quoted. Nevertheless, any estimate must be realistic, based on a knowledge of the details of the transaction, and include all disbursements, e.g. stamp duty and VAT. No client will be favourably impressed if the quoted figure is greatly exceeded. If you offer a fixed charge, the prospective client should be told the length of time the offer will remain valid.

The Law Society recommends that any indication of charges should be either given, or confirmed, in writing, and has drawn up a form (the domestic conveyancing charges form) to be completed and given to the client. The use of this form is optional.

1.4 Preparing the Package

If the seller's solicitor is following the protocol he must now assemble a package of documents to be sent to the purchaser's solicitor. For a freehold property this involves:

1. Making what are called the pre-contract searches and enquiries. Traditionally these are made by the purchaser's solicitor, but it may save time if they are made instead by the seller's solicitor as soon as he is instructed by his client to act in the transaction. The results are forwarded to the other side. These searches are discussed in greater detail in Chapter 6.
2. In the case of an unregistered title, making a land-charges search against the name of the seller and any previous estate owners whose names are not already covered by a satisfactory search certificate. (see Chapters 4 and 9). Apart from the protocol, it is always sensible for a seller's solicitor to make this search before drafting the contract, as without it he cannot be sure that he has full knowledge of his client's title (see the workshop section of Chapter 5).
3. In the case of an unregistered title, preparing an epitome of title, and where possible, marking copies of all deeds that will not be given to the purchaser on completion as having been examined against the originals. (see Chapter 8).
4. If the title is registered, obtaining office copy entries of the register, and of copy documents filed at the registry.

   (Items 3 and 4 mean that the purchaser is at this stage being given evidence of the seller's ownership of the property – see later).

The package to be sent to the purchaser on the sale of a freehold consists of:

(a) the draft contract,
(b) the office copy entries or the epitome of title,
(c) the results of the pre-contract searches,
(d) a completed property information form,
(e) the completed fixtures, fittings and contents form.

(For the sale of a leasehold see Chapter 15.)

1.5 Drafting the Contract

When you have seen your client and obtained either the deeds or an up-to-date office copy of the entries on the register of title, you should be able to draft the contract. The essential thing is that you do not allow your client to enter into a contract which he has no hope of fulfilling. Remember that it is essential that you thoroughly investigate your client's title. Your investigation must be every bit as thorough as if you were buying, rather than selling, on his behalf. The contract will contain express or implied promises as to the title, and if you find that your client cannot live up to these promises, because there is something wrong with his title, the promises must be altered.

The contract is prepared in duplicate, usually on a standard printed form (see Chapter 5). Both copies are sent to the purchaser's solicitor for approval. The purchaser's solicitor may make amendments. If so, a copy of the amended contract will be returned to you for your consideration.

When the contract is finally approved on behalf of both parties, one part will be signed by the seller and one part by the purchaser. The signature must usually be that of the client, not the solicitor. It is not generally part of the solicitor's authority actually to sign the contract. So if you find that the contract *has* been signed by the purchaser's solicitor, you need evidence that his client has given him express authority to do this.

The reason why the contracts are in duplicate is that the parties intend to *exchange* the two parts. The seller will then have the part signed by the purchaser, and the purchaser will have the part signed by the seller. As exchange is contemplated by the parties, the contract will not come into existence until exchange takes place.

1.6 Exchanging Contracts

Once the purchaser's solicitor is satisfied that the results of all the pre-contract searches and enquiries are satisfactory and that his client can safely enter into the contract, exchange will take place. Once contracts are exchanged, the parties are bound: the seller to transfer ownership, and the purchaser to pay the purchase price.

(*a*) *Personal Exchange*

This is where the seller's solicitor meets the purchaser's solicitor and the two parts of the contract are exchanged. This method of exchange is rare because a solicitor cannot usually spare the time involved in travelling to a colleague's office.

(*b*) *Exchange through the Post*

The purchaser's solicitor posts his client's part of the contract to the seller's solicitor, together with a cheque for the deposit. When he receives these, the seller's solicitor posts the part of the contract signed by the seller back to the purchaser.

Despite the long use of this method of exchange, there is still controversy as to the exact moment that the exchange takes place. One view is that exchange has occurred (and that the contract therefore exists) as soon as the second part of the contract is put in the post. The other view is that exchange has not taken place until the second part of the contract is actually received by the addressee. If the contract incorporates the standard conditions (see Chapter 5) the contract will provide that exchange is to be treated as taking place on the *posting* of the second part, not on its receipt. (See standard condition 2:1.1.) If Robert is not buying a new house, this method of exchange would be satisfactory. If he is buying a new house, the exchange of contracts on his sale needs to be synchronised with the exchange of contracts on his purchase, and this is not easily done if contracts are exchanged by post.

(*c*) *Exchange by Telephone*

In this case, exchange takes place by an agreement over the telephone that the contracts are to be *treated* as exchanged.

Suppose that this method of exchange is contemplated on Robert's sale. The purchaser's solicitor might send his part of the contract, together with a cheque for the deposit, to you. The accompanying letter is likely to say that these are not sent by way of exchange, but that you are to hold them to the order of the purchaser. This means that you cannot foist an exchange on the purchaser by posting the part of the contract signed by Robert. Exchange cannot take place until the purchaser is ready. When the purchaser is ready, his solicitor will telephone you, and say that he is ready to exchange contracts. It will then be agreed on the telephone that contracts are now exchanged. You, as Robert's solicitor, will agree that you now hold his part of the contract to the order of the purchaser, and that you will post it that day.

It is possible that exchange could be agreed over the telephone before either seller or purchaser has parted with his part of the contract. In such a case, the purchaser's solicitor will give an undertaking to post his client's part of the contract and deposit cheque that day, and you will undertake to post Robert's part of the contract.

You can see that although the exchange takes place when agreement is reached on the telephone, this is always followed (or possibly preceded) by the exchange of the documents themselves.

The drawback to this method of exchange is that it has taken place through a conversation, which might later be denied. For this reason, the Law Society recommends that written notes be taken by both parties as to what was said. It also recommends that the solicitors should agree that the telephone exchange be governed by either Law Society formula A (to be used where the purchaser has already sent a signed contract to the seller's solicitor) or formula B (to be used when each solicitor still holds his own client's part of the contract).

Both formulae provide for the insertion in the contract of an agreed completion date, for confirmation that the contracts are in the form agreed, and for the giving of the undertakings outlined above.

(An attempt to explain Law Society formula C is made in Chapter 17.)

Warning **Whatever method of exchange is used, exchange will not be treated as having taken place unless the contents of the two parts of the contract are identical. This is why it is essential that any alteration to the draft contract is written into *both* parts before they are exchanged. It is salutory to read the case of *Harrison* v. *Battye* [1974].**

1.7 The Deposit

On exchange of contracts, the purchaser will normally have to pay a deposit of 10 per cent of the purchase price (see Chapter 5). This is part-payment of the purchase price, but it is also something more. It is a pledge of the purchaser's intention to fulfil the contract. If the purchaser unjustifiably refuses to complete, the deposit is forfeited to the seller.

If the contract provides for payment of a deposit, and the purchaser fails to do this (either because no payment is ever made, or because his cheque is dishonoured) the purchaser is considered to have broken the contract in such a fundamental way as to enable the seller to treat the contract as discharged (see standard condition 2:2.4). The seller is released from the contract, and can also sue for the unpaid deposit (see *Damon Cia Naviera SA* v. *Hapag-Lloyd International SA* [1985]).

1.8 Insurance

If nothing is said to the contrary in the contract, the risk of capital loss passes to the purchaser as soon as contracts are exchanged. So if, for example, the house burns down, the purchaser bears the loss and remains liable for the full purchase price. Two things might mitigate his loss:

1. after exchange the seller owes the purchaser a duty to take reasonable care of the property until completion of the sale. So if the fire could be traced back to the negligence of the seller, he would be liable to compensate the purchaser;
2. if the seller had maintained his own insurance on the house (which is likely, although he is under no duty to the purchaser to do so), then the insurance money due under the policy is held by the seller on trust for

the purchaser. (This is the effect of s.47 of the Law of Property Act 1925.)

If the contract incorporates the standard conditions of sale (see Chapter 5) standard condition 5.1 alters these rules entirely. In Condition 5.1.1 the seller promises the purchaser to transfer the property in the same physical state as it was at the date of the contract (with the exception of fair wear and tear, i.e. ordinary dilapidation). This means that the risk of physical damage remains with the seller. It is therefore essential for the seller to continue to insure the property until the sale is completed, for his own protection. (Condition 5.3 makes it clear that the seller does not owe a duty to the purchaser to insure the property, and s.47 of the Law of the Property Act 1925 is excluded.)

If, for example, the house burns down before completion, or is in any way physically damaged, the seller must compensate the purchaser, which will amount to the purchaser paying a reduced purchase price.

Condition 5.1.2 creates rights to rescind the contract, i.e. set it aside as if it had never existed. It applies when, before completion, the change in the physical state of the property makes the property unusable for its purpose at the date of the contract. In these circumstances the purchaser can rescind the contract, i.e. he does not merely pay a reduced price; he need not buy the property at all, unless he wishes.

In the same circumstances, a right of rescission is also given to the seller, but in his case only if the damage is of a sort that he could not reasonably have insured against, or if it is damage that it is not legally possible for him to make good. For instance, this could be because he could not get planning permission. Why should a seller wish to rescind if the property is severely damaged? Presumably because faced with a greatly reduced purchase price, he prefers not to sell at all, perhaps because it will leave him without enough money to buy a new house. (Remember that the seller has the right of rescission if he *could not* insure; not because he *did not* insure.)

Condition 5.1 applies only to an alteration in the physical state of the property, but this is not the only thing that can decrease its value. The fact that the property is listed as being of exceptional historical or architectural merit can remove any development value from the land for instance. The risk of this sort of capital loss continues to pass to the purchaser on exchange of contracts.

Despite Condition 5.1 some purchasers will still prefer to insure the property themselves as from the date of the contract, preferring to have a claim against an insurance company rather than against the seller. If a purchaser does this the property will be doubly insured, i.e. by both seller and purchaser. The effect of double insurance is that each insurance company will pay only part of the claim, so the seller may find that his insurance company will pay only, say, half the loss, leaving the other half to be paid by the purchaser's insurer. The seller should consider putting into the contract a condition saying that if the seller's payment from the insurance company is reduced for this reason, then the compensation to be paid by him to the purchaser will be reduced by the same amount. The purchaser will recoup himself from the proceeds of his own policy.

Note: the position as to risk and insurance changes if the purchaser is allowed to occupy the house before completion – see standard conditions 5.2.3 and 5.2.2.

1.9 Proving Title

If the seller is following the protocol, the package of documents sent to the purchaser before contract will have included details of the seller's title. If the transaction is following a more traditional route, the purchaser may not be sent details of the seller's title until the contract is in existence. This is explained more fully in Chapter 5. However, in case you are asking yourself how it is at all possible that investigation of title could be left until after contract, it is because the contract will contain a promise (usually implied rather than expressed) by the seller that he has a good title. If the purchaser does not investigate title until after exchange of contracts, he agrees to buy in reliance on this promise. If after contract his investigation of title reveals that there are defects in the title that he was not told about at the time of contract, he can say that the defect is a breach of contract, and possibly that the contract is discharged by the breach. The purchaser is then released from his obligation to buy.

Of course, there is considerable inconvenience for a purchaser in this position, who is probably committed to a contract to sell his existing house, and so you may be asking yourself 'why does the purchaser not always investigate title *before* the contract'? He *can* do so if he is given the necessary evidence of title at that stage. Whether he *has* to, depends on the terms of the contract. If the purchaser is entitled to raise requisitions on the title (i.e. object that the title is not as promised in the contract) after exchange of contracts he can leave investigation of title until then if he wishes to do so. This is the position envisaged by the standard conditions of sale (see Chapter 5). If a special condition in the contract precludes the purchaser from raising requisitions after exchange, the purchaser *must* investigate title before contract, as it will generally be too late to object to the title after the contract is made.

Chapter 5 explains the promises as to title given by the seller and Chapters 7 and 8 explain the evidence of title that the seller must supply.

1.10 Dealing with the Purchaser's Requisitions on Title

If the purchaser is dissatisfied either with the soundness of the title or with the evidence of the title that is given, he will 'raise a requisition on title'. In other words, he will complain to you about what is wrong and ask you to put it right. When faced with the purchaser's complaint, the seller may be able to put the matter right. He may, for example, be able to supply a missing document, or prove that a third-party interest is no longer enforceable against the land.

If the seller cannot put the matter right, his position depends on whether the purchaser is investigating title before or after contract. If the former, the purchaser will not enter into the contract. If the purchaser is investigating title after contract, then generally the seller must face the fact that he is in breach of his contract. He cannot live up to his promise as to title. He awaits the purchaser's decision. The purchaser may be able to treat the contract as discharged by the breach, and cease to be under any obligation to buy. He may also be able to sue for damages. The damages may be heavy.

It is unfortunately true that the fact that your client is in breach of contract *may* be your fault. Why did you not notice that his title was defective when you investigated it prior to drafting the contract? You could then, by a special condition in the contract, have disclosed the defect and prevented the purchaser from raising the requisition (turn to Chapter 5).

1.11 Checking the Draft Conveyance or Transfer

Assuming that you are able to deal with any requisition, you now read the draft conveyance or transfer. This is drawn up by the purchaser's solicitor, but has to be approved by the seller's solicitor, who must check that it is not drawn so as to give the purchaser more than the seller contracted to give.

Once the draft has been approved by you, the purchaser's solicitor will 'engross' it, i.e. prepare a fair copy of it. This will be sent to you so that you can arrange to have it executed by your client.

1.12 Completion Statement

When you send to the purchaser's solicitor your replies to his requisitions on title, and the approved draft conveyance, you will also send him a completion statement, setting out the sum that the purchaser must pay on completion. This may consist merely of the purchase price, less the deposit already paid. There may sometimes be other items, for example:

(a) *apportionments of outgoings*. At one time it was usual to apportion the water and sewage charges, gas and electricity bills, so that if the seller had paid for a period extending beyond the completion date, he was credited with an apportioned part of the payment. This is not now usually done. The seller usually tells the relevant authorities of his date of departure and ensures that the meters are read as close as possible to the date of completion. He is then sent bills from the bodies concerned. The purchaser is responsible for the charges arising from the date of completion. The community charge is a personal matter. It does not relate to the property and cannot be apportioned.

An apportionment is still usual in an assignment of a lease. The rent might have to be apportioned, and so might payments made to the landlord in respect of insurance or maintenance.

(b) *interest*. If completion takes place later than the date agreed in the contract, either seller or purchaser might be liable to pay interest on the unpaid balance of the purchase price. The amount involved will be deducted from, or added to, the purchase price (see Chapter 18).

1.13 Completion

Completion at its simplest is a swop. The purchaser pays the balance of the purchase price in return (in the case of an unregistered title) for the deeds and the conveyance to him. The purchaser will then own the legal estate and the beneficial interest. If the seller's title is registered, the purchaser will receive the land certificate and the transfer. He will then own the beneficial interest, but will not own the legal estate until he is registered as the new proprietor (see Chapter 3). In our case, Robert's title is mortgaged. The purchaser will want evidence that the mortgage has been paid off. In unregistered title, he will demand that a receipt be endorsed on the mortgage deed, and executed by the mortgagee. In registered title, he will be given the charge certificate (or charge certificates, if there is more than one registered charge) and a form 53 for each charge. This is discussed further in Chapters 7 and 9.

1.14 After Completion

(a) You should now account to Robert for the proceeds of sale. You will usually have secured your client's authority to deduct from them your fees and disbursements, and any fees due to the estate agent. The balance, with a statement showing clearly how the balance is arrived at, is remitted according to your client's instructions.

(b) Any undertakings that have been given to the purchaser's solicitor must be complied with, e.g. in connection with the redemption of your client's mortgage.

2 Stages in a Conveyancing Transaction: The Purchaser's Point of View

2.1 Introduction

This chapter takes you through a transaction again, but this time from a purchaser's point of view. Imagine that you are acting for Susan Holt in her purchase of a house. She has applied for a mortgage loan from a building society, and you find that the society is prepared to instruct you to act for it in the creation of the mortgage. You have, therefore, two clients (see Chapter 2, section 2.18 on conflict of interest).

2.2 Gathering Information

(a) Susan must give you details of the bargain that has been struck so that you can judge if the draft contract prepared by the seller represents that bargain. Were fittings included in the sale, and at what price? What sort of completion date has been arranged between the parties?

(b) Was there anything about the property that struck her? Did anyone appear to have any sort of access over the property? Who appeared to be living on the property apart from the seller?

2.3 You Need to Know your Client's Financial Position

(*a*) *Total Purchase Price*

The first point is that you must make sure that she realises the *total* cost of the purchase. This may well take her by surprise. She needs an estimate of your fees and details of your foreseeable disbursements. These will include stamp duty (currently at 1 per cent of the entire purchase price, if this exceeds £30 000) and land registry fees. Again, you may decide to use the Law Society's domestic conveyancing charges form (see Chapter 1, section 3(f).

(*b*) *Mortgage Offer*

The second point is that as she is buying with the aid of a mortgage loan, you must be sure that the lender has made a *formal* offer of a loan before you commit your client to the contract to buy.

When you read the formal offer, check the amount of the loan. Is this the amount your client expects? Is there any retention clause (see Chapter 17). Is there any condition that must be satisfied before the loan is made? (An example might be that the Society wants a specialist survey done on some part of the house, e.g. for risk of subsidence. The money will only be available when the survey is done, and if the Society considers the result to be satisfactory.) If the mortgage is an endowment mortgage, the offer will be conditional on the life policy being on foot before completion. The proposal form for the assurance should be completed now and forwarded either to the lender or the assurance company, and confirmation that the proposal has been accepted by the company is needed *before contract*.

(*c*) *Deposit*

A contract usually provides for a deposit of 10 per cent of the purchase price to be paid on exchange of contracts. Your client must realise that this may be forfeited to the seller if it is your client's fault that completion does not take place. So any failure by her to complete will involve her in severe financial loss, even if the seller is in fact able to sell the house to someone else at the same, or even an increased, price. Of course, if the failure to complete is the seller's fault, Susan will be entitled to the return of the deposit.

If Susan does not have enough money to pay a 10 per cent deposit on exchange of contracts, there are various solutions:

(i) If she is selling her existing house to buy the new one, she will be receiving a deposit from her purchaser, and this may be used to finance the deposit which she has to pay to her seller (see Chapter 5 for details on the drafting of the contract for sale). However, if she is trading up – e.g. selling an £80 000 house and buying a new one for £120 000, she will still have to find £4000.

(ii) She may be able to persuade the seller to accept a smaller deposit, e.g. on the above example £8000 rather than £12 000. The seller may be unhappy with this, as he knows that if she fails to complete she will be forfeiting to him a significantly smaller sum.

However, he may be comforted by Standard Condition 6.8.4. This gives a seller who accepts less than the 10 per cent deposit a right to sue for the balance if he is forced to serve a completion notice because of the purchaser's delay in completion. So if things go wrong, the seller may be able to recover the missing £4000, always provided, of course, that Susan is not insolvent.

(iii) She may have to borrow the deposit, the loan either to be repaid when the mortgage loan is forthcoming at completion, or to be added to the mortgage debt. The customer's bank is a traditional source for such a loan, but building societies now have the power to lend on unsecured loans, as well as secured ones, so the building society may provide the deposit at exchange of contracts, instead of withholding the entire advance until completion. The mortgage, when made, will then charge the land with repayment of the total loan, including the amount lent to fund the deposit;

(iv) She may be able to use a deposit insurance scheme. The idea is that an insurance company, in return for a one-off premium (to be paid by the purchaser), promises the seller that if the contract is not performed owing to the purchaser's default, the company will pay the seller the 10 per cent deposit. It usually costs less to pay the premium than to pay the interest on a loan for the deposit. It is often not possible to use such a scheme in a chain transaction (see Chapter 17).

2.4 The Pre-contract Searches and Enquiries

As you will see in Chapter 5 the seller has a limited duty to tell the purchaser about defects in his title to the property and about third-party rights over it, such as restrictive covenants or easements. The duty stops there. So there is a great deal of information which might well affect the purchaser's decision as to whether or not to buy the property and which she must find out for herself, and she must do this *before* the contract. To take a simple example, the seller may know that the Motorway M1001 is to be built on the far side of the garden fence. The purchaser, however, does not learn this interesting fact until after she has agreed to buy the house. It is too late. The seller was under no duty to inform the purchaser about the proposed motorway. He has not broken a term of the contract, so the purchaser must either complete or lose her deposit and face a claim for damages. This is why it is so important for the purchaser to make enquiries about the property *before* contract.

Pre-contract searches and enquiries are dealt with in Chapter 6.

You will realise, having read Chapter 1, that if the seller's solicitor is following the National Protocol, these searches will be provided for the purchaser as part of the pre-contract package. It still remains the responsibility of the purchaser's solicitor to check the results of the searches, and to consider if any further searches need to be made.

2.5 Consideration of the Draft Contract

Once the draft contract has been received in duplicate from the seller, you must consider if it represents the bargain that your client expects. If there is any doubt, Susan must again be consulted. She should also be asked on what date she wishes to complete as the completion date will be put in the contract on exchange.

2.6 The Deposit

The deposit payable on exchange must now be obtained from the client. (The need to provide this deposit has already been discussed with her.) If your client is to give you a cheque, you should receive it sufficiently early for the cheque to be cleared before you draw on it to pay the seller. According to standard condition 2.2.1. (see Chapter 5) the deposit should be paid to the seller by banker's draft or by a cheque drawn on a solicitor's bank account. This, if complied with, should remove any possibility that the cheque will bounce. Condition 2.2.4 provides that if any cheque for the deposit is dishonoured, the seller can treat the contract as discharged.

2.7 Exchange of Contracts

Once you are satisfied:

(a) that the purchaser will have the necessary funds on completion to buy the property and to pay all attendant expenses;
(b) that the replies to all the pre-contract searches and enquiries are satisfactory;
(c) that the draft contract is satisfactory;
(d) if it is to be investigated before contract, that the title is satisfactory;

you may exchange contracts on behalf of your client. On exchange, a date for completion, previously settled between the parties, will be put in the contract.

2.8 Insurance

We have seen that if the contract incorporates the standard conditions, the risk of physical damage to the property no longer passes to the purchaser on exchange of contract. It is therefore not essential for a purchaser to insure against that risk until completion. However, as Susan is buying with the aid of a mortgage loan, you must check the *lender's* requirements as to insurance. The lender may require the borrower to take out comprehensive insurance as from the time the money is made available, which may be earlier than actual completion.

2.9 Investigation of Title

Once the contract is made, the purchaser will investigate title (see Chapters 7 and 9) and may raise requisitions on title. (Remember, though, what was said in Chapter 1, section 10. If the contract, by a special condition, prevents the purchaser from raising requisitions after contract, the purchaser *must* investigate title before exchange of contracts.)

The contract will, through the general conditions, provide a timetable for the stages of the transaction. Standard condition 4 says that requisitions must be raised within six working days of receipt of the seller's evidence of title, or if this was provided with the contract, within six days of the contract. The purchaser must be careful to observe this particular time limit as the condition provides that the purchaser's right to raise requisitions is lost after the six days have passed. In other words, if the purchaser does not object to the title *within* the time limits, she may be unable to object at all, and will have to accept the title with its defects. This condition will not prevent requisitions being raised out of time in some circumstances. A requisition can be raised out of time if it is as to a defect that is only revealed when the original title deeds themselves are seen, which may not be until completion. An example would be a memorandum of severance endorsed on a conveyance to joint tenants (see Chapter 11) if the abstract of title did not disclose the existence of this memorandum. Another exception is where the pre-completion search reveals a defect which was not disclosed by the abstract of title. Again, a requisition can be raised out of time.

The purchaser's solicitor must also remember that there is a time limit in standard condition 4 for the purchaser to raise observations on the seller's replies to the requisitions, and that this limit must be strictly observed.

2.10 Report on Title to the Building Society

You are investigating title not only on behalf of Susan Holt, but also on behalf of her mortgagee. Once you are satisfied that the title, and the evidence of the title, are satisfactory, you will report to that effect to the Building Society.

You might, however, have found a defect in title, and one that you consider to be sufficiently serious to affect the value of the property. Susan, because she likes the house so much, might be willing to press ahead. You owe a duty to the Building Society. You must report on the defect to the Society, with the possible result that the offer of the mortgage will be withdrawn. (This should not leave Susan Holt stranded, as if the defect is sufficiently serious to lead to the withdrawal of the mortgage offer, it will probably be a ground for Susan treating the contract to buy as discharged by the seller's breach.)

If Susan Holt will not consent to your informing the Society, you will have to tell the Society you can no longer act for it. The Society will instruct another solicitor, who will investigate title and discover the defect. So Susan might as well accept the inevitable.

2.11 Drafting the Conveyance or Transfer

It is your task to draft the purchase deed, and two copies of your draft will be sent, with your requisitions on title, to the seller's solicitor. Drafting is discussed in Chapters 13 and 14.

The seller's solicitor will return one copy of the draft, either approved or amended. Once any amendments have been negotiated and agreed, you will have the deed engrossed. You must then consider whether or not it is necessary for your client to execute it. It is often unnecessary for the purchaser to execute the deed, but she should do so if the deed contains covenants given to the seller. The deed should also be executed by co-purchasers, if it contains a declaration as to how they own the beneficial interest, i.e. whether as joint tenants or in shares. Execution of the deed makes this declaration binding upon them.

The deed is then sent to the seller's solicitor for execution by his client. The deed will then be retained by the seller's solicitor until completion.

2.12 Drafting the Mortgage

Your client will have a choice of mortgage. There are two main types, the repayment mortgage, and the endowment mortgage.

Under the repayment mortgage, the borrower promises monthly payments of capital and interest over a period of years. The maximum is usually 40 years. The capital debt is therefore slowly reduced. If the borrower expects to be survived by a spouse or by dependants for whom a home must be provided, he would be well advised to take out a mortgage protection policy. If the borrower dies before the mortgage loan is repaid, the policy will provide the money to pay off the balance due.

For an endowment mortgage, the borrower must take out an assurance policy on his life. The premiums are calculated so that at the end of the agreed number of years, the policy will yield at least sufficient money to repay the capital loan. When the mortgage over the land is created, the policy is assigned by the borrower to the lender. Over the term of the mortgage, the borrower pays the interest on the loan and the premiums on the policy. At the end of the mortgage term, the policy matures, and provides the money needed for redemption of the mortgage. The premiums can be calculated so that the policy yields more than the sum needed to redeem the mortgage. This means that the borrower will also have a capital sum for his own use. The endowment policy is then called a 'with profits' policy. If the policy will yield only the amount needed to repay the loan, it is called a 'minimum cost' policy. As the policy also matures if the borrower dies before the loan is repaid, there is no need for a mortgage protection policy.

Which mortgage is best for your client depends on his circumstances, and it is difficult to generalise. A 'with profits' endowment mortgage is sometimes preferred as it offers an effective means of saving. However any sort of life assurance must be looked upon as a long-term investment, as a borrower who attempts to surrender a policy in the early years (i.e. who asks the assurance company to end the contract early) will receive back from the company less than he has paid into it in premiums). This is no disadvantage if the mortgagor wishes to sell his house to buy another, as the same policy will be used as security for repayment of the new loan, and will not be surrendered. It is a disadvantage if the mortgagor, perhaps because of financial difficulties or marriage, wishes to sell his house and not buy another. The policy must be kept alive for several years if the assured wants anything like a real return for the premiums paid.

There is often no advantage at all in taking out a minimum-cost endowment policy. It has no savings element and the overall cost can be higher than a straight repayment mortgage. You must realise that your client is coming to you from the estate agent who has probably arranged the mortgage finance and possibly a life policy. Many estate agents are now owned by insurance companies, building societies or banks, and so may not, or perhaps cannot (because of the Financial Services Act 1986) give a choice of lender or assurance policy to the customer. Consider the suitability of the financial package that has been arranged, and whether a straight repayment mortgage might not be more suitable for your client than an endowment mortgage (see the statement of the Council of the Law Society on the 1986 Act in connection with life policies and tied agents, published in the *Guardian Gazette*, 23 March 1988).

A mortgagor who pays interest on a loan for the purchase of his principal residence is entitled to income-tax relief. This relief can only be claimed on the first £30 000 of the loan. If two or more people are responsible for the repayment of the loan, the relief is shared between them. Relief is usually given under what is known as the MIRAS scheme (mortgage interest relief at source). This provides that the borrower pays interest to the lender after deduction of the tax relief. The lender claims the balance from the Inland Revenue. So, for example, if the monthly interest is £100, and income tax is 25p in the £1, the borrower pays the lender £75. Relief is only given against basic-rate tax, not against higher rate.

As, in this case, you are also the solicitor for the Building Society, it will be your task to draft the mortgage documents. The Society will send you its standard form of mortgage, and you will only have to fill in the blanks with details of the property, the borrower, amount of loan, etc. In the case of an endowment mortgage you may have to prepare the deed of assignment of the assurance policy. (The policy will, of course, be reassigned when the loan is repaid.) It will also be necessary after completion to give notice to the assurance company that the policy has been assigned. This is important for two reasons. It ensures that when the policy monies are payable they will be paid to the Building Society rather than to Susan. It also preserves the priority of the mortgage, and prevents a later mortgagee of the policy gaining priority over the Society's mortgage. Two copies of the notice are prepared. After completion, both copies are sent to the assurance company which is asked to receipt one copy of the notice and return it. This is then carefully preserved for fear the company might one day deny having been given notice. (Increasingly, lenders do not ask the borrower actually to assign the policy, but only *to promise* to assign it if required to do so. Nor is any notice of the assignment given to the assurance company. This is because it is likely that the house will be sold before the policy matures, and the loan repaid from the sale proceeds rather than the policy proceeds.)

Susan will have to execute the mortgage and the assignment of the policy as well as, possibly, the conveyance or transfer (see earlier). Your instructions from the Building Society may tell you to ensure that the mortgage documents are signed in the presence of a solicitor, or legal executive, or licenced conveyancer. This will mean that she will have to come into your office. So ensure that she has had your completion statement (see Chapter 2, section 13) and can bring the balance of the purchase price with her when she comes, and be sure that the appointment leaves time for any personal cheque of hers to be cleared before completion.

2.13 Obtaining the Balance of the Purchase Money

(a) From the Building Society. When you reported to the Society that the title was in order, you would also have asked them to send you the advance in time for completion.
(b) From your client. You need to send a statement to Susan, setting out the sum needed from her to complete the purchase. It will consist of the purchase price (less the deposit paid on contract) plus any apportionment of outgoings, plus your fees for acting in the purchase and in the mortgage, plus all the disbursements, minus the net mortgage loan.

2.14 The Pre-completion Search

Shortly before completion, you must make the pre-completion search. This really represents the final step in the investigation of the seller's title.

Completion must not take place until the results of the search are known, and must then take place before the priority period given by the official search certificate expires.

If you are buying a registered title, the search is made at the appropriate District Land Registry. If you are buying an unregistered title, the search is made at the Land Charges Registry at Plymouth (see Chapters 7 and 9 for a further explanation of these searches).

2.15 Completion

On completion you will pay the balance of the purchase price to the seller's solicitor. This will usually be paid by banker's draft or it may be telegraphed directly to the bank account of the seller's solicitor.

You will expect to pick up:

(a) if the title is unregistered, the deeds and the conveyance to Susan executed by the seller. If the seller had a mortgage, the purchaser is entitled to see that this is discharged. The mortgage deed itself will be handed over, properly receipted by the lender, or instead the solicitor acting for the mortgagee (who will probably be the same solicitor as is acting for the seller) will give you 'the usual undertakings' (these are explained in Chapter 7);

(b) in registered conveyancing, the land certificate and the transfer executed by the seller. If the seller had a mortgage, you will pick up the charge certificate, the transfer, Land Registry Form 53, or the usual undertakings in respect of it (see Chapter 7).

If the parties' solicitors are actually going to attend completion, it will usually take place at the offices of the seller's solicitor. (On this point, see standard condition 6.2.) (If this involves a long journey for the purchaser's solicitor, he can instruct another solicitor to act as his agent.) These civilised meetings are becoming things of the past, and completion increasingly takes place through the post. The purchaser's solicitor telegraphs the purchase price to the seller's solicitor, and in return the seller's solicitor posts the deeds to the purchaser's solicitor. Certain tasks have to be undertaken by the seller's solicitor as agent for the purchaser's solicitor, e.g. the examination and marking of the deeds, and endorsement of memoranda. An important point for the purchaser's solicitor to have confirmed is that the seller's solicitor has authority from the seller's mortgagee to receive the money to be used to redeem the mortgage. Otherwise, if the seller's solicitor disappears with the money, the seller's mortgagee can refuse to discharge the mortgage (see *Edward Wong Finance Co. Ltd* v. *Johnson Stokes and Master [1984]*).

The Law Society has published a code for postal completions, designed to define the solicitors' responsibilities and to reduce risk. If the solicitors are following the protocol, they must agree to adhere to the code, but otherwise do not have to do so.

2.16 After Completion

(a) You must report to your client that completion has taken place and that she can now move in. Keys are usually left with the estate agents, rather than with the solicitors.

(b) You can now transfer the sums paid to you by Susan Holt in respect of your fees and disbursements from your clients' account to your office account.

(c) If your client has bought the property subject to a lease, the tenant should be given written notice of the identity of his new landlord. If you fail to give this notice to a residential tenant, any rent or service charge due from him will be treated as not being due, and so no action for non-payment can be taken (section 48 of the Landlord & Tenant Act 1987).

(d) Perfecting the title. As purchaser's solicitor, ask yourself two questions:

  (i) does the conveyance or transfer need stamping with *ad valorem* stamp duty, and/or the 'particulars delivered' stamp?
  (ii) is the purchaser affected by the Land Registration Act 1925?

If you have bought an unregistered title, you need to consider whether or not you must apply for first registration of your client's title (see Chapter 3). You have two months in which to apply. You will be applying for registration of Susan as proprietor, and also for registration of the Society's mortgage.

If you have bought a registered title, you must apply for registration of the transfer to your client. Only when registered will your client obtain the legal estate. The application for registration should be made before the priority period given by the pre-completion search expires (see Chapter 7). You will also be applying for registration of the Society's mortgage as a registered charge.

2.17 A Note on the Stamping of Documents by the Purchaser after Completion

(*a*) *Rates of Duty*

(i) *Ad valorem* and fixed-rate stamp duty A conveyance or transfer on sale of a freehold or existing leasehold estate is liable to *ad valorem* stamp duty at the rate of 1 per cent of the consideration. The conveyance or transfer will be exempt from stamp duty if it contains a certificate to the effect that the consideration does not exceed £30 000. (For full wording of this certificate, see the conveyance in Chapter 13.)

(ii) Stamp duty does not have to be paid on mortgages or vacating receipts executed after 1971.

(iii) A conveyance or transfer by way of gift executed after 30 April 1987 is exempt from stamp duty, provided it contains a certificate that it is an instrument within one of the categories of exempt documents under Stamp Duty (Exempt Instruments) Regulations 1987 (SI 1987/516).

(iv) An assent executed as a deed, an appointment of a new trustee, a conveyance or transfer in consideration of marriage, or as part of rearrangement of property on a divorce are now exempt from the 50p deed stamp, provided they are certified as in paragraph (iii) above.
(v) A power of attorney is not liable for stamp duty (s.85 of the Finance Act 1985).
(vi) An assent not executed as a deed is not liable for stamp duty.

(*b*) *Time Limit for Stamping*

The conveyance or other document should be presented for stamping within thirty days of its execution. The date of execution is taken as the date which the conveyance bears (i.e. usually the date of completion). There are financial penalties (which can be severe) if a document is presented for stamping after the thirty-day period, and the Land Registry will not register any conveyance or transfer that is not properly stamped.

(*c*) *'Particulars Delivered' Stamp*

The Finance Act 1931 provides that certain documents must be produced to the Inland Revenue, together with a form giving particulars of the documents and any consideration received. The form is kept by the Inland Revenue (it provides useful information for the assessment of the value of the land) and the document is stamped with a stamp (generally called the PD stamp) as proof of its production. Without this PD stamp the document is not properly stamped and the person who failed in his responsibility to produce it (i.e. the original purchaser) can be fined.

The documents that need a PD stamp are:

(i) a conveyance on sale of the freehold;
(ii) a grant of a lease for seven years or more;
(iii) the transfer on sale of a lease of seven years or more.

If a conveyance or transfer is being sent to the Land Registry for registration, and it is not liable for *ad valorem* stamp duty but does need a PD stamp (i.e. the sale was for £30 000 or less) the document need not be produced at the Inland Revenue before the application for registration is made. Instead, the form giving particulars is sent with the application for registration to the Land Registry, which forwards the form to the Inland Revenue.

2.18 Acting for Both Parties

We have treated acting for the seller and acting for the purchaser as alternatives. Is it possible for a solicitor to act for both?

The usual answer is 'no' because Rule 6 of the Law Society Practice Rules 1990 forbids it. Similarly, the same solicitor (or two or more solicitors acting in partnership or association) cannot act for both landlord and tenant. However, Rule 6 does permit a solicitor to act for both parties in a very limited number of cases. Even in one of these cases, a solicitor cannot act for both parties if there is a conflict of interest between them, or if the solicitor is acting for a builder or developer selling as such. A licenced conveyancer cannot act for both parties if there is a conflict of interest between them.

A conflict of interest may become apparent to you when you are drafting the contract for sale. As soon as you find yourself putting in a special condition that is to the disadvantage of the purchaser, e.g. cutting down his power of investigating title or preventing him from objecting to a defect in title, you should realise that you cannot also advise the purchaser on the wisdom of accepting the condition.

There is no rule of professional conduct to prevent a solicitor acting for co-sellers, or for co-purchasers unless there is a conflict of interest between them. Usually there will not be a conflict, but see Chapter 17 for an example of how this might arise.

There is not usually a conflict in acting for the seller and the seller's mortgagee as they both have the same objective in mind, i.e. successful redemption of the mortgage. Nor is there usually a conflict of interest in acting for the purchaser, and the purchaser's mortgagee, if the mortgagee is not a private person. However, there are two points that might arise:

(i) any defect in title that might affect the value of the property or the security of the mortgage must be made known to the mortgagee even though this might result in the mortgage offer being withdrawn;
(ii) any renegotiation in the terms of sale must be made known to the mortgagee, particularly any reduction in the purchase price. If the purchase price is reduced, a lender who is lending a substantial part of the price may also wish to reduce the amount of the loan.

If the mortgagee is a private person rather than an institutional lender, you cannot act for him and for the purchaser. This is because of the need to negotiate the terms of the mortgage.

3 Registered Title

Note: Unless it is otherwise indicated, a reference in this Chapter to 'the Act' is a reference to the Land Registration Act 1925.

3.1 Introduction

Conveyancing is bedevilled by the fact that the title to a legal estate may be either unregistered, or registered under the Land Registration Act 1925.

Whether or not the title is registered has no great effect on conveyancing procedure. The stages in the transaction remain the same. It does greatly affect investigation of title. It is also true to say that on some matters, such as the question of third-party interests in land, there is a different land law for registered title than there is for unregistered title.

If a title is unregistered, ownership of the legal estate is proved by the production of past conveyances, which show a transfer of the legal estate from one owner to another, and ultimately to the seller. The conveyances cannot guarantee ownership. To take a simple – although unlikely – example, a deed may be forged. A deed may also be voidable, for example, because it is a purchase of trust property by a trustee. However, the production of deeds, coupled with the fact that the seller is in possession of the house, i.e. either living there or receiving rent, usually offer assurance of ownership.

Just as the conveyances cannot guarantee ownership, neither can they guarantee that there are no third-party rights other than those mentioned in them. Some third-party rights may have been created by deeds predating those which the purchaser sees. Other third-party rights may have arisen independently of conveyances of the legal estate. A contract for sale, an option, an equitable interest arising from a resulting trust, would all be examples, as would an easement or restrictive covenant granted not in a conveyance of the land, but in a separate deed.

The Land Charges Act 1972, by providing for registration of some third-party interests affecting an unregistered title, does assist a purchaser who wishes to check on the existence of third-party rights. However, not all interests need to be registered under that Act. Nor can all interests that are registered necessarily be discovered by a purchaser. (Chapter 4 elaborates both these points.)

The purpose of the Land Registration Act 1925 is to simplify the investigation of title to a legal estate. If the title to, say, the freehold estate in Blackacre is registered, there is what amounts to a guarantee that the person named in the register as proprietor of the estate really does own it. This guarantee comes from what is known as the 'statutory vesting' (see later). As regards third-party interests, a transferee for value of the registered title will take the estate subject only to interests that are protected by an entry on the register, or that are 'overriding' interests. The reading of the title deeds in unregistered conveyancing is, therefore, replaced by the reading of the register.

Unfortunately, from the point of view of a purchaser, even in registered conveyancing, reading the register is not enough. A transferee will take the title subject to overriding interests, and an overriding interest is, by definition, an interest that is not entered on the register, but which will bind anyone who acquires the title (s.3 of the Act). You will see that it is the existence of overriding interests that introduce risk into registered conveyancing.

3.2 How does a Title Come to be Registered?

Since 1925, bit by bit, counties or parts of counties have been designated as areas of compulsory registration of title by Order in Council. (To tie this down to a concrete example, Rochester upon Medway, in Kent, became an area of compulsory registration on 1 March 1957). Indeed, as from 1 December 1990, the whole of England and Wales finally became an area of compulsory registration.

The mere fact that an area is one of compulsory registration does not mean that all the titles have to be registered. Only certain transactions necessitate an application for first registration of the title to the legal estate. These transactions are:

(i) a conveyance on sale of the freehold estate;
(ii) an assignment on sale of a leasehold estate, provided the lease has over twenty-one years to run at the date of assignment;
(iii) the grant of a lease having over twenty-one years to run at the date of the grant (s.123 of the Act as amended by s.2(1) of the Land Registration Act 1986).

Some examples may make this clearer.

Example 1

Samuel owns Blackacre, a house in Rochester. The title to it is unregistered. This is because it has not been sold since 1957. Patience, the purchaser, is now buying the freehold. Samuel will prove his ownership of the legal estate by producing past conveyances of it, ending with a conveyance to him. The legal estate will vest in Patience at completion of the sale. Patience, having stamped the conveyance to her (see Chapter 2, sections 16 and 17) must now consider the effect of s.123. She has *bought* Blackacre, and it is in an area of compulsory registration. She must now apply for first registration of the freehold title. She will apply to the District Land Registry that deals with Kent, i.e. the one at Tunbridge Wells.

The Act does not *compel* her to apply for first registration, but there is a sanction if she does not bother. Section 123 provides that if she does not apply within two months of the date of the conveyance, then the conveyance at the end of the two months will become void for the purpose of passing the legal estate. She will retain the equitable interest, and so have every right to live on the property. She will feel the pinch, however, when she decides to sell. Her title will be defective, as she will not own the legal estate. She can acquire the legal estate by applying for late registration of her title. Late applications are accepted by the Registrar, and the effect of registration will be to revest the legal estate in her.

Example 2

Terry owns the lease of a house in Kent. The lease has fifty years to run. The title to it is unregistered. Terry dies, and the lease vests in his personal representative, who vests it in Ben, the beneficiary named in Terry's will.

Neither the personal representative nor Ben has to apply for first registration. Neither bought the lease. The title to it will, quite properly, remain unregistered.

If the personal representative had instead sold the lease to Peter, Peter would have had to apply for first registration of the title to the lease.

Notice that it is only the title to the estate that has been sold that has to be registered. The freehold will remain unregistered, until this is itself sold.

'Sale' is not generally defined by the Act. It seems to have the usual meaning of a disposition for money. A conveyance or assignment by way of exchange for other land is specifically defined as a 'sale' if equality money is paid (s.123(3) of the Act).

It is doubtful if a conveyance for consideration other than money, e.g. in return solely for shares, or solely for other land, is a conveyance on sale.

Example 3

Len owns the freehold of a house in Kent, the title to which is unregistered. He grants a lease of thirty years to Teresa. Within two months of the grant of the lease Teresa must apply for registration of the title to it, otherwise, at the end of the two months, the lease will become equitable. The title to the freehold will not be registered until the freehold is sold.

(Suppose that Len granted a lease of twenty-one years and one month. The title should be registered by virtue of s.123. However, s.8 of the Act provides that it is impossible to register a lease that has twenty-one years or less to run. So Len would seem to be in difficulties if he delays his application for registration. He is compelled to register the unregistrable. This is why s.8(1A) provides that a lease that has less than twenty-one years to run when the application for first registration is made will be registered, if it had over twenty-one years to run when granted or assigned.)

Example 4

Although all areas are now areas of compulsory registration, it is still important when buying an *unregistered* title to know when the area became subject to compulsory registration. To return to Rochester and Example 1, if Patience finds that Samuel had bought Blackacre after Rochester became an area of compulsory registration she knows that his title is bad. It should not have remained unregistered. His failure to apply for first registration within two months of his purchase means that he has lost the legal estate. It can only be restored by registration of the title.

3.3 Voluntary Registration

It is always possible for an estate owner to volunteer for registration of his title. Voluntary registration would clearly be convenient for an owner, such as a developer, who intends to sell his land off in parts. It will be easier to prove title to several purchasers, if the title is registered.

3.4 What Titles Can be Registered?

It is possible to register the title to

(a) the freehold estate
(b) a legal leasehold estate. It is not however, possible to register the title to a lease granted for twenty-one years or less. Nor is it possible to apply for first registration of a lease that has less than twenty-one years to run at the time the application is made (but see s.8 (1A) of the Act previously mentioned).

These titles can be independently registered. It is also possible to register the title to an easement and to a mortgage or charge by deed. Such a registration will not be independent, but will be a registration against the title of the land affected. Registration of easements is discussed in Chapter 12. A mortgage or charge by deed can be registered as a registered charge in the charges register of the land affected.

3.5 The Effect of First Registration of a Title

The registration of a purchaser as proprietor of a legal estate automatically vests the legal estate in him (ss. 5 and 9 of the Act). This statutory vesting ensures that if you are dealing with the registered proprietor, you must be dealing with the owner of the estate.

Usually, the purchaser who has applied for first registration will already have acquired the legal estate on completion, so the statutory vesting merely confirms the pre-existing position. However, if, for example, the conveyance to the purchaser had been a forgery, no legal estate would have vested in him at completion, but will vest in him as soon as he is registered as proprietor. This example shows that registration can 'cure' a title.

3.6 Classes of Title

A proprietor can be registered with different classes of title. The class of title warns a purchaser about the extent of risk in dealing with that proprietor.

(*a*) *Absolute Title to a Freehold Estate*

Look at Example 1 in section 3.2. Patience has acquired the legal freehold estate on completion and must now apply for first registration of her title to it. She will do this by sending to the District Land Registry:

(i) all the conveyancing documents, i.e. the pre-contract searches and enquiries (but not the local land charge search and additional enquiries), the contract, the requisitions on title, the land charge search certificates and the title deeds, together with a list in triplicate of all these documents;
(ii) the Land Registry application form;
(iii) the fee.

The title will be investigated by the Registry staff. If there is nothing greatly wrong with the title, the Registrar will register Patience as proprietor of the freehold estate, with absolute title. (The date of registration is backdated to the date of application for first registration, Rule 42 of the Land Registration Rules 1925).

Section 5 of the Act says that a proprietor registered with an absolute title takes the legal estate, together with all rights appurtenant to it, subject only to:

(i) *Incumbrances protected by an entry on the register* Suppose for instance, that on investigation of Patience's title, the Registrar realises that the title is subject to restrictive covenants, created by a past conveyance, and properly registered as a DII land charge. When he draws up the register of Patience's title, a notice of these covenants will be entered on the charges register. Patience now owns the legal estate subject to these covenants.

Notice that when Patience's title was unregistered, she was bound by the covenants because they had been protected by registration as a land charge. Once her title is registered, she is bound by the covenants because they are entered on the charges register of the registered title. The registration as a land charge is now completely irrelevant. This is why it is so important for incumbrances existing at the date of first registration to be entered on the register (that is, unless they can take effect as overriding interests, e.g. legal easements). If the restrictive covenants were not entered on the charges register they would cease to bind Patience, as they would not be protected by an entry on the register, nor would they be overriding interests. The person with the benefit of the covenants would have been seriously prejudiced by the registration of the title. His remedy would be to apply for rectification of the title, to ensure that the covenants are entered in the charges register. (but see *Freer* v. *Unwins Ltd* [1976]).

Adverse interests entered on the register carry no risk to a purchaser of the registered title from Patience, as the interests are discovered by reading the register.

(ii) *Overriding interests* This is the area of risk. An overriding interest is one that is not on the register, but which will bind a purchaser. These are discussed in 3.15. Some may be discovered by inspecting the land.

(iii) *Interests of beneficiaries, if the proprietor is not entitled to the land for his own benefit, but is holding it as a trustee* These interests should not present a risk to a purchaser. If the proprietor holds as a trustee, this should be disclosed by a restriction on the proprietorship register. The purchaser can then arrange for the beneficiaries' interests to be overreached (if they exist behind a trust for sale or settlement under the Settled Land Act 1925) or otherwise satisfied. Even if there is no restriction on the register to warn the purchaser of the beneficiaries' interests, they may fail against him as being unprotected minor interests.

The danger is the presence of a beneficiary's interest which is not overreached, and which is an overriding interest because the beneficiary is occupying the land (see 3.16).

(*b*) *Absolute Title to a Leasehold Estate*

By virtue of s.9 of the Act a person who is registered as proprietor of a lease with absolute title owns 'the legal leasehold estate, subject to the same rights as those affecting a freehold absolute title, but subject in addition to the covenants and obligations of the lease'.

The registration of an absolute leasehold title amounts to a guarantee not only that the proprietor owns the leasehold estate, but also that the lease was validly granted. Clearly, that guarantee can only be given if the Registrar knows that the landlord had the power to grant the lease. In other words, the Registrar needs evidence of the title to the freehold and to any superior leases. If the superior titles are registered, the evidence of title is in the registry and no further evidence need be deduced to the Registrar. For example, if L is registered as proprietor of the freehold estate with absolute title and grants a thirty-year lease to T, T will be registered as proprietor of the leasehold estate with absolute title.

(*c*) *Good Leasehold Title*

If a person is registered as proprietor of a leasehold estate with good leasehold title, his position is the same as a proprietor of a lease with absolute title, but with an important exception. The registration does not guarantee that the lease is valid (s.10 of the Act). A purchaser knows that the proprietor owns the lease, and the purchaser can read the register and inspect the land to discover third-party rights, but the purchaser does not know if the lease is worth anything at all.

Why does an applicant for first registration only obtain a good leasehold title? Look at Example 3 in 3.2. Len cannot be forced by Teresa to give details of his freehold title, unless there is a contract between them that the title will be deduced. When Teresa applies for first registration she will be unable to give details of Len's title to the Registrar.

The Registrar, being unable to investigate the freehold title, cannot guarantee that the lease is valid. He can only give Teresa good leasehold title. Look also at Example 2, where Peter is buying the lease from the personal representative. Terry may have obtained no details of the landlord's title when he was granted the lease. No details can therefore be supplied by the personal representative to Peter. Peter will be registered with good leasehold title.

You can see that a good leasehold title is unattractive both to a purchaser and a purchaser's mortgagee. The problem is discussed in greater detail in Chapter 15.

(*d*) *Possessory Title to a Freehold or Leasehold Estate*

A proprietor will be registered with a possessory title when the registrar is not satisfied with the documentary evidence of ownership. This may be because the applicant's title is based on his adverse possession (a squatter's title) or because he has lost his title deeds.

The drawback of a possessory title is that the registration is subject not only to everything to which an absolute title would be subject, but is also subject to any estate or interest that is adverse to the first proprietor's title and that exists at the date of first registration (ss. 6 and 11 of the Act). In other words, the title is subject to the risk that X might pop up and claim that the registered proprietor has not been in adverse possession sufficiently long to extinguish X's estate or interest in the land. X's rights are overriding, so that a purchase from the registered proprietor may also be unable to deny X's superior claim to the land.

(e) *A Qualified Title*

An applicant for registration with an absolute or good leasehold title may find that although the title is granted the Registrar wishes to put a qualification on it. This will be because the Registrar has found a particular flaw in it. For example, the Registrar may find that one of the conveyances was a purchase of trust property by one of the trustees. The beneficiaries of the trust could apply to the court to have this conveyance avoided. The Registrar would qualify the title, by stating that registration did not affect the rights of the beneficiaries.

A qualification can only be put on the title with the applicant's consent, but if the applicant refuses he may instead find himself registered with only possessory title. This is no more attractive to a purchaser than a qualified absolute title, as it is subject to *all* pre-registration claims. Qualified titles are rare.

3.7 Upgrading of Title

The rules for upgrading a title are contained in s.77 of the Act, as amended by s.1 of the Land Registration Act 1986.

(a) A good leasehold title can be upgraded to an absolute leasehold title if the Registrar has satisfactory evidence of the freehold and any superior leasehold title.

Look again at Example 3 in section 3.2. If Len sells the freehold title, the purchaser will have to apply for first registration. Details of the freehold title will then be available to the Registrar. He may register the purchaser from Len as proprietor of the freehold with absolute title, and change Teresa's title to the lease from good leasehold to absolute. Teresa could apply for the upgrading, or the Registrar could upgrade on his own initiative.

(b) A possessory title can be upgraded to an absolute freehold title, or a good leasehold title, if either:

(i) the Registrar is given satisfactory evidence of title; or
(ii) if the title has been registered for at least twelve years and the Registrar is satisfied that the proprietor is in possession.

(c) a qualified title can be changed to an absolute or good leasehold title if the Registrar is satisfied as to the title.

3.8 The Form of the Register

The register of the title is, confusingly enough, divided into three registers. (In Chapter 5 you will see a rather simplified version of a register of title.) Each registered title has its own title number.

The Property Register

This describes the property, e.g. 1 Smith Avenue. The description usually refers to the Land Registry filed plan. This plan only indicates the general boundaries of the land, but does not fix them exactly (rule 278 of the Land Registration Rules 1925). It describes the estate – i.e. freehold or leasehold. If the estate is leasehold, the register will include brief details of the lease (the date, parties, the term and its starting date).

The Proprietorship Register

This gives the name and address of the registered proprietor. It also gives the class of title, e.g. absolute, possessory, etc. You must realise that the class of title may change with a change of proprietor. O may be registered with an absolute title. If S enters into adverse possession against O, S may eventually be registered as the new proprietor, but possibly only with possessory title.

Any restriction will be entered on the proprietorship register. This is because a restriction reflects some sort of limitation on the proprietor's power to dispose of the land. Cautions are also entered here.

The Charges Register

Here are noted adverse interests such as restrictive covenants, easements and leases (unless the lease is an overriding interest). Also appearing here are registered charges (i.e. mortgages).

3.9 The Land Certificate

As has been seen in 3.6, when Patience applies for first registration of her title, she will send the title deeds to the Registry. When the registration of her as proprietor is completed, the deeds will be returned to her. These deeds no longer prove her title, and provided she has obtained an absolute title, there is no legal reason for preserving them, unless they reveal positive covenants (see Chapter 12). There will also be sent to her a land certificate. This is a copy of the register of title, sewn up in an imposing cover. This, in a sense, now plays the role of the title deeds – i.e. it is evidence of the registered proprietor's title. No transfer of the title, or other dealings, will be registered, unless the application for registration is accompanied by the land certificate. It can be deposited with a creditor to give security for the loan, as can title deeds. The land certificate is not quite the same as the title deeds, however. The register is the real evidence of title. Often the entries in the land certificate are exactly the same as the entries on the register as whenever the land certificate is deposited in the registry, the certificate will be brought up to date with the entries on the register. However, there are some entries which can be put on the register without the land certificate having to go into the Registry. These include cautions, and a notice protecting a spouse's rights of occupation under Matrimonial Homes Act 1983.

3.10 The Charge Certificate

You may know that when an unregistered title is mortgaged for the first time, the lender nearly always takes control of the title deeds. It was felt necessary to reflect this practice in registered conveyancing. If a registered title is mortgaged by deed, the lender can register the mortgage as a registered charge. The application for registration is accompanied by the borrower's land certificate. The land certificate is then retained in the registry and a charge certificate is issued to the lender. The charge certificate will contain a copy of the entries in the register and a copy of the mortgage deed. If the title is mortgaged a second time, the proprietor of the second registered charge will have a second charge certificate.

3.11 Dealings with a Registered Title

The principle is this; that every registrable dealing with a registered title must itself be registered, or it will not pass a legal estate. What does this mean?

The following are registrable dealings:

(a) a transfer of the registered title. This may be on sale or by way of gift.
(b) a transmission of the title, e.g. to a personal representative on the death of the registered proprietor (see Chapter 10).
(c) a grant of a lease out of the registered title, if the lease is for over twenty-one years (see Chapter 16).
(d) the grant of a mortgage or charge by deed.
(e) the grant of an easement (see Chapter 12).

Here is a simple example. Susan owns the freehold estate in Blackacre. The title is registered. Susan sells Blackacre to Petunia. On completion, Susan will hand to Petunia the land certificate and a land registry transfer, executed by Susan. Petunia now owns the equitable interest in the land. She does not own the legal estate. Why not? Because no legal estate will pass until the transfer is registered. So the next step, once the transfer has been stamped with any *ad valorem* stamps necessary, and with the 'particulars delivered' stamp (see 2.16) is to apply for registration of the transfer. She will do this by sending the certificate, the transfer, application form and fee to the District Land Registry. Once Petunia is registered as the new proprietor the legal estate vests in her. There is no time limit for the registration of a dealing with the registered title, but Petunia should apply for registration before the priority period given by her pre-completion search expires (see 7.5).

3.12 Third-party Rights in Registered Title

A registered title can be subject to the same third-party rights (e.g. restrictive covenants, contracts, easements, mortgages, etc.) as unregistered title.

When the registered title is sold, will the purchaser be bound by these third-party interests? Does an owner of the third-party interest have to do anything to protect it?

Third-party interests in registered title fall into two categories, overriding interests and minor interests.

(*a*) *An Overriding Interest*

This is defined by s.3 of the Act as an interest that is not entered on the register, but subject to which registered dispositions are by the Act to take effect. An overriding interest thus binds every purchaser of the title, yet cannot be discovered by reading the register. Most overriding interests are listed in s.70 of the Act and will be dealt with later.

(*b*) *Minor interests*

These are defined by s.2 and s.3 of the Act. The definition creates three categories:

(i) *Registrable dealings that have not been registered* So, looking at 3.11, we see that the equitable interest which Petunia acquires at completion is a minor interest until she registers the transfer.

(ii) *Equitable interests existing behind a trust of the legal estate* The interest of a beneficiary behind a settlement of the legal estate under Settled Land Act 1925 is a minor interest. The interest of a beneficiary behind a trust for sale of the legal estate may be a minor interest as may the interest of a beneficiary behind a bare trust. (A bare trust exists when the legal estate is held on trust for one adult beneficiary, without any trust for sale being declared. See the case of *Hodgson* v. *Marks* [1971]).

(iii) *Interests that are not created by registrable dispositions and which do not exist behind a trust.* Into this category will fall restrictive covenants, equitable leases, easements, contracts for sale, options, etc.

Notice that the categories of overriding and minor interest are not mutually exclusive. If a beneficiary behind a trust for sale is living on the property, his interest will be overriding, by virtue of s.70(1)(g) of the Act 1925. (However, the interest of a beneficiary behind a Settled Land Act settlement is always a minor interest, despite occupation. This is laid down by s.86(2) of the Act.)

Similarly, a lease granted for twenty-two years out of a registered title is a registrable disposition. Pending registration, the tenant will have a minor interest but if he goes into occupation, it will be an overriding interest, again because of s.70(1)(g).

3.13 The Need to Protect a Minor Interest

A minor interest, unlike an overriding interest, is at risk. It should be protected by some form of entry on the register. The reason for this can best be given by quoting part of s.20 of the Act.

> In the case of a freehold estate ... a disposition of the registered land or a legal estate therein, including a lease thereof, for valuable consideration, shall, when registered, confer on the transferee or grantee an estate ... subject to the incumbrances and other entries, if any appearing on the register; and ... to the overriding interests, if any, affecting the estate transferred ... but free from all other estates and interests whatsoever.

S.23 is a similar provision dealing with the transfer of a registered leasehold title.

In other words, a transferee for value whether taking an outright transfer, or a mortgage, or a lease, will, when the disposition is registered, take free from any minor interest that is not protected by an entry on the register.

The transferee takes free of the minor interest, even though he knows of its existence. S.59(6) of the Act provides that a purchaser acquiring title under a registered disposition is not to be concerned with any matter or claim (not being an overriding interest) which is not protected on the register, whether he has or has not notice thereof, express, implied or constructive (but see *Lyus* v. *Prowsa Developments Ltd* [1982]*, the facts of which are given in the case notes to this chapter, for circumstances in which a purchaser did take subject to an unprotected minor interest because a constructive trust was imposed on him).

Note: When in a chapter an asterisk appears besides the name of a case, it signifies that the case is mentioned in the case notes to that chapter.

3.14 Methods of Protecting Minor Interests

(*a*) *Registration*

A registrable dealing should be registered. Until this is done, no legal estate is created or transferred.

(*b*) *Notices*

A notice is an entry of the interest on the charges register of the title affected. The land certificate must be deposited at the Registry before any notice is put on the register. This is why, generally speaking, the consent of the registered proprietor is needed before a notice can be used. However, we have seen that if the title is subject to a registered charge, the land certificate is retained in the registry. This makes it possible for a notice to be put on the register without the consent of the registered proprietor. The proprietor is told of an application to enter a notice, so he has an opportunity to object. (As an exception to this rule, a proprietor is not, for obvious reasons, told of a spouse's application for a notice to protect his/her rights of occupation under the Matrimonial Homes Act 1983.)

A notice ensures that *if the interest is valid*, any transferee will take subject to that interest. The registered proprietor is, of course, always able to challenge the validity of the interest, as a notice cannot change a void or unenforceable interest into a valid one.

(*c*) *Cautions*

If a notice cannot be used, because the land certificate is not deposited at the Registry, a caution must be used. When a cautioner applies for a caution to be entered, the application has to be accompanied by a statutory declaration, briefly describing the interest or right claimed by him. Unlike a notice, the caution itself does not set out the interest. A person reading the register will see merely 'Caution dated 1 April 1992 registered on 6 April 1992 in favour of Avril Printemps'.

The effect of lodging a caution is that the Registrar must inform the cautioner before he registers a dealing with the land. This gives the cautioner an opportunity to assert his claim in a hearing by the Registrar with usually one of three results:

(i) the Registrar registers the dealing, but subject to the interest or rights of the cautioner;
(ii) the Registrar refuses to register the dealing at all;
(iii) the Registrar registers the dealing free of the cautioner's claim.

Theoretically, a caution is not as effective a protection as a notice. A notice ensures that the purchaser will, without more ado, take subject to the protected interest. A caution merely gives the cautioner a right to defend himself against a transferee by disputing the registration. A caution is intended to be used as a temporary form of protection only, for example to defend the cautioner's rights pending litigation between himself and the proprietor. Practically speaking, a caution on the register can paralyse dealings with the title, as no sensible purchaser will pay over the purchase price until the caution is removed from the register. The proprietor is thus forced either to come to terms with the cautioner or to litigate.

Warning off a caution A registered proprietor can apply to the Registrar to 'warn off' a caution. Notice is served on the cautioner, and if he does not object within the time-limit specified in the notice, the caution is cancelled. If the cautioner does object, the dispute will be settled by the Registrar or the court.

(*d*) *Restrictions*

A restriction is an entry on the proprietorship register that reflects the fact that the proprietor's powers of disposing of the land are in some way limited. It ensures that the proprietor complies with certain conditions before any transfer by him is registered. Take, as an example, a proprietor who holds the legal estate on trust for X, an adult. Let us assume that it is a bare trust and not a trust for sale. This would be because no express trust for sale was ever created, and there are no grounds, such as co-ownership of the beneficial interest, for one to be implied.

In unregistered conveyancing, a purchaser for value of a legal estate from a bare trustee would take subject to the beneficiary's interest if the purchaser had notice of it. As soon as a purchaser learns of a bare trust, therefore, he should obtain the consent of the beneficiary to the sale.

This is reflected in the restriction that goes onto the proprietorship register if the title is registered. It will say, in effect, that no disposition by the proprietor will be registered unless the consent of X (the beneficiary) is obtained. It is the duty of the proprietor (the trustee) to ensure that this restriction is on the title (but of course, not every person does his duty).

You can see from this example that a restriction may exist as much for the protection of a purchaser as for the owner of the third-party interest, as the restriction ensures that the necessary conditions are fulfilled to clear the third-party interest from the title. To labour the point, you must realise that the absence of the restriction does not prejudice a purchaser if the interest that should have been protected by it is a minor interest. However, failure to enter the restriction will prejudice the purchaser if the interest that should have been protected by it is an overriding interest. The purchaser has been deprived of the warning that there were conditions to be satisfied that *if* satisfied, would have cleared the interest from the title. To return to the example of the bare trust. If no restriction is entered, the purchaser will take free of X's interest if X is not in occupation. The purchaser can plead s.20 of the Act. The purchaser will take subject to X's interest if X is in occupation, as the occupation will make X's interest overriding. A restriction would have ensured that the purchaser either obtained X's consent to the transfer, or did not proceed.

A restriction would have saved the bank (i.e. the purchaser) in *Williams and Glyn's Bank* v. *Boland* [1981]*, but would have saved the parents (i.e. the beneficiaries) in *City of London Building Society* v. *Flegg* [1988]* (see case notes at the end of this chapter).

A proprietor whose powers of disposition are limited does have a duty to apply for the appropriate restriction to be registered. The restriction can also be applied for by a person interested in the land. In some circumstances, the registrar is under a duty to put a restriction on the register, e.g. in the case of co-ownership. Examples of restrictions are given in Chapter 11.

(*e*) *Inhibitions*

An inhibition prevents any dealing with the land at all. The only common one is the bankruptcy inhibition, which is put in the register when the receiving order is made.

3.15 Overriding interests

Most overriding interests are set out in s.70 of the Act. Only the most common are dealt with here.

(*a*) *Easements*

To quote s.70(1)(a) of the Act in full:

> Rights of common, drainage rights, customary rights (until extinguished), public rights, profits *a prendre*, rights of sheepwalk, rights of way, watercourses, rights of water and other easements not being equitable easements required to be protected by notice on the register.

The paragraph has been quoted in full, because the wording of it has led to controversy.

It is clear that a legal easement is overriding. Is an equitable easement? S.70(1)(a) excludes equitable easements 'required to be protected' on the register. It is not clear what this means. There is no *requirement* in the Act that equitable easements be protected by an entry on the register, although such protection is possible, using a notice or caution. It may be that 'required' means 'needing', i.e. an equitable easement that needs protection cannot be overriding. In *Celsteel* v. *Alton House Holdings Ltd* [1985] it was held that an equitable easement, openly exercised, is an overriding interest by reason of rule 258 of the Land Registration Rules Act 1925. Therefore, the only equitable easement that needs protection by an entry on the register is one not openly exercised, because such an easement is not an overriding interest. The need to register easements granted out of registered land is discussed in Chapter 12.

(*b*) *Rights Acquired, or being Acquired under the Limitation Act 1980 (s.70(1)(f) of the Act)*

If a title is unregistered, the effect of a squatter being in adverse possession of land for the limitation period is to extinguish the original owner's title, both to the equitable interest and to the legal estate. If the title is registered, the adverse possession extinguishes the claim of the registered proprietor to the equitable interest. However, because of the principle that only registered dealings can transfer a legal estate, the registered proprietor will retain the legal estate until the register is rectified by entering the squatter as registered proprietor. Until rectification, the original proprietor will hold the legal estate on trust for the squatter.

If the original proprietor sells the title before rectification, the purchaser will take subject to the rights of the squatter. In other words, the transferee will be in no better position than the transferor.

(*c*) *The Rights of a Person in Actual Occupation of the Land (s.7(1)(g) of the Act)*

This is dealt with in 3.16.

(*d*) *Local Land Charges (s.70(i)(i) of the Act)*

As local land charges are overriding interests, it is as important for a purchaser of registered title to make a local land charge search, as it is for a purchaser of unregistered title. Details of the search are given in chapter 6.

(e) *Leases Granted for a Term Not Exceeding Twenty-One Years (s.70(1)(k)*

The title to a lease granted for twenty-one years or under is not registrable. The lease however, will be overriding, so that if the landlord's title is registered, any transfer of it will take effect subject to the lease.

In the case of *City Permanent Building Society* v. *Miller* [1952] the word 'granted' was seized on, and held to mean the creation of a legal estate. An informally created lease, taking effect only in equity, cannot, therefore, be overriding under s.70(1)(k). It could be overriding under s.70(1)(g).

It seems that as s.70(1)(k) makes the lease overriding, it will also make overriding any provision in the lease that affects the parties in their relationship of landlord and tenant. This would include an option to renew the lease, but would exclude an option to buy the landlord's reversion, as this is looked upon as a personal covenant (*Woodall* v. *Clifton* [1905]). However, such an option could be overriding under s.70(1)(g) (*Webb* v. *Pollmount* [1966]).

3.16 Section 70(1)(g) of the Act – Dangerous Occupiers

By virtue of s.70(1)(g), overriding interests include 'the rights of every person in actual occupation of the land, or in receipt of the rents and profits thereof save where enquiry is made of such person and the rights are not disclosed'.

At the start, it must be stressed that s.70(1)(g) does *not* say that occupation *creates* any rights. It is saying that *if* the occupier owns an interest in land arising under ordinary principles of property law, then occupation by the owner of the interest protects the interest and makes it overriding.

Uncle George who has been invited to live with the registered proprietor as a matter of family feeling is not a dangerous occupier, at least not to a purchaser. Uncle has no interest to assert against the purchaser, so his occupation is irrelevant.

However, an Uncle George who has contributed to the original purchase price, or who has paid for substantial improvements to the property and as a result of the work or contribution *owns part of the equitable interest*, is a dangerous occupier. He has an interest to assert, and his occupation makes the interest an overriding one. A purchaser who takes subject to the interest will be faced with the choice of living in the house with uncle, or re-selling the property and sharing the proceeds with him.

S.70(1)(g) makes not only an interest belonging to an occupier overriding, but also an interest belonging to anybody receiving rent from the land. So, for example, if the registered proprietor grants a lease to T, and T sublets to ST who lives on the property, both the sublease and lease are overriding interests.

Section 70(1)(g) can only make an interest overriding if it is one that by its nature is capable of surviving through changes in ownership. Neither a bare licence nor a contractual licence can, for this reason, be overriding interests (see *Strand Securities Ltd* v. *Caswell* [1965]). A licence backed by an estoppel could be overriding.

Although s.70(1)(1)(g) can make an interest overriding it does not otherwise change its character. It is now clear, for example, that the interest of a beneficiary behind a trust for sale remains overreachable, even though the beneficiary is in occupation. Once the interest has been overreached, it cannot be asserted against the purchaser and s.70(1)(g) is irrelevant (*City of London Building Society* v. *Flegg* [1988]).

All interests belonging to the occupier are overriding, not just the interest which entitled him to occupy in the first place. So if a tenant is in actual occupation, not only is his lease overriding, but also an option in the lease for the purchase of the landlord's reversion (*Webb* v. *Pollmount* [1966]).

3.17 The Meaning of 'Actual Occupation'

What does 'actual occupation' mean? In unregistered title, the occupation of land by someone who claims on equitable interest is relevant because it may give constructive notice of the equitable interest to the purchaser. If the purchaser, after diligent enquiry and after inspection of the land, fails to discover the occupation, he will take free of the occupier's interest because he does not have notice of it.

Section 70(1)(g) has no such concept of notice within it. In *Williams and Glyn's Bank Ltd* v. *Boland* [1981] it was said that a person is in actual occupation of the land if 'physically present' there. Lord Scarman in his judgement stressed that the statute had substituted a plain factual situation for the uncertainties of notice. Lord Wilberforce stated that in registered land, if there was actual occupation and the occupier had rights, the purchaser took subject to them, and that no further element was material.

The result of the decision clearly is that a purchaser should make enquiry of any occupier that he discovers on the land, to ascertain if that occupier has an interest in it. The enquiry should be made of the *occupier* not the seller. It is only where enquiry is made of the occupier and the rights are not revealed, that they cease to be overriding.

Yet even if a purchaser makes the most diligent search for occupiers, this may not be enough. Even if an occupier is undiscoverable, (for example, deliberately concealed by the seller) his interest may bind the purchaser, if the occupier can be said to be physically present. It is the fact of occupation that matters, not its discoverability.

The meaning of occupation has recently been discussed by the House of Lords in *Abbey National Building Society* v. *Cann and ors* [1990] (see the case notes to Chapter 11). Mrs Cann claimed that she was in actual occupation on the day that the purchase of the house by her son, financed by a mortgage loan from the Building Society, was completed. On that day she was abroad, but her husband and son began to move her belongings into the house as the seller moved out. Her belongings were on the property for 35 minutes before completion of the purchase.

It was said by Lord Oliver that what was necessary for occupation might vary according to the nature and purpose of the property, but that occupation always involved some degree of permanence and continuity, and not a fleeting presence. A purchaser who before completion was allowed to go in to plan decorations or measure for furniture could not be said to be in occupation.

Mrs Cann's claim that she had been in occupation therefore failed.

3.18 When Must the Occupier be in Occupation?

It has been held that if his interest is to be overriding under s.70(1)(g), the occupier must be in occupation at the time the title is transferred to the purchaser (see again *Abbey National Building Society* v. *Cann and ors*, the facts of which are given in Chapter 11). Once the purchaser has taken subject to the interest, it is not necessary that the owner of the interest remain in occupation. His interest will continue to bind the purchaser, even though the owner of the interest then leaves. However, his interest will not bind a later transferee from the purchaser unless the owner of the interest resumes occupation before the transfer takes place (*London and Cheshire Insurance Co. Ltd* v. *Laplagrene Property Co. Ltd* [1971]).

3.19 The Undisclosed Trust for Sale

Much of the litigation involving s.70(1)(g) has been in the context of an undisclosed trust for sale, and is further discussed in Chapter 11.

Case Notes

Williams and Glyn's Bank Ltd. v. *Boland*

[1981] AC 487, [1980] 2 A11 ER 408, [1980} 3 WLR 138, 124 Sol Jo 443, 40 PCR 451.

Mr Boland was the registered proprietor of the family house. His wife had contributed a substantial sum towards the purchase of the house and as a result owned part of the equitable interest. Mr Boland, therefore, held the legal estate on trust for sale for himself and his wife as tenants in common. No entry had been put on the register to protect the wife's interest. Mr Boland later borrowed money from the bank, and mortgaged the house to it. The bank made no enquiries of Mrs Boland. Mr Boland failed to keep up his mortgage payments, so the bank started an action for possession, with a view to selling the house. Could the bank obtain possession against Mrs Boland, or was it bound by her interest?

The bank could only be bound if her interest was an overriding one, under s.70(1)(g) of the Act. Counsel for the Bank raised two arguments in favour of the view that her interest could not be overriding.

The first was that s.70 defined overriding interests as interests subsisting in the registered *land*. The interest of a beneficiary behind a trust for sale is traditionally regarded as being not in the land, but in the proceeds of sale. This is due to what is known as the equitable doctrine of conversion, based on the maxim that 'equity looks upon that as done which ought to be done'. As a trust should be carried out, land subject to a trust for sale is regarded as already sold, and the interests of the beneficiaries as subsisting in the entirely mythical proceeds of the mythical sale.

The House of Lords nevertheless held that Mrs Boland's interest was capable of being overriding. It was said to be 'unreal' to describe her interest as existing merely in the proceeds of sale. Reliance was placed on the earlier Court of Appeal decision in *Bull* v. *Bull* [1955] 1QB 234, [1955] 1 A11 ER 253, [1955] 2 WLR 78. In that case, the son held the legal estate on trust for sale, the beneficiaries being himself and his mother as tenants in common. The son brought an action for possession against his mother. It was held that when a house is bought for joint occupation, each tenant in common has the right to be there, and neither is entitled to turn the other out. So an interest of a beneficiary behind a trust for sale, while it may not be technically an interest in land, is something more than an interest in the proceeds of sale.

However, it appears that if the purpose behind the trust for sale is not to provide a home for the beneficiaries, but instead an investment, an interest of a beneficiary will be regarded as being only in the proceeds of sale, and he will not have any right of occupation. In *Barclay* v. *Barclay* [1970] 2QB 677, [1970] 2 A11 ER 676, [1970] 3 WLR 82, a testator devised his house on trust for sale, with a direction that the proceeds be divided among five beneficiaries. One beneficiary wished to continue to live there. The court ordered that he relinquish possession, as his interest gave him no right to occupy the land. The purpose of the trust was that the land should actually be sold, and his interest was only in the proceeds. It follows that if the land had been sold to a purchaser, the interest of the beneficiary in *Barclay* v. *Barclay* could not have been overriding under s.70(1)(g). It would not have subsisted in reference to the land. So the purpose of a trust for sale is significant in deciding whether a beneficiary's interest is capable of binding a purchaser, either under s.70(1)(g), or if the title is unregistered, under the doctrine of notice.

The second argument used by counsel in the Boland case was that Mrs Boland was not in 'actual occupation'. This argument was based on the view that underlying s.70(1)(g) were the old rules about notice, so that the occupation must be such as to make a purchaser suspicious. A purchaser would not be suspicious when he found a wife occupying a husband's house, as the marriage would be a sufficient explanation. This argument was resoundingly rejected. The section was to be interpreted literally. A person is in actual occupation of the house if physically present there.

City of London Building Society v. *Flegg [1988] AC 54, [1987] 3 A11 ER 435, [1987] 2 WLR 1266*

Mr and Mrs Maxwell-Brown, and Mrs Maxwell-Brown's parents, Mr and Mrs Flegg, proposed to buy a house for the four of them to live in. The Fleggs contributed £18 000 towards the purchase price. The title was registered. The legal estate was transferred into the names of the Maxwell-Browns only, who held on trust for sale for themselves and their parents. Later, without the authority of the Fleggs, the Maxwell-Browns mortgaged the legal estate. The payments were not kept up, and the Building Society sought possession of the property. The parents claimed that they had an equitable interest in the house, by reason of their contribution towards its purchase, and that their interest bound the Society as the parents were in actual occupation. It was held in the House of Lords that the parents' interest could not be asserted against the Society, as the mortgage had been created by two trustees for sale and that consequently the interests of the beneficiaries had been overreached. Once the interests of the Fleggs had been overreached, they had no interest left in the land to be overriding.

Note that s.17 of the Trustee Act 1925 provides that a mortgagee lending money to trustees is not concerned to see that the trustees are acting properly. The validity of the mortgage, therefore, was not affected by the fact that the Maxwell-Browns were acting in breach of trust when creating it. The Fleggs could, perhaps, have put a restriction on the register, to the effect that no mortgage by the registered proprietors was to be registered without the Fleggs's consent (see Chapter 11).

Lyus v. *Prowsa [1982] 1 WLR 1044*

Land was sold by S to P expressly subject to X's contract to buy. The title was registered, but X was not in occupation and had not protected his minor interest by any sort of entry on the register. P then sold the land to Q, again expressly subject to the contract.

Q claimed that he was not bound by the contract, as it was an unprotected minor interest. It was held, however, that X could enforce the contract against Q.

The reason given was that P had held the land on a constructive trust for X. The judgement stressed that this was because it had been stipulated between S and P that P should give effect to the contract. No trust would have arisen if the sale had been said to be subject to the contract merely for the protection of S. The Land Registration Act 1925 could not be used as an instrument of fraud, so P could not claim to be released from the trust on the grounds that the contract had not been entered on the register. Q was bound by the trust, because he had bought with notice of it.

The decision has been criticised as having ignored provisions of the Land Registration Act. Section 74 of the Act, for example, states that a person dealing with a registered estate shall not be affected by notice of a trust. So Q should not have been affected by his notice of the constructive trust imposed on P. The decision was approved by the House of Lords, however, in *Ashburn Anstalt* v. *Arnold* [1987].

The same reasoning would apply to a conveyance of unregistered land. X's failure to protect his contract by registering it as a C(iv) land charge would usually ensure that the contract did not bind P, even though the conveyance by S to P said the land was conveyed subject to it. P would, however, be bound if the circumstances justified the imposition of a constructive trust.

Workshop

Attempt this problem yourself, then read the specimen solution at the end of the book.

Problem 1

You act for two brothers, Bill and Ben Brown, who have bought a freehold house, 15 Flowerpot Lane, for £45 000. They bought with the aid of a mortgage loan from the Bleaklow Building Society, for which you also act. The house was conveyed to the two brothers as tenants in common. In the conveyance they covenanted with the seller that no further buildings of any kind would be erected on the land. The transaction was completed yesterday.

1 What steps should you now take to ensure that the brothers will have a good title to the house?
2 What document will finally issue from the District Land Registry?

---

4 Unregistered Title: Third-Party Rights

This chapter serves as a reminder of the principles which decide whether or not a purchaser of *unregistered* land takes subject to a third party interest.

4.1 Is the Third Party's Interest Legal or Equitable?

When deciding whether or not the interest will bind a purchaser, the first question to decide is whether the interest is a legal interest or an equitable one. The reason is that generally speaking a purchaser of an unregistered title will take subject to legal estates and interests, whether he knows of them or not.

Interests capable of being legal include:

(a) A lease. Remember, however, that a lease is *capable* of being legal. In order to be so, it must have been granted by deed. A lease created by signed writing which does not amount to a deed will be equitable only (See Chapter 13 for the rules which now determine whether or not a document is a deed). The exception to this is a lease for 3 years or less at best rent without a premium, and giving an immediate right to possession. This can be created as a legal estate without a deed (Sections 52–4 of the Law of Property Act 1925.) So a periodic lease e.g. a weekly tenancy, will be legal, even though granted informally.

(b) An easement which is either perpetual, or granted for a term of years. (An easement for life can only be equitable.) Again, if the easement is to be legal, it must have been granted by deed.

(c) A legal mortgage or legal charge. However, if the mortgage or a legal charge is not protected by a deposit of title deeds with the lender, it is registrable under the Land Charges Act 1972, and will not bind a purchaser merely because it is legal (see later).

4.2 Is It Overreachable?

Equitable interests do not automatically bind a purchaser. So if faced with an equitable interest, the next questions will be, is the interest overreachable, and was it overreached?

Interests of beneficiaries behind a trust for sale of the legal estate, or behind a settlement under the Settled Land Act 1925 are overreachable. If, for example, the legal estate is vested in two or more trustees for sale, and they all convey, the interests of the beneficiaries will be overreached, and it is irrelevant whether the purchaser knew of their existence or not (see Chapter 11). If the sale had been by a single trustee for sale, the interests would not be overreached, and would bind a purchaser who had notice of them.

4.3 Does the Land Charges Act 1972 Apply?

Once you have decided that the equitable interest has not been overreached, the next questions to ask are, was the equitable interest registrable under the Land Charges Act 1972, and if so, was it registered? The principle is that if an interest is registrable, then if it is registered, it will bind a subsequent purchaser. If it is not registered, it will not. Registration is all. Of course, it is not quite as simple as that, and the principle is elaborated in section 4.5.

4.4 Notice

If you are left with an equitable interest that has not been overreached, and is not registrable as a land charge, you come to the well-known rule that the equitable interest will bind anyone who acquires the land with the exception of a *bona fide* purchaser for value of the legal estate without notice of the equitable interest.

Many equitable incumbrances are registrable under the Land Charges Act 1972, and if an interest is registrable under that Act, the concept of notice is irrelevant (see *Midland Bank Trust Co. Ltd* v. *Green* [1981]). The rule about the *bona fide* purchaser covers only those interests that do not fall within the Act. These interests include:

- restrictive covenants created before 1926;
- the interest of a beneficiary behind a trust for sale that has not been overreached;
- an interest created by proprietory estoppel.

If a purchaser wishes to escape such an interest, he must prove that he bought a legal estate for value (this would exclude a donee, someone acquiring property by a gift in a will, and a squatter) without *notice*.

(*a*) *Actual Notice*

Notice can be actual, i.e. the purchaser actually knows of the third-party interest. A purchaser may have actual notice of pre-1926 restrictive covenants because they are mentioned in the title deeds, and he reads them. (If he escapes actual notice because of his careless failure to read the title deeds, he will be fixed with constructive notice.)

(*b*) *Constructive Notice*

The purchaser will be treated as having constructive notice of anything he does not know about but would have discovered had he made such enquiries as he ought reasonably to have made. It follows from this that if despite all reasonable conveyancing enquiries the equitable interest remains undiscovered, the purchaser takes free from it.

A purchaser risks constructive notice if he fails to see all the title deeds which he is entitled to see; for example, if he accepts title traced from a document that is not a good root, or accepts title traced from a good root less than 15 years old. He risks constructive notice if he fails to inspect the land.

Occupation If someone other than the seller is occupying the land, that occupation gives constructive notice of any equitable interest the occupier owns. The occupation is suspicious; it throws doubt on the seller's claim of ownership, and should be investigated. (Do remember that if the occupier's equitable interest is registrable under Land Charges Act 1972, occupation is irrelevant. The interest will only bind the purchaser if it is registered.)

Not only is it possible to have constructive notice of the interest, it is also possible to have constructive notice of the occupation. In other words, if the purchaser, through his failure to make proper inspection of the property, fails to discover the occupier, he has constructive notice of the occupation, and through it, constructive notice of any equitable interest the occupier owns (see *Midland Bank Ltd* v. *Farmpride Hatcheries Ltd* [1980] and *Kingsnorth Trust Ltd* v. *Tizard* [1986]).

If the seller is in occupation, but with another, the occupation by that other may also give constructive notice of any equitable interest he owns. It still depends, of course, on the occupier being discoverable by ordinary conveyancing enquiries. It was said in *Kingsnorth Trust Ltd* v. *Tizard* that a purchaser is not under a duty to pry into drawers and wardrobes in a search for signs of occupation. However, it was also said that a purchaser who inspected the property by a pre-arranged appointment with the seller had not made proper enquiries, as the seller had been given an opportunity to conceal signs of occupation. Apparently, according to the judgement, only by calling on the seller unawares, and thoroughly inspecting the property, can a purchaser escape constructive notice.

The case also suggests that if the purchaser has reason to believe that the seller is married, then an enquiry must be pursued as to the possibility that the spouse may have an equitable interest, whether the spouse is in occupation or not.

(*c*) *Imputed Notice*

Any notice, actual or constructive, received by the purchaser's agent (e.g. solicitor, licenced conveyancer or surveyor) in the course of the transaction is imputed to the purchaser.

4.5 The Land Charges Act 1972 (Formerly 1925)

(*a*) *Registrable Interests*

The Act permits registration of certain interests affecting the title to unregistered land. Not all the interests registrable under the Act are listed here but only those most likely to be revealed by a search made by a purchaser.

(i) *A petition in bankruptcy* This is registered in the register of pending actions. A search certificate will reveal the entry PA(B).
(ii) *A receiving order in bankruptcy* This is registered in the register of writs and orders, and a search certificate will reveal the entry WO(B).
(iii) *A land charge class C(i)* This is a legal mortgage unprotected by a deposit of title deeds with the lender. A mortgage protected by deposit of title deeds cannot be registered as a land charge, the idea being that the absence of the title deeds is itself enough to alert the purchaser to a possible claim against the land.
(iv) *A land charge class C(iii)* This is defined as an equitable charge not protected by deposit of title deeds. This class includes the purchaser's lien for a deposit paid to the seller or seller's agent, and the seller's lien for any unpaid purchase price provided that he parted with the deeds on completion. It is uncertain whether an equitable mortgage of the legal estate should be protected by being registered as a C(iii) land charge, or as a C(iv) (being a contract for the grant of a legal mortgage).
(v) *A land charge class C(iv)* This is defined by the Act as 'a contract by an estate owner or by a person entitled at the date of the contract to have a legal estate conveyed to him to convey or create a legal estate, including a contract conferring expressly or by statutory implication a valid option to purchase, a right of pre-emption or any other like right'.

(aa) This covers a contract to sell the freehold. It also includes a subcontract. Suppose Sarah contracts to sell Blackacre to Pauline, who immediately contracts to resell it to Rosemary. Pauline can register a C(iv) against Sarah. Rosemary can also register a C(iv), as Pauline is a person entitled to have the legal estate conveyed to her. However, registration of the contract must be not against Pauline's name, but against Sarah's, as the Act requires a land charge to be registered against the name of the estate owner. It is Sarah who owns the legal estate (see *Barrett* v. *Hilton Developments Ltd* [1975]).
(bb) A contract to assign a lease.
(cc) A contract to grant a lease.

(dd) An option to buy the freehold or a lease, an option to renew a lease, and an option given to a tenant to acquire his landlord's reversion.

(ee) A right of pre-emption. A right of pre-emption is created, for example, when X contracts that if he wishes to sell the land, he will first of all offer it for sale to Y, before putting it on the open market. By contrast, an option is the right for Y to buy X's land, whether X wishes to sell or not. It was decided in *Pritchard* v. *Briggs* [1980] that a right of pre-emption, unlike an option, does not in itself create any interest in land capable of binding a purchaser. It is a personal right. However, when the circumstances occur which make the right of pre-emption exerciseable, (for instance, in the above example, when X puts the land up for sale) the right of pre-emption ripens into an option. A C(iv) land charge registered when the *right of pre-emption was created* will protect the option, and ensure that the option binds the purchaser.

(ff) A contract by a tenant to surrender his lease before seeking to assign it (*Greene* v. *Church Commissioners for England* [1974]).

(gg) An equitable lease.

(hh) A contract for the grant of a legal easement.

(vi) *Class D(ii) A restrictive covenant created after 1925* (but not one made between landlord and tenant).

(vii) *Class D(iii) An equitable easement* If the easement is equitable solely because it was not granted by deed, the correct head of registration appears to be C(iv), as the defective grant is treated as a contract for the grant of a legal easement. It is for the same reason that an equitable lease is registered as a C(iv) land charge. Class D(iii) seems to cover only an equitable easement that is incapable of being legal, e.g. an easement for life.

(viii) *Class F A spouse's rights of occupation under the Matrimonial Homes Act 1983* Section 1 of the 1983 Act gives a spouse who does not own the legal estate in the matrimonial home rights of occupation in that home. These rights are capable of binding a purchaser, provided (in the case of an unregistered title) they are protected by the registration of a class F charge.

(*b*) *System of Registration*

The system of registration adopted in 1925 was not registration against the land affected, but against the name of the owner of the legal estate who had burdened his land. This is unfortunate as a registration can only be discovered by a search against the right name. For example, suppose that since 1925 the freehold in Blackacre has been conveyed by the following deeds:

1928 a conveyance by A to B
1954 a conveyance by B to C

1969 a conveyance by C to D
1973 a conveyance by D to E

A purchaser from E sees only the 1973 conveyance, as this is fifteen years old. He enquiries of the Chief Land Registrar if any land charges are registered against the names of D and E. The reply is 'no'. Suppose, though, that in 1928, in the conveyance from A, B gave a restrictive covenant to A, burdening the land that B had just acquired from him. A, being the person with the benefit of the covenant, would have hastened to register a D(ii) land charge against B's name. Only a search against B's name will reveal that registration. The purchaser cannot search against B's name because he does not know it, yet the covenant will bind the purchaser, as it is registered. So a purchaser takes subject to all land charges registered since 1925, but only has the opportunity to discover the recent ones.

This is the problem of what is called 'the pre-root land charge'. It is mitigated by:

(i) The practice of every deed mentioning existing incumbrances in the habendum. It is likely that the 1973 conveyance would say that Blackacre was conveyed to E 'subject to the covenants created by a deed dated 29 February 1928 made between A of the one part and B of the other part'. The purchaser can add these two names to his search.
(ii) The duty of the seller to disclose all incumbrances affecting the present title, even those created pre-root.
(iii) The possibility of compensation under s.25 Law of Property Act 1969 (see Chapter 19).

(*c*) *Name*?

Although the Act requires registration against the 'name' of the estate owner it does not say what is meant by 'name'. The case of *Diligent Finance Co. Ltd* v. *Alleyne* (1972) established the convenient rule that the name against which registration is to be effected is the name contained in the conveyancing documents.

A registration against an incorrect version of this name will not bind someone who searches against the correct name, and obtains a clear certificate of search. In the Alleyne case, a wife registered a class F charge against Erskine Alleyne. This registration did not bind a mortgagee, who searched against the husband's full name Erskine Owen Alleyne, the version of the name that appeared in the deeds. This shows how the rule in the Alleyne case can catch out a person who cannot see the deeds.

Although a registration against an incorrect version of the name will not bind someone who searches against the correct version, it has been said that it will bind someone who does not search at all, or someone who searches against *another* incorrect version. In *Oak Co-operative Building*

Society v. *Blackburn* [1968] the name against which the land charge should have been registered was Francis David Blackburn. The charge was registered against the name of Frank David Blackburn. The purchaser applied for a search to be made against the name of Francis Davis Blackburn and obtained a clear search certificate. It was held that the purchaser could not rely on the search certificate, but took subject to the charge.

(*d*) *Effect of Non-Registration*

An unregistered land charge is void against a purchaser for value of any interest in the land. Exceptions to this are land charges C(iv), and D(i)(ii) and (iii), which are void against a purchaser for money or money's worth of a legal estate. The only difference in the two types of consideration is marriage, which provides value but not money's worth.

The difference between a purchaser of any interest, and the purchaser of a legal estate is of more significance. An unregistered class F land charge is void against both a legal and an equitable mortgagee. An unregistered estate contract is void for non-registration only against a legal mortgagee.

It seems that once a land charge is void against a later purchaser, it is also void against anyone who claims through the purchaser. For example, suppose that Morgan owns Blackacre, and gives Owen an option to buy it. Two weeks later, Morgan conveys Blackacre to Pritchard. Then Owen registers a C(iv) land charge. Pritchard sells Blackacre to Ross. Does Ross take subject to the option? It was registered before he bought it. However, he probably shares Pritchard's immunity. After all, it means little to Pritchard that he *owns* free of the option if he cannot also *sell* free of it.

(*e*) *A Search at the Land Charges Registry*

This is dealt with in Chapter 9.

Workshop

Questions needing a knowledge of the Land Charges Act will be asked at the end of later chapters.

---

5 Drafting the Contract

5.1 Introduction

In order to draft the contract, the seller's solicitor must have a thorough knowledge of his client's title, information about the property (almost invariably culled from the client rather than by looking at the property) and must know anything that has been agreed between his client and the purchaser, for example the fact that the sale includes curtains (see 1.3).

5.2 Drafting a Contract to Sell a Registered Title

(*a*) *Introduction*

Suppose that you are the solicitor or licensed conveyancer instructed by Harry Mark to sell his house, 232 Main Road. It is clear from the estate agent's particulars and from what Harry tells you, that he owns a small semi-detached house, built about 1900, that fronts onto the road. Harry lives alone there. In response to your questions about the possibility of any neighbours having rights over the property, he tells you that his neighbours, who live at 234, have the right to cross his backyard in order to reach the side entrance which runs between numbers 232 and 230. This side entrance belongs to number 230, but Harry tells you that a right to use it was granted in 1980 to the then owners of 232 and 234, in return for the surrender by them of a right-of-way across the back garden of 230 to Ship Lane.

The house is mortgaged to Harry's bank, but the bank has told you that the title is registered and you have obtained office copy entries.

Harry wants to take various plants from the garden when he moves, particularly some shrub roses. The purchase price of the house is £72 000 but he is also selling the curtains and the wardrobes. These are not fitted wardrobes, but are being left behind because they are too big to get down the stairs without being dismantled. The price agreed for the curtains and wardrobes is £1,000.

Look at the office copy entries shown overleaf.

Office Copy Entries

HM LAND REGISTRY

Title Number K000000

A. PROPERTY REGISTER

County: Kent District: Hope's Bottom

(17 October 1951) The freehold land shown edged with red on the plan of the above title filed at the Registry known as 4 Andrews Cottages, Main Road.

(19 March 1979) Property now known as 232 Main Road.

(30 April 1981) The property has the benefit of a right-of-way granted by a deed dated 15 April 1980 made between (i) Express Developments Limited and (ii) Betty Booper.

B. PROPRIETORSHIP REGISTER

Title Absolute

Proprietor

1. (19 March 1981) Harry Mark of 232 Main Road, Hope's Bottom, Kent.

C. CHARGES REGISTER

---

1. (17 October 1961) by an agreement dated 21 February 1961 made between Lilian Hopwood and the County Council of the Administrative County of Kent, a strip of land fronting Main Road comprising three square yards was dedicated as part of the public highway.
2. (19 March 1981) charge dated 20 January 1981 to secure the monies including the further advances therein mentioned.
3. (19 March 1981) Proprietor – Midland Bank plc of 19 Pessimist Street, Hope's Bottom, Kent.

The property register mentions the right of way over number 230. As this was granted to benefit registered land, the deed granting it was sent to the Land Registry, and the easement was registered in the property register of the benefited land. (If the title to number 230 was also registered, the easement should also appear in the charges register of that title (see Chapter 12). As the grant is not set out in full in the property register, the purchaser will want to see a copy of this deed. We can obtain an office copy of it from the Registry.

There is no mention of the right of way belonging to number 234 over the backyard of our client's house. Remember the age of the property. The right was probably never expressly granted, but arose by prescription, i.e. by virtue of long use. It would have existed as a legal easement when the title to number 232 was first registered, but as there was no documentary evidence of it, no entry was put on the charges register. Nevertheless, it will still be enforceable against a purchaser from Harry, as it is an overriding interest (see 3.15).

Now you can start to draft the contract.

(*b*) *The Form of the Contract*

Look at the form of agreement in the Appendix to this book. This is the standard contract which must be used if you are following the protocol. You are likely to use it even if you are not. It incorporates what are known as the Standard Conditions of Sale (2nd Edition). (These supersede the two separate sets of conditions known as the Law Society's Conditions of Sale and the National Conditions of Sale).

The front page of the contract, when completed, will give details of the property, the seller's title to it, and other terms of the bargain. The back page lists the conditions of sale. The conditions are the terms upon which the property is sold. There is a distinction to be drawn between the standard conditions and the special conditions. The standard conditions have been drawn up by the Law Society and the Solicitors' Law Stationery Society Ltd who own the copyright. They are designed to be suitable for both domestic and commercial conveyancing, and cover eventualities likely to be common to most transactions. The special conditions are those written into the contract by the person drafting it, to deal with matters peculiar to the particular transaction (although some special conditions are already printed onto the contract form in a helpful manner).

Read the printed special condition 1. It expressly incorporates the standard conditions into the contract. The Law Society recommends that if the standard conditions are not actually printed on the form of contract, then a copy of them should be attached to it. This will ensure that s.2 of the Law of Property (Miscellaneous Provisions) Act 1989 is satisfied (see 5.10).

(*c*) *Date and Parties*

Still looking at the form, you will see that the first blank to be filled in is the date. *Do not fill this in*. The contract will be dated when the two parts are exchanged, probably with the date of exchange.

The next part to fill in shows the names of the parties. Your investigation of title, and enquiries of Harry have satisfied you that he is the beneficial owner of the legal estate. There seems to be no equitable interest to overreach, and no need for the appointment of another trustee to act with him (see Chapter 11 for circumstances in which the appointment of a second trustee would be necessary). Harry or the estate agents will have told you the purchaser's name.

(*d*) *The Property*

You then have to draft the description of the property. This must be done carefully, for if the seller misdescribes the title (e.g. calls a sub-lease a head-lease) or the property (e.g. says it is 100 acres when it is only 75) he will inevitably break his contract. He will not be able to convey what he has contracted to convey. This particular breach of contract is called misdescription and is dealt with in Chapter 18.

The three things to bear in mind are:

(i) stating the estate;
(ii) describing the extent of the property;
(iii) stating any rights that benefit the property.

So, if number 232 had been an unregistered title, a satisfactory description would have been, 'The freehold property known as 232 Main Road, Hope's Bottom, Kent, together with the benefit of a right-of-way over part of number 230 Main Road, so far as the same was granted by a deed dated 15 April 1980 made between (i) Express Developments Limited and (ii) Betty Booper'. Of course, a copy of the 1980 deed would have to accompany the draft contract, otherwise the purchaser's solicitor would find that part of the description meaningless. No plan would be used. The boundaries of number 232 are well-established and no map is needed to determine them. Most urban properties can be described by postal address alone.

In fact the title to number 232 is registered. This need not make any change to the particulars at all. However, in registered title, it is usual to see the particulars drafted in this way: 'the freehold property known as 232 Main Road, Hope's Bottom, Kent, as the same is registered at HM Land Registry with absolute title under Title Number K000000'. This has the advantage of making it clear that the seller is only contracting to convey the land that is registered under the title. (If the registered title does not include all the land that the purchaser hoped to buy, the seller cannot be accused of misdescription.) An office copy of the entries on the register will accompany the draft contract, and a copy of the 1980 deed. Nothing is said about the 1980 right-of-way in the particulars, as the contract is promising the land described in the property register, and the property register mentions the easement. (Notice that it is in fact never essential to mention easements that benefit the land. They will pass to the purchaser on completion anyway, as being part of the land conveyed. If there is any doubt about the enforceability of the easement against the neighbouring land, the easement should not be mentioned at all, or else the doubt should be made clear in the contract.)

(*e*) *Root of Title/Title Number*

A contract only specifies a root of title if the seller's title is unregistered. Your client's title is registered, so you merely state the title number. Had Harry's title been other than absolute, you might have felt it desirable, although not essential, to state the class of title. It would not be essential, because almost invariably office copy entries of the register are sent to the purchaser with the draft contract. The reason that it would have been desirable is that it has been held that if a title is described in the contract merely as registered, the purchaser is entitled to assume that it is registered with absolute title. If the seller is registered only with possessory or good leasehold title, it is true that that will be disclosed by the accompanying copy entries, but a special condition puts the question of disclosure beyond doubt.

If you have already stated the title number and class of title in your description of the property (see b), nothing need be written here at all.

(*f*) *Incumbrances*

Look at condition 3.1.1. The seller is selling the property free from incumbrances other than those that are listed in condition 3.1.2. This says that the property is being sold subject to incumbrances that are mentioned in the agreement, and also those that are discoverable by inspection of the property before the contract. Harry might argue that this right-of-way is discoverable by inspection, perhaps because of a gate in the wall dividing number 234 from number 232, but the buyer may later dispute this. The safest thing to do is to mention the easement in the contract. You will do this by giving details of it under the heading 'Incumbrances' on the front page of the contract. You might say something like 'a right belonging to the owners and occupiers of number 234 to walk across the backyard of the Property to and from the side entrance running along the boundary of the Property and number 230, Main Road'. You could also add that there is no documentary evidence of the right-of-way, but that it has been exercised for many years, and is believed to have arisen through prescription. Now read special condition 2. The sale is now subject to this right-of-way.

The subject of disclosure of incumbrances is dealt with in greater detail later in this chapter.

(*g*) *Capacity in which the Seller Sells*

Here you state the capacity in which the seller will be expressed to convey in the later conveyance or transfer. There are four capacities in which the seller can say he conveys – i.e. beneficial owner, trustee, personal representative, or mortgagee (s.76 of the Law of Property Act 1925). Your investigation of title has shown that Harry owns the legal estate for his own benefit, so you will state that he will convey as 'beneficial owner'. This is then the capacity which will be stated in the transfer. The point about the statement of capacity is that certain covenants for title will be implied into a conveyance or transfer according to which capacity is stated (see Chapter 19).

(*h*) *Completion Date*

The completion date will be inserted when contracts are exchanged, and is obviously a matter of negotiation between the seller and purchaser. If this clause is not completed, standard condition 6.1.1 provides that the date for completion will be 20 working days after the date of the contract.

Whether the completion date is fixed by a special or by the standard condition, standard condition 6.1.2 states that if the money due on completion is received after 2.00 p.m. on that day, completion is for the purposes of standard conditions 6.3 and 7.3 to be treated as taking place on the next working day. Working days are defined by standard condition 1.1.1 to exclude weekends and bank holidays. So, for example, suppose completion date is Friday, 30 April. The purchase price is not received from the purchaser until 3.30 p.m. on Friday. For most purposes – e.g. the dating of the conveyance or transfer – completion took place on Friday. However, under condition 6.3 the outgoings will be apportioned as if completion took place on Monday, 3 May and the purchaser will under condition 7.3 have to pay interest for late completion.

(*i*) *Contract Rate*

This clause is used to agree a rate of interest for the contract. This rate of interest is relevant to calculate the interest payable on late completion (see standard condition 7.3). The rate of interest can be specified by a special condition. It must not be too high, or it may deter a prospective purchaser from entering into the contract. Remember too that if Harry is responsible for the delay in completion, he will be paying the same rate. The point is to have the contract rate something higher than the rate charged by banks for a bridging loan. This encourages a purchaser to complete promptly, as it will be cheaper for him to obtain a bridging loan than to delay completion. If a special condition is felt necessary, it will probably specify a figure that is something above the base rate from time to time of a chosen bank, e.g. '4 per cent per annum above the base rate from time to time of the Midland Bank plc'.

If a rate is not set by a special condition, standard condition 1.1.1 says that the rate is 'the Law Society's interest rate from time to time in force'. The Law Society sets a rate for this purpose which is published in every issue of the *Law Society's Gazette*. It is a figure 4 per cent above the base rate of the Law Society's own bank, which is Barclays. The rate set by the standard condition will, therefore, generally be acceptable, and only peculiar circumstances will make it necessary to set the rate by a special condition.

If conveyancers are prepared to accept the standard condition, it will have the advantage of ensuring that every contract in a chain of transactions will have the same interest rate applying to it. However, this is not always desirable if there is a big disparity in the purchase prices (see Chapter 17).

(*j*) *The Purchase Price, Deposit and Amount Payable for Chattels*

The purchase price is the amount payable for the land, so in Harry's case it is £72 000. Land includes fixtures. Standard condition 2.2.1 provides for the payment by the purchaser of a deposit of 10 per cent of the purchase price. Unless this is altered by a special condition (it is now quite common for the purchaser to pay less than 10 per cent) the figure here will obviously be £7200.

There is then added the price payable for the chattels (£1000) so the balance payable on completion is £65 800.

It is important for the purchaser that the total of £73 000 to be paid is correctly apportioned between the land and the chattels. One reason is that stamp duty is only paid by the purchaser on the consideration paid for the land. Another reason is that the deposit is 10 per cent of the purchase price paid for the land, not for the chattels.

(*k*) *The Agreement*

The front page concludes with the promise of the seller to sell, and the purchaser to buy.

(*l*) *Printed Special Conditions*

Now turn to the second page of the form. There is no reason in this transaction to change the first three of the four special conditions already printed here.

(*m*) *Special Condition 3 – Fixtures and Chattels*

You know that it has been settled between Harry and the purchaser that Harry can remove the roses, but is selling the carpets and wardrobes.

The underlying law is that once Harry has contracted to sell the land, he cannot remove any part of it, unless the contract permits him to do so. Plants are generally part of the land, so the contract must give Harry the right to remove the roses. A dispute can arise as to whether a particular item is a chattel (and not therefore part of the land, so removable before completion unless the contract says otherwise) or a fixture (and therefore part of the land, so not removable). The legal definition of a fixture is that it is a chattel which is fixed to the land and has lost its identity as a chattel and become part of the land. The definition is easy to state, but not to apply. The initial test is that of fixing. If the chattel is fixed to the land or to the house on the land, it is presumed to be a fixture. If not fixed, it is presumed to be a chattel. This test can however, be upset by a finding of intention. An item may not be fixed, yet rank as a fixture because it was intended to become part of the land. A dry stone wall would be a fixture. On the other hand, an item may be fixed yet remain a chattel, because there was no intention that the chattel should become part of the land, e.g. a tapestry fixed to a wall for display. In other words, there is plenty of scope for argument.

It is always possible to evade argument by special conditions in the contract. You could have a condition saying that the sale excludes the shrub roses, but includes the carpets and wardrobes. Fine, but this specific condition is of no use when the purchaser bitterly complains that Harry has taken the sundial from the garden. Was Harry justified? Was it a chattel or a fixture?

In its national protocol the Law Society encourages the use of a fixtures, fittings and contents form which lists in detail which items are, or are not, included in the sale. You will have sent this form to Harry for completion or have asked him to complete it at the initial interview. This completed form is then attached to the contract and forms part of it (see special condition 3). Harry will spend a pleasant half-hour filling in the form, stating against each item listed in the form whether the sale includes it, or excludes it. The sundial? It is one of the items noted in the form (garden ornaments). So the dispute will be settled by reading the form to see if Harry said he would be leaving it, or taking it.

(*n*) *Special Condition 4*

This offers alternatives. Harry is selling with vacant possession, so you will cross out the alternative statement that the sale is subject to existing tenancies.

(*o*) *Other Special Conditions*

The facts do not seem to justify any other special conditions. The gaps in the agreement – e.g. remedies for late completion – are filled in by the standard conditions incorporated into the contract. Most of the standard conditions are mentioned in other chapters of this book.

Before practising the drafting of another contract, we shall pause to consider the drafting of special conditions relating to the seller's title.

5.3 The Implied Promise as to Title

Although the seller's promise as to his title is the most important of the promises he gives in the contract, you will rarely see the promise expressed in the contract. The parties rely on the fact that the promise is *implied.*

The implied promise is that the seller has a good title to the freehold estate free from incumbrances. Clearly, if he cannot live up to this promise, it must be changed by an express condition in the contract.

It is because of this promise in the contract that it is said that the seller has a duty to disclose latent defects in title. However, this duty of disclosure is perhaps better understood as a *precaution* of disclosure. If there is a flaw in the seller's title, and this is not disclosed to the purchaser before the contract is made, then inevitably the seller is breaking his promise as to title. The purchaser, on discovering the defect before completion, may be able to say that the breach is serious enough to discharge the contract, or may be able to claim a reduction in the purchase price by way of damages. If, however, the seller discloses the defect before the contract is made, the contractual promise is altered. If the defect is disclosed, the purchaser has, by implication, agreed to buy subject to it. The promise by the seller is now 'good title, free from incumbrances, with the exception of this particular matter which has been disclosed to the purchaser'. Disclosure cuts down the seller's promise as to title.

What follows will be easier to understand if you realise that a defect in title may consist of a third-party right enforceable against the land – for example, an easement, covenant or lease. The seller cannot then give title free from incumbrances. Alternatively, it may be what is known as a 'paper' defect – i.e. that there is something wrong with the documentary evidence of title. The deeds may not show that the seller owns the legal estate, or may show that his ownership could be challenged. He would not then have a good title.

What Must the Seller Disclose?

Unless the contract says otherwise, the answer is '*latent* defects in *title*'. So from this we can see that:

(a) *He need not disclose physical defects* There is no implied promise in the contract about the physical state of the property. This is why the purchaser should consider having the property surveyed before he decides to buy. However, a physical defect *may* give the purchaser a cause of action against the seller:

(i) if before contract the seller states the property is free from physical defect, and the statement is untrue. The purchaser would have remedies for misrepresentation (see Chapter 19);
(ii) if the contract *does* make an *express* promise about the physical state of the property;

(iii) if the property being sold is a leasehold, rather than a freehold estate. The physical defect, if a breach of covenant in the lease, may also be a defect in title (see Chapter 15);
(iv) if the seller has taken active steps to conceal a physical defect before contract. This may amount to fraud;
(v) if the seller built the house and did it negligently (*Anns* v. *Merton London Borough Council* [1978] and see Defective Premises Act 1977).

(b) *The seller need not disclose patent defects in title* A patent defect has been defined by case law as a defect that is visible to the eye or can reasonably be inferred from something that is visible to the eye (*Yandle & Sons* v. *Sutton* [1922]. The logic of this is that as the land discloses the defect to the purchaser, there is no need for the seller to do it. A path across the property might mean that the private right of way along the path would be a patent defect. It was held in the Yandle case however, that a *public* right of way was not necessarily to be inferred from the existence of a pathway. Few defects will be patent. A defect in the paper title will always be latent as it will be discoverable only by looking at the deeds. A lease is a latent defect, even though the tenant is living on the property. In the case of unregistered title, s.24 of the Law of Property Act 1969 makes it clear that the fact that an incumbrance is registered as a land charge under the Land Charges Act 1972, does not make it into a patent defect.

(Do not allow yourself to become confused at this point. Remember we are talking about the responsibility of the seller to tell the purchaser about third-party rights. We are *not* discussing whether or not the rights will bind the purchaser on completion, when registration or occupation might be very relevant).

(c) *The seller need not disclose third-party rights that will not bind the purchaser on completion* They are not defects in title. If the seller is a trustee for sale, he need not disclose the interests of the beneficiaries behind the trust, as he can, by conveying with another trustee, overreach them.

Another example would be an option to buy that has not, in unregistered title, been registered as a C(iv) land charge, or, in registered title, been protected by an entry on the seller's register. The non-registration will make the option void against the purchaser. The same would hold true of unprotected restrictive covenants, although in fact these would have to be mentioned in the contract if an indemnity covenant were required (see Chapter 12).

It should now be made clear that although generally the disclosure of the defect to the purchaser means that he has agreed to buy subject to it, this does, in fact, only apply to an irremovable defect. If a defect is removable – for example, as above, by the appointment of a second trustee – then the purchaser is entitled to assume that it will be removed. This is why it is the duty of the seller to ensure that all mortgages and other financial charges are paid off before completion, even though the purchaser knew of the charges before contract. If, in fact the sale is to be subject to the financial charges, there must be a special condition saying this. (Remember that if it is a financial charge in favour of a local authority, the contract may say that the sale is subject to it, see standard condition 3, discussed later).

Notice two further things about the duty of disclosure:

1. The seller is under a duty to disclose *all* incumbrances, even those he does not know exist. Remember the promise is freedom from *all* undisclosed incumbrances. Therefore, if the purchaser, before completion, discovers a third-party interest over the property which the seller has not told him about, the seller would, in the absence of a condition in the contract, be in breach of contract. It would be no excuse for the seller to say that the non-disclosure was due to his complete ignorance of the interest. The only way that he could escape liability would be to establish that the interest was a patent, rather than a latent, incumbrance (but notice the effect of standard condition 3, discussed later).
2. In unregistered title, the duty of disclosure covers all defects in the paper title, except a pre-root defect which the seller did not know about. The exception arises from s.45 of the Law of Property Act 1925, which is explained in Chapter 8.

5.4 When Do we Need to Alter the Implied Promise as to Title?

(*a*) *When We are Not Selling the Freehold, But the Leasehold*

It must be made clear that it is a leasehold estate that is being sold. The particulars will generally give details of the lease, and a copy of the lease will accompany the draft contract (see Chapter 15).

(*b*) *When the Seller Does Not Have a Good Title to the Estate*

The seller's promise that he has a good title is not a promise that the title is completely flawless, but that it is a title that will lead to quiet possession of the land, without any real threat of dispute or litigation.

If there is a defect in his title, the first thing for the seller to consider is putting his title into order. If the conveyance to him was void – for example, because it was not properly executed – he may be able to ask for a confirmatory conveyance. He may be able to trace a plan lost from a past deed, or to contact a past mortgagee to obtain a receipt that should have been previously endorsed on a redeemed mortgage.

However when faced with a defect in the paper title that cannot be put right, the last resort of the seller is a special condition which details the defect, and then says that the purchaser cannot raise any objection to the title on that ground. It is a last resort, because if the defect is serious, a purchaser will reject the draft contract, and look for a different property to buy. However, if the defect is there, and cannot be put right, a special condition is the only answer to the problem. A reluctant purchaser might be tempted into the contract by a reduced price, or by arranging insurance against third-party claims.

A condition saying that a purchaser cannot object to some part of the title, or indeed saying that the purchaser cannot object to the title at all, is valid, but only *provided* that the seller is honest. He must disclose defects in the title either that he knows about or that he ought to know about, and then preclude the purchaser from objecting to the title (*Becker* v. *Partridge* [1966]). After such disclosure, the purchaser is bound by the contract, even if the seller's title is not just questionable but non-existent.

This problem of paper defects is peculiar to unregistered title. The only comparable points in registered title would be:

(i) the fact that the registered title is not absolute, but is possessory or qualified. The class of title should be detailed in the contract, and a copy of the entries in the register will accompany the draft contract. The purchaser can be prevented by a special condition from requiring any other evidence.

(ii) The possibility of someone having the right to apply for rectification of the register, e.g. a squatter who has been in adverse possession for over twelve years. This defect, being latent, would have to be disclosed. (Remember that the fact that an interest is overriding has nothing to do with the seller's duty to tell the purchaser about it.)

(c) When the Seller's Land is Subject to Third-Party Rights (e.g. easements, restrictive covenants, options, etc.)

A special condition in the contract will state that the sale is subject to them. The purchaser, before accepting a term that says the sale is subject to a third-party right, will naturally want details of it, and if it was created by a document, will want a copy of that document. This will be supplied with the draft contract.

5.5 The Effect of Standard Condition 3.1

Read this condition. How does it alter the position outlined in 5.3?

Condition 3.1.3 says that the seller is selling free from incumbrances. It then retreats from this general promise by saying that the sale is however subject to the incumbrances listed in 3.1.2.

Those listed in 3.1.2 are:

(a) Incumbrances mentioned in the agreement. Remember that when drafting Harry's contract we mentioned the right-of-way on the first page. The sale then became subject to the incumbrance. The incumbrance must be mentioned in the contract if the sale is to be subject to it. If it is not mentioned, the sale is not subject to it, even though it is revealed by the evidence of title that accompanies the draft contract.

(b) Incumbrances discoverable by inspection of the property before contract. This reflects the open contract rule about patent defects. However, when we were considering patent defects we saw that most defects in title are latent. The only safe thing for a seller to do is to mention in the contract a defect of which he knows and never to assume that it is a patent defect.

(c) Incumbrances that the seller does not and could not know about. You may remember that the *implied* promise is that there are *no* undisclosed incumbrances, and that it would be no defence for a seller to say that he did not disclose the incumbrance because he did not know it existed until the purchaser discovered it. Condition 3 alters this. The seller promises freedom only from incumbrances he knows about. So if an undisclosed incumbrance is discovered by the purchaser, the seller is not in breach of contract if the seller did not know of the incumbrance. The condition talks of those the seller 'does not and *could not* know about', so the seller must not only have been ignorant of the incumbrance when he entered into the contract, but must also have lacked the means of discovering the defect. If the defect were discoverable by the seller, e.g. by reading his own deeds or inspecting his own property, he is treated as knowing of it. It brings in the idea of constructive knowledge.

(d) Entries on any public register. 'Public register' is defined to exclude the register kept under the Land Charges Act 1972, the register of title kept under the Land Registration Act 1925, and entries of a company file kept at Companies House. Thus if there is a registered land charge (unregistered title) or a caution or notice (registered charge) affecting the property that is not disclosed in the contract the seller will be in breach of contract.

(e) Public requirements. These are defined in condition 1.1.1 as 'any notice order or proposal given or made (whether before or after the date of the contract) by a body acting on statutory authority'. This means for example that the sale is subject to all local land charges. Condition 3.1.5 emphasises this by stating that the purchaser must bear the cost of complying with all public requirements, and must indemnify the seller against any liability arising from a public requirement.

5.6 Barring Requisitions

According to standard condition 4.1.1 the purchaser must raise requisitions on title within six working days of the date of the contract or the date of delivery of the evidence of title, whichever is the later. So it is still contemplated by the standard conditions that the purchaser can leave investigation of title until after exchange of contracts, and then object to the title because it is not a good title, or because it is subject to incumbrances not mentioned in the contract but known to the seller.

If the seller wants to force the purchaser to investigate title before contract he can alter the standard conditions to prevent the purchaser raising requisitions on the evidence of title supplied, once contracts are exchanged. In other words, the purchaser will contract to accept title as deduced pre-contract.

A special condition such as this would not present a purchaser from objecting to the title on the ground of the concealment by the seller of a defect known to him (see 5.4 (b) and *Becker* v. *Partridge* [1966]) or because of a defect not revealed by the evidence of title supplied (Re *Haedicke* v. *Lipski*'s Contract [1901]).

5.7 Drafting a Contract for the Sale of an Unregistered Title

(*a*) *Introduction*

While bearing all this in mind, attempt the drafting of a contract for the sale of an unregistered freehold title. You are using the same form of contract incorporating the standard conditions of sale. Your clients are Harry and Martha Hill. The estate agent's particulars and the information given by your clients disclose that the house is a large detached house, standing in two acres of ground. It is in a poor state of repair. There is a public footpath cutting across the far corner of the garden.

You have the following deeds:

(i) a deed dated 1940 conveying the freehold estate on sale, made between B and C as sellers and D as purchaser. It describes the property as being 'Blackacre, in the village of Little Hove and in the parish of St James the Vernacular, in the County of Kent, as the same is bounded to the North by Mr Fitzgerald's property, to the West and South by the park paling of Lord Footscray, and to the East by the London to Folkstone Road'. It also says that Blackacre is more particularly described on the plan attached to a conveyance dated 1 April 1910 and made between A of the one part and B and C of the other part. It says that the property is conveyed subject to restrictive covenants contained in the 1910 deed. (You do not have a copy of this deed.) B and C are expressed to convey as trustees for sale.

(ii) A deed dated 1980, conveying the estate on sale from D to your clients. It describes the property simply as 'Blackacre, Lower Hove, Kent'.

(iii) A mortgage dated 1980 by your clients to the Champagne Building Society.

Notice that you do not have any search certificates against the names of the past estate owners. This means that you cannot be certain that there are not land charges against those names that may have been created by documents that you do not have in your possession.

A cautious solicitor would feel that he did not really know his clients' title without certificates of search, and might now make searches against the names of A, B, C, D, Harry and Martha. (It is certainly always worth thinking about making a search against your own client's name. This might reveal a class F registration (spouse's rights of occupation under Matrimonial Homes Act) and a C(i) or C(iii) (a mortgage unprotected by deposit the deeds, i.e. a second mortgage). It is better to know about these before contract than after, when their existence may mean that your client is in breach of contract). If you are following the protocol, you must do these searches now, anyway, as the certificates must be sent to the purchaser as part of the pre-contract package (see section 1.4). You should have no difficulty in completing the first page of the contract, apart, perhaps, from the particulars.

(*b*) *Particulars*

In unregistered conveyancing, there is often a temptation simply to copy out a description from a title deed. In this case, it would be foolish to use the verbal description in the 1940 deed, as it is clearly now out of date. Also the 1940 deed describes the land by reference to a plan. The plan is lost. For that reason alone, you obviously cannot refer to the plan in the particulars of sale. Even if you had the plan, it would not necessarily form a good basis for the contract description. You would certainly need to confirm that the plan actually represents the present boundaries. In fact, if there is no doubt about where the present boundaries lie, there is unlikely to be any need for a plan to form part of the contract description. (A plan might be vital when a client is selling only part of his property. For example, he might be selling the end of his large garden to a developer. It is necessary to establish the new boundary and a plan is the only way to do it. Of course, the plan must be professionally prepared, and it will be used in the conveyance or transfer as well as in the contract.) In our case, it is probably sufficient to describe the land as the freehold land known as Blackacre, Lower Hove, Kent. (There is no *need* to add, 'and the house built on it' as the house is a fixture and forms part of the land.) The difficulty most often lies in checking that the title deeds are dealing with all the land that is *now* recognised as forming part of Blackacre. Boundaries move. (Look at the problem in the workshop section of Chapter 9.)

(*c*) *Root of Title/Title Number*

You now have to state how title shall be deduced.

Here, of course, you are dealing with an unregistered title, so what you must do is specify the document with which your evidence of title will start, i.e. the root of title.

If a contract for the sale of an unregistered title says nothing about the commencement of title, the rule is that the seller must start his evidence of title with a 'good root' at least 15 years old. (Again, do not get confused here. For both registered and unregistered title, the promise as to title is the same, i.e. that the seller has a good title to the freehold. Here, however, we are talking about the *evidence* that he must produce to substantiate that claim. As has been seen, in registered conveyancing, the evidence is the register of title. In unregistered conveyancing, the evidence comes usually from the past deeds.) A good root is a document which shows the legal and equitable interest passing from one owner to another, which identifies the land, and which does not itself make the title seem doubtful in any way. Both a conveyance on sale and a deed of gift can be good roots. A purchaser would probably *prefer* to find that the good root is a conveyance on sale, as the purchaser under that conveyance would have investigated the title before he bought. A donee might not have done this. However, if the contract is silent about the start of the title, the purchaser will have to accept a deed of gift as a root of title.

Usually, a contract will not be silent as to the start of the evidence of the title. It will specify the document that is to form the root. Usually, the seller will specify what would have been a good root anyway, and will choose a document that is at least fifteen years old. The reason is that if he proffers a document that is not a good root, or one that is immature, the purchaser may simply say that the condition in the draft contract is unacceptable. There is a risk in a purchaser agreeing to accept evidence starting with a root less than fifteen years old. The risk is that the purchaser misses seeing a section of the title that he would otherwise see, and he may miss a name that he could otherwise search against in the Land Charges Registry.

To illustrate this, suppose that you, as purchaser's solicitor in 1992, see in the draft conveyance a condition that title will be traced from a conveyance dated 1 May 1980 made between John Williams and Albert Black. You notice that the condition does not say whether the conveyance was on sale, or by way of a gift, and that the conveyance is only twelve years old.

If the contract had not specified a root, you would have been entitled to one at least fifteen years old. Accepting a root only twelve years old does not mean that you are missing an investigation of three years of ownership. You might be missing considerably more. The conveyance by which John Williams obtained the property might be dated 1930, and it would have been from that that you could have traced title.

Before completion, you will be making a search at the Central Land Charges Registry against the names of past estate owners revealed by the abstract of title. By accepting an immature root, you cannot add the name of the person who conveyed the land to John Williams. If anything is registered against that name, for example, a land charge D(ii) because he (the person who sold to John) burdened the land with restrictive covenants when he bought it, you will take subject to the land charge, and you will have no right to compensation from the Chief Land Registrar (see Chapter 19).

Suppose the conveyance to John was dated 1920, and created restrictive covenants. Again you would take subject to these covenants, even though the later deed might make no mention of them. As they arose before 1926, the covenants are not registrable, but bind people who have actual or constructive notice of them. Your failure to see the 1920 conveyance, when under an open contract you would have been entitled to do so, fixes you with constructive notice of anything you would have discovered had you done so.

To return to the drafting of the Hills' contract, which deed will you specify as the root of title? You know that the purchaser will object if you put the 1980 conveyance forward as a root, as it is not yet fifteen years old. What about the 1940 deed? It *is* fifteen years old. It does show the legal estate and equitable interest passing from B and C to D. (Although B and C, being trustees, may not themselves have *owned* all the equitable interest, they could still pass it to D, because of their powers of overreaching beneficiaries' claims.) It does not disclose anything suspicious about the title. However, it does not by itself describe the property. It refers to the 1910 plan for a better description. Most purchasers, seeing the description in the 1940 conveyance, would instantly demand a copy of the 1910 plan, on the basis that the description in the 1940 deed is inadequate without it. This point of view may not be correct, as the verbal description in the 1940 conveyance might well be a sufficient description, but the point in drafting a contract is to anticipate difficulties.

So, if you had a copy of the 1910 deed, you would have a choice. You could still state that the root of title is the 1940 deed, but supply a copy of the 1910 plan with the draft contract. (Strictly speaking, you should supply a copy of the entire 1910 conveyance, so the purchaser can check if the plan is said to describe the land in detail, or merely provide a general identification.) Or, you could state that the 1910 conveyance is itself to be the root of title.

In this case, it would scarcely matter which course you adopted. It would have made a difference if there had been documents of title between 1910 and 1940 as they would not have to be abstracted if the root were the 1940 conveyance, but would have to be abstracted if it were the 1910 conveyance.

However, you do not have a copy of the 1910 conveyance. So nip objections in the bud. Say in the contract that title will be traced from the 1940 deed, and that no copy of the plan on the 1910 conveyance can be supplied, and that the purchaser shall not be entitled to ask for it. There seems to be no need here for any clauses to be added on the second page.

Notice that nothing is said in the contract about the disrepair of the property. There is no duty on the seller to disclose physical defects, and standard condition 3.1.3 states that the purchaser accepts the property in the physical state it is in when the contract is made.

(*d*) *Incumbrances*

The public right-of-way must be mentioned here. Do not assume it is discoverable by inspection of the land.

You must also mention the 1910 restrictive covenants.

However, as soon as the purchaser sees a condition in the draft contract saying that the sale is subject to the covenants, he will naturally demand a copy of the 1910 conveyance, to see what they are. We cannot supply him with a copy. The deed appears to have been lost forever. All we can do is to say in the contract that no copy of the covenants can be supplied, and that the purchaser can raise no requisition as to what the covenants are, nor as to whether or not they have been broken. (Faruqi v. English Real Estates Ltd [1979]).

Of course, this is a condition that may deter our prospective purchaser. However, there is nothing else we can do. The purchaser probably need not be unduly concerned with the existence of the covenants if he does not intend to change the existing use of the land. If our clients can confirm that no objection to the existing use has been made by neighbouring landowners in the past, it is unlikely there will be one in the future. The purchaser should be concerned if he intends to develop the land – for example, pull down the house and build a block of flats. This might be breaking the covenants (which bind the purchaser in this case because of actual notice) and a furious neighbour who has the benefit of them may object. One solution for a purchaser who does want to buy the land is to insure against the risk of the covenants being enforced.

(*d*) *Capacity*

To complete the first page of the contract, you must decide in what capacity your clients will be selling. As they co-own the equitable interest in the house, the legal estate will be held by them on trust for sale. The capacity can, therefore, be stated as 'trustees'. It will mean that there will not be implied into the conveyance by the Hills the wide-ranging covenants for title that are implied when a seller conveys as beneficial owner, but only the covenant that the sellers have not themselves incumbered the title (see Chapter 19).

5.8 Other Conditions that it Might be Necessary to Add to a Contract

(*a*) *Deposit*

Standard condition 2.2 provides for a 10 per cent deposit to be paid on exchange of contracts by the purchaser to the seller's solicitor as stakeholder. We have already considered the possibility that a purchaser might ask to pay a smaller deposit (see section 2.3). The point here is the capacity in which the deposit is held by the solicitor. A stakeholder holds a deposit as agent for both seller and purchaser, so cannot release it to either until the contract is discharged. Usually the contract will be discharged by the successful completion of the contract, when the deposit is released to the seller. It is possible for the contract to be discharged (i.e. terminated) by one party breaking the contract. If the breach is the purchaser's, the seller is entitled to call for the deposit to be forfeited to him. If it is the seller who has broken the contract, the purchaser can ask for the deposit to be returned to him. While the contract still exists, the deposit is frozen.

The exception to this is standard condition 2.2.2. This applies when the seller is buying another house. The seller would like to use the deposit paid on his sale to finance the deposit he must pay on his purchase. This is possible, as the condition provides that the deposit may be released to the seller to be used *for that purpose only*. If the seller would like to have the use of the deposit before completion for some other purpose, the standard condition does not permit this. A special condition would have to be substituted saying the deposit is to be paid to the seller's solicitor as agent for the seller. This change is likely to prove unpopular with the purchaser. A deposit paid to a stakeholder is safe if the seller goes bankrupt, as the trustee in bankruptcy has no better right to the deposit than the seller, i.e. usually, only if and when the sale is completed. A deposit paid to an agent of the seller is not safe; it belongs to the seller. To recover it, a disappointed purchaser would have to prove in the bankruptcy. The only safeguard is that if a deposit is paid to a seller or seller's agent, the purchaser has a lien on the seller's land for its recovery. The lien is in the nature of an equitable charge, so the purchaser is a secured creditor. However, the lien offers no comfort if there are prior mortgages that exhaust the value of the property.

You must also consider the need for a special condition if the deposit is to be held by someone other than the seller's solicitor. A special condition must provide for this, and state in what capacity the deposit is to be held. It seems that a deposit paid on exchange of contracts to the seller's estate agent will be held by him as agent for the seller unless the contract says otherwise. (Note that 'solicitor' for the purpose of the standard conditions is defined to include a licensed conveyancer.)

At common law a stakeholder is entitled to keep any interest earned by the deposit. Higher standards are, however, expected of a solicitor. The Law Society has recommended (*Law Society's Gazette*, 29 April 1987) that interest earned by a deposit should belong to the client, not the solicitor. Standard condition 2.2.3 reflects this, as it provides that on completion the deposit is to be paid to the seller with 'accrued interest' (this term is defined in standard condition 1.1).

What if, as events turn out, the deposit has to be returned to the purchaser? The purchaser will then receive accrued interest paid by the seller – see standard condition 7.2.

(*b*) *Sale of Part*

We have seen that if the seller is selling only part of his land, the drafting of the particulars will require care. He must also consider the grant and reservation of easements, and the giving or imposition of restrictive covenants. This topic and the effect of Standard Condition 3.4 are considered in Chapter 12.

(*c*) *The Need for an Indemnity Covenant*

This is considered in Chapter 12.

(*d*) *Sale Subject to an Existing Tenancy*

If the land is to be sold subject to an existing tenancy, this should be stated in the special conditions, for example, 'the sale is subject to the weekly periodic tenancy of the top floor, the tenant being Mr Alex Brown'. A copy of the tenancy agreement should be supplied to the purchaser with the draft contract. The purchaser is then treated as entering into the contract with full knowledge and acceptance of the terms of the tenancy (condition 3.2.2).

The sale may be to the sitting tenant himself. If this is so, the tenancy will probably end on completion, as it will merge into the freehold that the purchaser has acquired. However, this is a matter for the purchaser. The contract will still say that the sale is subject to the purchaser's own tenancy, and that as he is the tenant, he is taken to buy with full notice of terms of the tenancy.

The purchaser must, of course, read the tenancy agreement. He must not lose sight of the fact that if it is a residential tenancy, the agreement will not in fact reflect all the rights of the tenant. These may be considerably increased by statute.

If the tenancy was created before 15 January 1989 it may be protected by the Rent Act. This Act gives the tenant considerable security of tenure, and may limit the amount of rent that can be recovered from him.

If the tenancy was created on or after 15 January 1989, the Housing Act 1988 will apply, and the tenant will have some degree of security of tenure, but little rent protection.

Standard condition 3.3.7 emphasises that the purchaser must satisfy himself as to whether the tenancy is protected by either Act and as to what rent is legally recoverable.

(*e*) *Sale of a Matrimonial Home when the Legal Estate is Owned by only One of the Spouses*

This is dealt with in Chapter 11.

(*f*) *Sale of a Leasehold Estate*

Additional matters to be borne in mind when drafting a contract for the sale of a leasehold property are dealt with in Chapter 15.

(*g*) *Absence of Title Deeds*

If the title is unregistered, and the seller bases his title on adverse possession, or while having documentary evidence of his title does not have either the original or a marked copy of every title deed, he should alter standard condition 4.2.3 and 4.2.4.

5.9 Conditional Contracts

The seller and the purchaser may agree to the sale of the property, but 'subject to' some matter being first of all settled. This qualification can have different results:

(a) It may mean that there is no contract at all. The phrase 'subject to contract' nearly always has this effect.

(b) It may simply be one of the terms in a concluded contract. In this sense, it is possible to say that the contract is 'subject to' the purchaser paying the price, or 'subject to' the seller making good title. In *Property and Bloodstock Ltd* v. *Emerton* [1967], the contract was expressed to be subject to the seller obtaining his landlord's consent to the assignment of the lease. It was held that this was a promise by the seller as to title. It did not create a 'conditional contract' in the sense that the phrase is used in the next paragraph.

(c) It may create a conditional contract. This term is used here to mean a concluded contract, but one which cannot be enforced by either party until a condition is fulfilled. If the condition is not fulfilled within its time limit, both parties are released from the contract.

    If the parties wish to create a conditional contract, they must make their intention clear, and must ensure that the condition is sufficiently certain.

    A condition is void for uncertainty if it is impossible for the court to decide the circumstances in which it could be said to be fulfilled. If the condition is void, the contract is void. If the contract is to be conditional on planning permission, for example, the condition should give details of the permission being sought, and whether or not it will be fulfilled by an outline planning permission, or by one with conditions attached.

    A contract subject to the results of a local land charge search and additional enquiries should say that it depends on the results being satisfactory to the purchaser or his solicitor acting reasonably. This is a standard that can be objectively tested by the court. (See *Janmohamad* v. *Hassam* (1976) and *Smith and Olley* v. *Townsend* [1949].)

5.10 Formalities for the Creation of a Contract for the Sale of Land

Nothing has been said as to the legal formalities until this late stage, because if the usual conveyancing procedures are followed, the formalities will inevitably be observed.

Section 2 of the Law of Property (Miscellaneous Provisions) Act 1989 states that a contract for the sale or other disposition of an interest in land must be in writing. The contract must incorporate all the terms which the parties have expressly agreed. It will incorporate the terms if it actually contains them or if it refers to some other document which contains them.

The contract must be signed by or on behalf of each party to the contract.

If, in the usual way, contracts are prepared in duplicate with a view to exchange, s.2 will be satisfied if *both* copies incorporate all the agreed terms, and if each party signs one copy, even though they sign different copies.

The result of s.2 is that there can no longer be an oral contract for the sale of land. Under the previous law (s.40 of the Law of Property Act 1925) an oral contract was unenforceable. Now, there can be no such thing as an oral contract.

Interest in land is defined to include an interest in the proceeds of sale of land – i.e. an equitable interest existing behind a trust of sale of the legal estate.

Section 2 does not apply to a contract to grant a lease for a term not exceeding 3 years at best rent without a premium nor to a contract made at auction. At auction, the contract comes into existence at the fall of the auctioneer's hammer. Both seller and purchaser are in fact then invited to sign a written contract, but the contract exists without the writing.

Section 2 provides that the document must incorporate all the terms agreed between the parties, so that if one party can point out that a head of agreement is *not* contained in the written contract, the contract becomes void. One answer to this could be rectification of the contract on the ground that the written document by mistake does not express the true agreement of the parties (see *Joscelyne* v. *Nissen* [1970].

Workshop

Attempt this problem yourself, then read the specimen solution at the end of the book.

Problem

(This problem is best attempted after you have read Chapter 11.)

You have been instructed to act for Ada Faulkener in the sale of her cottage. You have borrowed the title deeds from Doom Building Society, Ada's mortgagee. There is a memorandum on the conveyance to Ada to the effect that part of the garden was later sold by Ada to a neighbour in June 1980. You did not act for Ada then. You have taken the precaution of obtaining a land charges search against her name. The search reveals a D(ii), a C(i) and an F land charge registered against her name, all apparently affecting the cottage. None of the entries can be explained by the documents in your possession. What action will you need to take in respect of the matters disclosed by your search and when?

N.B. An exercise in drafting a contract is set at the end of Chapter 12.

6 Pre-contract Searches and Enquiries

6.1 Introduction

You now know that a seller has a duty either implied or expressed in the contract to disclose certain defects in his title to the purchaser. Much information which might affect the value or the enjoyment of the property, and make it unattractive to the purchaser is not within this duty of disclosure. He should seek out this information before contract. As the seller is not under a duty to disclose it, it is too late for a purchaser to discover it after the contract, as there will be no breach of contract to offer him a remedy.

The solicitor for the purchaser therefore always makes, or ensures that he has the results of, what are known as the 'usual' pre-contract searches and enquiries. They are called 'usual' because they are applicable to nearly every transaction. There are also 'unusual' searches which might have to be made because of the property's location. A purchaser's solicitor who fails to obtain the usual searches, and whatever other searches are considered necessary as a matter of good conveyancing practice, will have failed in his duty to his client.

Again we revert to the protocol. The *seller's* solicitor, if following the protocol, will be making the pre-contract searches, and supplying the results to the purchaser's solicitor as part of the pre-contract 'package' (see section 1.4). Keep this in perspective. The protocol states that the searches are to be done by the seller's solicitor solely because this will save time, particularly if, as the protocol hopes, the seller consults his solicitor as soon as he decides to put his house on the market. The protocol, of course, produces the result that the expense of the searches initially falls on the seller rather than the purchaser. If the negotiations fall through, and the purchaser never enters into the contract the seller will be out of pocket. If the purchaser does enter into the contract, the protocol requires him to re-imburse the seller for the search fees, but only if the purchaser has relied on the searches. If he rejects the searches done by the seller, because they are incorrect or too old, there is no re-imbursement.

The fact remains that whoever *does* the searches, it is the responsibility of the purchaser's solicitor to decide if the searches are adequate, if the replies are satisfactory, and if any necessary ones have been omitted. That it is the seller who actually puts the searches in train is a matter of procedure; the rule remains '*caveat emptor*' for matters that do not fall within the seller's duty of disclosure.

6.2 The 'Usual' Searches and Enquiries

(*a*) *Enquiries of the Seller (the Seller's Property Information Form)*

Making the Enquiries There have been until the introduction of the protocol and perhaps will continue to be, many standard lists of enquiries to be asked by the purchaser of the seller. At one time the Oyez form reigned supreme, but in recent years has been challenged by others. The number of questions grew steadily and the answers given by the seller's solicitor became increasingly non-committal and unhelpful. To quote from the Law Society's introduction to the protocol:

> if any one part of the conveyancing process over the past years has caused criticism within the profession it has been the use of ever-lengthening forms of enquiries before contract, some being a repeat of those included in the standard form and others being irrelevant to the particular transaction or relating to the structure or condition of the property.

The protocol documentation now includes what is called the 'Seller's Property Information Form'. Part I of this form is completed by the seller, and part II by the seller's solicitor. The form is then sent to the purchaser's solicitor as part of the pre-contract package. The form reads as a series of questions and answers. Why? To quote again from the Law Society:

> the property information form continues to be set out as replies to a series of standard questions. Since the seller's solicitor will be providing this information it might be seen as more logical at a future date to develop this as a simple statement of information without the question and answer format. However there are two reasons for retaining this. First it is a system with which the profession is familiar and secondly, it is hoped that even in those instances where for any reason the protocol is not being followed the buyer's solicitors will still use the property information form rather than revert to other forms for raising enquiries before contract.

The form is in the Appendix for you to read. Below are a few of the questions in Part I of the form.

(i) Question 4 asks if the property has the benefit of any guarantees. This might cover guarantees given after damp or timber treatment or in respect of double glazing. A purchaser should ensure that the benefit of the guarantees is expressly assigned to him on completion.

According to the protocol, if there are any such guarantees, the seller's solicitor should obtain copies of them and send them to the purchaser's solicitor with the property information form.

This enquiry may also reveal the fact that the house is protected by the National House Building Council's Scheme (known as 'Buildmark'). This scheme covers houses, bungalows flats or maisonettes built by a builder or developer who is registered with the Council. The scheme protects a purchaser for ten years against the developer's failure to build the house properly and against structural defects. It is backed by insurance cover. The purchaser from the developer must ensure that he has the protection of the scheme and that he receives the necessary documentation, i.e. offer of cover form, the booklet that explains the scheme and the warranties that are given by the developer, and the 'ten year' notice, which is issued by the NHBC and which brings the scheme into operation. Any subsequent purchaser who buys while the ten year protection period is still running should ensure that the booklet and the ten year notice are handed over to him. The benefit of the scheme will pass to him without having to be expressly assigned.

If the house is built before 1 April 1988 the NHBC documentation will be different.

There is another scheme known as Foundation 15 that also protects purchasers of newly built houses. This scheme is not yet as widely used as the NHBC scheme.

(ii) Question 5 asks what services (e.g. gas and electricity) the property has and the routes taken by the pipes, wires, etc., and whether they have to cross anybody else's land to reach the property. The point of this is to investigate whether any necessary easements exist.

(iii) Question 8 asks the names and ages of any person in actual occupation of the land, and what legal or equitable interest such an occupier has. Having read Chapters 3 and 4 you know why a purchaser is concerned about anybody other than the seller occupying the land. The age of the occupier is relevant because it is suggested that if the occupier is so young that he cannot be considered as independent of his parent, the child is not in actual occupation for the purposes either of constructive notice, or s.70(i)(g) of the Land Registration Act 1925. An answer denying that anybody else is in occupation is usually accepted in practice, unless the purchaser knows better, but an untruthful denial by the seller that Uncle George is in occupation does not clear any interest that Uncle might have from the title, although there would be a cause of action against the seller. (This is elaborated in Chapter 11.)

(iv) Question 10 is checks on compliance with planning requirements (see section 6.5).

Part II of the form that is completed by the seller's solicitor asks more technical questions, for example as to easements benefiting the property, the existence of overriding interests and as to who has the benefit of restrictive covenants burdening the land. The solicitor is also asked if the sale is dependent on the seller buying another property, and if so, whether he needs and has arranged a mortgage loan to finance the purchase. This is to check if there is likely to be a delay before the seller is in a position to exchange contracts. The seller's solicitor owes a duty of confidentiality towards his client, and must not reveal these details without his consent.

The protocol also recommends that the purchaser's solicitor tell the seller's solicitor about the position of the purchaser's own sale, and the progress of his mortgage arrangements to finance the purchase, but again only if the purchaser consents.

Having received the pre-contract 'package' the purchaser's solicitor may make additional enquiries but according to the protocol only those specific additional enquiries which are required to elucidate some point arising out of the documents submitted or which are relevant to the particular nature or location of the property or which the purchaser has expressly requested, but omitting any enquiry, including one about the structure of the building, which is capable of being ascertained by the purchaser's own enquiries or survey or personal inspection.

If the sale is of a leasehold property, the purchaser's solicitor must also be sent a completed 'additional property information form'. This is discussed in Chapter 15.

Replying to the enquiries Imagine now that you are the seller's solicitor. The replies to the questions on both parts of the form are the seller's. You formulate and sign the replies to the questions in Part II of the form as his agent. An incorrect answer may mean that the seller can be held liable for misrepresentation (see Chapter 19).

If it is due to your carelessness that the answer is wrong, you will be liable to your own client for any loss you cause him. In *Sharneyford Supplies Ltd* v. *Edge* (Barrington Black Austin & Co [a firm], third party) [1987] an enquiry was raised as to the existence of tenancies. The solicitor for the seller, *without consulting his client*, said that the tenants had no security of tenure. The purchaser successfully sued the seller when the tenants were found to be irremovable, and the seller's solicitors were ordered to indemnify their client.

(*b*) *The Local Land Charge Search*

Each district authority (or for Greater London, each London Borough or the Common Council of the City of London) maintains a register of local land charges affecting the land within its area. It is difficult to define a local land charge, except to say generally that it is something designated as a local land charge either by the Local Land Charges Act 1975 itself or by some other Act. They are matters affecting land that are public matters, rather than private ones, and are registrable either by the district authority itself, or some other statutory body. Their name is legion, but they include:

(i) *Financial charges* Examples would be charges to recover the cost of street works, or the cost of emergency repairs to unsafe buildings, or to recover some forms of improvement grant.
(ii) *Planning matters* These include conditions imposed after July 1977 on planning permissions, enforcement notices actually in force, tree preservation orders.
(iii) *The listing of buildings as being of special architectural or historic interest* This listing restricts demolition and alteration of the building, and so can remove any development potential from the land (see *Amalgamated Investment and Property Co. Ltd* v. *John Walker & Sons Ltd* [1976]).

It is not clear to what extent the existence of a local land charge will constitute a defect in the seller's title. A financial charge and probably an order requiring demolition of the property will be a matter of title and therefore fall within the seller's duty of disclosure. (In this context, consider the case of *Rignall Developments Ltd* v. *Halil** [1987].) If a local land charge, or other local authority matter, is not a defect in title, it does not have to be disclosed. These rules are affected by the standard conditions. Consider again standard condition 3.

As many local land charges are not matters of title, and so not within the seller's duty of disclosure and as standard condition 3.1.2 makes the sale subject to all of them anyway, the purchaser will ask the authority to make a search of the local land charges register *before* he enters into the contract. The official search certificate will list any land charges registered at the date of the certificate, but the certificate is not conclusive nor does it give the purchaser any priority period. (See Local Land Charges Act 1975.) The purchaser will take subject to all charges in existence at the date of the search, whether revealed by the certificate or not, and subject to all charges coming into existence after the date of the search. What the certificate does do is give a limited right to compensation. A purchaser who relies on an official search certificate before entering into a contract can claim compensation if he is adversely affected by a land charge that existed at the date of the search but was not registered, or by a charge that was registered but was not disclosed by the search certificate. (A purchaser who relies on a *personal* search of the register can claim compensation only in respect of a local land charge that existed, but was not registered.)

To claim compensation the purchaser need not have ordered or made the search himself. It is sufficient if he or his solicitor had notice of the contents of the search certificate before exchange of contracts (s.10 of the Local Land Charges Act 1975). This is why the protocol is able to require the seller's solicitor to make the search. Notice, however, that no compensation is payable in respect of local land charges that come into existence after the date of the search, so certificates become increasingly useless with age.

In connection with the introduction of the protocol, the Law Society has arranged a Search Validation Scheme. This protects a purchaser for six months from the date of the search against new entries being registered against the property. The protection comes from an insurance policy backed by the Lombard Continental Insurance plc and Eagle Star. The insurance can be taken out by either seller or purchaser, as an alternative to repeating the search.

It is usually pointless for a purchaser to repeat a local land charge search after contract but before completion, because, if any new matter has arisen, standard condition 3 will have thrown the burden of it onto the purchaser anyway. However, the purchaser's intended mortgagee may ask for the search to be repeated, and may withdraw or reduce the loan if anything adverse is discovered.

It is because the certificate is not conclusive that Enquiry 3 on the property information form asks the seller if he has received any notices or communications from the local authority or other statutory body.

(*c*) *The Enquiries of the District Authority*

The district authority will know much that will not be revealed by the local land charge search, for the simple reason that the information is not registrable as a land charge. This information can be extracted from the authority by raising enquiries. There is a standard form of enquiries, approved by local authorities. The form is divided into two parts. The first contains questions that are always answered by the authority. The authority will only answer those questions in the second part which the enquirer has ticked, and for which he has paid an extra fee. The enquirer may also add further questions of his own devising, but the authority can refuse to answer these.

Examples of Part I Enquiries

(i) *Roads* The Authority is asked if the road and paths giving access to the property are maintained at the public expense, and if not, whether the authority has passed a resolution to make up the roads, etc., at the cost of the frontagers. It is also asked if it has entered into any outstanding agreement relating to the adoption of any such road or path, and if any such agreement is supported by a bond.

If you are buying a house that is reached by a road that is not maintained by the local authority, the following problems arise;

(aa) *Easements* Does the house have easements over the road, so that the purchaser will have the right to walk and, if relevant, drive over the road without relying on someone's permission?

(bb) *Maintenance* At the moment, is anyone under an obligation to repair the roadway? The answer may be 'no', as the owner of land subject to a right of way does not generally have a duty to keep the way in repair. Sometimes, there is an agreement between the people who use or own the road to maintain it.

(cc) *Future expenses* Has the local highway authority resolved to 'make up' the road? Under the Highways Act 1980, the local authority can pass a resolution to 'make up' a road not previously maintained at the public expense. When the road has been repaired to a suitable standard it is 'adopted' by the authority and from then on will be maintained out of public funds. This sounds like good news to the owners of houses reached by the road. The drawback, however, is that the authority can apportion the cost of the work that brings the road up to standard in the first place among the owners and occupiers of premises which have a boundary adjoining the road. This can involve an owner in considerable expense. The owner (and his successors) can be sued for debt by the authority, and in addition the amount due is a charge on the property and registrable as a land charge.

A developer building estate roads will normally enter into an agreement with the authority under s.38 of the 1980 Act. The developer promises the authority to build the estate roads to a certain standard. The authority agrees that once the roads are completed, it will adopt them. The developer may be selling the completed houses before the roads are adopted. If he breaks the agreement, and does not build the roads to the required standard, the authority can do the work, and charge the houseowners. So the purchaser might find that he is having to pay a substantial amount towards the creation of the road. The developer may have covenanted in the conveyance to the purchaser that he would complete the roads, but the problem has probably arisen in the first place because of the developer's insolvency.

To avoid the problem, the s.38 agreement is supported by a bond, given by, for example, an insurance company. The insurance company promises the authority that if the developer does not make up the roads, the cost of the authority doing it will be paid by the insurers. This does not remove all risk, as if the sum promised under the bond is insufficient to cover the costs of the roads, there will again be a charge to the frontagers.

So a purchaser of a house on a new estate where the roads have not yet been adopted, will want to be satisfied as to the existence of the s.38 agreement, and as to the existence and adequacy of the bond.

(ii) *Sewers* The authority is asked if the property is served by a sewer maintained at the public expense.

In the case of a new building estate, there may be an agreement between the developer and the authority under s.104 Water Industry Act 1991, similar to the agreement under the Highways Act. The authority is asked to disclose the existence of any such agreement and supporting bond.

(iii) *Various planning matters* designed to gauge the authority's planning intentions for the area.

(*d*) *Search in the Public Index Map, and Parcels Index*

This search is usually only relevant when the purchase is of unregistered title. It is made at the District Land Registry that serves the area in which the land lies. It will reveal:

(i) whether the title is unregistered, or registered. It is apparently possible for it to be forgotten that a title has been registered, and for subsequent owners to deal with it as if it were unregistered. None of these unregistered dealings will have passed the legal estate. It may also warn the purchaser that there has been a previous sale of part of the land dealt with by the title deeds.

(ii) if the title is registered, the title number, and whether the title is freehold or leasehold.

(iii) any caution against first registration. This can be lodged by anyone who fears that an application for first registration will prejudice his rights over the land. The effect of the caution is that the Registrar must inform the cautioner of any application for first registration. The cautioner then has an opportunity of claiming that his interest should be noted on the register, or perhaps that registration should not take place at all.

(*e*) *A Search in the Land Charges Register against the Seller's Name*

This will only be relevant when buying an unregistered title. It is usually unnecessary to make a search of the central land charges registry before contract, as any registered land charge should be disclosed by the seller (See section 5.3 of this book, s.24 of the Law of Property Act 1969 and standard condition 3.)

If the seller's solicitor is following the protocol, a search against the seller's name and against the names of the other estate owners revealed by the evidence of title will have been supplied to the purchaser as part of the pre-contract package (see section 1.4).

If the protocol is not being followed, and the purchaser's solicitor is not given evidence of title before exchange of contracts, it is impossible to make the search pre-contract. The purchaser's solicitor does not know the names of the estate owners. However, in these circumstances, a cautious purchaser might consider making a search before contract against the seller's name. It might give early warning of his bankruptcy, or the registration of a Class F land charge. The purchaser might then decide that the least troublesome thing to do would be to buy a different house.

(*f*) *Inspection of the Property*

The property should be inspected before contract

(i) to look for physical defects (see section 6.4).
(ii) to look for patent defects in title (see section 5.3).
(iii) to look for dangerous occupiers (see sections 3.16 and 4.4).

This inspection is far more likely to be done by the purchaser, than by his solicitor.

6.3 The 'Unusual' Searches

There are searches that will be made only for certain localities (for example, areas where minerals have been won, or limestone or salt extracted) or particular problems (for example, where the land is cut by a rail line or a canal). Details of the searches required can be found in specialised textbooks on conveyancing searches.

One of the more common is the search made when buying land in a coal-mining area. The search is sent to British Coal Mining Reports in Burton on Trent. Information will be obtained as to the whereabouts of existing workings, plans for new workings, whether a claim for subsidence has already been made, and whether any compensation has been paid. British Coal has published a directory setting out the areas where a coal-mining report should be obtained. (For further details see *Law Society's Gazette* (1991) No. 39.)

Another search worth mentioning is the commons registration search. Each County Council maintains a register of common land in its area, and a search in this register might reveal that rights of common exist over the property. The search should be made if land has never been built on, or only recently built on, particularly if it is in open country or on the edge of a village.

6.4 The Survey

As the contract promises nothing about the physical condition of the property, it is sensible for a purchaser to have the property surveyed before he agrees to buy it. He can instruct a surveyor to carry out a full structural survey. Even this cannot guarantee the complete soundness of the property, as inspection is limited by problems of access to floorboards, rafters, etc. The cost of a full survey is currently about £500 for a three-bedroomed house, and few purchasers commission one. A cheaper alternative is a house-buyer's report, which comments on the condition and value of the property, and lists visible serious defects.

If the purchaser is borrowing money to buy the house, the prospective lender will instruct a surveyor to carry out a valuation report. The Royal Institute of Chartered Surveyors stresses that this is not a survey. Its purpose is only to value the property to decide if it offers sufficient security for the loan. Some lenders let the purchaser see this report, others do not, although in all cases it is the purchaser who pays for the inspection to be carried out. Well over three-quarters of house-buyers rely on this report alone. Whether or not the purchaser sees the report, he assumes that the lender would not lend unless the report was satisfactory. It is now settled that on the purchase of a 'modest' house, the lender's surveyor owes a duty of care to the purchaser and cannot protect himself from liability for negligence by a disclaimer of responsibility. (See *Smith* v. *Eric S. Bush* [1987]*, and *Harris* v. *Wye Forest District Council* [1987]*.)

6.5 Town and Country Planning

Planning matters feature in the preliminary enquiries, the local land charge search and the additional enquiries of the district authority. For this reason a brief outline of planning law is given here.

(*a*) *Development of Land*

Note: A reference in this section to 'the Act' is a reference to the Town & Country Planning Act 1990 as amended by the Planning and Compensation Act 1991.

Planning permission is needed for the development of land (s.57 of the Act). Development is defined as:

(i) the carrying out of building engineering, mining or other operations in, on, over or under the land;
(ii) the making of any material change of use of any buildings or other land (s. 55 of the Act).

Buildings and other operations It is clearly development to build a house or to extend an existing house. It is development to add a garage, or a potting shed. It is development (because it is an engineering operation) to make an access way from the house to the highway.

However, the Act expressly provides that internal or external improvements or alterations to a building are not development if they do not materially affect its external appearance (s.57(2) of the Act).

Change of use A *material* change of use is development. As a guideline, a change in the kind of use will be material, but a change in the degree of use will only be material if it is substantial. Thus, to change the use of a house from residential to a business use would require planning permission. For an owner-occupier of a house to take in a lodger would not be a material change of use, but for the owner-occupier to turn his house into a boarding-house probably would be.

It is specifically provided that it is a material change of use if a single house is used as two or more separate dwellings. This point is of concern to a purchaser of a flat created by the conversion of a house (s.55(3) of the Act).

It is not a material change of use if a building or land within the curtilage of a dwelling house is used for any purpose incidental to the enjoyment of the house as such. That is why no permission is needed to start using an existing outhouse as a garage. (Remember it *is* development to build a new garage.)

To assist in the decision of whether or not a change of use is material, there exists the Town and County Planning (Use Classes) Order 1987. This specifies various classes of use. For example, Class A1 is use for the purpose of most sorts of shop. Class A2 is use for the provision of financial or professional services to the visiting public (e.g. the offices of Building Societies, or banks). Class B1 is use as an office other than as in Class A2.

A change of use from one use to another is not development, provided that both uses are within the same class. A change from use in one class to a use outside that class may be development. It will depend on whether the change is considered to be material. For example, to change from a clothes shop to a grocery store will not be development, as both uses are within class A1. Similarly, a change from an accountant's office to a solicitor's office will not need permission, as both uses are within Class B1. A change from a clothes shop to use as a branch office of a Building Society would need permission as it would be a change of use that would be considered material.

(*b*) *Applying for Planning Permission*

(i) If you are not sure whether the proposed activity constitutes development, you can apply to the local planning authority for a decision on the point (s.64 of the Act).

(ii) If planning permission is needed, you must consider whether express permission is needed, or if the General Development Order can be relied on.

(iii) The Town and Country Planning (General Development) Order 1988 (as amended) itself gives planning permission for certain developments.

For example:

Part I Class A – development within the curtilage of a dwelling-house
This includes enlarging a house, (subject to limitations on the volume and the height of the extension), and building a new garage (subject to limitation on size and situation). If the proposed development is

outside the limitations imposed by the order, express planning permission will be needed. Class I also permits the erection of greenhouses, sheds, chicken-houses, etc.

Part II Class A – minor operations These include erecting fences (subject to limits on height) or painting the outside of the building.

Before relying on permission given by the general development order, you must check if an 'article 4' direction exists. This will be revealed by the additional enquiries of the local authority. The local planning authority can direct that all or any of the permissions granted by the General Development Order shall not apply to the whole or part of its area. For example, the authority may withdraw the permission granted for the erection of chicken-sheds. Anybody wanting to build one would then have to apply for express planning permission.

(iv) If express planning permission is needed, the application must be accompanied by detailed plans. If the applicant does not own the land, he must certify that he has notified every owner of the land. 'Owner' includes an owner of the freehold, and anyone owning a lease with seven or more years to run. (s.66 of the Act).

(v) If you propose to build on land and want to check that there is no objection in *principle* to the development, you can apply for outline planning permission. This commits the authority to allowing that type of development while allowing it to control any matter that is expressly reserved in the outline permission for later approval, such as the exact siting of the buildings, or their appearance. This procedure avoids the delay and expense of preparing detailed plans, when the application in fact never had any chance of success. (Outline planning permission is not available for a proposed change of use.)

(vi) The planning authority must give written notice of its decision within 2 months of the application. If the decision is not made within this period, the applicant can, if he wishes, treat the failure to give a decision as a refusal of permission, and appeal to the Secretary of State (ss.78 and 79 of the Act).

Once a planning permission has been given, it enures for the benefit of the land, so that a purchaser of land will acquire the benefit of existing permissions. That is why one often sees a house advertised for sale with the benefit of a planning permission. However, a purchaser must remember that planning permissions do lapse (see next paragraph).

Duration of Planning Permission

(i) A planning permission is subject to a condition that development will be begun within five years of the date of the grant or whatever period is specified by the authority. If development is not begun, the permission lapses.

(ii) An outline planning permission is subject to a condition that application for approval of the reserved matters be made within three years of the grant of the outline permission and that development be begun within either five years of the grant of the outline planning permission, or two years of the approval of the reserved matter, whichever is the later (Sections 91 and 92 of the Act).

(*c*) *Enforcement of Planning Control*

(i) If development is carried out without permission, or is in breach of a condition imposed on the planning permission, the local planning authority can issue an enforcement notice (s.172 of the Act). The notice has to be served on the owner and on the occupier of the land, and any person who has a property interest in the land which might be affected by the notice. The notice is first of all issued; it may then be served not more than 28 days after its issue. It will specify a date on which it is to become effective, and this must be at least 28 days from the date of service.

(ii) *Time limits for service*
These time limits have been changed by provisions of the Planning and Compensation Act 1991 which came into effect on 27th July 1992. The new time limits are as follows:

(aa) If the breach consists of an unauthorised building, mining or other operation, the notice must be served within four years of the breach.
The four-year rule also applies to an unauthorised change of use *from* any building to use as a single dwelling-house.

(bb) If the breach consists of any other unauthorised change of use or is a breach of a condition attached to a planning permission, the notice must be served within ten years of the breach.

Once the time limit for service of an enforcement notice has passed, it is possible to obtain a certificate of lawfulness of the existing use or development. This certificate will not only establish that the development or change of use is immune from an enforcement notice, it will also amount to a grant of planning permission so that the development or new use becomes legal.

(iii) Failure to comply with an enforcement notice is a criminal offence, and there is liability for fines and other severe financial penalties. In addition, if the enforcement notice specifies steps such as the demolition of an unauthorised building, or reinstatement of the land to its previous condition the authority can enter onto the land and do the work itself, recovering the expense from the owner of the land (s.178 of the Act). This means that if a purchaser buys land that had, say, a garage built on it by the seller without planning permission, it is the purchaser (as the current owner) who will have to pay the authority's costs of demolition. The purchaser will be able to recover this expense from the seller (see s.178 of the Act). The authority cannot enter onto land to force discontinuance of an unauthorised use.

(*d*) *Planning and the Property Information Form*

Having digested all this, we can return to the property information form and question 10 on it.

The protocol requires the seller's solicitor to send with the property information form all planning decisions and building regulation approvals that the seller possesses. If he is buying a new house, the purchaser will want a copy of the planning permission for its erection. He will also want a copy of the building regulations consent given by the Local Authority under the Public Health Acts.

Even if he is not the first purchaser of the house, he will want to see a copy of the planning permission, as he will want to check not only that permission was obtained to build the house, but also if conditions were imposed on the permission, and if these conditions have been broken within the previous ten years. He will also require details of any further building on the land, or any improvements or alterations made in the previous four years. You can now see why the enquiries as to building works are confined to this period. If a garage was built or altered more than four years ago, no enforcement notice can be served.

If the purchaser is hoping to acquire the benefit of an existing permission for future development, he will want to check that the permission has not lapsed, or will not shortly lapse. If the purchaser intends to enlarge the house under the authority of the general development order, he must ask for details of any previous extensions carried out. The point is that the *original* volume of the house can only be increased within specified limits, so previous additions may already have exhausted those limits. If the house has been in existence since 1 July 1948, any enlargement since that date will be relevant.

(e) *Building Regulation Approval*

Apart from planning permission, a purchaser of a new house, or of a house recently substantially altered, needs evidence that the Building Regulations were met. The purpose of these regulations is to ensure that houses are safe and provide a decent living standard. Major alterations must comply with them, but smaller improvements such as conservatories are exempt.

Building Regulations approval must be obtained from the local authority. The current regulations are the Building Regulations 1991, which replace the 1985 regulations.

Case Notes

Smith v. *Eric S. Bush [1989] 2 WLR 790*

In this case, a firm of surveyors was instructed by a building society to carry out a visual inspection of a house and to report on its value. The surveyor noticed that two chimney-breasts had been removed, but failed to check if the chimneys had been left adequately supported. His report said that the house needed no essential repairs.

The application form for the mortgage loan and the valuation report both contained a disclaimer of liability for the report's accuracy, both on behalf of the building society and the firm of surveyors. The borrower, Mrs Smith, was warned that the report was not a full survey, and that she should seek independent advice. The building society supplied her with a copy of the report, and in reliance on it she bought the house. One chimney collapsed. She sued the surveyors for negligence, who relied on the disclaimer.

Harris v. *Wyre Forest District Council [1989] 2 WLR 790*

In this case, the Council lent money to Mr and Mrs Harris. It instructed one of its employees to value the property. The application form for the mortgage said that the valuation report was confidential, and that the Council accepted no responsibility for the value or condition of the house by reason of the report. The Council's valuer recommended minor repairs. Three years later it was discovered that the house suffered from serious structural faults. The Harrises sued the Council, as being responsible for the negligence of its employee. They had not seen the report, but had assumed, when the Council continued with the loan, that it must have been favourable.

It was held in both cases that a valuer instructed by a prospective lender to carry out a valuation of a house at the 'bottom end' of the market to decide if it offered sufficient security for the loan, owed a duty of care to the borrower to exercise reasonable skill and care in carrying out the valuation, if he realised that the borrower would probably buy the house in reliance on the valuation, without having an independent survey.

It was stressed that this principle applied on the purchase of a 'modest home', when there was great pressure on a purchaser to rely on the valuation report, because he might be unable to afford a second survey fee. Lord Griffiths expressly reserved his position in respect of valuations of industrial property, large blocks of flats, and very expensive houses. In these cases, it would be more reasonable to expect the purchaser to arrange his own full structural survey.

In neither of these two cases had the surveyor exercised reasonable skill and care as, although only a limited appraisal was expected, it was by a skilled professional person, and each surveyor was guilty of an error which the average surveyor would not have made.

It is possible for a surveyor to disclaim liability for negligence, but the disclaimer would be ineffective under s.2(2) of the Unfair Contract Terms Act 1977 unless it was fair and reasonable to allow reliance on it, under s.11(3) of the Act. Since a surveyor was a professional person, whose services were in fact paid for by the borrower, it would not be fair and reasonable for him to rely on a disclaimer. Also, the disclaimer was unfair in that it was imposed on a person who had no power to object to it.

Rignall Developments Ltd v. *Halil [1987] 3 WLR 394*

The property was subject to a local land charge. It was a financial charge to recover an improvement grant made by the district authority. The seller knew that this charge existed. The property was sold by auction. One of the conditions of sale was that the purchaser was deemed to have made local searches and enquiries and that the property was sold subject to anything that might be revealed thereby.

After contract, the purchaser learned of the charge, and refused to complete. The seller argued that the condition in the contract prevented the purchaser from objecting to the charge. However, the validity of the condition depended on the seller disclosing any matter she knew of, and as she had not disclosed the charge she could not rely on the condition (see section 5.4). It was, therefore, her duty to remove the charge by paying the local authority.

It was argued as that s.198 of the Law of Property Act 1925 says that registration of a charge amounts to actual notice for all purposes, registration was equivalent to disclosure. (You will remember that this argument could not have been used had it been a *central* land charge, but s.24 of the Law of Property Act 1969 does not apply to local land charges.)

It was held that where there was such a condition, and the seller knew of the charge, s.198 could not discharge her duty of expressly disclosing the existence of the charge.

Workshop

Attempt these problems yourself, then read the specimen solutions at the end of the book.

Problem 1

Your client tells you that he has signed a written contract to buy 'Fools Paradise', a freehold house at the price of £90 000. He shows you a copy of the contract. It incorporates the standard conditions. He entered into the contract without having made or seen any local land charge search certificate or answers to enquiries of the local authority. He has now discovered that the house is burdened with a financial charge in respect of the cost of road works prior to the adoption of the road on which the house fronts. The charge existed before he signed the contract, but he tells you he knew nothing of it. Advise him.

Problem 2

You have been consulted by Mr David Jones who proposes to purchase a semi-detached house which was built sixteen years ago on a small private residential estate. The house occupies a corner site on the edge of the estate and the side road is a private unmade road. Mr Jones is particularly attracted to this house because the present owner built a very large garage five years ago at the bottom of the garden and fronting onto the side road. Since that time he has been using the garage for repairing motor vehicles and Mr Jones wishes to do the same. The present owner has said that he has been using the garage for this business since it was built although he admits that he did not get planning permission either to build the garage or to use it for business purposes.

(a) Explain the issues, other than planning matters, with which you will be concerned in your perusal of the contract, the property information form, the searches and the evidence of title, in the particular circumstances of this case.

(b) Can the Local Planning Authority require the garage to be demolished?

(c) If the garage is not demolished, can the Local Planning Authority prevent its continued use for business purposes?

(This question is based on one in the Law Society Summer paper 1983.)

Problem 3

Joan is thinking of buying a house, but she would need to build an extension to provide a bedroom for her elderly mother. The seller's solicitor has provided her with the pre-contract package in accordance with the protocol. It includes the local land charge search certificate and the replies to the additional enquiries. They are four months old.

1. If Joan decides to buy, will she need to repeat the search and enquiries?
2. Will she need planning permission for the extension?
3. If she does need express planning permission, when should she apply for it?

7 Deducing and Investigating a Freehold Registered Title

7.1 Deduction of Title

As we have seen, the seller promises in the contract that he has a good title to the freehold estate, free from incumbrances (other than those, if standard condition 3 applies, mentioned in the contract or of which the seller was ignorant). At some stage the seller must prove that he does indeed have that title. He must 'deduce' his title, i.e. give evidence of it. Traditionally title was deduced after contract. If the seller's solicitor is following the protocol, title will be deduced *with* the draft contract.

So we are now considering what evidence of title the seller must produce, if he is contracting to sell a registered freehold title.

7.2 Section 110(1) of the Land Registration Act 1925

In the case of a registered title, s.110 of the Land Registration Act 1925 stipulates that the seller *must* supply the purchaser with

- a copy of the entries on the register;
- a copy of the filed plan;
- copies or abstracts of documents noted on the register of title.

Note

(a) The register of title is no longer private. It is unnecessary to give the purchaser an authority to inspect the register.

(b) S.110 only requires the seller to provide *a* copy of the entries on the register. So the seller could merely photocopy the contents of his land certificate. This would provide the purchaser with details of the register of title as at the date when the land certificate was last brought up to date with the register. This date is printed inside the cover of the certificate, and the purchaser would need to be told this date, for the purpose of his pre-completion search.

Alternatively, the seller can provide the purchaser with an office copy of the register, filed plan, etc. (and this is made obligatory by standard condition 4.2.1). Office copies are obtained from the District Land Registry. They are dated and are as admissible in evidence as to the state of the register at that date as is the register itself.

It is preferable for the seller's solicitor to obtain *up-to-date* office copy entries for his own sake. He might be caught out if he relies on the land certificate when drafting the contract. A caution, and a notice protecting a spouse's rights under the Matrimonial Homes Act 1983 can be entered on the register without the Land Certificate being put on deposit at the Registry, and so will not appear on the Land Certificate.

(c) Subsection (1) of s.110 cannot be altered by the contract. These documents *must* be supplied by the seller.

7.3 Section 110(2) of the Land Registration Act 1925

This provides that the seller must provide 'copies, abstracts and evidence (if any)' in respect of matters as to which the register is not conclusive. However, s.110(2) *can* be altered by contract.

Remember that the register is not conclusive:

(a) as to overriding interests. If the seller knows of an overriding interest, the effect of condition 3 is that the sale is only subject to the interest if it is mentioned in the contract. The purchaser would at the draft contract stage have been given whatever documentary evidence existed, and may have been prevented by a special condition in the contract from requiring any other evidence.
(b) in the case of a possessory title, as to matters affecting the pre-registration title. The seller may have no evidence as to this title, and again a contractual condition would prevent the purchaser from asking for any.
(c) in the case of a leasehold title, as to the provisions of the lease and in the case of a good leasehold title, as to the validity of the lease. The points are dealt with in Chapter 15.

7.4 Investigation of Title

The protocol requires the copies of the register, etc., to be sent to the purchaser with the draft contract, so some of the matters dealt with below would in fact have been dealt with before the purchaser decided to enter into the contract.

Suppose that as the purchaser's solicitor, you have the office copy entries and filed plan in front of you. Read them.

(*a*) *The Property Register and Filed Plan*

(i) Check the title number, estate and description of the property against the contract details. Care will be needed if there have already been sales of part of the land originally comprised in the title. The property register will indicate that part of the land has been sold off, and the filed plan will have been amended. Check that the seller is not contracting to sell land he has already transferred to someone else.

(ii) Check any reference to appurtenant rights. If the property register includes an appurtenant right, such as an easement, as part of the description of the property, you can be certain that the easement exists. The registration indicates ownership of the easement just as it indicates ownership of the estate to which it is appurtenant. If the register merely says that right is 'claimed' by the proprietor or that a deed 'purports' to grant the easement, the register is not conclusive as to its existence. The existence of the easement should be proved by the proprietor, unless the contract says otherwise.

(*b*) *The Proprietorship Register*

(i) Check that the seller is the person who is registered as proprietor. Suppose he is not? The solution may be that:

(aa) the seller is the personal representative of the dead registered proprietor (see Chapter 10).

(bb) the seller is the trustee in bankruptcy of the registered proprietor (see section 9.10).

(cc) the seller is a trustee for sale, who has been appointed, but who has not been registered as proprietor (see Chapter 11).

However, the solution may be that the seller has contracted to sell a legal estate that is in fact vested in someone else.

The principle here is that a seller shows good title only by establishing that he owns the legal estate, or that the legal estate is owned by someone who can be *compelled* by the seller to convey it to the purchaser. This is illustrated by the case of *Elliott* v. *Pierson* [1948] in which it was held that the seller had proved a good title to the freehold when he established that it was owned by a limited company which he controlled. If he had not had control of the company he would not have made good title, even if the company had been willing to convey to the purchaser. This would not have created any difficulty if the purchaser had been equally willing to accept a conveyance by the company, but the flaw in the seller's title would have given a reluctant purchaser the opportunity to treat the contract as discharged.

(ii) Look for restrictions. Either the seller must have the restriction removed before completion, or he must comply with it. Otherwise, the transfer to the purchaser will not be registered.

(iii) Cautions. If a caution is discovered on the register, do not accept an explanation of why the protected interest is in fact void, and so could not be asserted against the purchaser. Insist that the caution must be removed from the register before completion.

(*c*) *The Charges Register*

(i) Are there any entries on the charges register of incumbrances that are not mentioned in the contract?

(ii) Registered charges. Unless the contract expressly says otherwise, a purchaser is entitled to a title free from any mortgage. There are two usual methods by which a registered charge can be removed from the register.

(aa) *through its redemption* – i.e. the loan is repaid. The seller will be using part of the purchase price to pay off the mortgage. In the case of registered title the evidence that the mortgage loan has been repaid is Land Registry form 53 executed by the mortgagee (see s.35 of the Land Registration Act 1925). In essence, the form says that the proprietor of the registered charge admits that the charge has been discharged.

In an ideal world, this form would be handed to the purchaser on completion. However, some banks and building societies refuse to seal form 53 in advance of payment, so it is not available at completion. The solicitor acting for the purchaser is often prepared to accept what are called 'the usual undertakings' from the solicitor acting for the mortgagee, who will usually also be the seller's solicitor. The undertakings are guarded in form, because the solicitor will only undertake to do things that are within his own control. So he will not undertake that form 53 will be sealed. He will only undertake that he will forward the money necessary for redemption to the mortgagee, and that if and when the form 53 is sent by the mortgagee to him, he will send it on to the purchaser.

The purchaser accepts these undertakings, because it causes too much fuss and delay to object to an established practice. However, a purchaser does not have to accept the undertakings, and should not do so if there is a possibility that the execution of form 53 might be delayed. The undertakings should not be accepted, for instance, if the mortgagee is a private person. A building society does not die, or go on an extended holiday. A private mortgagee might. Form 53 must be available at completion.

An undertaking should only be accepted from a solicitor or licenced conveyancer. If the seller is acting for himself, an undertaking from him should not be accepted, and the form 53 should be available at completion.

If part of the land in the title is being transferred, and the mortgagee is releasing only the part being transferred from his mortgage, form 53 will say that the mortgage is discharged as regards the part of the land identified by the plan accompanying form 53. This plan would also be executed by the mortgagee.

(bb) *through being 'overreached'*. The proprietor of a registered charge has a statutory power of sale. (s.101 of the Law of Property Act 1925 and s.34 of the Land Registration Act 1925).

The power arises when, under the terms of the mortgage, the money is due and owing. This means that someone purchasing from a registered chargee must read the mortgage. He may, in an old-fashioned mortgage, find a promise to repay on a specified date, usually six months from the date of the mortgage. It is on this date that the money is technically due, and the power arises. Other mortgages may say that the money is repayable on demand (in which case evidence is needed that the mortgagee has requested repayment), or that the money is deemed to be due as from the date of the mortgage. The only check that a purchaser need make is that the power exists and has arisen. The power should only be used by the mortgagee when it has become exercisable. It may become exercisable under s.103 of the Law of Property Act 1925 (because of failure to repay capital, pay interest, or because of a breach of a provision in the mortgage) or under the terms of the mortgage. Some mortgages exclude s.103 and specify the defaults on which the power of sale becomes exercisable, or even say that the power becomes exercisable without default as from the date of the mortgage. Whatever the mortgage may say, this question of exercisability is an internal matter between the mortgagee and mortgagor (s.104 of the Law of Property Act 1925). Someone purchasing from the mortgagee need not enquire as to whether the power of sale is exercisable, and will get a good title from the mortgagee even if it is not. (However, it is said that a purchaser who learns that the power of sale is not exercisable should not complete, as he will not get a good title.)

Equally, a mortgagee when selling must take reasonable precautions to obtain the true market value at the time of sale. Failure in this duty to the mortgagor will not invalidate the sale to a purchaser who is innocent of fraud or collusion. The mortgagor must sue the mortgagee for damages.

The power is to sell the mortgagor's legal estate, free from the mortgage of the mortgagee who is selling and from any mortgage later in priority. These mortgages cease to be claims against the land and become instead claims against the purchase money paid to the mortgagee who sold. The mortgages are not cleared from the title through their redemption, so the purchaser will not receive forms 53 in respect of them. Even if the purchase price is not enough to repay the mortgages, the purchaser takes free of them. They no longer affect the land. Therefore, a purchaser from the proprietor of the first registered charge will receive on completion a transfer signed by the mortgagee, and the mortgagee's charge certificate. When the transfer is registered, all registered charges will be cancelled.

A mortgagee has no power to overreach a mortgage which has priority over his own. Therefore, if the seller is the proprietor of say, the second registered charge, there is a choice. The sale must either be subject to the first mortgage (unlikely) or the mortgagee who is selling will redeem the first mortgage.

(*d*) *Overriding Interests*

These, of course, will not be discovered from looking at the entries on the register. Any known to the seller should have been disclosed in the contract. If any overriding interest not disclosed by the contract and known to the seller is discovered before completion, the seller has broken his contract. (This is assuming standard condition 3 applies to the contract.)

A transfer signed by the seller's attorney This is discussed in 9.4.

7.5 The Pre-Completion Search: Form 94

This is the final step in the investigation of the seller's title.

The purchaser has evidence of the state of the title up to a certain date. If he was given office copy entries, it is the date of the office copies. If he was given a copy of the entries in the Land Certificate, it is the date that the certificate was last officially brought up to date with the register.

The object of the pre-completion search is to bring the purchaser's information up to date. The search form (Land Registry form 94A if a purchase of all the land in the title, 94B if a purchase of only part) consists in essence of an enquiry addressed to the Land Registrar, as to whether any adverse entry has been made on the register since one of the two dates mentioned above.

On receipt of the search form, the Registry will issue an official search certificate, saying whether or not adverse entries have been entered on the register since the date specified in the search form. This official search certificate gives a purchaser a priority period of 30 working days (i.e. excluding weekends and bank holidays) the first day of which is the date of delivery of the search at the Registry. Any entry made on the register during this period is postponed to the purchase, provided the purchase is completed, and an application to register the purchaser's title is delivered to the registry, before the period expires. So a purchaser is protected against last-minute registrations made after the date of his search.

It is important to apply for registration before the period expires, as otherwise anything that was being postponed to the purchase (e.g. an application to enter a caution) will cease to be postponed, so that when the purchaser does eventually apply for registration, the registration will be subject to it.

The priority period cannot be extended by another search. The second search will simply give a different priority period, and can only postpone applications made after the second search, but not ones made after the first search but before the second.

Subject to this limitation, a second search is worth making. It will give the second priority period, and will also reveal if an adverse entry has been put on the register since the date of the first search.

The priority period protects a purchaser. 'Purchaser' includes a prospective mortgagee or tenant. A search made by a prospective transferee acquires a priority period for the transferee, but not for the transferee's mortgagee. A search by the prospective mortgagee, however, does give a priority period both to the mortgagee and to the transferee. In other words, if Jane is the solicitor both for Bill, who is buying the house, and for the Larkshill Building Society which is lending Bill the money to do it, Jane will make only one search, on behalf of the Building Society. The priority period given by the search will protect both Bill and the Society against last-minute entries on the register, provided the application to register the transfer and the mortgage is delivered to the registry before the 30 days expire. (This is the effect of the Land Registration (Official Searches) Rules 1990).

A search certificate is not conclusive in favour of the purchaser, so if it is wrong (for example, if it fails to reveal an adverse entry) the purchaser will take subject to the entry. He will, however, be able to claim compensation from the registrar (s.83(3) of the Land Registration Act 1925).

7.6 Other Pre-Completion Searches

(*a*) *At the Companies Registry*

If the registered proprietor is a limited company, it appears unnecessary to search the company file at the Companies Registry.

(i) *Fixed charges* A fixed charge will not bind the purchaser unless protected by an entry on the register of the title at HM Land Registry, even though it is registered at the Companies Registry (s.60(1) of the Land Registration Act 1925).

(ii) *Floating charges* A floating charge will not bind a purchaser unless protected by an entry on the register of title. If it is so protected, the purchaser will need to obtain a certificate of non-crystallisation signed by the company secretary, or, preferably, by the owner of the floating charge. This certificate should be dated as at the date of completion.

(iii) A company going, or gone, into liquidation. It is suggested (see Ruoff and Roper – Registered title) that there is no need to search for this purpose, because so long as the company remains registered proprietor, it has the ability to transfer the legal estate, provided there is no caution on the register.

(*b*) *A Bankruptcy Search in the Land Charges Registry Against the Name of the Purchaser*

This search has nothing whatsoever to do with the investigation of the seller's title, but is added to the list of pre-completion searches for the sake of completeness.

If the solicitor for the purchaser is also acting for the purchaser's mortgagee, it is his duty, as the mortgagee's solicitor, to discover if the purchaser is, or is about to become, insolvent. This can be done by making a search against the purchaser's name at the Land Charges Registry, to see if there is a PA(B) or WO(B) registered (see sections 4.5(a) and (b)). This is not a title search, and it has nothing to do with the seller's ownership of the property being sold. It is a status search, to prevent the mortgagee lending money to a bankrupt. It is done by sending to the Land Charges Registry a search form K16, which asks the Registrar to search only for bankruptcy entries against the names listed.

Of course, this search is not necessary if the loan is not to the purchaser of a registered title, but to the existing registered proprietor. In the latter case, entries as to the bankruptcy of the proprietor will appear on the register of title, and will be revealed by the Land Registry Search.

Workshop

Attempt this problem yourself, then read the specimen solution at the end of the book.

Problem

You are acting for William and Mary Thompson, who are buying a freehold dwelling-house, number 34 Holly Avenue, at the price of £34 000. They are obtaining an advance of £30 000 from the Best Building Society (for whom you act) by way of an endowment mortgage. The seller is the Z Finance Company Ltd, which is selling as second mortgagee free from incumbrances, the first mortgagee being the Y Building Society.

List the documents you will send to the Best Building Society after completion.

---

8 Deduction of Unregistered Title

8.1 Form of Evidence

In the case of an unregistered title, a seller deduces his title by providing evidence of what his title deeds say. At one time, he would have sent the purchaser an abstract of the deeds. This amounted to a précis of their contents, prepared in a stylised form. Nowadays, the simplest method of letting a purchaser know the contents of deeds is by sending him photocopies of them. The photocopy deeds must be accompanied by an epitome i.e. a chronological index of the accompanying deeds. The epitome should state whether each original deed will itself be available on completion, and whether it will be handed over then to the purchaser. In this book, 'abstract' is used to mean both the traditional abstract and the epitome.

8.2 What Deeds and Other Documents Should be Abstracted?

The abstract will start with the deed that the purchaser is entitled to see as the root of title. Usually there will have been a term in the contract specifying what deed this is to be. If not, the document must be one that is a good root of title at least 15 years old (see section 5.8(e)). The abstract may start with an earlier document in circumstances in which the purchaser is entitled to see a pre-root deed (see section 8.3(e)). Having started with the root, the abstract must then give details of every deed, document or event that passes the legal estate from owner to owner, and eventually to the seller. Notice again that he must establish either that he owns the legal estate, or that it is owned by someone who can be compelled by him to convey it to the purchaser. This has been discussed in the context of registered title in section 7.4(b).

8.3 Which are Not Abstracted?

(a) An abstract should not contain *information about equitable or other interests that will be overreached by the sale*, and so will not affect the purchaser. So, for example, on a sale by trustees for sale the purchaser need not be given information about the interests of the beneficiaries. On a sale by a mortgagee, the purchaser need not be given details of mortgages later in priority to that of the seller's.

(b) *A lease that has expired by effluxion of time* For example, if a lease was granted in 1975 for ten years, and the tenant left at the end of the term in 1985, the purchaser need not be given a copy of that lease. If the lease ended by any other means, the purchaser should be given whatever information is available to prove its termination, so if the tenant surrendered the lease in 1980, the purchaser should see a copy of the lease, and of the deed of surrender.

(c) *Birth, death or marriage certificates* These are matters of public record, and the strict rule is that if a purchaser wants a copy he can get one for himself. What the purchaser must be given is the information he needs to do this, e.g. the date of the marriage. In fact, if the seller has these certificates, it would be churlish of him to refuse the purchaser a copy.

(d) Strictly, *equitable mortgages should be abstracted*, so that the purchaser can check on their redemption. Remember though, that an equitable mortgage can be created with little formality. So equitable mortgages are not usually abstracted if they have in fact been paid off. If however, an equitable mortgage has been protected by the registration of a C(iii) land charge, the registration should be cancelled, otherwise the purchaser is alerted to the existence of the mortgage, and will need evidence of repayment of the loan.

Any legal mortgage created after the root of title should be abstracted, together with any relevant vacating receipt.

A legal mortgage created before the root of title, but discharged at a date after the date of the root of title should be abstracted, together with any vacating receipt. If it was not redeemed or otherwise discharged until after the date of the root of title, it is part of the post-root title, no matter when it was created.

A legal mortgage created and discharged earlier than the date of the root of title need not be abstracted.

(e) *Pre-root deeds and documents* Generally, a purchase has no right to see any deeds or documents that are dated earlier than the root of title.

Section 45 of the Law of Property Act provides that 'a purchaser shall not:

(i) require the production, or any abstract or copy of any deed, will or other document, dated or made before the time prescribed by law, or stipulated, for the commencement of the title, . . .;

(ii) require any information or make any requisition, objection or enquiry, with respect to any such deed, will or document, or the title prior to that time . . .'.

This section prohibits the purchaser from making any objection to the soundness of the pre-root title. It is as if there were an express term in the contract itself preventing the purchaser from raising requisitions on title. We have seen that any such contractual stipulation is valid only if the seller has shown good faith, i.e. has revealed to the purchaser any defect he knows about or ought to know about (see section 5.4). The same is true of the s.45 interdiction. So the purchaser can object to the pre-root title if he establishes the existence of a defect that was known to the seller at the time of contract and not disclosed. For this reason, a seller cannot use the section to escape his duty of disclosure. Any pre-root defect known to the seller should be expressly disclosed, and the purchaser expressly prohibited from raising a requisition in respect of it. Further, an incumbrance that is still enforceable is a matter of the post-root title, even though created pre-root.

There are four exceptions to s.45, when a purchaser can insist on seeing a pre-root document. The first three are laid down by s.45.

(i) a purchaser can see a power of attorney, no matter what its date, if it authorised the execution of a document that is part of the title;
(ii) a purchaser can see a document no matter what its date which created an interest or obligation which still subsists, if one of the documents on the title conveys the land subject to the interest;
(iii) a purchaser can see a document which creates a trust, if one of the documents on the title disposes of the land by reference to that trust. This does not however apply to a trust deed of a settlement by way of trust for sale, or one governed by the Settled Land Act 1925, the reason being that the equitable interests created by those sorts of trust deeds should be cleared from the title by being overreached. So this exception is only likely to apply to a conveyance by a trustee of a bare trust at the direction, or with the consent, of the beneficiary.
(iv) the fourth exception comes not from s.45 but from the definition of a good root, i.e. that it must describe the property that is being conveyed. If the root of title describes the property it is conveying by a reference to a description in an earlier deed, or to a plan in an earlier deed, it is possible that a purchaser can either insist on a copy of the deed being produced, or can claim that the root of title is not a good root, as not containing an adequate description.

These rights of a purchaser can be removed by a special condition in the contract, with the exception of the pre-root power of attorney. Section 125(2) of the Law of Property Act 1925 makes it impossible for the purchaser's right to any power of attorney affecting his title to be excluded by the contract.

(f) *Past land charge search certificates* These are not documents of title, and the purchaser is not entitled to the results of past searches. However, if the seller has any, it is courteous to send copies to the purchaser, as it may save him from repeating searches against the names of past estate owners. The protocol requires the seller's solicitor to provide a certificate of search against 'appropriate' names which must mean the names of all the estate owners revealed by the abstract.

8.4 Verification of the Abstract

The abstract or epitome is only *prima facie* evidence of the seller's ownership of the property. The abstract might be inaccurate, omit vital documents or memoranda, or, of course, be a complete fabrication. Either at or before completion the purchaser must see the original deeds.

If the seller will be retaining the title deeds, it is usual for the purchaser's solicitor to 'mark' the abstract (or the copy deeds, in the case of an epitome) i.e. to write on it the fact that it has been examined against the original, and that the abstract is correct. This statement is signed by the solicitor, who adds the date, and sometimes the place where the examination was made. In later transactions the marked abstract or marked deeds may be acceptable as evidence of title, without recourse to the original deeds. However, a solicitor who relies on a marked abstract or marked copies which then turn out to be inaccurate, might be accused of negligence. (The protocol requires the seller's solicitor to mark any copy or abstract of a deed that will not be given to the purchaser on completion before sending the copy or abstract as part of the pre-contract package.)

8.5 Retention by the Seller of Deeds at Completion

On completion, a seller must generally hand to the purchaser all title deeds in his control. The seller can, however, retain the title deeds if he is also retaining part of the land to which they relate (s.45(9) of the Law of Property Act 1925). In such a case the purchaser should:

(a) mark the abstract as examined against the original deeds (if not already done);
(b) ensure that a memorandum of sale of part is endorsed on the conveyance to the seller;
(c) ensure that the conveyance to him contains an acknowledgement and undertaking in respect of the retained deeds.

It will often be wise for a seller of part to retain a copy of the conveyance to the purchaser with his deeds. It will identify exactly what part was sold and disclose any easements or covenants given by the purchaser in favour of the retained land.

Workshop

Attempt this problem yourself, then read the specimen solution at the end of the book.

Problem

You are acting for Patrick O'Connor who is selling his freehold house. You have the documents listed below:

1. 4 July 1970 – a conveyance on sale from A to B, said to be subject to covenants contained in a deed dated 1950.
2. 4 July 1970 – a mortgage given by B to the Foundation Building Society, with a receipt endorsed on it dated 30 September 1973 executed by the Society.
3. 6 July 1970 – a lease by B to T for 30 years.
4. 20 September 1973 – land charges search against B and O'Connor.
5. 30 September 1973 – a conveyance on sale from B to O'Connor, subject to the 1950 covenants.
6. 30 September 1973 – a mortgage given by O'Connor to the Roof Building Society.
7. 9 February 1975 – a surrender of lease by T to O'Connor.

(a) When you are drafting the contract, which document will you specify as the root of title?

(b) What documents will you abstract when deducing title to the purchaser?

9 Investigating an Unregistered Title

9.1 Introduction

When investigating an unregistered title, we are looking for a flaw in the soundness of the seller's claim to own the legal estate, and for any third-party right that will bind the purchaser after completion but to which the sale has not been made subject by the contract. This is easier said than done.

It does not matter for present purposes whether we are investigating the title before exchange of contracts or after. In the former case we will ask for any defect to be put right before we agree to buy; in the latter case we shall raise a requisition on the basis that the seller has not proved that he has the title promised in the contract. Of course, if we agree by a special condition in the contract to accept the title as deduced, we must investigate the title before exchange of contracts, as our power to object to the title after contract will be very limited (see Chapter 5).

We will start by considering the basic points of the root of title, the stamping of the title deeds, the identification of the property, execution of the deed, and the 'missing link'.

Suppose we are acting for Paula Prentiss, who is contracting to buy the freehold of Sandy Cottage from Ian Lane.

We receive an epitome of title, accompanied by the photocopies of two documents.

9.2 The First Document of Title

The first document is a deed of conveyance on sale dated 3 June 1971, and this deed is now going to be considered.

(*a*) *The Root of Title*

If the contract does not specify what document is to be the root of title, we will consider our right to have title traced from a good root at least 15 years old, and we will check that this conveyance satisfies the definition of a good root (see section 5.8(e)). Our contract doubtless specifies from what document title is to be traced, so the question as to whether this document is adequate as a root was considered before accepting the contractual condition. We will be wary of any condition compelling us to trace title from an immature root. The 1971 conveyance appears to be a good root, and is, of course, over 15 years old.

(*b*) *Stamping*

(i) If the 1971 deed is not properly stamped, this is a defect in the seller's title. A document that is not properly stamped cannot be produced in court, and a title that cannot be defended in court is not a good title. If the deed is not properly stamped, we shall insist that the seller have it stamped. (We can do this even though there is a condition in the contract saying that no objection can be raised to an insufficiency of stamps, as the condition is void, by virtue of s.117 of the Stamp Act 1891).

As the conveyance is on sale, we would expect to see the 'particulars delivered' stamp. We also need to check that the conveyance bears the correct *ad valorem* stamps. The difficulty is that the thresholds for stamp duty have changed over the years, as have the rates of duty. In the past, rates of stamp duty were graded, so the certificate of value (see section 2.17) was used not just as now, to claim total exemption from duty, but also to claim a reduced rate, e.g. 0.5 per cent rather than 2 per cent. So it is possible for a conveyance to have a certificate of value and also *ad valorem* stamps. Details of past rates of duty should be kept to hand, so that the stamping of past conveyances and other documents can be checked.

One thing must always be wrong, namely the absence from a conveyance on sale of both a certificate of value and *ad valorem* stamps. Total exemption from *ad valorem* stamp duty could only ever be claimed through a certificate of value. If the conveyance contained no certificate, *ad valorem* duty was payable at the then full rate, no matter how low the consideration.

(ii) *A note about particular documents* In the past, not only conveyances on sale had to be stamped *ad valorem*. A deed of gift was also liable, the duty being calculated on the value of the land. A certificate of value could be used to claim a nil or a reduced rate. The deed had to be sent into the Stamp Office for the duty to be adjudicated, so the deed should bear a blue adjudication stamp. A deed of gift made on or after 25 March 1985 was liable for a 50p deed stamp. A deed of gift made after 30 April 1987 bears no stamp duty, provided it is certificated (see section 2.17).

An assent under seal was liable for a 50p deed stamp if made before 25 March 1985.

Mortgages and vacating receipts (with the exception of a building society receipt) were liable to stamp duty if made before 1 August 1971.

(*c*) *The Parties to It*

Suppose the seller in the 1971 deed is John Smith, and the purchaser is Alice Hardy. John is a mystery to us and will remain so. We may never know how he obtained the legal estate, as that can only be revealed by investigating the pre-root title.

(*d*) *The Parcels Clause*

We are hoping to establish that the land conveyed in the 1971 deed did include the land that Ian has contracted to sell to our client. Under an open contract, the seller must prove that the property he has contracted to sell is the same as that being dealt with by the title deeds. This obligation does not appear to be altered by the standard conditions, although condition 4.3.1 absolves the seller from having to prove the exact boundaries of the property or the ownership of the boundary fences.

The proof usually comes merely from the description in the deed, i.e. that it says it is conveying Sandy Cottage. If the deed did not make it clear that it was dealing with Sandy Cottage, further evidence would be needed, for example, a declaration from Ian that the land has been occupied since 1971 under the authority of the title deeds without challenge from anyone.

(*e*) *Incumbrances*

Reading the parcels clause in the 1971 conveyance might reveal the reservation of an easement not disclosed in the contract but known to the seller. Reading the habendum might disclose incumbrances already existing before 1971 but not mentioned in the contract.

(*f*) *Execution of the Deed*

The formalities for execution of a deed by an individual changed on 31 July 1990 when s.1 of the Law of Property (Miscellaneous Provisions) Act 1989 came into force. The new formalities are set out in Chapter 13, where the drafting of a deed is considered. The old formalities are set out here, as they remain important when checking the due execution of a past title deed.

A deed executed before s.1 of the 1989 Act came into effect had to be signed and sealed by its maker, and delivered as his deed (s.73 of the Law of Property Act 1925). If these formalities were not observed, the document was not a deed, and could not create or convey a legal estate (s.52 of the Law of Property Act 1925).

We are unlikely to query the authenticity of a signature on a deed. In theory we could ask Ian to provide evidence that what purports to be John Smith's signature is indeed that very thing. In practice we would not do that. Anyway, in respect of the 1971 deed, any requisition by us would be countered by Ian quoting the rule that a deed or document 20 years old proves itself, provided it is produced from proper custody and there are no suspicious circumstances. A suspicious circumstance would be a startling difference between two signatures both purporting to be that of John.

Section 73 did also require a seal. The days of personal seals are long past, and a seal became only a red wafer disc to be obtained from any law stationer. However, it was still essential that a seal be on the conveyance *before* the maker signed. So if the 1971 conveyance does not bear a seal, evidence is needed that a seal was in position at the time of execution. If a seal was never there, nor anything such as a printed circle which might have served as a seal, then the document is not a deed, and could not have conveyed the legal estate (see *First National Securities* v. *Jones* [1978]; and *TCB Ltd* v. *Gray* [1986]).

The delivery of a deed is a matter of intention. A deed is delivered when it is signed by the maker with the intention that he shall be bound by it. If a person signs and seals a deed, it is inferred from this that the deed is also delivered, so we will not call on Ian for evidence that John delivered the deed.

9.3 The Second Document of Title

We now turn to the second and final document of title. This is a conveyance on sale dated 1 March 1987.

(a) We again check stamping.

(b) We again consider the parties, looking particularly for the 'missing link'. If in 1971 the property was conveyed to Alice Hardy, we expect to see Alice Hardy conveying it in 1987. Suppose for the sake of argument, that we find that the seller in the 1987 deed is, in fact, Christopher Camp. We need an explanation. Perhaps Alice had died, and Christopher was her personal representative. If so, we would ask for a copy of the grant of representation, identifying Christopher as executor or administrator, and would turn to Chapter 10. Alternatively Alice might have gone bankrupt, and Christopher was the trustee in bankruptcy, in which case we would ask to see a copy of the bankruptcy order and the certificate of appointment of Christopher as trustee.

If the ownership of the legal estate had not passed to Christopher by operation of law, then it must have passed by conveyance. In the absence of such a conveyance, the title is bad. The legal estate remained in Alice, and only she had power to convey it to Ian. To put his title right, Ian must either procure a conveyance by Alice to himself, or prove to us that he can compel Alice to convey the property directly to our client (see sections 7.4(b)).

(c) *The Parcels Clause*

We expect to see a description similar to that in the 1971 deed, or at least linked to it. For example, the 1971 deed might talk about 'Farmer Giles's 10-acre field', but (we hope) also refer to an annexed plan which shows that the field covered the site of what is now Sandy Cottage. The 1987 deed may talk about Sandy Cottage forming part of the land 'conveyed by the 1971 deed'.

(*d*) *Incumbrances*

We are again looking to see if the 1987 deed created new incumbrances not disclosed in the contract.

There now follows a list of diverse points to be considered on investigating the title. The list is not complete, and must be read in conjunction with Chapters 10, 11 and 12.

9.4 Execution of a Deed by a Company

Again, the formalities for the execution of a deed by a company changed on 31 July 1990, but this time by virtue of s.130 of the Companies Act 1989, brought into force on that day. The present formalities are set out in Chapter 13. The previous formalities are set out here.

If a conveyance was executed by a limited company, the execution was valid if the conveyance was executed in accordance with the company's articles of association. If the company's articles incorporated Table A of the Companies Act 1985, its articles provided for a deed to be executed by the affixing of the company seal by the authority of the directors in the presence of a director and the secretary, or the presence of two directors.

By virtue of s.74 of the Law of Property Act 1925, if the company seal had been affixed in the presence of the secretary and director, the deed was deemed to have been duly executed, even if in fact the articles demanded different formalities. Further, a purchaser could assume that the deed had been executed so as to satisfy s.74 if there was on the deed a seal that purported to be the company seal, and signatures that purported to be that of secretary and director. So a purchaser could take these matters at face value.

It follows from s.74 that the company was bound by its deed executed in accordance with the section, even though the seal was affixed without the authority of a resolution from the board of directors (*D'Silva* v. *Lister House Development Limited* [1971] Ch 17 [1970] 1 A11 ER 858).

9.5 Execution of a Document by an Attorney

(*a*) *Power of Attorney*

A seller who will, for example, be out of the country when the sale of his property is to be arranged, may authorise someone else to sign all the necessary documents on his behalf. If it is to confer the power to execute a deed (i.e. sign as well as deliver) the authority must itself be given by deed. The authority is called a power of attorney. We will call the seller, who confers the power, the principal, and we will call the person on whom the power is conferred, the attorney.

(*b*) *Scope of the Power*

A purchaser, before accepting a conveyance or transfer signed by the seller's attorney, must consider whether the attorney has the necessary authority under the terms of the power to sign the conveyance. This is decided by reading the power, and seeing what acts it does authorise.

A power may be specific, i.e. may authorise the attorney to do only those things which are enumerated in the power. A power 'to do all things, and execute all documents connected with the sale of 10 Cherry Avenue' is clearly useless if an attorney seeks to establish his authority to execute a mortgage of 10 Cherry Avenue.

Alternatively, a power may be general. The power may say simply that the attorney is appointed in accordance with s.10 of the Powers of Attorney Act 1971. This confers on the attorney authority to do on behalf of his principal anything that can lawfully be done through an attorney. So this attorney can execute a mortgage or conveyance of 10 Cherry Avenue, or of anything else that the seller owns beneficially. (Section 10 does not apply to any function which the principal has as a trustee or personal representative.)

(*c*) *Revocation of the Power*

The purchaser must also consider the possibility that the power had been revoked before the attorney executed the deed. Most powers of attorney are given solely because the principal is not able himself to sign the documents. The attorney has no proprietary interest in the land that is to be conveyed. This type of administrative power can be revoked by the principal at any time. It is also automatically revoked by the death of the principal, or by his bankruptcy or mental incapacity.

By contrast, the attorney may have an interest in the property to be conveyed, and the power might have been given to protect that interest. An example would be a power of attorney given to an equitable mortgagee authorising him to execute a legal mortgage in his own favour. This type of power is called a security power, and can be made irrevocable. Section 4(1) of the Powers of Attorney Act 1971 provides that if a power of attorney is *expressed* to be irrevocable and is given to protect a proprietary interest of the attorney, then so long as the attorney has that interest the power is not revoked by any event, nor can it be withdrawn by the principal unless the attorney consents.

(*d*) *Protection for the Purchaser from the Attorney*

But for the 1971 Act (and earlier Acts) the rule would be that if the power had been revoked before the attorney executed the conveyance or transfer, the conveyance would be void. Section 5 of the Powers of Attorney Act protects the person dealing with the attorney from the possibility of previous revocation of the power. It provides that even if the power has been revoked, the transaction by the attorney is nevertheless valid, provided that the person dealing with the attorney (i.e. the purchaser from the principal) did not know of the revocation. So it is not the fact of revocation that matters, so much as whether or not the purchaser from the principal *knew* of the revocation. (It must be remembered that knowledge of a revoking event – for example, the death of the principal – amounts to knowledge of the effect of that event, i.e. the consequent revocation of the power.)

Section 5 also provides that if the power is *expressed* to be irrevocable and is *expressed* to be given by way of security, the person dealing with the attorney is entitled to assume that the power can only be revoked with the consent of the attorney. Knowledge of the donor's death would in such a case be irrelevant. The person dealing with the attorney does not receive this protection if he knows that the power was not in fact given by way of security. The Powers of Attorney Act 1971 applies to all powers of attorney whenever created but only to transactions completed by the attorney on or after 1 October 1971. For the validity of transactions completed before that date, the effect of ss.123 – 128 of the Law of Property Act 1925 must be considered.

(*e*) *Evidence of the Power*

On completion, the attorney will not part with the deed creating the power if it is a general power, or if it authorises any disposition other than that to the purchaser. What he will give the purchaser is a facsimile copy (e.g. a photocopy) certified by the solicitor as being an accurate copy. This copy is then conclusive evidence of the contents of the original power. This means that anyone later investigating title need never see the original power; he need only see the copy, which has been handed from purchaser to purchaser with the title deeds.

(*f*) *Protection of Later Purchasers*

We can see that the validity of the title that the attorney gives to the person dealing with him may depend on whether or not that person knew of a revocation of the power. There are two occasions when it is conclusively presumed in favour of any subsequent purchaser that the person dealing with the attorney did not know of a revocation.

One is where the transaction between the attorney and the person dealing with the attorney is completed within 12 months of the date of the power. The other is where the person dealing with the attorney makes a statutory declaration before or within 3 months of the subsequent purchase that he did not at the material time know of the revocation of the power (s.5(4) of the 1971 Act).

Example An example might help. Vimto has agreed to sell Blackacre to Pedro. Vimto gives his solicitor, Alexis, a power of attorney to execute a deed of conveyance and to complete the transaction.

Alexis executes the deed and completes on 1 October 1989. The conveyance to Pedro will be valid unless Pedro knew that Vimto had by then revoked the power, or become bankrupt or insane or had died.

Pedro later sells to Quentin. Quentin can conclusively presume that Pedro did not know of any revocation, provided that the power came into effect in the 12 months preceding 1 October 1989. Quentin will *not* raise any requisition as to Pedro's knowledge. He will simply compare the date of the power and the date of the conveyance. If the 1989 conveyance was executed by Alexis more than 12 months after the date of the power, Pedro will be asked to make the statutory declaration.

Again, the requisition to Pedro is not 'did you know of any revocation?' but is 'supply the statutory declaration'. Pedro may be lying in his teeth when he makes the declaration, but the title he gives to Quentin will be sound.

(*g*) *A Power of Attorney Delegating a Trust*

Section 25 of the Trustee Act 1925 (as amended by s.9 of the Powers of Attorney Act 1971) provides that a trustee (including a trustee for sale) can by a power of attorney delegate the exercise of his trust and powers for up to 12 months.

The power of attorney must be executed in the presence of a witness, and notice of it must be given to the other trustees.

A trustee cannot delegate to his fellow-trustee if there are only the two of them. One of three or more trustees can delegate to a fellow-trustee. Nor can a trustee use the statutory form of power of attorney under s.10 of the Powers of Attorney Act 1971 even if the trustee is also a beneficial owner (see *Walia* v. *Michael Naughton Ltd* [1985]).*

So if A and B own the legal estate on trust for sale for themselves as beneficial co-owners:

(i) A cannot appoint B as his attorney;
(ii) If A appoints X as his attorney, the power must comply with the Trustee Act 1925, otherwise it will be void.

(*h*) *The Application of these Rules to Registered Title*

Although this chapter is on the subject of unregistered title, this is a convenient time to consider the application of these rules to a registered title.

A transfer by the attorney of the registered proprietor will again be valid, provided that the person dealing with the attorney did not know of the revocation of the power. The transferee will then apply for registration of the transfer. It is now the *Registrar* who is concerned as to whether the transferee did or did not know of any revocation. Therefore, if the transfer did not take place within 12 months of the power, the Registrar will require the transferee to provide the Registrar with a statutory declaration that at the time of completion the transferee did not know of the revocation of the power. If the power is a security power, the transferee must declare that he did not know that the power was not in fact given by way of security, and did not know of any revocation with the attorney's consent. The power, or a certified copy of it, must also be filed (Rule 82 of Land Registration Rules 1925, as substituted by Land Registration (Powers of Attorney) Rules 1986).

This declaration must also accompany an application for first registration.

(*i*) *The Enduring Powers of Attorney Act 1985*

The purpose of this Act is to enable a principal to appoint an attorney whose authority will not be revoked by the principal becoming mentally incapable. The power must be created while the principal is of sound mind, and so long as he remains mentally capable the power operates as an ordinary power of attorney. It may confer a general authority on the attorney, or empower him to do only those things specified by the power. An enduring power is effective from the moment it is executed, so the attorney is empowered to dispose of the principal's property even while the principal is still mentally capable. It can be made clear in the power that it is only to become effective when the principal becomes mentally incapable if this precaution is felt to be necessary. The power must be in a prescribed form (see the Enduring Powers of Attorney (Prescribed Form) Regulations 1990 SI No. 1376). It must, for example, contain an express statement that the principal intends the power to continue notwithstanding any later mental incapacity, and the principal must confirm that he has read this statement. The power must be executed by the principal and the attorney in the presence of a witness.

When the donor becomes mentally incapable, the attorney is under a statutory duty to register the power with the court, and his authority to deal with the principal's property is suspended until the power is registered. Once the power is registered, the principal cannot revoke the power unless he recovers mental capacity *and* the court confirms the revocation. The power, although not revoked by the mental incapacity of the principal, is revoked by his death or bankruptcy.

The risk for the person dealing with the attorney is not so much the risk of *revocation* of the power, as of its invalidity, or its suspension through non-registration. The Act contains provisions to protect the person dealing with the attorney against such possibilities. The protection depends on the ignorance of these matters. Subsequent purchasers have the benefit of a conclusive presumption that the transaction between the attorney and the person dealing with him is valid if either it took place within one year of the power being registered, or the person dealing with the attorney makes a statutory declaration that he had no reason to doubt the existence of the attorney's authority to enter into the transaction.

As an exception to the rule set out in (g), a power under the 1985 Act will delegate any powers which the principal had as a trustee, even though the attorney is the sole fellow-trustee. So, if A and B were co-owners of land, a power given by A to B under the 1985 Act would enable B to sell the property effectively on his own (although in the name of A and B) and by himself to give a good receipt for the purchase price (s.3(3) of the Enduring Powers of Attorney Act 1985).

This is one reason why a power of attorney is often drawn up as an enduring power rather than an ordinary one. A second reason is that a delegation of a trust under s.25 Trustee Act 1925 lasts for only 12 months. A delegation of a trust under the 1985 Act lasts indefinitely. A third reason is that the presumption as to the validity of the transaction is applied to any dealing within 12 months of the registration of the power rather than of its execution. So no statutory declaration is needed even though the power may have been executed more than 12 months before the attorney executes the conveyance.

9.6 Clearing a Mortgage off the Title

In unregistered title, there are three usual ways of removing a mortgage from the title.

(*a*) *Redemption*

The purchaser is entitled to evidence that the mortgage loan has been repaid. Section 115 of the Law of Property Act 1925 provides that a receipt for all the money due under the mortgage endorsed on the mortgage and executed by the lender will discharge the mortgaged property from all interest and principal secured by the mortgage. The section also provides that the receipt should name the person making the payment. When investigating the discharge of the mortgage, you need to check that the person named in the receipt as making the payment was the person who then owned the mortgaged property. If he was, the receipt does discharge the mortgage. If he was not, the receipt does not discharge the mortgage; instead it transfers ownership of it from the original lender to the person named as making the payment. This is why care is needed in dating the receipt. Suppose that Bella owns Blackacre, which is mortgaged to the Northlands Bank. She contracts to sell Blackacre free of the mortgage to Catherine, and the sale is completed on 6 March. Part of the purchase price is used to pay off the Bank. The Bank endorses the receipt on the mortgage deed and names Bella as having made the payment. It is correct to name Bella rather than Catherine as the arrangement in the contract was that the mortgage was to be discharged by the seller before Blackacre was conveyed to Catherine. The receipt must be dated either 6 March or earlier. If it is dated 7 March, Bella is not at that date the owner of the land. The receipt transfers the mortgage from Northlands Bank to Bella. Although in theory

Bella would have taken a transfer of the mortgage, probably nothing would have to be done to clear the title. If the conveyance to Catherine said that Bella's title was 'free from incumbrances', Bella would be estopped from asserting the mortgage (see *Cumberland Court* (Brighton) Ltd v. *Taylor* [1964].

A receipt will not operate as a transfer if the receipt provides otherwise.

A building society will use the form of receipt allowed by the Building Societies Act 1986. This merely acknowledges receipt of the money. It does not name the person making the payment, and cannot operate as a transfer.

The seller's mortgage As has already been mentioned, banks and building societies sometimes refuse to execute the receipt in advance of completion. The purchaser's solicitor may accept undertakings as discussed in section 7.4(c).

(*b*) *By Release*

This is discussed in Chapter 13.

(*c*) *By Overreaching*

This is discussed in section 7.4(c). A purchaser will not see a receipt on the mortgage of the mortgagee who is selling, nor on any subsequent mortgage. In unregistered title, the power of sale is implied into any mortgage by deed (s.101 of the Law of Property Act 1925).

9.7 Establishing a Title by Adverse Possession

A seller can establish that he has a good title by proving adverse possession. However, he must establish not only that he (and possibly his predecessors) have been in possession of the land, but also that the possession has extinguished the title of the true owner (see Re *Atkinson and Horsell's* contract [1912]). This means that the title of the true owner must be deduced, and the extinction of that title must be proved. It is not sufficient merely to prove possession, for however long, as the effect of the possession cannot be gauged unless it is known whom the possession has been against. If, for example, the land is subject to a ninety-nine year lease, possession for over twelve years may have extinguished the tenant's title to the lease, but will not have extinguished the landlord's title to the reversion, as time does not start running against a landlord until his right to possession arises at the end of the lease.

It will often be impossible for a seller to prove the title of the true owner, and a special condition in the contract will be required, limiting the evidence of title to, for example, a declaration by the seller that he has been in undisputed possession of the land for however long it is. If the condition specifies what evidence of title will be supplied, the seller will be in breach of contract unless he supplies that very evidence. In the case of *George Wimpey & Co Ltd* v. *Sohn* [1987] the sellers promised in the contract to give the purchaser a statutory declaration that they had been in undisputed possession of the land for twenty years. However, the sellers could not make the declaration, as their possession had been disputed. The sellers then claimed that they had been in adverse possession for twelve years, and had thereby extinguished the title of the true owners. The purchaser could refuse this title, as he had not been given the evidence of title he had been promised.

9.8 Minors

It is not usual to raise a requisition as to the age of a purchaser under a past title deed. This is because there is a *presumption* that a party to a deed is adult. If, however, it becomes known that land was conveyed to a minor then the following principles apply:

(a) A minor cannot hold a legal estate, either beneficially or as a trustee.

(b) If land is conveyed to a minor for the minor beneficially, he does obtain the equitable interest. The legal estate remains with the transferor, who holds it in trust for the minor. The transferor is under an obligation to create a settlement on the minor under the Settled Land Act 1925 (s.27 of the Settled Land Act 1925). It will be necessary to do this if the land is to be sold while the minor is still under 18. This will mean drawing up a trust deed, and a vesting deed, transferring the legal estate to the trustees of the settlement. They can then convey it, and overreach the minor's equitable interest.

    If the minor has reached 18, there is no need to create a settlement. The transferor can execute a confirmatory conveyance of the legal estate.

(c) If the legal estate is conveyed to an adult and a minor as beneficial co-owners, the legal estate will vest only in the adult. He will hold it in trust for sale for himself and the minor. He can overreach the minor's interest by appointing a second trustee for sale (see Chapter 11).

9.9 A Voluntary Conveyance

A deed of gift can be set aside under the Insolvency Act 1986. A donee has therefore a voidable title. Under s.339 of the Insolvency Act 1986, a trustee in bankruptcy can apply to have the deed set aside if made within the two years prior to the presentation of the petition in bankruptcy. If the two years are past, but five years have not yet passed, it can be set aside providing the donor was insolvent at the time of the gift, or became insolvent as a result. It will be up to the trustee to prove the insolvency, unless the donee was an associate of the donor (as defined by s.435 of the Act) e.g. a spouse, in which case there is a rebuttable presumption of insolvency.

However, s.342 provides that the gift cannot be set aside if this would prejudice an interest in the property acquired in good faith without notice of the relevant circumstances.

Rider It is doubtful if s.342 offers a purchaser of an unregistered title any protection if the purchaser buys from the donee within two years of the gift. The purchaser is bound to know that the seller acquired the property by way of gift, simply by reading the conveyance to him, so will have notice of the 'relevant circumstances'. The solution, pending the promised amendment of the Act, is to arrange title insurance. (If a registered title is given away, the donee will be registered as the new proprietor. The purchaser will not know that the transfer was by way of gift, so will be protected by s.342). If two years have passed since the gift, but not five years, the purchaser should ask for a statutory declaration by the donor that he was solvent at the time he made the gift.

9.10 Bankruptcy of the Seller

Bankruptcy proceedings are started by the presentation of the petition in bankruptcy, usually by a creditor. If the court is satisfied that the debtor is unable to pay his debts it will make a bankruptcy order. This has the effect of vesting the bankrupt's property in the official receiver. This would be followed by an appointment of a trustee in bankruptcy. When the trustee is appointed, the bankrupt's estate vests in the trustee and it is his duty to collect and distribute the bankrupt's assets (ss. 305 and 306 of the Insolvency Act 1986).

As soon as the court makes the bankruptcy order, any disposition by the bankrupt made between the time of the presentation of the petition and the time when his assets vest in his trustee in bankruptcy is void (s.284 of the Insolvency Act 1986). Therefore, a conveyance made by the bankrupt in this period would be void. So a purchaser who is alerted as to the presentation of the petition will not accept a conveyance from the seller, but will await the appointment of the trustee and take a conveyance from him. This may mean delay, and a purchaser who is unwilling to accept the delay could terminate the contract by serving a completion notice (see Chapter 18). If the purchaser suffers loss through the delay he will have to prove in the bankruptcy. If he ends the contract, he will also have to recover his deposit. There will be no difficulty if this is held by a stakeholder. If it had been paid to the seller's agent the purchaser would have to prove in the bankruptcy, unless he can rely on his lien (see section 5.9(a)).

It is possible for the trustee in bankruptcy to disclaim the contract and as a result cease to be under any obligation to fulfil it. However, it is unlikely that the seller's trustee would do this. The equitable interest in the land would have vested in the purchaser as a result of the contract and disclaimer of the contract would not restore this interest to the trustee, who would, therefore, lose both property and price.

The purchaser should be alerted to the bankruptcy of the seller by the pre-completion search. If the title to the bankrupt's land is unregistered, the petition in bankruptcy is registrable under the Land Charges Act 1972 in the register of pending actions and the order in bankruptcy is registrable in the register of writs or orders. If the title to the bankrupt's land is registered under the Land Registration Act 1925, when the petition is presented *and* it is ascertained that the bankrupt does own the registered land, a creditor's notice will be registered in the proprietorship register. When the order in bankruptcy is made, a bankruptcy inhibition is entered preventing the registration of any disposition other than by the trustee (s.61 of the Land Registration Act 1925).

It is very unlikely, in the case both of unregistered and registered title, that the registration will not be made, as the registration is applied for by the staff of the Bankruptcy Court on the filing of the petition in bankruptcy. If it should happen, however, a purchaser would as the result of the non-registration take the property free from the claims of the creditors and of the trustee in bankruptcy (see s.6 of the Land Charges Act 1972 and s.61 of the Land Registration Act 1925).

9.11 Bankruptcy of the Purchaser

The trustee in bankruptcy could disclaim the contract if it is unprofitable (s.315 of the Insolvency Act 1986). Otherwise, he will have to complete it.

Section 284 of the Insolvency Act 1986 again presents a danger. A payment by the purchaser of the purchase price will be a disposition and therefore void, so that the trustee could reclaim the purchase price. The seller might be able to claim the protection of s.284(4) which provides that a payment received by a person before the order in bankruptcy is made, in good faith, for value and without notice that the petition has been presented, shall be valid.

9.12 The Purchaser's Pre-completion Search – The Last Stage in the Investigation of Title

(*a*) *The Search at the Central Land Registry*

A search should be made against the name of every estate owner revealed by the abstract of title. The search form (K15) must:

(i) Specify the name against which the search is to be made. If variations of a name appear in the abstract, a search should be made against every variation of the name, e.g. Edward Smith, Edward John Smith, Eddie Smith, Edward Smyth.

(ii) Specify the county in which the land is situated. This means not just the county in which the land is now, but also any county in which it has been during the period covered by the search. The difficulty can be illustrated by looking at Sidcup. The postal address of a house in Sidcup is Sidcup, Kent. But Sidcup is in the London Borough of Bexley, not in Kent. It was however in Kent until the creation of Greater London in 1965.

(iii) Specify the years to be searched. For example, if Edward Smith bought the house on 1 June 1960, and sold it on 12 August 1964, the form would specify 1960 to 1964 inclusive.

The registry will issue an official search certificate, saying either that there is no adverse entry against the name or that an entry does exist:

e.g: Edward Smith
Dii No 40 dated 1 June 1960
Land at Greenstairs, Kent

If the purchaser's solicitor finds an unexpected entry, he can ask the seller's solicitor to certify that the entry does not affect the land contracted to be sold. (This could be because it affects other land in the county owned by this Edward Smith, or because the registration is against a different Edward Smith.) If either solicitor feels doubt on the matter, he can obtain an office copy of the entry on the register, and from this find the name and address of the person who owns the benefit of the interest that has been registered.

Advantage of an official search certificate

(i) The official search certificate gives the purchaser a priority period of 15 working days from the date of the certificate. If the purchaser completes his purchase within that period, he will take free of any entry made on the register after the date of the search and before completion. Purchaser is defined to include someone who takes a lease or a mortgage. It also presumably includes anyone who claims through the purchaser. So suppose Vera owns a freehold house. She arranges to borrow money, and to grant a mortgage of her house in return. On the Monday before the completion of the mortgage, the lender obtains a certificate saying there is no entry against Vera's name. On Tuesday, Vera's husband Horatio registers a class F land charge. The mortgage is completed on the Friday. The mortgage is not subject to Horatio's rights of occupation. If Vera fails to keep up her mortgage payments, the mortgagee may exercise his statutory power of sale. The purchaser from the mortgagee also takes free from Horatio's rights.

(ii) The certificate is conclusive (s.10(4) of the Land Charges Act 1972). This means that if the Registry staff makes a mistake, so that the certificate fails to reveal the D(ii) registration against the name of Edward Smith, the purchaser will take free of the covenants leaving the incumbrancer to the chance of redress from the Chief Land Registrar. There is no statutory right to compensation in these circumstances, which seems strange, but it seems that an action against the Registrar for negligence would be possible. However a purchaser can only rely upon the certificate if his application for the search was in order. If the D(ii) is properly registered against the name of Edward Smith, a certificate issued in the name of Edward Smyth, because that was the version of the name supplied by the purchaser, confers no protection against the registration. The purchaser will take subject to the covenants (see section 4.5).

Section 10(6) states that there is no liability on the part of the registry staff for a discrepancy between the particulars in the application for the search, and the search certificate itself. So if the purchaser searches against the name of Edward Smith, and receives a certificate saying there is no registration against the name Edward Smyth, the purchaser must realise that this certificate is not reliable, and ask for the search to be repeated. So when reading a certificate of search, you must ask yourself, 'Is this the name I asked for the search to be made against?'

Past search certificates As a matter of courtesy, the seller's solicitor usually sends with the abstract of title any past search certificates that exist. If the protocol is being followed, the seller's solicitor must supply search certificates against the names of past owners revealed by the evidence of title. The purchaser's solicitor needs to check on the reliability of any such certificate. He must check that the search is against the correct name, that it covers the period of estate ownership and that completion took place within the priority period given by the search. Try problem 1 in the workshop section.

(*b*) *If the Seller (or a Past Owner) is a Limited Company, is a Search of the Companies Registry Necessary*?

A search at the companies registry in the file of the company concerned may be essential. A fixed charge created by a company before 1 January 1970 could be protected against a purchaser *either* by its registration at the companies registry, *or* (if unprotected by deposit of title deeds) by its registration as a land charge. Therefore, a clear land-charge search certificate against the company's name does *not* clear away the possibility of there being a pre-1970 fixed charge capable of binding a purchaser on completion. A fixed charge created by a company after 1969 and unprotected by deposit of title deeds must be registered as a land charge if it is to bind a purchaser for value.

A floating charge created by a company at whatever date is not registrable as a land charge. The purchaser will require a certificate of non-crystallisation signed by the company secretary, or better, by the chargee, to be handed over at completion.

A search must also be made for evidence of the commencement of winding-up proceedings. In a winding-up by the court, any disposition of the company's property after the commencement of the winding-up is void (s.127 of the Insolvency Act 1986). The winding-up of a company by the court is deemed to commence at the time of the presentation of the petition for winding up (s.129(2) of the Insolvency Act 1986). The *order* for the winding-up will be filed in the company's file, but the petition is advertised in the *London Gazette*, so a search must also be made in the *London Gazette*.

It is also important to discover the appointment of an administrator or administrative receiver.

The company's file can only be searched personally, so this will be done either by the solicitor, or by a law agent instructed by the solicitor. The search gives no priority period, so should be done only shortly before completion.

(*c*) *A Bankruptcy Search at the Central Land Charges Registry against the Name of the Purchaser*

This has been explained in section 7.6(b). It is made on behalf of the mortgagee who is lending money for the purchase. It has nothing to do with the seller's title, and has been added here simply to complete the list of pre-completion searches.

(*d*) *Repetition of Local Land Charge Searches*

The solicitor acting for the purchaser's mortgagee may have instructions to repeat the local land charge search before completion if it is by then more than, say, 3 months old. This applies equally to registered title. Use of the Law Society's Search Validation Scheme would be an alternative (see section 6.2(b)).

Case Note

Walia v. *Michael Naughton Ltd*

[1985] 1 WLR 1115

Three people, X, Y and Z owned the legal estate in land on trust for sale for themselves beneficially. X appointed Y to be his attorney. The power of attorney was expressed to be given 'in accordance with s.10 Powers of Attorney Act 1971'. A transfer of the land in favour of P was executed by Y personally, by Y as X's attorney and by Z. The transfer was held to be void as the power did not authorise Y to execute the transfer on behalf of X. Although X owned part of the equitable interest and to that extent was a 'beneficial owner' the function that he was delegating was his power to convey the legal estate, and his ownership of the legal estate was that of a trustee. The power of attorney, being given in accordance with s.10 of the 1971 Act, was not effective to delegate his function as a trustee.

Workshop

Attempt these problems yourself, then read specimen solutions at the end of the book.

Problem 1

You are investigating an unregistered freehold title. The seller Anthea Grumble has supplied you with a search certificate. The date of the certificate is 1 June 1969. It reveals that the search was against the names of William Faulkner and Anthea Grumble, and says that there were no subsisting entries against these names. She also supplies you with a copy of the conveyance dated 1 July 1969 by which William Faulkner conveyed the property to her. Does the search have to be repeated against these two names?

Problem 2

Alan Brown is acting for Vesta Smith, who is selling Rosedene, a large property in the village of Leadlode. The title is unregistered. The conveyance to Vesta, dated 1940, describes the property as the 'piece of land together with the dwelling-house standing thereon known as Rosedene, as the same is for the purpose of identification only outlined in red on the plan annexed hereto'. Alan used this description in the contract, and a copy of the 1940 plan and deed were sent with the draft contract to Paula Prentiss, the purchaser, for approval. Paula looked at the plan, and has told Alan that it does not show the current boundaries of Rosedene. She feels that the site of the large water-garden and summer-house is not, according to the plan, part of the property conveyed by the 1940 deed. What should Alan do?

Problem 3

You are investigating the title to Blackacre. The abstract of title gives you details of the following deeds:

1. 1 October 1973 – a conveyance on sale from Agnes to Bertha.
2. 4 December 1979 – a power of attorney given by Bertha to Sarah, her solicitor, authorising Sarah to execute all documents and deeds connected with the sale of Blackacre.
3. 23 December 1980 – a conveyance on sale from Bertha, executed by Sarah as Bertha's attorney, to Charles.
4. 14 March 1981 – grant of letters of administration to the estate of Charles, the administrator being Delia. Delia is the seller.

Is this title in order?

Problem 4

This question is taken from the Law Society Examination, Winter 1985.

Your firm acts for James Brown who has just contracted to purchase 23 Chestnut Grove from the West Building Society. The contract incorporates the standard conditions. The Building Society is selling the property in exercise of the power of sale given by a mortgage dated 24 June 1982 executed in their favour by Donald Smith. The root of title is a conveyance on sale dated 6 July 1974. The XY Building Society is to lend Mr Brown £20 000 towards the purchase price of £25 000 and your firm has been instructed to act for them. You have taken over the conduct of the transaction from a colleague who is on holiday and you have just received the replies to his requisitions on title which include those shown below.

(a) Comment on these requisitions and the replies and briefly explain whether or not the replies are satisfactory. If not, state what further action is necessary and whether or not this can be left until your colleague returns from holiday.

(b) List and briefly explain the steps you will take up to the completion of the transactions once you are satisfied with the replies to the requisitions on title.

Requisitions on Title

1. The conveyance of 23 August 1974 is insufficiently stamped and this must be rectified before completion.
2. A land charges search has revealed a C(i) entry against Donald Smith registered on 10 September 1982. This must be discharged on or before completion.
3. Please supply a copy of the plan annexed to the conveyance dated 4 March 1960 to which reference is made in the conveyance of 6 July 1974.

Replies to Requisitions on Title

1. See the special condition in the contract prohibiting requisitions on stamping of documents.
2. The Purchaser is not concerned with this.
3. This plan is annexed to a pre-root conveyance and the purchaser is not entitled to a copy.

10 Personal Representative: The Passing of a Legal Estate on Death

10.1 The Death of a Sole Beneficial Owner

Suppose that Albert is the sole owner of the legal estate in Blackacre, and he owns it for his own benefit – i.e. not as trustee for someone else. When Albert dies, Blackacre will be owned by his personal representative. His personal representative may be his executor, i.e. the person appointed by Albert in his will to manage his affairs. If Albert has not appointed an executor, his personal representative will be the person, probably a member of his family, who applies to the probate registry for a grant of letters of administration. Both executors and administrators are known as personal representatives, and their statutory powers of disposing of Albert's assets are the same. The powers include a power of sale (s.39 of the Administration of Estates Act 1925).

10.2 Buying from the Personal Representative

If you are buying Blackacre from Albert's personal representative, when investigating his title you must check his identity, the number of personal representatives, and if any memoranda are endorsed on the grant.

(*a*) *The Identity of the Personal Representative*

Look at the grant of representation to confirm the identity of the personal representative. The grant is the only evidence that is acceptable.

An executor would actually have become the owner of Albert's property as soon as Albert died, as his position of executor derives from his appointment by the will. Despite this, you must not complete the purchase until the executor has obtained a grant of probate of the will, naming him as executor. The grant is conclusive evidence of his status. The will is *not*. (Remember the will may turn out to be void, or to have been revoked by a later one. Of course, the will may be challenged after probate has been granted, and as a result, the grant of probate itself revoked, but a dealing with an executor who has obtained a grant usually remains valid despite the later revocation of the grant, s.37 and s.55(1)(xviii) of the Administration of Estates Act 1925). It is possible to enter into the contract with the executor before probate, but the grant must be obtained before completion.

An administrator would not have become the owner of Albert's property, nor would he have any powers over it, until he had obtained the grant of letters of administration. The point is that it is *the grant* which makes him the administrator. Therefore, both contract and completion should wait until the grant is obtained.

(*b*) *The Number of Personal Representatives*

The grant may be to a single personal representative. If so, it is perfectly safe to deal with him alone. He can on his own give a good receipt for the purchase money (s.27(2) of the Law of Property Act 1925). (Do not confuse a personal representative with a trustee for sale. A receipt must be given by at least two trustees for sale, but personal representatives and trustees for sale are different animals.)

The grant may be to two or more personal representatives. The authority of personal representatives to *convey* is joint *only*, i.e. they must *all* execute a conveyance or assent if it is to be valid (s.68 of the Administration of Estates Act 1925). (Their authority to *contract* to convey is several, i.e. they can act independently of one another, so in theory, if A and B are the two personal representatives, A could sign the contract alone, and thereby bind himself and B to convey.)

(*c*) *Memoranda Endorsed on the Grant*

When looking at the grant, check that no statement has been written on it, to the effect that Blackacre has already been transferred by the personal representative to someone else. If there is such a memorandum, if you have any sense you will realise that the personal representative can no longer transfer Blackacre to you. Completion will not take place, and you will turn hurriedly to Chapter 18 to consider remedies for breach of contract.

If there is *no* such memorandum, this is probably for the simple reason that the personal representative has *not* already disposed of Blackacre to someone else and that is why he now feels free to convey it to you.

However, the interesting thing is that if the personal representative *has* already disposed of the legal estate to someone else (let us call him Ben), and Ben has failed to put a memorandum warning of this on the grant, then, in some circumstances, when the personal representative later conveys to you, you *will* get the legal estate, and Ben will lose it.

The reason for this is s.36(6) of the Administration of Estates Act 1925. There is now set out a simple, and *so far as it goes*, accurate version of s.36(6) – if a personal representative conveys the legal estate in Blackacre to a purchaser for money, and the conveyance contains a statement that the personal representative has not made any previous conveyance or assent in favour of someone else and the purchaser relies on that statement, then the conveyance will vest the legal estate in the purchaser, despite the fact that the personal representative has already passed the legal estate on to a beneficiary of the will or intestacy, provided that the beneficiary has not by then put a memorandum about the disposition to him on the grant. The disposition to the beneficiary is overridden. The personal representative cannot override any earlier disposition to another purchaser for money, be he a purchaser from the personal representative himself, or from the beneficiary. So the protection given to a purchaser from a personal representative by s.36(6) is really very narrow.

If you think this through slowly, the following points will occur to you:

1. any sensible beneficiary, having had the legal estate vested in him by the personal representative, will immediately insist on a memorandum about it being put on the grant. This makes it impossible for him to lose the legal estate to a later purchaser for money from the personal representative. Section 36 gives the beneficiary the right to insist on this. The memorandum does not have to be in any particular form; it will probably say something like 'By an assent dated . . . , Blackacre was transferred by the personal representatives named in this grant to Ben Brown.'
2. any sensible purchaser who is buying from a personal representative will:
   - when drafting the conveyance to himself, put in a statement (usually a recital – see section 13.2(b)) that the seller (i.e. the personal representative) has not made any previous assent or conveyance in respect of the property being conveyed. Without this statement, s.36(6) does not apply.
   - on completion, ask to see the original grant to check there is no memorandum on it. He must see the original, and not allow himself to be fobbed off with an office copy, which for this purpose is useless;
   - after completion, put a memorandum on the grant about the conveyance to himself. This is said to be good conveyancing procedure, in all circumstances. It certainly is in the case of a sale of part of the land owned by the deceased, when the personal representative is retaining the deeds. In this case, a memorandum about the sale should be endorsed either on the conveyance to the deceased, as in any sale of part, or on the grant. However, failure on the part of a purchaser from the personal representative to put a memorandum of the sale on the grant cannot prejudice his title by virtue of s.36(6). Remember that a personal representative cannot override a previous conveyance to a purchaser for money, and if you are still in doubt look at problem 3 at the end of this chapter.

3. s.36(6) is perhaps relevant only to unregistered title. If the title is registered, the problem will be solved by provisions of the Land Registration Act 1925. Again for an explanation, look at problem 3.

10.3 The Use of an Assent

Once the personal representative has the grant, he can convey the legal estate. Nothing further is needed if he intends to convey in the capacity of personal representative. The contract will say that he *will* convey as a personal representative, and the conveyance will say that he *does* convey as a personal representative. No assent will be needed.

An assent is needed (a) to transfer ownership from the personal representative to a beneficiary, or (b) to change the capacity in which the personal representative holds the estate.

(*a*) *To Transfer Ownership from the Personal Representative to a Beneficiary*

This is an area where it is easy to become confused, and it really may be helpful to look first of all at the pre-1926 law, and then to realise the nature of the changes made by the Administration of Estates Act 1925.

Suppose that Albert died in 1924. His will appointed Edward as his executor, and gave the legal estate in Blackacre to Ben. On Albert's death two titles to Blackacre were created. Ben had a title to Blackacre by virtue of the gift in the will. That is why, if Ben had decided to sell the property, the will would have appeared on the abstract. However, the death also gave the executor a title to Blackacre, for the purpose of administering the estate. This meant that if, for instance, money had to be raised to pay the deceased's debts, Edward could have sold Blackacre, and so defeated Ben's title. The title of the executor was the better or 'paramount' title. If it had become clear that the executor would not need to sell Blackacre, he could have allowed the gift to the beneficiary to take effect. In other words he could have 'assented' to the gift. The use of the word 'assent' for what the executor was doing made sense before 1926 as it means 'consent'. The executor consented to the gift, and so released his own superior title to the property. As the assent was not in any way a conveyance to the beneficiary, it could be informal, and the mere fact that a beneficiary was allowed to take possession could indicate assent to the gift. When you consider the nature of a pre-1926 assent, it becomes clear why an administrator could not assent when the deceased died intestate. There was no gift to which to assent, so the administrator would convey the legal estate to the beneficiary by deed.

In 1925, the Administration of Estates Act made considerable changes. An assent made after 1925 is quite different from an assent made pre-1926, and it is a pity that this was not made quite clear by giving a different name to the thing.

On a death after 1925, no title is conferred by the will on the beneficiary. This is why a will of a person who dies after 1925 no longer appears on the abstract of title to prove change of ownership of the legal estate. The title belongs only to the personal representative. If he conveys the legal estate to a purchaser, he will use a deed of conveyance or a land registry transfer. If a sale is not necessary, the personal representative will wish to vest the legal estate in the person entitled to it under the terms of the will or under the intestacy rules. The document that he will use is what is now called an assent. You can see now how an assent has changed its character. It is now actually a document of transfer, passing ownership from the personal representative to the person in whose favour the assent is made. As it does transfer ownership, it can no longer be allowed to be informal; and it can be used by administrators as well as executors, because it no longer depends upon there being a gift in a will.

Form of a post-1925 assent Section 36(4) demands that an assent that relates to a *legal estate* in land be in writing, be signed by the personal representatives (i.e. it need not be delivered as a deed) and name the person in whose favour it is made.

An assent says something like 'I Alice Grace as the personal representative of May East as personal representative assent to the vesting in fee simple of Blackacre in Ann Hyde and I acknowledge the right of Ann Hyde to production of the probate of the will of May East and to delivery of copies thereof. Signed this 4 day of July 1989.'

The assent is by deed if the beneficiary gives a covenant to the personal representative, e.g. an indemnity covenant.

So an abstract of title tracing a change of ownership of the legal estate by virtue of death would now, for example, give details of the following deeds and events:

1 January 1960 Conveyance of Blackacre by W to X.

1 January 1980 Statement that X died on this date.

1 July 1980 Grant of probate to Y + Z.

[If you were buying from Y + Z as personal representatives, the abstract would end here.]

1 January 1981 Assent signed by Y + Z, saying that they assent to the vesting of Blackacre in Ben.

1 January 1981 A memorandum of the assent endorsed on the grant of probate.

On this basis would we be happy to buy from Ben? Yes, because on the evidence we have here, Ben could convey to us as beneficial owner. If there were no memorandum on the grant, we would have cause for concern (see problem 3).

Points which Might Occur to You

(i) Do we need to see X's death certificate? Realistically, the answer is 'no'. A grant of probate of his will, or a grant of letters of administration to his estate is usually taken as being satisfactory evidence that X really is dead.

(ii) How do we know that Ben was the right person to be given the legal estate? We do not know, and we will not usually enquire. The reason for this is s.36(7) of the Administration of Estates Act 1925, which says that the assent itself is 'sufficient evidence' that the assent has been made to the correct person, and has been made upon the correct trusts, if any. So we can take an assent at face value. That is why we are safe in buying from Ben, and why we will assume he is a beneficial owner, as the assent makes no mention of the legal estate being transferred to him on any sort of trust. If we did have reason to suspect that Ben were not the person entitled to have the legal estate passed to him, or that he ought to be holding it on some sort of trust, *then* we could no longer take the assent at its face value, and we would have to enquire about its correctness. If we did not do this, we would risk being fixed with constructive notice of other beneficiaries' rights. This is because s.36 says that the assent is 'sufficient' evidence, but it does not say it is 'conclusive' evidence. So no enquiry is made *unless* we have cause for suspicion (see Re *Duce* and *Boots Cash Chemists (Southern) Ltd's* Contract [1937]).

(iii) What if the title were registered? The use of the assent is exactly the same. The events would be, for example:
(aa) X is registered proprietor.
(bb) X dies. There is a grant of representation to Y + Z. They have a choice, so,
(cc) *either* Y + Z register themselves as the new proprietors, by producing an office or certified copy of the grant to the Chief Land Registrar. Y + Z could then sign the assent in favour of Ben.

or Y + Z could choose not to be registered. Indeed, there is little point in the personal representatives registering themselves as proprietors if they intend to assent to a beneficiary, or convey to a purchaser, within a reasonable time. Y + Z could sign an assent to a beneficiary, who could register himself by producing a copy of the grant, and the assent, and the land certificate.

(*b*) *To Change the Capacity in which the Personal Representative Holds the Legal Estate to that of Trustee for Sale, or Beneficial Owner*

Suppose that Albert's will says 'I appoint X and Y as the executors and trustees of this my will. I give Blackacre to X and Y to hold on trust for sale, the proceeds of sale to be held by them on trust for my widow for life, and after her death for my daughter Sara absolutely.'

On Albert's death, Blackacre vests in X and Y as *personal representatives*. If they have to sell it, that is the capacity in which they will convey. When X and Y have administered the estate, they will be ready to change their capacity to that of trustees for sale. They must change their capacity as the final step in the administration of that asset, as there can be difficulties if a personal representative dies with property still vested in him as such (see section 10.4). Re *King's Will Trusts* [1964] decided that s.36(4) of the Administration of Estates Act 1925 (which demands a written assent) applies not only when a personal representative is actually going to transfer ownership of the legal estate, but also when he is going to retain it but wishes to change the capacity in which he holds it. So in order to become trustees for sale, X and Y must sign a written assent in their own favour, e.g. 'We X and Y hereby assent to the vesting of Blackacre in ourselves, upon trust for sale.' Until this written assent is made, there is no change of capacity, and X and Y continue to hold the legal estate as personal representatives.

A similar case would arise if Albert's will said 'I give all my property to X, and appoint him the executor of my will.' X holds the legal estate in Blackacre as personal representative. He does not hold it as beneficial owner until he signs a written assent in his own favour. It is important that this is done if he intends to keep Blackacre, as if he dies with the legal estate still vested in him as personal representative, his own personal representatives may not be able to deal with Blackacre at his death (see problem 2). Even if he intends to sell Blackacre, although he could convey as personal representative, a purchaser might prefer to take a conveyance from him as beneficial owner, rather than personal representative as wider covenants for title would be implied (see Chapter 19), and if the purchaser persists in this point, an assent will again be necessary.

10.4 The Death of a Personal Representative

A personal representative is himself mortal. If he dies before he has finished administering the estate, there may be difficulties if he is the sole personal representative.

Suppose that Albert dies, and X and Y are his personal representatives. Albert's assets are vested in X and Y jointly, so that if X dies, Y will have the whole of Albert's property vested in him alone, and he can happily continue administering Albert's assets as the sole surviving personal representative. So X's death, although a serious blow to his many admirers, has not caused any difficulty in the administration of Albert's estate.

Suppose now that Y dies, while still in the course of administering the estate, so that on his death there are still assets vested in him as personal representative.

The difficulty now is that Albert has run out of personal representatives. The estate can only be administered by new personal representatives *of Albert*. Where will these new personal representatives come from? There are two possibilities:

1. That there exists what is known as a 'chain of representation' under s.7 of the Administration of Estates Act 1925. It may save you from error

if you think of it as a chain of *executorship*. Section 7 provides that on the death of a sole, or last surviving proving executor, *his* proving executor takes over his unfinished executorship. The chain only forms through *proving executors* (i.e. who obtain probate. It is a general rule that executors who are appointed by the will but who do not obtain probate can be ignored.) It only forms through the death of the last proving executor to die. It is best explained through an example. Suppose Albert dies, and Betty and Carol obtain probate of his will. If Betty dies before all of Albert's assets are administered, you do not consider the chain of executorship at all. Albert still has an executor, and Carol will simply carry on alone. Betty's personal representatives do not come into the picture at all. On Carol's death, as she is the last surviving executor of Albert, you will look to see if any of her executors obtain probate of her will. Suppose she has appointed David as her executor, and he obtains probate. The effect of s.7 is that when David becomes Carol's executor, he automatically becomes Albert's executor as well, with power to dispose of his assets. He does not need a further grant to Albert's estate.

If Carol had died without appointing an executor, so that David had been her administrator, having applied for a grant of letters of administration, then David would not acquire any power over Albert's assets. Remember, it has to be a chain of *executorship*.

2. If a chain of executorship does not exist (for instance, as in the last example, if either Betty and Carol, or David, were administrators) the only way that Albert could acquire a new personal representative is by a new grant of representation to his estate. This would be a grant of letters of administration (if relevant, with will annexed) '*de bonis non administratis*' – that is, it gives the person who obtains the grant the power to deal only with the unadministered part of Albert's estate. Who will be entitled to this grant? It depends on the Non-contentious Probate Rules 1987. Their effect can be summed up very briefly by saying that the grant will be to a person who is in some way entitled to the assets. The grant must be made to create the new personal representative. Without it, no one has power to pass title to the assets.

Workshop

Attempt these problems yourself, then read specimen solutions at the end of the book.

Problem 1

You have contracted to buy an unregistered title from Eric. He has contracted to convey it as beneficial owner, and to trace title from a conveyance on sale dated 1 April 1970. The abstract gives details of the following documents:

1 April 1970 Alan conveys as beneficial owner to Bertha.

1 April 1982 Bertha dies.

1 April 1983 Grant of probate to Charles and David, the executors of Bertha's will.

1 April 1985 Conveyance on sale by David to Eric. Is Eric's title acceptable?

Problem 2

We have contracted to buy Blackacre from Fred. The abstract gives details of the following transactions:

1 April 1975 Alice conveys Blackacre as beneficial owner to Bill.

1 April 1980 Edward conveys it as personal representative to Fred.

The recitals in the 1980 conveyance make the following statements to explain why Edward is the seller:

(i) that Bill died in 1977, and a grant of letters of administration was made to his wife Carol;

(ii) that Carol died in 1978, and a grant of probate of her will was made to Edward.

Was Edward able to convey Blackacre to Fred in 1980?

Problem 3

Consider the following abstract of title:

1970 Albert conveys Blackacre to Bryn as beneficial owner.

1972 Bryn dies.

1973 Grant of probate of his will to Cathy and Drew.

1974 An assent, signed by Cathy and Drew, in favour of Elaine.

1980 Elaine conveys to Fred.

Should we raise a requisition on Fred's title?

11 A Sale by Trustees for Sale

11.1 How Do You Know the Sellers are Trustees for Sale?

Suppose you are buying an unregistered title. You are buying it from Abel and Bertha. You read a copy of the conveyance to them. A clause in it says 'the purchasers declare that they hold the property hereby conveyed on trust to sell the same (with power to postpone sale), and to hold the net proceeds of sale, (and pending sale, the income of the land) on trust . . .'. It does not require a great mental effort to deduce from this that Abel and Bertha hold the legal estate as trustees for sale. The trust to sell is expressly declared.

Suppose instead that you read the conveyance and it says 'the seller . . . hereby conveys . . . Blackacre to hold unto Abel and Bertha in equal shares'. This also tells you that Abel and Bertha hold the legal estate as trustees for sale. Why? It is because they co-own the beneficial interest. When two or more purchasers co-own the equitable interest, then if no express trust for sale of the legal estate is declared, the legal estate vests in them on an implied trust for sale (ss.34–36 of the Law of Property Act 1925). They will always hold the legal estate as joint tenants, whether they hold the equitable interest as joint tenants or tenants in common.

If the conveyance had been to Abel, Bertha, Charles, Deirdre and Edna in equal shares, the difficulty would have arisen that although the equitable interest is owned by five people, a legal estate can only be held by four. The legal estate would vest in the first four adult co-owners named in the conveyance (s.34 of the Law of Property Act 1925). So although the conveyance simply says that the land is conveyed to the five people, it has the same effect as if it read 'to A B C and D on trust to sell, proceeds of sale to be held by them on trust for A B C D and E equally'. You can see from this that if you were buying the legal estate, you would need a conveyance signed only by A B C and D. E does not own the legal estate. He is sacrificed in the interests of limiting the number of estate owners, but he has not lost his share of the beneficial interest, which is what really matters.

Now suppose that the title is registered. When Abel and Bertha bought from the then registered proprietor, the transfer would either have declared an express trust for sale, or have disclosed the circumstances which gave rise to an implied trust for sale, e.g. the co-ownership of the beneficial interest by the two of them. Abel and Bertha, as the trustees for sale, are entitled to apply to the Registrar to have themselves registered as proprietors. As they are trustees for sale they are under a duty to apply for a restriction to be entered on the register. (The one exception to this is where they hold on trust for sale for themselves as beneficial joint tenants – see later). The restriction will read 'No disposition by a sole proprietor of the land (not being a trust corporation) under which capital arises is to be registered except under an order of the Registrar or of the court' (Land Registration Rules 1989).

If they do not apply for the entry of the restriction, the Registrar is nevertheless under a duty to enter it whenever it is clear to him that a trust for sale exists (s.58(3) of the Land Registration Act 1925).

The restriction reflects the fact that a sale by a sole trustee for sale has no overreaching effect, so should not be accepted by the purchaser.

If Abel and Bertha, under an expressly declared trust for sale, hold on trust for people other than themselves, they will only have those powers to deal with the legal estate which statute gives them (see s.28 of the Law of Property Act 1925). They have a power of sale, but only limited powers of leasing and mortgaging. It is a principle of registered conveyancing that the registered proprietor has *unlimited* powers of disposition, unless an entry on the register says otherwise. If their powers are limited, they should apply for a further restriction to be entered on the register, preventing the registration of unauthorised leases or mortgages.

It is possible for a conveyance or transfer to trustees to increase their powers to deal with the legal estate to those of a sole beneficial owner, i.e. their powers become unlimited. If this has been done, this second restriction will not appear on the register.

If Abel and Bertha are holding a trust for sale for *themselves* as *tenants in common*, the first restriction, preventing a sale by the sole survivor, will appear on the register, again reflecting the fact that a sole trustee cannot make good title. However, as in this case the trustees are also the only beneficiaries, their powers of dealing with the legal estate are unlimited, as what they cannot do by reason of their powers as trustees, they can do by virtue of their beneficial ownership. The second restriction will not, therefore, appear on the register.

If Abel and Bertha hold on trust for themselves as beneficial joint tenants, there will be no restriction at all on the register. This reflects the fact that the sole survivor of Abel and Bertha will be able to sell by herself/himself, without any need to appoint another trustee.

Note that a trust for sale can be created by will, and is implied on an intestacy. The vesting of the legal estate in the personal representatives, and later in the trustees for sale, is dealt with in Chapter 10.

11.2 Who Are the Current Trustees?

If you are buying a legal estate that is held by trustees for sale, the first obvious question to ask yourself is 'who are the current trustees?' In unregistered conveyancing, the original trustees are identified by reading the conveyance which created the trust for sale. In registered conveyancing, the original trustees will have been registered as the registered proprietors. Of course, trustees, like all mortal things, are transient. They come and go. The important thing is to check that when a trustee goes, he parts with all his interest in the legal estate, and that when a new trustee arrives, the estate is vested in him.

11.3 Changes of Trustees

(*a*) *Death of a Trustee Leaving At Least One Trustee Behind*

Suppose that Alice, Beryl and Catherine are the three trustees when the trust for sale first arises. The legal estate is vested in them jointly, no matter how they, or anyone else, might share the equitable interest. If Alice dies, the legal estate remains vested in the surviving trustees. (Remember that it is a characteristic of a *joint* tenancy, as opposed to a tenancy in common, that when a joint tenant dies, the surviving joint tenant(s) continue to own the entire interest.) Beryl and Catherine, therefore, can convey the legal estate. As there are two trustees for sale, the effect of the conveyance will be to overreach the equitable interests, so that they become claims against the purchase price. The only thing that the purchaser has to check is that Alice really is dead. (If she is still alive, a conveyance or transfer by Beryl and Catherine alone will be void; see later.) This is done by seeing a copy of her death certificate.

Note that in registered conveyancing, Beryl and Catherine could have had Alice's name removed from the proprietorship register by sending to the Registrar a copy of the death certificate (Rule 172, Land Registration Rules 1925). They need not do this. They can prove Alice's death to a purchaser from them by a copy of the death certificate, and when registering the transfer the purchaser will send to the Registrar the Land Certificate, copy of death certificate, and the transfer signed by Beryl and Catherine.

Appointment of new trustee Should Beryl now die, Catherine will be left as sole trustee, owning the legal estate. She cannot sell alone, as a conveyance by a single trustee has no overreaching effect, so another trustee must be appointed to act with her. (As an exception to this general rule, she could sell alone if she and Alice and Beryl had been not only joint tenants of the legal estate, but also the only joint tenants of the beneficial interest; see later.)

Who can appoint this new trustee? An expressly created trust for sale may give a particular person a power to appoint new trustees. Otherwise, for both express and implied trusts for sale, it is the surviving trustee(s) who can appoint the new one (s.36 of the Trustee Act 1925). In other words the new trustee will be appointed by Catherine.

Method of appointment In unregistered title, a trustee can be appointed by writing, but a *deed* of appointment should be used. This is to take advantage of s.40 of the Trustee Act 1925, which provides that if a new trustee is appointed by deed, the deed vests the trust property in the people who become, or are, the trustees after the appointment, without any need for a separate conveyance. For example, Catherine can execute a deed saying that she appoints Deirdre to be the second trustee. The effect of that will be that the legal estate will be vested in Catherine and Deirdre.

If the title is registered, the appointment of Deirdre as a new trustee will not in itself vest the legal estate in her. The legal estate will vest when, after seeing the appointment, the Registrar adds Deirdre's name to the proprietorship register. The appointment can be carried out by Catherine executing a Land Registry transfer to herself and Deirdre. Notice that if Deirdre is appointed solely for the purpose of selling the land, it is not necessary that her name be entered on the register before completion. The purchaser will be registered as proprietor by including in the application copies of the death certificates of Alice and Beryl, the appointment of Deirdre, and the transfer signed by Catherine and Deirdre.

(*b*) *Death of the Sole, or Last Surviving, Trustee for Sale*

Suppose Catherine dies, without having appointed another trustee? There are three ways in which title could now be made to the legal estate:

(i) Section 36 of the Trustee Act 1925 provides that on the death of a sole trustee, her personal representative(s) can appoint new trustees. So suppose Catherine's executor is Dorothy, then Dorothy could appoint Edna and Florence as new trustees of the trust. Edna and Florence could then convey the legal estate to a purchaser.

(ii) Sections 18(2) and (3) of the Trustee Act 1925 provide that on the death of a sole trustee, her personal representatives can actually carry out the trust, i.e. stand in for her and convey the legal estate to a purchaser. However, because the personal representatives, when they do this, are acting in the role of trustees for sale, rather than as personal representatives, there must be at least two of them if the conveyance is to overreach the equitable interests. So, in the above example, Dorothy could not sell the property herself; she could only appoint the new trustees. If Catherine had left two executors, say Dorothy and Deborah, they could themselves exercise the trust by conveying the legal estate under s.18(2).

(iii) If Alice, Bertha and Catherine had been holding on trust for themselves as beneficial joint tenants, then Catherine's personal representative(s) could make title, relying in unregistered conveyancing on the Law of Property (Joint Tenants) Act 1964, or in registered title, on the absence of any restriction on the register (see later).

(*c*) *Retirement of a Trustee*

A trustee might wish to retire from the trust whilst still alive. For example, Alice, Bertha and Catherine might be partners in the running of a grocery business. The shop premises would be owned by them jointly on trust for sale. They would probably own the equitable interest as tenants in common. Alice might wish to retire from the partnership and Bertha and Catherine agree to buy her out. Alice must divest herself of all interest in the legal estate, otherwise, if Bertha and Catherine later wish to sell it, Alice would have to be traced to her retirement home, as her signature to the conveyance or transfer would be needed. If the title to the shop is unregistered, the retirement will be by deed and the effect of s.40 of the Trustee Act 1925 will be that the legal estate will vest in Bertha and Catherine. If the title is registered, the simplest procedure is again for the three registered proprietors to sign a transfer in favour of Bertha and Catherine. On registration of the transfer, the name of Alice will be removed from the register.

11.4 How Many Trustees Are There?

Having identified your current trustees, you must now consider how many there are.

If there are two or more, you must remember that their powers are joint. In other words *all* the trustees must sign the conveyance or transfer. If the legal estate is vested in three trustees, you will not obtain it if only two of these three trustees convey it to you. If there are three registered proprietors of the registered title, all three must sign the Land Registry transfer. Otherwise it is totally void.

If the conveyance is by all the trustees, and there are at least two of them, a conveyance (or mortgage) by them will overreach the interests of the beneficiaries, which become claims only against the purchase price (ss.2 and 27 of the Law of Property Act 1925). If there is only one trustee for sale, then generally, as has been said, a second trustee for sale must be appointed. A conveyance by a single trustee will pass the legal estate to the purchaser, but will not overreach the equitable interests.

11.5 Consents

It is possible for the person creating the trust for sale to say that the trustees can only sell if they first obtain the consent of some person named by the settlor.

For example, a wealthy testator may in her will give her property to her husband for his lifetime and provide that on his death the capital is to go to the children. As a life interest is being created, the legal estate in any land will have to be settled. The testator will usually choose a trust for sale so the legal estate will be held by trustees for sale on trust for the husband and children. (If a trust for sale is not created, the land will be settled under the Settled Land Act 1925.) The power of sale is, therefore, exercisable by the trustees, but the testator may wish to ensure that her husband will have some control over whether or not the family home is sold. One solution is to appoint the husband as one of the trustees. The will may also say that the husband's consent must be obtained to any sale.

If there is a requirement that a consent be obtained, the purchaser from trustees must ensure that the consent is obtained, otherwise he will not get a good title. (In registered conveyancing the need for consent will appear as a restriction on the register.)

However, s.26 of the Law of Property Act 1925 may make life easier for the purchaser. First, it says that if the person whose consent is necessary is under age, or mentally incapable, the purchaser need not obtain that consent. Second, if that still leaves the purchaser faced with the task of obtaining more than two consents, only two need be obtained. The provision does not exist to make life easier for the trustees. If they sell without obtaining all consents they are breaking their trust.

11.6 Investigating the Equitable Interests

Usually, a purchaser has no need to investigate the equitable interests behind a trust for sale, as the conveyance by the trustees for sale will overreach the interests. If, however, the trustees dispose of the legal estate to the beneficiaries, then when the title is examined subsequently, the equitable interests do have to be brought into the title.

Suppose, for example, that Bill and Ben hold the legal estate on trust for sale for Xavier for life, remainder to Yvonne absolutely. On Xavier's death, Bill and Ben may convey the legal estate to Yvonne. A later purchaser from her will know that this conveyance had no overreaching effect, as it was not a *sale* by the trustees. The purchaser will have to investigate the equitable interests to check that Yvonne was entitled to have the legal estate conveyed to her. Otherwise he risks having constructive notice of outstanding equitable interests.

If the title is registered, it is the Registrar who will have to be satisfied that Yvonne should be registered as proprietor without any restriction appearing in the proprietorship register.

11.7 Co-ownership of the Equitable Interest

(*a*) *The Equitable Interest*

If two people are, between them, buying a house, they must decide how they are to own the equitable interest. There are two possibilities. They could own it as beneficial *joint* tenants. If people own property jointly, it is as if they have been fused together to form a single unit. Between them there is what is called the right of survivorship. When one joint tenant dies the entire property belongs to the survivor(s). This is why a joint tenancy is considered apt for a married couple. If H and W own property jointly, say a joint bank account, then on the husband's death, the wife automatically owns the entire property. Her entitlement does not depend on her husband's will. For this reason, she does not need to get probate of her husband's will in order to prove her ownership of the property. She merely has to prove that he is dead, by producing his death certificate.

The other possibility is that the couple could own the equitable interest as tenants in common, i.e. they own shares in the property, although the property has not as yet been physically divided between them. There is no right of survivorship in a tenancy in common, so when one tenant in common dies, his share passes to his personal representative, and from him to the beneficiary named in the will, or the next-of-kin under the intestacy rules.

(*b*) *The Legal Estate*

They must also decide as to who is to own the legal estate. If X and Y own the equitable interest, whether jointly or in common, and are both adult, it is common sense that they should both own the legal estate. This makes it impossible for either to sell the house without the consent of the other, as both signatures are needed on the conveyance. So the conveyance or transfer to X and Y:

(i) will say that the legal estate is conveyed to them;
(ii) will say how they own the equitable interest, i.e. either jointly or in shares, and if in shares the size of each share;
(iii) may declare an express trust for sale of the legal estate. We have already seen that if an express trust for sale is not created, a statutory trust for sale will be implied;
(iv) may increase the statutory powers of dealing with the legal estate.

So, as a tiresome recap, you must appreciate the following matters, otherwise you will always be in a muddle in this area:

1. If you read a conveyance that says the legal estate in Blackacre is conveyed to Ann and Bill, as beneficial joint tenants, the result is that Ann and Bill hold the *legal estate jointly*, on trust for sale, and they hold the proceeds of sale, or pending sale the income of the land, on trust for themselves as *beneficial joint tenants*. So that on Bill's death Ann owns the entire legal estate and, prima facie, the entire equitable interest. The provisions of Bill's will are irrelevant to the ownership of Blackacre.
2. If the conveyance says the legal estate is conveyed to Ann and Bill to hold in equal shares, the result is that they hold the legal estate *jointly* (remember that co-owners always hold the legal estate jointly) on trust for sale, but that they hold the *equitable interest as tenants in common*. The word 'equally' shows that they have *shares* and so cannot hold the

equitable interest jointly. On Bill's death, Ann will own the entire legal estate, but only half the beneficial interest. The other half is owned by Bill's personal representatives. The provisions of Bill's will are relevant to the ownership of his share of the equitable interest, but still irrelevant to the ownership of the legal estate.

3. If registered title is transferred to Ann and Bill, they will apply for registration of the transfer. The Registrar will read the transfer. The transfer will say how Ann and Bill own the beneficial interest. It may say expressly that the survivor of them can give a valid receipt for capital money (i.e. that they are joint tenants) or that the survivor cannot give a good receipt for capital money (i.e. that they are tenants in common). If the Registrar believes them to be joint tenants of the beneficial interest he will not put a restriction on the register. Otherwise, he will enter a restriction, preventing a sale by the survivor of Ann and Bill.

Bear this in mind when you read the following section.

11.8 A Conveyance or Transfer by the Sole Surviving Co-owner

The problem is this – Ann and Bill hold the legal estate on trust for sale for themselves. Do you accept a conveyance or transfer from Ann alone after Bill's death?

(*a*) *Ann and Bill Hold on Trust for Themselves as Tenants in Common*

You do *not* accept a conveyance from Ann alone. She now holds the legal estate on trust for herself and Bills's personal representative. Again, if the title is registered, there will be a restriction on the register. The solution is for Ann to appoint another trustee.

It may be, of course, that Bill left his share of the beneficial interest in the house to Ann by his will, so that in fact she does now own the entire beneficial interest. However, title should not be proved to a purchaser by tracing ownership of the equitable interest, and the purchaser should not agree to make the investigation. Never mind who now owns Bill's interest, the interest should be overreached. Bill's will is only of relevance to the trustees, when they divide the proceeds of sale. (Note that if the title is registered, and Ann has succeeded to the ownership of Bill's share, she could apply to the Registrar for the removal of Bill's name from the register, and for the removal of the restriction. She would have to provide the Registrar with a copy of Bill's death certificate, and a statutory declaration as to how she became solely and beneficially interested. Once the restriction is removed from the register, a purchaser would accept a conveyance from Ann alone.)

(*b*) *Ann and Bill Hold on Trust for Themselves as Beneficial Joint Tenants*

This is the only occasion when the purchaser would consider taking a conveyance from Ann alone. *Prima facie*, on Bill's death, because the right of survivorship applied to both the legal estate and the beneficial interest, Ann became sole beneficial owner. Why only *prima facie*?

The difficulty is that the joint tenancy of the equitable interest can be severed and changed into a tenancy in common. This destroys the right of survivorship. There are various ways in which Bill could have severed the equitable joint tenancy before he died: for example, by selling his equitable interest, by serving written notice on Ann under s.36 of the Law of Property Act 1925, by going bankrupt, or by mutual agreement with Ann. Suppose, for instance, that Bill, before his death, served a notice on Ann, saying that henceforth they were to be tenants in common of the equitable interest. The result would be that Ann and Bill would remain joint tenants of the legal estate, as it is impossible to sever the legal joint tenancy, but they would become tenants in common of the equitable interest. Bill could make sure that the severance came to the notice of any prospective purchaser. In registered title, he could apply to the Registrar for the restriction to go on the register, ensuring that Ann could not transfer the house after his death without appointing another trustee. In unregistered title, he could write a memorandum on the conveyance to himself and Ann, saying that the severance had taken place. This again would prevent Ann from selling the property after his death without appointing a second trustee (see the later discussion of the Law of Property (Joint Tenants) Act 1964).

Bill, however, might do nothing at all, so that on his death Ann would look like a beneficial owner, but would in fact be a trustee for sale holding on trust for herself and for Bill's estate. Traditionally, the answer to the *possibility* of severance of the equitable interest was always to insist that Ann appoint a second trustee, so that if there were a half share of the equitable interest to be overreached, this would be done. It is now usually unnecessary to appoint a second trustee, for the following reason.

Registered title When Ann and Bill were first registered as proprietors, there would have been no restriction on the register, because of their *joint* ownership of the beneficial interest. So there is nothing on the register to forbid a transfer by Ann alone after Bill's death. A purchaser from Ann need only see Bill's death certificate, to check that he really is dead, and not just locked away somewhere in a cupboard.

Suppose Bill had severed the joint tenancy of the equitable interest before he died? Suppose when he was alive he sold his equitable interest to Xerxes? Or suppose he served notice of severance on Ann and then left his half-interest to Xerxes in his will. Xerxes could then have applied for the entry of a restriction on the register, or, if Ann would not cooperate in this, he could have lodged a caution. Either would alert the purchaser to the situation and lead to the appointment of a second trustee. Suppose Xerxes does not do this. He is then in the position of having an unprotected minor interest. Remember section 3.13. A transferee for value takes free of an unprotected minor interest. That is why a purchaser is safe in taking a transfer from Ann alone. The absence of a restriction or caution generally ensures that an interest belonging to someone other than Ann will fail to bind the purchaser. However, remember that a transferee for value *does* take subject to overriding interests. If Xerxes has moved in, his interest will be overriding under s.70(1)(g) of the Land Registration Act 1925. So it is the absence of an entry on the register *and* the absence of anyone else in occupation that enables the purchaser to buy from Ann alone in complete safety.

Unregistered title If a purchaser buys from Ann alone after Bill's death, he cannot claim that Bill's interest has been overreached. However, there remains the traditional defence of a purchaser against an equitable interest, namely that of being a *bona fide* purchaser for value of the legal estate without notice of the equitable interest. However, no purchaser likes to rely on this defence, because of the difficulty of proving absence of notice, particularly of constructive notice. This is why, before 1965, a purchaser from Ann would have preferred her to appoint another trustee and rely on the defence of overreaching, rather than that of being without notice.

The Law of Property (Joint Tenants) Act 1964 aimed at making this precaution of having a second trustee unnecessary. This Act builds on the defence of being without notice, by providing that if the purchaser takes certain precautions he can assume that the sole survivor of the joint tenants does own all the beneficial interest. The actual wording of the Act is that in favour of the purchaser the sole survivor shall 'be deemed to be solely and beneficially interested if he conveys as beneficial owner or the conveyance includes a statement that he is so interested'.

It is not certain if the assumption that the purchaser can make it irrebuttable. In other words, can the purchaser rely on the Act even if he *knows* that Ann and Bill had become tenants in common before Bill's death? As the doubt exists, it would be unsafe for a purchaser who actually *knows* that Ann is not solely and beneficially entitled, to rely on the Act. Instead, Ann should be asked to appoint a second trustee, so that the equitable interests can be overreached. Indeed, should a purchaser rely on the Act if he merely *suspects* that someone other than Ann might be interested in the house? A purchaser might be suspicious because he finds that Xerxes occupies the house with Ann, although there could be other explanations for Xerxes's presence, apart from his owning an equitable interest. The Act is presumably designed to protect a purchaser against constructive notice of severance, even if not against actual notice. However, as there is doubt on this point, perhaps a purchaser who is merely suspicious should not rely on the Act either, but should insist on a second trustee.

The 1964 Act specifically says that it does not apply if there is a notice of severance endorsed on the conveyance to the joint tenants, nor if there is an entry in the Central Land Charges Registry as to the bankruptcy of Ann or Bill. On both these occasions a second trustee must be used. (The effect of Bill's bankruptcy would have been that the joint tenancy of the beneficial interest would have been severed, and half would belong to Bill's trustee in bankruptcy.)

So, to sum up, if you are buying from Ann after Bill's death, and wish to shelter behind the protection of the 1964 Act, you should take these precautions:

(i) read the copy conveyance to Ann and Bill, sent to you as part of the abstract of title. Only rely on the Act if the conveyance says they are beneficial joint tenants. Do not use the Act if the conveyance says they are tenants in common, i.e. have shares. If the conveyance does not say whether they are joint tenants or tenants in common, then it is wiser not to rely on the Act;
(ii) look at Bill's death certificate;
(iii) make a land charge search against the names of Bill and Ann, and check there is no registration as to bankruptcy;
(iv) raise a requisition asking for confirmation that there is no memorandum of severance on the conveyance to Ann and Bill, and check the original deed when you see it at completion;
(v) be sure that the conveyance from Ann says that she conveys as beneficial owner.

You are then entitled to assume that Ann is the sole owner of the equitable interest, and can plead that you took free from Xerxes's claim because you had no notice of it. The Act also applies when it is not Ann who is conveying, but Ann's personal representative. If Bill dies, and then Ann dies, the Act entitles you to assume that Ann at her death owned the legal and all the equitable interest. In this case you must:

(i) read the copy conveyance to Ann and Bill to check that it was to them as beneficial joint tenants;
(ii) look at Bill's death certificate;
(iii) look at a copy of the grant of probate or letter of administration to Ann's estate. This is to confirm the identity of her personal representative;
(iv) make a land charge search as above;
(v) check for a memorandum of severance as above;
(vi) be sure that the conveyance by Ann's personal representatives says that Ann was solely and beneficially interested in the land at her death;
(vii) as the sale is by a personal representative, you should also ensure that the conveyance says the personal representative has not made any previous assent or conveyance in respect of this property, that there is no memorandum on the grant of representation about a previous

disposition by the personal representative, and that a memorandum about the conveyance to you *is* endorsed on the grant (see Chapter 10).

Do not forget that the Law of Property (Joint Tenants) Act 1964 Act does *not* apply to registered title. It does apply to a conveyance of unregistered title even before 1965, as the Act is retrospective to the beginning of 1926.

11.9 The Wolf in Sheep's Clothing, or the Problem of the Disguised Trustee for Sale

Suppose that X and Y both contribute towards the purchase price of the house. X contributes £30 000 and Y contributes £42 000. As a result, they share the equitable interest. The legal estate, in an ideal world, would have been conveyed or transferred to both of them. As we have seen, they would hold the legal estate on trust for sale. Any disposition would have to be by the two of them, be it a sale or a mortgage, and the purchaser or mortgagee would be safe from any claim that he took subject to X's and Y's beneficial interests, as these would have been overreached.

Suppose, however, that the legal estate is conveyed into the name of X alone. This could occur because, for example, Y is under 18 so cannot hold a legal estate, or because Y does not have his wits about him and does not realise that he is being put at a disadvantage, or perhaps because Y has not made a direct financial contribution, but a contribution, for example, in the form of considerable works of improvement. In a case such as that, Y may not consider the possibility of his owning part of the house beneficially until he has to defend that ownership against a third party.

X will hold the legal estate on trust for himself and Y, and the trust will be the statutory trust for sale, already considered in other cases of co-ownership (*Bull* v. *Bull* [1955]). (We are assuming that no express trust for sale is created.) X, of course, is a sole trustee for sale. The trouble is that he is a disguised trustee. There is no express trust for sale declared, and there is nothing in the conveyance or transfer to X that reveals the contribution made by Y and his co-ownership of the equitable interest. If X is registered as proprietor, no restriction will appear on the register. To the world at large, X looks like a beneficial owner.

Suppose now that X decides to sell the property or to mortgage it. The purchaser will want to move in. In the case of a mortgage, if X does not keep up the mortgage repayments, the lender will want to sell with vacant possession. Y might go quietly, but it is now that Y might decide to assert this equitable interest and to claim that it binds the purchaser or mortgagee, who as a result can only claim ownership or a mortgage of part of the property, and may not be able to get possession. As X is a sole trustee, the sale or mortgage could not have overreached Y's equitable interest. However, the purchaser or mortgagee may be able to raise the other defence, of having taken free of the interest because he 'had no notice of it'. We now meet 'the dangerous occupier'.

11.10 The Dangerous Occupier

(*a*) *Unregistered Title*

If the title to the house is unregistered, the purchaser or mortgagee will be raising the classic defence that an equitable interest does not bind a *bona fide* purchaser for value of a legal estate without notice of the interest (re-read Chapter 4 and remember that Y's interest, being an interest of a beneficiary behind a trust, is not registrable under the Land Charges Act 1972). If Y is not living on the property and is not X's spouse, the purchaser may well be able to claim that his ignorance of Y's interest means that the purchaser takes free from it. This would leave Y with no claim against the land, but only with the right to pursue X for a share of the purchase price or mortgage loan.

If Y is living on the property, the purchaser will find it difficult to prove lack of notice, as the occupation would give the purchaser constructive notice of the occupier's rights (see section 4.4).

(*b*) *Registered Title*

The doctrine of notice has no place in registered conveyancing. It is s.70(1)(g) of the Land Registration Act 1925 that presents the problem. As we have seen, if Y has an interest in the land, and is in actual occupation, Y's interest is overriding and will bind the purchaser, unless *Y* is asked if he has an equitable interest and he denies it.

(*c*) *Case Law*

Litigation in this area shows a seesaw between the desire to protect Y and the desire to protect the innocent purchaser or lender. There is, at the moment, no way of reconciling their claims. The state of play at the moment seems to be this:

(a) it is now quite clear that the usual overreaching provisions apply, whether or not Y is in occupation. So X could overreach Y's interest by appointing a second trustee to join with X in selling or mortgaging (see *City of London Building Society* v. *Flegg* [1988]).

(b) If X mortgages the house to the lender as part of the process of buying the house, i.e. the bank provides the purchase price, and Y *knows* of the intention of X to mortgage, the lender takes precedence over Y's interest and is not bound by it. One reason is that Y's equitable interest arises from a trust that is imputed to X and Y, i.e. the courts impute an agreement between them that as each has contributed towards the purchase price, then each will have a share of the beneficial interest. However, when imputing this agreement, the court will, when the balance of the purchase price is to be raised by a mortgage loan, also impute an intention by both X and Y that their interests are to be postponed to the mortgage (see *Bristol and West Building Society* v. *Henning* [1985]). Another way of putting the argument is to say that Y has authorised X to mortgage the house and to give the mortgage priority over Y's interest (see *Abbey National Building Society* v. *Cann and anor* [1990]).* The principle has been extended to the case of a re-mortgage (see *Equity & Law Home Loans Ltd* v. *Prestridge* [1991] 1 All ER 909).

The principle applies in both registered and unregistered title, and the fact that Y is living there at the time of the mortgage makes no difference. The lender cannot be affected by Y's interest, as the nature of the interest is one that is postponed to the mortgage. The principle seems to offer the lender an excellent defence against Y, because it is unlikely that Y will not know that the balance of the purchase price is being raised by a mortgage loan. However, this has happened, and it has been held (see *Lloyd's Bank plc* v. *Rosset* [1988] in the Court of Appeal) that the courts cannot impute to Y an intention that his interest should be postponed to the mortgage, when Y does not know that the mortgage will exist.

The lender may still not be affected by Y's interest, however, because of the principle stated in the next paragraph.

(c) When the mortgage loan finances the purchase of the house another reason why Y's interest will not bind the lender is that the conveyance or transfer of the property to X and X's immediate mortgage of it to the lender will be looked on as one indivisible transaction, so that the estate that vests in X is, from the outset, subject to the lender's mortgage, and it is only from that encumbered estate that Y can derive his equitable interest. It follows from this that the mortgage will have priority over Y's equitable interest, whether Y knew of the mortgage or not (*Abbey National Building Society* v. *Cann and anor* [1990]).

(d) If X already owns the house, and then later mortgages it or sells it, then Y's interest might well bind the lender or purchaser, because of Y's occupation (as already shown).

(*d*) *What Do We Do about the Dangerous Occupier?*

From the purchaser's point of view Not surprisingly the property information form asks the seller if any other person is living on the property, and if that person has any claim of ownership.

If the answer is 'Yes, my Auntie Beryl, and she co-owns the equitable interest', then at least the purchaser knows what to do about it. The seller is disclosed as a single trustee for sale, and must be asked to appoint another trustee for sale. This can be done before contract, so that the two trustees will be the sellers in the contract, or it can be done after the seller has entered into the contract, as the final step in his establishing the soundness of his title. Auntie Beryl would be a good choice as the second trustee, because if she is one of the sellers in the contract, she will be personally promising good title, and vacant possession.

If the seller answers 'No, there is no one in occupation but me', or 'Yes, Auntie Beryl is here, but she has no interest in the property', then this is not a satisfactory answer from the purchaser's point of view. If it is a lie, he will have an action against the seller for misrepresentation, but it will not clear Auntie Beryl's interest from the title. It is *Auntie Beryl's* statement that she has no interest that in unregistered conveyancing will save the purchaser from notice, or in registered title, will ensure that her interest is not overriding. So it is still advisable, once Auntie Beryl is discovered, to have her appearing in the contract. However, her role may be different. She is there to put *her* signature to the statement that she has no equitable interest.

From the seller's point of view If the seller knows that there is an equitable interest to be overreached, the mechanism is simple enough. He must appoint another trustee to act with him. The cost of preparing the deed of appointment cannot be thrown onto the purchaser. Any condition in the contract saying that the purchaser must pay the cost is void (s.49 of the Law of Property Act 1925). Nor can the seller say that instead of overreaching the equitable interest, the owner of it will join in the conveyance or transfer to assign it. Any such condition in the contract would also be void (s.49 again). Anyway, a purchaser of the legal estate should never take the trouble and risk of investigating ownership of equitable interests if the equitable interests can be overreached.

The seller should remember that it is not enough to overreach the equitable interest. He is, in the contract, promising vacant possession. So, to revert to our two friends X and Y, X must be sure (if X is selling, rather than mortgaging) that Y actually leaves the house before completion. It is true that if Y remains in occupation after his interest has been overreached, the purchaser could successfully sue him for possession, but there will be delay and expense, for which X will have to compensate the purchaser.

From the point of view of the seller's legal representative Suppose that you are acting for the seller, and he tells you that his mother owns part of the property. If she is co-owner of the legal estate, it is impossible for your client to sell alone, and instructions to sell are also needed from the mother. You must ask your client to discuss the matter with his mother, and explain to her that her cooperation is needed if the property is to be sold. If, as a result, she also instructs you to act in the sale, you would still be unable to act for her if you had any suspicion that the instructions were not given of her own free will. Otherwise, you can act for your original client and his mother, unless it transpires there is some conflict of interest between them. (These are rules of professional conduct. See *The Professional Conduct of Solicitors*, published by the Law Society.) You would expect any house bought from the proceeds of the sale also to be put in both their names, and the beneficial interest to be shared in the same way that it was shared in the house just sold.

If you discover that your client is the sole owner of the legal estate, but that his mother owns the entire equitable interest, your client is holding the legal estate on what is called a bare trust. In this case, no sale should take place without the mother's consent. It is her decision, not that of the estate owner as to whether or not the house is sold.

If you discover that your client is sole owner of the legal estate but that he and his mother share the equitable interest, her interest can be overreached, but as previously said, her consent is needed as your client is promising that the house will be unoccupied at completion. You can approach her to explain that her cooperation is necessary, either as the second trustee, or to join in the contract to promise vacant possession, but you cannot advise her to cooperate, and you should suggest she obtains legal advice. If, in fact, she is quite happy to move, she may instruct you. You can then act for her and her son provided that there is no conflict of interest.

11.11 The Dangerous Spouse

The problem of the concealed trustee for sale and the dangerous occupier is particularly likely to occur in the case of a married couple, and judging from the litigation on the subject, it usually takes the form of the husband holding the legal estate on a concealed trust for sale for himself and his wife, who co-own the equitable interest. That is why the facts in the next paragraph take that form, but of course everything said is equally applicable where the wife owns the legal estate on trust for herself and her husband.

Let us imagine the Henry and his wife, Winifred, are living together in the matrimonial home, 1 South Avenue. Henry is sole owner of the legal estate. It is true that Winifred may well own an equitable interest in the house. Her interest is overreachable, but as has been said earlier, her consent to any sale by her husband is in fact necessary, because Henry has to promise in the contract that the house will be empty on completion. However, this point about vacant possession would not apply if Henry were mortgaging the house, so that he could, by appointing a second trustee, create a mortgage that would override Winifred's interest.

However, an occupying *spouse*, whether or not she (or he) has an equitable interest, has another string to her (his) bow, namely the statutory right to occupy a house that is or has been the matrimonial home. The right is given to a spouse who does not own the legal interest in it. To put it at its simplest, as Henry owns the legal estate in the home, and Winifred does not, Winifred has this statutory right to remain in occupation until the right is destroyed by an order of the court (Matrimonial Homes Act 1983).

Winifred's right is capable of binding any purchaser from Henry, or any mortgagee. So you can see that Winifred has the power to prevent any disposition of the house without her consent. (You can see from this why the Matrimonial Homes Act 1983 does not apply when both spouses own the legal estate. No disposition is then possible anyway, without both spouses signing the deed.)

However, Winifred's right must be protected if it *is* to bind a purchaser or mortgagee. If the title to the home is registered she *must* put a notice on the register. (The 1983 Act specifically provides that the right of occupation is not overriding under s.70(1)(g) of the Land Registration Act 1925 even though the spouse is living in the home.) If the title to the home is unregistered, Winifred must register a class F land charge against Henry's name. So you can see that if Xerxes is buying from Henry, or lending money to him, Xerxes must be concerned about the possibilities:

(a) that Winifred owns part of the equitable interest;
(b) that Winifred will protect her statutory right of occupation by registering a notice or land charge before completion.

If Xerxes is buying, and is worried about the threat of the Matrimonial Homes Act, he can before contract check whether or not Winifred has already protected her right. If she has, and refuses to join in the contract for sale, it would be best for both Henry and Xerxes to abandon the idea of sale. Henry will be entering into a contract that he is probably doomed to break. He promises vacant possession and can only give it if Winifred cancels the registration, or if he obtains a court order for the ending of the right of occupation. (By virtue of s.4 of the 1983 Act, a seller who promises vacant possession is also deemed to promise the cancellation of any registration protecting the statutory right of occupation, or that he will on completion give the purchaser an application for its cancellation signed by the spouse.)

However, even if Henry and Xerxes satisfy themselves that Winifred has not registered her right before exchange of contract, there is nothing to prevent her from registering after contract. The last moment for registration would be the date of Xerxes's pre-completion search. The priority period given by the search would protect Xerxes from any registration after the date of the search. Therefore, both Henry and Xerxes must protect themselves against this registration: Henry, because he faces being liable for breach of contract; Xerxes, because he wants to acquire a house, rather than a right to damages for breach of contract.

The answer is to have Winifred as a party to the contract, in which she will promise not to register the right of occupation, or to cancel any registration that already exists.

To sum up, on the sale of a matrimonial home, you will expect to see both spouses appearing in the contract and signing it, either:

(a) because they both own the legal estate, and are, therefore, joint sellers. This will dispose of their equitable interests, as they will be overreached and no rights of occupation under the Matrimonial Homes Act will exist;

(b) because one spouse is sole beneficial owner, but the other spouse is joining in to confirm that he/she has no equitable interest, and will be releasing any rights under the Matrimonial Homes Act 1983.

(a) *Protecting the Purchaser's Mortgagee*

To recap, you can see that the purchaser's mortgagee faces *two* dangerous spouses, and may be bound by an equitable interest and/or right of occupation belonging to the seller's spouse, and by an equitable interest belonging to the purchaser's spouse.

Any claim by the seller's spouse should be cleared away by the drafting of the contract of sale between seller and purchaser (see above).

It now seems unlikely, following the House of Lord's decision in *Abbey National Building Society* v. *Cann and anor* [1990] (see section 11.10 and case notes) that the mortgagee will be bound by an equitable interest belonging to the borrower's spouse, providing that the money is lent to finance the purchase. If the mortgage is created *after* the house has been acquired, the mortgagee will feel safe if:

1. both the purchase and the mortgage is by both spouses (overreaching); or
2. the purchase and the mortgage is by one spouse, but the other spouse, before completion, gives written confirmation to the lender that he/she knows of the mortgage and agrees that it takes precedence over his/her equitable interest (but see the next section).

11.12 Undue Influence

It has been previously suggested that if the home is in the name of, say, husband alone, the wife should nevertheless be made a party to any disposition of it, or at least give written confirmation that she does not claim any interest in it. Suppose you are the solicitor for someone lending money to the husband on the security of his existing house. You ask the husband to obtain the wife's signature to the mortgage papers. On the face of it, her signature should ensure that she would have no defence to a possession action by the lender, but this is not necessarily so. Her signature will be worthless if she can prove:

(a) that she was induced to sign by the undue influence of her husband, or by his fraudulent misrepresentation;
(b) that the transaction was manifestly disadvantageous to her; and
(c) that when he persuaded her to sign, her husband was acting as agent or representative of the lender, *or* that the lender had notice of the undue influence, or circumstances that might give rise to undue influence (see amongst others, *Kingsnorth Trust Ltd* v. *Bell** [1986]; *Midland Bank*

Ltd v. *Shephard* [1988] and *Bank of Credit and Commerce International SA* v. *Aboody & anor*) [1989].

It is important, therefore, that neither the lender nor his solicitor impliedly constitute the husband as their agent to secure the wife's signature. The papers needing the wife's signature should be sent direct to the wife, and it should be suggested that she seek legal advice. (See *Barclays Bank plc* v. *O'Brien* [1992], in which it was suggested that a borrower's wife was particularly likely to be influenced by her husband, and that a lender must take reasonable steps to ensure that the wife understands the transaction.)

This is not a problem that arises only in the context of spouses. It could arise in the context of a child having undue influence over his parents (*Coldunell* v. *Gallon* [1986]). Nor is it a problem confined to the context of a mortgage. An occupier who is induced by the seller to sign a document that he does not claim any equitable interest in the property may be able to use the same defence, if the seller could be said to be acting as the purchaser's agent in obtaining the signature.

Case Notes

Bristol and West Building Society v. *Henning and anor*

[1985] 2 A11 ER 606, [1985] 1 WLR 778, 50 P & CR 237

Mr and Mrs Henning had lived together as man and wife for several years. They decided to buy a house. The title to the house was unregistered. It was bought with the aid of a mortgage loan. The legal estate was conveyed into the name of Mr Henning alone, and only he created the mortgage. Mrs Henning did not directly provide any of the purchase money, but it was agreed that she should run a self-sufficiency project using the large garden.

The relationship broke down, and Mr Henning left the house and ceased to make the mortgage payments. The Building Society claimed possession. Mrs Henning claimed that she had an equitable interest in the house, and that her interest bound the society, as she was living in the house when the mortgage was executed, and so the Society had notice of it.

It was held that any equitable interest she might have arose from a resulting trust, on the basis of an imputed agreement between herself and Mr Henning that she should have such an interest. If so, it must also be a term of that agreement that her equitable interest should be postponed to the mortgage. She knew and supported the proposal that the purchase price of the house should be raised on mortgage. It was their common intention that the man should have the power to create the mortgage, and it must also have been their intention that the mortgage should have priority over any equitable interests in the house. The mortgagee was, therefore, entitled to possession.

Equity & Law Home Loans Ltd v. *Prestridge and anor*

[1992] 1 A11 ER 909

Mr Prestridge was sole registered proprietor of the house in which he lived with Mrs Brown. She had contributed £10,000 towards the purchase price and the balance had been raised by a mortgage loan of £30,000 taken out by Mr Prestridge with the Britannia Building Society with Mrs Brown's knowledge. Some time after the original purchase, Mr Prestridge applied to Equity & Law to remortgage the house for £43,000. Equity & Law knew that Mrs Brown was living in the house but nevertheless lent the money on the security of a mortgage given by Mr Prestridge alone. He used the money to pay off the money owing to the Britannia, pocketed the balance, left the house and failed to make any payments due on the mortgage. Equity & Law claimed possession.

It was held that

- That Mrs Brown owned all the equitable interest in the house. (The reasons for this do not concern us.)
- That her interest had not bound the Britannia Building Society. Applying the reasoning in the *Henning* case led to the conclusion that she had agreed that her interest should be postponed to the Britannia mortgage.
- That her interest did not bind Equity & Law either. This is because the court was prepared to impute to her not only an agreement that her interest should be postponed to the mortgage she knew of, but also to any mortgage that replaced it on no less advantageous financial terms. Note that the imputed agreement only extended to the amount of the original loan, i.e. £30,000. Equity & Law could only enforce the mortgage against the house for that amount, not for the additional £13,000.

Abbey National Building Society v. *Cann and anor*

[1990] 1 A11 ER 1085 [1990] 2 WLR 832

Mr Cann proposed buying a house. He told the Society that he intended to live there by himself, although in fact he was buying the house for his mother to live in. The Society made a formal offer of loan, which was accepted. Contracts for the purchase were then exchanged, and at 12.20 p.m. on 13 August 1984 the purchase and the mortgage were completed. Mrs Cann (the mother) was then abroad on holiday, but at 11.45 a.m. her son started to move the furniture into the house and carpets were laid.

On 13 September 1984 Mr Cann was registered at HM Land Registry as proprietor, and the mortgage was registered as a registered charge. By that date Mrs Cann was living in the house. Mr Cann failed to make the mortgage payments, and the Society sought possession of the house. Mrs Cann claimed an equitable interest in the house (for reasons based on a contribution towards the purchase price and proprietory estoppel) and that this interest was overriding by virtue of s.70(1)(g) of the Land Registration Act 1925 and therefore bound the Society. Her claim failed for the following reasons:

1. That although a purchaser or mortgagee took subject to overriding interests existing at the date of the registration of the dealing, nevertheless if it was claimed that the interest was overriding by virtue of s.70(1)(g), the claimant must prove that she was in occupation not at the date of registration but the earlier date of completion (i.e. in this case, at 12.20 p.m. on 13 August). Mrs Cann was not in occupation at that time (see section 3.17).

2. Alternatively, where the purchase of a property is financed by a mortgage loan, then although in theory there is a tiny gap in time between the completion of the transfer to the purchaser and his subsequent mortgage, so that it might be arguable that an equitable interest could arise after the transfer but before the mortgage and therefore potentially bind the mortgagee, realistically no such gap exists, or certainly not in the case where the loan has been made pursuant to an earlier agreement that it would be secured by a mortgage. It is all one transaction. The only thing ever available to Mr Cann to hold on trust for, or share with, his mother was a *mortgaged* property. For this reason, even if Mrs Cann *had* been in occupation on 13 August, her interest would still not have bound the mortgagee.

Kingsnorth Trust Ltd v. *Bell*

[1986] 1 A11 ER 423

Mr Bell owned the legal estate in the matrimonial home, but his wife shared the equitable interest. Mr Bell wished to buy a new business, and to raise money to buy it by a mortgage on the home. The solicitors to the Kingsnorth Trust Ltd asked Mr Bell's solicitors to arrange for the execution of the mortgage deeds, and they asked Mr Bell to obtain his wife's signature. He lied to his wife, telling her he needed the money for his existing business. She did not instruct solicitors to act for her, and had no independent advice.

It was held that Kingsnorth Trust, through its solicitors, had instructed the husband to obtain his wife's signature. He had, in effect, been acting as Kingsnorth's agent, and the lenders were bound by his fraudulent misrepresentation.

Workshop

Attempt these problems yourself, then read the specimen solutions at the end of the book.

Problem 1

The legal freehold estate was conveyed in 1970 to three brothers, Albert Brick, Robert Brick and Sidney Brick. The conveyance declared that they were to hold the legal estate on trust for themselves as tenants in common as part of their partnership assets.

In August 1975 the legal estate was conveyed by Albert and Sidney Brick to Jennifer Cooper. A recital in the 1975 conveyance stated that Robert Brick had retired from the partnership.

You have a copy of a search certificate (the search having been made by Miss Cooper when she bought the land from the two Bricks) which reveals that a C(iv) land charge was registered against the name of Robert Brick and Albert Brick on 3 July 1975, but that there is nothing registered against the name of Sydney Brick.

If you are acting for a purchaser from Miss Cooper, is there anything on this title to cause you concern?

Problem 2

You have been instructed by Mrs Anne Mason to deal with a loan she is obtaining from the County Building Society for the purpose of installing central heating and double glazing in her house. The house was erected thirty years ago and is not in a mining area. She has handed you the land certificate which she explains she and her late husband were given because the title deeds were lost. You have also been instructed to act for the building society, and have obtained office copy entries. There are no entries on the charges register, and the proprietorship register looks like this:

B. *PROPRIETORSHIP REGISTER*
Title: Possessory.
First registered proprietors
Alan Mason and Anne Mason
both of 48 Queens Road, Loamster, Loamshire
registered on 13 September 1974.

She has also handed you her late husband's will which has not been proved. It leaves all his property to her absolutely.

1. Does the will have to be proved in order to complete the mortgage? What steps do you need to take to have the title registered in her sole name?
2. What is the significance of registration with possessory title, and will this fact create any problems in dealing with the mortgage?
3. What searches will you make on behalf of the building society?

12 Easements and Restrictive Covenants

These two incumbrances have been mentioned in nearly all the previous chapters. This chapter discusses them in greater detail.

12.1 Sale of Land that Already has the Benefit of an Easement Over a Neighbour's Land

Simple. Before you draft the particulars in the contract, re-read Chapter 5. Before you draft the conveyance, read Chapters 13 and 14.

12.2 Sale of Land that is Already Burdened with an Easement

Simple. When drafting the contract, list the easement as an incumbrance on the property (see the topic of disclosure in Chapter 5). When drafting the conveyance of unregistered title, mention the easement in the habendum (see Chapter 13).

12.3 Sale of Land, when the Seller will Continue to Own Land Nearby

Unfortunately, this is not simple. There are two dangers from the seller's point of view:

(a) that he may unintentionally give the purchaser rights over land that he is retaining:
(b) that he may not reserve a right to use the land he is selling, for example as a means of access, even though that use would add considerably to the enjoyment or value of the land he has retained.

Study Figure 12.1.

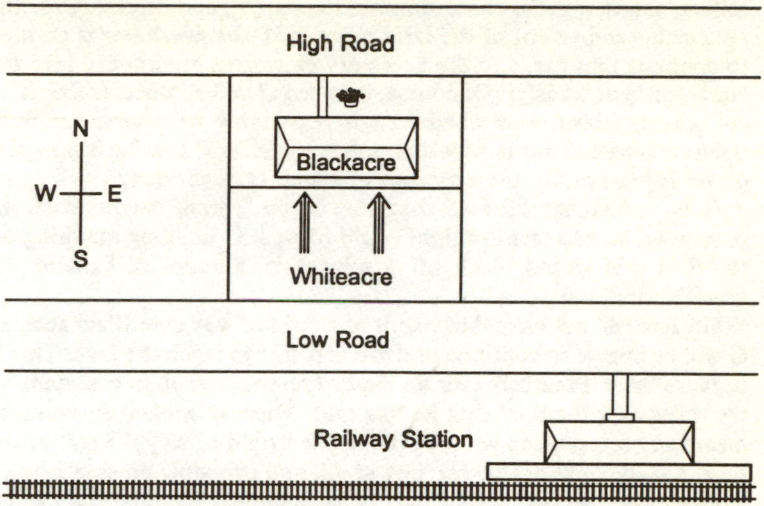

Figure 12.1

Blackacre is a house and surrounding garden. Whiteacre is a field. They are both owned and occupied by O. The house fronts on to the High Road, and if you look carefully you can see the front path, with a tub of flowers beside it. However, O often takes a short cut across Whiteacre to reach the railway station and surrounding shops.

The field is usually reached from Low Road, but O has often driven farm machinery along the edge of Blackacre as a short cut to and from Whiteacre, instead of going the long way round by road.

The arrows indicate light streaming across Whiteacre into the windows of the house on Blackacre.

At the moment there are no easements over either property, as a person cannot have an easement over land which he owns and occupies himself.

Suppose, however, that O now sells Blackacre to P. We will ignore the contract for sale for the moment, and concentrate on the conveyance or transfer. We will assume that it is a silent conveyance, i.e. it makes no express mention of easements. The result of the silent conveyance could be this:

(a) Blackacre may acquire an easement of light, and a right of way over Whiteacre.

There are various reasons why a sale of part of the seller's land may contain an implied grant of easements to the purchaser. The reason for the implied grant in these circumstances is what is known as the rule in *Wheeldon* v. *Burrows* [1879]. This says that if at the time O conveys, he is using the land he is retaining to the advantage of the land he is selling, and that use is continuous and apparent, and necessary for the reasonable enjoyment of the land being sold, the purchaser is entitled to continue that use, and the necessary easements are implied into the conveyance or transfer. Of course, between O and P, whether the short cut was apparent, and whether it is reasonably necessary, are both open to debate. That is why it is unfortunate for P that he has to rely on an *implied* grant, the existence of which O might deny.

It is unfortunate for O that the implied grant might exist. In particular, an easement of light could prevent O building anything on the field that would block off a substantial amount of light to the house's windows.

(b) Whiteacre will not have the benefit of a right of way over Blackacre, so O will be unable to continue to drive across it to reach the field. This is because there is scarcely ever an *implied* reservation of an easement by the seller over the land that he has sold. There is implied an essential means of access, when without the implied right of way the rest of the seller's land could not be reached at all, and probably an easement of support when an owner sells part of his building. Nothing else can be relied on. The short cut across Blackacre is *not* an essential means of access, as the field can be reached from Low Road.

From O's point of view, we can now see that he would have preferred the conveyance or transfer *not* to be silent. He would have liked to see in it:

(a) a clause saying that there was no implied grant of easements to P (*Wheeldon* v. *Burrows* can be ousted by agreement) or at least that there was not an easement of light.
(b) a clause saying that he did reserve a right of way over Blackacre.

From P's point of view, we can see that P would have preferred an express grant of, say, the right of way over Whiteacre. The existence of this right would then be beyond dispute, and could easily be proved when P re-sold. In other words, the conveyance should not have been silent. Instead, it should have spoken up.

Of course, neither party can insist on anything going into the conveyance, unless the preceding contract says that it can go in. It is the contract that governs the drafting and contents of the conveyance. So O and P, when agreeing the terms of the contract, should have decided on special conditions settling what easements were to be reserved expressly in the conveyance, what easements were to be granted expressly, and that the conveyance should state that no others were to be granted by implication.

The conditions in the contract are not creating the easements, but merely providing that the easements will be created by the conveyance or transfer. Therefore it is essential to have the necessary grant and reservation in the conveyance, together with the statement preventing any implied grant. If through carelessness, the conveyance was drafted without any reference to easements, the seller would have no easements over the part sold to the purchaser, and the purchaser could perhaps claim easements other than those that had been intended by the contract.

If O and P forget to put in special conditions to deal with the grant and reservation of easements but the contract incorporates the standard conditions, standard condition 3.3 will govern the drafting of the conveyance or transfer. Condition 3.3.2 states first of all that the buyer will not have any right of light or air over the retained land. This prevents there being any implied grant by the contract to the purchaser of such rights, and also entitles the seller to put a clause in the conveyance preventing there being any implied grant by the conveyance.

Subject to this, condition 3.3.2 then provides that the seller as owner of the retained land and buyer as owner of the land being sold will each have the rights over the land of the other which they would have had if they were two separate buyers to whom the seller had made simultaneous transfers of the land being sold and the retained land. Condition 3.3.3 adds that either party can request that the conveyance or transfer contain the necessary express grant or reservation.

At first sight this is incomprehensible, but it is based on this point of law; that if – in the case of Blackacre and Whiteacre – instead of selling Blackacre and retaining Whiteacre O had sold the two properties simultaneously, Blackacre to P and Whiteacre to Q, P would have had an implied grant of easements over Whiteacre and Q would have had an implied grant of easements over Blackacre. So P might well have had a right of light and way over Whiteacre and Q a right of way over Blackacre (not a right of light, as there were no windows on Whiteacre receiving light at the time of the conveyance). Condition 5 is, therefore, saying that you must imagine that O, instead of retaining Whiteacre, is buying it. What easements would have been impliedly granted to O? Answer – *Wheeldon* v. *Burrows* easements and possibly others. Then those are the easements that O can expressly reserve in the conveyance of Blackacre for the benefit of Whiteacre and himself. Similarly, P is entitled to have inserted in the conveyance as express easements those that would have been implied into the conveyance with the exception of easements of light and air. So the condition decreases P's right to easements, but does mean that P can ask for an *express* grant to be written on the face of the conveyance, instead of having to rely on an implied grant. O's right to easements is increased and put on a par with P's. Indeed O's rights are better than P's, because there is nothing in the condition to prevent O expressly reserving rights of light or air, providing that the facts justify it.

There are considerable drawbacks in relying on the standard condition. It may not represent the parties' intentions. The seller, for instance, might not want the purchaser to have any easements at all over his land. Another point is that if one party wants to insist on his rights under it, and have the express grant or reservation written into the conveyance, the other party can deny that the easement in question would have been the subject matter of an implied grant, e.g. because it is not continuous and apparent. If it would not have been the subject matter of an implied grant, it cannot, under condition 4.3 be the subject matter of an express grant. So the condition is a breeding ground for dispute.

(*Note*: A grant of easements is not only implied under *Wheeldon* v. *Burrows*. Easements of necessity are implied, and there may be a grant implied into the conveyance or transfer by s.62 of the Law of Property Act 1925. The rules are not dwelt on, as the purpose of this chapter is to urge you to replace an implied grant by an express grant, following a special condition in the contract.)

12.4 Particular Points about Easements and the Land Registration Act 1925

The Land Registration Act seems particularly obscure on the question of easements.

The principles *seem* to be as follows:

(a) If land has the benefit of a legal easement when the title to that land is first registered, then the easement remains legal. It will therefore bind a later purchaser of the servient tenement (the land over which the easement is exercised). If the title to the servient tenement is unregistered, the easement will bind the purchaser of it because the easement is legal. If the title to the servient tenement is registered, the purchaser of it will be bound by the easement, because the easement, being legal, is overriding under s.70(1)(a) of the Land Registration Act 1925;

(b) If an easement is granted out of a registered title, the creation of the easement must be followed by its registration. The principle involved here is one that has been met already in section 3.11. The creation of an easement out of registered title is a registrable dealing. The easement will not be legal until it is registered. Pending registration, the easement is only equitable, and possibly is only a minor interest (see section 3.15).

If an easement is granted out of registered title, and the servient tenement is also registered land, the registration of the easement has two aspects. The benefit of the easement must be registered on the title to the dominant tenement, and the burden must be registered on the title to the servient tenement.

The Registrar can only register the benefit if he is sure that the grant of the easement is valid. As the title to the servient tenement is registered, it should be quite clear that the servient owner has the power to grant the easement, providing that the servient owner is registered with absolute title. If there is doubt, the registrar may only be able to state in the register to the dominant tenement that the easement is *claimed.*

For the burden to be registered against the servient tenement, the servient owner should be asked to put his land certificate on deposit at the registry. If the land certificate is not put on deposit, a caution will have to be entered on the register to protect the easement.

If this situation – of an easement being granted out of, and for the benefit of, a registered title – occurs on the occasion of a sale of part of the land in the title, registration of the benefit and burden of the easements should present no difficulty. The title is known to the Registrar and the seller's land certificate will have been put on deposit to await the registration of the transfer of part. The Registrar can, therefore, check the validity of the grant, and can register the burden of the easements reserved by the seller on the purchaser's new title, and can register the burden of the easements given to the purchaser on the seller's title.

It is possible, however, that the easement could be granted by a deed of grant, quite independently of any transfer, e.g. by one neighbour to another. In this case it must be remembered that it is insufficient for the benefit to be registered. The burden must also be registered on the title to the servient tenement. If this is not done, there is the possibility that when the servient tenement is sold, the new owner may be able to claim that the easement does not bind him, as it is an unprotected minor interest.

Could this unregistered easement bind the purchaser because it is an overriding interest? There is no certain answer. Remember that the easement is only equitable, because it has not been registered. There is considerable controversy over whether an equitable easement can be overriding under s.70(1)(a) (see 3.15). Respected authors of leading textbooks differ on the point. In view of the uncertainty, it is clearly important that the easement be properly registered.

(c) If an easement is created by a deed of grant, and only the servient tenement is registered, the burden should be registered on that title. If only the dominant tenement is registered, the benefit will be entered on the register, provided that the registrar is satisfied that the grant is valid. He can only be satisfied if the title to the servient tenement is proved to him. Otherwise, at best he can only put a note to the effect that the easement is claimed.

(d) If part of the land in a registered title is sold, the purchaser may acquire easements over the seller's retained land by virtue of an implied grant, e.g. under *Wheeldon* v. *Burrows*, or by virtue of s.62 of the Law of Property Act 1925. These easements take effect as overriding interests, under rule 258 of Land Registration Rules 1925, and do not have to be noted on the servient tenement in order to bind a purchaser of it.

12.5 Covenants

When the seller will continue to own land near the property he is selling, he will also consider whether it is desirable to insist that the purchaser, in the conveyance or transfer to him, give covenants back to the seller.

One purpose of the covenants will be that the seller can control the use of the land he has sold. If he has sold the end of his garden to a developer, he may be prepared to accept the building of a bungalow, but will want a covenant by the developer not to build anything else, for example, a block of flats.

Another purpose might be to force the purchaser to carry out work, for example, repairs or fencing. Of course, the covenant might equally well be given by seller to purchaser.

12.6 The Contract

Suppose that Sarah owns both Blackacre and Whiteacre. She contracts to sell Whiteacre to Patricia. The contract provides that in the conveyance or transfer Patricia will covenant:

(a) to use Whiteacre only as a single dwelling-house;
(b) to fence the boundary between Whiteacre and Blackacre.

Notice that the covenant is going to be given in the conveyance or transfer. The contract is merely giving Sarah the right to insist that the conveyance does contain the covenant. The contract can, and should, prescribe the exact wording to be used in the conveyance, because for example:

(a) The benefit of a covenant can be 'annexed' to the benefited land (in this case, Blackacre) by – amongst other possibilities – saying that it is given 'for the benefit of each and every part of Blackacre'. The result of the covenant being worded in such a way is that the benefit and the land become inseparable, so that a later purchaser of any part of Blackacre that does in fact benefit from the covenant, acquires not only the land but the power to enforce the covenant. There is then no need to show that the benefit of the covenant has been expressly assigned.

    It is true that the benefit of a covenant may be annexed without any express wording, owing to the wording implied into the covenant by s.78 of the Law of Property Act 1925 (as interpreted in the case of *Federated Homes Ltd* v. *Mill Lodge Properties Ltd* [1980]) but as the benefited land should be identified in the conveyance, express words of annexation might as well be used.
(b) A covenant to repair or to fence should define the obligation exactly, so the wording should be settled in the contract.

12.7 The Conveyance or Transfer

In the conveyance, the covenant is actually given by purchaser to seller, or seller to purchaser, using the wording already settled by the preceding contract.

12.8 Protecting the Covenant

We must now distinguish between the two covenants in our imagined contract. The fencing covenant is positive, as it requires labour or the spending of money to perform it. The user covenant is negative. Nothing has to be *done* to observe it, it is rather the case of not doing anything to change the existing use.

The point of the distinction is, of course, that the negative covenant (or, as it is generally called in a conveyancing context, the *restrictive* covenant) is capable of becoming an incumbrance on the land and so may be enforceable not only against Patricia but against whoever claims the land through her (*Tulk* v. *Moxhay* [1848]). However, the incumbrance is an equitable one and so will not automatically bind a purchaser from Patricia. If Sarah's title is unregistered, and if the disposition to Patricia does not necessitate an application for first registration, for example because it is a gift, then the covenant is registerable as a D(ii) land charge. If Sarah does not register the charge against Patricia's name, the covenant will not bind a later purchaser of the land. If the disposition by Sarah to Patricia is a sale, Patricia will have to apply for first registration of title. In this case Sarah will not register a D(ii) land charge. Instead, the covenant will be protected by an entry on the register of title at HM Land Registry (s.14 Land Charges Act 1972).

If Patricia's title to Whiteacre is registered under the Land Registration Act 1925, the negative covenant is a minor interest, and will only bind a transferee for value of the title if the covenant is protected by an entry on the register, either a notice or a caution. Usually, a covenant is given when part of the seller's land is sold (although this does not have to be so). For this reason a restrictive covenant is usually protected by a notice. Suppose that Sarah sells part of her registered title to Patricia, and Patricia covenants in the transfer to use the property only as a dwelling-house. Patricia will lodge the transfer in the Registry, to be registered as proprietor of the part she has bought. The Registrar, when registering the transfer, will also put a notice on the charges register of Patricia's title. If Sarah had given a negative covenant to Patricia, this covenant should be noted on the charges register of Sarah's title. This needs the deposit of Sarah's land certificate but in these circumstances it will already be on deposit to await registration of the transfer of part.

A positive covenant does not create an incumbrance on land, so that when Patricia conveys Whiteacre to Quentin, he will not have to perform the fencing covenant, at least not in the sense that it can be enforced against him directly by Sarah. Sarah could only enforce the user covenant against him.

However, Quentin may be affected by the enforcement against him of an indemnity covenant.

12.9 Indemnity Covenants

Return to Sarah and Patricia. When Patricia gave the two covenants she undertook a perpetual liability. She will have covenanted not only that *she* would perform the covenants but that *anyone* who later succeeded to the land would also perform them (s.79 of the Law of Property Act 1925). Therefore, when Patricia sells Whiteacre to Quentin, if he does not fence or does not observe the user covenant, Sarah can sue *Patricia* for breach of contract.

Sarah may not bother to sue Patricia if it is the negative covenant that is being broken. If the burden of that covenant has run with the land and Quentin has taken subject to it, Sarah's most effective remedy will be to proceed against *him* and obtain an injunction to prevent the breach being continued. However the possibility of being sued remains to haunt Patricia.

As regards the positive covenant, Patricia is the only person who can be sued by Sarah, as Sarah cannot take any action against Quentin.

As she is aware of this possibility of being sued at some time in the future, perhaps long after she has parted with the land, Patricia, when she sells to Quentin, will want a covenant from him to indemnify her against any consequences of a future breach of either covenant. Patricia can only insist on the conveyance or transfer to Quentin containing an indemnity covenant if the contract says that it will.

Condition 4.5.3 of the standard conditions provides for the insertion of an indemnity covenant into the conveyance or transfer, if despite the sale, the seller will remain liable on any obligation affecting the property. The covenant is given only in respect of future breaches so that Quentin will not be liable for breaches committed before the land was conveyed to him. The condition also requires Quentin to promise to perform the obligation. This means that Patricia would not herself have to be sued before insisting that Quentin fence in accordance with the covenant given by her to Sarah.

A special condition in the contract is therefore not needed unless the standard condition is considered unsatisfactory. Again, remember that the contract does not create the indemnity covenant. The covenant is put in the conveyance or transfer as a result of the condition in the contract.

As Quentin has undertaken a perpetual responsibility to indemnify Patricia, when Quentin sells to Rosemary, he needs an indemnity covenant from Rosemary. He needs an indemnity against his promise to indemnify. The indemnity given by Rosemary should have the same wording as the indemnity given by Quentin. For example, if Quentin promised to *perform* and indemnify, Rosemary should be required to give the same promise to him. If Quentin only promised to indemnify, but not to perform, Rosemary should alter standard condition 4.5.3, so that in the conveyance *she* will only promise to indemnify.

A long chain of indemnity may eventually stretch from Patricia to the current owner of Whiteacre. The older the covenant and the longer the chain, the more ineffective the chain becomes. If Sarah, or Sarah's successor to Blackacre, decides to sue Patricia, Patricia may be untraceable. If Patricia is dead, while it is in theory possible to sue her estate, the expense and difficulty of finding her personal representatives and of tracing her assets into the hands of the beneficiaries will make the remedy impracticable. If Patricia is successfully sued, Patricia may not be able to find Quentin. Remember the only person who can sue Rosemary by virtue of the indemnity chain is Quentin, so if Patricia is unable to sue Quentin, Rosemary will not be called upon for an indemnity, so is unconcerned at the continuance of the breach either by her or her successor. However, if you are acting for a seller who gave an indemnity when he originally bought the land, you make certain that he is indemnified when he sells. You do this, even though it seems very unlikely that your client would ever be sued on the chain.

12.10 Particular Points about Covenants and Registered Title

The restrictive covenants will be set out in the charges register of the burdened land. They may be set out in full or if they are long the register may refer to the document that created them. This document or a copy will be filed at the Registry and a copy bound up in the land certificate.

If positive covenants are created in a transfer of registered title, they will also appear on the register. If in the transfer they were mixed in with negative covenants, the Registrar will not divide them, but will put both the negative and the positive covenants in the charges register. If the transfer contains only positive covenants, their existence will be noted on the proprietorship register. The positive covenants are not really part of the title to the land. They are only noted on the register as a matter of convenience. Without a note on the register their existence could be easily forgotten, as the transfer that created them is filed in the registry. If they were forgotten, the original covenantor or his successors might forget the necessity for an indemnity covenant when retransferring.

Notice that it is not the practice to enter on the register those positive covenants that already exist when the title is first registered. The registry considers this to be unnecessary. The original deeds are returned to the registered proprietor and *these* reveal the existence of the covenants. This is the one reason why the title deeds remain important, despite registration of the title.

Indemnity Covenants

An indemnity covenant given by the applicant for first registration will not be mentioned on the register of title. This is because when he resells, he can recall the fact that he gave, and therefore needs, an indemnity covenant by looking at the title deeds. If an indemnity covenant is given by a later registered proprietor, a note is put in to the proprietorship register, referring to the existence of the indemnity covenant.

Workshop

Attempt these problems yourself, then read the specimen solutions at the end of the book.

Problem 1

Your client is buying a freehold detached house, 21B Landsdown Crescent, from Alice Brown. Alice Brown also owns 21A. She used to own number 21, but this was sold by her to Catherine Douglas in 1986. Figure 12.2 is a plan of the three properties.

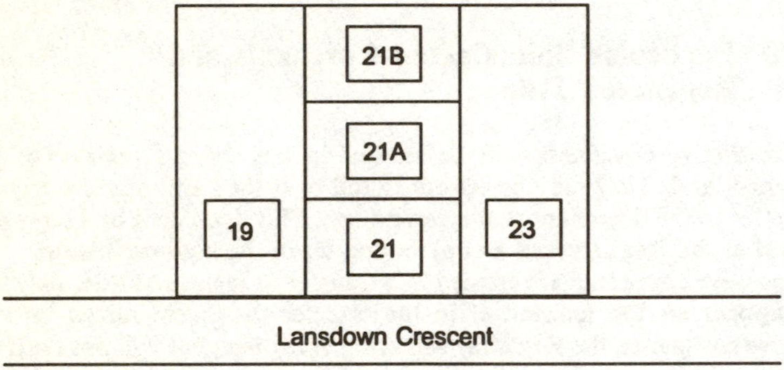

Figure 12.2

Enquiries of the district authority and the property information form reveal that Landsdown Crescent is a public road and that the pipes and wires serving 21A and 21B lead from Landsdown Crescent across number 21.

You are considering the draft contract prepared by Alice Brown's solicitor. You have to decide whether your client will obtain all the easements necessary for his enjoyment of 21B. Do you think he will? What documents should you read?

Problem 2

You are acting for Hebe, the seller of 1 Rosemary Avenue. You are investigating the unregistered title. You have the following title deeds.

- A conveyance dated 1 May 1940, made between the seller A and the purchaser B. This conveyance contains a covenant given by B to A that no buildings whatsoever would be put on the land other than one detached house.
- A conveyance dated 1 June 1980, made between the seller B and the purchaser C. This conveyance contains an indemnity given by C to B against breach of the 1940 covenant.
- A conveyance dated 1 July 1988 made between the seller C and Hebe the purchaser. The conveyance contains an indemnity given by Hebe to C against breach of the 1940 covenant. As soon as Hebe bought the property, she built a large garage.

1. Can the covenant be enforced against Hebe?
2. How do these facts affect your drafting of the contract of sale?

Problem 3

You are acting for Jacob Green, whose wife, Naomi Green, has just died. He has decided to sell 9 Havelock Street, where he has lived all his married life, and move in with his widowed sister. He has asked you to act for him in the sale.

He has handed you Naomi's will, which divides everything she owns equally between Jacob and their daughter, Dr Ruth Green.

The title to the house is registered. The land certificate is in the possession of the Equine Bank, but you have obtained an office copy of the entries on the register. The property register describes the property as '9 Havelock Street, Spa on Wells, together with the rights granted by but subject to the exceptions and reservations contained in the conveyance dated 1 April 1965, referred to in entry no.2 of the register.'

The proprietorship register names Jacob and Naomi as proprietors, and contains the restriction that no disposition by the sole survivor under which capital money arises will be registered.

Entry no.1 on the charges register states that a conveyance of 1922 contains restrictive covenants affecting the land, but that neither the original conveyance, nor a certified copy or an examined abstract of it was produced on first registration. Entry no 2 says that the conveyance of 1 April 1965 contains restrictive covenants affecting the land, and that a copy of the conveyance is in the certificate. Entries 3 and 4 relate to the registered charge in favour of the Equine Bank.

Jacob tells you that the sale is to include the fitted carpets and all curtains, but is to exclude the garden shed. You how have to draft the contract. How will the facts set out above affect the drafting of the contract.

13 Drafting a Conveyance of Unregistered Title

13.1 Introduction

When called upon to draft a conveyance, your first instinct might be to turn immediately to a precedent book. You must remember that a precedent is your servant, not your master. You must know what sort of clauses your conveyance needs before you turn to the precedent for an appropriate form of words. You should not rely on the precedent to alert you to the necessity for the clause in the first place.

This chapter will introduce you to a standard form of conveyance, discuss the effect and purpose of the various clauses, and then consider what changes should be made to suit particular circumstances. The clauses are not put forward as precedents, but serve only to illustrate the purposes that must be achieved by clauses in the conveyance.

It must be emphasised that it is the contract that governs the contents of the conveyance or transfer made in performance of the contract. Clauses affecting the rights of seller and purchaser against one another, e.g. easements, covenants, or the cutting down of an implied grant, can only be put in the conveyance if justified by a provision in the contract. The person drafting the conveyance on behalf of the purchaser must ensure that the conveyance gives the purchaser the rights which the contract promised would be given. The person checking the draft conveyance on behalf of the seller must check that it gives the purchaser nothing more.

Not only the *special* conditions in the contract must be considered. Some of the standard conditions affect the drafting of the purchase deed. These are:

Condition 3.3 possibly justifying the inclusion of an express reservation of easements by the seller, and an express grant to the purchaser. It also enables a seller to put in a declaration negating any implied grant of an easement of light or air to the purchaser. (These conditions are discussed in Chapter 12.)

Condition 4.5.3 justifying the inclusion of a covenant to perform and indemnify (see Chapter 12). This could be relevant not only when the property is sold subject to covenants, but also when the property is sold subject to, for example, a legal mortgage or rent charge.

Condition 8.1.4 this applies on the assignment of a lease, and justifies the seller who is conveying as a beneficial owner in amending the implied covenants for title so that they do not include a promise that the repairing obligations in the lease have been performed by him (see Chapter 15).

Condition 4.5.4 enabling a seller who is conveying as a trustee or a personal representative to refuse to give an undertaking for the safety of a deed retained by him (see later).

13.2 A Specimen Conveyance

This is a draft conveyance of a freehold. It takes a form that some would consider to be old fashioned, although it is still often used today. It is useful to consider this type of conveyance, despite its cobwebs, as this is the sort of deed that you will meet when you investigate an unregistered title, and because the principles of drafting that it illustrates hold true even if you decide to follow more modish precedents. (See 14.4 for the possibility of drafting a conveyance of an unregisted title in the form of a land registry transfer.)

This Conveyance is made the .... day of .... 19..... between Amy Baker of .... (hereinafter called the seller of the one part) and Catherine Douglas of .... (hereinafter called the purchaser) of the other part

Whereas the seller owns the freehold estate in the property hereinafter conveyed free from incumbrances, and has agreed to sell the same to the purchaser at a price of £76 000

Now this deed witnesses that in consideration of £76 000 now paid by the purchaser to the seller (receipt whereof the seller hereby acknowledges) the seller as beneficial owner hereby conveys all that property known as 39 Woodbrooke Avenue Nineoaks Kent to hold unto the purchaser in fee simple

In witness thereof the parties hereto have hereunto set their hands the day and year first above written

Signed as a deed and delivered
by the said Amy Baker in
the presence of .... }

Now look at the parts of the conveyance separately.

(*a*) *The Parties*

The two essential parties to the deed will be the seller and the purchaser.

If four people were buying the property, they would still be one party as they are all performing the same role.

Sometimes, other parties will be introduced into the conveyance.

(i) If trustees for sale have to obtain a consent to the sale (see section 11.5) the person whose consent is needed can be made a party, so that the giving of the consent appears on the face of the conveyance.

(ii) If the seller is a tenant for life of a settlement under the Settled Land Act 1925, the trustees of the settlement will be joined as parties to give a receipt for the purchase price. (By virtue of s.18 of the Settled Land Act 1925, a conveyance by a tenant for life is void unless the purchase price is paid, not to the tenant for life, but to the trustees.)

Notice that the sale by the trustees for sale or by the tenant for life is capable of overreaching the interests of the beneficiaries. The beneficiaries would not, therefore, appear as parties to the conveyance.

(iii) Sale of a property subject to a mortgage.

(aa) If the mortgage is to be redeemed on completion, the mortgage is treated as redeemed *before* completion, so the property is conveyed free from it. The conveyance does not, therefore, mention the mortgage, and the mortgagee is certainly not a party to the conveyance.

(bb) If the mortgage is *not* to be redeemed on completion, so that the house is conveyed subject to it, the mortgagee does not *have* to be joined as a party (although it would be wise to obtain his prior consent to the conveyance, in case the conveyance prompts him to call in the mortgage). He is often joined in as a party since this has two advantages. He can confirm the exact amount owing on the mortgage, and can take a personal covenant from the purchaser for the repayment of the mortgage loan. The conveyance will also contain a promise by the purchaser to indemnify the seller against any claim by the mortgagee.

(iv) A sale by a mortgagee under his power of sale If the sale is by a mortgagee under his statutory power of sale, he and the purchaser will be the parties to the conveyance. The mortgagee has the ability to convey the mortgagor's estate, and to give a good receipt for the purchase price. The mortgagor is not a party to the conveyance.

(v) *Subsales* If by the time completion arrives the purchaser (Paul) has already contracted to resell to someone else (Barnabas) the seller can be compelled to convey direct to Barnabas unless either this would prejudice the seller or the contract gives the seller the right to refuse.

It will be necessary for Paul to be a party to the conveyance if he has resold to Barnabas at a higher price, as a receipt clause for the increase in price will be needed from him.

The conveyance to Barnabas will be by the seller but will be expressed to be by the direction of Paul. The wording would be 'the seller as beneficial owner at the direction of the purchaser as beneficial owner hereby conveys unto' the sub-purchaser.

The point is that if a person *directs* a conveyance as beneficial owner, that person will thereby give covenants for title. Barnabas therefore has the benefit of covenants for title given by both the seller and by Paul (see s.76(2) of the Law of Property Act 1925, and Chapter 19 of this book).

(*b*) *The Recitals*

The words 'whereas . . .' introduce the part of the conveyance known as 'the recitals'. These are increasingly omitted in modern conveyances. The first recital in our form of conveyance explains that the seller is able to convey the property. It is usually pointless to recite how he came to be in this position as anyone later entitled to investigate the matter has only to read the earlier title deeds.

The second fact recited is the fact that the seller has contracted to sell the property to the purchaser. This explains the reason for the conveyance taking place, and what it is intended that the conveyance shall achieve. Recitals, although their purpose is largely explanatory, do have a legal effect.

(i) A recital of fact will create an estoppel against the person making it, and against that person's successors in title. This can be important. For instance, Amy Baker cannot now deny her ownership of the legal estate at the date of the conveyance. If she did not in fact have it then, but acquired it *after* the date of the conveyance, the legal estate would automatically vest in Catherine Douglas, without any need for a fresh conveyance by Amy. The estoppel is said to have been fed.

(ii) A recital of fact in a document 20 years old at the date of the contract must be taken to be sufficient evidence of the truth of that fact (s.45(6) of the Law of Property Act 1925). The assistance of this rule is not usually needed in modern conveyancing.

(iii) If the conveyance is by a personal representative, a recital that he has not made any previous assent or conveyance will give the purchaser the protection of s.36(6) Administration of Estates Act 1925 (see Chapter 10).

(iv) If the conveyance is by the personal representatives of a sole joint tenant, a recital that the deceased was at his death solely and beneficially interested in the property will give the purchaser the protection of the Law of Property (Joint Tenants) Act 1964 (see Chapter 11).

(*c*) *Consideration and Capacity*

The words 'Now this deed witnesses' introduce what is known as the 'operative' part of the deed, that is, the part that actually does the job of transferring ownership from seller to purchaser

(i) It traditionally starts with the statement of the consideration. Section 5 of the Stamp Act 1891 makes it essential for the consideration to be stated on the face of a conveyance. It is also convenient, as the statement will be accepted by the Stamp Office, and the calculation of stamp duty based on it.

(ii) This is followed by the seller's acknowledgement of the receipt of the purchase price. There are two reasons for inserting this:

(aa) Section 67 of the Law of Property Act 1925. If a receipt is contained in the body of the deed, the purchaser cannot ask for any other receipt.

(bb) Section 69 of the Law of Property Act 1925. Where a solicitor (or by virtue of s.34(1)(c) of the Administration of Justice Act 1985, a licensed conveyancer) produces a deed that has in it a receipt for the consideration money, and that deed is executed by the person entitled to give the receipt (i.e. usually the seller) the deed is sufficient authority to pay the money to the solicitor or licensed conveyancer, without the recipient having otherwise to prove that he has been authorised to receive it. In other words, if the solicitor then decamps with the money, the loss is the seller's, not the purchaser's.

It is sometimes argued in textbooks that s.69 authorises the purchaser to pay only the solicitor, and not the solicitor's employee. The argument has never impressed conveyancing practitioners, who happily hand over the purchase price to whatever representative of the seller's solicitor's firm materialises before them.

(iii) The conveyance will then state in what capacity the seller conveys (see Chapter 19).

(*d*) *The Parcels Clause*

Introduced by the words 'all that . . .', a parcels clause falls into three sections, (i) the descriptive, (ii) the 'plus factor' and (iii) the 'minus factor'.

(i) *The description of the property being conveyed* Ideally, an accurate and adequate description was settled at the time of the contract, and this can now be reproduced in the conveyance. However, the purchaser, when drafting the conveyance, does not have to use the contract description. The drafting of a description of the property has been discussed in Chapter 5 in the context of the drafting of a contract.

Use of a plan On the sale of part of the seller's land, a plan will usually be necessary in order to define the new boundary. A seller cannot refuse to convey by reference to a plan, unless one is unnecessary for the description of the property. (The reason why he might wish to refuse is that it involves him in checking the accuracy of the plan.)

It need scarcely be said that if a plan is to be used then that plan must be accurate and professionally prepared. It must also be on a sufficiently large scale. As well as the plan being physically attached to the conveyance, reference should be made to it in the conveyance (otherwise it is not strictly part of the deed at all).

There should, of course, be no conflict between the verbal description in the conveyance and the plan. The main role of the plan will be to supplement the verbal description, particularly in the role of defining boundaries, where it is difficult to frame a sufficiently clear verbal description. In such a case, where the plan is to prevail as it gives the more precise description, the plan should be referred to as 'more particularly' describing the property.

The verbal description will prevail if the plan is inadequate, or unclear, or is referred to as only being for the purpose of identifying the property. (You might ask yourself before using such a plan of what use it is if it does not make the position clearer than the verbal description does.)

Fixtures Fixtures are part of the land, and pass automatically with a conveyance of it. There is, therefore, no need to mention such things as garages, as they will pass to the purchaser anyway. The same could be said of the house, but it is usual to include the house in the description of the land being conveyed. Indeed the description of the house often stands as the description of the land, for example, 'all that house and garden known as 1 Roseberry Crescent . . .'.

(ii) *The 'plus factor'* The second part of a parcels clause may be called 'the plus factor', and is introduced by the words 'together with . . .'. There are then listed:

(aa) existing easements that the property already enjoys over neighbouring land;
(bb) new easements, being granted in this conveyance by the seller over land that he is retaining nearby.

The existing easements would pass to the purchaser anyway, as they are part of the land being conveyed. The benefit of listing them is that they are not later forgotten.

(iii) *The 'minus factor'* The final part of the parcels clause may be called 'the minus factor' and is introduced by the words 'except' and 'reserving'. There are then listed any *new* easements that the seller is reserving for the benefit of his land over the property he is conveying.

A reservation takes effect as a grant by the purchaser. Thus, if the conveyance says 'reserving to the seller a right of way on foot over the property hereby conveyed along the route marked green on the said plan . . .' this is in fact a right of way granted by the purchaser over the property which he is acquiring. This has the result that as an ambiguous grant is always construed against the grantor, any ambiguity in the reservation of the easement will be construed against the purchaser and in favour of the seller.

The reservation takes effect even if conveyance is not executed by the purchaser (s.65(1) of the Law of Property Act 1925).

Any exception, for example, of mineral rights, also appears in this part of the parcels clause. (Strictly, an exception is where the seller retains something from the land that is already in existence, for example, mineral rights. A reservation is where the seller acquires a right not previously existing, such as an easement or a profit. In practice, the distinction is unlikely to be of importance, as the two are always put together.)

(*e*) *The Habendum*

The words 'to hold . . .' introduce what is known as the *habendum*. This describes the title that is to be conveyed, that is, the estate, and the incumbrances to which the estate is subject.

Further points about the habendum are made in sections 13.4(a) and 13.4(d).

(*f*) *The Testimonium and Execution*

The testimonium (in witness, etc.) introduces the signatures of the parties. In many cases, there is no need for the purchaser to execute the conveyance (for exceptions, see section 13.5).

13.3 Formalities of Execution

(*a*) *By an Individual*

What is written here applies to deeds executed after the coming into effect of s.1 of the Law of Property (Miscellaneous Provisions) Act 1989 on 31 July 1990. (The formalities for execution of deeds before that date are set out in section 9.2(f).

A conveyance of a legal estate must be by deed. A document will only be a deed if:

- it is signed by its maker;
- if that signature is witnessed and attested;
- if it is clear that the document is intended to be a deed. That intention can be made clear either by describing the document as a deed (e.g. 'This Deed of Conveyance is made 1 September 1990 _____) or because the document is expressed to be executed or signed as a deed (e.g. the attestation clause might say 'signed by the seller as his deed in the presence of _____');
- if the deed is delivered as a deed.

The delivery of a deed may be a matter of intention only. A deed is delivered by a seller when it is signed by him with the intention that he shall be bound by it.

Signature by another The Act makes it possible for an individual to direct another person to sign a deed on his behalf, provided that the signature is made in his presence and there are *two* attesting witnesses.

Delivery by another A deed may be delivered by its maker, or it may be delivered by someone on his behalf.

Escrows A deed may be delivered absolutely, and is then of immediate effect. Alternatively, it may be delivered conditionally, and is then known as an *escrow*.

Until the coming into effect of s.1 of the 1989 Act, conveyancing practice had been that the conveyance was signed and *delivered* by the seller some days before completion. This ensured that every conveyance was delivered conditionally. Had the delivery been absolute, the legal estate would there and then have vested in the purchaser, although he had not yet paid the purchase price. Delivery was conditional upon completion taking place and the purchase price being paid. The conveyance came into full effect when the condition was fulfilled.

So every sale produced an escrow but escrows create difficulties. One is the so-called doctrine of 'relation back', which has the effect that the true date of the conveyance (whatever date it might bear on its face) is the date of the conditional delivery (i.e. some days before completion) rather than the date the condition is fulfilled (i.e. the actual date of completion). Another is that delivery in escrow is binding. It commits the seller; he cannot withdraw from the deed while the time limit for fulfilment of the condition is still running. Only if completion does not take place in due course can he renounce the escrow (see *Glessing* v. *Green* [1975]). One suggested solution to the problem of an escrow is that the seller should sign the conveyance only, and authorise his solicitor to deliver the deed at completion. Up until 1990 the idea was not put into practice as the authority would have had to be given by a power of attorney. This difficulty is now swept aside by s.1 of the 1989 Act, for the section abolishes the rule that the authority to deliver can only be given by deed. It is now, therefore, possible for the deed to be delivered at completion by the seller's solicitor. The purchaser need not check the solicitor's authority to deliver the deed, as the Act provides that where a solicitor or licensed conveyancer (or his agent or employee) delivers an instrument on behalf of a person for whom he is acting, it shall be conclusively presumed in favour of the purchaser that such a person *is* authorised to deliver the instrument. The aim is, therefore, to make it unnecessary for a deed to be delivered by the seller in escrow. What can now happen instead is that before completion the seller will sign the deed, without any intention of being then bound by it. He will then send it to his solicitor. At completion, the solicitor will hand or send it to the purchaser's solicitor, and thereby manifest the seller's intention to be bound. The deed will at the same time be both physically and legally delivered.

(*b*) *By a Company*

What is written here applies to a deed executed by a company after the coming into effect of s.130 of the Companies Act 1989, i.e. again 31 July 1990. (The formalities for the execution of a deed before that date are set out in section 9.4.) For a document to be executed as a deed by a company, it is necessary that the document be executed (i.e. signed or sealed) and delivered as a deed.

Execution Section 36A Companies Act 1985 (inserted by s.130 of the 1989 Act) provides that the document can be executed *either*

- by the affixing of the company seal, *or*
- by being signed by a director and the secretary, or by two directors of the company, provided that the document is expressed to be executed by the company. In other words, it must be made clear that the signatures amount to execution by the *company*, rather than execution by the directors *personally*.

Delivery If the executed document makes it clear on its face that it is intended to be a deed, it will be a deed when delivered as a deed. It is presumed, unless the contrary appears, to be delivered at the time it is executed.

Protection of third parties Section 36A(6) provides that a purchaser for value can presume (a) that the document has been properly executed as a deed by the company if it bears two signatures purporting to be those of a director and the secretary, or those of two directors, and (b) that it has been delivered as a deed, providing it is clear on its face that it is intended by the signatories to be a deed.

The purchaser will be content, therefore, if he sees a statement in the document that it is signed *as a deed by the company*, and sees accompanying this statement two signatures purporting to be those of directors or director and secretary.

13.4 Variations to our Standard Form of Conveyance

(*a*) *Where the Sale is of an Incumbered Freehold*

Suppose that the contract states that the sale is subject to restrictive covenants contained in a conveyance dated 1 July 1950.

First, the recital as to the seller's ownership should be changed. It should not say that he owns an unincumbered estate. It will instead say something like 'the seller owns the freehold estate in the property hereby conveyed subject as hereafter mentioned, but otherwise free from incumbrances . . .'.

Second, the habendum must be changed. It will now read 'to hold unto the purchaser in fee simple, subject to the restrictive covenants contained in a conveyance dated 1 July 1950, made between Mark Old of the one part and Ian Stone of the other part'. In the case of covenants, there are also often added the words 'so far as the same are valid and subsisting and can be enforced against the land hereby conveyed'.

There are two reasons for listing incumbrances in the habendum. One is that it keeps remembrance of them alive. The other is that it modifies the covenants for title given by a seller who conveys as beneficial owner (see Chapter 19).

It must be pointed out that whether or not the incumbrance is mentioned in the conveyance has no effect on whether or not the incumbrance will bind the purchaser. In the case of the 1950 covenant, its enforceability depends on whether or not it is registered as a D(ii) land charge. If it is not registered it will not bind a purchaser, even though the conveyance is said to be subject to it (but see *Lyus* v. *Prowsa* [1982]). Similarly, if the land were subject to a legal easement, the easement would bind a purchaser because it is legal, and whether or not the conveyance mentions it is irrelevant to the issue.

We have seen that new easements are reserved by the seller in the parcels clause, but note that existing easements burdening the land are mentioned in the habendum. The same point can be made in respect of restrictive covenants. A covenant is not, of course, created by a reservation. It takes the form of a promise, and will be created by a separate clause following the operative part of the conveyance.

Example

1 April 1970 Conveyance from Alice to Beryl. Parcels – except and reserving to Alice a right of light. Covenant clause – Beryl promises Alice to use only as a dwelling-house.

1 April 1990 Conveyance from Beryl to Carol. Parcels – no reservation (unless Beryl *is* reserving a *new* easement). Habendum – subject to easement of light and 1970 covenant. No covenant clause, unless Carol is giving Beryl a *new* covenant.

As soon as you find yourself writing that the property is conveyed subject to covenants, you should also think about the inclusion of an indemnity covenant, whereby the purchaser promises to indemnify the seller against breach of the covenants. The standard conditions will justify the inclusion of an indemnity covenant, and also govern its wording (see Chapter 12).

(*b*) *Sale of Part of the Seller's Land*

The fact that it is a sale of part will cause the following alterations:

(i) The parcels clause:

- particular care must be taken in describing the land conveyed. If a new boundary is to be defined, a plan is probably essential. Great care must be taken if a building is being divided (see *Scarfe* v. *Adams* [1981].

- the contract may justify the inclusion of a reservation or grant of an easement. These new easements will be created in the parcels clause. (This point has already been discussed.)

(ii) The contract may provide for the inclusion of positive and restrictive covenants. The wording of restrictive covenants is discussed in Chapter 12.

(iii) The contract may justify the inclusion of a clause preventing an implied grant of easements.

(iv) The inclusion of an acknowledgement and undertaking. The seller, if selling only part of the land covered by the title deeds, is entitled to, and will, retain the title deeds in his possession. (The normal rule is, of course, that the seller must hand over the title deeds to the purchaser on completion. However, s.45(a) of the Law of Property Act 1925 enables the seller to retain title deeds if they relate to land he is retaining, or to a subsisting trust.) The purchaser may need access to the original title deeds if on first registration the Registrar raises a query as to the accuracy of the marked copies.

When the seller retains deeds, the purchaser is entitled to a written acknowledgement of his rights to have the retained deeds produced and to an undertaking that the seller will keep them safe. This does not depend on any stipulation in the contract. It is a matter of general law.

The seller's acknowledgement, by virtue of s.64 of the Law of Property Act 1925, gives the purchaser the right to ask for the production of the documents covered by the acknowledgement, at the purchaser's expense. This right can be enforced by a decree for specific performance.

The undertaking for safe custody gives the purchaser a right to damages if the documents are lost, destroyed or injured, unless, to quote s.64, this is due to 'fire or other inevitable accident'.

The burden of these obligations runs with the deeds, so it can be enforced against whoever at the time has control or possession of them. The benefit of the obligations runs with the land, so can be enforced by the purchaser's successors (but not by a tenant of the land at a rent).

A person selling as personal representative or as a trustee, or a mortgagee selling under his power of sale, will be prepared to give the acknowledgement, but would prefer not to give the undertaking, because of the possible liability to damages. The refusal is probably pointless, as the seller has the burden of undertakings given by his predecessors. Furthermore, he has no right to refuse the undertaking, although the traditional refusal has been traditionally accepted. Standard Condition 4.5.4, however, *entitles* a fiduciary seller to refuse to give the undertaking.

Section 64 demands that the acknowledgement and undertaking be in writing. They are invariably put in the conveyance itself. The usual wording is 'the seller hereby acknowledges the right of the purchaser to the production of the documents specified in the schedule hereto (the possession of which documents is retained by the seller) and to delivery of copies thereof and undertakes with the purchaser for the safe custody of the said documents'.

This wording actually extends the statutory rights, which do not include the right to take copies. The documents will be described in the schedule by their nature, date and parties, for example:

1 April 1980	Conveyance	Ian Williams (1) Percy Bishop (2)
3 March 1989	Mortgage (with receipt endorsed	Percy Bishop (1) Norward Bank (2)

Section 49 refers to documents. This clearly gives the purchaser the right to an acknowledgement and undertaking in respect of the title deeds. It probably does not cover such things as search certificates, marriage or death certificates, nor is there any reason why a purchaser should want it to do so, as they are documents of public record.

In the absence of an acknowledgement, it seems that there is an equitable right for a person the proof of whose title depends on deeds, to require production of those deeds. Section 45(7) of the Law of Property Act 1925 says that if the purchaser has an equitable right to production of the title deeds, he cannot object to the seller's title on the ground that the seller cannot give him the benefit of a statutory acknowledgement. So suppose, for example, that when Alan sells part of his land to Bill and retains the title deeds, Bill carelessly fails to obtain an acknowledgement from Alan. When Bill contracts to sell to Charles, Charles can demand production of the deed from Alan by virtue of the equitable right, so he cannot say that Bill's failure to get the statutory acknowledgement is a flaw in Bill's title. Bill however, should, have altered standard condition 4.5.4 in the contract or he would otherwise have promised that Charles would have the benefit of a written acknowledgement.

(*c*) *Sale of Part of the Seller's Land when the Title is Mortgaged*

Suppose that Alec owns the whole of Blackacre and it is mortgaged to the Elephant Building Society. He is thinking of selling the north-east corner to Benjie, but Benjie will only buy if he can get the property free from the mortgage. That is no difficulty if Alec has the funds to pay off the entire mortgage debt. If he has not, he must approach the Society and ask if it will release the corner from its security, leaving the rest of Blackacre still subject to the mortgage. If the rest of Blackacre offers good security for the loan, the Building Society may agree, or it may agree in return for receiving part of the proceeds of sale towards reduction of the debt. (If the Society does not agree, there is nothing Alec can do, if he cannot pay off the entire loan. That is why Alec must ensure that the Society will cooperate *before* he enters into the contract.)

In order to release the land from its mortgage, the Society will usually be joined into the conveyance, so the following differences will be made to our conveyance:

(i) the parties will be the seller of the first part, the Building Society of the second part and the purchaser of the third part;
(ii) the recitals will include the statements that the property is mortgaged to the Society, and that the Society has agreed to join in the conveyance for the purpose of releasing the land from its mortgage;
(iii) the operative part of the conveyance will say something like 'the seller as beneficial owner hereby conveys, and the Society *hereby releases* all that property known as . . .';
(iv) the acknowledgement and undertaking clause will read something like:

'The Society hereby acknowledges the right of the purchaser to production of the documents specified in the schedule hereto and to delivery of copies thereof
The seller covenants with the purchaser as to the said documents that as and when any of them come into his possession, he will when requested at the cost of the purchaser or his successor in title execute a statutory undertaking for their safe custody'

What lies behind this clause is the fact that an acknowledgement is only effective if given by the person who then has custody of the deeds, in other words, the Building Society. That is why the Society and not the seller, gives the acknowledgement. The Society will refuse to give the undertaking. This again cannot be given at the moment by the seller, because he does not possess the deeds. Hence the covenant that he will give the undertaking when the deeds return to him, that is, on redemption of the mortgage.

(*d*) *A Purchase by Co-Owners*

If the property is to be owned by more than one person, the conveyance (or perhaps a separate trust deed) must declare how the equitable interest is to be held by them. This may be done, in simple cases, in the habendum. For example, if two people are buying the property, the habendum might read 'to hold unto the purchasers in fee simple as beneficial joint tenants'. If they wish to be tenants in common, the habendum might read 'to hold unto the purchasers in equal shares'. (The creation of shares means that there is a tenancy in common.)

It is clearly important to the purchasers that the conveyance declares how they own the equitable interests. This declaration will be binding on them, and in any later dispute will be decisive as to their ownership. The declaration is also important from the point of view of making title. If one co-owner dies, the declaration of ownership will decide whether the surviving owner can convey the property by himself, or must appoint a second trustee for sale to act with him. Unless there is a declaration that the co-owners held as beneficial joint tenants, no purchaser will be prepared to accept a conveyance from the survivor alone (see Chapter 11).

The purchaser's solicitor needs instructions from his clients as to how they intend to own the equitable interest. A married couple may well choose to own it as joint tenants, as the right of survivorship will ensure that the whole house belongs automatically to the surviving spouse. However, some married couples choose otherwise. Two people joining together to buy a house for the simple reason that neither could afford to buy a house alone, will wish to be tenants in common, so that there will be no right of survivorship. They will not necessarily wish to be tenants in common in equal shares, as the size of the shares should reflect the size of the contributions towards the total purchase price. The size of the shares should always be stated. It is insufficient merely to say that the purchasers are tenants in common.

The co-ownership of the equitable interests will automatically mean that a statutory trust for sale is imposed on the legal estate (see Chapter 11). There is often little point in creating an express trust for sale to replace the statutory trust for sale, although this is frequently done.

A clause is also often inserted increasing the powers of the purchasers (who will be the trustees for sale) to deal with the legal estate. This is because the powers of trustees for sale are limited, and in particular trustees can only mortgage the property if it is to raise money for authorised purposes, e.g. for the improvement of the property. In a simple case, where the trustees and the beneficiaries are the same people, there is no real need for such a clause, as what the owners cannot do as trustees they can do by virtue of their beneficial ownership. A bank or building society does not hesitate to lend money to, for example, a husband and wife on the security of their house, no matter for what purpose they need the money, as the bank looks beyond their ownership of the legal estate, to find that they are the only owners of the beneficial interest. However, this does involve investigation of the equitable interests, so many draftsmen would feel it desirable expressly to extend the powers.

(*e*) *A Sale by a Personal Representative*

If the sale is by a personal representative, the following changes will be made to our form of conveyance:

(i) the recitals will generally explain the seller's ability to convey the legal estate. The facts that will be noted are:

- (aa) that Digby (the deceased) died, the date of his death, and the fact that probate (or letters of administration) was granted to the seller;
- (bb) that Digby at the date of his death, owned the freehold estate free from incumbrances (or as appropriate);

(cc) that the seller has contracted to sell the property to the purchaser;

(dd) there must then be added the recital that the seller has not made any assent or conveyance in respect of this property. This recital gives the purchaser the protection of s.36(6) of the Administration of Estates Act 1925 (see Chapter 10).

(ii) The seller will be retaining the grant, so the conveyance will contain an acknowledgement for production of the grant.

13.5 A Specimen Conveyance of Part

There are now outlined the clauses that might appear in a conveyance of part of the seller's land:

(a) The date of conveyance
(b) The parties. Let us suppose there is one seller and two purchasers.
(c) The standard recitals as to the seller's ownership of the freehold estate, and the contract to convey it to the purchasers.
(d) The operative part:

(i) consideration and receipt clause;
(ii) the fact that the seller conveys, and his capacity;
(iii) the parcels clause;
(aa) the description of the land being conveyed, possibly 'as more particularly delineated and outlined in red on the plan annexed hereto'
(bb) 'together with' existing easements and new easements justified by the terms of the contract.
(cc) 'except and reserving' to the seller any new easements justified by the terms of the contract.
(iv) the habendum, that is, the fact that the freehold is being conveyed, and details of all existing incumbrances. Let us suppose it is said that the land is subject to restrictive covenants created in 1950.

(e) A clause declaring that the purchasers are not by virtue of the conveyance to become entitled to any right to light or air over the land retained by the seller, and any enjoyment of light or air by the purchasers from the retained land is deemed to be had by the consent of the seller.
(f) New covenants given by the purchasers to the seller, or vice versa.
(g) A covenant for indemnity and performance given by the purchasers to the seller in respect of the 1950 covenants.
(h) A declaration by the purchasers that the land has been conveyed to them on trust for sale for themselves as beneficial joint tenants.

(i) A declaration that the purchasers have the same powers of dealing with the land as if they were a sole beneficial owner.
(j) The seller's acknowledgement and undertaking in respect of the deeds retained by him.
(k) A certificate that the consideration does not exceed £30 000.
(l) Execution of the deed by the seller and both purchasers. The signatures will be witnessed.

The provisions of this conveyance should now be clear, but the following points should be noted:

1. Clause e – the purpose of the first part of this clause is to negative any grant of an easement of light or air to the purchasers that might otherwise have been implied into the conveyance, for example by *Wheeldon* v. *Burrows* or by s.62 of the Law of Property Act 1925 (see Chapter 12). It can be included in the conveyance by virtue of a special condition in the contract, or by virtue of standard condition 3.3.2.

   The second part of the clause prevents any future acquisition of an easement of light or air by prescription, because it provides evidence that the receipt of light or air from over the seller's land is by virtue of his written consent, and not as of right. This part of the clause could be included by virtue of a special condition in the contract, but it is doubtful if its inclusion is justified by the standard condition.
2. Clauses h and i create an express trust for sale, declare the equitable ownership, and extend the powers of the purchasers to those of a sole beneficial owner – that is, without restriction. They will not, therefore, have to prove their equitable ownership before borrowing money on the security of the land.
3. In this case, the conveyance has been executed by the purchasers as well as the seller. Although it was said earlier that the execution of the conveyance by the purchaser is not generally necessary, execution of *this* conveyance by the purchasers is important. There are two separate reasons:

   (i) a purchaser should execute a conveyance if he is giving covenants to the seller. If the purchaser does not execute the conveyance, the seller could not bring an action in law for damages for the breach, although the covenant might be enforceable in equity;
   (ii) if there are two or more purchasers, and the conveyance declares how they own the equitable interests, the purchasers should execute the conveyance. If the conveyance is executed, the declaration binds the parties, and will be treated by the courts as being decisive of their ownership. It has been said that if the conveyance is not executed, then a party can give evidence that the declaration is incorrect (see, for example, *Robinson* v. *Robinson* (1976) – but for the opposite view see *In re Gorman (a bankrupt)* [1990]).

4. Notice the traditional order of the clauses. Matters affecting the relationship between seller and purchaser are dealt with first (clauses a to g). Then come the clauses affecting the purchasers *inter se* (clauses h and i).

The acknowledgement and undertaking clause is traditionally the last before the attestation, yielding this place of honour only to the certificate of value. The certificate is of course only included if the purchase price is £30 000 or less.

Workshop

Attempt to solve this problem yourself, then read the specimen solution at the end of the book.

Problem 1

The contract is for the sale of the northern half of Blackacre.

The sellers are Vera Brown and William Brown (her husband). The purchasers are Phyllis and Pauline White, two sisters, who have contributed to the purchase in equal shares, and wish to own as tenants in common. The purchase price is £30 500 of which £500 is being paid for carpets, curtains, and a refrigerator.

The contract incorporates the standard conditions. The special conditions provide that:

1. the sale is subject to restrictive covenants contained in a conveyance dated 19 September 1960 made between Ann Rogers of the one part and Buck Thompson of the other part;
2. the sellers and their successors in title will have the right to walk along the eastern boundary of the plot being sold as a means of access to the southern half of Blackacre, which they are retaining; but they are not entitled to any other right.
3. standard condition 3.3 is excluded;
4. the purchasers will covenant not to build or allow to be built on the land conveyed to them more than one bungalow, and that to be built in accordance with plans approved by the sellers.

List the provisions that should be contained in the conveyance.

---

14 Drafting a Transfer of a Registered Title

14.1 A Transfer of Whole

The form of a land registry transfer is prescribed by the Land Registration Rules 1925. A completed land registry form 19 (transfer of title) would look like this:

HM LAND REGISTRY
Transfer of Whole

County and District or London Borough	Kent, Nineoaks
Title No.	KT 00007
Property	39 Woodbrooke Avenue
Date	19 —

In consideration of SEVENTY SIX THOUSAND POUNDS (£76 000) the receipt of which is acknowledged I AMY BAKER of 39 Woodbrooke Avenue Nineoaks Kent civil engineer as beneficial owner hereby transfer to CATHERINE DOUGLAS of 39 Woodbrooke Avenue Nineoaks Kent market gardener the land comprised in the title above mentioned

Signed as a deed and delivered
by the said Amy Baker in
the presence of: } (signed) Amy Baker
Norma Hopeless
40 Woodbrooke Avenue
Nineoaks Kent

Compare this with the conveyance in section 13.2:

(a) There are no recitals.
(b) The address of the purchaser should be the address at which he will be living after the registration of the transfer (often the address of the property that is being transferred). This is because the address on the transfer is the address that will be entered on the proprietorship register, and that will be the address to which the Registrar writes, e.g. giving warning of the application for entry of a caution.

(c) There is a statement of consideration, receipt clause and statement of capacity. They appear in a transfer for the same reasons as they appear in a conveyance.
(d) There is no parcels clause, nor habendum. These are unnecessary because of the phrase 'comprised in the title above mentioned'. The description of the land being conveyed and the title comes from the register, not from the transfer.

14.2 Variations

(*a*) *A Transfer to Co-Purchasers*

Land Registry form 19(JP) can be used for a transfer to co-owners. It varies from the standard form 19 by adding a clause which says either that the sole survivor of the transferees *can* give a good receipt for capital money arising on a disposition of the land, or alternatively, that he *cannot*. This clause amounts to a declaration as to whether or not the transferees are beneficial joint tenants and will govern whether or not a restriction is put on the proprietorship register (see Chapter 11).

However, while the declaration that the survivor cannot give a good receipt shows that the transferees are tenants in common, it does not establish the *size* of their shares. It is quite possible to declare the size of the share in the transfer, so that the transfer will state, for example that the registered proprietor transfers to Catherine Douglas and Charles Deering 'as tenants in common in equal shares the land comprised in the title above mentioned'. It is then unnecessary to state that the survivor cannot give a valid receipt, as that is clearly evident from the statement that they are tenants in common. However, remember that the transfer is sent to the Registry for registration, and is retained there. It is, therefore, a sound idea not to depend on the transfer for a declaration of the shares, or at least not if they are in any way complicated. A separate document should be signed by the transferees setting out their equitable ownership. This is not sent to the Registry as the Registrar is not concerned with the ownership of the equitable interests. He will merely see the statement in the transfer that the sole survivor cannot give a good receipt for capital money.

(*b*) *Transfer of Part of the Land in the Title*

(i) It is essential for the transfer to describe which part of the land within the registered title is being transferred.

The transfer will read something like 'the land shown and edged red on the annexed plan and known as . . . being part of the land comprised in the title above mentioned'. The Land Registration Rules 1925 require that a plan be used, unless the part being transferred can be clearly defined by means of a verbal reference to the filed plan. If a plan is used in the transfer, it must be signed by the transferor and by or on behalf of the transferee (see rule 98 and Land Registry form 20).

(ii) No acknowledgement or undertaking are required. On completion the seller will hand the purchaser the transfer of part, but not the land certificate, as the seller is retaining some of the land in the title. The seller should, before completion, send his land certificate to the registry. He will be given a deposit number, which he passes on to the purchaser. The purchaser, on applying for registration of his transfer, will quote this number. The transfer and the land certificate will meet at the registry. The seller's register and land certificate will be noted with the fact that the land has left the title, the filed plan will be amended and the land certificate returned to the seller. The part transferred to the purchaser will be registered under a new title number, and the new land certificate relating to that title will be sent to the purchaser.

(iii) A transfer of part may create new easements in favour of seller or purchaser, or new restrictive and positive covenants (see Chapter 12 for the question of their registration).

(*c*) *Indemnity Covenant*

A transfer may contain an indemnity covenant, either because the seller gave positive or restrictive covenants when he bought or because he gave an indemnity covenant. (For disclosure by the register of personal covenants, see Chapter 12.)

14.3 A Transfer of Part

To illustrate the points made, there now follows a form of a transfer of part (based on Land Registry Form 20). It is usually easier when drafting a transfer of part to abandon the first-person approach used in a transfer of whole.

HM LAND REGISTRY
Land Registration Act 1925 and 1971
Transfer of Part of Freehold Land

County	Kent
Title No.	K000007
Property	2 River View Hoo St Werburgh
Date	4 June 19—

1. In consideration of TWENTY EIGHT THOUSAND POUNDS (£28 000) the receipt of which is acknowledged ALEC HERBERT and ANN HERBERT (his wife) both of 2 River View Hoo St Werburgh Kent (hereinafter called the sellers) as trustees hereby transfer to Ian Bigge and Belinda Bigge

(his wife) both of 1 Marshy Close Cliffe Kent (hereinafter called the purchasers) the land shown and edged with red on the annexed plan being part of the land comprised in the title above mentioned

2. The sellers reserve the right set out in the first schedule to this transfer for the benefit of the remainder of the land comprised in the above mentioned title (hereinafter called the retained land)
3. This transfer does not include any right to light or air over the retained land
4. The purchasers jointly and severally covenant with the sellers that the purchasers will at all times observe and perform the covenants contained in the conveyance dated 1 February 1980 referred to in entry number 1 of the charges register of the above mentioned title so far as they are still enforceable against the land transferred hereby and will to the same extent indemnify the sellers against all claims in respect of any future breach of the said covenants
5. The purchasers jointly and severally covenant with the sellers so as to benefit each and every part of the retained land and so as to bind the land hereby transferred and every part thereof into whosesoever hands the same might come to observe and perform the covenants contained in the second schedule hereto
6. The purchasers declare that the survivor of them is entitled to give a valid receipt for capital moneys arising on a disposition of the land
7. It is hereby certified that the transaction hereby effected does not form part of a larger transaction or of a series of transactions in respect of which the amount or value or aggregate amount or value of the consideration exceeds THIRTY THOUSAND POUNDS (£30 000)

The First Schedule
(details of reserved easements)
The Second Schedule
(covenants)

Signed and delivered as a deed by all parties, with each signature attested.

14.4 Using a Form of Transfer for an Unregistered Title

Nowadays, a purchase of an unregistered title will lead to an application for first registration. It is common, but not obligatory, for the purchaser of an unregistered title to draft the conveyance in the form of a Land Registry transfer rather than in the traditional form. There is no point to this unless it produces a simpler, shorter document. It may do this if the purchaser is buying all the seller's land. If he is only buying part so that there are grants,reservations, covenants and other special clauses, the change in form does not necessarily lead to any greater simplicity. If the draftsman does decide to model the deed on a Land Registry transfer, the resulting document will *not* be 'a rule 72 transfer' even though it is commonly called one.

Look again at the conveyance at the start of Chapter 13. If we had decided to draft this document in the form of a transfer, it would say this:

HM LAND REGISTRY

County and District — Kent, Nineoaks
Title No.
Property — 39 Woodbroke Avenue
Date — 19—

In consideration of Seventy Six Thousand Pounds (£76,000) the receipt of which is acknowledged I Amy Baker of 39 Woodbroke Avenue Nineoaks Kent civil engineer as beneficial owner hereby transfer to Catherine Douglas of 39 Woodbroke Avenue Nineoaks Kent market gardener [the freehold property 39 Woodbroke Avenue Nineoaks Kent] or [the property conveyed to myself by a deed dated 4 June 1975 made between Guy Javert (1) and Amy Baker (2)]
Signed (etc.)

Notice that there is no title number, nor is there any reference to 'the land comprised in the title above mentioned', which is replaced either by a traditional parcels clause or by a reference to the conveyance to the seller, this conveyance accompanying the application for first registration.

14.5 Rule 72 of the Land Registration Act 1925

This rule provides that a person who has the right to apply to be registered as first proprietor of the land can deal with the land before he is in fact registered as proprietor in the same manner as he could do if he were registered. So, for example, imagine that Pauline buys an unregistered title in an area of compulsory registration of title. She intends to re-sell to Queenie. She may do so, without herself applying for first registration. However, the document that she uses to convey to Queenie should be in the same form as it would have been had Pauline been a registered proprietor, i.e. it should be drawn up as a land registry transfer, rather than as a conveyance of unregistered land. Of course, it will not be quite the same as a land registry transfer, as no title number can be quoted and the transfer must describe the property rather than referring to it as that comprised in the registered title.

Queenie will then apply for first registration of title, proving by the title deeds that Pauline had the right to be registered as proprietor and also proving by the transfer drawn up under rule 72, her own right to be registered as first proprietor instead.

15 Buying a Leasehold

15.1 Introduction

The procedure for buying or selling a leasehold house differs little from the procedure for buying a freehold house. This chapter, therefore, serves only to point out those parts of a conveyancing transaction which are peculiar to leaseholds, and which have not yet been mentioned. [Note that this chapter is dealing with the purchase of an *existing* lease. The grant of a *new* lease will be dealt with in Chapter 16]

Three topics will be discussed generally first, and then set in the context of the transaction.

15.2 Title to be Shown

(*a*) *What the Purchaser May See*

Unless the contract says otherwise, s.44 of the Law of Property Act 1925 provides that a person who has agreed to buy an existing leasehold is entitled to two things:

1. He is entitled to see the document (i.e. the lease) which granted the estate he is buying. The reasons for this are obvious. The lease must be seen to check that the estate was ever granted in the first place. It must also be seen to discover the terms of the grant, e.g. the covenants, forfeiture clause, etc. Although an open contract allows the purchaser to call for production of the lease, it is a point rarely considered in practice, as a copy of the lease will be provided with the draft contract. No purchaser will contract to buy a leasehold estate without seeing the lease.
2. He is also entitled to evidence that the seller owns the leasehold estate. This is the same as in freehold conveyancing, and the nature of the evidence is the same.

So how will the seller prove his ownership of a lease registered under the Land Registration Act 1925? By providing a copy of the entries on the register, a filed plan, etc., to comply with s.110 of the Act. The fact that the seller is registered as proprietor of the leasehold estate, whether with absolute or with good leasehold title, means that he owns the legal estate. The register may warn us of third-party interests by disclosing a notice, caution, restriction or registered charge. (Remember that the register is not conclusive as to the contents of the lease, so the lease must be seen, as well as the entries on the register.)

Suppose the title is unregistered. Title to an unregistered freehold is proved by producing past conveyances of it. Equally, title to an unregistered leasehold is proved by the production of past conveyances, although for some reason a conveyance of a leasehold estate is usually called an assignment. To take some examples:

(i) Peter is buying a leasehold from Tom. Tom is the person to whom the estate was granted by landlord Len. Peter will see the lease. Tom establishes his ownership of the leasehold simply by the fact that he is the tenant named in the lease.

(ii) Some years later, Quentin is buying the leasehold from Peter. As Peter is not the original tenant he must produce the assignment of the lease into his name. As the assignment was by the original tenant, that is the only document that can be produced.

(iii) Robert is buying from Quentin. Quentin must produce the assignment into his name. If this assignment between Peter and Quentin took place more than fifteen years ago, Quentin need *only* produce this assignment. This is because he has traced title to the lease from a good root at least fifteen years old. So once Robert has seen an assignment that is fifteen years old, he cannot demand to see any earlier ones, as these would be pre-root (s.44 of the Law of Property Act 1925). This will mean that Robert may not know how the leasehold ever came to be vested in Peter.

If the assignment between Peter and Quentin took place less than fifteen years ago, Robert would be entitled to see the preceding assignment, between Tom and Peter. As this is an assignment by the original tenant, investigation would end there.

(*b*) *What the Purchaser May Not See*

Section 44 does not permit the purchaser of a leasehold to demand evidence of any reversionary title. This means that Robert cannot investigate Len's title to grant the lease. This carries considerable risks.

(i) Robert does not know if Len owned the freehold estate, or a leasehold estate, or indeed any estate at all.

(ii) Robert does not know in what capacity Len held the estate. Fiduciary owners such as trustees for sale or a tenant for life under the Settled Land Act 1925 may have only limited statutory powers of leasing.

(iii) Robert does not know if Len's estate was mortgaged when he granted the lease. Section 99 of the Law of Property Act 1925 empowers a mortgagor who is in possession of the mortgaged property to grant a lease which will bind the mortgagee. In other words, the mortgagee will not be able to obtain possession against the tenant, and will only be able to sell subject to his lease. This statutory power is naturally unpopular with mortgagees, and it can usually be, and usually is, excluded by a clause in the mortgage deed. It may either exclude the power altogether, or make it exercisable only with the mortgagee's consent. Either provision ensures that any lease granted by the mortgagor after the date of the mortgage will not bind the mortgagee, unless the mortgagee consents to its grant. A tenant can, therefore, find himself with no security at all should his landlord fail to keep up with the mortgage payments. If the mortgagee wishes to exercise his power of sale he will evict the tenant if a better price could be obtained by selling the property with vacant possession.

So Robert would like to know if Len's estate was mortgaged when he granted the lease to Tom, and if it was, if the mortgagee consented to the grant. Yet s.44 prevents this enquiry.

(iv) As Robert does not know if Len owned the freehold or a leasehold estate when he granted the lease to Tom, Robert does not know if he is buying a headlease or an underlease. If he is buying an underlease, he would like to see copies of the superior leases. This is because Robert does not want inadvertently to break a covenant – for example, a user covenant – in a superior lease. This is explained in Problem 1 in the Workshop section.

(v) Robert does not know if there are third-party rights affecting the superior titles – for example, any restrictive covenant on the freehold, if it is protected by being registered as a land charge D(ii), or by the entry of a notice or caution on the register of title, will bind the tenant or undertenant, as the registration amounts to actual notice (see s.198 of the Law of Property Act 1925, s.50(2) of the Land Registration Act 1925, and *White* v. *Bijou Mansions* [1938]). Yet the registration cannot be discovered, as s.44 prevents investigation of the freehold title.

The risks that s.44 presents do not exist only on the purchase of an unregistered lease. They are the same when buying a registered lease *if* it is registered only with good leasehold title. The title does not guarantee that the landlord had power to grant the lease, nor will it contain details of incumbrances on the superior titles, which may nevertheless bind the purchaser of the lease.

Section 44 has never presented the same risks to a purchaser of a lease registered with absolute title. This class of title follows investigation of all the superior titles by the Registrar. It guarantees that the lease is valid, and incumbrances affecting the superior titles will be noted on the register of title.

N.B. If the landlord's title is registered under the Land Registration Act 1925, the fact that s.44 Law of Property Act 1925 does not compel the seller to give details of the landlord's title to the purchaser is mitigated by the fact that the landlord's register of title is open to public inspection. (Land Registration Act 1988). The purchaser will be able to obtain office copies of the register for himself. The only effect of s.44 will be that the purchaser, rather than the seller, will have to pay for these copies.

Section 44 remains a difficulty if the landlord's title, or, if relevant, any superior title, is not registered.

A public index map search will disclose whether or not the titles are registered, and the title numbers. (See section 6.2.)

(*c*) *A Special Condition in the Contract*

A purchaser can oust s.44 by a special condition in the contract which compels the seller to give details of the freehold title and of any superior leasehold titles. The seller, of course, will not accept the inclusion of such a condition if he has no evidence of the superior titles to supply. The lack of such evidence may discourage a purchaser from entering into the contract, and a mortgagee from lending on the security of the leasehold estate.

15.3 Consent to Assignment

A lease may contain a prohibition against assignment or subletting. If this prohibition is absolute, i.e. it says simply 'no assignment', then assignment cannot take place unless the landlord agrees to waive the covenant, and permit the particular assignment. An assignment without his consent would be valid, in the sense that ownership of the lease would pass, but the proud new owner would probably face a forfeiture action, as it is most unusual for a fixed-term lease not to contain a clause allowing the landlord to forfeit the leasehold estate for breach of covenant.

A lease usually contains a qualified covenant against assignment. It says that the tenant covenants not to assign or sublet *without the landlord's consent*. As soon as the covenant is qualified in this way, a statutory proviso is automatically added, whether the landlord likes it or not, to the effect that the landlord cannot unreasonably withhold his consent (s.19(1) of the Landlord and Tenant Act 1927).

The proviso still makes it necessary for a tenant proposing to assign or sublet to seek his landlord's consent. An assignment made without asking for the consent is a breach of covenant even if the landlord had no grounds for withholding it. If the landlord refuses his consent when asked for it, the tenant must consider the reasons for the refusal. If the landlord has reasonable grounds for refusing, the tenant can do nothing. Any assignment without the consent would be a breach. If the grounds are unreasonable, the tenant:

(a) is now free to assign or sublet without the landlord's consent, and there will be no breach of covenant. The risk is that if the landlord then threatens forfeiture of the lease, the court may disagree with the tenant, and consider that the landlord *was* acting reasonably. In order to persuade a purchaser to buy the lease, the tenant may have to go to court, and obtain a declaration that the landlord's grounds for refusal of consent are unreasonable.

It is outside the scope of this book to consider what may or may not be considered reasonable. An instructive case is *International Drilling Fluids Ltd* v. *Louisville Investments (Uxbridge) Ltd* [1986].

(b) may be able to obtain damages from the landlord. The Landlord and Tenant Act 1988 places a statutory duty on a landlord who is asked for consent to an assignment or subletting to give a decision within a reasonable time, and to give his consent, unless there are reasonable grounds for withholding it.

If the tenant can prove a breach of this duty, he will be able to obtain damages, and an injunction that consent be given. This on the face of it still involves a disappointed tenant in litigation but the hope is that the threat of damages will dissuade a reluctant landlord from acting unreasonably in the first place.

Purchaser's Position

A purchaser of a lease (or a prospective subtenant) will not complete the purchase without the consent of the landlord to the assignment. Ideally, the consent should be obtained before exchange of contracts. However the purchaser and the seller may safely enter into the contract *before* the consent is obtained. Under standard condition 8.3, if the consent is not given by the landlord at least three working days before the contractual completion date, either party can rescind the contract. This means that the contract will be wiped out, no damages will be recoverable by either party against the other, and the deposit will be returned to the purchaser. Of course, this is cold comfort to a purchaser who has already contracted to sell his present house, and such a purchaser would have been better advised to have ensured before contract that the landlord's consent would be given.

The condition places an obligation on the seller to use all reasonable efforts to obtain the landlord's consent and he cannot rescind the contract if he fails in this duty. He would face a claim for damages by the purchaser.

15.4 Breach of Covenants

If the seller of the lease has broken a covenant in it, the purchaser can object to the seller's *title* to the lease. A breach of covenant is a matter of title, because the breach will usually give the landlord the right to forfeit the lease. A title liable to forfeiture is not a good title.

Therefore, strictly, on completion a purchaser is entitled to ask for evidence that the covenants in the lease that he is buying and in any superior lease, have been performed and observed (forfeiture of a headlease leading to forfeiture of underleases). However, s.45(2) of the Law of Property Act 1925 provides a rule of great convenience for the seller. It states that if on completion he produces a receipt for the last rent due before completion under the lease that the purchaser is buying, the purchaser must assume, unless the contrary appears, that the rent has been paid, and all the covenants have been performed, both in the lease that he is buying and all superior leases. Therefore, the purchaser *cannot* ask for evidence that the covenants have been performed and observed, unless there are grounds for suspecting that they have not. One reason for suspecting a breach of covenant by the seller would be the disrepair of the property. However, the purchaser will probably find himself barred from complaining about the seller's breach of the repairing covenants in the lease by the terms of the contract. Standard condition 3.1.3 provides that the purchaser accepts the property in its present physical state. The effect of this when a leasehold is being sold is that the purchaser has no right to complain of the breach of a repairing covenant in the lease. This leads to a consideration of standard condition 8.1.4 and consequent care in drafting the assignment or transfer of the lease (this will be considered later).

15.5 Changes in Procedure

(*a*) *The Property Information Form*

The seller will supply the purchaser with the usual property information form used in freehold transactions, and will also supply the additional information form (part of the protocol documentation) which contains questions peculiar to leasehold sales. They cover areas such as:

(i) *Service charges* On the purchase of a flat (or indeed a suite of rooms in an office block) the lease may provide for each tenant to contribute towards the cost of the maintenance and repair of the common parts of the building, e.g. the entrance hall, stairs, lift, roof, etc.

The payment of the service charges can be as burdensome as payment of the rent, and the amount to be paid is unpredictable, as it will depend from year to year on the amount of repairs to be done and their cost. A service charge is often expressed to be payable as additional rent, so that non-payment may lead to forfeiture of the lease.

A tenant of a residential flat or dwelling is protected against unjustified and excessive claims for such charges by ss.18 – 30 of the Landlord and Tenant Act 1985 as amended by the Landlord and Tenant Act 1987. For the purposes of these sections, a service charge is defined as an amount payable by the tenant of a dwelling for services, repairs, maintenance, insurance, or the landlord's costs of management. The landlord can only recover his costs to the extent that they are reasonably incurred, and if the costs relate to the provision of services or to works, only if the services and works are of a reasonable standard. If the cost of the proposed works will exceed an amount prescribed from time to time by statutory regulations, the landlord must obtain at least two estimates of the cost (one of the estimates must be from a person unconnected with the landlord) and copies of the estimates accompanied by a notice, must be given to the tenants for their comments.

A tenant may require information as to the costs incurred by the landlord. When the information is given, it must be certified by a qualified accountant unconnected with the landlord.

A landlord may ask for service charges to be paid in advance. This enables a fund to be built up in expectation of future repairs. However, a sum can only be requested in advance if there is provision to that effect in the lease, and only to the extent that the sum is reasonable.

The information form will therefore:

(aa) give details of past service charge payments over the previous three years, and copies of all accounts invoices or certificates relating to these payments.
(bb) say if past service charges have been challenged by the seller or his predecessors.
(cc) give details of any substantial expenditure incurred or contemplated by the landlord likely substantially to increase the contribution by the tenants.

On completion, consideration will have to be given to the apportionment of the service charges. Apportionment will be difficult, as the amount to be charged by the landlord may not be known on completion. An apportionment may be made on the basis of the figures for the previous period, with an agreement to readjust when the figures for the current period are known. Otherwise, one party may agree to pay the whole amount for the current period, with the other party promising an appropriate reimbursement.
Standard condition 6.3.5 provides for apportionment on the best estimate available, with a later adjustment.

(ii) complaints by the landlord of a breach of any of the covenants contained in the lease, or complaints by the seller of a breach of covenant by the landlord or management company.
(iii) details of insurance The lease may provide for insurance by the landlord, with the right for him to recover premiums from the tenant, or may require the tenant to insure, possibly with a particular company specified by the landlord. The purchaser's mortgagee will want details of the insurance arrangements to check that they are sufficient to protect his security. If it is a sale of a flat, the landlord will often have arranged a block policy, on which the interest of each tenant will be noted. The purchaser will ask for a copy of this policy, any current schedule to it, and a copy of the receipt for the last premium.
Note: whereas on the sale of a freehold property the seller is under no duty to insure the property, on the sale of a leasehold property

condition 8.1.3 compels the seller to comply with any obligation to insure imposed on him by the lease.

(*b*) *Drafting the Contract*

(i) the seller's solicitor must consider the question of deducing title to the freehold and to any superior leases (see section 15.2).
(ii) the seller's solicitor must consider the need for the landlord's consent to assignment. The landlord will ask for references, and the necessary details of referees should be obtained from the purchaser.
(iii) the particulars of sale will refer to the description of the property in the lease, and a copy of this lease will be supplied with the contract. Standard condition 8.1.2 provides that before the contract is made, the seller must provide the purchaser with full details of the lease. The purchaser is then treated as entering into the contract knowing and accepting the terms of the lease.

(*c*) *Approval of the Draft Contract by the Purchaser's solicitor*

As well as approving the contract, he will also be considering the provisions of the lease, such as the repairing obligations and the outgoings, to check that they will not be too heavy a burden on the purchaser.

The solicitor must consider his client's future plans. If it is a lease of business premises, the solicitor must know what use his client intends to make of the premises. If this will be a change from the existing use, the lease must be checked for any covenant to the effect that the use cannot be changed, or can be changed only with the landlord's consent. In the latter case, there is *no* statutory provision that the consent cannot be unreasonably withheld, so the purchaser must ensure that the landlord's consent is obtained before exchange of contracts.

The lease may also contain a covenant against alterations and additions. If the consent is qualified, i.e. is one not to alter 'without the landlord's consent', the landlord cannot unreasonably withhold his consent but can require that the property be reinstated before the end of the lease. (s.19(2) of the Landlord and Tenant Act 1927.)

(*d*) *The Drafting of the Assignment or Transfer*

This is a form of assignment of an unregistered lease.

This Assignment is made the _ day of __ Between AB (hereinafter called the seller) of the one part and CD (hereinafter called the purchaser) of the other part.

Whereas

(1) By a lease dated 1 September 1986 and made between Mary Short of the one part and the seller of the other part the property known as

1 Shortlands Grove in the City of York was demised to the seller for a term of 50 years from 1 September 1986 at a yearly rent of £104 subject to the performance and observance of the covenants on the part of the tenant therein contained.

(2) The seller has contracted to sell the said property for all the residue now unexpired of the said term at the price of £75 000.

Now this deed witnesseth

(1) that in consideration of £75 000 now paid by the purchaser to the seller, (the receipt whereof the seller hereby acknowledges) the seller as beneficial owner hereby assigns to the purchaser all the property comprised in the said lease to hold unto the purchaser for all the residue now unexpired of the term granted by the said lease subject to payment of the rent reserved by the said lease, and to performance and observance of the covenants on the part of the tenant contained in it.

(2) The covenants implied by the seller assigning as beneficial owner are hereby modified so that it shall not be hereby implied that the covenants contained in the lease and on the part of the tenant to be performed and observed which relate to the repair of the above mentioned leasehold property have been observed and performed up to the date hereof.

In Witness whereof etc.

You can see that is very similar to a conveyance of an unregistered freehold, except, of course, that the recitals and the habendum change. However, clause 2 needs explaining.

As we have seen, by virtue of the standard conditions in the contract a purchaser is not entitled to object to the fact that the seller has broken the repairing covenants in the lease. However, when a seller conveys for value as beneficial owner, there is implied into the conveyance a covenant by him that all the covenants in the lease have been performed (see Chapter 19). Hence the purchaser would be able to sue under the terms of the conveyance when he could not have sued under the terms of the contract. This is why standard condition 8.1.4 provides that the assignment is to record that no covenant implied by statute makes the seller liable for any breach of the lease terms about the condition of the property. This is what clause 2 is doing.

A transfer of a registered leasehold title differs little from a transfer of a registered freehold title. A transfer of a registered lease, by virtue of s.24 of the Land Registration Act 1925 has implied in it a covenant that the transferor has performed the covenants in the lease. This implication is made whatever the capacity in which he conveys. The transfer will therefore contain a clause negativing the effect of s.24 and if necessary the effect of the beneficial-owner covenants, so that no promise is given as to the performance of the repairing obligations. This is again to give effect to condition 8.1.4.

Covenants for indemnity On assignment of a lease, the seller will wish to be indemnified by the purchaser against the consequences of any future breach of the obligations of the lease. Such an indemnity will be implied into a conveyance for value by virtue of s.77 of the Law of Property Act 1925, and in the case of a transfer of registered title, additionally by s.24 of the Land Registration Act 1925. The covenant is not, therefore put in expressly, unless an unregistered lease is disposed of by way of a gift.

(*e*) *The Pre-Completion Searches*

If the lease being transferred is registered with absolute title, the pre-completion search will be made at the District Land Registry, in the same way, and with the same results, as if it were a transfer of a freehold with absolute title.

If the lease being transferred is registered with good leasehold title, then again a land registry search will be made. If the superior titles are unregistered and have not been deduced the purchaser will know the name of at least one superior owner, i.e. the landlord. It is worth making a land-charges search against that name. If the landlord is a freeholder, it might reveal a registration of restrictive covenants. It might also reveal a second mortgage, leading to the query as to whether the lease binds that mortgagee. (It will not reveal a first mortgage, as this will be protected by deposit of title deeds, and not registrable as a land charge). Of course, if the superior titles are unregistered and have been deduced, the land charges search will be made against the names of all the estate owners revealed by the copy documents.

If the lease is unregistered, a land-charges search will be made against the name of the landlord, original tenant, seller and any other estate-owners revealed by the abstract of title to the lease. A search will also be made against the names of superior owners if the superior titles are deduced.

(*f*) *Completion*

At completion, the purchaser of an unregistered lease will pick up the lease, past assignments of it, and the assignment executed by the seller. He may also, if appropriate, pick up the landlord's written consent to the assignment and a marked abstract of the title to the freehold and superior leases. The purchaser of a registered lease will pick up the lease, the land certificate and the transfer executed by the seller. He may also pick up the landlord's consent to the assignment, and if the title is good leasehold, a marked abstract of the freehold title and superior leases.

If the leasehold estate is mortgaged, the purchaser will want a receipt on the mortgage deed or Land Registry form 53 as appropriate, or undertakings in respect of them.

The purchaser will also want to see a receipt for the last rent due (see section 15.4).

(g) *Post Completion*

The purchaser must consider:

(i) Whether the transfer of the assignment needs stamping with *ad valorem* stamps, and a PD stamp (see section 2.17).

(ii) If it is an assignment of an unregistered lease, whether the purchase must be followed by an application for first registration (see section 3.2).

(iii) If it is a transfer of a registered lease, the need to apply for registration of the transfer, before the priority period given by the Land Registry search expires (see section 3.11).

(iv) The assignment of a share in a management company. Where the landlord has let flats, the upkeep of the common parts and enforcement of the covenants of the leases are often managed through a management company, in which each tenant has a share. The share will be transferred on completion and the transfer must then be registered with the company.

(v) Notice of assignment The lease may provide that any assignment of the lease, or mortgage of it be notified to the landlord's solicitors, and a fee paid. A failure to do this will be a breach of covenant.

Workshop

Attempt these two problems yourself, then read specimen solutions at the end of the book.

Problem 1

You act for Pamela who is considering buying a lease from Vera. The lease was made between Len as landlord and Vera as tenant for a term of eight years. It contains

1. a covenant against assignment without the landlord's consent;
2. a covenant against change of use without the landlord's consent;
3. an option for the tenant to renew the lease for a further term of eight years.

The premises are currently being used as an office, but Pamela would like to use it as a shop for selling her designer knitwear.

Consider:

(a) What consents should be obtained before Pamela contracts to buy the premises?
(b) Whether Pamela will be able to exercise the option for renewal?

Problem 2

A leasehold estate of ninety-nine years was granted in 1965 by Lena to Alice. The title to the lease remains unregistered. In 1969 Alice assigned the lease to Beatrice. In 1971 Beatrice assigned the lease to Carol. In 1973, she assigned it to Deirdre. In 1988 Deirdre assigned it to Enid, Enid has just contracted to sell the leasehold to Pamela. What assignments is Pamela entitled to see?

16 The Grant of a Lease

16.1 Procedure

The grant of a lease is often not preceded by a contract that it will be granted. There is then no legal tie between the parties until the leasehold term itself comes into existence. The lease is usually prepared in duplicate, one part being executed by the landlord (the lease), the other part being executed by the tenant (the counterpart lease). The leasehold term comes into existence on the exchange of the two parts.

If there is a contract, standard condition 8.2.6 provides for the seller to engross both lease and counterpart, and to send the counterpart to the purchaser for signature at least five working days before completion.

16.2 Title

(*a*) *A Lease to be Granted Out of the Freehold Estate*

If the title to the freehold is unregistered s.44 of the Law of Property Act 1925 provides that the prospective tenant is not entitled to any evidence of the freehold title. This is really buying a pig in a poke. The same problems arise as have been discussed in 15.2(b). The purchaser may be sinking a large premium into the purchase of a void lease, an encumbered lease or a lease that does not bind the landlord's mortgagee. However, remember that s.44 implies a term into the *contract*. So if the proposed tenant has not entered into a contract to accept the grant of the lease, he is free to break off negotiations for the lease if the landlord refuses details of his title. If there is to be a contract, the tenant must beware of s.44, and must have a condition in the contract promising deduction of the freehold title (see later).

Section 110(1) Land Registration Act 1925 does not apply to the grant of a lease, so if the title to the freehold is registered, the prospective tenant cannot insist that the landlord supply a copy of the entries on his register of title. However, the register of title is public, and a prospective tenant will be able to obtain office copy entries for himself from the Registry.

(*b*) *The Grant of an Underlease*

1. *Out of an unregistered lease* If there is a contract for the grant of an underlease s.44 Law of Property Act 1925 provides that the prospective undertenant is entitled to see

(i) the document creating the leasehold term out of which the underlease is to be granted;
(ii) evidence of the prospective landlord's ownership of the leasehold term (in other words his power to grant the underlease).

He is not entitled to see any evidence of superior titles.

So imagine that Len is the freeholder and Tom is the head tenant. Susan is to be granted an underlease by Tom. Susan is entitled to see the headlease and evidence of Tom's ownership of the leasehold estate granted by it. If Susan later contracts to subunderlet to Ursula, and the contract does not alter the effect of s.44, Ursula may see a copy of Susan's underlease and require Susan to prove her ownership of it (in other words, exactly the same evidence as if Ursula were buying Susan's underlease rather than taking a term granted out of it). Ursula could not ask for a copy of the headlease, nor for proof that Tom had power to grant the underlease; nor can she ask for evidence of the freehold title.

2. *Out of a registered lease* A sensible person would think that the position of a prospective undertenant would be the same, whether his lease was to be granted from an unregistered or a registered lease. A sensible person would be wrong. We have seen that s.110(1) of the Land Registration Act 1925 does not apply on the grant of a lease. It seems that this covers not just the grant of a headlease, but also that of an underlease. So a prospective tenant whose underlease is to be granted from a registered leasehold estate cannot insist on being supplied with either a copy of his landlord's register of title or a copy of his lease. If we look at the previous example, we can see that if Tom's lease were registered and he contracted to grant an underlease to Susan, she could not ask for a copy of the lease Len granted to Tom, nor require Tom to prove his ownership of the leasehold estate. As has been said, she could acquire a copy of the register of Tom's title from the Registry, but not a copy of his lease. The Registry does not always keep a copy of a lease when registering a leasehold title. Even if the Registry has in Tom's case, the lease, unlike the register of title, is not a public document, and the Registry will not supply a copy. A condition in the contract should require Tom to provide an office copy of the entries on his register and a copy of his lease, and possibly to provide evidence of Len's freehold title.

3. *The effect of condition 8.2.4* This alters the statutory rules, as it provides that the prospective landlord (called 'the seller' by the standard conditions) must deduce a title that will enable the prospective tenant (the purchaser) to register his lease at HM Land Registry with absolute title. The condition only applies if the lease is to be granted for a term of over 21 years. The restrictions of s.44 continue to apply to a short lease. What is the effect of the condition?

(i) If the lease is to be granted out of the freehold title, the seller must prove he owns the freehold by supplying evidence of his title in accordance with usual conveyancing practice. So if the freehold is registered, the purchaser must be given office copy entries of the title, or if the freehold is unregistered, a marked epitome and copy title deeds starting with a good root of title at least 15 years old. In both cases, if the freehold is mortgaged, the purchaser must be given a copy of the mortgagee's written consent to the grant of the lease.

(ii) If an underlease is to be granted out of a leasehold estate that is registered with absolute title, the seller has to prove his ownership of that leasehold estate by supplying office copy entries of his title. He must also supply a copy of his lease and, if necessary, the consents of his mortgagee and of his own landlord to the grant of the underlease. He does not have to supply any evidence of the freehold title nor of any superior leasehold title. Remember that the registration of the seller's leasehold with absolute title guarantees its validity, so this is not something that he has to prove.

(iii) If an underlease is to be granted out of a leasehold estate that is registered only with good leasehold title or that is not registered at all, the purchaser must be given not only evidence of the seller's ownership of his leasehold estate but also evidence that his lease is valid. This will mean that the purchaser is entitled to

- Office copy entries (registered lease) or past assignments (unregistered lease – see section 15.2(a)).
- The seller's lease.
- Consent of the seller's mortgagee to the grant of the underlease.
- Evidence of the freehold title. If this is unregisterd, title must be traced from a good root that was 15 years old *when the headlease was granted.* The purchaser wants to check the title of the person who granted the lease, not the title of the current freeholder.
- Evidence of any leasehold title superior to that of the seller. This means copies of the leases themselves and evidence of the ownership of each superior leasehold when the underlease was granted out of it.
- Evidence of any necessary consents by superior landlords to the grants of underleases.

Let us apply this to a simple example(!) Suppose that Ann in 1940 bought a freehold house. The locality of the house did not become a compulsory area until 1991. In 1960 Ann granted a lease of 300 years to Beryl. In 1962 Beryl assigned the lease to Carol. In 1993 Carol is contracting to grant an underlease of the house to Don. If condition 8.2.4 applies, Carol must

- Deduce title to the freehold in order to prove the validity of the headlease. This means providing an examined copy of the 1940 conveyance.

- Provide a copy of the 1960 headlease.
- Prove her ownership of the headlease by producing a copy of the 1962 assignment to her.

Should Carol's solicitor alter the standard condition?

(i) Definitely, if Carol does not possess these examined copies. If she did not insist on being given evidence of the freehold title in 1962, she cannot obtain any evidence now. The condition must be excluded. She must not promise what she cannot perform. The exclusion of the condition may discourage a purchaser from entering into the contract. Beryl suffers now from her carelessness in 1962.

If she did investigate Ann's title, but her copies of the freehold deeds are not marked as having been examined against the originals, she must exclude standard condition 4.2.4 so that she promises only unexamined copies.

(ii) Even if she feels she does have the necessary evidence of title, she might still be unwilling to offer what is in effect a guarantee that if that evidence is sent to the Registry, an absolute title will result. Why should she rather than the purchaser have to evaluate the sufficiency of the evidence? If she feels any doubt on the matter, she could replace the standard condition by a special condition which promises deduction of the freehold title from the 1940 conveyance, but does not promise registration with absolute title.

To end with a more difficult example, suppose that Carol granted the sublease to Don in 1970. After a few years Don assigned his sublease to Ed, and Ed now contracts to grant a sublease out of his own subterm. Ed would have to produce copies of

- the 1940 conveyance of the freehold
- the 1960 headlease
- the 1962 assignment
- the 1970 sublease
- the assignment of the 1970 sublease to him.

16.3 Stamping a New Lease

The lease must be stamped with *ad valorem* stamp duty. This is calculated on the amount of the premium and the rent payable. There will be no duty payable on the premium if the lease contains a certificate that the premium does not exceed £30 000 and the rent does not exceed £300 per annum.

If the lease is granted for seven years or more, the lease must be impressed with a 'particulars delivered' stamp.

The counterpart lease must be stamped with 50p duty.

16.4 Registration

After the lease has been granted, you must decide if the title to the leasehold should be registered under the Land Registration Act 1925. Do you remember the contents of Chapter 3? If not, the points are made again here.

(a) If the landlord's title is unregistered, a tenant who is granted a lease of over twenty-one years should, within 2 months of the grant apply for first registration of the title to the leasehold estate (s.123 of the Land Registration Act 1925). If he can give details of all the superior titles to the Registrar he will be registered with absolute title. Otherwise, he will be registered with good leasehold title. If the landlord then sells his reversion any purchaser of it will be bound by the lease as a purchaser of an unregistered title is bound by all legal estates.

   If the lease is for twenty-one years or less, the title to it cannot be registered.

(b) If the landlord's title is registered, a tenant who is granted a lease of over twenty-one years must apply for registration of his title. This is because it is a registrable dealing with a registered title. If the tenant made a pre-completion search, he should apply for registration before the priority period expires. It is not sufficient that the title to the lease is registered. A notice of the lease should also be entered on the landlord's register, to ensure that if the reversion is sold, the purchaser of it will be subject to the lease. There is no need for the tenant to apply for this entry. It is done automatically by the registry staff, as part of the process of registering the title to the lease.

   There is some dispute as to whether the landlord's land certificate must be put on deposit to perfect the tenant's application. It is clear that if the lease is granted at a rent but without a premium, the application does not have to be accompanied by the landlord's land certificate. This is under the authority of s.64(1)(c) of the Land Registration Act 1925. If the land certificate is not deposited, the Registry will put a notice on the landlord's register. This is an example of how there can be a discrepancy between the register of title and the land certificate. If the lease is granted at a premium, the Land Registry takes the view that the tenant's application for registration is incomplete unless the landlord's land certificate is deposited in the Land Registry, despite the criticism of this viewpoint in the judgements in *Strand Securities Ltd* v. *Caswell* [1965]. It should therefore be agreed between the parties before completion that the landlord will put his certificate on deposit.

(c) If there is no entry on the landlord's title as to the existence of the lease, a purchaser will still be bound by the lease if it is an overriding interest. It may be overriding either under s.70(i)(k) or s.70(i)(g) of the Land Registration Act 1925 (see Chapter 3).

16.5 The Contents of the Lease

If there is a contract that a lease will be granted, standard condition 8.2.3 provides that the lease is to be in the form of the draft attached to the contract. The solicitor for the prospective tenant must, therefore, check that the terms of both the contract and the lease are acceptable before contracts are exchanged. After that date, the tenant will be unable to ask that the terms of the draft lease be altered.

It is outside the scope of this book to consider the drafting of the lease in any detail, but the following is an outline of some of the major matters you should consider when acting on behalf of a prospective tenant of a house or flat.

(*a*) *The Parcels Clause*

If the lease is of a flat or part of a house, the exact boundaries of the flat should be stated in the lease, even to the joists below the floor and above the ceiling. The vertical division of the flat's walls should be clear. This is important as it may determine where the tenant's repairing responsibilities end, and the landlord's (or another tenant's) begin.

You should check that the tenant is given any necessary rights of access, car parking, use of communal garden, etc.

(*b*) *Repairing Obligations*

You must check that the repairing and decorating obligations to be imposed on the tenant are not too onerous. If the lease of a house will contain a covenant by the tenant to do internal and external repairs (or if the tenant of a flat will have to contribute towards the cost of external or structural repairs via a maintenance charge) the tenant should consider having a survey done before he agrees to take a lease on those terms.

If the property is a flat, you must check that the landlord does covenant to repair the exterior and the common parts of the building such as the entrance hall, stairways, lifts, etc. It is true that the cost of doing this will probably be channelled back to the tenant through a service charge, but it is better for a tenant to contribute towards the cost of repairs than face the dilapidation, danger and devaluing of the property if the repairs are not done at all. Check also that the landlord covenants to provide the services for which any service charge will be levied, e.g. central heating.

(*c*) *User*

There are likely to be clauses restricting the tenant to residential use, and preventing immoral use. In the case of a flat, it is important that the landlord promises to put the same covenants in all the leases, and to *enforce* them. Then, indirectly, your client will be able to control the use of the neighbouring flats by suing the landlord if the landlord does not insist on residential use. A lease of a flat may also contain rules about the keeping of pets, playing of musical instruments, etc. These may seem restrictive to your client, but on the other hand they will protect him from the thoughtlessness of his neighbours, provided the landlord promises to enforce the rules. Alternatively, the lease may say that the rules (in so far as they are negative – i.e. what *not* to do) can be enforced directly by tenant against tenant, creating a leasehold equivalent of a development scheme.

(*d*) *Restrictions on Assignment and Subletting*

In a long lease of a house (e.g. ninety-nine years) you may consider it unreasonable for the landlord to restrict in any way the assignment or subletting of the entire house. Even so, the landlord could justifiably:

- Restrict the assignment or subletting of *part* of the house, either by totally forbidding it, or by making it subject to his consent;
- Say that any assignment, even of the whole, in the last, say, seven years of the term must be with his consent. It is important for the landlord that the person who is tenant at the end of the lease be solvent, as it is against him that the landlord will be enforcing the tenant's covenant to leave the premises in repair.

In the case of a flat, the landlord may wish to make a disposal even of the whole of the flat subject to his consent. The character of any proposed assignee and his intended use of the property is important not only to the landlord, but also to the tenants of the other flats in the building.

(*e*) *Insurance*

If the landlord covenants to insure, he should also covenant to use any insurance monies to reinstate the damaged premises.

If the lease is of a flat, the landlord will probably arrange the insurance of the entire building, each tenant promising to reimburse part of the premium. The tenant should check that his interest in the building is noted on the policy.

(*f*) *Forfeiture*

In a fixed-term lease the tenant will have to accept the inclusion of a clause permitting the landlord to forfeit the lease for non-payment of rent or breach of covenant. You should not permit the inclusion of a right for the landlord to forfeit should the tenant become bankrupt, as lenders will not lend on the security of a lease containing such a clause.

(g) *Management Companies*

If a management company has been formed to manage the block of flats, check that the reversions to the leases are vested in the company. If they are, the company is the landlord and there is no difficulty about enforcement of covenants by the tenant against the company nor by the company against fellow tenants. If the company does not own the reversions it is not the landlord. The prospective tenant should ensure that either he becomes a party to a contract with the company or that he will have remedies against whoever is the landlord if the management company does not do its job.

17 Chain Transactions

In domestic conveyancing, the seller and purchaser are likely to be part of a chain. X's purchase depends on his sale as it is the proceeds from the sale of his present house that will be helping to finance the purchase of his new house. The chain presents problems to the conveyancer.

17.1 Drafting the Contract

The following points arise.

(*a*) *The Deposit*

We have already seen in section 5.9 that standard condition 2.2.2 allows the deposit paid to the seller to be used by him as a deposit on his own purchase. The seller should resist any attempt by the purchaser to change that condition.

(*b*) *The Rate of Interest*

As we have seen (in Chapter 5) the contract will provide a rate of interest to be paid in the event of late completion. The interest is paid on the balance of the purchase price by the person responsible for the delay. (See Chapter 18 for further detail). It is desirable, if *possible*, for the interest rate to be the same in all the contracts in the chain. For example, suppose Q is selling Blackacre to R (Contract 1) and at the same time R is selling Whiteacre to S (Contract 2). Both contracts contain the same completion date. Suppose Q fails to complete on the agreed date, but completes ten days later. As a result R completes the sale to S ten days late as well. R is going to have to pay interest to S under contract 2 but is entitled to interest from Q under contract 1. There is no problem for R if the amount he has to pay is roughly the same as the amount he will receive. If the amount that R has to pay to S is more than the interest he will receive from Q, R suffers a loss, which he will have to recover from Q by way of damages for delayed completion.

The problem is that having the same rates of interest in contracts 1 and 2 will not necessarily safeguard R if the purchase prices are substantially different.

On the assumption that it is Q who causes the delay, R is all right if he is 'trading up', i.e. buying a property that is more expensive than the one he is selling. He will be receiving interest on the higher sum, and paying interest on the lower sum.

If he is trading down, and selling his large house to replace it with a smaller one, he will be receiving interest on a lower sum, and paying it on a higher sum.

If it is S who causes the delay, R faces a problem if he is trading up. S will pay him interest on the smaller price, and R will have to pay Q interest on the higher price. The loss would have to be recovered by R claiming damages for delay from S.

Ideally, the contract with the lower price should contain a higher rate of interest to remove this sort of imbalance, but this may not be possible. Assuming that R is trading up, we would want a higher rate of interest in contract 2 than in contract 1. However, if we raise the interest in contract 2 this may produce a rate too high for S to accept. If we decrease the interest in contract 1, this may produce a rate too low for Q to accept. It will certainly become impossible to juggle the rates of interest in this way if there are other links in the chain, at different prices.

(*c*) *The Time for Completion*

The time for completion should also be considered. A special condition can be put in contract 1 that completion takes place before, for example, 11.30 a.m. so that funds can be transferred to finance the purchase in the afternoon. (Remember that standard condition 6.1.2 permits completion at any time up to 2.00 p.m.)

17.2 Synchronisation of Exchange of Contracts

There should be no time-lag between the exchange of the contracts to sell, and the exchange of the contracts to buy, or as little time-lag as is practically possible. Otherwise, the purchaser faces two unpleasant possibilities:

(a) He might exchange contracts on his sale but find that the exchange of contracts on his purchase falls through at the last moment. He then has a choice of temporary homelessness, or delaying completion of his sale beyond the agreed completion date, and so becoming liable for financial penalties (see Chapter 18).

(b) Alternatively, he might exchange contracts on his purchase, and then find that the exchange of the contracts on the sale falls through. This is a worse problem. He might find temporary finance to complete his purchase on time, but bridging loans are expensive. He might attempt to delay completion of the purchase until he has found a new buyer for his own house, but any attempt at delay can be thwarted by the seller serving a completion notice. If completion does not take place by the date specified in the notice the seller can withdraw from the contract, and keep the 10 per cent deposit. So it is probably better for your client to run the risk of having no house than of having two houses, *if* there has to be a risk at all.

A straightforward method of synchronising exchange of contracts is set out in the answer to problem 1 at the end of this chapter, which would be adequate when only two transactions are involved. Undertakings are given in accordance with Law Society Formula A (see section 1.6). If the chain had been longer, this method would not have been satisfactory. For chain transactions the Law Society has recently devised a formula C. Like formulae A and B it rests on undertakings given by solicitors or licensed conveyancers which, as a matter of professional conduct, they have to fulfil.

Formula C works in two stages, cunningly named by the Law Society as Part 1 and Part 2. Imagine a chain of sales. W is selling his home to X. X is selling his present home to Y. Y is selling *his* present home to Z, a first-time buyer. It is Monday. The order of events is as follows:

1. Z's solicitor telephones Y's solicitor. They agree a latest time that contracts can be exchanged that day, say 5.00 p.m. They agree that formula C Part 1 shall apply. This means that each confirms that he holds a part of the contract signed by his client, and Z's solicitor confirms that if Y's solicitor wishes to exchange contracts by 5.00 p.m., Z's solicitor will exchange. Notice the effect of this. Z's solicitor has undertaken that he will exchange contracts today if Y's solicitor wishes it. Obviously Z's solicitor needs his client's authority to give that undertaking.
2. Y's solicitor now telephones X's solicitor. Again they agree that formula C Part 1 shall apply but that the latest time for exchange shall be, say 4.30 p.m. So now Y's solicitor must exchange contracts on the purchase if X's solicitor asks him to do so, before 4.30 p.m. Y's solicitor can give his undertaking, because he knows that if a contract for the purchase is forced on him, he can force the sale contract on Z.
3. X's solicitor now phones W's solicitor. W is at the top of the chain, as he has no related purchase. So exchange between W and X can take place, using formula B.
4. X's solicitor phones Y's solicitor. Part 2 of formula C now applies. It is agreed that each solicitor holds the part of the contract in his possession to the order of the other (so exchange has taken place) and each promises to despatch it to the other today.

   What if Y's solicitor has gone out when X's solicitor tries to phone him? Within Part 1 of the formula is an undertaking by the purchaser's solicitor that he or a colleague will be available until the agreed time, in this case 4.30 p.m. in order to exchange. So Y's solicitor cannot go out, unless his colleague remains in.
5. Y's solicitor now phones Z's solicitor. Part 2 of the formula applies, and contracts are exchanged.

What about the deposit? Formula C envisages a deposit travelling up the chain, so that any deposit paid by Z helps to fund the deposit to be paid by X to W. This is the way it works.

Each contract will contain the standard condition stating that the deposit shall be paid to the seller's solicitor (or licensed conveyancer) as stakeholder, but that the seller may use it to pay a deposit on his own purchase.

Suppose W is selling to X for £80 000, X is selling to Y for £75 000. Y is selling to Z for £60 000. To go through the events again:

1. When Z's solicitor and Y's solicitor speak to one another on the telephone, Y's solicitor will ask Z's solicitor to pay the deposit of £6000 to X's solicitor (Y's solicitor knowing nothing yet of W). The Part 2 undertakings that will be given on exchange of contracts include an undertaking by the purchaser's solicitor to despatch the deposit to the seller's solicitor, or some other solicitor specified by the seller's solicitor to be held in formula C terms (i.e. according to the standard condition that should be in the contract, discussed above.)
2. X's solicitor will ask Y's solicitor, in the course of their conversation, to pay the deposit of £7500 to W's solicitor on the same terms, or to *procure its payment*. An undertaking to that effect will be given on exchange of contracts, in accordance with Part 2 of the formula.
3. On the exchange of contracts between W and X, X's solicitor will undertake that he will send £500 to W's solicitor and ensure that £7500 is sent by Y's solicitor.
4. Y's solicitor will undertake that he will send £1500 to W's solicitor, and procure payment of the remaining £6000.
5. When contracts are exchanged with Z's solicitor, Y's solicitor will now ask him to send the £6000 not to X's solicitor but to W's solicitor.

All these payments should be despatched on the day of exchange. W's solicitor will receive £500 from X's solicitor, £1500 from Y's and £6000 from X's. If the money is not forthcoming from Y's or Z's solicitors X has broken his undertaking to W's solicitor, which is a serious matter. But then Y and Z's solicitors are in breach of their undertakings to X's solicitors.

If the full 10 per cent deposits are not being paid, or if the deposit guarantee scheme is to be used, the undertakings in respect of the deposits will have to be changed.

The deposit held by W's solicitor will be held by him as stakeholder, as there is no related purchase. (If Z had been paying more for Y's house than Y was paying for his, so that Y was receiving a deposit larger than he needed for his related purchase, the excess would be held by Y's solicitor as stakeholder.) You must realise that if Y delays in completion of the sale, perhaps because there is something wrong with his title, so that Z discharges the contract by a completion notice, Z has no claim against the deposit held by W's solicitor. Z's deposit was paid to Y (no matter how Y may have utilised it) and must be recovered from him.

17.3 The Transfer of Funds

Funds can be transferred from the sale to the purchase by split banker's drafts. (A banker's draft is an order by a bank to itself to pay the stated sum to the payee named in the draft. It is inconceivable that a bank would dishonour its draft.)

Suppose that the solicitors for Q, R and S all have offices in the same town.

Q is selling his house to R for £40 000. It is mortgaged to B Building Society, and the redemption money needed is £15 000.

R is selling his present house to S for £34 000. R's house is mortgaged to C Building Society for £14 000. S's solicitor can arrive at R's solicitor's office with banker's drafts, one for £20 000 and one for £14 000.

R's solicitor sets the £14 000 draft aside for C Building Society, and hastens off to the offices of Q's solicitor. He takes with him the draft for £20 000 which he will endorse over to Q's solicitor, plus a second draft for £20 000.

Exciting manoeuvres such as these are becoming increasingly rare, as completions by post become the normal thing (see section 2.15). Funds are telegraphed from one solicitor's bank account to another solicitor's bank account, through the Clearing House Automated Payments System.

17.4 The Client's Finances Generally

Your client's finances should be checked at an early stage before he is committed to any contract. The object is to contrast what he will have coming in to finance the purchase, with the total cost of the purchase. If the former is less than the latter, the result, as foreseen by Mr Micawber, will be misery. So do this sum.

Coming in

A *Net* proceeds of sale, i.e. contract price *less*:

(i) money needed to redeem first mortgage. Obtain an approximate redemption figure now from the lender.
(ii) money needed to redeem a second or later mortgage. The possibility of a second mortgage should be checked. Your client may forget to tell you about it, or may not have realised the significance of the piece of paper he signed some time ago. A search of HM Land Registry or the Land Charges Registry should be made if there is any doubt.
(iii) solicitor's fees and disbursements.
(iv) estate agent's fees.

B *Net* loan to be secured by mortgage. Check the amount offered, and deduct

- any arrangement fee.
- in the case of an endowment mortgage, the first premium on the life policy, if this is payable on completion.
- any retention money. If the lender wants substantial work done to the property, the practice is for part of the loan to be withheld until the work is done. The borrower cannot usually do the work before completion, for the simple reason that he has not got possession of the house, so he will have to budget without that part of the loan. He should also consider whether he will have the money to do the work after completion. If the work to be done is minor, the lender will not make a retention, but the borrower may have to undertake to do the work fairly soon after completion, and again he should consider whether he will have the money to do it.
- any legal fees.
- any other payment indicated by the lender. Some lenders deduct the first month's payment of interest.

C Other sources – e.g. client's savings.

Going out

Purchase price, plus:

- solicitors fees and disbursements, including Land Registry fees and search fees;
- stamp duty if the consideration is over £30 000;
- money for all the general expenses like removal costs.

Workshop

Attempt these problems yourself, then read the specimen solutions at the end of the book.

Problem 1

(This is based on the 1983 Law Society examination question.)

You have been instructed by Mr John and Mrs Arabella Archer to act for them in connection with their sale for £40 000 of 5 King Street, Ledsham. You have also been instructed to act for them in the purchase for £60 000 of 'Greenbank', Juniper Close, Ledsham, and you have been instructed by the West Kirby Building Society to act for

them in connection with the mortgage advance on 'Greenbank' and the discharge of the mortgage on 5 King Street. The offer of advance from the Building Society states that it is willing to lend £32 000, but subject to a retention of £2000 until the house has been rewired, and a new damp course put in.

The draft contract for the sale of 5 King Street has been approved by the purchaser's solicitors who have just informed you that their client is now ready to exchange contracts. You have obtained the title deeds to 5 King Street from the Building Society, and they include the first mortgage to the Society, and a notice of a second mortgage to Grasping Bank plc. Your clients inform you that approximately £10 000 is owing on the first mortgage and that the second mortgage to the Bank is security for various loans made to Mr Archer's business. You have established that the second mortgage to the Bank has been registered as a Class C(i) land charge.

What advice would you give your clients regarding the financial arrangements? Is it necessary for you or your clients to make any further enquiries or arrangements regarding the financial aspects of either transaction before exchange of contracts?

It is necessary that exchange of contracts on both sale and purchase be as simultaneous as possible. Explain how this can be achieved in view of the fact that all the firms of solicitors involved are some distance from each other.

Problem 2

You are acting for Mr Fawkes who is selling his house called The Plot, and buying a house called The Tower. He has arranged a loan from the Parliamentary Building Society (for which you will also be acting), and that and the net proceeds of sale of The Plot will ultimately finance the purchase of The Tower. However, although the purchaser of The Plot is prepared to exchange contracts now, he will not agree to a completion date earlier than three months away. As Mr Fawkes wishes to buy The Tower immediately, he has arranged a bridging loan from his bank. The bank will require an undertaking from you to pay the proceeds of the sale of The Plot into Mr Fawkes's account to discharge the loan.

You have received the deeds of The Plot, and you have noticed that the house is owned jointly by Mr Fawkes and his wife.

Mr Fawkes tells you that nearly all the proceeds of sale will be needed to pay off the bridging loan, but says that his wife accepts this and wishes you to act for her as well as himself in connection with the sale.

Will you accept the instructions to act for Mrs Fawkes? What advice will you give, either to her or to Mr Fawkes, and to the Building Society concerning the arrangements? How will you word the undertaking to the bank?

Problem 3

(This is based on the 1984 Law Society examination question.)

Samuel Savage and his wife Sara instructed you some days ago that they wished you to act in the sale of their present property, 22 Mount Road, Mixford. Your clients have come to see you again, and on this occasion they are accompanied by Mr and Mrs Coward who are Sara's elderly parents. Mr and Mrs Savage inform you that they have received two firm offers of £25 000 for Mount Road, and Mr and Mrs Savage and Mr and Mrs Coward inform you that they also wish you to act for them in connection with the purchase by them all of 'The Knoll', 2 Little Acre, Southmaster, Loamshire for £72 000.

Mr and Mrs Coward are retired, and have no property to sell. They live mainly on the income from £50 000, their life savings. They had intended to move to a private nursing home and use their savings to pay the fees, but their daughter has offered to look after them if a suitable house can be found to accommodate both families. The Knoll is a large detached house and the two couples intend to convert the property into two separate flats. Mr Coward tells you that he thinks the cost of conversion will be about £5000 and that he and his wife will bear all this cost, and in addition they have agreed to contribute £40 000 towards the purchase price. Both Mr and Mrs Coward have made Sara a beneficiary under their wills. After the purchase of The Knoll they wish Sara to remain the only person who will benefit from their death. Mr and Mrs Savage are to raise the balance of the purchase price of £32 000 and to pay all the legal costs and disbursements, and have agreed to make all payments due under any mortgage which may be required to raise this sum. Mr and Mrs Savage expect to receive approximately £7000 as the net proceeds of their sale after repayment of the outstanding mortgage and all the expenses of these transactions. Mr and Mrs Savage and Mr and Mrs Coward have received an offer of advance of £25 000 from the Omega Building Society, and the Society have instructed you to act in connection with the mortgage advance.

(a) Explain to Mr and Mrs Savage and Mr and Mrs Coward whether or not you can act for all four of them.
(b) Explain whether the intended financial arrangements are satisfactory and whether any further information is necessary.
(c) Explain whether the interests and wishes of either couple need protection or explanation, and if so, what steps are recommended by you.

18 Remedies for Breach of Contract

18.1 Introduction

Either seller or purchaser may fail to meet his obligations under the contract. The seller may fail to show the good title he has promised; may be found to have wrongly described the land in the contract; may not be ready to complete on the agreed date. The purchaser may fail to find the money in time for completion.

We are assuming, therefore, in this chapter, that completion has not taken place, and that one party has established that the other party has broken a term of the contract. What remedies has the injured party?

As in any contract, the remedies for the breach will depend on the gravity of the breach.

(a) A breach may be so serious that it gives the right to the innocent party to treat the contract as discharged by the breach. The choice is the innocent party's. He may decide to continue with the contract and confine his claim to damages. If he does decide to treat the breach as discharging the contract, and tells the other party of his decision the contract is terminated as regards future obligation of both parties. So the purchaser is released from his obligation to buy, and the seller can now sell the house to someone else. It is not discharged as regards responsibilities that have already arisen. This is why a seller who elects to treat a contract as discharged can sue to recover any part of the deposit not paid on exchange of contracts (see *Dewar* v. *Mintoft* [1912] approved in *Damon Cia Naviera SA* v. *Hapag-Lloyd International SA* [1985]). The discharge of the contract can also be accompanied by a claim for damages.

(b) If the breach is not considered by the court to be sufficiently serious to enable the innocent party to treat the contract as discharged, he can only claim damages.

18.2 Assessment of Damages

Damages for breach of contract are designed to put the innocent party in the same position as if the contract had been performed. However some loss suffered may be irrecoverable, as being considered too remote from the breach. The rule governing remoteness of damage for breach of contract is *Hadley* v. *Baxendale* (1854). The innocent party can recover loss that arises naturally from the breach (i.e. that anyone could reasonably have contemplated arising), and loss that was actually in the contemplation of the parties at the time the contract was made.

Let us look at this from the seller's point of view. He may be able to claim loss of bargain. This would arise if the contract price was £80 000, but the property was worth only £76 000. He would have lost £4000. Remember, however, that he will be entitled to treat the deposit as forfeited. The deposit of £8000 will be set against any loss he suffers. (Note that s.49(2) of the Law of Property Act 1925 empowers the court to order a seller to repay the deposit to the purchaser and will apparently do so if that would be the fairest course – see *Universal Corp* v. *Five Ways Properties Ltd* [1979].)

If the property were worth only £70 000 the loss of bargain would be £10 000, so he could claim £2000 actual loss, having taken into account the forfeited deposit.

Common-law damages are usually assessed at the date of the breach, so the value of the property at that date will be used in the calculation. However, in *Johnson* v. *Agnew* [1980] this was said not to be an invariable rule, and circumstances may lead the court to consider that a different date would be fairer. In the case, the purchaser obtained a decree of specific performance, which proved to be unenforceable, as the seller's mortgagees sold the property to someone else. The purchaser returned to the court, and asked for an award of common-law damages. Damages were awarded, assessed on the value of the property at the date the decree proved to be unworkable.

It may not be possible for a seller to prove loss of bargain, because the property has been steadily appreciating in value. He can then claim wasted conveyancing expenses, e.g. legal fees incurred both before and after contract. He cannot claim both loss of bargain and wasted conveyancing costs, as the costs would have been necessary to secure the bargain.

Looking at it from the purchaser's point of view, we can see that the purchaser will be entitled to the return of his deposit, and can claim either loss of bargain, or wasted costs. Suppose that the purchaser was a developer, buying the land with a view to building on it, and then reselling land and house at a large profit. Can the developer recover this profit? The profit will not be treated as loss flowing naturally from the breach (*Diamond* v. *Campbell-Jones* [1961]) and so can only be recovered if the seller knew when the contract was made of the purchaser's intention to develop. Damages will be given to compensate the purchaser for the profits that both parties contemplated he would make (*Cottrill* v. *Steyning and Littlehampton Building Society* [1966]).

18.3 The Seller Breaking his Promise as to Title

Damages for this particular breach used to be limited by the rule in *Bain* v. *Fothergill* (1874). This rule was abolished by the Law of Property (Miscellaneous Provisions) Act 1989, and damages are now assessed as they are for any other breach, under the rule in *Hadley* v. *Baxendale* (1854).

18.4 Misdescription

A misdescription occurs when the property is not as described on the face of the contract. There is clearly a breach of contract as the seller will not be able to convey what he has promised to convey. Usually, the misdescription will be as to the physical characteristics of the property, e.g. a misstatement of the area, or land that is not suitable for development because of an underground culvert being described as valuable building land (re *Puckett and Smith's Contract* [1962]). It can, however, also be of title, as when a sublease is wrongly disclosed as a headlease (re *Beyfus and Master's Contract* (1888)).

In an open contract, the purchaser's remedies depend on whether or not the misdescription is considered to be 'substantial'. The classic definition of a substantial misdescription comes from *Flight* v. *Booth* (1834) which defines it as one that so far affects the subject matter of the contract that 'it may reasonably be supposed that, but for such misdescription, the purchaser might never have entered into the contract at all'. (In the case, a lease was described in the contract as prohibiting offensive trades. In fact it prohibited many inoffensive trades as well, including that of vegetable- and fruit-selling, a serious matter, as the shop was in London's main vegetable market. The misdescription was substantial.)

If the misdescription is substantial, the purchaser can escape the contract. He can claim his deposit back, and specific performance will not be awarded against him. If the purchaser wishes to continue with the contract, he can ask for specific performance at a reduced price. If the misdescription is insubstantial and not fraudulent, the purchaser can only claim a reduction in the purchase price by way of damages. He is not released from the contract.

Standard condition 7 restricts the remedies available for misdescription. It has been held (see, for example, *Flight* v. *Booth* (1834)) that no exclusion clause can prevent a purchaser escaping from the contract if the misdescription is substantial. The standard condition does not attempt to do this, as it permits the purchaser to rescind the contract if the error is due to fraud or recklessness, or if the property differs substantially from what the misdescription led the purchaser to expect and the difference prejudices him. The condition also permits the seller to rescind the contract if there is a substantial difference prejudicial to him, but favouring the purchaser. The seller can thus escape a decree of specific performance, but will not escape liability for damages.

Whether or not the contract is or could be, rescinded, a 'material' difference between the property as described and as it is will entitle the affected party to compensation. The condition differentiates between 'substantial' differences, and 'material' ones, so that some errors will lead to a claim for compensation, because material, but will not justify rescission, because not substantial. 'Material' is not defined. The provision for compensation means that just as the purchaser is entitled to a reduction in the price if the property is worse than as described, the seller is entitled to an increase if the property is better than its description. So a purchaser who finds he is getting more than he expected must either pay compensation, or refuse to accept a conveyance on the ground that the difference is substantial.

18.5 Delayed Completion

(*a*) *Specific Performance*

(i) *The nature of the remedy* A party who wishes to force completion through, despite the reluctance of the other party, can apply to the court for a decree of specific performance. This decree, if obtained, will order a reluctant seller to execute a conveyance to the purchaser, or will order the reluctant purchaser to pay the agreed purchase price. It is particularly a purchaser's remedy. If the seller refuses to complete as agreed, the purchaser may be able to treat the contract as discharged, and recover damages for breach of contract, but this is cold comfort for a purchaser who wanted the house rather than compensation for failure to get it. A decree of specific performance will secure the house itself. If the seller refuses to comply with the order to convey, the court can order someone to execute the necessary conveyance on his behalf, or can make an order automatically vesting the property in the purchaser.

A seller who is faced with a reluctant purchaser may not want a decree of specific performance. He can, instead, after service of a completion notice treat the contract as discharged, and treat the deposit as forfeited. He may then be able to resell at the same or a higher price, or if forced to sell at a lower price, recover compensation from the purchaser. The occasion when a seller would consider specific performance is when he has succeeded in selling a white elephant which he sees little chance of selling to anyone else.

(ii) *A discretionary remedy* Specific performance is an equitable remedy, and the court has therefore, a discretion as to whether or not to award it. However, in the case of a contract for the sale of land, the decree will be awarded as a matter of course, unless there are special circumstances. Factors which might lead a court to refuse the decree include:

(aa) impossibility of performance. The court will not order the seller to convey the property if he has already conveyed it to someone else.

(bb) The badness of the seller's title. If the seller is in breach of contract because his title is bad, he cannot obtain specific performance, because he cannot fulfil his own part of the contract. However, it may be that the purchaser agreed in the contract not to raise requisitions on the title. As we have seen, such a condition is valid provided the seller fully disclosed any defect known to him, so the purchaser should complete, notwithstanding the fact that the title is defective. If the title is totally bad, however, equity will not force the purchaser to accept a conveyance. The purchaser does not thereby escape common-law damages. If the title, although defective, seems to offer the right to undisturbed possession the seller will be granted the decree (see Re *Scott and Alvarez's Contract*, *Scott* v. *Alvarez* [1895]).

(cc) Delay. A plaintiff who is tardy in applying for the decree may be refused it, certainly if the delay has prejudiced the defendant.

(dd) Hardship. The decree may be refused if to grant it would cause undue hardship to the defendant. Usually, the court will only consider hardship that arises from circumstances at the time the contract was made, or from its terms. In *Wroth* v. *Tyler* [1974] for example, the purchaser failed to get the decree, because the seller could only comply with the contractual promise of vacant possession by litigating against his own wife for the discharge of her rights of occupation under Matrimonial Homes Act 1983. The outcome of the litigation would be uncertain and unlikely to have an improving effect on the marriage.

Hardship arising from a change in circumstances after the contract was made is not usually considered – for example, the fact that the purchaser has lost his money. This is not an absolute rule, and was not applied in *Patel* v. *Ali* [1984] where the grave illness of one of the sellers arising after the date of the contract would have had meant great hardship had she been compelled to move from her home, and specific performance was not, therefore, awarded against her.

(iii) *Failure to obtain a decree* A plaintiff who is refused the decree may still be able to pursue the common-law remedies e.g. common-law damages for breach of contract. Alternatively, if the plaintiff had a proper case to apply for the decree, but the court refuses it – for example, because of hardship to the defendant – the court can order what are often known as 'equitable damages' which are in substitution for the decree (s.50 of the Supreme Court Act 1981.) These damages were awarded in the case of *Wroth* v. *Tyler* [1974]. In that case, the damages were assessed on the value of the house at the date the decree was refused, rather than the date on which the contract was broken; a logical choice as the damages were to compensate for not obtaining the decree. It resulted in a substantial increase in the size of the award, as the value of the house had been increasing throughout the litigation.

(iv) As has been said, enforcement by the purchaser is comparatively easy, as the court can order transfer of ownership to him. It is not so easy for the seller to enforce the decree. He has in some way to obtain the purchase price. The methods available to any judgement creditor are available to him. He may proceed against other property of the purchaser, or may present a petition for the purchaser's bankruptcy.

When the seller realises that the purchaser is not prepared to comply with the decree he may regret his choice of remedy. If so, he can return to court, and ask it to terminate the contract as having been discharged by the purchaser's breach, and to award common-law damages for breach of contract (see *Johnson* v. *Agnew* [1980].)

(*b*) *Completion Notice*

(i) Any delay in completion, even a single day, is a breach of contract. However, delay in itself is not necessarily a breach that is sufficiently grave for the non-delaying party to claim that the contract has been discharged.

Time of the essence If time is 'of the essence of the contract' any delay is a sufficiently serious breach to lead to termination of the contract. Time will only be of the essence if a special condition in the contract makes it so, or if it is made so by implication. The fact that the sale is of a wasting asset, so that delay affects its value, would lead to such an implication.

Time not of the essence In such a case, the delay must be unreasonably long if it is to lead to the right to treat the contract as discharged.

The difficulty is in establishing whether or not the delay is unreasonable. The unreasonableness of the delay is traditionally established by the service of a completion notice by the innocent party on the guilty party. Under an open contract, the rule is that the innocent party can serve a notice at any time after the agreed completion date has passed demanding completion on a date that is a reasonable time from service of the notice (*Behzadi* v. *Shaftesbury Hotels* Ltd [1991] 2 All ER 477). The new date is 'of the essence' in the sense that if completion does not take place then, delay has been established as unreasonable, and sufficient to discharge the contract.

In view of the uncertainty as to the calculation of a reasonable period, it is not surprising that the conditions in a contract provide for the service of a contractual completion notice.

Standard condition 6.8 provides that if the sale is not completed on the agreed date, then either party, provided he is himself ready able and willing to complete, can at any time on or after that date give the other party notice to complete. It then becomes a term of the contract that completion will take place within ten working days of the giving of the notice, and that time shall be of the essence in respect of that period.

(ii) *Its validity*

(aa) The notice is only valid if the person serving it is himself ready to complete the transaction. A person is ready to complete if there are only administrative matters to finish, such as the preparation of a completion statement or the execution of a conveyance. He is not able and ready to complete if there are matters of substance still to be dealt with, so a seller who has not shown good title cannot serve a valid notice. (These examples are taken from the case of *Cole* v. *Rose* [1978].)

(bb) A notice to complete must be clear and unambiguous and leave no reasonable doubt as to how and when it is to operate. (*Delta Vale Properties Ltd* v. *Mills and ors* [1990]). It need not, however, specify an exact date for completion. A letter requiring the recipient to 'treat this letter as notice to complete the contract in accordance with its terms' has been held to be sufficient (*Babacomp Ltd* v. *Rightside Properties Ltd*) [1974]. It is probably better not to specify the date on which the period for completion expires, in case the wrong date is specified. If this misleads the recipient of the notice, the notice may be declared void.

(iii) the completion notice makes time 'of the essence' for both parties, not just for the party who served the notice. In *Finkielkraut* v. *Monahan* [1949] the completion notice was served by the seller, but it was the seller who failed to complete on expiry of the notice. It was held that the purchaser could treat the contract as discharged, and recover his deposit.

The recipient of the notice need not wait to complete until the last day of the specified period. He can complete on any day before the period expires, so can choose whatever date is convenient to himself. However, it seems that any date chosen within this period is not of the essence for either party. It is only the final expiry date of the period that is of the essence (*Oakdown Ltd* v. *Bernstein & Co.* (1984)). For example, if the ten-day period under the standard condition expires on 1 April and the notice is served by the seller, the purchaser can say that he intends to complete on 27 March. If completion does not take place on that day, neither party could treat the contract as discharged, as the obligation of both parties remains that of completing on or before 1 April.

(iv) *Remedies for non-compliance with completion notice*

(aa) Non-compliance by purchaser The seller can forfeit the deposit, and is free to sell the property to someone else. Any loss incurred on the resale can be recovered as damages, a point repeated by standard condition 7.5.2.

(bb) Non-compliance by the seller The purchaser can recover his deposit, (and, under standard condition 7.6.2, interest on it) and can also recover any loss caused by the seller's breach of contract.

(v) *Use of the completion notice* The true function of the completion notice is to establish a ground on which the contract can be treated as discharged by breach. It is not designed to force an unwilling party to complete, although it is often used as such, in the sense that, say, a purchaser serves a completion notice in the hope that the seller will be forced to complete for fear of losing the contract. If the seller is undismayed, and still refuses to complete, the notice has achieved nothing if in fact the purchaser still wants to buy the property.

The remedy to be used against a seller who is unwilling to complete at all is specific performance. Application for a decree may be made as soon as the agreed completion date has passed, whether or not time is of the essence. Indeed, application for a decree can be made before the completion date has arrived, if the seller has already indicated that he does not intend to complete the sale (see *Hasham* v. *Zenab* [1960]).

(*c*) *Compensation for the Fact that Completion has Taken Place Later Than Agreed*

Damages To repeat, any delay is a breach of contract. So if completion takes place, but later than agreed, the innocent party can claim damages from the guilty party, even though time is not of the essence. This was established in the case of *Raineri* v. *Miles* [1981]. Suppose that Alan has contracted to sell Blackacre to Bill, and that Bill has contracted to sell his existing house, Whiteacre, to Charles. If Alan delays completion, Bill will either have to live in a hotel, or delay in completing the sale to Charles, so becoming liable to Charles for damages (or possible interest, see later). The expense to which Bill is put can be recovered by him from Alan. If it is Charles who delays completion, Bill will either have to obtain a bridging loan, or delay the purchase from Alan, becoming liable to Alan for damages or possibly interest. Bill can recover this expense from Charles.

Interest Standard condition 7.3.1 obliges the party responsible for the delay in completion to pay interest at the contract rate on the purchase price (or, if it is the purchaser paying interest, on the price less the deposit). The condition does not remove the right to claim damages for the delay, but any claim must be reduced by the amount of interest paid under this condition.

Workshop

Attempt this problem yourself, then read the specimen solution at the end of the book.

Problem

(This question is based on a question in Law Society Summer 1980 paper.)

You are acting for Green who has contracted to purchase a dwelling-house number 27 Leafy Lane from Black. The contract includes the standard conditions of sale. He has also contracted to sell his present house with completion on the same date, and this contract also incorporates the standard conditions. Black has gone abroad and will not return for another three months. The contract has been signed by his attorney White who is appointed by a power of attorney dated 31 March 1990 in the form set out in the Powers of Attorney Act 1971.

(a) Can White execute the conveyance? What special documents would you require White to hand over on completion?
(b) A few days before completion, your client tells you that he has heard from White that Black has been killed in an accident. He is concerned that there should not be any delay in completing the purchase and asks what will happen now. Advise Green whether White can complete the sale, and if not, what steps will have to be taken to enable completion to take place.
(c) Assuming there is a delay in the completion of either transaction:
    (i) explain the rights which Green's purchaser will have;
    (ii) what will Green's own rights be under his contract to buy number 27 Leafy Lane?

19 Remedies Available to the Parties after Completion

19.1 For Breach of Contract

(*a*) *Open Contract*

The principle is that on completion of the sale, the contract ceases to exist. It is said to 'merge into the conveyance'. It has been discharged through its performance.

If the sale is of registered title, it is not clear whether the merger takes place on completion (at which point the seller has fulfilled his contractual obligations) or when the transfer is later registered, (which is the point at which the legal estate vests in the purchaser).

If the contract has ceased to exist, there cannot be an action brought on it. So, after completion, it is generally speaking impossible for a disappointed purchaser to sue for breach of contract. However, some terms of a contract do survive completion, and do, therefore, continue to offer a purchaser a remedy. The principle is that a condition will survive if that is what the parties intended. Examples are:

(a) *The promise for vacant possession* This promise must survive completion, as it is only after completion that a purchaser will discover that it has been broken. In *Beard* v. *Porter* [1948] the seller was unable to give vacant possession on completion, because of his inability to evict a tenant. The purchaser nevertheless completed the purchase. He was awarded damages which consisted of:

- (aa) the difference between the purchase price, and the value of the house subject to the tenancy;
- (bb) payment for somewhere to live until a second house was bought;
- (cc) legal fees and stamp duty connected with the purchase of the second house.

(b) *An express condition* giving the right to compensation for misdescription (*Palmer* v. *Johnson* (1884)).

(c) *A promise by the seller* to build a house on the land (*Hancock* v. *B.W. Brazier* (Anerley) Ltd [1966]).

(d) *Possibly, damages for late completion* This was stated to be the case in *Raineri* v. *Miles* [1981] although in that case the plaintiff had issued his writ for damages before completion took place.

(*b*) *Standard Condition 7.4*

This says that completion will not cancel liability to perform any outstanding obligation under the contract. Clearly this means that if there is any sort of financial obligation or any work to be done on the house, there will be a remedy for breach of contract even after completion, if the obligations are not met. Indeed, as regards compensation for late completion or apportionment of outgoings, these sums are by standard condition 6.4 made part of the amount to be paid on completion, so that if the purchaser does not add these amounts to the purchase price and proffer them on completion, the seller can refuse to complete

The effect of condition 7.4 does not seem clear if it is a defect in title or an undisclosed incumbrance that is discovered after completion. Are promises as to title that are not satisfied by the conveyance or transfer outstanding contractual obligations? If they are, the condition has completely overturned the open contract position.

19.2 On the Covenants for Title

(*a*) *The Right to Sue on the Covenants*

The right to sue on the contract, lost through merger, is said to be replaced by a right to sue on the conveyance, i.e. on the covenants for title implied into it. Much can be written about these covenants, but little is going to be written here, as the main point of the following paragraphs is to show how rarely these covenants will provide an effective remedy for a disappointed purchaser.

(i) *The beneficial owner covenants* By virtue of s.76 of the Law of Property Act 1925, when a seller 'conveys and is expressed to convey' a freehold estate as beneficial owner, there will be implied into the conveyance covenants by him as to his title. He does not categorically covenant that he has a good title. He promises that he has the power to convey the property, that the purchaser will be able quietly to enjoy the property, for freedom from incumbrances, and to do anything further that is necessary for vesting the property in the purchaser.

If the conveyance is of a leasehold property, there are also implied covenants that the lease is valid and subsisting, and that the seller has not broken any of the covenants in the lease.

So why do these covenants only rarely offer a remedy? It is because they are qualified in two ways:

(aa) the covenants 'relate to the subject matter of the conveyance as it is expressed to be conveyed'. The basis of an action on the covenants, therefore, is a discrepancy between what the conveyance promises by way of title, and what the purchaser actually gets. If the conveyance is expressly said to be subject to a defect or incumbrance there can be no action under the covenants in respect of that matter. Hence the importance in unregistered conveyancing of setting out incumbrances in the habendum, e.g. 'To hold unto the purchaser in fee simple subject to the restrictive covenants continued in a conveyance of 2 February 1954 made between Alice Baynes of the one part and Christine Davis of the other part' (see Chapter 13).

(bb) the seller is not giving absolute covenants as to the soundness of his title. He is covenanting only in respect of defects or incumbrances arising from the acts or omissions of persons for whom he is responsible.

He is responsible for himself; for his predecessors in title, but not if he claims through those predecessors through a conveyance for money or money's worth; for people who dcrive a title through him, e.g. his tenants and mortgagees; and for people claiming in trust for him.

An example may make this qualification clear. Suppose that Alex owns Blackacre, and incumbers the land by granting a right of way over it. Alex conveys Blackacre for £75 000 to Vera, and the conveyance says he conveys it as beneficial owner. Vera later conveys Blackacre for £80 000 as beneficial owner to Paul. Neither conveyance says the land is conveyed subject to the easement.

After completion, Paul is irritated to discover a stranger strolling across his backyard.

The first thing for Paul is to consider is whether or not he did take subject to the easement. If the title is unregistered, and the easement is legal, Paul is bound by it.

If the title is registered, Paul is bound by the easement if it is overriding under s.70(1)(a) of the Land Registration Act 1925, or if it registered on the title (a fact which surely would not have escaped Paul's attention until now).

If Paul is bound by the easement he will naturally feel a sense of grievance towards Vera. He cannot sue her for breach of contract even if she is guilty of non-disclosure because the contract no longer exists. He must therefore, sue her for breach of her covenants for title. The covenants have been implied because Vera conveyed as beneficial owner and for value. However, Vera did not create the right of way herself and she is not liable for the acts of Alex, because she claims ownership from him through a conveyance for money.

This is why the covenants given by Vera turn out to be worth so little. As she bought the property from Alex, she is not liable for any defect in title at all, unless she created it. (She is liable for her own omissions, as well as acts, so it seems she would be breaking her own covenants for title if she failed to pay off a mortgage created by a predecessor, but only, it seems if she knew of the mortgage when she conveyed (*David* v. *Sabin* [1893]. She is not liable for a failure to get rid of the easement as this is not something she has power to do.)

Although Paul could not sue Vera, he could sue Alex.

Covenants for title were implied into the conveyance between Alex and Vera; the benefit of the covenants has passed to Paul as the benefit of the covenants runs with the covenantee's estate in the land; and Alex has broken the covenant because he is liable for his *own* acts. Of what use, though, is a right of action against a seller's predecessor in title, when the predecessor is probably untraceable?

If Alex had given the property to Vera, Vera would have broken her covenants, as she would have been responsible for anything done by Alex, as no conveyance for money separates her from Alex. This does not necessarily mean that she is also liable for things done by Alex's predecessors. If Alex bought the property for money, she derives title from *them* through that conveyance, and so is not responsible for their acts.

If a borrower mortgages his property to the lender, and the mortgage deed says he does this as beneficial owner, the covenants for title are absolute, not qualified, so the borrower cannot escape liability to the mortgagee by proving that the incumbrance or default was created by another person.

(ii) If the seller conveys and is expressed to convey as *trustee*, *personal representative* or as *mortgagee*, he impliedly covenants only that he has not himself incumbered the property. A purchaser who wants the benefit of the beneficial owner covenants, but who is in fact buying from a personal representative or a trustee, might ask the seller to state in the conveyance that he conveys as beneficial owner. It is doubtful if that is sufficient to imply the covenants into the conveyance, as s.76 uses the phrase 'conveys and is expressed to convey as beneficial owner'. It seems it is not sufficient for the seller to *say* he is conveying in that capacity, he must actually be doing it. If the purchaser in these circumstances wants the benefit of the beneficial-owner covenants, it would be better expressly to incorporate them.

If co-owners convey as beneficial owners, the covenants may be implied. Although the capacity in which they hold the legal estate is that of trustees for sale, they could also fairly be described as beneficial owners as they do between them own the entire beneficial interest. A purchaser who greatly desires the benefit of the beneficial-owner covenants, and who feels doubtful about this point, should again expressly incorporate the covenants.

(*b*) *Covenants for Title and Registered Title*

The covenants for title would also seem to be implied into a transfer of registered title. Rule 76 of the Land Registration Rules 1925 recognises this:

> For the purposes of introducing the covenants implied under ss.76 and 77 of the Law of Property Act 1925, a person may in a registered disposition, be expressed to execute, transfer or charge as beneficial owner....

Rule 77 states that the covenants take effect subject to all charges and other interests appearing on the register when the transfer is executed and to all overriding interests of which the purchaser has notice. So no action can be bought on the covenants for title in respect of these matters. Rule 77 therefore seems to envisage a purchaser being able to bring an action in respect of an overriding interest of which he did not know.

Although that seems clear to the average person it has been the subject of considerable academic controversy. The argument, put briefly, is this. A transfer of registered title transfers 'all the property comprised in the above title' (see Chapter 14). The transfer promises the title as registered. That is what the purchaser obtains, so there is never any discrepancy between what the transfer promises and what the purchaser gets, and there can be no action on the covenants for title.

There has been a successful case on the covenants for title. In *Dunning (AJ) & Sons (Shopfitters) Ltd* v. *Sykes and Son (Poole) Ltd* the defendants had previously sold part of the land comprised in their registered title. This land was described in the case as the 'yellow land'. The defendants then sold another part of the land to the plaintiffs. The transfer contained two descriptions of the land being transferred. One verbal description said it was part of the land comprised in the defendants' title. This description did not include the yellow land, as it was no longer part of that title. The other description was by reference to the plan annexed to the transfer, and the plan clearly purported to include the yellow land. The transfer also said that the defendants conveyed as beneficial owners.

When the plaintiffs realised that they had not acquired the yellow land they sued the defendants for breach of the covenants for title and were successful.

It is held that the description in the plan prevailed over the description by title number. The transfer did, therefore, promise a title to the 'yellow' land, and the defendants could not give that title by virtue of their own act in conveying it elsewhere. If no plan had been used the plaintiffs would have failed. The transfer would have promised the land in the title, and that is what they would have got, albeit less than they expected. Nor does the case destroy the above argument so far as it relates to overriding interests. The transfer is silent as to incumbrances on the property. It promises the title as registered and registration is subject to all overriding interests.

Nevertheless, any decision that there is no right of action in respect of an undisclosed overriding interest makes nonsense of rules 76 and 77.

19.3 Under s.25 of the Law of Property Act 1969

This remedy is only available to a purchaser of an unregistered title. We saw in Chapter 4 that it is possible for a purchaser to take subject to a registered land charge without having an opportunity to discover the fact of registration, as it is against a pre-root name. If the purchaser had discovered the land charge before completion he would have had remedies for breach of contract. When he discovers it after completion he may have no remedy against the seller under the covenants for title, because of the qualified nature of the covenants.

In recognition of the fact that it is the system of registration that is at fault, a purchaser who is affected by a pre-root land charge can claim compensation from the Chief Land Registrar under s.25 of the Law of Property Act 1969. The conditions are (a) that the purchaser must have completed in ignorance of the existence of the charge and (b) that the charge is not registered against the name of an estate-owner appearing as such in the title which the seller was entitled to investigate under an open contract. If a document in the title that the purchaser is entitled to investigate refers to an incumbrance, the document creating that incumbrance is treated as part of the title open to investigation by the purchaser.

Consider this example: The title deeds are:

- A 1940 conveyance made from A to B. B gave restrictive covenants to A which were duly registered against B's name.
- A 1950 conveyance from B to C. C later gave an option over the property to D, which D registered against C's name.
- A 1952 conveyance from C to E.
- A 1979 conveyance from E to F.

Under a contract made in 1990, F contracts to sell to G, and G agrees to accept a title traced from the 1979 conveyance. The contract does not disclose the covenants or the option. G completes, and then discovers their existence. G cannot claim compensation for the fact that he has bought subject to the option. Had he not accepted the contractual condition cutting short his investigation of title he could have traced title back to a root at least fifteen years old, so back to the 1952 conveyance, and would have been able to search against C's name.

F can claim compensation for the covenants. Even had he traced title back to 1952, he would still not have discovered B's name. However, he cannot claim compensation if either the 1952 or 1979 conveyance says that the property is conveyed subject to the covenants.

No compensation can be claimed in respect of a land charge registered against a name appearing on a superior title which the purchaser or grantee of a lease cannot investigate because of s.44 of the Law of Property Act 1925. The purchaser's loss is caused by s.44, not by the system of registration under the Land Charges Act 1972.

19.4 For Misrepresentation

A representation is a statement of fact made by the seller or his agent before the contract comes into existence, which helps to induce the contract and on which the purchaser relies. (It is possible for a misrepresentation to be made by a purchaser, but this is likely to be rare.)

If the statement is incorrect, the purchaser will have remedies, both before and after completion. He may be able to rescind the contract or claim damages. A question on misrepresentation appears in the workshop section of this chapter.

Workshop

Attempt this problem yourself, then read the specimen solution at the end of the book.

Problem 1

Pauline has contracted to buy Roger's house. The contract incorporates the standard conditions. She is told by Roger's estate agent before contract that the house has the benefit of a planning permission for the ground floor to be used as a shop but in fact the permission had expired the previous year. Pauline has just discovered this, and she asks if she has any remedies against Roger.

Appendix A Agreement

AGREEMENT

(Incorporating the Standard Conditions of Sale (Second Edition))

Agreement date: ____________________

Seller: ____________________

____

Buyer: ____________________

Property (freehold/leasehold): ____________________

Root of title/Title Number: ____________________

____

Incumbrances on the Property: ____________________

____

____

Seller sells as: ____________________

Completion date: ____________________

Contract rate: ____________________

Purchase Price: ____________________

Deposit: ____________________

Amount payable for chattels: ____________________

Balance: ____________________

The Seller will sell and the Buyer will buy the Property for the Purchase Price.

The Agreement continues on the back page.

WARNING	
This is a formal document, designed to create legal rights and legal obligations. Take advice before using it.	SIGNED ____________________ SELLER/BUYER

(*The following text is the back page of the Agreement.*)

SPECIAL CONDITIONS

1. (a) This Agreement incorporates the Standard Conditions of Sale (Second Edition). Where there is a conflict between those Conditions and this Agreement, this Agreement prevails.

   (b) Terms used or defined in this Agreement have the same meaning when used in the Conditions.

2. The Property is sold subject to the Incumbrances on the Property and the Buyer will raise no requisitions on them.

3. The chattels on the Property and set out on any attached list are included in the sale.

4. The Property is sold with vacant possession on completion.

(or)

4. The Property is sold subject to the following leases or tenancies.

Seller's Solicitors: ______________________________

Buyer's Solicitors: ______________________________

Appendix B Standard Conditions of Sale

STANDARD CONDITIONS OF SALE (SECOND EDITION)

(National Conditions of Sale 22nd Edition, Law Society's Conditions of Sale 1992)

1 General

1.1 Definitions

1.1.1 In these conditions:

(a) "accrued interest" means:

(i) if money has been placed on deposit or in a building society share account, the interest actually earned

(ii) otherwise, the interest which might reasonably have been earned by depositing the money at interest on seven days' notice of withdrawal with a clearing bank

less, in either case, any proper charges for handling the money

(b) "agreement" means the contractual document which incorporates these conditions with or without amendment

(c) "banker's draft" means a draft drawn by and on a clearing bank

(d) "clearing bank" means a bank which is a member of CHAPS and Town Clearing Company Limited

(e) "completion date", unless defined in the agreement, has the meaning given in condition 6.1.1

(f) "contract" means the bargain between the seller and the buyer of which these conditions, with or without amendment, form part

(g) "contract rate", unless defined in the agreement, is the Law Society's interest rate from time to time in force

(h) "lease" includes sub-lease, tenancy and agreement for a lease or sub-lease

(i) "notice to complete" means a notice requiring completion of the contract in accordance with condition 6.6.1

(j) "public requirement" means any notice, order or proposal given or made (whether before or after the date of the contract) by a body acting on statutory authority

(k) "requisition" includes objection

(l) "solicitor" includes barrister, duly certificated notary public, recognised licensed conveyancer and recognised body under sections 9 or 32 of the Administration of Justice Act 1985

(m) "transfer" includes conveyance and assignment

(n) "working day" means any day from Monday to Friday (inclusive) which is not Christmas Day, Good Friday or a statutory Bank Holiday.

1.1.2 When used in these conditions the terms "absolute title" and "office copies" have the special meanings given to them by the Land Registration Act 1925.

1.2 Joint parties

If there is more than one seller or more than one buyer, the obligations which they undertake can be enforced against them all jointly or against each individually.

1.3 Notices and Documents

1.3.1 A notice required or authorised by the contract must be in writing.

1.3.2 Giving a notice or delivering a document to a party's solicitor has the same effect as giving or delivering it to that party.

1.3.3 Transmission by fax is a valid means of giving a notice or delivering a document where delivery of the original document is not essential.

1.3.4 Subject to conditions 1.3.5 to 1.3.7, a notice is given and a document delivered when it is received.

1.3.5 If a notice or document is received after 4.00pm on a working day, or on a day which is not a working day, it is to be treated as having been received on the next working day.

1.3.6 Unless the actual time of receipt is proved, a notice or document sent by the following means is to be treated as having been received before 4.00pm on the day shown below:

(a) by first class post:	two working days after posting
(b) by second class post:	three working days after posting
(c) through a document exchange:	on the first working day after the day on which it would normally be available for collection by the addressee

1.3.7 Where a notice or document is sent through a document exchange, then for the purposes of condition 1.3.6 the actual time of receipt is:

(a) the time when the addressee collects it from the document exchange or, if earlier

(b) 8.00am on the first working day on which it is available for collection at that time.

1.4 VAT

1.4.1 An obligation to pay money includes an obligation to pay any value added tax chargeable in respect of that payment.

1.4.2 All sums made payable by the contract are exclusive of value added tax.

2 Formation

2.1 Date

2.1.1 If the parties intend to make a contract by exchanging duplicate copies by post or through a document exchange, the contract is made when the last copy is posted or deposited at the document exchange.

2.1.2 If the parties' solicitors agree to treat exchange as taking place before duplicate copies are actually exchanged, the contract is made as so agreed.

2.2 Deposit

2.2.1 The buyer is to pay or send a deposit of 10 per cent of the purchase price no later than the date of the contract. Except on a sale by auction, payment is to be made by banker's draft or by a cheque drawn on a solicitor's clearing bank account.

2.2.2 If before completion date the seller agrees to buy another property in England and Wales for his residence, he may use all or any part of the deposit as a deposit in that transaction to be held on terms to the same effect as this condition and condition 2.2.3.

2.2.3 Any deposit or part of a deposit not being used in accordance with condition 2.2.2 is to be held by the seller's solicitor as stakeholder on terms that on completion it is paid to the seller with accrued interest.

2.2.4 If a cheque tendered in payment of all or part of the deposit is dishonoured when first presented, the seller may, within seven working days of being notified that the cheque has been dishonoured, give notice to the buyer that the contract is discharged by the buyer's breach.

2.3 Auctions

2.3.1 On a sale by auction the following conditions apply to the property and, if it is sold in lots, to each lot.

2.3.2 The sale is subject to a reserve price.

2.3.3 The seller, or a person on his behalf, may bid up to the reserve price.

2.3.4 The auctioneer may refuse any bid.

2.3.5 If there is a dispute about a bid, the auctioneer may resolve the dispute or restart the auction at the last undisputed bid.

3 Matters affecting the property

3.1 Freedom from incumbrances

3.1.1 The seller is selling the property free from incumbrances, other than those mentioned in condition 3.1.2.

3.1.2 The incumbrances subject to which the property is sold are:

(a) those mentioned in the agreement

(b) those discoverable by inspection of the property before the contract

(c) those the seller does not and could not know about

(d) entries made before the date of the contract in any public register except those maintained by HM Land Registry or its Land Charges Department or by Companies House

(e) public requirements.

3.1.3 The buyer accepts the property in the physical state it is in at the date of the contract, unless the seller is building or converting it.

3.1.4 After the contract is made, the seller is to give the buyer details without delay of any new public requirement and of anything in writing which he learns about concerning any incumbrances subject to which the property is sold.

3.1.5 The buyer is to bear the cost of complying with any outstanding public requirement and is to indemnify the seller against any liability resulting from a public requirement.

3.2 Leases affecting the property

3.2.1 The following provisions apply if the agreement states that any part of the property is sold subject to a lease.

3.2.2 (a) The seller having provided the buyer with full details of each lease or copies of the documents embodying the lease terms, the buyer is treated as entering into the contract knowing and fully accepting those terms

(b) The seller is to inform the buyer without delay if the lease ends or if the seller learns of any application by the tenant in connection with the lease;

the seller is then to act as the buyer reasonably directs, and the buyer is to indemnify him against all consequent loss and expense

(c) The seller is not to agree to any proposal to change the lease terms without the consent of the buyer and is to inform the buyer without delay of any change which may be proposed or agreed

(d) The buyer is to indemnify the seller against all claims arising from the lease after actual completion; this includes claims which are unenforceable against a buyer for want of registration

(e) The seller takes no responsibility for what rent is lawfully recoverable, nor for whether or how any legislation affects the lease

(f) If the let land is not wholly within the property, the seller may apportion rent.

3.3 Retained land

3.3.1 The following provisions apply where after the transfer the seller will be retaining land near the property.

3.3.2 The buyer will not have any right of light or air over the retained land, but otherwise the seller and the buyer will each have the rights over the land of the other which they would have had if they were two separate buyers to whom the seller had made simultaneous transfers of the property and the retained land.

3.3.3 Either party may require that the transfer contains appropriate express terms.

4 Title and transfer

4.1 Timetable

4.1.1 The following are the steps for deducing and investigating the title to the property to be taken within the following time limits:

Step	Time Limit
1. The seller is to send the buyer evidence of title in accordance with condition 4.2	Immediately after making the contract
2. The buyer may raise written requisitions	Six working days after either the date of the contract or the date of delivery of the seller's evidence of title on which the requisitions are raised whichever is the later.
3. The seller is to reply in writing to any requisitions raised	Four working days after receiving the requisitions.
4. The buyer may make written observations on the seller's replies	Three working days after receiving the replies

The time limit on the buyer's right to raise requisitions applies even where the seller supplies incomplete evidence of title, but the buyer may, within six working days from delivery of any further evidence, raise further requisitions resulting from that evidence. On the expiry of the relevant time limit the buyer loses his right to raise requisitions or make observations.

4.1.2 The parties are to take the following steps to prepare and agree the transfer of the property within the following time limits:

Step	Time Limit
A. The buyer is to send the seller a draft transfer	At least twelve working days before completion date.
B. The seller is to approve or revise that draft and either return it or retain it for use as the actual transfer.	Four working days after delivery of the draft transfer
C. If the draft is returned the buyer is to send an engrossment to the seller	At least five working days before completion date.

4.1.3 Periods of time under conditions 4.1.1 and 4.1.2 may run concurrently.

4.1.4 If the period between the date of the contract and completion date is less than 15 working days, the time limits in conditions 4.1.1 and 4.1.2 are to be reduced by the same proportion as that period bears to the period of 15 working days. Fractions of a working day are to be rounded down except that the time limit to perform any step is not to be less than one working day.

4.2 Proof of title

4.2.1 The evidence of registered title is office copies of the items required to be furnished by section 110(1) of the Land Registration Act 1925 and the copies, abstracts and evidence referred to in section 110(2).

4.2.2 The seller authorises the buyer's solicitor and the buyer's mortgagee's solicitor to inspect the register.

4.2.3 The evidence of unregistered title is an abstract of the title, or an epitome of title with photocopies of the relevant documents.

4.2.4 Where the title to the property is unregistered, the seller is to produce to the buyer (without cost to the buyer):

(a) the original of every relevant document, or

(b) an abstract, epitome or copy with an original marking by a solicitor of examination either against the original or against an examined abstract or against an examined copy.

4.3 Defining the property

4.3.1 The seller need not:

(a) prove the exact boundaries of the property

(b) prove who owns fences, ditches, hedges or walls

(c) separately identify parts of the property with different titles

further than he may be able to do from information in his possession.

4.3.2 The buyer may, if it is reasonable, require the seller to make or obtain, pay for and hand over a statutory declaration about facts relevant to the matters mentioned in condition 4.3.1. The form of the declaration is to be agreed by the buyer, who must not unreasonably withhold his agreement.

4.4 Rents and rentcharges

The fact that a rent or rentcharge, whether payable or receivable by the owner of the property, has been or will on completion be, informally apportioned is not to be regarded as a defect in title.

4.5 Transfer

4.5.1 The buyer does not prejudice his right to raise requisitions, or to require replies to any raised, by taking any steps in relation to the preparation or agreement of the transfer.

4.5.2 The seller is to transfer the property in the capacity specified in the agreement, or (if none is specified) as beneficial owner.

4.5.3 If after completion the seller will remain bound by any obligation affecting the property, but the law does not imply any covenant by the buyer to indemnify the seller against liability for future breaches of it:

(a) the buyer is to covenant in the transfer to indemnify the seller against liability for any future breach of the obligation and to perform it from then on, and

(b) if required by the seller, the buyer is to execute and deliver to the seller on completion a duplicate transfer prepared by the buyer.

4.5.4 The seller is to arrange at his expense that, in relation to every document of title which the buyer does not receive on completion, the buyer is to have the benefit of:

(a) a written acknowledgement of his right to its production; and

(b) a written undertaking for its safe custody (except while it is held by a mortgagee or by someone in a fiduciary capacity).

5 Pending completion

5.1 Responsibility for property

5.1.1 The seller will transfer the property in the same physical state as it was at the date of the contract (except for fair wear and tear), which means that the seller retains the risk until completion.

5.1.2 If at any time before completion the physical state of the property makes it unusable for its purpose at the date of the contract:

(a) the buyer may rescind the contract

(b) the seller may rescind the contract where the property has become unusable for that purpose as a result of damage against which the seller could not reasonably have insured, or which it is not legally possible for the seller to make good.

5.1.3 The seller is under no obligation to the buyer to insure the property.

5.1.4 Section 47 of the Law of Property Act 1925 does not apply.

5.2 Occupation by buyer

5.2.1 If the buyer is not already lawfully in the property, and the seller agrees to let him into occupation, the buyer occupies on the following terms.

5.2.2 The buyer is a licensee and not a tenant. The terms of the licence are that the buyer:

(a) cannot transfer it

(b) may permit members of his household to occupy the property

(c) is to pay or indemnify the seller against all outgoings and other expenses in respect of the property

(d) is to pay the seller a fee calculated at the contract rate on the purchase price (less any deposit paid) for the period of the licence

(e) is entitled to any rents and profits from any part of the property which he does not occupy

(f) is to keep the property in as good a state of repair as it was in when he went into occupation (except for fair wear and tear) and is not to alter it

(g) is to insure the property in a sum which is not less than the purchase price against all risks in respect of which comparable premises are normally insured

(h) is to quit the property when the licence ends.

5.2.3 On the creation of the buyer's licence, condition 5.1 ceases to apply, which means that the buyer then assumes the risk until completion.

5.2.4 The buyer is not in occupation for the purposes of this condition if he merely exercises rights of access given solely to do work agreed by the seller.

5.2.5 The buyer's licence ends on the earliest of: completion date, rescission of the contract or when five working days' notice given by one party to the other takes effect.

5.2.4 The buyer's right to raise requisitions is unaffected.

6 Completion

6.1 Date

6.1.1 Completion date is twenty working days after the date of the contract but time is not of the essence of the contract unless a notice to complete has been served.

6.1.2 If the money due on completion is received after 2.00pm, completion is to be treated, for the purposes only of conditions 6.3 and 7.3, as taking place on the next working day.

6.1.3 Condition 6.1.2 does not apply where the sale is with vacant possession of the property or any part and the seller has not vacated the property by 2.00pm on the date of actual completion.

6.2 Place

Completion is to take place in England and Wales, either at the seller's solicitor's office or at some other place which the seller reasonably specifies.

6.3 Apportionments

6.3.1 Income and outgoings of the property are to be apportioned between the parties so far as the change of ownership on completion will affect entitlement to receive or liability to pay them.

6.3.2 If the whole property is sold with vacant possession or the seller exercises his option in condition 7.3.4, apportionment is to be made with effect from the date of actual completion; otherwise, it is to be made from completion date.

6.3.3 In apportioning any sum, it is to be assumed that the seller owns the property until the end of the day from which apportionment is made and that the sum accrues from day to day at the rate at which it is payable on that day.

6.3.4 For the purpose of apportioning income and outgoings, it is to be assumed that they accrue at an equal daily rate throughout the year.

6.3.5 When a sum to be apportioned is not known or easily ascertainable at completion a provisional apportionment is to be made according to the best estimate available. As soon as the amount is known, a final apportionment is to be made and notified to the other party. Any resulting balance is to be paid no more than ten working days later, and if not then paid the balance is to bear interest at the contract rate from then until payment.

6.3.6 Compensation payable under condition 5.2.6 is not to be apportioned.

6.4 Amount payable

The amount payable by the buyer on completion is the purchase price (less any deposit already paid to the seller or his agent) adjusted to take account of:

(a) apportionments made under condition 6.3

(b) any compensation to be paid or allowed under condition 7.3.

6.5 Title deeds

6.5.1 The seller is not to retain the documents of title after the buyer has tendered the amount payable under condition 6.4.

6.5.2 Condition 6.5.1 does not apply to any documents of title relating to land being retained by the seller after completion.

6.6 Rent receipts

The buyer is to assume that whoever gave any receipt for a payment of rent or service charge which the seller produces was the person or the agent of the person then entitled to that rent, or service charge.

6.7 Means of payment

The buyer is to pay the money due on completion in one or more of the following ways:

(a) legal tender
(b) a banker's draft
(c) a direct credit to a bank account nominated by the seller's solicitor
(d) an unconditional release of a deposit held by a stakeholder.

6.8 Notice to complete

6.8.1 At any time on or after completion date, a party who is ready able and willing to complete may give the other a notice to complete.

6.8.2 A party is ready able and willing:

(a) if he could be, but for the default of the other party, and
(b) in the case of the seller, even though a mortgage remains secured on the property, if the amount to be paid on completion enables the property to be transferred freed of all mortgages (except those to which the sale is expressly subject).

6.8.3 The parties are to complete the contract within ten working days of giving a notice to complete, excluding the day on which the notice is given. For this purpose, time is of the essence of the contract.

6.8.4 On receipt of a notice to complete:

(a) if the buyer paid no deposit, he is forthwith to pay a deposit of 10 per cent
(b) if the buyer paid a deposit of less than 10 per cent, he is forthwith to pay a further deposit equal to the balance of that 10 per cent.

7 Remedies

7.1 Errors and omissions

7.1.1 If any plan or statement in the contract, or in the negotiations leading to it, is or was misleading or inaccurate due to an error or omission, the remedies available are as follows.

7.1.2 When there is a material difference between the description or value of the property as represented and as it is, the injured party is entitled to compensation.

7.1.3 An error or omission only entitles the injured party to rescind the contract:

(a) where it results from fraud or recklessness, or
(b) where he would be obliged, to his prejudice, to transfer or accept property differing substantially (in quantity, quality or tenure) from what the error or omission had led him to expect.

7.2 Rescission

If either party rescinds the contract:

(a) unless the rescission is a result of the buyer's breach of contract the deposit is to be repaid to the buyer with accrued interest
(b) the buyer is to return any documents he received from the seller and is to cancel any registration of the contract.

7.3 Late completion

7.3.1 If there is default by either or both of the parties in performing their obligations under the contract and completion is delayed, the party whose total period of default is the greater is to pay compensation to the other party.

7.3.2 Compensation is calculated at the contract rate on the purchase price, or (where the buyer is the paying party) the purchase price less any deposit paid, for the period by which the paying party's default exceeds that of the receiving party, or, if shorter, the period between completion date and actual completion.

7.3.3 Any claim for loss resulting from delayed completion is to be reduced by any compensation paid under this condition.

7.3.4 Where the buyer holds the property as tenant of the seller and completion is delayed, the seller may give notice to the buyer, before the date of actual completion, that he intends to take the net income from the property until completion. If he does so, he cannot claim compensation under condition 7.3.1 as well.

7.4 After completion

Completion does not cancel liability to perform any outstanding obligation under this contract.

7.5 Buyer's failure to comply with notice to complete

7.5.1 If the buyer fails to complete in accordance with a notice to complete, the following terms apply.

7.5.2 The seller may rescind the contract, and if he does so:

(a) he may
  (i) forfeit and keep any deposit and accrued interest
  (ii) resell the property
  (iii) claim damages.

(b) the buyer is to return any documents he received from the seller and is to cancel any registration of the contract.

7.6 Seller's failure to comply with notice to complete

7.6.1 If the seller fails to complete in accordance with a notice to complete, the following terms apply.

7.6.2 The buyer may rescind the contract, and if he does so:

(a) the deposit is to be repaid to the buyer with accrued interest

(b) the buyer is to return any documents he received from the seller and is, at the seller's expense, to cancel any registration of the contract.

7.6.4 The buyer retains his other rights and remedies.

8 Leasehold property

8.1 Existing leases

8.1.1 The following provisions apply to a sale of leasehold land.

8.1.2 The seller having provided the buyer with copies of the documents embodying the lease terms, the buyer is treated as entering into the contract knowing and fully accepting the lease terms.

8.1.3 The seller is to comply with any lease obligations requiring the tenant to insure the property.

8.1.4 The transfer is to record that no covenant implied by statute makes the seller liable to the buyer for any breach of the lease terms about the condition of the property. This applies even if the seller is to transfer as beneficial owner.

8.2 New leases

8.2.1 The following provisions apply to a grant of a new lease.

8.2.2 The conditions apply so that:

"seller" means the proposed landlord

"buyer" means the proposed tenant

"purchase price" means the premium to be paid on the grant of a lease.

8.2.3 The lease is to be in the form of the draft attached to the contract.

8.2.4 If the term of the new lease will exceed 21 years, the seller is to deduce a title which will enable the buyer to register the lease at HM Land Registry with an absolute title.

8.2.5 The buyer is not entitled to transfer the benefit of the contract.

8.2.6 The seller is to engross the lease and a counterpart of it and is to send the counterpart to the buyer at least five working days before completion date.

8.2.7 The buyer is to execute the counterpart and deliver it to the seller on completion.

8.3. Landlord's consent

8.3.1 The following provisions apply if a consent to assign or sub-let is required to complete the contract.

8.3.2 (a) The seller is to apply for the consent at his expense, and to use all reasonable efforts to obtain it.

(b) The buyer is to provide all information and references reasonably required.

8.3.3 The buyer is not entitled to transfer the benefit of the contract.

8.3.4 Unless he is in breach of his obligation under condition 8.3.2, either party may rescind the contract by notice to the other party if three working days before completion date:

(a) the consent has not been given or

(b) the consent has been given subject to a condition to which the buyer reasonably objects.

In that case, neither party is treated as in breach of contract and condition 7.2 applies.

9 Chattels

9.1 The following provisions apply to any chattels which are to be sold.

9.2 Whether or not a separate price is to be paid for the chattels, the contract takes effect as a contract for sale of goods.

9.3 Ownership of the chattels passes to the buyer on actual completion.

Appendix C Seller's Property Information Form

SELLER'S PROPERTY INFORMATION FORM

Address of the Property: ______________________________

____

____

IMPORTANT NOTICE TO SELLERS

* Please complete this form carefully. It will be sent to the buyer's solicitor and may be seen by the buyer.

* Incorrect information may mean you have to pay compensation to the buyer. For many of the questions you need only tick the correct answer. Where necessary, please give more detailed answers on a separate sheet of paper. Then send all the replies to your solicitor so that the information can be passed to the buyer's solicitor.

* The answers should be those of the person whose name is on the deeds. If there is more than one of you, you should prepare the answers together.

* It is very important that your answers are correct because the buyer will rely on them in deciding whether to go ahead.

* It does not matter if you do not know the answer to any question so long as you say so.

* Do not the buyer anything about the property unless you are willing to accept legal liability for what you say. This applies to this questionnaire and to anything else you tell him, even in casual conversation.

* The buyer will be told by his solicitor that he takes the property as it is. If he wants more information about it, he should get it from his own advisers, not from you.

* If anything changes after you fill in this questionnaire but before the sale is completed, tell your solicitor immediately. This is as important as giving the right answers in the first place.

* Please pass on to your solicitor immediately any notices you have received which affect the property. The same goes for notices which arrive at any time before completion.

* If you have a tenant, tell your solicitor immediately there is any change in the arrangements but do nothing without asking your solicitor first.

* You should let your solicitor have any letters, agreements or other documents which help answer the questions. If you know of any which you are not supplying with these answers, please tell your solicitor about them.

* Please complete and return the separate Fixtures, Fittings and Contents Form. It is an important document which will form part of the contract between you and the buyer. Unless you mark clearly on it the items which you wish to remove, they will be included in the sale and you will not be able to take them with you when you move.

IF YOU ARE NOT SURE ABOUT ANYTHING, ASK YOUR SOLICITOR

Part I – to be completed by the seller

1 Boundaries

"Boundaries" mean any fence, wall, hedge or ditch which marks the edge of your property.

1.1 Looking towards the house from the road, who either owns or accepts responsibility for the boundary:

Please tick the right answer

(a) on the left?	WE DO	NEXT DOOR	SHARED	WE DON'T KNOW
(b) on the right?	WE DO	NEXT DOOR	SHARED	WE DON'T KNOW
(c) at the back?	WE DO	NEXT DOOR	SHARED	WE DON'T KNOW

1.2 If you have answered "we don't know", which boundaries have you actually repaired or maintained?

(Please give details) ____________________

____

____

1.3 Do you know of any boundary being moved in the last 20 years?

(Please give details) ____________________

____

____

2 Disputes

2.1 Do you know of any disputes about this or any neighbouring property?

NO	YES (PLEASE GIVE DETAILS)

____

____

2.2 Have you received any complaints about anything you have, or have not, done as owners?

NO	YES (PLEASE GIVE DETAILS)

2.3 Have you made any such complaint to any neighbour about what the neighbour has or has not done?

NO	YES (PLEASE GIVE DETAILS)

3 Notices

3.1 Have you either sent or received any letters or notices which affect your property or the neighbouring property in any way (for example, from or to neighbours, the council or a government department)?

NO	YES	COPY ENCLOSED	TO FOLLOW	LOST

3.2 Have you had any negotiations or discussions with any neighbour or any local or other authority which affect the property in any way?

NO	YES (PLEASE GIVE DETAILS)

4 Guarantees

4.1 Are there any guarantees or insurance policies of the following types:

(a) NHBC or Foundation 15 (for houses less than 15 years old)?	NO	YES	COPIES ARE ENCLOSED	WITH DEEDS	LOST
(b) Damp course?	NO	YES	COPIES ARE ENCLOSED	WITH DEEDS	LOST
(c) Double glazing?	NO	YES	COPIES ARE ENCLOSED	WITH DEEDS	LOST
(d) Electrical work?	NO	YES	COPIES ARE ENCLOSED	WITH DEEDS	LOST
(e) Roofing?	NO	YES	COPIES ARE ENCLOSED	WITH DEEDS	LOST
(f) Rot or infestation?	NO	YES	COPIES ARE ENCLOSED	WITH DEEDS	LOST
(g) Central heating?	NO	YES	COPIES ARE ENCLOSED	WITH DEEDS	LOST
(h) Anything similar? (e.g. cavity wall insulation)	NO	YES	COPIES ARE ENCLOSED	WITH DEEDS	LOST

(i) Do you have written details of the work done to obtain any of these guarantees?

NO	YES	COPIES ARE ENCLOSED	WITH DEEDS	LOST

4.2 Have you made or considered making claims under any of these?

NO	YES (PLEASE GIVE DETAILS)

5 Services

(This section applies to gas, electrical and water supplies, sewerage disposal and telephone cables.)

5.1 Please tick which services are connected to the property.

GAS	ELEC.	WATER	DRAINS	TEL	CABLE T.V.

5.2 Do any drains, pipes or wires for these cross any neighbour's property?

NOT AS FAR AS WE KNOW	YES (PLEASE GIVE DETAILS)

5.3 Do any drains, pipes or wires leading to any neighbour's property cross your property?

NOT AS FAR AS WE KNOW	YES (PLEASE GIVE DETAILS)

5.4 Are you aware of any agreement which is not with the deeds about any of these services?

NOT AS FAR AS WE KNOW	YES (PLEASE GIVE DETAILS)

6 Sharing with the neighbours

6.1 Do you and a neighbour share the cost of anything used jointly, such as the repair of a shared drive, boundary or drain?

YES (PLEASE GIVE DETAILS)	NO

6.2 Do you contribute to the cost of repair of anything used by the neighbourhood, such as the maintenance of a private road?

YES	NO

6.3 If so, who is responsible for organising the work and collection of contributions?

6.4 Please give details of all such sums paid or owing, and explain if they are paid on a regular basis or merely as and when work is required.

6.5 Do you need to go next door if you have to repair or decorate your building or maintain any of the boundaries

YES	NO

6.6 If "Yes", have you always been able to do so without objection by the neighbours?

YES	NO PLEASE GIVE DETAILS OF ANY OBJECTION UNDER THE ANSWER TO QUESTION 2 (DISPUTES)

6.7 Do any of your neighbours need to come onto your land to repair or decorate their building or maintain the boundaries?

YES	NO

6.8 If so, have you ever objected?

NO	YES PLEASE GIVE DETAILS OF ANY OBJECTION UNDER THE ANSWER TO QUESTION 2 (DISPUTES)

7 Arrangements and rights

Are there any other formal or informal arrangements which give someone else rights over your property?

NO	YES (PLEASE GIVE DETAILS)

8 Occupiers

8.1 Does anyone other than you live in the property?

YES	NO

If "No" go to question 9.1.
If "Yes" please give their full names and (if under 18) their ages.

8.2(a)(i) Do any of them have any right to stay on the property without your permission?

NO	YES (PLEASE GIVE DETAILS)

(These rights may have arisen without your realising, e.g. if they have paid for improvements or if they helped you buy the house.)

8.2(a)(ii) Are any of them tenants or lodgers?

NO	YES (PLEASE GIVE DETAILS AND A COPY OF ANY TENANCY AGREEMENT)

8.2(b) Have they all agreed to sign the contract for sale agreeing to leave with you (or earlier)?

NO	YES (PLEASE GIVE DETAILS)

9 Restrictions

If you have changed the use of the property or carried out any building work on it, please read the not below and answer these questions. If you have not, please go on to Question 10

Note The title deeds of some properties include clauses which are called "restrictive covenants". For example, these may forbid the owner of the house to carry out any building work or to use it for the purpose of a business – unless someone else (often the builder of the house) gives his consent.

9.1(a) Do you know of any "restrictive covenant" which applies to your house or land?

YES	NO

(b) If "Yes" did you ask for consent?

NO	YES (PLEASE GIVE DETAILS AND A COPY OF ANY CONSENT)

9.2 If consent was needed but not obtained, please explain why not.

9.3 If the reply to 9.1(a) is "Yes", please give the name and address of the person from whom consent has to be obtained.

10 Planning

10.1 Is the property used only as a private home?

YES	NO (PLEASE GIVE DETAILS)

10.2(a) is the property a listed building or in a conservation area?

YES	NO	DON'T KNOW

(b) If "Yes", what work has been carried out since it was listed or the area became a conservation area?

10.3 Has there been any building work on the property in the last 4 years?

NO	YES (PLEASE GIVE DETAILS)

10.4 Have your applied for planning permission, building regulation approval or listed building consent at any time?

NO	YES	COPIES ENCLOSED	TO FOLLOW	LOST

10.5 If "Yes", has any of the work been carried out?

NO	YES (PLEASE GIVE DETAILS)

11 Fixtures

11.1 If you have sold through an estate agent, are all the items listed in its particulars included in the sale?

YES	NO

If "No" you should instruct the estate agent to write to everyone concerned correcting this error.

11.2 Do you own outright everthing included in the sale?

(You must give details of anything which may not be yours to sell, for example anything rented or on HP)

NO	YES (PLEASE GIVE DETAILS)

12 Expenses

Have you ever had to pay anything for the use of the property?

(Ignore rates, water rates, community charge and gas, electricity and phone bills. Include anything else: examples are the clearance of cess pool or septic tank, drainage rate, rent charge.)

NO	YES (PLEASE GIVE DETAILS)

13 General

Is there any other information which you think the buyer may have a right to know?

NO	YES (PLEASE GIVE DETAILS)

Signature(s) ....

....

Date ....

THE LAW SOCIETY

SELLER'S PROPERTY INFORMATION FORM

Part II – to be completed by the seller's solicitor and to be sent with Part I

A Boundaries

Does the information in the deeds agree with the seller's reply to 1.1 in Part I?

YES	NO (PLEASE GIVE DETAILS)

B Relevant Documents

(i) Are you aware of any correspondence, notices, consents or other documents other than those disclosed in Questions 3 or 4 of Part I?

NO	YES

(ii) If "Yes", please supply copies of all relevant documents.

C Guarantees

If appropriate, have notices of assignment of any guarantees been given in the past?

NO	YES

D Services

Please give full details of all legal rights enjoyed to ensure the benefit of uninterrupted services, e.g. easements, wayleaves, licences, etc.

E Adverse Interests

Please give full details of all overriding interests affecting the property as defined by the Land Registration Act 1925, s.70(1)

F Restrictions

Who has the benefit of any restrictive covenants? If known, please provide the name and address of the person or company having such benefit or the name and address of his or its solicitors

____

____

____

G Mechanics of Sale

(a) Is this sale dependent on the seller buying another property? | YES | NO |

(b) If "Yes", what stage have the negotiations reached?

____

____

(c) Does the seller require a mortgage? | YES | NO |

(d) If "Yes", has an offer been received and/or accepted or a mortgage certificate obtained?

____

____

Seller's Solicitor ....

Date ....

Reminder

1. The Fixtures, Fittings and Contents Form should be supplied in adddition to the information above.
2. If the property is leasehold, also complete the Additional Property Information Form.

THE LAW SOCIETY

Specimen Solutions to Workshop Problems

Chapter 3

Problem 1

1. Re-read section 2.17. The conveyance must be stamped with *ad valorem* stamps and a PD stamp. The stamping must be done within 30 days of completion.

   Re-read section 3.2. You must apply for first registration of your client's title within 2 months of completion.

   Now consider what entries will appear on the proprietorship and charges registers of your clients' title.

   The proprietorship register will presumably say that the title is absolute. Under the names of Bill and Ben as registered proprietors will appear a restriction. If you do not yet know why, you will do so when you have ploughed through Chapter 11.

   A notice of the restrictive covenant will be entered on the charges register and the mortgage will be registered there as a registered charge.
2. It will send a charge certificate to you, as you are acting for the lender, and you will forward this to the Building Society.

Chapter 5

Problem

(i) D(ii). You must first find out what these restrictive covenants are. You do not seem to have a copy of the deed which created them. A copy of the application for registration of the land charge can be obtained from the registry, and the name and address of the person with the benefit of the covenants discovered. They might have been given by Ada to her neighbour when she sold him part of the garden in 1980. Once it is known what the covenants are, they must be listed in the contract as incumbrances on the land.

(ii) C(i). This is probably a second mortgage. Again, the name of the lender can be discovered, and you can find from him the sum that will be necessary to redeem the mortgage. You must be satisfied that there will be enough money available at completion to discharge both mortgages, before you commit your client to the contract.

(iii) The contract will promise vacant possession yet Ada's husband has protected his rights of occupation under the Matrimonial Homes Act 1983. The husband must be approached before contract, and asked if he will join in the contract to release his rights of occupation, and if he will cancel the registration of the Class F. He should be warned to obtain independent advice before agreeing to do this. If he will not cooperate, Ada must not enter into the contract, as she will not be able to fulfil her promise, and might be liable to pay heavy damages.

Now that you know that Ada is married, you should also consider the possibility that her husband has an equitable interest in the house. If he says that he does not, he can be joined in the contract to repeat that statement. If he says he does, he should be joined in the contract as a second trustee. Again, it should be suggested that he obtain independent advice unless it is clear that there is no conflict between himself and Ada, and that he is prepared to instruct you to act for him in the sale as well.

Chapter 6

Problem 1

It is usually the seller's responsibility to pay off all financial charges before completion, as they are removable defects. However, do not forget the general conditions. Look at standard conditions 3.1.1 and 3.1.2. The sale is subject to all public requirements. Your client has agreed to buy subject to the road charges. Also read 3.1.5. Your client is to bear the cost of complying with any outstanding public requirement.

However, the seller must have known about the adoption of the road and the road charges. The seller's failure to disclose the charge means that he cannot rely on the conditions and he must remove the charge by paying the authority (see the *Rignall* case).

Problem 2

(a) With regard to the side road, re-read section 6.2(c). Will Mr Jones have the right to walk and drive cars along the side road, or will he have to depend on a permission? If this is not made clear by the documents supplied, an additional enquiry must be made of the seller. Is there any possibility of the road being adopted, with consequent expense to your client? What do the local land charge search and enquiries of the local authority reveal? What is the answer to question 6 on the property information form? With regard to the use of the garage, you need to check the title to see if the land is subject to any restrictive covenant prohibiting business use. Such a covenant may have been imposed when the developer sold the houses sixteen years ago. The developer might have created a development scheme, so that the covenants are enforceable not by the developer but by the owners of the other houses in the estate.

(b) Re-read section 6.5(d). Four years have passed since the garage was built, so no enforcement notice can be served requiring the garage to be demolished.

(c) There has been a change of use in the land from residential to business. There is a 10 year time limit for the service of an enforcement notice.

Problem 3

1. It does not matter that Joan did not make the searches and enquiries herself. Remember that compensation can be claimed under the Local Land Charges Act 1975 by anyone who knew of the contents of the search certificate before entering into the contract. Equally, if the replies to the additional enquiries are wrong because of negligence on the part of the district authority, damages will be recoverable in tort by anyone who could have been expected to rely on the answers. However, the search and enquiries were made four months ago. Joan

would be sensible to repeat them. No compensation is payable in respect of matters coming into existence after the date of the search. Alternatively, she could ask the seller's solicitor if he is willing to repeat the searches at his client's expense, or to arrange insurance under the Search Validation Scheme. If he refuses, she will have to repeat the search or arrange insurance.

2. The extension will certainly be development, so permission will be needed. What she must check is whether or not the development comes within the General Development Order. If it does, she will not need express planning permission. This is providing that the effect of the Order has not been negatived by an article 4 direction.
3. She should apply for it before exchange of contracts, so that if her application is rejected, she is not committed to the purchase of the house. Alternatively, she could enter into a contract that was conditional on her application for permission being successful (see section 5.10).

Chapter 7

Problem

The Finance Company is selling free from incumbrances. Both charges must, therefore, be cleared from the title. As it is the proprietor of the second registered charge, it cannot overreach the first mortgage, which will have to be redeemed by it from the proceeds of the sale. In respect of the first mortgage, therefore, there will be handed over the first charge certificate, and either form 53 or undertakings given by the solicitor to the Y Building Society in respect of it.

The second and any later registered charges will be overreached by the sale. All the Finance Company needs to hand over therefore is its own (i.e. the second) charge certificate, and a transfer executed by it.

Within 30 days of completion (i.e. the priority period given by the search) and having had the transfer stamped with a PD stamp and *ad valorem* stamps, you must apply for registration to the District Land Registry. The application will be for the discharge of the two registered charges, registration of the transfer to the Thompsons, and of the charge in favour of the Best Building Society. There will, therefore, after some months, issue forth from the Registry a charge certificate, containing in it a copy of the mortgage to the Best Building Society.

As it is an endowment mortgage, there must be sent to the society with the charge certificate a copy of the life policy, a deed executed by the Thompsons assigning it to the building society, and a notice of assignment receipted by the assurance company. (Re-read 2.12 and note that the instructions of the Best Building Society may have made it clear that it did not consider an assignment of the policy to be necessary, the Thompsons as a condition of the mortgage promising to execute an assignment if called upon to do so by the Society.)

Chapter 8

Problem 1

(a) You could specify either the 1970 or the 1973 conveyance as the root, since both are at least fifteen years old. If you specify the 1970 conveyance, you will have to abstract the 1970 mortgage, and the receipt endorsed on it. If you specify the 1973 conveyance, these documents can be omitted. The 1973 conveyance, therefore, seems the better choice.

(b) Assuming that the 1973 conveyance is used as the root, you will have to abstract:

(i) the 1950 deed creating the covenants. (See the exceptions to s.45 of the Law of Property Act.)
(ii) the 1970 lease. Although this was created pre-root, it did not end until 1975, and so is part of the post-root title.
(iii) the 1973 conveyance.
(iv) the 1975 surrender. Remember that it is only leases that expire by effluxion of time that do not have to be abstracted. The purchaser is entitled to check on the validity of the surrender.
(v) the 1973 mortgage.

If you are not following the protocol, you do not have to abstract the 1973 land charge search certificate, as it is not a document of title, but it would be courteous to do so. It will save the purchaser having to repeat the search against B, but not, you realise, against O'Connor.

Chapter 9

Problem 1

Yes. There is no discrepancy in the name of William Faulkner as it appears on the certificate and in the conveyance. But look at the dates. The priority period given by the search had lapsed before the conveyance was completed. Therefore, the search gives no protection against registrations against William's name that were made after the date of the search, and before the completion of the sale by him, i.e. between 1 June and 1 July. We therefore need to repeat the search to see if there is any such entry.

The search certificate against the names of Anthea Grumble is completely useless. It does not cover any part of her period of ownership, as it was made against her when she was buying. The search would have been made on behalf of the person making the mortgage loan to her, and would have been solely to find whether or not there was a bankruptcy entry against her name.

If Anthea is following the protocol, she should supply you with a recent land-charge search certificate against her name. This is of use, because it might give an early warning of trouble ahead, e.g. a class F land charge. However, another search will have to be made against her name just before completion, to cover her full period of ownership. If this reveals a new entry, she will be in breach of her contract.

Problem 2

Alan needs to check his client's title to that part of the land. There are three possibilities:

1. That the 1940 conveyance did not include the site of the water-garden, but that this extra land was bought by Vesta or her predecessor at some other time. Vesta must be asked if this is so, and asked where the title deeds are. If they are found, the transaction will proceed normally, except that two separate titles will be abstracted.
2. That the 1940 conveyance did include the site of the water-garden. Remember that the 1940 plan was said to be 'for identification only' and it might be completely

unreliable. Evidence may be obtained from Vesta, neighbours, or large-scale maps of the area, as to what was occupied as 'Rosedene' in 1940. A special condition can be put in the contract that, for example, a statutory declaration will be supplied by Vesta that she has occupied Rosedene, including the water-garden, for the past fifty years under the authority of the conveyance. This may satisfy Paula.

3. That the 1940 conveyance did not include the site of the water-garden, nor was it ever conveyed to Vesta by some other deed. Over the years Vesta has simply encroached on her neighbour's land. In this case, it is most unlikely that Vesta can make good title to the piece of land, as she will not be able to deduce the true owner's title. A special condition should be put in the contract saying that the purchaser must be satisfied with a declaration by Vesta that she has occupied the land for however many years it is.

   It is lucky for Vesta that this problem came to light before exchange of contracts. Otherwise, she would have promised good title to the water-garden, and then perhaps been unable to establish it.

Problem 3

The only difficulty is the question of revocation of the power. The Powers of Attorney Act 1971 does not entitle the purchaser to assume that Charles did not have any notice of revocation of the power. The conveyance took place more than 12 months from the date of the power, and there seems to be no statutory declaration made by Charles that he did not have notice of the revocation.

Charles can scarcely be asked to make one now. So the Act is useless. You cannot *presume* that Charles did not know of any revocation, and it is not something that can be *proved*, as no one knows what Charles knew, except Charles himself. What you now need is proof that the power was never in fact revoked, and the only person who can give evidence as to that is Bertha. If Bertha cannot be traced, there is a flaw in the paper title. You could take comfort from the fact that the conveyance took place several years ago, and no one has yet challenged its validity. If the conveyance of 1980 is void, because of the prior revocation of the power, Charles has been in adverse possession, and his successors will eventually acquire a title under the Limitation Act 1982.

These facts do show a loophole in the protection given by the Powers of Attorney Act 1971. The problem could have been avoided if Charles had made the statutory declaration as soon as he completed his purchase.

Problem 4

(a) *Requisition 1* Is this condition valid? Re-read section 9.2(b).

Requisition 2 The reply is quite correct. Re-read section 9.6(c).

Requisition 3 The 1960 conveyance is pre-root.

However, it is arguable that the description in the 1974 deed is not complete without a copy of the 1960 plan.

You cannot leave these problems until your colleague's return. See standard condition 4.1.1. You have three working days after receiving the replies to the requisitions in which to respond to them.

(b) An opportunity to revise Chapter 2. You will have to draft the conveyance, if you have not already done this, and send it to the seller for approval. When it is approved you must engross it, and send the engrossment to the seller for execution (see standard condition 4.1.2 for the time limits).

You must report on title to the XY Building Society, and ask them to provide the money in time for completion. You will draft the mortgage deed, and have it executed by your client. You must prepare a completion statement for your client, showing the balance of the purchase price that he must provide for completion.

Shortly before completion, you will do a search at the Central Land Charges Registry against the names of all the estate-owners revealed by the abstract of title and against which you do not already have a satisfactory search certificate. This will include the seller's name. You will also search against the name of James Brown, on behalf of the XY Building Society, to check that he is not bankrupt. You will complete within the priority period given by this search.

Chapter 10

Problem 1

You should not consider it acceptable without further explanation from Eric. In 1973 the legal estate was owned by two personal representatives. We would, therefore, expect to find the next conveyance to be by both of them, bearing in mind that the authority of personal representatives to convey is only joint.

The clue may be in the 1985 conveyance. A conveyance usually states the capacity in which the seller conveys. If the 1985 conveyance says that David conveys the estate 'as personal representative', there are two possibilities:

(i) Charles was still alive on 1 April 1985. If this is so, the conveyance is void. The legal estate remain where it was, in Charles and David jointly. The legal estate can only be obtained by a conveyance from them both.

(ii) Charles was dead on 1 April 1985. If so, the conveyance is valid. David, as the sole surviving personal representative, was competent to convey alone. Proof is needed of Charles's death. Strictly speaking, we cannot insist on seeing the death certificate itself, as it is a document of public record, but we can insist on being given the date of death, so that we can obtain a certificate for ourselves. In fact, if the seller has a copy of the certificate, he would be very churlish not to let us see it. We are not, of course, in the slightest bit interested in seeing the grant of representation to Charles's estate. We only want to check his death, not the identity of his personal representatives.

Suppose that the conveyance says that Charles conveys as 'beneficial owner'. How could his capacity have changed from being one of two personal representatives to being the sole beneficial owner?

The probable answer is that David was also the beneficiary, so that when Bertha's estate had been administered, the land was vested in David. If this is so, we must see the document of transfer. It is likely to be an assent, which under s.36(4) of the Administration of Estates Act 1925 must be in writing signed by Charles and David. So our requisition would be 'Provide an abstract of the assent made in favour of David'. (If an assent is produced, we still have to worry about whether or not a memorandum of it was endorsed on the grant – see problem 3.)

If David and Charles had overlooked the necessity for a written assent – not having read chapter 10 carefully enough – the legal estate remained with them, and the 1975 conveyance by David alone is void. (An interesting point is that the equitable interest might have passed to David, and thence to Eric. Section 36(4) applies only to a legal estate. An assent in respect of an equitable interest can still be informal and inferred from circumstances (see Re *Edward's Will Trusts* [1982]). However, a purchaser requires the legal estate, not just the equitable interest.)

Suppose that having requisitioned for the missing assent, we receive instead an abstract of a conveyance whereby Charles and David convey the land on sale to David as purchaser? This would certainly explain why David was later able to convey as beneficial owner: it would be because he had bought the property. It does not, however, increase our confidence in the title. It is a conveyance on sale by two personal representatives to one of themselves. Do you remember the principle of trust law that a purchase of trust property by a trustee can be voided by the beneficiaries, no matter how fair the purchase price might be? Eric's title is voidable, and as we will be buying with notice, our title will be voidable too. It is possible that the only beneficiaries are David and Charles themselves, or that any other beneficiaries have, after independent advice, consented to the sale. If, however, no solution can be found, the title is bad, we could refuse it, and consider remedies for the seller's breach of contract in failing to make good title to the land.

Problem 2

The first thing that might occur to us is that we should have copies of the two grants, the one to Carol, and the one to Edward. Even with these, the title is unacceptable. Apparently Carol died still owning Blackacre in her capacity of Bill's personal representative. She was an administrator, so there can be no chain of executorship. When Edward became Carol's personal representative, he did not thereby become Bill's. So he had no power to convey any of Bill's unadministered assets, including Blackacre. Blackacre can only be conveyed by the person who obtains a grant *de bonis non administratis* to Bill's estate. The person entitled to the grant might possibly be Edward; this would be due to his status as personal representative to the beneficiary entitled to Blackacre, Carol being entitled under the intestacy rules. The fact remains that Blackacre cannot be dealt with until the fresh grant to Bill's estate is obtained, and only the person who obtains that grant can convey Blackacre to Fred. (Had Carol been an executor, the chain of executorship would have existed. Edward could have conveyed Bill's assets because by becoming Carol's executor and proving her will, he would also have become Bill's executor.)

There is a final possibility. We have assumed that when Carol died, she owned Blackacre as personal representative. This is because the recitals make no mention of any assent. If, before she died, she signed an assent in her own favour, then she held Blackacre as beneficial owner, in which case Edward, as *her* personal representative, would be entitled to deal with it. The assent, however, would have had to be in writing.

Problem 3

What we should ask for is confirmation that a memorandum of the assent was endorsed on the grant in 1974. If it was, no subsequent conveyance by Cathy and Drew could have diverted the legal estate from Elaine in favour of a purchaser from themselves.

If it were not, there is, at least in theory, the possibility that Cathy and Drew, between 1974 and 1980, conveyed Blackacre to a purchaser for money or money's worth, who relied on a statement made under s.36(6) of the Administration of Estates Act 1925 that the personal representatives had not made any previous assent. If this were so, Elaine no longer had the legal estate in 1980. She could not convey it to Fred. (We do not have to worry about the possibility of the personal representatives having conveyed Blackacre after 1980 – remember that s.36(6) cannot remove the legal estate from a purchaser for money – i.e. Fred.)

So a requisition would have to be raised that Cathy and Drew confirm that no conveyance was made. They are, after all, the only people who can confirm it. Of course, they might now be dead or untraceable. In that case, the fact that Fred is living in Blackacre and has the title deeds is reassuring, and we might feel that we could advise our client-purchaser that the risk of the title being bad is very small.

Notice that the absence of a memorandum has been important because we were deriving title through the *beneficiary* who never protected her assent by a memorandum. Contrast the following abstract:

1972	Albert conveys to Bruce
1973	Bruce dies
1974	Grant of probate to Bruce's will to Carl
1975	Carl conveys on sale as personal representative to David
1976	David conveys to Elaine

Again we may query the absence from the grant of any memorandum of the conveyance. However, in this case the absence of a memorandum is not a defect in title. Even if Carl did convey to another purchaser after 1975, David would not lose the legal estate. So although it is important for a *beneficiary* to endorse a memorandum, it is not a matter of title if a *purchaser* from the personal representatives fails to do so. Nevertheless, as has been mentioned earlier, it would be sensible if he did.

NB

1. As you read about s.36(6), you may have been asking yourself, *why* do the personal representatives, having transferred the property to A, then seek to transfer it to B? Does the Act consider personal representatives peculiarly liable to lapses of memory? A double conveyance can occur in the case of badly drawn parcels clauses and maps, so that a border strip is conveyed twice. It can also happen that the deceased has two consecutive and separate personal representatives, e.g. on the making of a grant *de bonis non administratis*. It is possible that the administrator *de bonis non administratis* may not know of an assent made by his predecessor. However, if you feel that s.36(6) is a lot of fuss about nothing much, you have my sympathy. Still, if s.36(6) offers protection to a client who is buying from a personal representative, it is a conveyancer's job to procure it for him by putting the correct recital in the conveyance to him.
2. Another point worth mentioning here is that when reading an assent or a conveyance by a personal representative, check if it contains an acknowledgement for the production of the grant. Although the grant is a public document and copies can be obtained by anyone from the Probate Registry, a later purchaser will want to see the original because of the importance of checking for memoranda. Acknowledgements are discussed in Chapter 13, and you will see that the absence of an acknowledgement is not a defect in title.
3. Section 36(6) is sometimes said to have no relevance to registered title. Suppose you are buying from the personal representative of the dead registered proprietor, and you are considering the possibility of there having been a previous assent to a beneficiary. There are two possibilities:
   (i) the beneficiary has registered himself as the new proprietor. If he does this, your pre-completion search of the register will disclose the new proprietor, and you will not complete the purchase from the personal representatives.
   (ii) if he has not registered himself as the new proprietor, he has an unprotected minor interest, and your defence will be based on the Land Registration Act 1925 (a transferee for value taking free from an unprotected minor interest). However, if the beneficiary is living on the property, his interest is overriding, not minor. So you must realise that the Land Registration Act will not protect you against the earlier assent if the beneficiary is living in the house. So s.36(6) may be of use, and certainly no harm is done by putting the statement in the transfer that the personal representative has not made any previous assent.

Chapter 11

Problem 1

Do you remember the principle that *all* the trustees for sale must execute the conveyance? The fact that Robert retired from the partnership did not of itself divest him of the legal estate. You need to see a conveyance of the legal estate from Albert, Robert and Sidney to Albert and Sidney. This might take the form of a deed of retirement (see section 11.3(c)). Alternatively, you need evidence that Robert died before 1975, in which case the legal estate would have vested automatically in the surviving Bricks. If the legal estate was still vested in all three Bricks in 1975, the conveyance by two of them was void.

The search certificate is, at first sight, puzzling. The contract, or whatever it is that is protected by the C(iv) registration, would have had to be created by all three of them. The power of trustees (unlike personal representatives) to enter into a contract is joint only. Even if all of them entered into the contract, registration against only some of the estate-owners is not effective. Re-read section 4.5(c). Do you notice the discrepancy between the name on the deed, 'Sidney', and the name on the certificate, 'Sydney'? The certificate of search is useless, the search having been made against an incorrect version of the name. If we search again we probably shall find a C(iv) registered against Sydney.

If this is so, you must approach Miss Cooper's solicitor, and ask for an assurance that this land charge does not affect the land you are buying. There is a possibility that it does not, as it might be a contract in respect of other land owned by the Bricks. Another possibility is that it is protecting the contract by the Bricks to convey to Jennifer. If this is so, you can ask her solicitor to apply for cancellation of the registration. This should have been done by the solicitor as soon as the purchase by Miss Cooper was completed.

The solicitor may argue that the registration is protecting a void contract, an unenforceable contract, or one that was discharged by breach, and that he was satisfied as to this when he bought the land for his client. The answer should be that it is not your task to pass judgement on the validity of the contract; it is the seller's task to have the registration cancelled.

(This question is taken from part of the Law Society Summer 1988 paper.)

Problem 2

1. As both the Masons are registered as proprietors, you know that both owned the legal estate. They must have held it as joint tenants. There is no restriction on the register, so you can assume that they owned the beneficial interest jointly, too. Therefore, when her husband died, Mrs Mason became sole owner of the legal estate and the beneficial interest *simply because her husband had died*. She does *not* trace her claim to ownership of even the equitable interest through the will. The will is completely irrelevant, therefore. To have the title registered in her own name, she need only produce her husband's death certificate.
2. The drawbacks of registration with a possessory title are set out in section 3.6(d). You can imagine that the building society will be reluctant to lend on the security of such a title. Notice, though, that the title was registered in 1974. Re-read section 3.7. Mrs Mason can apply to have the title upgraded to absolute.
3. The building society needs to know as much about the property as a purchaser would, so the searches made are the same as if the building society were actually

buying the house. So you start by doing what in the context of a purchase would be called 'the pre-contract' searches and enquiries. Re-read Chapter 6, find the answers to the questions in the property information form, and make the local land-charge search and additional enquiries of the district authority. (For inspection of the property, you will be relying on the building society's surveyor.)

In this case there will be no contract for the grant of a mortgage, but these usual searches and enquiries may reveal things that would affect the value of the property. When the results of the searches are known, you will investigate the title and draft the mortgage deed. Before completion, you will make your pre-completion search at the district land registry, to enquire if there are any adverse entries on the register, either since the date of office copy entires obtained by you, or since the date when the land certificate was last officially compared with the register (re-read section 7.5).

You will complete the mortgage within the priority period given by the search. Completion will consist of your asking Mrs Mason to execute the mortgage and give you custody of the land certificate in return for the advance. It will have been part of the arrangement between herself and the society that you be able to deduct your fees and disbursements from the loan. You will then have to apply for registration of the mortgage as a registered charge, again before the priority period expires.

Note the searches you did *not* make:

(i) the coal board search, for obvious reasons;
(ii) the commons registration search – the house was built 30 years ago;
(iii) the public index map search – the title is registered;
(iv) the 'bankruptcy only' search at the Land Charges Registry. In this case the registered proprietor and the borrower are one and the same person. If Mrs Mason is insolvent, the register of her title will warn us. If the land registry search discloses no bankruptcy entry, you can safely lend money to her.

Suppose there had been a restriction on the register to the effect that no disposition by the sole survivor of the registered proprietors would be registered. You know that Mrs Mason has succeeded to her husband's share of the equitable interest under the terms of the will. Nevertheless, if she were *selling* the house, the simplest thing would be for her to appoint another trustee to act with her, so that the equitable interests are overreached. So again, for the purpose of making title to the house, the will would be irrelevant. It would only be of relevance when it had to be decided by the trustees how the proceeds of the sale were to be accounted for.

However, in this case Mrs Mason is keeping the house. It is probably better, therefore, to have the restriction removed, by proving to the Registrar the fact that she does now own the whole of the equitable interest. Probate of the will must be obtained, an assent in respect of the equitable interest made in her favour (but *not* in respect of the legal estate, as she owns this by virtue of the right of survivorship) and a statutory declaration made to the Registrar of these facts (see section 11.8(a)).

Chapter 12

Problem 1

You can see the problem. 21B has no direct access to the public road. The house can only be reached by crossing others' land. Pipes and wires must cross others' land to reach the public sewers and to obtain electricity, gas, telephone services, etc.

To deal with number 21, the question we have to ask here is 'What easements already exist over number 21 for the benefit of 21A and 21B?' In other words, what easements were reserved by Alice Brown when she conveyed to Catherine, because it is only the benefit of these easements that can be passed on to us. To stress a point that is obvious but can be forgotten in the heat of the moment, Alice can only pass to us the benefit of easements that already exist over number 21. She cannot create *new* easements over land she no longer owns.

If the title to number 21 is unregistered, you need a copy of the conveyance to Catherine. You will be looking in it for an express reservation over number 21 for the benefit of 21A and 21B of rights of way for pedestrians and vehicles, rights of drainage, and rights for all other necessary pipes and wires. You would also expect to see a right for the owners of 21A and 21B to enter number 21 for the purpose of inspecting and repairing the pipes, etc., and you would not be surprised to see a promise by the owners of 21A and 21B to contribute towards the cost of maintenance of the pipes, etc. If these rights were reserved, our client will succeed to the benefit of them. (If the conveyance to Catherine did contain a reservation, a copy of the conveyance – or even perhaps a duplicate – should have been kept with Catherine's deeds.)

If the conveyance does not contain an express reservation, there will have been a reservation implied into it, but, as we have seen, possibly only an essential means of access, so the pipes, wires, drains, and sewers would seem only to be there by virtue of Catherine's permission.

If the title to these properties had been registered at the time of the sale of number 21 to Catherine, any reservation of an easement in the transfer of part to Catherine would have been entered on the register of Catherine's title, and the benefit of it would have been entered on the register of Alice's title to 21A and 21B.

The absence of easements over number 21 would be a difficult problem to solve. The only person who can now grant an easement is Catherine, who may be unwilling to encumber her land. *She* may be willing to allow the pipes, etc., to remain where they are, but a purchaser from her may not be. The problem may be serious enough for our client to decide against buying number 21B.

If Alice finds that her failure expressly to reserve the necessary easements is making 21A and 21B unsellable, she should consider the contract that preceded her conveyance of number 21. As has been seen, the conditions in that contract might well have allowed her to put an express reservation of easements in the conveyance or transfer. She might now be able to apply to the court for rectification of the conveyance as it is not carrying out the terms of the contract but this right of rectification, if it exists, will not bind any purchaser of number 21 from Catherine, unless that purchaser has notice of it.

Number 21A presents a quite different problem. This is owned by the seller, so any easements your client needs over 21A can be granted by Alice. It is really a question of settling special conditions in the draft contract. Alice should promise your client in the contract that the conveyance will contain all the rights needed for access and services. These rights should be specified. She may wish to reserve easements, although from the plan it is difficult to see why she would require any. The contract should also agree shared obligations as to maintenance and rights of entry as previously mentioned.

The special conditions should replace the standard condition. If the standard condition is not expressly excluded, it might 'top up' what the parties have expressly agreed to grant and reserve, contrary to their real intentions.

Problem 2

The enforcement of the covenant against Hebe has two aspects. One possibility is that the covenant could be enforced against her by A, or whoever has succeeded to the benefited land together with the benefit of the covenant. For the burden of the covenant to have passed with the land, it would have been essential for the covenant to have been registered as a D(ii) land charge against the name of the original covenantor, B. You need to make a land charges search against B's name. If a land charge is registered, the person with the benefit of the covenant may take action against Hebe. If no land charge is registered, the covenant is not an incumbrance on the land. The covenant cannot be enforced directly by A against Hebe.

However, the fact remains that A *can* sue B, as B promised that the covenant would *always* be observed. B can sue C, and C can sue Hebe. So despite lack of registration, Hebe should not have ignored the covenant.

The Contract Clearly, if the covenant is registered, the covenant must be disclosed and the contract must list the covenant as an incumbrance on the property. What must also be disclosed is the *breach* of the covenant. (Even if it is not expressly disclosed in the contract, the seller must give an honest answer to the enquiry on the property information form which asks if the seller has observed all the restrictions affecting the property.)

Usually, Hebe, having promised an indemnity to C, would like an indemnity from her purchaser. However, the purchaser will not be prepared to promise a general indemnity for he knows that the covenant has already been broken. The standard condition promises an indemnity only in respect of breaches committed after the date of the conveyance, and the purchaser will not agree to an alteration to this.

If the covenant is registerd, the purchaser may be concerned about the consequences of an action brought by A. He does not want to find himself paying damages or having to dismantle the garage.

If a covenant has been broken, there are various ways to make the title acceptable to the purchaser. The seller might offer to indemnify the purchaser and his successors against the consequence of any breach (i.e. the seller will be promising to indemnify the purchaser against past breaches, and the purchaser will be promising to indemnify the seller against future breaches). This is not really satisfactory for either party if the consequences are likely to be serious, for example, if it had been the house itself, rather than a garage, that had been built in breach of covenant. The value of the indemnity depends on the seller's continued solvency (and traceability). The seller lives under a threat of one day having to find an unknown, but possibly large, sum of money.

Another possibility is taking out insurance against the risk of enforcement. The size of the premium will, of course, depend on the size of the risk.

(The purchaser will also be considering the planning position. Remember that express planning permission would have been needed, unless the garage came within the General Development Order. If the garage was built without planning permission, no enforcement notice can be served after four years have elapsed – see chapter 6.5.)

Problem 3

1. *The Restriction on the Proprietorship Register* Jacob must appoint another trustee, so that the transfer can be by two trustees. If the second trustee is appointed now, both will be named in the contract as sellers, and the contract will say that they will convey as trustees.

2. *The Property Register* The particulars in the contract may say '9 Havelock Street, Spa on Wells, as the same is registered with absolute title under title no KT1111111 at Tunbridge Wells District Land Registry'. An office copy of the entries on the register will accompany the contract, and naturally, the purchaser will want to know exactly what easements were granted and reserved by the 1965

conveyance. You must, therefore, obtain a copy of it. You could do this by asking the Equine Bank to photocopy the charge certificate. Alternatively, you could obtain an office copy of the deed from the Land Registry. The reservation of the easement certainly must be disclosed.

3. *Entry no.1 on Charges Register* If it was known what the 1922 covenants were, the contract could simply have said that the property was sold subject to entries 1 and 2 on the charges register of the title. (Not, notice 'subject to the entries on the charges register' as the sale is *not* subject to entries 3 and 4.) However, as no one knows what the 1922 covenants are, it is best for the contract to say not only that the sale is subject to the 1922 covenants, but also that there is no information about what the covenants are, and that no requisitions about them can be made by the purchaser.

   It is unfortunate that while it is quite clear that the covenants will bind the purchaser, as they are entered in the register, nobody knows what they are. This situation is not uncommon. The applicant for first registration produced the recent conveyances, all of which said the property was conveyed subject to the covenants, but the 1922 deed itself had been lost.

4. *Entry no.2* The contract will say that the sale is subject to the 1965 covenants. Again, the purchaser will see a copy of these before exchange of contracts.

5. *Entries 3 and 4* The sale is not subject to the mortgage, but there is no need to say this expressly in the contract because of the effect of standard condition 3 (see section 5.5).

6. *Fixtures and Fittings* Do not bother to rack your brain as to whether or not the shed is a fixture. Ask your client to fill in the fixtures fittings and contents form (in which all these items are included) and attach it to the contract.

7. *The Will?* Did you fall into the trap of thinking that the will was in some way relevant to the title to the home? It was not.

   After Naomi's death, Jacob was sole owner of the legal estate, by virtue of the right of survivorship. He owned it as sole trustee for sale. He could not however transfer it alone, because of the restriction on the register. The sale by two trustees would overreach the equitable interests.

   Naomi's will did affect the ownership of the equitable interests (but not the legal estate) but a purchaser does not have to investigate the interests of the beneficiaries. The will is of interest to the two trustees, as it determines how they should deal with the purchase price. It cannot all be given to Jacob. Some share of it must go to Ruth.

   Note: You need to check, when looking at the office copies, whether the Greens were the applicants for first registration. If they were, you will have to ask the bank to let you see the pre-registration deeds to discover if the Greens gave an indemnity covenant in respect of the covenants when they bought. If they did, Jacob will need an indemnity from the purchaser. You will not need a special condition to provide for the indemnity, unless you consider the standard condition to be inadequate.

   If the Greens were not the applicants for first registration, but were later transferees of the title, they apparently gave no indemnity covenant, as one does not appear on the proprietorship register. If they did not give an indemnity covenant, Jacob will not need one when he resells.

Chapter 13

Problem 1

1. the commencement – that is, 'This conveyance ...'
2. Date.
3. Parties. The two sellers will be one party; the two purchasers the other party.
4. Recital of sellers' ownership (in fee simple, subject as mentioned later in the conveyance, but otherwise free from incumbrances), and of the contract for sale.
5. Consideration – £30 000. (£500 is not being paid for the *land*, so exclude it.)
6. Receipt clause.
7. The fact that the sellers convey as beneficial owner. The capacity in which they hold the legal estate is that of trustees for sale, and the contract should have stated that they would convey in that capacity. The contract, however, seems to be silent on this point, so the effect of standard condition 4.5.2 is that they must convey as beneficial owners.
8. Parcels. A plan was probably used in drafting the particulars of the contract. If not, one should be used in the conveyance, unless the boundary between the northern and southern boundaries is well-established.
9. A reservation in the parcels clause of the right of way.
10. Habendum – to hold unto the purchasers in fee simple in equal shares subject to the 1960 restrictive covenants.
11. New restrictive covenant.
12. Indemnity and performance covenant *if* the sellers gave an indemnity covenant when they bought (standard condition 4.5.3).
13. Acknowledgement for production of retained deeds (this is a sale of part) and an undertaking for safe custody. (Query, could the sellers refuse the undertaking under standard condition 4.5.4 on the ground that they are fiduciary sellers? Perhaps not, as although they own the legal estate as trustees for sale, they hold on trust only for themselves.)
14. Certificate of value – consideration not exceeding £30 000.
15. Testimonium.
16. Any schedules referred to, for example, of retained deeds.
17. Execution of the document as a deed by sellers *and* purchasers, and attestation of their signatures.

Chapter 15

Problem 1

(a) *Consents*

1. *Assignment* The need for the landlord's consent for assignment is obvious. This will probably be obtained before contract, but could be sought after contract (see section 15.3).

2. *User*

   (a) The landlord's consent is needed.

   (b) We do not know whether this is a headlease (i.e. granted out of the freehold) or an underlease. If it is an underlease, we need to consider the user covenants in the superior leases. A superior landlord generally has no direct right of actior against an undertenant if he breaks a provision of the headlease. There is no privity of contract or estate between them. An exception to this rule is a restrictive covenant. A superior landlord can obtain an injunction against a subtenant who breaks a restrictive covenant in a superior lease if the subtenant had notice of the covenant when he obtained his sublease. This is because of the rule in *Tulk* v. *Moxhay* (1848) which has the effect of making a restrictive covenant an encumbrance on the land enforceable against anyone who takes with notice. However, as Pamela, by virtue of s.44 of the Law of Property Act 1925 is not entitled to see the headlease, she cannot be taken to have had constructive notice of its contents. This point can be pursued in any land law textbook, but it is not the major point which is as follows.

If the subtenant's activities on the premises cause the tenant to be in breach of the covenants of the superior lease, the superior lease may be forfeited for breach of covenant. Therefore, for practical reasons a subtenant has to observe the user restrictions not only in his own lease, but all superior leases, as the forfeiture of a superior lease causes the end of all inferior leases derived from it. It is for this reason that user-covenants in a superior lease are often reproduced in the sublease. The tenant, knowing he can be controlled by his landlord, needs the same sort of control over his subtenant.

So, to return to Pamela, she should ask if the lease she is buying is the headlease, or an underlease. If Vera's landlord is not the freeholder, he can be asked if any consent to change of use is needed under the terms of his own lease, and if it is, it should be obtained. It is as much in the interest of the landlord that consent is obtained as it is in Pamela's.

Of course, it is also possible that there is a covenant on the freehold preventing use as a shop. If this covenant is registered either under the Land Charges Act 1972 or under the Land Registration Act 1925, it will bind Pamela as she will be treated as having actual notice of it. The risk of an unknown covenant is diminished if the contract between Vera and Pamela provides for deduction of the superior titles (diminished, not removed, because of the spectre – if the freehold title is unregistered – of the pre-root land charge).

(c) The proposed change of use will need planning permission. It is a change from one class of use to another within the Use Classes Order (see section 6.5).

3. *Alterations* Pamela will probably want to alter the inside of the premises. The lease should be checked to see if the landlord's consent is needed to alterations.

(b) *The Option*

An option to renew a lease is one that 'touches and concerns the land'. When a lease is assigned the new owner of it succeeds automatically to the benefit of such covenants. Therefore, the mere fact that Pamela becomes the new owner of the lease ensures that she has the benefit of this option. If Len is still the landlord, the option will be enforceable against him, and he will have to renew the lease. However, it is possible that Len has assigned the reversion to the lease. Let us assume that we have checked on this point and we find that he sold the reversion to Mary last year. Can Pamela enforce the option against Mary? It is true that a purchaser of a landlord's reversion takes subject to the burden of the landlord's obligations that touch and concern the land (s.142 of the Law of Property Act 1925), but the option is affected by other rules as well. We need to know if the title to the reversion is registered under the Land Registration Act 1925. If the title is registered, Mary will have taken free of the option unless it was a minor interest that was protected by an entry on the register, or was an overriding interest. The option is probably overriding. It is probably overriding under s.70(1)(g) as an interest belonging to a person in actual occupation of the land. So s.70(1)(g) ensures that Mary is bound by the lease and by the option. It is also possibly overriding under s.70(1)(k) (see section 3.15(e)).

If the title is unregistered, the option comes within the definition of an 'estate contract' and is registrable as a C(iv) land charge. If Vera did not register the land charge before Mary bought the reversion, Mary is not bound by the option and cannot be forced to renew the lease. The only remedy would be to sue Len for breach of contract. He promised to renew the lease if asked, but now cannot do so.

Notice that if Len had sold to Mary under a contract incorporating the standard conditions, Len could claim an indemnity against Mary if he were sued in such circumstances. Condition 3.2.2d provides that a purchaser of property subject to a lease shall indemnify the seller against all claims arising under the tenancy 'even if void against a purchaser for want of registration'. Mary might prefer to renew the lease, rather than face the cost of indemnifying Len.

Note Suppose the option had not been to renew the lease, but instead to buy the landlord's reversion. Would this have made any difference? This option is one of the few covenants generally found in a lease that is not considered to touch and concern the land, but is treated as a personal agreement between the original landlord and the original tenant. For this reason, Pamela cannot claim she owns the benefit of the option merely because she owns the lease. However, unless the option is so drafted that it is exercisable *only* by Vera, there is nothing to stop Vera expressly assigning the benefit of the option at the same time as she assigns the lease. It has been held that if the option is drafted so that it is expressed to be exercisable by the original tenant and by assignees from her, then the assignment of the lease will also impliedly assign the benefit of the option (see *Griffith* v. *Pelton* [1958]).

The option creates an equitable interest in land which is capable of binding Mary but again it must either have been registered as a C(iv) land charge, or, in the case of a registered title, be protected by notice or caution, or be an overriding interest. The option could be overriding under s.70(1)(g) but probably not under 70(1)(k), as it is a provision in the lease that does not touch and concern the land and stands outside the relationship of landlord and tenant.

Problem 2

She is entitled to see the assignment to Enid. She must always see the assignment to the seller. This assignment is not yet fifteen years old. So Pamela is also entitled to see the assignment by Carol to Deirdre. This is over fifteen years old. Enid therefore satisfies her obligations under s.44 of the Law of Property Act 1925 by producing the 1940 lease and the 1973 and 1988 assignments. Pamela has no right to insist on investigating ownership of the lease between 1965 and 1973.

Note Pamela has no right to investigate the superior titles unless s.44 of the Law of Property Act 1925 has been altered by a term in the contract for sale.

Chapter 17

Problem 1, possible solutions

You need to work out how much the Archers will need to buy Greenbank, and the money they will have coming in.

Coming in

A. Sale proceeds

Contract price		£40 000
Less		
• redemption of first mortgage	£10 000	
• redemption of second mortgage	(unknown)	
Solicitor's fees and disburse ments in connection with sale, purchase and mortgages say	£ 400	
Estate agent's fees say	£ 600	
at least	£11 000	£11 000
Less than		£29 000

Urgent step – to confirm redemption figure on first mortgage and to obtain redemption figure on second mortgage.

B. Net Mortgage offer

Amount of loan		£32 000
Less retention moneys	£ 2000	£ 2 000
		£30 000

So less (perhaps, *considerably* less) than £60 000 coming in

Going out

Purchase price		£60 000
Add stamp duty @ 1%		£ 600
Miscellaneous expenses, say		£ 200
	Total – something over	£60 800

There is a shortfall. There are possible solutions.

1. Your clients must reconcile themselves to remaining in 5 King Street.
2. The Grasping Bank might be willing to transfer its mortgage from 5 King Street to Greenbanks. It will not then be necessary to find money to redeem it. The fees of the Bank's solicitors will have to be paid. You must check whether the Building Society's mortgage contains a covenant not to create a second mortgage without the Society's consent.
3. Increase the size of the loan from the Building Society. Your clients, before seeking to increase their borrowing, must consider their ability to repay.

If the transaction can continue, you must think about the deposit of £6000 to be paid on the exchange of contracts for the purchase of Greenbanks. Your clients will want to use the £4000 coming in from the sale of 5 King Street so make sure that the 5 King Street contract incorporates standard condition 2.2.2 unaltered. This leaves £2000 to find. Your clients do not appear to have any savings. Possibly the seller can be persuaded to accept a smaller deposit. Otherwise, your clients will have to arrange temporary finance, or use the deposit guarantee scheme. Both involve expense.

The two sets of contracts must now be exchanged as simultaneously as possible. This can be done by arranging exchange over the telephone. A simple method would be this:

Suppose Q is selling Greenbanks to the Archers, and the Archers are selling 5 King Street to S. S's solicitors will send S's part of the contract concerning 5 King Street to the Archers' solicitors, together with the payment of the deposit. (If the standard conditions apply, this will have to be by way of banker's draft, or a cheque on the solicitors' clients' account.) The accompanying letter will make it clear that the contract is not sent by way of exchange, but that the Archers' solicitors are for the present to hold it to the order of S. The Archers' solicitors then send their clients' part of the contract concerning Greenbanks to Q's solicitor, and the deposit, again making it clear that it is not sent by way of exchange. This is necessary because otherwise Q could force a contract on˜the Archers by returning his part of the contract. When they are ready to exchange, the Archers' solicitors will phone Q's solicitors, to say that they are about to exchange contracts on 5 King Street, and asking if they will be able to exchange the contracts on Greenbanks immediately afterwards. If the answer is 'yes', the Archers' solicitors phone S's solicitors, and the exchange of the contracts on 5 King Street is agreed, and the Law Society undertakings given, in this case, according to formula A. The Archers' solicitors immediately phone Q's solicitors, and contracts are exchanged for the purchase of Greenbanks.

This method does not remove all risk. It is possible that at the last minute while the Archers' solicitors are exchanging contracts on 5 King Street, Q may telephone his solicitors and withdraw his instructions to exchange. The Archers' solicitors will then find that when they telephone back to Q's solicitors, exchange does not take place. The risk of this happening in the small amount of time involved is small, and probably acceptable.

Notice the order of events. The contracts for sale are exchanged before the contracts for purchase, so there is no risk of the Archers being bound by a contract to buy, while not having disposed of their own house.

Problem 2: Possible Solution

The point about finances here is that Mrs Fawkes presumably owns part of the beneficial interest in The Plot, so *her* money will be partly financing the purchase of The Tower. If this is so, then The Tower should be conveyed into both their names, and the conveyance should declare how they hold the equitable interest.

Provided that there is no conflict of interest between Mr and Mrs Fawkes, you can act for them both, but you must receive Mrs Fawkes's instructions from her, not from her husband, and the point about the conveyance being to them both must be explained. If they cannot agree as to the ownership of the equitable interest there is a conflict between them, and you cannot act for them both.

Another reason why the conveyance should be to them both is that the mortgage to the Building Society should be by both of them. If the conveyance were to Mr Fawkes alone the Building Society would have to be warned that Mrs Fawkes contributed to the purchase price, and so has an equitable interest in The Tower. The Building Society would then be reluctant to accept a mortgage from Mr Fawkes alone, lest it be subject to the wife's interest.

An undertaking such as you have been asked for is common in chain transactions where a bridging loan has been obtained from a bank. If you are a solicitor or licensed conveyancer you are under an absolute duty to honour your professional undertaking, and any failure to do this would be looked upon as serious misconduct. For this reason you must only undertake to do what is within your own control. So the following precautions must be taken:

1. You must obtain your client's irrevocable instructions to give the undertaking.
2. You must only undertake to the bank to pay the net proceeds of the sale to it if and when they come into your hands. This covers the possibility that you may never receive the proceeds, e.g. because your client decides to transfer the transaction to another solicitor.
3. The undertaking is only in respect of the net proceeds after, e.g. deduction of your own costs, and redemption of mortgages, etc. Tell the Bank what deductions you will be making.
4. Undertake only to pay the proceeds into the account. Do not undertake to discharge the bridging loan from the proceeds. Otherwise, if the proceeds are insufficient, you may have to discharge the bridging loan from your own money. If the bank does not accept an undertaking in these guarded terms, you refuse to give an undertaking to the bank.

Problem 3

(a) Usually there is no conflict of interest between co-purchasers, and so it is possible to act for them all. However, if there is a conflict of interest the purchasers will have to be separately represented. So your answer depends on whether you can see the probability of a conflict of interest between the Savages and the Cowards. We will return to this point when we answer part (c).

(b) To begin with, check the overall position to see if there will be sufficient money to buy 'The Knoll'.

Coming in

A. Net proceeds of sale of 22 Mount Road (This is an estimate made by the Savages, and should be checked.)	£ 7 000
B. Contribution by the Cowards	£40 000
C. The mortgage loan	£25 000
	£72 000

Going out

Purchase price of The Knoll	£72 000

(The expenses connected with the purchase, e.g. stamp duty of £720 and solicitors' fees and disbursements seen to have been taken into account in estimating the net proceeds of the sale, but this must be checked.)

The figures here seem to balance, but there is no surplus to meet any expenses that have been overlooked. The figure given for the net proceeds of the sale of Mount Road must be carefully checked to see if the Savages have foreseen all the expenses connected with both transactions.

Second, what about the position of the Savages? They have life savings of £50 000. They are going to contribute £40 000 towards the purchase and pay for the costs of conversion which are approximately £5000. This leaves them with only £5000. They need to obtain firm estimates for the costs of conversion. They must also be sure that they will have sufficient income to live on after most of their capital has been tied up in the house. Apparently they will have little more than their old age pension. The problem could become even more acute when one of them dies, and the other is living on the reduced pension. It will be difficult to realise their capital investment if they need to do so, unless the Savages cooperate.

(c) A decision must be reached as to how the equitable interest in The Knoll is to be shared. There must be a division of it into two shares, one for the Cowards and one for the Savages. Each couple will then be a tenant in common with the other couple. The Cowards' share can then be held by them jointly. This ensures that when one dies, the entire share will be automatically owned by the survivor. When the survivor dies, the share will pass over the terms of his or her will, i.e. to Sara. This will carry out the Cowards' wishes that only Sara will benefit from their deaths. The Savages' share will also probably be owned by them jointly, as again the right of survivorship, which is inherent in a joint tenancy, seems appropriate to the matrimonial home. (Notice that even if the couples' contributions had been equal, it would have been wrong for the conveyance to them to declare that they held the whole as beneficial joint tenants. This would not have carried out the Cowards' wishes, as it would mean that after their deaths their interests would be owned by their son-in-law and daughter jointly, rather than entirely by their daughter.) The problem lies in deciding the size of the two shares. The Cowards are contributing £40 000 of the total purchase price of £72 000, so possibly should have a share in proportion to their contribution, i.e. a five-ninths share. They are also paying for the costs of the conversion, but it is debatable if this adds anything to the capital value of the house. On the other hand, the Savages are bearing the expenses of the purchase.

The mortgage is another difficulty. The understanding between the Savages and the Cowards is that the Savages are to be solely responsible for the repayment of the loan. However, as they are giving the legal estate as security, not just the Savages' equitable interest, they will all sign the mortgage and covenant to repay. In other words, as far as the Building Society is concerned, all four of them are responsible, and the Cowards could be sued for debt. What would certainly happen if the Savages failed to make the monthly repayments is that the Society would sell the house, and the Cowards would lose their home.

It is possible to draw up the conveyance so that the legal estate is conveyed to the Savages alone on trust for sale for themselves and the Cowards. The mortgage of the legal estate would then also be solely by the Savages, and only the Savages would covenant to repay. This would mean that the Cowards could not be sued by the Building Society for debt, but it otherwise offers no solution, and indeed, creates other problems. The Cowards remain at risk if the Savages should fail to repay, as the Building Society would sell the property. The Cowards' equitable interests would not have bound the Building Society, as they would have been overreached by the mortgage (see *City of London Building Society* v. *Flegg* [1988]). It would be possible for the Savages to create a second mortgage without the concurrence of the Cowards. A safeguard against this in the case of registered title would be a restriction on the register, saying that no disposition by the registered proprietors would be registered unless the consent of the Cowards was obtained.

We can now see that the proposed arrangement is not completely satisfactory from the Cowards' point of view and as a result it is probably impossible for us to act for them as well as for the Savages without a conflict of interest. The Cowards should be separately advised.

Chapter 18

Problem

(a) Does the power authorise White to execute the conveyance? Yes. Re-read section 9.4(b).
White should hand over a facsimile certified copy of the power. Re-read section 9.4(e).

(b) This is not a security power, so death revokes it. More importantly, Green *knows* of the revocation, and for this reason any conveyance by White to him would be void. The person who will have the power to convey is Black's personal representative. He will be bound by the contract, as the contract for the sale of land is not discharged by the death either of the seller or of the purchaser. Can the personal representative convey *now* however? No. He must first obtain the grant, either of probate or letters of administration (see section 10.2). So there will be delay before the sale to Mr Green is completed.

(c) (i) The fact that his purchase may be delayed is no excuse for Mr Green to delay his sale. So he may decide to convey his present house on the agreed date, and find temporary accommodation. Mr Green may be tempted to stay where he is, and postpone completion of his sale until he completes his purchase. He may be thwarted by the purchaser, who can issue a writ for specific performance as soon as the agreed completion date has passed, or serve a completion notice and threaten to end the contract. If Green's purchaser is prepared to accept a delayed completion, when it takes place he may have a claim for interest under standard condition 7.3, or for damages.

(ii) It would be pointless for Mr Green to try to speed completion on by applying for a decree of specific performance. The personal representative cannot give a good title until he has obtained the grant, so the delay is inevitable.

If Mr Green does wish to discharge the contract, he could serve a completion notice. However, there are difficulties. It is not possible, whatever means are used, to serve notice on a dead man. Nor can the notice be served on his solicitors. A corpse has no solicitors, and death ends the retainer. Service would have to be on the personal representative. If Mr Black died without having appointed an executor he has no personal representative until letters of administration are granted. However, the rule is that pending the grant, an intestate's property is vested in the President of the Family Division. Could notice be served on him? If Mr Black died having appointed an executor, notice could be served on him. The trouble is that Mr Green cannot be sure who is the executor until he has seen a grant of probate. If the delay looks as if it is going to be substantial Mr Green would probably be forced to court for a declaration that the delay is unreasonable, being unable to serve a completion notice to establish that fact (see *Graham* v. *Pitkin* [1992] 2 A11 ER 235).

If Mr Green waits for the personal representative to obtain a grant, when completion takes place, he will be able to claim either interest or damages, and the claim will include any compensation he has had to pay to the purchaser from him.

A possible solution is for the personal representative to allow Mr Green to move in before completion. The rights of the parties will then be defined by standard condition 5.2.

Chapter 19

Problem

Presumably the contract does not repeat the statement as to the existence of the permission. So there is no possibility for action for breach of contract. Pauline will have to establish that the statement was a misrepresentation. If it is, the next question to decide is whether the representation was fraudulent or not, as this affects Pauline's remedies. To be fraudulent, the statement must have been made with the knowledge that it was false, or without belief in its truth, or reckless of whether it was false or true. A fraudulent misrepresentation could give Pauline the right to rescind the contract and to claim damages for the fraud. It seems difficult here for Pauline to prove fraud. Her remedies for non-fraudulent misrepresentation come from the Misrepresentation Act 1967. She has a right of rescission, (subject to the court's power under s.2(2) of the Act to award damages instead). She has a right to damages unless the representation was made without negligence.

The contract incorporates the standard conditions, and condition 7.1 restricts remedies for misrepresentation. (The condition has already been considered in this chapter in the context of misdescription, but it applies to misrepresentations as well.) When considering its effect, remember that a condition removing or restricting remedies for misrepresentation is void unless the condition is a fair and reasonable one to have been included in the contract having regard to all the circumstances known to the parties when the contract was made (s.3 of the Misrepresentation Act 1967). It is up to Roger to establish the validity of the condition. If he cannot do so, *or* if Pauline can establish that the misrepresentation makes a *substantial* difference, she will be able to rescind the contract. The right to rescission survives completion (s.1(b) of the Misrepresentation Act 1967) so it is possible that even if the house had actually been conveyed to Pauline, she could still ask for her money to be returned. This may make things very awkward for the seller, who may have used it to buy his new home, or otherwise put it beyond easy reach, and that sort of difficulty could be a reason for the court to exercise its discretion to award damages in place of rescission.

The remedy of rescission is an equitable one, and there are so-called 'bars' to obtaining an order for it. One is delay. Another is that rescission will not be awarded if it would prejudice innocent third parties who have acquired an interest in the property for value. If Pauline bought with the aid of a mortgage loan, rescission would destroy the mortgagee's security for repayment of the loan. This difficulty should be solvable by an arrangement being made for redemption of the mortgage when Pauline reconveys the land to Roger, in return for the purchase price.

If the exclusion clause is valid, and the misdescription makes a material difference, but not a substantial one, Pauline could not rescind, but could only claim damages.

Index